Brohdan's Quest is an exhilarating account of a common dragon who discovers his birthright – a thrilling realization, yet also a daunting one. And while he accepts his destiny, he's unsure if he can live up to the lofty standard set by his predecessors, nor the culmination of events that first plagued the world over seven thousand years ago.

When Belkidar had lived a mere millennium, he fought in the War, waged to forever rid the world of Jenkar's masterpiece, the root of incredible prosperity – and the seed of endless corruption. He narrowly prevailed, yet despite his victory, the evil escaped and festered unseen.

Time is short. *Now* is the time to act. Belkidar recruits five other creatures, Brohdan among them, to once and for all rid this world of Jenkar's evil before it's too late. With sincere, heartfelt characters similar to those that defined Rothfuss' *The Name of the Wind*, inspiring character arcs reminiscent of Abercrombie's *The First Law*, an intricate plot littered with titanic battles resembling Tolkien's *The Lord of the Rings*, and compelling struggles that fundamentally connect each character to an underlying purpose, *Brohdan's Quest* is a testament to how unyielding perseverance, self-sacrifice, and the strength of friendship can overcome any evil.

Brohdan's Quest

by

Todd A. Ivener

Brohdan's Quest

by

Todd A. Ivener

We'd love to hear from you! Please leave us your thoughts at:
https://BrohdansQuest.com

The Motive

A story is eternal.
    Struggle through your Quest,
    Fight to pass the Test.
A piece a father leaves behind.

A story is alive.
    A soul relentless,
    A heart resentless.
A peace a father leaves behind.

I'm grateful beyond words for having so many loved ones support me throughout this process. I'm sorry I can't list everyone, but please know you will forever have my gratitude.

To those who tirelessly sacrificed to help make this the best story possible, THANK YOU...

... to **my wife**, for steadfastly supporting me in this quest.

... to **my parents**, for raising us right.

... to **Terry**, for challenging me, for helping to make this story a memorable one...

... to my proofreaders: **Timothy, Jeff, Marko, and Kasia**, for sticking with Brohdan through the good...and sometimes not-so-good...

...to **Sharon Graham Smith**, for creating the artwork on the cover and title page – and for quietly reminding us that there will always be beauty in this world. Discover more of her fantastic work at:

www.sharongrahamsmith.com

...and finally, to **YOU**, the reader, for offering more than I ever had a right to expect.

Prologue

Most people don't realize that dragons and humans are very much alike. Dragons are a tremendously proud species with a rich cultural and social history. An unyielding loyalty defines their character, and their behavior reflects a profound sense of duty. Dragons, like humans, have interests that vary from science to art to philosophy. A dragon's sense of humor is diverse, ranging from quick sarcasm to downright silliness. However, perhaps the most fundamental similarity between humans and dragons lies in the fact that neither is born with the knowledge of what he can become.

Katja

Kaarlo

Celomorin Ocean

Tymotheu

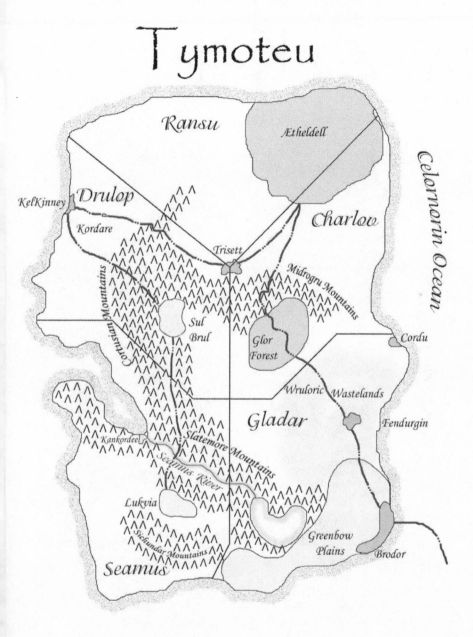

Tymoteu

Katja

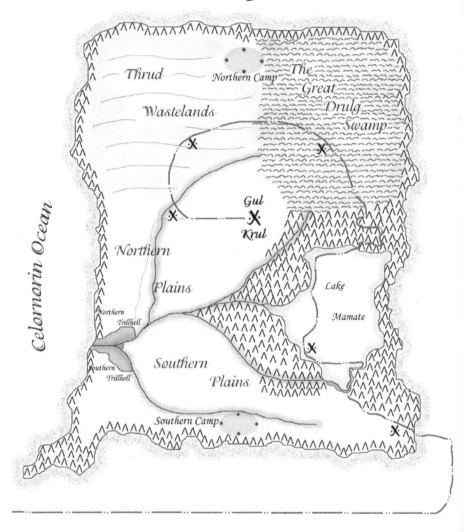

Glossary

Measurements of Time

Dru. The shortest measurement of time. One thousand *drus* comprise a link. Derived from <u>Dru</u>lop, the location where twenty clans were united after Edward rode Legend at a canter for an entire day with no rest.

Link. Twenty *links* comprise a day. Derived from the twenty clans united after Edward rode Legend at a canter for an entire day with no rest.

Mooncycle. Thirty-six days comprise a *mooncycle*.

Cycle. Ten mooncycles comprise a *cycle*.

Decacycle. Ten cycles comprise a *decacycle*.

Centacycle. One hundred cycles comprise a *centacycle*.

Kilacycle. One thousand cycles comprise a *kilacycle*.

Measurements of Distance

Elye. The shortest measurement of distance, an *elye* is the distance between Edward's Legend's eyes. Derived from <u>E</u>dward's <u>L</u>egend's <u>eye</u>s.

Elad. The second shortest measurement of distance, an *elad* is the length of Edward's Legend's head. Derived from <u>E</u>dward's <u>L</u>egend's he<u>ad</u>.

Linak. The second longest measurement of distance, a *linak* is the distance Edward's Legend could walk in a half link. Derived from <u>lin</u>k w<u>alk</u>. Through the centacycles, the word *linalk* evolved into *linak*, probably for simplicity of pronunciation.

Linop. The longest measurement of distance, a *linop* is the distance Edward's Legend could gallop in a half link. Derived from <u>lin</u>k gal<u>lop</u>. Through the centacycles, the word *linlop* evolved into *linop*, probably for simplicity of pronunciation.

Introduction

*Conflict is change, a marriage of cunning and
violence. War, perhaps the ultimate mortal conflict,
begets heroes and villains – martyrs, who transcend
ages, and pawns, whom history is destined to forget.
The difference between the two is not one's actions,
but the inspiration they evoke. How, then, do we
inspire hard-hearted warriors, creatures capable of
untold cruelty?*

A brilliant sun warmed the calm waters of the vast Celornorin
Ocean. The day was unusually pleasant for so early in spring. Twenty
linaks beyond the southwestern shores of Seamus, an old dolphin
detected the dark silhouettes of several marlin diving deeper into the
shadowy depths. He sprinted toward the surface, a fine mist erupting
from his blowhole the instant he emerged. He seemed to hover, his
trajectory cresting the sun's shimmering reflection, then fell, tiny
bubbles swirling as he gave chase.

But they had no need to fear Belkidar. More than most, he
understood life's fragile nature, and so he simply enjoyed being a
dolphin, savored the sensation of remaining true to what he was,
content with what he was not.

Over the course of the next several links, Belkidar leisurely
mingled with many of the sea's inhabitants until eventually
encountering a small group of humpback whales. The dolphin
considered these gentle giants as he maneuvered in the spaces that
separated one whale from the next. For as long as he could remember,
Belkidar enjoyed their company. They moved casually enough for him
to navigate through the group while still matching the pod's overall

pace, and he found their general indifference to his playful intrusions refreshing. But perhaps more than anything, the old dolphin found humpback whales to be the finest conversationalists of all the ocean's creatures.

"Good afternoon," Belkidar greeted the eldest female.

"Back for more fun, are we Belkidar?"

"Oh, you know how it is. I'd been stuck on land far too long. What have you heard?"

The huge creature studied her old friend for several moments. "Something very interesting. I expected you sooner."

The dolphin's expression turned curious.

"Have you not heard? An evil invaded Kaarlo. The Indifferent failed. The Jewel is lost."

The dolphin cursed softly, yet his muffled expressions carried for linops through the ocean's depths.

"My, I haven't heard talk like that in cycles."

Belkidar grunted. "I learned those persevere particular words from you, as I recall. Who stole the Jewel from the Indifferent?"

"Need you ask? Hildegard now possesses the Headpiece *and* the Jewel – that's two of the three Artifacts in case you've lost count. You'd better make sure he doesn't get the third."

"He won't get the Staff. I'm curious, though – how did you discover so much about events that happened so far from the water?"

"Oh, it wasn't difficult. Hildegard took the form of a brown forest fox and stole into the village where the Jewel was kept. Riikka and his people had really grown lax in their protection. I know they're the Indifferent, but he really should've been more careful."

"My dear, what happened to the Jewel?"

"Oh yes," the huge creature continued, slowly pacing her large fluke once for every dozen of the much smaller dolphin's. "The fox slipped into the village not long after midnight. From what I was told, he had little trouble finding the Artifact. He silently leaped through a window and found no resistance as he approached Riikka's treasury. It wasn't until mid-afternoon the following day when a guard noticed the

Jewel's absence. By then, Hildegard had assumed a wolf's form and had traveled well beyond Riikka's reach."

"Are you sure this information is accurate?"

"I'm afraid so. An owl saw this 'fox' steal the Jewel. Because this unique trio of Artifacts ultimately affects us all, the owl became concerned and followed him for a few linaks before witnessing his transformation into a wolf." She turned and regarded the dolphin. "You realize, of course, humans aren't the only ones who would be affected by the reunification of the Staff of Power?"

"Yes, my dear," he sighed. "Please continue."

"Very well. The owl followed the thief for linaks. When he finally reached the coast, he changed his form once again. It was Hildegard. He boarded a ship and headed toward Katja."

"The owl knew he must send for help, so he talked to a nearby seagull and explained what had happened. After finally calming the smaller bird – seagulls are quite excitable, you know – the owl told him to relay the news to the first whale or dolphin he could find. Not many people realize that seagulls are the only birds that can communicate with sea mammals. Very strange accents, though."

"Continue, please," Belkidar prodded.

"Right. The owl understood that oceans offered the fastest way to share this information. For instance, I often speak with whales that are more than fifty linops away."

"Yes, dear. I *am* a dolphin," Belkidar replied with unusual patience.

"Perhaps. Anyway, a blue whale diving beyond the coast of Kaarlo relayed this information to me yesterday evening. Evidently, the blue heard it from a killer whale earlier that morning. From what I understand, it was this orca with whom the seagull first talked."

Belkidar was flabbergasted. After a few more curses, he thanked her before sprinting toward the surface. Still accelerating, the dolphin exploded into the air, soaring a dozen elads above the water before a peaceful white-blue light consumed his body. In an instant, the aura vanished to reveal a large eagle coasting upward along the same path as had the glistening dolphin. After a few thrusts of his powerful wings, Belkidar felt the warm salt breeze pass over his immaculate feathers as he navigated toward a young friend.

Chapter 1
Home

Our doubts are traitors,
And make us lose the good we oft might win,
By fearing to attempt.

William Shakespeare, <u>Measure for Measure</u>

Lukvia was an ancient province, one of the few places dragons still called home. All of Brohdan's short life had been spent there, and until recently he'd been content. He had loving parents who spoiled him beyond measure. Grediva and Brohdeck loved to treat him as though he were still an infant, but to Brohdan's dismay, his incessant reminders to the contrary continually fell on deaf ears. Despite their coddling, Brohdan loved his parents, and their annoying habits did little to lessen the enormous respect he held for them.

Brohdan was a Dalluvian Green, a common dragon. Nearly his entire body was covered with hard scales of deep emerald. His long, muscular neck was perfectly balanced by an even lengthier tail. Both of his legs were equipped with powerful talons, and a pair of large, seemingly oversized wings grew from his long, slender body. They appeared relatively narrow at his shoulders, but their size grew as they traveled outward, especially near his wingtips. When he walked, the outer half of his wings pointed skyward, his tough, leathery wing hooks at his elbows the only parts that touched the ground. A spiny armor made from many small horns lined the bridge of his long nose, then split into two rows as they traveled above his eyes, forming brows. Similar armor ran the length of his neck, back and tail.

Brohdan's earliest memories were of his father trying to prepare him for his grombit. He recalled countless times when Brohdeck explained the finer points of flying, but as hard as he tried, Brohdan just couldn't convince his wings to support his weight. Most parents instructed their children as best they could, but there's really nothing that can prepare young dragons for their grombit. As with most trials in life, a grombit is simply something you must experience to understand. Now approaching the fiftieth anniversary of his birth, the knowledge that his grombit would soon begin was the source of his mounting anxiety.

All dragons enter their grombit during the first three mooncycles of their fifty-first cycle. It has always been so, but Brohdan had an unpleasant feeling his grombit would be hopeless. He was widely known as a clumsy dragon, and even he admitted there was a certain truth in that. He'd always felt as though his body was foreign to him, and he certainly had no confidence that it would be any different now, at the very moment he was to begin the transformation into an adult dragon, capable of fire-breathing and flight. He knew he'd also physically mature, gaining as much as half of his adolescent weight. Most of this gain could be attributed to the muscle development in his shoulders, chest, and back, affording him the ability to fly, but an adult dragon was also several elads longer than a youngling. He knew these changes would come soon, and that knowledge only deepened his concern.

In the morning, he would travel south to the Sichundar Mountains. Because he could not yet fly, the journey would take him five days. Once there, he'd become the newest member at the Lukvian grombit camp, a place where 'younglings walk in and adults fly out.' Brohdan desperately hoped he wasn't the first dragon destined to walk out.

All of the adult dragons Brohdan knew had not attended a grombit camp. Instead, they learned adult skills from their parents, and through practice, they mastered flying, fire-breathing, and the stamina required for each. Brohdan was different. His father told him several mooncycles ago that he was to undergo formal grombit training. Brohdan couldn't blame him, everyone knew he was uncoordinated. But understanding that didn't lessen his anxiety.

It was well past midnight, but even the pleasant spring breeze failed to soothe him. Brohdan rose from his cave and walked into the starlight. He had always been enamored with the stars, in part because they never failed to rouse his imagination. There were so many, and no two looked exactly alike. The depths of the night sky fascinated him, and he understood that no matter how painful the next few mooncycles might prove, he'd at least have the company of these long-time friends. Comforted, Brohdan returned to his cave and hoped sleep would find him.

Dawn came quickly. He recalled vivid dreams of profound loneliness, where he was the only dragon in the world, searching for comfort he would never find. He'd had no friends or family he could talk to, nobody who could understand his anguish. He was destined to wander through life alone, always watching others interact with friends and loved ones, but never realizing those precious moments himself. He unsuccessfully shook off those lingering thoughts as he joined his parents outside their cave.

"Are you excited?" Grediva asked a bit too enthusiastically as her son emerged into dawn's light.

"Yes, mother."

Brohdeck laughed. "You should be, Brohdan. The Lukvian grombit camp is thousands of cycles old. Hundreds of generations used the cave you'll sleep in every night. Just think of it – some of your ancestors learned adult skills there! Doesn't that excite you?"

Brohdan grunted softly, but his father was too excited to wait for an answer.

"I think there are only three younglings at the camp, not including yourself," Brohdeck continued. "That's good, because you shouldn't have to share a cave with anyone. All three instructors are stern, but I've heard they're excellent teachers. Do you remember their names?"

"Instructors Dorumir, Rossing, and Loryck," Brohdan repeated automatically.

"Good. Dorumir is the Chief Instructor, so try to get on his good side. I don't know much about Loryck, other than he arrived from Sul Brul a few cycles ago. Rossing is a fair instructor, but she really likes to work the younglings, so make sure you're prepared. All three are Gorduvians, but don't let that spoil your impression of them."

Brohdan nodded. He hated good-byes, and considering this particular journey likely involved equal parts frustration and humiliation, this one was especially difficult.

"I know you'll do fine," his father offered. "Just do your best, and we'll be proud of you, regardless of what may or may not happen."

Brohdan grimaced. Even his father expected the worst. But who could blame him? Considering the blundering manner of his first fifty cycles, it was easy to assume his grombit would be a catastrophe. Learning to fly and breathe fire are demanding tasks for any dragon, but for one who struggled during his mundane, pre-grombit life? That could only lead to disaster, and his father knew it. And despite his determination to succeed, so did Brohdan.

Grediva went to her son. "Brohdan, I want you to promise me something. If you happen to struggle, don't ever give up. Sometimes, becoming an adult takes longer for some dragons, that's all. If yours does, it's for a reason. I know you're destined for great things."

Brohdan nodded. "I should get started."

"Yes," Brohdeck agreed. "Go well, my son!"

Brohdan completed a Hongi with his parents – he kissed them in the way of dragons by touching his nose and forehead to his mother's and father's – before turning to leave. It was going to be a long journey, and he'd always despised the drawn-out periods before pain and sorrow. Better to just get it over with.

And so Brohdan departed the only home he'd ever known. He made his way south to the Sichundar Mountains, to a foster home that lacked any of the compassion and solace of his true home. His trepidation grew with each step, and he knew beyond any doubt that his life would never be the same.

Chapter 2
Grombit Camp

*Courage is not having the strength to go on; it is
going on when you don't have the strength.*

Napoléon Bonaparte

Brohdan had been at grombit camp for over three mooncycles,
summer had come and gone, and his experience there was even worse
than he'd feared. No one could predict exactly when a dragon's
grombit would start, so those chosen for grombit camp arrived on the
fifty-first anniversary of their birth. At some point over the next three
mooncycles, their grombit would begin. The instructors diligently
taught the dragons who'd entered their grombits, and those who hadn't
were expected to assist wherever they could.

The dragon pack living in Lukvia wasn't large, so the Sichundar
grombit camp was a relatively small one. Because of this, Brohdan
knew the other three younglings at the camp, having spent the majority
of his life interacting with them to various degrees. As the newest
member, he was the only one who hadn't yet entered his grombit.

Albrogu and Methren were Klonduvian Reds, the world's most
common dragon. Brohdan, a Dalluvian Green, was the second most
common of the four dragon subspecies. Albrogu and Methren had
entered their grombits over four mooncycles ago, and although their
flying needed much improvement, they could both breathe fire almost
as well as some adults.

Limbrin was a Gorduvian Gold, the second rarest subspecies of
dragon after only the mighty Broglia Black. Gorduvians have
traditionally held the highest honors in dragon society. The Chief
Dragon, historically the leader of all dragons, had been a Gorduvian
Gold for the past ten kilacycles. Although their domineering hold
appeared to be diminishing, they nevertheless remained influential in

all dragon societies. Limbrin was very proud of his heritage, and if he was smug before he entered his grombit, he'd been absolutely arrogant since.

Limbrin had been at the camp for nine mooncycles, and his grombit was nearly complete. Unlike the other three subspecies, Gorduvians spit acid instead of breathing fire. This distinction only added to their belief that they joined the Broglia Black as 'greater' dragons, while Klonduvians and Dalluvians comprised the 'lesser' dragons.

The end of the three-mooncycle window where all dragons entered their grombit had passed, yet Brohdan had thus far shown no signs that his would ever begin. The strength and stamina required for flight eluded him, and his fire-breathing was still nonexistent. He was eager to start, diligently watching the others for lessons he could apply to his own grombit, but his body simply would not cooperate.

"I thought I told you to bring me food!" Limbrin told him after completing a rigorous flight around camp. Methren and Albrogu had just finished fire-breathing exercises and approached the camp commons area from the eastern mountain pass.

Brohdan silently did as he was told, knowing better than to anger the instructors with his 'defiance' again. Limbrin completed his meal in short order, then turned back to Brohdan. "You're a disgrace. If I were you, I'd at least have the decency to leave Lukvia. Don't you have *any* self-respect?"

Brohdan's anger grew, but he suppressed it – again – and said nothing. He'd promised his parents that he'd do his best, and getting into more fights with this arrogant dragon wouldn't help. Past experience told him it'd only make matters worse, and he'd suffered enough already. Besides, Limbrin was nearly an adult, so he was larger and more powerful than Brohdan. He always stuck up for himself, even though nobody else did, but in truth he could do nothing except further anger the Gorduvian.

"Answer me!" Limbrin shouted, flying toward him. He climbed several elads into the air, tucked his wings along his back and landed hard on top of the Dalluvian. The collision knocked Brohdan onto his back, his wings trapped awkwardly beneath him. Limbrin clamped his talons into Brohdan's chest, blood escaping between his claws.

His anger swelling, Brohdan fought against the weight of the larger dragon, his rage demanding release, but he was trapped.

"Admit it! You're a worthless excuse for a dragon! You shame our entire pack!"

It took every ounce of Brohdan's self-control to keep the promise he'd made to his parents. And so he said nothing as he felt his blood trickle down his sides and pool beneath his wings.

"That's what I thought. You have no honor, and you'll never be a leader of dragons." Limbrin retracted his talons. "You may think I'm cruel, but it's for your own good. I'm a Gorduvian Gold, and I must help those who cannot help themselves. One day, you may understand."

Brohdan got to his feet, wincing slightly from his wounds. Albrogu sneered at him as he made his way to the pens. Methren's expression remained impassive.

"Did you finish your meals yet?" Instructor Dorumir demanded as he emerged from his cave. He was an older Gorduvian, evidenced by the loose skin below his jaws and upper neck. "You have a lot of work ahead of you today. Limbrin, you must still fly to the Southern Peak and back before sunset. Flying short distances is fine, but adults must have the stamina to fly linops if needed."

"At once!" Limbrin said, his false enthusiasm making Brohdan sick. He took to the air and headed south to the tallest mountain in the Sichundars.

"Albrogu, warm up with five laps around camp. Make it swift, because you've got a lot of fire-breathing to do afterward."

"Yes, Instructor Dorumir," the Klonduvian said, unsteadily lifting into the air.

"Methren, have you burned those trunks yet?"

"No, Instructor Dorumir."

"Then why are you here?"

Although he was still hungry, Methren wasn't about to admit that to his instructor. Instead, he bolted toward the fire pits.

Dorumir then turned to Brohdan. "Why are you bleeding? Did you try to fly by yourself again?"

"No, Instructor Dorumir."

"Good. I told you to have an instructor present whenever you try. Have you made any progress?"

"Not yet. I can glide a few elads when I get a running start, but that's all."

Lukvia's Chief Instructor shook his head in frustration. "No fire?"

"No, Instructor Dorumir."

"Brohdan, I've been instructing grombits for six decacycles, and not once have I had a youngling fail to complete his grombit, let alone *start* it. You will learn to fly and breathe fire, or you will die trying!"

Brohdan nodded in total agreement, his own irritation far exceeding his instructor's.

"Go to the stream and see to those wounds."

"Yes, Instructor Dorumir."

Brohdan watched as he went to confer with Loryck and Rossing, trying to detect anything in his instructor's technique that he could apply to his own. Yet he was fuming at Limbrin and frustrated with Dorumir. If it was up to him, he would've started his grombit long ago. But it wasn't. He was a slave to his body, and he couldn't force his grombit to begin any more than he could change the color of his scales. For three mooncycles now, he was mocked, threatened, beat, and punished for something that was beyond his control, and he was tired.

He remembered a promise he made to his mother, and her words instantly came back to him.

"Sometimes, becoming an adult takes longer for some dragons, that's all. If yours does, it's for a reason. I know you're destined for great things."

Brohdan wanted to believe that, but how could he be destined for greatness if he couldn't even become an adult?

Brohdan's life grew worse over the next two mooncycles. It had been a warm autumn, but that did little to raise his spirits. He was already older than any youngling in the history of the Lukvian pack, and he still hadn't shown any signs of beginning his grombit. His instructors had grown increasingly impatient, and Brohdan's perpetually aching body reflected Limbrin's growing distaste.

Brohdan limped from his cave early one morning to prepare the fire pits. Limbrin had beaten him badly the night before, and his right leg was stiff.

Albrogu emerged from his cave, but said nothing. Methren wasn't far away, near the center of camp.

"Where are you going?" Methren asked.

"To add trunks to the fire pits."

Methren looked around, then spoke quickly, his voice low. "Brohdan, why don't you try harder? At your age, if you tried hard enough, surely you could fly a *little*. Or at least breathe *some* fire."

Brohdan smothered his annoyance. "I *am* trying, Methren, harder than any of you. Do you really think I enjoy this life?"

"Of course not. But perhaps Limbrin's right. Maybe you do need to be motivated."

"Exactly!" Limbrin said as he stepped from the shadows of his cave above and behind where Brohdan and Methren talked. "That's precisely what I've been trying to do, Methren, but Brohdan resists me at every turn. Grombit isn't supposed to be easy, and some just don't have the courage to face it. That's when greater dragons must provide what the lesser dragons lack."

Limbrin took to the air, flew several elads overhead, then breathed acid on top of him. Brohdan leapt out of the way, but it still overwhelmed him. He backed away as his stomach retched, the powerful flumes burning his nose and blurring his vision.

Limbrin took advantage of his blindness, landed hard on top of him. With his right leg already injured, Brohdan didn't have the strength to compensate for the unexpected collision. He collapsed, a loud snap muffled beneath the weight of both dragons.

Brohdan roared in pain. "Get OFF of me!"

But the Gorduvian didn't move, his talons imbedded deep into Brohdan's back. "But I've only just started."

"Maybe you should get off," Methren said. "I think he's really hurt."

Limbrin did, reluctantly. "Maybe, but it can't compare to the suffering he's caused the rest of us."

Despite the searing pain, Brohdan managed to stand, leaning heavily on both wing hooks, his right leg useless.

"What's going on?" Dorumir asked, emerging from his cave.

"Brohdan fell. Again." Limbrin explained.

Dorumir looked from Limbrin to where Brohdan stood, his right leg held above the ground. "Get some food, Limbrin. You'll need it."

"Yes, Instructor Dorumir." Limbrin took flight, never once looking back. Methren and Albrogu took the hint and followed him to the pens.

Dorumir sighed. "You've been falling more and more, Brohdan. Perhaps it's time to send you home."

Brohdan shook his head, defiant. "I won't quit. If you want to send me back, do it – but it'll be your decision, not mine."

Dorumir understood. If Brohdan left, it would be because his instructors quit on him, not the other way around. "Very well," Dorumir conceded. "But you're useless in that condition. Go to the river and spend a few nights in solitude. Perhaps that'll help improve your balance."

Brohdan limped toward the large river that served as the camp's northern border. It took him nearly a link to reach it, and once there, he gratefully submerged his injured leg in the freezing water, the cold immediately soothing his injury. He lay on the bank, his leg slack in the sluggish current, the scent of pine a welcome change from the acid's lingering sulfuric bite.

This was his favorite place in the camp. The sound of the stream calmed him, and the soft breeze swept away his concerns. There were plenty of trees nearby, so he had shade whenever he wanted. More than anything, though, this place offered seclusion. Seclusion from Limbrin, from his instructors, from the tedium of his life. And from his constant failures. Here, he was alone. Free.

"Are you going to lie there all day?"

Brohdan abruptly raised his head, swung his long neck toward the voice, expecting the worst. Instead, he discovered a very old, frail human standing among the trees behind him. He'd only seen a human once before, several decacycles ago when his parents hunted near Kankordee. That one had been a female, and he remembered her being only slightly skinnier than this man.

The human wasn't even two elads tall and appeared incredibly feeble. His hair was the color of snow, and a matching beard fell halfway to his waist. He saw compassion in his steel-blue eyes, their color an ocean blending into a winter sky. He supported himself with an old, thick staff, and his tattered garments somehow exacerbated his already wretched appearance.

His father had long ago warned him of humans, explaining that although they were quite small and fragile, they were capable of feats no other species could comprehend. Brohdan hadn't fully understood his father's warning, but he trusted his judgment, and so with only a little remorse, he raised his tail and whipped it toward him.

To his amazement, a white-blue aura enveloped the human an instant before his tail struck. His bewilderment grew when his scales thudded against it, as though they'd crashed into the stone walls of his cave.

The aura remained, and within it the old man smiled, displaying a father's patience. Alarmed, Brohdan stood and faced him.

"What happened?" he asked, indicating the leg Brohdan held above the ground.

"I fell," he answered, distracted by his sincerity.

Skeptical, the human let the white-blue aura vanish. "I'm sure you did. Hold still while I have a look."

Brohdan stared at him, surprised, saying nothing. He was used to pain now and, truthfully, he no longer cared how much suffering he was forced to endure.

The human approached, seemingly without a concern in the world, least of which was an injured dragon that was nearly four times longer than he was tall. He placed his hand softly against the scales of his leg, then closed his eyes. A faint white-blue light flashed from beneath his palm, then disappeared just as quickly.

"You've broken both bones in your lower leg. One severed some muscle tissue, causing it to bleed internally."

Brohdan snorted. "It's what I deserve."

The human's expression turned curious. "I can mend this if you wish, but it'll be painful."

"You can heal this?" Brohdan asked, stunned. Then he surprised himself by nodding.

The old man's smile returned. "Very well." He replaced his hand on his leg, but this time, the white-blue light that escaped his touch was anything but faint, yet its singular brilliance somehow didn't hurt his eyes. If anything, it beckoned his gaze. Unfortunately, the blazing pain that spread through his leg wasn't as merciful. He could feel where his bones were broken, and it felt as though the old human used fire to fuse them back together.

And then it was over, the pain vanishing a moment before the light. Brohdan flexed his talons, shock still written across his face. He put his weight on it, again felt nothing. He turned toward the human, his eyes wide. "How did you – ?"

"That, my young friend, would require more time than I have."

"Thank you."

"You're very welcome. But I must admit, I'm surprised. That was no trivial injury. How did it really happen?"

Brohdan couldn't lie to him again, not after what he'd just done. "Limbrin."

"Limbrin?"

He nodded. "A Gorduvian Gold who's embarrassed that I haven't started my grombit yet."

The human grew visibly angry. "Another dragon did this to you? What else has he done?"

"It doesn't matter."

"It matters. Tell me."

The debt he owed the old man surpassed his reservations. His shame forced his eyes to the ground, but in his periphery, it seemed as though the human grew slightly larger as Brohdan described his past. A sense of undeniable power emanated from him, silencing nearby birds, the stream the only complement to Brohdan's deep voice.

After he'd finished, the human forced his gaze from his face, immediately noted the swelling, the scars. "Did you fight back?" he asked, a tremor in his voice.

"Of course I did! Every time! But he's nearly an adult, and I haven't even started my grombit yet."

"Do the other younglings beat you?"

"No."

"What about the instructors?"

"No. They punish me for not having started my grombit, but I deserve that."

"Brohdan, you deserve no such thing! Nobody should be punished for things they can't control."

Brohdan silently nodded, then abruptly stopped. "How did you know my name?"

The small human smiled. "I'm surprised how much you've grown."

Brohdan cocked his head. "Who are you?"

"I'm sorry, I've forgotten my manners. My name is Belkidar. I first saw you when you were ten. You were so small, but now you must be nine elads long!" He went to a nearby tree, sat in its shade. "Since then, I've kept an eye on you, and do you know what I learned? That you dreaded your grombit. Most can't wait to become adults, but you're different. If I didn't know better, I'd guess you were frightened."

"Frightened?" he snorted. "Why would I be afraid of learning to fly, or breathe fire?"

"No, not afraid of learning those – afraid of what you might learn about *yourself*."

Brohdan was speechless. He wasn't afraid of anything, even Limbrin. "That's not true, Belkidar. Staying a youngling is the last thing I want."

"I know, Brohdan. But sometimes what you want conflicts with what you're ready for. I promise, when you're truly ready, your grombit will begin. And whether you know it or not, it will include challenges few dragons ever have to face."

"I don't understand. My grombit will be no different than Methren's. Or Albrogu's."

"If that were true, you would've already started it, and Limbrin would treat you with respect. Brohdan, your fate lies along a much different path than theirs. Your grombit will begin when you're ready. And once it does, your work will have just begun."

"What do you mean?" But he was gone. Brohdan searched for him in the trees surrounding the river bank, but he was nowhere to be found. Then he noticed a small parchment on the ground next to where he'd sat. He carefully lifted it with his wing hooks and read the message Belkidar had left him.

Over the course of your grombit, you will be
confronted with many challenges. Much of what you
endure will be disappointing, and there will be times
when you will wish you had never begun.

*You will experience many events that will surpass
your wildest imagination. Strive for patience and
determination, for they will see you to the end. Only
near the end will you understand.*

Your friend

Something deep inside him disliked anybody who would call
himself 'your friend' before he even had a chance to know the person.
But then he realized that although he didn't know Belkidar, it was
becoming obvious that Belkidar *did* know him.

Interrupted by the protesting grumbles of his stomach, Brohdan
made his way downstream to a deeper part of the river. After eating
several fish, he returned to the river bank and considered the day's
events. If that strange old man was correct, he'd eventually begin his
grombit, hopefully sooner rather than later. But that reprieve would
only lead to more challenges, challenges that most never had to face.

Finding no answers, he reluctantly turned and made his way back
to his instructors, anxious with what his future might entail.

Chapter 3
Revelations

Sow a thought and you reap an act;
Sow an act and you reap a habit;
Sow a habit and you reap a character;
Sow a character and you reap a destiny.

Ralph Waldo Emerson

Despite what Belkidar told him, Brohdan's time in the Sichundars didn't improve. His instructors were just as frustrated with his lack of progress, and Limbrin's actions did little to help.

"Instructor Dorumir expects me to graduate in a few days," Limbrin declared as they took their midday break in the commons area.

"What does that involve?" Albrogu asked.

"I'm not sure. Some sort of test, I think."

"Instructor Loryck said it's nothing," Methren explained. "It's just a confirmation of your adult skills. No dragon has ever failed it."

"I know somebody who can fail any test," Limbrin said with a sneer.

Brohdan ignored him, instead headed for the fire pits to make sure they were stocked with fresh tree trunks for their afternoon training sessions.

"Where are you going?" Limbrin asked, taking flight. "Did I hurt your feelings?" He landed in front of Brohdan, blocking his path.

Brohdan forced himself to remain calm, veered to his left to avoid a collision.

Limbrin whipped his tail, striking Brohdan hard on the left side of his head, the impact echoing from the nearby cliffs. "Look at me when I talk to you!"

Something in Brohdan snapped. He'd always treated others with respect, regardless of whether they were Klonduvian Reds, Dalluvian

Greens, Gorduvian Golds, or – even though he had never seen one before – a Broglia Black. But now, after five mooncycles of constant bullying, Brohdan reached the limit of his patience, experienced a fury that he'd never before known.

Brohdan launched himself at Limbrin. Before he could react, Brohdan knocked him backward and landed on his chest, pinning the larger dragon to the ground. Then he lunged to sink his long, sharp teeth into the base of the Gorduvian's neck.

Limbrin laughed before rolling to his left, throwing Brohdan off balance. He immediately regained his feet, but the Gorduvian was ready. He swept Brohdan's legs with his tail, then fled into the air, spraying the younger dragon with acid. "That was impressive, youngling! With more practice, you may actually scare a human!"

Brohdan reeled from the fumes, clamped his eyes closed, raised his long neck to free himself from the excruciating acid. Limbrin landed next to him, and while still blinded, sank his teeth deep into Brohdan's neck. Blood flowed from the wound, drenching the green grass of the commons area. Suppressing a roar, Brohdan took a step back, attacked blindly with his wing hooks.

Limbrin still held Brohdan's neck in his jaws, partially blocking his view, but Brohdan couldn't see either. His left wing hook glanced off Limbrin's chest, opening a small wound. His right struck Limbrin solidly below his ribcage, knocking the air from his lungs, causing him to release his jaws.

Brohdan didn't waste the opportunity. He swung around, whipping his tail. Limbrin jumped high into the air, his wings preserving the momentum of his leap, Brohdan's tail swinging harmlessly below.

"What's going on here?" Dorumir asked, returning from a meeting with the other instructors.

"Brohdan tried to hit me with his tail!" Limbrin said, landing beyond Brohdan's reach.

"And I'm sure it was unprovoked. Limbrin, you still owe me five laps." He turned to Brohdan, his neck bleeding from Limbrin's attack. "Make it ten," he added, not taking his eyes off Brohdan.

Limbrin mumbled something under his breath, gave Brohdan a seething look as he flew away. The Klonduvians left hastily toward the fire pits.

Dorumir said nothing for several drus. When he finally spoke, frustration was evident in his voice, but Brohdan couldn't determine if it was the result of Limbrin's malice or his own ineptitude. "I've discussed your situation – at length – with the other instructors. We're at a loss. You've received proper instruction, and you're of age. The only possible reason for your incompetence is a lack of motivation. We are therefore forced to provide that on your behalf."

Brohdan met his instructor's eyes, said nothing.

"Henceforth, you shall practice your grombit skills in front of the instructors, as well as your peers. You will succeed or fail in public."

Brohdan's face remained impassive, his irritation boiling just below the surface.

"We'll begin tomorrow at sunrise. In the meantime, I suggest you make whatever preparations you can." Dorumir took off and headed toward where Albrogu and Methren practiced their fire-breathing.

Brohdan was stunned more than enraged. After how hard he'd tried – how hard he'd *fought* – how could his instructors still believe he lacked the dedication needed to start his grombit?

He made his way back to the river, but the journey only increased his frustration. His instructors jumped to the only conclusion that took the burden off of their responsibilities. He wasn't the grombit expert, they were! At least they were supposed to be, yet they offered him no constructive solutions, only public humiliation.

Before he knew it, he found himself standing where he'd last seen Belkidar. He paused there, recalling their brief conversation.

"I promise, when you're truly ready, your grombit will begin."

What did Belkidar mean? He *was* ready – he'd never wanted anything so badly in his life!

More of his words came to him.

But sometimes what you want conflicts with what you're ready for."

Brohdan *wanted* to start his grombit, but Belkidar implied he wasn't *ready* to start it yet. But what dragon truly is? He'd heard how Methren and Albrogu had failed miserably when they first began, yet they improved with practice, as all do.

"And whether you know it or not, it will include challenges few dragons ever have to face."

Suddenly, things became a little clearer. Brohdan had no idea what challenges Belkidar referred to, but whatever they were, he must still lack the skills to overcome them. But more importantly, these challenges were unique, ones that few dragons ever had to face. Knowing this made him feel a little better, because they'd likely prevent any dragon from starting his grombit, not just him.

What failed to comfort him was the solution that still evaded him. What must he do to prepare himself? As Instructor Dorumir stated, Brohdan had received adequate training, and he was old enough. And he knew himself to be dedicated beyond measure, despite what others assumed. So what was he missing?

Nothing came to him. As far as he could tell, he had everything he needed to begin. And yet he somehow didn't.

It was dark by the time he left the river. The others were already in their caves, and Brohdan was relieved to find the camp quiet. He entered his dwelling and laid on the cool stone floor. Closing his eyes, he hoped for sleep, but his thoughts had a different agenda, reliving the past five mooncycles he'd spent in camp. The failures. The helplessness. The humiliation and frustration. The loneliness. Despite Belkidar's wishes, Brohdan hated himself for his futility.

No, that wasn't true. He didn't hate himself, because he knew he gave everything he had to succeed. If he tried his best, he knew he could live with the consequences, regardless of what they may be. He only hoped those consequences wouldn't bring shame to his parents.

Brohdan woke before the others. When Limbrin, Methren, and Albrogu emerged from their caves a quarter link before dawn, Brohdan was already waiting for them at the center of camp. Instructors Dorumir, Loryck, and Rossing arrived shortly thereafter. All save the Chief Instructor took a seat just inside of the trees that encircled the commons area.

"Are you ready?" Dorumir asked as he approached Brohdan.

Limbrin snickered but otherwise remained silent.

Brohdan nodded. He still didn't know what prevented him from starting his grombit, but all he could do was keep trying.

"Very well. As you've been taught, breathing fire is the simplest adult skill you'll eventually learn. Flying takes much more practice, so we'll keep it simple. Do you see the target Instructor Rossing placed there?" he asked, using his left wing to point toward a tree trunk standing on its end several elads away.

Brohdan nodded.

"Burn it."

Brohdan turned toward it. He knew what he was supposed to do. Like all fire-breathers, glands in the back of his throat produced a thick, flammable liquid. Powerful muscles sprayed it toward the front of his mouth, and four igniters, one located behind each row of dagger-like teeth, lit the fuel as he exhaled to accelerate the flames toward his target.

Brohdan opened his jaws and exhaled as he flexed the muscles of his fuel glands.

Nothing happened.

He relaxed and tried again, desperately imploring his body to comply.

Again, nothing.

Limbrin initially giggled at his futility, but as Brohdan's struggles continued, his snickers evolved into unconstrained laughter.

The instructors said nothing, offering neither assistance nor judgment. They simply watched as Brohdan failed.

After several drus, Brohdan stopped. Limbrin's constant laughter rang in his ears, enraging him. He was trying his best, yet nobody offered advice. If they weren't mocking him, they were ignoring him.

Brohdan tried to suppress his fury with logic. He knew their opinions made no difference. The only things that mattered were his opinion of himself and the respect of his loved ones. *His* belief in his own character was what was important, not others' *estimations* of it. True, he hoped his loved ones respected him, because they wanted what was best for him. But Limbrin? Why should he care if he questioned him? It certainly didn't make him a better dragon, and he knew unquestionably that his integrity was beyond reproach.

Limbrin's laughter stopped abruptly as a strange rhythmic sound permeated the camp. Brohdan glanced at Limbrin and was surprised by his terrified expression. Methren and Albrogu appeared just as frightened, and all three were awkwardly backpedaling away from him. Still facing the three younglings, Brohdan turned his head toward the instructors. Though less alarmed, they were obviously stunned by the same thing that had frightened the others.

Brohdan suddenly realized why. His once useless wings flapped smoothly at his sides as he effortlessly hovered above them, bright orange and yellow flames rising from his mouth. Despite his better judgment, he opened his jaws wide and released a long stream toward Limbrin. The Gorduvian barely jumped out of the way, his terrified high-pitched screech eclipsing the rumble of Brohdan's fire.

"That's enough!" Dorumir called loudly. "You three to the fire pits. Prepare six trunks each. Brohdan, wait for us here while Instructors Loryck, Rossing and I discuss your...breakthrough."

"Yes, Instructor Dorumir," Brohdan managed as he dropped back to the ground.

The three instructors left Brohdan standing in the middle of the camp while they talked near the trees. After several drus of hushed discussion, the trio returned.

"Have you breathed fire before this morning?" Loryck asked.

"No, Instructor."

"Never?"

"No, Instructor Loryck."

"What about flying?" Rossing asked.

"No, Instructor. Never."

The three seemed incapable of speech for several drus before Dorumir broke the silence. "Do you expect us to believe that, after all your struggles over the past five mooncycles, you suddenly know how to breathe fire and fly? All without practice?"

It was now Brohdan who was speechless. The only other possibility was that he preferred embarrassment, bullying, and ridicule. "That is *exactly* what I expect you to believe," he managed through clenched teeth.

Several drus passed while Brohdan's instructors considered the possibilities.

"It's possible," Dorumir eventually said to no one in particular. "Instructors Rossing and Loryck, come with me. We have much to discuss." The three hurriedly departed, leaving Brohdan alone in the middle of the camp.

Brohdan was ecstatic. Not wanting to forget how, he again opened his jaws. He tasted the thick, pungent fuel squirt from the glands in the back of his throat, sensed the heat surge through his mouth as the igniters set the fuel aflame, and spewed a wide column of fire toward the tree trunk. Nodding to himself, Brohdan turned and attempted flight.

He flapped his wings and rose unsteadily from the ground. He hovered five elads above the commons area, carefully adjusting for changes in the wind. He slowly spun around so that he faced the burned target. Spinning the opposite way, he leaned forward and flew the length of the small field. Although not moving very fast, the sensation thrilled him. He was flying! And it wasn't even difficult! If it was this easy, he should've started his grombit mooncycles ago!

And then it came to him. The only difference between his earlier failures and his recent success was his attitude. Ever since he came to camp, Brohdan tried his best to begin his grombit, but he'd always been concerned by what others thought of him. If he was honest with himself, he knew in his heart that it had bothered him when they questioned his motivation. Their perceptions must've somehow affected him. Learning to ignore the judgments of others must've been the last piece he needed to begin.

Well. If he had known it would be that simple... But why aren't other dragons forced to learn such lessons? Surely Methren or Albrogu care what others think of them. Why did these limitations only affect *his* grombit? He carefully flew to his cave and searched the back chamber. After finding Belkidar's parchment, he slowly re-read the human's words.

> *Over the course of your grombit, you will be confronted with many challenges. Much of what you endure will be disappointing, and there will be times when you will wish you had never begun.*
>
> *You will experience many events that will surpass your wildest imagination. Strive for patience and determination, for they will see you to the end. Only near the end will you understand.*
>
> *Your friend*

Brohdan then recalled Belkidar's insinuation that his grombit would be different, that he'd face more challenges than other dragons.

Of course! *That's* why his grombit was affected by things other dragons never had to consider! Even Limbrin never had to worry about how other dragons' perceptions affected him. This had to be one of the obstacles Belkidar had alluded to.

Feeling infinitely better, Brohdan left his cave and flew – flew! – to his favorite place in the Sichundars. He landed on the river bank and searched for fish. The more he thought about what Belkidar told him, the more confident he became.

Yet one detail still eluded him – why was his grombit different than everyone else's? What made *him* different? More of Belkidar's words came to him:

"Brohdan, your fate lies along a much different path than theirs. Your grombit will begin when you're ready. And once it does, your work will have just begun."

So far, Belkidar's explanations, although cryptic, had proven accurate. Trusting in his wisdom, Brohdan returned to the commons area, eager to begin his first real training session. He arrived to find the grounds empty. The instructors were nowhere to be found and, judging by the smoke rising from the fire pits, his peers were practicing fire-breathing.

Brohdan's frustration grew, but he didn't have long to wait. Loryck and Rossing landed a few elads away, concerned expressions written on their faces.

"Where is Instructor Dorumir?"

"He had urgent business in Sul Brul," Rossing answered curtly. "With luck, he'll return in four or five days."

Brohdan knew better than to question her, so he dropped the subject.

"I see you've improved already," Loryck commented, nodding to the burnt wooden target.

"I believe so, Instructor Loryck."

"I'm pleased, Brohdan. Although we all wished for an earlier start to your grombit, I see we have much to work with."

"Thank you." Brohdan had no idea why his instructors were being so uncharacteristically pleasant with him, but he certainly didn't intend to ruin a good thing.

Loryck remained with Brohdan and began teaching him the basics of flight. Rossing went to the fire pits and instructed the other three dragons. After several links, the students switched locations, and Brohdan learned fire-breathing fundamentals from Rossing.

Four days passed. The instructors paired Brohdan with Methren, while Limbrin practiced with Albrogu. Although he never had an opportunity to compare his progress against the latter dragons, he grew pleased with how well his skills measured up against Methren's.

Methren had been in camp for nearly nine mooncycles, so his grombit was likely nearing completion. Brohdan, on the other hand, had been in his grombit all of five days. Yet Brohdan's adult skills seemed to come naturally to him, so much so that he'd matched Methren's after the third day. His progress did nothing for his ego; that fateful lesson that unlocked his grombit would always be with him. He wanted only to build on each of his successes.

During their breaks, all four younglings ate and rested together. Limbrin no longer mocked him; in fact, he generally avoided him altogether. Methren acted normal when it was just the two of them, but he was more withdrawn when Limbrin was around.

Brohdan didn't care. He would've liked to call them friends, but he was too busy with his grombit to concern himself with their childishness. He occasionally felt an urge to avenge the way Limbrin had treated him over these past five mooncycles, but his better judgment always prevailed.

Brohdan made sure to heed the advice of his two instructors, and they seemed pleased with his improvement. Despite his workload, Brohdan frequently wondered why Dorumir had gone to Sul Brul. It was a strange decision considering the Lukvian camp now had an additional youngling to instruct, but he trusted Dorumir's business was important enough to warrant his absence.

Chapter 4
Krepli

*There are two kinds of teachers: the kind that fill you
with so much quail shot that you can't move, and the
kind that just gives you a little prod behind and you
jump to the skies.*

Robert Frost

Dorumir returned from Sul Brul late in the morning on the fifth day
after Brohdan had entered his grombit. Another Gorduvian
accompanied him, and together they landed gracefully in the center of
camp. Their arrival triggered an early midday break, the four
younglings and two instructors greeting them shortly after landing.

"Welcome back, Instructor Dorumir."

"Thank you, Instructor Loryck. It's good to be back." He turned
to address all of the dragons at the camp. "May I present Master
Krepli, Sul Brul's Chief Instructor."

This news silenced the entire camp. Sul Brul was the largest
dragon community in Drulop, and Master Krepli was known to every
pack. He was renowned for his teaching abilities, and it was even
rumored that he was instructed by Chuvous, the personal tutor to
Balthasar, the world's last Broglia Black who died just over one
hundred cycles ago.

Dorumir turned toward his guest. "Master Krepli would like to
address you."

The old instructor stepped forward. He slowly regarded each of
the dragons, his expression unchanging as his eyes passed over student
and instructor alike. Finally, in a deep, gravelly voice, he spoke. "All
younglings save Brohdan may return to your packs. Immediately," he
added before turning to Dorumir. "We'll begin this afternoon." With
that, he turned and headed for the largest cave in the nearby cliffs.

The seven remaining dragons stood there, shocked.

"What does he mean?" Limbrin asked. "We're not finished with our training yet! And why does Brohdan get to stay? He only started his grombit a few days ago!"

Dorumir sighed. "Limbrin, you heard Master Krepli. And he did say immediately."

Limbrin's anger was palpable, but he managed to depart without making a scene. Albrogu and Methren looked uncertainly at their instructors. After a few drus, they too left, heading back to their homes.

"Brohdan, you've got a few links before we begin this afternoon. Don't be late," Dorumir added, glancing toward the cave now inhabited by Krepli.

Brohdan nodded before flying to the river. He landed among the shadows of the enormous trees, laid on the cool riverbank and considered the morning's events. Dorumir approached Krepli only after Brohdan had entered his grombit, and sending the others home confirmed that the old instructor was here specifically to help with his training. But judging by the reactions on his instructors' faces, nobody expected the other students to be dismissed.

He wondered if outside help was really needed. Surely he could make up for lost time, especially considering the progress he'd made over the past five days, most of which took place during Dorumir's absence.

Then he reminded himself of the lesson that triggered his grombit. Although it was becoming simple to ignore the judgments of his peers, it wasn't so easy with his instructors.

Putting his ego aside, the possibility of learning from such a renowned instructor intrigued him. If the stories were true, Chuvous tutored Krepli as an instructor, and Chuvous had taught Balthasar, a Broglia Black! He could think of no higher honor.

Brohdan made up his mind. He would try his best regardless, he only hoped it would be enough to please his instructors, whomever they may be.

He returned to the commons area just in time to see the four instructors returning from their midday meal.

"I'll work with Brohdan alone this afternoon," Krepli began. "Please continue his preparations for the coming mooncycles."

Brohdan watched them leave, then turned to his new instructor

"Hello, Brohdan. I'm Krepli."

"It's a pleasure to meet you, Instructor Krepli."

"Likewise, Brohdan. I think there may be much to learn, for us both. Where would you like to begin?"

His question seemed strange to Brohdan; it was the first time he'd been asked to evaluate his own progress. "Instructor Krepli, I'd like to be a stronger flier."

"Very good, but please call me Krepli when the other instructors aren't around. I don't wish to be a poor influence, but I find the formal traditions tiring. And we may be together for quite some time."

That surprised him, and he nodded uneasily. With the rate he'd been progressing, he'd surely complete his grombit in half a cycle, not *that* long considering the grombits of most dragons.

They worked on flying techniques, concentrating first on hovering. He did well near the ground, but wasn't able to repeat that success when he tried it higher in the air.

"Don't worry, Brohdan, you'll get there. Hovering is much easier near the ground, because whether you know it or not, the ground itself helps you. But when you're higher, you no longer have that advantage, so you must compensate with strength and stamina. Those will come with practice."

Brohdan spent four more links training with Krepli, and he was relieved when he saw the other three instructors return. He was exhausted, but he didn't miss the brief eye contact that passed between Dorumir and Krepli.

"Brohdan, take a half link to regain your strength."

"Yes, Instructor Krepli."

Brohdan took off and flew to the river. He drank from the bank and laid on the cool grass, curious how their discussions would affect his grombit. He liked his new instructor, despite how hard he worked him. He was stern, but respectful.

Not wanting to be late, Brohdan returned to the commons area. The break was well-timed; he needed the rest, and now he felt ready for more links of hard work.

When he arrived, he noticed the instructors deep in conversation near the trees that surrounded the commons area. Not wanting to disturb them, he landed quietly in the center of camp. He waited there, awkwardly, stuck between wishing to neither interrupt nor eavesdrop. He was successful in the former, but failed somewhat in the latter.

"But we're still not sure," Dorumir said in hushed tones.

"I'm fairly certain," Krepli answered. "He's different, surely you see that."

"Of course, Master Krepli. I've witnessed his awkwardness for five mooncycles now. But what if we're rushing to the wrong conclusion? I don't wish to disturb Dre for a fool's errand."

"I appreciate your concerns. And don't worry about Dre, he's an old friend."

"Are you sure now's the time?" Rossing asked. "You've only spent half a day with him."

"I've seen enough. And we must act swiftly, before it's too late."

Dorumir nodded. "Very well. I'll find Dre."

"No, but thank you. It'd be more appropriate for me to meet with him."

As Krepli spread his wings, Brohdan quickly turned away. He felt ashamed for listening to their conversation, but at the moment his primary concern was Dre. Who was he, and why did Krepli seek his opinion?

"Oh, there you are," Dorumir said as he approached the commons area. "How long have you been here?"

"Only a few drus, Instructor Dorumir. I finished my break, and I'm ready for more training."

"Very good, Brohdan. Please meet Instructor Rossing in the pits."

"Is Instructor Krepli joining us? I assumed he had more flying exercises for me."

"No, Instructor Krepli has other business to attend."

Brohdan nodded. Rossing took flight, and Brohdan followed her to the fire pits. She was a very good teacher, but his thoughts kept returning to Krepli and his purpose for needing yet another opinion.

"Brohdan, you must focus your fire into a tighter stream! When you keep it wide like that, you lose much of the heat. Try again."

The tedious session finally ended, and Brohdan ate two deer before returning to his cave. His quick progress energized him, even his exhaustion failed to dampen his enthusiasm. But he was becoming increasing preoccupied with his instructors' concerns. He vowed to talk with Krepli about it as soon as he returned.

Brohdan was the first to wake. He flew to the river, drank, and steadied his resolve. Then he returned to the commons area just as the sun emerged above the eastern horizon. Krepli was the only one there to greet him.

"Good morning, Brohdan."

"Good morning, Krepli. I'd like to talk to you about my grombit."

"I'm afraid that'll have to wait. I want you to fly to a large cave on the southern edge of the Sichundars. A friend of mine lives there, and he wants to talk to you this morning."

"Of course."

"His name is Dre. I wanted to bring him here last night, but he's quite old and prefers his solitude. It's very important you see him."

Brohdan nodded. After receiving more detailed instructions, he took off and headed south. A little more than a link later, he reached the foothills of the southern Sichundar range and began searching for

Dre's cave. He immediately realized the difficulty with flying over such rugged landscape, having to constantly make tiny adjustments to keep himself headed where he wanted. Before long, though, it became second nature, allowing him to focus his attention on finding Dre's cave.

The view was incredible. Patches of snow lined the tops of the taller mountains and blanketed areas in perpetual shadow. Despite his altitude, he detected the scent of pine, the brisk air numbing his nose. A few hundred elads below and to his right, he watched a gray wolf crouch in tall grass, waiting to pounce on an unsuspecting rabbit. Directly below him, he saw the tiny twitches of dragonflies as they danced along the surface of a mountain lake.

He discovered many smaller caves, then finally spotted one that was large enough for a dragon. He swooped down, folding his wings along his back to increase his speed. As he neared the ground, he leaned back and flapped his wings downward to control his descent and forward to decrease his speed. With a few more strokes, he touched down, remaining upright as he peered inside.

At first, he saw nothing, but then two golden eyes returned his gaze from the darkness. He took a few steps back as he leaned forward onto his wing hooks.

"You must be Brohdan," the owner of the eyes asked as they slowly emerged from the darkness.

Brohdan immediately realized that Dre was indeed quite elderly. The Gorduvian's scales were unusually pale, appearing more yellow than gold. He moved slowly, savoring the warmth of the morning sun. Yet as he regarded him, Brohdan perceived a profound wisdom, an aura that spoke to untold experience lying just behind those golden eyes.

"Good morning. Master Krepli sent me."

"Yes, he had some questions and wanted a second opinion. Tell me about your grombit," Dre asked as he sat with his back toward the sunlight.

"How much do you know?"

"Only what Krepli told me, but I prefer to hear about a dragon's life from the dragon himself."

Brohdan nodded. So far, he liked Dre. "I took a long time to start my grombit, much longer than I would've liked. It wasn't a pleasant time," he added softly.

"I understand. But you did start your grombit, just recently from what I understand."

"Six days ago."

"Six days ago! And you flew here? Over these mountains?"

"Yes, sir."

"If I didn't know better, I'd say you started your grombit over a half cycle ago."

Brohdan remained silent; he had always felt uncomfortable when complimented.

"And from what I hear," Dre continued, filling the silence, "breathing fire wasn't too difficult either. How did it happen – starting your grombit I mean?"

"Another youngling at camp mocked me, thinking I humiliated our pack. I was frustrated, bitter – but that forced me to realize that I really didn't care what they thought of me anymore. Then, before I knew it, I was hovering and breathing fire at him."

"You *hovered*? Before you even flew?"

"Yes, sir."

"And you breathed fire?" he asked, still puzzled.

"Yes, sir."

"That's enough of those 'sirs' if you don't mind. Call me Dre. That's my name, after all."

Brohdan nodded, suppressing a smile.

"Anything else about your grombit that you'd consider strange?"

"Not really. Well, maybe. While searching for your cave, I saw things I normally wouldn't have noticed before."

"Like what?"

He described the prowling wolf and dancing dragonflies. "It seemed like I could make out details better up there than I ever could on the ground. But I've never flown so high before, so I assumed I just wasn't used to it."

Dre was deep in thought. He rose, began pacing. "I suppose it *could* be," he muttered, turning and retracing the steps he'd just taken. "I mean, the timing is just about right. But of all the grombit camps, what are the odds it would happen here?"

Brohdan became uncomfortable.

Dre stared at him intently, and Brohdan felt he was looking *through* him rather than merely *at* him. "Are you clumsy?"

"I, uh, suppose."

Dre retreated back into his thoughts, renewing Brohdan's anxiety.

"I believe there's a very simple reason for that. Your body thinks it's larger than it actually is. At least, larger than it is right now."

"Well, that's understandable, isn't it? Every dragon has some growing to do when he enters his grombit."

"That's true, but if I'm right, you've got substantially *more* growing to do."

Brohdan immediately thought of Belkidar's insinuation that he would face challenges other dragons never had to consider. "It may be true that I'm a bit small for my age," he offered weakly.

"You don't understand," Dre sighed. "Have you ever heard of Balthasar?"

"Of course. Everyone has. He was the last Broglia Black."

"That's right. There have never been two Broglias alive at the same time. Usually, a centacycle separates the death of the last Broglia with the birth of the next." Dre's ancient eyes bored into Brohdan's young ones. "Balthasar died just over one hundred cycles ago. He lived to be eight hundred eighty-four. He was the wisest dragon I've ever known."

Brohdan's eyes grew wide. "You knew him?"

He nodded. "I worked for the Chief Dragon at the time, and we often had need to talk with Balthasar. Broglia Blacks are the wisest of us, after all. Most creatures believe the Chief Dragon is the most influential dragon in the world, but if there's a Broglia alive, the Chief

Dragon takes a very distant second. If he knows what's good for him, that is," he added with a chuckle. Then his expression turned sad. "It really is a shame he died so young."

"Who? The Chief Dragon?"

"No, of course not. Balthasar!"

"Young? I've never heard of any dragon living that long. Not even you!"

"Yes, but he was a Broglia Black. They usually live twelve hundred cycles or more."

Brohdan stared at Dre, blinking frequently as he considered the life of a Broglia. "That's a long time."

"Yes, it is, but there are other creatures whose lifespans dwarf that."

Brohdan considered that as Dre continued.

"Balthasar endured a very difficult grombit, just as all Broglias must. My father was an adolescent friend of his, and later I too became friends with that incredible dragon. Piecing together what they explained to me, I think I have a pretty good idea what a Broglia's grombit is like, especially in how they differ from those of lesser dragons. Simply put, Broglias have much more to learn. For instance, they must learn to use their barz, a weapon at the tip of their tail. They're quite large when fully developed, about the size of a lesser dragon's head. A single blade will grow from the bone inside, but it's much harder than bone, and not nearly as brittle. In fact, a Broglia's blade is said to be indestructible."

"What does it look like?"

"Oh, it's flat, measuring just over an elad at the base and extending nearly three elads from the barz. It has two sharp edges that never dull. Once fully formed, it'll automatically extend from the tip of the barz, slicing it open from the inside. After it heals, a Broglia can extend or retract the blade whenever he wants. The barz itself becomes very hard, allowing a Broglia to wield it like a club. But with the blade extended, it becomes considerably more effective, as I'm sure you can imagine."

Brohdan nodded, considering how such a weapon could be used in battle.

"Broglia Blacks are also immune to all sorcery. In fact, they even have the ability to *cast* a few spells."

That surprised Brohdan. "I never knew that."

"Not many do. Learning how to resist magic is rather simple – once that ability matures during grombit, it's yours forever. The same is true for Broglias, but they resist all types of harmful sorcery."

"Harmful sorcery? Is there any other kind?"

"Of course. Incantations, or cants, are offensive spells, wards are defensive, but most are neither." He laughed. "Everyone hears stories about these tiny human sorcerers lighting each other on fire, but most spells are just the opposite. Some make a sorcerer's life a little more comfortable, others heal wounds that can't be treated any other way."

Brohdan instantly recalled his first encounter with Belkidar and how easily he'd healed his broken leg. Interesting.

"But *casting* spells is completely different than *resisting* them. A region of the brain must develop first, and for dragons, only Broglias gain that ability. Despite that, sorcery doesn't come naturally to them. In fact, it took three full cycles before Balthasar felt comfortable using sorcery."

"Can I interrupt you?" Brohdan asked, looking confused.

"Obviously."

Brohdan continued, oblivious. "Why are you telling me about a Broglia's grombit? I'm a Dalluvian Green. Krepli wanted me to talk to you about *my* grombit."

Dre stared at him. "Have you ever heard stories about a Broglia Black youngling?"

"No," Brohdan admitted.

"That's because they don't exist. Since the beginning of time, Broglias have always been born as one of the three lesser dragons, probably so they can always relate to those they lead. When a young Broglia enters his grombit, he enters a metamorphosis. His scales slowly change color, and horns emerge from his head. And a Broglia begins to grow. And grow. When his grombit's over, a Broglia will be completely black and typically three times the size of lesser dragons."

A look of terror suddenly crossed Brohdan's face. "You can't be serious."

"Actually, I'm quite serious, but there's no way to prove it. We'll just have to wait and see if we're right," Dre explained with a calmness that terrified Brohdan all the more.

"But – I mean – if I *were* a Broglia Black, I think I'd know it!"

"Not necessarily. It all fits together, you know. You're clumsy from time to time because, even if your mind doesn't know it yet, your body understands it's supposed to be much larger than it is."

Brohdan looked helplessly at the old dragon as he continued.

"Your eyesight is already becoming more acute. That's another Broglia trait – incredibly unique eyesight. Did I tell you the story about when I was flying with Balthasar and he saw a beautiful young female just when she... Well, maybe later I suppose."

"So, I have good eyesight and I'm clumsy. That doesn't prove that I'm a Broglia!"

"No, it doesn't. I have proof of nothing. Then again, how do you explain how easily you learned to breathe fire and fly? And hover?"

"I don't know. Maybe I'm just talented in those particular areas."

"Right. A dragon who's admittedly been clumsy his whole life just happens to be extremely talented when it comes to flying?" Dre asked as he got up and slowly walked to a nearby boulder.

Brohdan watched as he leaned back and stretched against the huge rock. "I'm feeling every bit of my seven hundred cycles this morning. That cave is just a little too damp for these aching bones. It might be time to find a warmer one."

Brohdan didn't hear a word as he tried to digest everything he'd heard, but he couldn't think of another explanation. "If I *am* a Broglia – which I'm not saying I am – but *if* I am, when will I know?"

"That all depends on you, Brohdan. You probably could've started this grombit of yours mooncycles ago."

A chill traveled down Brohdan's spine. "What do you mean?" he asked nervously, remembering what he'd learned on the morning of his public training session.

"A Broglia, just like any dragon, must be physically mature before beginning his grombit. This occurs sometime in the first three mooncycles of a dragon's fifty-first cycle, as you already know. When a lesser dragon reaches that state of maturity, he simply enters his grombit, but when a Broglia reaches that same point, his grombit doesn't automatically begin. A Broglia's grombit is much more demanding, so he must not only prove ready physically, but mentally as well. Nothing can interfere with a Broglia's grombit – our entire species depends on it. Not until a he's completely prepared will he enter this final stage of maturation, even if lesser dragons of lesser maturity have already begun theirs. I suspect you've been physically capable for a while, Brohdan, but you may not have been mentally ready for the challenges ahead. That alone is an important lesson."

Brohdan looked into Dre's eyes and immediately understood. "I realized the same thing the morning I entered my grombit."

"Good, then you're on the right path. A Broglia Black is fundamentally a leader. He *must* be. There lives only one in the world at any given time, and all other dragons look up to him. Never sacrifice your instincts for the ignorance of others. Good leaders are not always liked, but they're always respected. Remember that."

"I understand," Brohdan said softly. "It's not easy though."

"That's got nothing to do with it."

"Is this why Krepli wanted us to talk? To get your opinion on whether I'm the next Broglia or not?"

"Yes. Krepli is an old friend, and he's an outstanding teacher. You couldn't have found a better tutor."

Brohdan felt embarrassed. He remembered eavesdropping on his instructors' conversation, yet they were only trying to help him. "Thank you, Dre. You've given me a lot to think about."

"You're welcome, Brohdan. It was truly an honor to meet you," he said, bowing.

Brohdan became immediately uncomfortable. After their farewells, he spread his wings and took flight. As he climbed into the sky, he considered the likelihood of Dre's prediction. He didn't know enough to agree or disagree with him, so he simply accepted the possibility that he may be the next Broglia Black dragon. With more questions than answers, he approached the center of camp and landed lightly on the grass. Krepli was there, waiting for him.

"What do you think?" his instructor asked.

"I think Dre is unique."

Krepli laughed. "That he is, but he's also wise."

"Do you think I may be a Broglia?" Even the word was difficult for Brohdan to say aloud.

"Yes, I do, Brohdan. That's why we have these grombit camps, after all. We recognized long ago the difficulties associated with Broglia grombits, so all dragon packs send any younglings that have shown signs of possibly being the next Broglia to these grombit camps. This allows experts to identify as early as possible which of us is destined to become the next Broglia. In doing so, we not only identify the dragon as early as possible, we also begin their grombits with proper instruction from the beginning. This process has proven invaluable, to the instructors, but more importantly to the Broglia himself."

Now Brohdan understood. He wasn't sent to this camp because of his clumsiness! He was sent here because others had seen more in him than he had seen in himself. He instantly remembered his mother's final words to him on the morning of his departure.

"If you struggle during your grombit, don't ever give up. Sometimes, becoming an adult takes longer for some dragons, that's all."

She knew! She knew back then! With a start, Brohdan suddenly came back to the present and realized with some guilt that Krepli was still talking.

"…Chuvous taught me well, and I'm pretty sure I can spot a Broglia youngling when I see one. Now get a midday meal so we can start your training sessions!"

Brohdan left the commons area and went to his favorite spot next to the river. He had a lot to consider, but very little experience to judge it by. His first thoughts went back to his encounter with Belkidar.

"Sometimes what you want conflicts with what you're ready for. I promise, when you're truly ready, your grombit will begin. And whether you know it or not, it will include challenges other dragons never have to consider."

More of Belkidar's words came to him.

"Brohdan, your fate lies along a much different path than theirs. Your grombit will begin when you're ready. And once it does, your work will have just begun."

It all seemed so clear now. Belkidar knew he was a Broglia before he even entered his grombit, long before his instructors suspected it. His parents obviously had suspicions, or he would've never been sent to this grombit camp. Krepli was sure of it, as was Dre.

When Brohdan woke this morning, he thought himself an ordinary Dalluvian Green. As such, the expectations of him – and those he held for himself – were readily attainable. But now he suspected that he'd one day become the leader of all dragons. To his horror, he realized he no longer knew how to meet the expectations that came with this new life. And while he accepted his fate, he didn't know what consequences were tied to it.

Brohdan wanted to find fulfillment in his life, wanted his life to mean something, and he hoped he was ready for the challenges Belkidar already knew lay before him.

Chapter 5
The Staff of Power

*Nearly all men can stand adversity, but if you want to
test a man's character, give him power.*

Abraham Lincoln

Brohdan's grombit continued, albeit under much different circumstances. Krepli tailored his instruction to a Broglia's adult skill set instead of a Dalluvian's, and his first day proved exhausting. Krepli's training routines consisted of several exercises, none of which Brohdan had expected. He spent several links hovering, then flew laps around the camp for what seemed like an eternity, all in an effort to improve his strength and stamina. Finally, well after sunset, Krepli allowed his pupil to eat a well-earned meal before getting some much-needed sleep.

Brohdan slept soundly that night, but when he woke, he suddenly realized just how many muscles he had. Each objected loudly as he stood, and by the time he staggered out of his cave, he thought today's lessons should consist of slow walking and long periods of rest.

But that was not his fate. By mid-morning, he grudgingly realized today's lessons would closely mirror those of the previous day. For his midday break, he returned to the river. He landed softly and, as he approached the water to drink, he heard a faint sound from the trees behind him. He stopped and peered over his shoulder. Unable to discover the source of the noise, he slowly turned back to continue drinking.

He nearly jumped out of his green scales. To his astonishment, Belkidar stood next to him.

"Nice work, Brohdan! Very impressive. You've certainly come a long way since the last time I saw you."

"Belkidar! Where have you been?"

"Ssshhh! Not so loud, my friend. I don't want the others to know I'm here."

"Why not?"

"I came to see you alone. How much time do you have before you're to meet Krepli again?"

"Maybe a link or so," he answered, unsurprised by Belkidar's knowledge of his new instructor.

"Good." Belkidar moved away from the river toward the trees. He sat on the ground, his back resting against the trunk of a large pine, his battered walking stick balanced across his lap. The sun crested the bright, blue sky, and although the shadows grew short, plenty of shade remained beneath the thick canopy.

"Brohdan, we have a problem." The old human sighed, his fingers working a spasm in his brow. "Have you ever heard of the Staff of Power?"

"No." Brohdan lowered himself onto his belly, his tail extending into the river's soft current.

"Then I'll start from the beginning. Several thousand cycles ago, the world was very different than the one you know today. The entire populace of Men and beasts lived in harmony. As far as our historians could determine, the world remained that way for many kilacycles. A natural, long-lasting peace linked every tribe, pack, and community of the world, and societies attained heights never before conceived. Composers wrote equaled masterpieces. Doctors discovered cures for countless diseases. Philosophers were free to debate every imaginable subject. Artists created works which, to this day, stir the soul, thousands of cycles later." The old man paused a moment, his eyes staring into the distance. "And sorcerers were free to experiment in wondrous, indescribable realms, bound only by their skill and imagination."

Belkidar paused again, his eyes eventually regaining their focus as they found the dragon. "One of the products of these experiments was the Staff of Power. Jenkar was a very powerful sorcerer, perhaps the most powerful the world has ever seen. Over the course of several hundred cycles, the Staff of Power occupied his every thought. His goal was to create an object powerful enough to cure even the world's most horrible disaster. Indeed, his motives were pure, in the beginning. At long last, Jenkar uncovered three Artifacts and used them to forge his Staff of Power. He was hailed by the entire sorcery community for his astonishing accomplishment, and rightfully so. For a millennium the world lived in absolute peace." Belkidar seemed to be lost in thought for a moment. "It was a very gratifying time."

"Unfortunately, Jenkar's behavior gradually changed. For instance, several representatives came to him, asking to help their communities, only to be turned away. After some time, when too many pleas were ignored, a movement formed to have Jenkar replaced, thus empowering another as caretaker of the Staff of Power. Looking back, that was probably our biggest mistake. Jenkar reasoned that because he'd created it, the Staff of Power was his to use in whatever manner he saw fit. Others viewed it not as a possession, but as a gift to the entire world."

"As the cycles passed, tensions escalated and the situation deteriorated. Several sorcerers disagreed with the way Jenkar wielded the Staff of Power, but he utterly refused to forfeit sole ownership of what was undeniably his creation. And so a vicious cycle ensued: the more he was pressed to relinquish the product of his life's work, the more selfishly he used it. Inevitably, war erupted."

"For the first time in history, the world had finally witnessed global despair. Several million perished. Countless more were maimed, the survivors carrying scars for the rest of their lives. Jenkar, completely mad by this point, promised personal rewards from the Staff of Power to all those who fought on his behalf. He recruited millions, multiplying his forces. Eventually, after two hundred cycles of war, his minions defeated, Jenkar was killed."

"Every species endured incredible casualties. As nearly as I can calculate, the dwarven population was cut in half. The elves fared only slightly better. Humans were hit the hardest, losing over sixty percent. Some of our kind suffered more than others, of course. Jenkar clearly understood the unique threat that sorcerers posed since we were the only creatures who could wield the Staff of Power, so he targeted us from the very beginning. Only three sorcerers survived the War." Belkidar had tears welling in his eyes now. "Krollum, Aelya, and I stood alone in what had recently been a community that numbered in the hundreds. Once a society founded in integrity, in teamwork and discovery, the guild of sorcerers became a fragmented shell of its former self. I lost so many friends…"

"I'm sorry," Brohdan said helplessly.

"Thank you, but there's nothing that can be done. I learned that lesson a very long time ago."

Brohdan considered Belkidar's story, and his eyes grew wide as he considered its implications. "You're over a thousand cycles old!"

"Oh, yes," he chuckled. "Much older than that. Jenkar forged the Staff of Power approximately seven thousand cycles ago. I was born a thousand cycles before that."

Brohdan's astonishment had overwhelmed his ability to speak. He did manage a few strangling sounds, though. "And to think I was impressed to learn that Dre was seven *hundred* cycles old!"

Belkidar laughed. "Good for that old Gorduvian! I haven't seen him in cycles."

"What happened after the War ended?"

Belkidar's smile slowly faded. "Krollum, Aelya and I suddenly found ourselves the world's only experts on the Staff of Power. In reality, though, we were anything but. Krollum's field of study centered on the elements – fire, water, and the like. Aelya concentrated on alchemy. At the time, I was very interested in the body and mind – things like shape-shifting and teleportation. None of us really knew much about the Staff of Power, so the three of us 'experts' held a council to determine our best course of action. In this meeting, we learned as much as we could about the Staff of Power and how it was created. At last, after a very tiring time, we finally settled on our best option."

"In this council, we learned that the Staff of Power somehow altered Jenkar's mind. For reasons we couldn't explain, the Staff changed him, corrupted him somehow, so we agreed on a new goal – to never let that happen again. If Jenkar had succeeded and defeated us in the War, he may very well have ruled forever. On the other hand, we couldn't simply destroy the Staff of Power. First of all, we weren't certain it was even possible to destroy such an Artifact. More importantly, we agreed that we wouldn't destroy something that had proven to be so beneficial. So we eventually decided on a compromise."

"The Staff of Power would survive, but not intact. We carefully disassembled it into its elements: the Headpiece, the Jewel, and the Staff, the three Artifacts Jenkar had used to forge it. Although it was theoretically possible for an extremely powerful sorcerer to reassemble them, it was highly unlikely that any one person would have the ability collect all three pieces, then assemble them unnoticed. We finally left our council chamber and reported our actions to the world."

"Few were pleased; they couldn't imagine a world that no longer included the Staff of Power. After all, those who survived the War – save Krollum, Aelya and I – knew no other way. Dozens of generations passed with the Staff of Power as their companion, and the cure-all they'd grown so dependent upon was suddenly gone. That was true enough, but it was also true that the Staff of Power would never again be the root of another war."

"Each Artifact remained very powerful, but none to the degree of the Staff of Power. In time, we knew the world would learn to live without Jenkar's infamous masterpiece, just as it had prior to its creation."

"Up until several mooncycles ago, the three Artifacts remained carefully secured. We hid the Staff on Tymoteu with me. The Headpiece we left in Krollum's possession who, after the last official gathering of sorcerers, departed to Katja. The Jewel was given to the nomadic kingdoms in Kaarlo. We agreed that by dispersing the three Artifacts, we'd ensure their power would benefit the entire world.

Also, if any unforeseen evil tried to collect them, we knew the distance that separated them would provide the time necessary to mount a defense."

"Time alters realities. One of the drawbacks of immortality is that sometimes you lose perspective of such things. Through the thousands of cycles from the time we dismantled the Staff of Power until only a few cycles ago, I remained ignorant of the events secretly taking place on Katja. I confirmed that Krollum still guarded the Headpiece, but I realized too late that my old friend had changed. He now calls himself Hildegard, and an evil has corrupted him in much the same way it had Jenkar."

Belkidar sighed deeply. "When Krollum, Aelya, and I deliberated after the War, we were convinced that society's proposal to remove the Staff of Power from Jenkar's control was the impetus that turned him toward selfishness and evil. Unfortunately, that premise was incomplete, and our error now appears to have claimed a dear friend. The fact that Krollum has turned proves to me that it was the Headpiece that originally corrupted Jenkar, and now it's done the same to Krollum."

"Riikka was the last of the nomad chiefs to care for the Jewel. He was its one hundred twenty-third caretaker. During that time, the nomadic kingdom had apparently become lax in their guardianship. Hildegard had little difficulty traveling to Kaarlo and slipping unnoticed into Riikka's camp. Before anybody became aware of the theft, Hildegard was presumably halfway back to Katja."

Belkidar's story fascinated Brohdan. "What happened to Aelya?"

The sorcerer's expression suddenly turned from displeasure to regret. "She is no more. Over three thousand cycles ago, she departed on a trip to visit Krollum. We hadn't heard from him for a while and grew concerned." His eyes took on a distant look as he continued.

"The sun had just risen when she left, such a beautiful sunrise. She wore her favorite robes – a simple purple garment with white accents. She kissed me so softly," he explained, his right hand touching his bearded cheek. "I now suspect that, under the enormous burden of the

Headpiece's influence, Krollum had already begun his journey down the path of evil. But at that time, neither of us was even remotely aware of that possibility. I haven't seen her since." Belkidar paused as he stared into the forest.

"I believe she discovered what he'd become," he finally continued, still gazing through the countless trees. "Whatever occurred after she left my side, she was lost. I've never been able to discover what happened to her, but I do know she's no longer with us." A single tear ran down his face, disappeared into his long, white beard.

"You two were friends."

A weak smile. "We were much more than that."

A long silence passed before Brohdan spoke. "What's to become of Hildegard?"

That roused him. "We know he has two of the Artifacts now, but he won't get the third."

"How do you know?"

Belkidar didn't respond, he just sat there, patting the thick walking stick that lay across his lap.

Brohdan looked at it, amazed. "That's the Staff?" he asked, his eyes wide.

Belkidar nodded.

Brohdan stared at the Artifact for several moments. "Why are you telling me this?"

He looked from the Staff to the eyes of his young friend. "If I depart without your help Brohdan, Hildegard will complete what Jenkar could not." Then he smiled. "You have some things to learn yet, but I'll be back to check on your progress. So far, I'd say you're doing quite well."

"Thank you," Brohdan replied automatically, "but I'm not sure I'm worthy of your confidence."

"Don't worry about that, my friend. Just pay attention to your lessons and try to master them as quickly as you can. It'll take me a couple cycles before I can resolve a few issues, so you've got plenty of time." Belkidar paused and looked deeper into his eyes. "If I don't have your help, Brohdan, Hildegard will prevail."

Brohdan returned his gaze, and there was no doubting the sincerity of his words.

"Now, get back to your instructor. I'll see you later." With that, Belkidar shimmered into a familiar white-blue light. An instant later, he was gone.

Brohdan felt gratified that Belkidar thought highly enough of him to need his help, but apprehensive that he may eventually be called upon to fight in battles that would doubtlessly determine the fate of the entire world. As he slowly made his way to Krepli and the training that awaited, he suddenly realized these lessons were critical to much more than his own destiny. With a determination he had never before realized, the Broglia Black sought out his instructor, desperate to maximize the day's remaining sunlight.

Brohdan was never the same after that meeting with Belkidar. Although he had known about human sorcerers, it never occurred to him that they could be so powerful, or so long-lived. It was hard enough believing his own life could span twelve hundred cycles, and now he learned that was only a fraction of a sorcerer's life.

Brohdan had previously paid little attention to the world outside of dragons. In fact, his thoughts rarely roamed beyond his Lukvian pack. But now he realized momentous events were unfolding in the world, a few of which would impact the fate of every civilization whether they knew it or not.

Perhaps the most important result of his conversation with Belkidar was his attitude toward his grombit. His original goal had been to start and finish it, preferably without making a fool of himself. Then, when he learned that he'd be the next Broglia, his goals changed; instead of just getting through his grombit, he wanted to master the skills of a Broglia Black so that he'd be a better leader of dragons. But now he realized he'd be needed for a much larger, more pivotal role. Without his help, Belkidar believed the world would suffer a terrible fate, and so Brohdan elevated his goals yet again. He utterly committed himself to finishing his grombit as early and successfully as possible. He did everything in his power to learn each lesson to its fullest extent so that he'd be prepared when Belkidar returned for him.

Brohdan's newfound dedication wasn't lost on Krepli, and to Brohdan's delight and exhaustion, he redoubled his training workload. The old instructor pushed Brohdan hard, his resulting progress both immediate and drastic.

It took Brohdan the rest of the winter and almost the entire spring to attain the conditioning Krepli desired. Looking back on the training, Brohdan was amazed at what he'd accomplished. He could hover near the ground literally all day if he wanted. He could perform a high hover for many drus at a time with little rest between sets. Now that he was beginning the next step of his grombit, it was all he could do to hold back his excitement.

"Are you going to show me how to use sorcery now?" Brohdan asked early one spring morning.

"No. I told you last cycle that I'd teach you sorcery toward the end of your grombit. And if you prove to have limited capabilities, those lessons will likely last only a few mooncycles."

Krepli led Brohdan to the center of the camp. "Now, as I told you last night, today we start the next phase of your grombit. But your physical conditioning won't just help you during the remainder of your grombit, it'll serve as the foundation for the rest of your life, affecting your well-being more than anything I could ever teach you. Never forget that, Brohdan. To help emphasize that point, we'll start each lesson with conditioning drills. Now, you've got a half-link to fly five laps around camp. I'm going to be watching, so no rounding the corners this time."

Brohdan nodded before taking off and heading south. Five hundred drus wasn't an awfully long time to complete five laps, but he'd previously accomplished it in four hundred fifty, so this would be a good warm-up. As he flew, he wondered what the next phase of lessons would entail. The more he thought about it, the more questions he had.

Brohdan finished with twenty drus to spare and gracefully glided to the field where he'd left Krepli. As he landed, he noticed a group of large logs planted neatly in several rows where there had previously been an empty field. When he touched down, he saw Krepli dragging another log from the forest nearby.

"Don't just stand there, grab that last one and follow me."

"Sure, but why are you dragging it? Why not just fly it over there?"

"In all the mooncycles since you began flying, haven't you never tried to carry anything?"

He thought about that. "No. I couldn't fly when I prepared the fire pits, and since then I've never had the need."

"Well then, go ahead and try," Krepli suggested as he continued dragging the trunk, his wing hooks embedded deep into the wood.

Brohdan flew to the fallen tree, hovered over it, then latched onto it with his talons. Satisfied with his grip, he flapped his wings harder, but before he realized what had happened, he found himself lying face-first, the bark cracked where his head had slammed against it. He stood quickly for fear his instructor would see his clumsiness, then tried again. He was shocked to learn that by trying to lift it, he had an uncontrollable urge to topple forward. He tried to compensate, hovered forward to lift it closer toward the end. He nearly fell forward again, despite the fact that nearly two thirds of the dead tree lay behind him. He finally abandoned the effort, sank his wing hooks into the log, and dragged it to the field.

"What kept you?" It was hard to miss the grin on Krepli's face.

"Why couldn't I lift it?"

"Take a look at me," Krepli said.

"You're a Gorduvian. I've seen several."

"Thanks for noticing. Look at my wings, and compare them to a bird's."

"Your wings are bigger?" Brohdan said uncertainly.

"That's right, but they're also further back. A bird's body is suited for flight, much more so than ours, that's why their wings are so much smaller compared to their body. We need much larger wings to offset our shortcomings."

"Like what?"

"Well, like our long neck and tail. And having scales instead of feathers. And for having our wings further back along our bodies. Our oversized wings are very powerful, they give us the ability to fly fast and accelerate quickly, but they can't offset the disadvantage we have in the delicate balance we're forced to maintain in flight. When you lifted that log, you upset that balance, which is what caused you to land on your face," Krepli said as he pointed to Brohdan's forehead with his right wing. "We can only carry a small burden, and even then, we must fly carefully."

"I never knew that."

"Well, that's why I'm here," he said, walking to the first of a long line of logs whose ends were planted in the ground. "Now, we move on to the next tier in your grombit: fire-breathing. What I have in mind is more...involved...than the fire-breathing you've seen in the pits."

Brohdan sighed, having thought he already knew how to breathe fire.

"As I've stated, your physical condition will largely determine how well you perform in battle. A dragon's second-most important skill is his ability to breathe fire or acid, whichever the case may be. Every dragon gains this ability during his grombit, but it takes considerable skill to employ it effectively."

"A Broglia's fire is different. It burns hotter, much hotter, than other dragon fire, so much so that if he's skilled enough, it can melt iron, or turn sand to glass. But a Broglia's fire is one of the last things to develop, so yours will still resemble a Dalluvian's for a while longer.

That's why we'll concentrate on your fire-breathing now, so that when your Broglia fire develops, you'll be ready."

Krepli shifted his attention to the nearest dead tree. "Let's see what I have to work with. I want a nice, tight stream, aimed halfway up. Try to cut it in half before your breath runs out."

Brohdan didn't even know it was possible to burn a tree in half with just one breath. He hardened his resolve, inhaled, then blew intense flames toward the tree. But it wasn't really doing much damage except singeing the thick bark. He blew harder, narrowed the stream, causing its rumbling to rise in pitch. Now the flames struck the wood more forcefully instead of curving around it as before. Finally, his breath spent, he stopped. As the smoke cleared, Brohdan inspected it, surprised that he hadn't even burned a third of the way through.

"Not bad for your first try, Brohdan, not bad at all. I think you started to get the hang of it toward the end. When you tighten the stream like that, the strength of your attack increases significantly. But it can get much tighter. Watch."

Krepli exhaled, and instead of the familiar orange and red fire that he'd just witnessed, Krepli breathed a stream of pungent, green acid. Though a body length away, Brohdan was forced to take several paces backward to prevent the fumes from burning his eyes and nostrils. About as round as a cow's rib, his acid stream was surprisingly narrow.

Krepli completed his demonstration, then looked back at his pupil. "It's a little easier working with acid, but you should still try to get yours as narrow as mine. You must practice several links each day to get the muscles in your jaw strong enough. Do you understand?"

"Yes," Brohdan managed as he suddenly realized these lessons would prove just as tedious as his conditioning drills.

"Good. Now, you've got two rows of twenty trees here. I'd say you'd better get busy." Krepli watched and offered advice over the course of the next several links. When Brohdan had burned through those, they went in search of more. Well after sunset, red and orange reflections glowed in the forest as they continued long into the darkness.

When they finally finished, Brohdan's mouth was so tired he could barely speak, his slurred words incomprehensible. With the taste of his fuel still fresh in his mouth, food wasn't even slightly appealing. He slowly staggered to the rear chamber of his cave and laid down, almost immediately falling to sleep.

Learning how to properly control his fire took much longer than he'd thought. His training routine generally went unchanged over the course of the next two mooncycles. Each day started with the same thing – conditioning. To his surprise, Brohdan enjoyed it. He was pleased with his endurance, and he loved watching the shadows grow shorter as he hovered high above the ground. He still felt the same freedom when he flew, and he never grew tired of the wind rushing across his scales.

After he completed the conditioning drills, things grew more tedious. Brohdan rummaged through the forest in search of fallen trees, but when they became scarce, Krepli led him to the mountains near his cave and practiced breathing fire against stone. Around midday, he was given a link to eat and rest, but afterward it was more fire-breathing until dusk. Just before he was released from the day's lessons, Brohdan completed a lap around camp to warm up before accomplishing a high hover for as long as his endurance would allow. After that, he ended with three more laps to cool down.

Now deep into summer, Krepli finally showed signs of becoming satisfied with Brohdan's progress. When he was convinced the muscles in Brohdan's mouth had developed sufficiently, Krepli led him back to the forest and had him retrieve one more fallen tree. After driving an end into the ground, Brohdan once again attempted to burn the log in half with a single breath. Because he'd been practicing against stone, he wasn't certain how much he'd improved.

He inhaled deeply and released his fire toward the tree, filling the surrounding area with a low rumble. The stream was very narrow, and

Brohdan exhaled harder as he tried to burn the log in half. With only a third of his breath expended, he was surprised to see the top of the log sway. An instant later, it bolted away, crashed and skidded across the ground.

The surprised expression still remained on Brohdan's face when the smoke finally cleared.

"There just may be hope for you yet," Krepli observed, his smile triumphant.

"I didn't think it'd be that easy!"

"Well, you do realize wood burns much easier than the stone we've been working with, don't you?" Krepli's expression revealed much more than mere joy. He was genuinely proud.

"I'd like to take this opportunity to mention one unique advantage fire-breathing has over acid attacks. Each time you breathed fire during our lessons, you unconsciously adjusted the volume of fuel that your glands released – the harder you exhaled, the more fuel you used. This time, I want you to attack that log," Krepli instructed, nodding toward the portion of the log that still remained, "but keep your stream wide."

Brohdan turned his attention to the charred log and released a wide breath of fire against it, unsurprised by its ineffectiveness.

"Good," Krepli began. "When you keep your stream wide like that, the damage is relatively weak, but with one minor adjustment, you can change that result substantially. I want you to attack the wood again using another wide stream, only this time, consciously increase the amount of fuel you use."

Brohdan nodded and turned back toward the wood. He inhaled deeply and launched a third attack against the log, this time deliberately increasing the volume of fuel that shot from the glands near the back of his throat. After only a few drus, he ceased his attack. There was no need to continue. As the rumble of his fire breath receded into the nearby woods, the crackling of fire persisted. The log that remained embedded into the ground stood ablaze, dense black smoke rising into the clear sky.

"As you can see," Krepli explained, "an attack that uses a wide stream can be very useful. That time, you applied more fuel than your fire could immediately consume, so it continued burning long after you stopped your attack. Most dragons call this liquid flames, and although less powerful than a tight stream of fire, it can engulf a significantly larger area. And because a Broglia's fire is so much hotter, their liquid flames are even more devastating."

"I understand."

"Good. Now take a break. This afternoon, I'd like to work on distance and accuracy." With that, Krepli flew off and left him alone in the field.

Autumn's arrival passed as Brohdan improved his fire-breathing abilities. While honing his liquid flames during one particularly chilly evening, Brohdan saw Krepli flying toward the center of camp with two dragons in trail. As the trio neared the commons area, Brohdan recognized Krepli's companions – his parents.

Brohdan immediately abandoned his fire-breathing practice, leaving the wood target burning and thick black smoke rising. His parents were waiting for him as he landed in the commons area.

"Brohdan!" Grediva shrieked. "You're so *graceful!*"

"And large," Brohdeck added. "You must've grown a two elads!"

"Thanks," he answered self-consciously, completing a Hongi with them.

Krepli, not wanting to intrude, awkwardly cleared his throat. "I'm sorry for interrupting. Brohdan, I brought your parents here because there are important matters to discuss, and I thought you'd value their opinions."

"Thank you."

"I think it best if we first share the discovery we made last cycle. Afterward, we must decide on your next phase of training. Of course, I have a recommendation in that regard."

"What happened?" Brohdan's parents asked in unison.

"You didn't tell them?" Brohdan asked Krepli, wondering how much they already suspected.

"Of course not, that should come from you."

Brohdan appreciated Krepli's thoughtfulness, but he wasn't sure how to tell his parents he was a Broglia Black dragon. Not only would it force unwanted attention on them, he also knew they'd worry constantly.

"Brohdan?" his mother said, overcome with curiosity. "Are you well?"

"Yes, I never felt better." He paused, trying to find the best way to begin. "Do you remember my life before I came here? I was clumsy, and I never really felt comfortable in my own body."

"Yes, sweetheart. But we told you not to worry, that your grombit would change that."

Brohdan nodded. "That's exactly what happened. My grombit *has* changed me. There was a reason for my clumsiness when I was young."

Brohdeck and Grediva glanced at each other before turning back to their son. "What do you mean?" Brohdeck asked.

"When my grombit's complete, I'll be much larger than I was as a youngling. Much larger than adults, even."

"But that means…" his father began, then paused.

"I'm the next Broglia Black dragon." He still felt self-conscious thinking those words, let alone saying them.

"Dre confirmed it last autumn," Krepli added. "The timing's right, and Brohdan's showed remarkable progress. There's no doubt that your son is our next Broglia Black."

Grediva looked askance at her husband. The moment lasted a little too long.

"You knew!" Brohdan said, his suspicions confirmed. "You knew before I ever came here that I was the next Broglia!"

Brohdeck looked uneasy. "Not exactly. It's true that we suspected as much, but we were far from certain." He looked again at his wife before continuing. "We just thought it best to send you here just in case."

"We're so proud of you!" Grediva shrieked, tears flowing down the green scales of her face.

Krepli approached them. "Brohdan's grombit has progressed rapidly. I hadn't expected him to achieve this level of competence for an additional cycle. In fact, if he continues at this rate, I really don't think his grombit will last another two cycles."

"Incredible, really. Five to six cycles is the accepted time for a Broglia grombit to run its course. I've heard of some lasting as long as eight and others lasting only four. Brohdan's pace is really off the scales – no pun intended."

"I'm pleased with his progress in his strength, stamina, flying skills, and fire-breathing. But we've done very little to develop his sorcery abilities. That's the main reason I've asked you here." Krepli looked at the three of them before continuing. "I want to take Brohdan to Sul Brul."

"What? Why?" Grediva asked before Krepli had a chance to explain.

"As a lesser dragon, I have no personal experience with casting spells. Although I've talked with those who do – Balthasar several times and a human sorcerer once – I have no first-hand knowledge that I can pass along to Brohdan. That's why I strongly recommend Brohdan accompany me to Sul Brul where he'll not only progress under my tutelage, but under the guidance of two other instructors as well. Between the three of us, I'm confident we can overcome any obstacles in his development."

Brohdeck nodded. "Grediva and I are impressed with the progress you and Brohdan have made so far. And I agree, he should learn from experts that are knowledgeable in Broglia grombits. But with your expertise, couldn't Dorumir and his instructors here finish his grombit?"

Brohdan agreed with his father and, judging by her intense nodding, so did his mother.

"I've been a grombit instructor for many centacycles. Although Brohdan is the first Broglia I've guided through his early grombit, I was an apprentice to Chuvous when he guided Balthasar through the latter stages of his. I was very young at the time and admittedly knew very little about Broglias, but I still vividly recall the difficulties Chuvous encountered when Balthasar began his sorcery training. I've said it many times since – sorcery does not come easily to dragons. I don't believe Brohdan will take to sorcery quickly, even in Sul Brul where he'll have three dedicated instructors concentrating specifically on his Broglia grombit."

Brohdeck nodded. "Brohdan, what do you think? The choice is yours after all."

Brohdan liked the idea of training close to Lukvia and his parents, but then he recalled his last conversation with Belkidar.

If I don't have your help, Brohdan, Hildegard will prevail.

That thought had been engrained in him ever since. He loved his parents more than anything in this world, but his sense of duty was even stronger than his desire to remain near his family. He met their eyes, and they knew at once what his answer would be. "I'll go with you to Sul Brul, Master Krepli."

Krepli understood duty and commitment, knew well Brohdan's sacrifice. "I'll see you tomorrow morning," he said before leaving them.

Their evening meal passed too quickly, each realizing the relationship between parent and child would be forever altered, knew that was the nature of life. They made the most of their final night together, talked of memories long passed, content in the quiet familiarity of close families.

Brohdan was fortunate if he slept a link that night. He was anxious to grow his sorcery skills to a level that may prove useful to Belkidar, but he was also heartbroken knowing in a few links he'd say goodbye to his parents. How could he do it? He realized that after tomorrow, it could be cycles, or even their lifetime, before he and Belkidar were finished with their task.

After the longest night of his life, Brohdan went outside. He watched the eastern skies glow violet before a red sun slowly emerged from behind the distant mountains. He'd dreaded this day ever since Belkidar hinted of his fate. After a few drus, Brohdan saw Krepli flying toward him, much earlier than he'd expected. He looked back, considered waking his parents, but the decision was made for him as they left the shadows of their cave, walking side-by-side into the dawn.

"We couldn't sleep either," his mother explained.

Brohdan just stared at the ground, refusing to look his parents in the eyes for fear his brave front might crumble.

Krepli had silently landed a good distance away in the field where he and Brohdan had tackled so many of his lessons.

"Brohdan," Grediva began, "you know this is your destiny. Do your best, and always remember we'll be here if ever you need us. We love you dearly, sweetheart," she sobbed, her sentence trailing into silence.

"My son, never forget where you came from, and always remember how proud we are of you."

Wordlessly, Brohdan completed a Hongi with them, then slowly headed for the practice field. He met Krepli there alone. "Let's go," he said, taking flight. Without looking back, he flew silently in the faint morning light toward Sul Brul, and to his destiny.

Chapter 6
Sul Brul

*A teacher affects eternity; he can never tell where his
influence stops.*

Henry Adams

Despite his vast improvements over the past half cycle, Brohdan
initially found it challenging to keep pace with the old Gorduvian. But
when he eventually grew comfortable, he shifted his focus to the
landscapes that passed below.

He followed Krepli first to the north and noticed how he avoided
the large human city of Kankordee. After a link or so, they turned
northeast toward Sul Brul, and soon the incredible heights of the
Slatemore Mountains came into view.

The vast Seamus River became visible a few links into the
mountains. Krepli led him down a box canyon lined with beautiful
pines and tall evergreens. The pair flew a few elads above the river as
they approached a small prairie that bordered the cold water.

"I thought we could use a break," Krepli explained after landing.

"It's amazing." The swiftly-running waters of the Seamus created
a soothing background, the sound reflecting off the sheer cliffs that
towered above them.

"I've come here countless times, yet this place never ceases to
amaze me. It's perfect for our midday meal. Stay here," he added as
he extended his wings. "I'll find some food."

The pair remained within the beauty of the Slatemores for the
better part of a link. They ate deer Krepli discovered a few passes to
the west, drank from the Seamus, and talked in the shade. Eventually,
they took flight and continued their journey.

Finally, after nearly fifteen links they landed in the outskirts of Sul
Brul, Brohdan immediately realizing it was home to a much larger pack

than he'd expected. Nearly sixty dragons lived in and around this bustling community. Numerous mountains bordered them to the north and east. Although significantly smaller than the Slatemores, they offered more than seventy dragon-sized caves. With a little advice from Krepli, he chose a large one knowing he'd grow considerably before he left.

As stars pierced holes in the darkening sky, he eventually rested his large body on the cool stone floor of the cave's rear chamber. Tired from the long flight, he closed his eyes and thought about his new home. It was a nice, spacious dwelling, but he nonetheless missed the little corner of his parents' cave, and the security that came with it.

Brohdan woke the next morning and realized the dreary weather was the perfect reflection of his mood. The sky was completely overcast, and rain poured relentlessly from low, dark clouds. With his heart still longing to return to his family, he slowly made his way to the cave's mouth.

"There you are! I was wondering if you'd already left!" Her voice came from just beyond the entrance.

Brohdan slowly peered outside, the rain drenching his head and upper neck. A female was seated on a rock formation just beside the cave entrance. She was the most beautiful thing he'd ever seen. Like all Klonduvians Reds, her scales were a deep crimson, but these were a more distinctive shade than any he'd ever seen.

"You must be Brohdan," she said, filling the awkward silence.

Her wings were sedately folded along either side of her back as she sat on her haunches. Her tail wagged – somewhat seductively Brohdan thought – side to side as she looked down at him from her elevated perch.

"Hellooooo?"

Her beautiful eyes curved slightly up at their outside tips, and her cheekbones were placed high on her face.

"Are you okay down there?" she asked, leaping from the rock and landing softly in front of him.

"Er – yes, I'm fine. Why do you ask?"

"I don't know. I thought you had a stroke or something," she replied, laughing. "I'm Mikka. My father asked me to show you to your training field."

Brohdan followed her into the air, once again marveling at her beauty as she flew gracefully ahead. After catching up, he found he desperately wanted to get to know her, but he could find nothing say. "Rainy weather. Very wet."

She laughed at his 'joke.' "So, tell me about yourself. You must be talented to have three instructors."

"That's not for me to say. I'm making progress, but we'll have to see if I can ever learn sorcery."

Mikka chuckled. "Sorcery? I think you mean sorcery *resistance*."

Brohdan didn't elaborate, wanting neither to correct her nor to openly state that he was the next Broglia Black.

His silence piqued her interest. "You mean – but that would make you…"

"So they say."

"Now it makes sense. I've seen some talented dragons come through Sul Brul before, but none had three instructors."

"I assume you've lived here awhile then?"

"All my life. I love it. Not everyone likes packs as large as Sul Brul, but things are so interesting here. I really don't think I could be happy anyplace else."

"It's funny you should say that, I was thinking the same about my home."

"How long have you been in your grombit?"

"About a cycle."

"And you're already flying like *that*?"

He snorted. "It took me a long time to start it, so I had some catching up to do. Plus, Krepli's training is brutal, so I did a lot of flying and hovering every day. I'm sure that helped."

"Hold on," Mikka said. "You can hover too?"

"That was one of Krepli's conditioning exercises. He wouldn't even let me practice breathing fire until I could maintain a high hover for thirty drus."

Mikka's expression progressed from surprise to frustration to deflation.

Brohdan changed the subject. "You're flying quite well yourself. Tell me about your grombit."

She did, reluctantly. "I just finished mine last winter. It took me three and a half cycles, but I still have some work to do. Dad told me to keep practicing and explained how all dragons have difficulties, but after listening to how quickly you learned, I think he was just being nice to me."

Feeling guilty, Brohdan thought of ways he could cheer her up. But before he could, she was already leading him down toward a large, open field. Still some distance away, Brohdan could already see several dozen wooden posts sticking out of the ground in three neat rows, each topped with a large, round rock.

The two landed in the meadow, the columns of wooden posts on their left, the entire right side of the field clear. "Looks like we're early," Mikka said, looking for the instructors.

"What are they for?" Brohdan asked, pointing to the posts with his left wing.

"The idea is to aim your fire at the rock sitting on the post. As you improve, you steadily increase the distance. When mastered, you'll be able to blow the rock off the pillar without singeing the wood."

"It's harder to keep your stream tight over a longer distance," Brohdan said automatically from Krepli's training.

She looked at him curiously. "Yes, exactly. They're also used to improve the power of your attacks."

Soon, three dragons approached from their right. After landing, Mikka made the introductions.

"Everybody, this is Brohdan. You already know Master Krepli, of course."

"Hello, Brohdan. Did you sleep well last night?"

"As well as can be expected, I suppose," Brohdan replied without embarrassment.

"Don't worry, you'll get used to being away from home, even if it sometimes takes longer than we'd like."

Mikka continued. "Brohdan, this is my father, Instructor Boseda."

Boseda was very similar in appearance to his daughter. He was a very handsome Klonduvian, and he too had a unique tint to his crimson scales.

"Nice to meet you, Instructor Boseda."

"Likewise, Brohdan. I've been looking forward to this ever since Master Krepli told me about you."

Turning to the third dragon, Mikka continued. "Finally, I'd like to introduce Instructor Rouldra."

Rouldra was a Gorduvian Gold and appeared very old. Her scales were in poor condition, and her flesh hung from her face and neck in much the same way Dre's had. With her head held high, she was forced to look down her snout to see anything of consequence. She stared into Brohdan's eyes long enough to make him uncomfortable. "Brohdan," she finally greeted him.

"Instructor Rouldra."

"I'll update everyone on Brohdan's progress over a meal," Krepli suggested.

The five dragons took off from the field with the three instructors leading the way. Brohdan deliberately lagged behind with Mikka so they could talk without the instructors overhearing.

"I get the distinct impression that Rouldra doesn't like me."

"Yeah, she takes a while to get used to. She's the sort that thinks Gorduvians are above all but Broglias." She paused as she said that final word and looked at Brohdan before continuing. "Because you're a Dalluvian – or you were a Dalluvian – she probably takes that as an insult."

"What? Why? How?"

"Rouldra, like many Gorduvian Golds, believes that a Broglia should come from two Gorduvian parents. They think it's inappropriate for a lesser dragon to be involved in the creation of something as authoritative as a Broglia. It has to do with bloodlines or something. I really don't understand it myself."

Well. "I think I've heard it all."

They ate on the banks of a beautiful mountain lake, their conversation beginning with the progress Brohdan had made thus far in his grombit.

"I understand you've mastered several lessons already, Brohdan," Boseda began.

"I've been able to get the basics," Brohdan replied, glancing at Mikka.

Krepli regarded Brohdan for a few moments. "Brohdan's being modest. He's an extraordinary dragon. But despite everything he's learned during the past cycle, he's far from mastering any of them. Indeed, I doubt any of us has mastered naught but breathing and eating." With that, he studied the available fish, eventually selected a rather large silver one and swallowed it whole.

"I tend to agree," Rouldra said flatly from where she ate. "From what I've seen thus far, Brohdan still needs considerable training."

"I don't agree," Krepli finally managed after having some trouble swallowing the fish. "We're still early in his grombit, yet his endurance and stamina are cycles ahead of schedule. Both his low and high hovers are progressing at an unparalleled rate. I'm pleased with his resistances and very impressed with how far he's come with his fire-breathing in such a short period. However, there's still one area we must focus on – his sorcery."

"As you know, I was Chuvous' apprentice when he trained Balthasar, just as Boseda will be mine during the remainder of Brohdan's grombit. I distinctly recall the difficulties Chuvous had with

Balthasar's sorcery, and I want to use what we learned to help Brohdan. I'm certain he'll have his own challenges, so he'll need all the expertise we can offer. That's where you two come in. Obviously, none of us has ever taught sorcery before, but we do have several centacycles of experience to draw upon."

Boseda nodded his agreement. "I've talked with several dragons who knew Balthasar. A few of them witnessed his use of sorcery, some even discussing it with him. That should help."

"Thank you, Instructor Boseda, I appreciate your thoroughness." Krepli turned and looked at the silent Rouldra. "Madam, you've remained uncharacteristically silent. I'm curious to hear your thoughts."

Rouldra looked down her nose at the four of them, drawing out the silence for several moments. Finally, and in no particular hurry, she began. "This won't work, not unless the student in question was a greater dragon, but he is only a Dalluvian. How are we supposed to teach *that*?" she demanded.

Before Brohdan could say a word in his defense, Krepli spoke. "Rouldra, not a single thing you said has merit." He too paused for effect. As he did, Brohdan noticed Rouldra's scales ruffle about her neck and back. "In case you've missed the significance of this meeting, I'll explain it to you. Brohdan is not a Dalluvian. He's a *Broglia Black*, our species' leader for the next millennium. Do not be fooled by his green scales and calm demeanor. And I believe a Broglia qualifies as a greater dragon, wouldn't you agree?"

Rouldra fumed, shooting to her feet. "You can instruct him all you wish, but I won't have any part of this nonsense." She abruptly spread her wings before briefly turning back to them. "Brohdan a Broglia? Please."

"Suit yourself," Krepli said as he returned his attention to Boseda and continued the conversation, albeit a little louder than was necessary. "As I was saying, Brohdan has already displayed certain Broglia characteristics."

Rouldra had no choice but to hear his statement, turning her head and neck as she continued flying away.

Krepli continued. "The problem lies in the fact that he's been limited in his instruction. We must teach him how to use his sorcery as he intends it, not as an emotional response."

This was too much for the Gorduvian. By the time Krepli had finished, she was already in the final stages of her landing. "Brohdan's already used sorcery?" she asked.

"Oh, yes," Krepli replied innocently. "A ward. Did I not mention that before?"

"No, you didn't."

"It must've slipped my mind."

She slowly turned her gaze from Krepli to Brohdan. "So, he really is a Broglia..."

"Yes, he is. You should've trusted my judgment, Rouldra." Krepli understood her sudden change of heart. Broglia instructors were revered above all others, and Rouldra coveted the reputation that would come with instructing Brohdan. Realizing her name would go down in history, she selfishly reconsidered. "Forgive me, Krepli. I did not fully understand the situation."

"You are with us then?"

"Yes."

"Good," Krepli remarked. "Your wisdom will be most valuable in the cycles to come."

Soon, all five dragons finished their meals. "You two take the rest of the day off. I want some time to finalize Brohdan's lesson plans with Boseda and Rouldra."

Not wanting to give Krepli an opportunity to change his mind, Brohdan was in the air before Mikka had a chance to spread her wings.

"Aren't you coming?" he asked her, tucking his legs beneath his body as he accelerated.

"Sure, I'm right behind you." After she caught up to him, they were nearly a linak from the others. "I can't believe it! I was never that lucky!"

"What would you like to do?"

Mikka's face lit up as she decided the day's events. "Follow me. I've got a few ideas," she added, her smile nearly causing Brohdan forget to flap his wings.

Mikka led Brohdan past her cave, following a fast-running river that wound along the base of the mountainside. After a half link, she descended along its far slopes toward a small lake, landing on a lone island near its center.

"This is my favorite place in the world. Those are the Serrald Mountains," she explained, nodding to the south. "Your cave lies further down the valley on the other side of that range," she added before turning her gaze back to her new friend.

"What's the name of the lake?"

She smiled. "I think it's too small to have one."

"It's beautiful here," Brohdan agreed, placing more emphasis on his company than their surroundings. "I can certainly understand why you like it so much."

Mikka beamed. But then her expression turned serious. "Brohdan, I'm sorry if I seemed upset before. I guess I became a little insecure at the thought of your grombit. When I was a youngling, I looked forward to mine more than anything in the world, and I was so excited when the day finally came. But that didn't last long. Despite everything, I still struggled. It was just a disappointing time for me."

"But you finished in just over three cycles. That's nothing to be ashamed of."

"It is for me. My father's one of the world's leading grombit instructors, yet his only child managed to complete her grombit in three and a half cycles. I'm afraid I embarrassed him."

"You have nothing to be embarrassed about. You obviously did the best you could, and that's never anything to be ashamed of."

"You don't understand. My father and I are Klonduvians, but all of his peers are Gorduvians. I can only imagine what his colleagues must've said behind his back." Tears welled in her eyes.

"And yet Krepli chose him as his apprentice."

Mikka considered that. "True."

Brohdan grunted. "I'm convinced that grombits are hard for everyone. It must be a punishment for something."

Mikka laughed. "I heard Broglia grombits are especially difficult."

He paused a moment, recalling his time in the Sichundars. "It took me five mooncycles before I even started it."

This stunned her, but she didn't comment. Nevertheless, Brohdan recognized the shock in her expression.

"I know, it's the longest any Lukvian dragon had ever taken to begin a grombit. At the time, none of my instructors ever seriously considered that I was a Broglia youngling, probably because of how useless I was. And so they assumed I was lazy and lacked proper 'motivation.' But that wasn't the worst part. A Gorduvian youngling at camp was nearly finished with his grombit, and he thought it was his duty to motivate me." Brohdan didn't elaborate. He didn't need to.

"I'm so sorry, Brohdan."

He remained silent for a few drus, then smiled. "It could've been worse. Besides, it taught me a valuable lesson."

"What was that?"

"That it doesn't matter what others think of you, unless you let it. Understanding that is what triggered my grombit."

Mikka suddenly realized why he chose to share this story with her, and she appreciated his thoughtfulness, especially since it was obviously a painful memory. "You're right, Brohdan. I just don't want to be an embarrassment to my father."

"You can't let that bother you, Mikka. Besides, who cares what some Gorduvian says, anyway? Your father knows how well you did, that's the only thing that matters."

Mikka looked at Brohdan. "I never considered that. I was so worried with what others were saying about him, I never considered what he'd think."

"Do you think it'd bother him?"

She snorted, thinking of her gruff father. "No!" Then she released a long breath, relieved, before leaning over and gently touching her nose to his. "Thank you. I feel better now."

The two spent the rest of the morning and early afternoon by the lake. Time passed quickly as they talked. Brohdan described his childhood in Lukvia, including everything about his parents. She was saddened when he talked of his time in the Sichundars, but then laughed when he described how he'd breathed fire at Limbrin.

But Brohdan was content to let Mikka do most of the talking. She described her life in Sul Brul, learning all about his two new instructors in the process. He watched as she spoke, entranced by the grace with which she accomplished even the most ordinary task. Eventually, as the sun descended behind the mountain peaks, they headed back and reluctantly returned to their caves.

Brohdan's grombit progressed over the next two cycles, albeit more slowly than he would've preferred. His sorcery skills gradually improved, but not without complications. Krepli and his assistants were often befuddled, spending links discussing methods to prod their student over each hurdle.

Unlike his stubborn sorcery skills, Brohdan's physique developed effortlessly. His distinctive horns began protruding from over his brows, and his barz grew swiftly, the blade at its center early in its development. Brohdan's scales were now a dark green, and his size nearly forced him to find a larger dwelling.

"It won't be long now," Krepli told him early one autumn morning as they landed near the back of the practice field. "Let's see how your barz is coming along."

The old instructor carefully inspected the bulge at the tip of his tail. "Does this hurt?" he asked, stepping on it gently.

Although Brohdan's reply wasn't technically common speech, the pitch of his roar and the volume of flames nonetheless communicated his thoughts.

"Sorry, I just needed to check the progress of your blade. Judging by your sensitivity, I'd say it's well on its way." Krepli suppressed a smile as he gave his student a little distance to practice his sorcery.

"Okay. Let's review your spells. Start with 'cloak.'"

"All right," Brohdan agreed, quickly regaining his composure as the subject thankfully turned from his sore tail. He closed his eyes and thought of the product of the spell – he pictured in his mind what a dragon would see if he looked at him while cloaked.

As Brohdan concentrated, Krepli verbally reviewed the spell. "Cloaking won't turn you invisible; instead, it's a form of camouflage. It takes the image of your background and projects it to the foreground, causing an onlooker to see a recreation of what lies behind the sorcerer instead of the sorcerer himself."

"When you're still, your background remains constant, increasing the spell's effectiveness. But like anything, it has its limitations, the most significant of which is the lag between the actual background and the image it projects. The more quickly you move, the less effective the spell becomes."

Krepli watched Brohdan as he described the spell from memory. Slowly, almost imperceptibly, Brohdan vanished.

"Good. Very good, Brohdan. I can still see you, but you're nicely cloaked to your surroundings. Now, maintain it until I return." With that, Krepli leapt into the air and flew away.

Brohdan became bored just twenty drus after his instructor's departure. Not wanting to move, he sat motionless, watching his surroundings.

Before long, animals returned to the meadow. Birds flew past his head and landed on a nearby tree, jostling loudly for position. Not long afterward, five deer timidly approached the field upwind from where

Brohdan sat. He could see them from the corner of his eye as they dropped their heads to the lush grass. Slowly, they bravely moved into the sunlight a few elads beyond the edge of the trees. The deer eventually made their way toward him, oblivious. They continued eating, their ears and tails twitching.

Brohdan watched them for what seemed like a link before his hunger finally got the better of him. Remembering that quick movements made his ward less effective, he slowly turned his head toward a doe that ate nervously a few elads away. His prey appeared to look straight through him, but somehow sensed the danger. In a flash, she darted away, the others immediately following.

"If you wanted to eat one, you should've struck swiftly," Krepli explained after he and the other instructors landed on the grass in front of him.

Brohdan didn't reply, but his growling stomach spoke in his stead. And then he noticed Rouldra's continued stare. "What is it?" Brohdan finally asked.

"You seem to have lost your tail," she remarked impatiently.

"Oh." Brohdan allowed his tail to reappear. "I guess I didn't release the spell completely."

"No. I guess you didn't."

With a sigh, Krepli continued the lesson. "Now, I'd like you to try 'steelskin.' Only this time, you must harden all of your skin and scales, not just where you don't happen to have an itch. Got it?"

"Yes, Master Krepli."

Again, as Brohdan concentrated, Krepli described the spell's effect for both review and to test his ability to focus while using sorcery. "This spell increases the hardness of your skin and scales. If cast correctly, no arrow, spear, or javelin will pierce your skin. But you must remain vigilant, for 'steelskin' may be insufficient to withstand a sword in hands of an expert."

As Krepli spoke, Brohdan thought about the effect 'steelskin' would have on his body. When he 'thought,' the part of the brain reserved for sorcerers cast the ward.

"I think I've done it," Brohdan managed through clinched jaws.

"Brohdan, you really must learn to relax when casting spells," Boseda explained. "It's much too tiring to remain rigid like that every time you use sorcery."

"I'm trying, but it's hard when your skin feels as heavy as mine does right now."

"Oh, I hadn't thought about that."

"All right, let's have a look," Krepli said to the instructors. They each extended a wing and carefully used their hooks to search for soft spots in his ward.

"Nicely done, Brohdan. I see that all of our hard work is paying off!" Krepli commented after several drus of probing. Rouldra, however, hadn't quite completed her inspection. "Hold still while I test the strength of the spell."

Brohdan instinctively tightened his muscles as Rouldra drove her hook into his ribs. He was surprised to find he scarcely felt the blow.

"Not bad," she allowed. "Let's try again." With that as her only warning, she drove it brutally into his side, then immediately winced in pain as her wing hook bent backward, stymied by Brohdan's spell.

"How'd I do," he asked, unable to completely conceal his grin.

"Satisfactorily."

"Brohdan, keep that spell in place until we return," Krepli said, turning toward his assistants. "I'm still not satisfied with how heavy this spell makes him feel. I'm not even sure he could fly in that condition."

Brohdan once again found himself alone. He didn't like these times because inevitably his thoughts drifted back to Lukvia. He enjoyed his time in Sul Brul, and he was pleased with the way his grombit was progressing, but he missed his family. Mikka had become his best friend, and although he felt comfortable talking to her about anything, he found it hard to express these feelings to someone who had spent her entire life among so many other dragons. Mikka simply passed it off as homesickness, and while that was true, it went much deeper than that.

He eventually noticed a large eagle circling overhead. Shaken from his daydream, he watched with interest as it spiraled lower and lower, gliding only a few elads above his head before landing on the lush grass behind him. Perplexed, he continued staring as it and strode confidently toward him. Without warning, it took Brohdan's tail in its beak just above his growing barz, pinching it savagely.

Brohdan jumped back with an equal amount of pain and shock.

"What's the matter?" the bird asked in a very understandable voice. "Haven't you cast 'steelskin?'"

"Yes," Brohdan answered, not yet realizing he was talking to a bird.

"Then why were you injured?"

"Because sorcery has its limits!"

"Are you sure?" the bird remarked as a faint aura grew around it. As Brohdan watched, the aura expanded, quickly consumed the bird's form. Within the light's brilliance, the blurred silhouette of the bird changed into a human's. Before he realized it, the white-blue light vanished and Belkidar stood before him.

Taking several moments to recover, Brohdan finally found his voice. "'Steelskin's' never been able to protect me from a bite like that."

"I understand, but a limited imagination is perhaps the greatest single factor that limits sorcerers. How can you ever improve your spells if you put limits on them? If cast properly, 'steelskin' makes it impossible for an enemy to injure your flesh – or scales, as the case may be," he quickly amended. "I see they're changing color. Good!"

"Why's that good?"

"It indicates your grombit is drawing to an end. Five transformations signal the final stages of a Broglia's grombit. First, his color changes to black. Next, his size increases dramatically, and horns around his head begin to grow. Next, his fire grows much hotter, and his barz completes its development. How's yours coming along, by the way?"

"It's getting there," Brohdan answered, moving his tail out of Belkidar's reach.

"What's the matter? I want to see it."

Reluctantly, Brohdan moved his tail closer. "Just don't step on it," he muttered almost to himself.

"It's coming along nicely, Brohdan. I'd say in another few mooncycles your grombit will be complete."

"What? That can't be! Krepli said that Broglia grombits last between five to six cycles. I've only been in mine for three."

"Be that as it may, your grombit is nearly finished. You should be excited!"

Brohdan was still in shock. He believed he had another cycle or two to prepare for whatever Belkidar required of him.

"Which spells have you learned?"

"'Steelskin' and 'cloak.' I'm pretty sure Krepli taught me 'fear' as well, but since dragons are immune to it, it's hard to know for sure."

"Try it on me."

"All right. Give me a dru to prepare myself," Brohdan said, closing his eyes.

Belkidar sighed impatiently as he waited.

After a moment, Brohdan opened his eyes. "That's it," he said, sounding a little deflated. "I guess it didn't work."

"No, it worked."

"It did? You were supposed to run away, preferably screaming."

"Ah. Would it help if I ran away now?"

Brohdan smiled. "Not so much."

"It wasn't your spell so much as my experience. 'Fear' is just like anything else that frightens you – after you've seen it enough, you become accustomed to it. Your spell was fine, but you should work on your delivery."

"My delivery?"

"Yes, that's an important ingredient to the strength of many spells. Let's say you wanted to play a joke on one of your friends and scare them as they walked through a forest, what would you do?"

"I'd surprise them," Brohdan replied, confused.

"Exactly. It's the same with sorcery, you want the spell to jump out at them. The way you cast 'fear' on me just now was the equivalent of slowly walking out from behind a group of trees. Understand?"

Brohdan nodded.

"Good. Try it again, but this time with a better delivery."

Again, Brohdan took a moment to gather his thoughts. Soon afterward, he opened his eyes and looked at the sorcerer. Belkidar's expression remained unchanged.

"Much better."

Brohdan gave up on the idea that he could ever scare the old human. "Did you discover anything since our last meeting?"

"Yes, and it's not good," Belkidar answered as he took a seat on the grass. "Hildegard isn't in a hurry to get the Staff, that's for sure." As he said this, Brohdan's eyes involuntarily drifted to the large walking stick that now lay across Belkidar's lap. "He remains in Gul Krul, his fortress home on Katja."

"Why would he steal the Jewel and not want the Staff?"

"Oh, I'm certain he wants the Staff, but you have to appreciate his perspective. Judging by his timing and his attention to every detail, it appears as though he's been planning this for a very long time. He patiently observed, waiting centacycles for the Indifferent to become complacent in their guardianship of the Jewel. When the time came, he simply walked in and carried it away."

"Hildegard's been preparing for this day ever since the Headpiece corrupted Krollum, over three millennia ago. I learned that he's bred enormous armies to secure his possession of both Artifacts. They're at least three times larger than any force we could summon, so we'd have no hope of assaulting his fortress in an attempt to steal back the Jewel. He seems perfectly content to sit there and wait for us to weaken, at which time I'm sure he'll take the Staff just as easily as he took the Jewel. Besides, he already has two of the Staff of Power's three Artifacts. That alone gives him a distinct advantage. When coupled with the size of his forces, we suddenly find ourselves in an extremely precarious position."

"Why not build up our own forces?"

"He already has too much of a head start. Remember, he *planned* this, and now the difference in population between our two continents is far too great to overcome. We have no hope in conquering him through a war of attrition."

"How are we to defeat him then?"

"I believe I've discovered a way to retake the Jewel, and possibly kill Hildegard in the process."

Brohdan's eyes lit up. "How?"

"It's simple, but risky. Hildegard plan relies on his superior numbers, his enormous armies are a testament to this fact. It's my hope that he feels so secure, so confident, that he never considered the idea that a small group could challenge him."

Brohdan nodded. "What will we face?"

Belkidar smiled. "Hildegard's erected Five Defenses, each designed to destroy entire armies, so they'll obviously be a challenge for our modest group. Once past them, we must face Hildegard himself."

"Is that all? I was getting worried there for a while."

"Actually, there's more. As I've said, Hildegard's been planning this for thousands of cycles. During that time, he's used his considerable sorcery skills to mold the landscape of Katja to better suit his plans. As a result, any army of significant size sent to recapture the Jewel would be hindered by the unforgiving terrain. To make matters worse, I'm sure he's placed each of his Five Defenses in precisely those locations that would most effectively handicap our armies." He paused, shook his head. "The fact that our armies would be forced to face his hordes is a challenging prospect in its own right, but to have the landscape give his Defenses an even greater advantage may very well prove insurmountable. But a small, elite group of highly-skilled warriors could traverse these lands more quickly than a large army could, possibly eliminating one of Hildegard's greatest advantages.

And we wouldn't need a supply train, letting us travel in stealth. Perhaps with a substantially nimbler army, we could also defeat his Defenses."

Brohdan considered this. A smaller force could make its way through Katja more swiftly, but it'd have to be an extraordinary group if it was to defeat Defenses that were designed to conquer armies.

Belkidar looked to the southwest. "They're returning. I think you'd better cast 'steelskin' again so you don't disappoint them," he offered, rising to his feet.

"I never released it."

Belkidar glanced at the young dragon for a moment. "Indeed you haven't," he agreed softly, a faint smile crossing his lips.

Brohdan's three instructors landed nearby, their expressions unreadable as they cautiously approached. "A human," Rouldra spat, disgusted. "I've not seen their kind here for centacycles." She looked down her nose at his small form. "Shall I crush him?" she asked Krepli, her gaze fixed on him.

Belkidar stood leaning against his Staff, a brow raised, his smile barely noticeable.

In a flash, Krepli broke the silence. "Venerable One, we are honored by your presence! On behalf of our pack, I welcome you to Sul Brul." He bowed formally toward the small, seemingly frail human.

"Thank you, Master Krepli. You honor me," Belkidar replied as his gaze returned to Rouldra.

The female Gorduvian turned her attention first to Krepli and then back to the human.

"What brings you to dragon country, Belkidar?" Boseda asked, rising from his bow.

Rouldra, finally realizing to whom they were speaking, stuttered an incoherent apology.

Belkidar ignored the stammering Gorduvian and instead answered Boseda. "I apologize, but I must steal Brohdan from your most capable instruction. I've discovered unsettling news and unfortunately need his help."

"It must be grave indeed if you cannot manage it alone," Krepli observed.

"I'm afraid it is."

"Might I ask you to delay your errand? At least until we've concluded Brohdan's training?"

"I wish that were an option, I truly do Master Krepli. Perhaps I could instruct him during our journey?"

Reluctantly, Krepli explained the state of Brohdan's grombit. "He's progressed very rapidly, and we're all very proud of him. But his sorcery skills are only adequate, and his barz remains too underdeveloped to teach him its uses. Finally, I was hoping to teach Brohdan the finer points of self-defense once he had physically matured."

Belkidar thought for a long moment. "I respect your wisdom in these matters, Master Krepli, and I certainly don't wish to seem insensitive, but perhaps I'm the best choice to instruct Brohdan's sorcery skills? It'd be my privilege to do so."

Krepli nodded, considered the idea.

Belkidar continued. "Brohdan will eventually adjust to his size – Balthasar adapted quickly, as did Kantor, Gorldalev, and Thordlow before him. And I have no doubt Brohdan will learn the uses of his barz in time, though I agree it'll take a bit longer without your valuable instruction."

The enormity of Belkidar's experience was tangible. Rouldra and Boseda stared openly, amazed, but Krepli simply nodded his reluctant agreement. "I trust you Ancient One, and I would respect your judgments long before I would trust my own."

"Thank you, Master Krepli. Can we further discuss Brohdan's sorcery development over a meal tonight?"

"We would be honored, Belkidar. Let's meet again this evening."

"I look forward to it, my friend."

After another bow, Krepli took off and departed toward his cave. Boseda and Rouldra silently followed.

"I didn't realize you wanted to take back the Jewel so soon," Brohdan admitted. "I'm not sure how much use I'll be facing Hildegard's Defenses right now."

"You don't have to worry about that for a while. Before we take on Hildegard and his Five Defenses, we must recruit the other members of our party. That'll take a while as it involves considerable traveling. By then, I have every confidence you'll be ready to face Hildegard's hordes."

Brohdan relaxed a little after realizing his first battle lay in the distant future. "Good."

Belkidar once again blurred in front of Brohdan's eyes as he returned to the form of the huge eagle. "Let's prepare for the feast," he squawked as he took flight and headed for Brohdan's cave.

"How do you know where you're going?" Brohdan asked, struggling to catch up.

"I have my ways. Now see if you can beat this old man to your home!"

With several powerful strokes of his large wings, the sorcerer opened a considerable lead. Brohdan was doing all he could just to keep pace when suddenly the bird folded his wings and dove toward the trees. Brohdan was amazed with his speed as he watched the large eagle level off only a few elads above the treetops. Brohdan mimicked his tactics, gained incredible speed in his dive, flew faster than he'd ever flown in his life. When he approached the treetops, he extended his wings to slow his descent just as the eagle had, but the force was more than he expected, his gigantic wings nearly forced together behind his back. Straining, he held them extended and regained control. Having narrowly avoided a horrific and somewhat embarrassing crash, Brohdan flew the remaining distance to his cave with considerably more care.

When he arrived, Belkidar stood waiting in his human form. After briefly looking inside, his eyes returned to his large friend. "I don't suppose you have any ale here?"

"Ale?"

"Never mind."

"Belkidar, how did you know about me? You know – not being a Dalluvian Green?"

"It's all right, Brohdan, you can say Broglia. You have nothing to be ashamed of. On the contrary, you should be proud that you're joining their storied lineage."

"That's just it, what if I'm the first one to fail? I have so many great dragons to live up to. What if I can't?"

"My dear Brohdan. All you must do is try. Try your best in all you do, and your concerns will never be justified. I promise."

"I will, Belkidar." For some reason, the sorcerer's words had a very comforting effect.

"How has your grombit gone thus far?"

"I think it's gone well. I mean, everybody told me how difficult it would be, so I expected the worst. I think sorcery is really the only aspect that's lived up to those expectations. It's just so difficult, especially maximizing its benefits while minimizing the drawbacks."

"What sort of drawbacks?"

"Well, several. For instance, when I cast 'steelskin,' my scales feel so heavy."

"I see," Belkidar said. "Let me give that some thought."

They continued discussing Brohdan's grombit over the next link and a half before Krepli joined them.

"Good evening," the old Gorduvian greeted them. "I trust I'm not too early?"

"Not at all," Belkidar answered. "We were just discussing his sorcery."

"Excellent. Why not continue that discussion over our evening meal? All is ready."

Brohdan saw that a great feast had been prepared a linak down the small river that ran southwest of his cave. He followed them, landing in a beautiful meadow alongside the river.

"Ancient One, please forgive me if I'm intruding, but I'm forced to wonder about the errand that requires Brohdan's grombit to be cut short. Can you tell me more about it? Perhaps I could help?"

Belkidar sympathized with him, respected the loyalty he bore his student. "Under normal circumstances, I know you'd be an enormous help, but we must keep our party small. Your presence, along with that of any other creature beyond what is required, would hinder our Quest beyond measure. I mean no disrespect, Master Krepli, I truly hope you understand."

"I do, Venerable One. Please forgive me for protecting Brohdan's interests."

"I'd do the same in your position, my friend. There is nothing to forgive."

Despite the premature completion of his formal grombit training, Brohdan was nonetheless relieved that the days of zealously preparing for Belkidar's arrival had ended and the occasion of putting those lessons to use had finally arrived.

Their hosts had arranged the feast toward the east end of the meadow, furthest from the creek. The sound of the running water was ever present, a perfect backdrop to their discussions. The crisp breeze was a welcomed change from the unusually warm autumn, and the smell of moss and evergreens mingled with the roasting meat, the smoke from the fires drifting lazily above the trees. Cattle, Brohdan's favorite, was being prepared in abundance.

"Good," Krepli began, "now that we're all here, I'd like to introduce our guests." The old Gorduvian extended his right wing toward the south end of the field. There, before Brohdan's startled eyes, were his parents. Without thinking, he half-flew, half-ran to greet them, then led them to the others.

"It's a privilege to see you again," Brohdeck greeted Belkidar, bowing low with his wife.

"You're too kind," Belkidar answered, returning his bow. "You've both done a remarkable job with Brohdan. I've met many Broglias in my life, yet Brohdan still manages to impress me."

Grediva beamed a parent's pride.

"Again?" Brohdan asked his father, confused by the insinuation that they'd previously met.

"Who do you think invited us?" Brohdeck answered. "Belkidar stopped through Lukvia on his way here."

Brohdan turned to the old man, saw his mischievous grin. He continued the introductions.

"Mom, Dad – I'd like to introduce you to Boseda. He's one of the instructors that assists Master Krepli with my grombit."

"Nice to meet you both," Boseda said. "You really have an exceptional son. It's been a pleasure instructing such a talented young dragon."

"Thank you, Instructor Boseda," Brohdeck said.

"This is Rouldra," Brohdan continued. "She's Master Krepli's other assistant. Instructor Rouldra's been most valuable testing my various spells for weaknesses," Brohdan remarked, desperate to find something pleasant to say.

"Hello," Rouldra said shortly.

"Very nice to meet you, Rouldra," Grediva said.

Brohdan swallowed. "This is Mikka. Mikka, these are my parents."

Although they hadn't seen their child for nearly two cycles, their separation wasn't long enough to have Brohdan's awkwardness to go unnoticed.

"Something tells me you're a very dear friend to Brohdan," Brohdeck began. "I'm sure your support has been invaluable."

Somewhat surprised by their sincerity, Mikka bowed low. "Brohdan's helped me understand a great many things about myself as well. I completed my grombit a few cycles ago, but it was only recently that I found contentment in it. I have Brohdan to thank for that."

"The bovine is ready," Rouldra interrupted. They all made their way to the east end of the meadow, the shadows of the trees growing long. Soon, a large portion of beef lay before each dragon while Belkidar started on a very thick porterhouse.

"Rouldra, this is the finest steak I've had in centacycles," he said between mouthfuls. "You're an excellent cook."

"Why, thank you, Belkidar," Rouldra replied with rare gratitude. "I wish some of the others were as appreciative," she added, glancing toward Krepli and Boseda.

"Yes, nicely prepared," Krepli said quickly. He then leaned over to Boseda. "I'd say something too, or you'll regret it for a mooncycle," he whispered a bit too loudly.

"Great food, Rouldra," Boseda said, though something in her icy stare told him his compliment had come a little too late.

Conversation was scarce during the rest of their meal. Thanks to Rouldra's preparations, all came to realize their eyes had larger appetites than their stomachs, but that's not to say they ate sparingly. Even Belkidar's performance was notable, although in the company of dragons it seemed modest even as an appetizer.

"I must thank you all for such a delicious feast," Belkidar said after he'd finished. "It's not often I see dragons eat cooked meat. I appreciate the gesture."

Rouldra inclined her head toward the surprising human. "You are quite welcome, Belkidar."

Not unexpectedly, the topic soon settled on Brohdan's grombit.

"Krepli, I'd like to better understand a few things before I remove Brohdan from your expert care," Belkidar began. "Most importantly, please elaborate on the areas that need the most attention."

Krepli thought a moment. "As I touched on this afternoon, he must work on his self-defense when he grows into his body. I agree that this shouldn't be an area of concern, it'll simply take time and practice. The one area I am concerned with is his sorcery. While there remains improvement to be made in the effectiveness of his spells, what really confounded us was eliminating their shortcomings."

"Brohdan mentioned that. Can you elaborate?"

"With 'steelskin,' Brohdan's skin and scales feel heavy, to the point where I'm not sure he could even fly. With 'cloak,' any movement at all makes his camouflage nearly useless."

"I see." Belkidar paused a moment. "What's his state of mind when he cast these spells?"

"We've emphasized that Brohdan must remain calm whenever he uses sorcery, that he should never cast a spell when he's angry. How can a Broglia control his sorcery if he can't even control his emotions?"

"I couldn't agree more."

Brohdan glanced at Mikka, and again his anxiety lessened. He didn't particularly enjoy his struggles being dissected in front of everyone, but he knew they were only trying to help him.

"Brohdan, when you cast your spells," Belkidar continued, his gaze fixed on the fire, "describe your frame of mind." The orange glow of the flames danced on the sorcerer's weathered face and long white beard, their playful reflections a stark contrast to his serious expression.

"It's difficult to explain," Brohdan began. He suddenly became aware of his voice as he realized all eyes rested on him. "First, I calm myself and try to remove all emotion from my thoughts. Next, I think about the spell's objective. When I think of hardening my skin and scales, for example, I cast 'steelskin.' As long as I remember that I want my skin to be hard, the spell is held in place. As soon as I become distracted, or if I think of my skin going back to normal, the spell is released."

Belkidar nodded slowly. "Let me start at the beginning." The human paused as he took his battered walking stick from his lap and placed it to his side as he leaned back against a tree trunk.

"All the world's sorcerers have at least one thing in common. A part of their brain, called the Linsilor Sorcerenic, has developed so that they can cast a spell; without this, sorcery is impossible. The more capable the Linsilor, the greater potential for the sorcerer, although good technique, a vast knowledge base, and lots of practice are also required, regardless the Linsilor's development."

Belkidar thought about Brohdan's situation. "You're a Broglia Black, so your Linsilor has obviously matured," he said, turning to face the dark green dragon. "That's been verified by your proven ability to cast spells. So the issues you're having must stem from your technique. I'll think about it."

Krepli smiled. "I appreciate your expertise, Belkidar. I fear there's little the three of us can teach him that you cannot."

"History doesn't lie," Boseda agreed, "his experience will benefit Brohdan the most."

"I agree," Rouldra offered. "Belkidar is the perfect instructor to finish Brohdan's training. Good luck," she added with a wry smile.

With the consent of Brohdan's instructors, Belkidar formally took over Brohdan's training. "Thank you all. I respect the loyalty, the accountability, that forever bonds teacher to student. And I understand how difficult it is for you to transfer that responsibility. I vow to do my best to finish what you started."

Brohdan thoroughly enjoyed the rest of the night. The moon made its entrance low in the clear sky and began its slow ascent. After its trek was nearly half completed, Belkidar rose and cut himself another large steak. As he carried it back to join the others, the steak began to sizzle, and Brohdan could only wonder at the depths of his tremendous gift.

The firelight gradually became more assertive as darkness filled the gaps between trees and dragons, casting a warm glow that sporadically danced across the varied faces around the fire. The intermittent pops of the burning wood broke the infrequent silence as their conversations covered periods of Belkidar's early childhood, Krepli's experiences with Balthasar, and Rouldra's first three husbands. Brohdan's parents, obviously enjoying their time outside of Lukvia, talked excitedly with Mikka as the others discussed Brohdan's progress, their pride obvious in the animated telling of their stories. But eventually, much closer to dawn than midnight, their imminent journey forced Belkidar and Brohdan to end the otherwise perfect evening.

"When will you leave?" Krepli asked, rising to his feet and wing hooks.

"In a few links," Belkidar replied. "Time is short, and we've much to do."

"Take care of him. He was a most rewarding student."

Belkidar smiled. "I will, old friend. Take care of yourself in our absence. There are ever too few instructors in the world, especially those with your wisdom."

He returned the sorcerer's smile, then turned to face his former student. "Brohdan, thank you for accepting my instruction. You've demonstrated an exceptional work ethic, and your dedication is infectious. It's been an honor and privilege to instruct such a gifted young dragon." For the first time since Brohdan had met him, the old Gorduvian bowed to him, acknowledging the Broglia Black's place in society. It was in this way that all Broglia instructors officially recognized the conclusion of a grombit. Brohdan was now considered an adult Broglia Black, instantly becoming the most respected dragon in the world.

"Thank you, Master Krepli. Thank you for seeing in me what other instructors couldn't, and for believing in me when nobody else did. Whatever I become, whatever services I can provide, I owe to you," Brohdan said, returning his bow.

Krepli nodded. His life's work successfully concluded, his expression conveyed a contentment Belkidar had rarely seen. With only the sound of his flapping wings, he rose slowly and disappeared into the darkness.

"Brohdan, I relished our relationship," Rouldra said shortly. "After all the work I've put into you, don't do something stupid like get yourself killed." She too bowed.

"I'll try not to, Instructor Rouldra," Brohdan said, bowing also. "Thank you for sharing your knowledge with me."

Rouldra looked at the large dragon, but said nothing. After a rare smile, she followed the Chief Instructor into the night.

Boseda was the last of his instructors to approach him. "I'll miss our time together. You may not realize it, but you taught me at least as much as I hope to have taught you." He smiled. "You've been a patient student, Brohdan. It's difficult for an instructor to teach a subject in which he himself has no experience. I hope we've been adequate."

"Sir, you've been much more than adequate. I understand the difficulties you faced – and overcame – and that makes me even more grateful. Master Krepli could've searched the world and never found a better successor than you," Brohdan said, bowing.

Boseda returned his bow before departing toward his home.

"I'll find a spot to hold up for the night down there somewhere," Belkidar said as he motioned further along the river with his walking stick. "I'll be ready to leave at sunrise. That's in a few links, in case you lost track of the time." Belkidar then transformed himself into a large wolf and silently trotted toward the river.

"Son, it was wonderful to see you again," Brohdeck began. "Your mother and I have to go back to Lukvia tonight. Dorchuva was quite sick when we left, and I'm not comfortable leaving him alone when he can't hunt."

"I understand."

"Don't worry, we'll be here when your Quest is over," his mother offered. "Just do your best, and be careful," she added, tears falling from her eyes.

"I will, Mom. Thank you both for coming to see me. I don't think you realize how homesick I've been."

"Oh, I think I do," Grediva muttered, her crying intensifying.

"Goodbye, son. Listen to Belkidar and you'll be fine."

"I will, Dad," Brohdan said as he touched his nose and forehead to his father's and then his mother's.

"Be careful," his mother repeated as her nose slowly left her son's. His parents, side-by-side, took off and headed south. His heart heavy, Brohdan watched until the darkness swallowed them. He couldn't be sure when he'd see them again, but he knew it'd be longer than he'd wish.

"Are you okay?" Mikka asked.

"I suppose so. It doesn't get any easier, does it?"

"I understand if you'd rather be alone."

"No, please don't leave. I've said goodbye to too many I love."

And so she stayed. They spent the night together, and Brohdan again experienced that helpless feeling of not wanting dawn to arrive. Inevitably, he knew it must, and he'd again be forced to say goodbye to someone he loved. Accepting this, he shed his loneliness and sorrow, cherished the moment. It was an experience built on companionship and love. It was a night he would never forget.

Chapter 7
Kiera

It is a great act of cleverness to be able to conceal one's being clever.

Francois de La Rochefoucauld

Brohdan woke to find a faint violet painting the skies above the eastern mountains. He had dreaded this day ever since he first met Mikka nearly two cycles ago, and now the moment stood before him. He wasn't surprised to find her awake, and side-by-side they watched the sunrise together.

"Promise me you'll be careful."

"I promise." He turned to look into her eyes. "I'll miss you more than you could possibly know."

She smiled sadly. "If anything happens to you…"

"Nothing will happen, I'll be with Belkidar."

"I know. But if anything does, I won't have a reason to live." She nestled into his chest.

"I love you, Mikka."

"I love you too, Brohdan," she sobbed, then touched noses with her mate. In tears, she flew away.

Brohdan's eyes followed her until she disappeared behind the trees of a distant ridgeline. When he forced his gaze from her, he saw Belkidar waiting respectfully near the foothills below his cave.

"It's never easy," he offered as Brohdan approached.

"How have you done it for so long?"

"One by one."

Brohdan nodded, understanding only a fragment of his past.

"If you're ready…"

"I'm ready."

"We're headed that way," Belkidar explained, motioning toward the northwest with his Staff.

Brohdan waited briefly as Belkidar prepared himself. Without speaking a word, the eagle spread his large wings and took to the air, Brohdan following closely behind.

It was a perfect day for flying. The sun's warmth slowly invaded Drulop's crisp morning air, and a light southern breeze quickened their progress. After flying nonstop for several links, Belkidar led them to a large field for a well-deserved meal.

Brohdan followed the eagle and landed next to him. Just as he touched down, he watched Belkidar transform himself into a creature he'd never seen before. Savage-looking with a bear-like head, shaggy black fur, and six powerful, lanky legs, the beast stood a full two elads at the shoulders.

He sniffed the air, then left with a growl so deep, Brohdan felt it resonate through his chest more than his ears. It moved effortlessly through the trees, accelerating on all six legs before smoothly transitioning into a four-leg gallop. Unlike its other paws, Brohdan saw that its front pair had opposable thumbs, resembling talons.

After only a few drus, Brohdan heard several cries pierce the once-peaceful forest. The creature returned a few moments later, his lips raised in a snarl, dragging an enormous elk carcass to where Brohdan sat.

"Thank you," Brohdan said as Belkidar shimmered back to his original self.

"Don't mention it," Belkidar replied, blood still matting his beard. "You can hunt tonight."

Brohdan nodded, distracted by what he'd just witnessed. "Tell me, what was that? I've never seen anything like it."

"Oh, Briz. I'm very proud of him. He's something I invented a long time ago to hunt large game, but it didn't take me long to realize I needed something more agile. I continued refining him over the next few centacycles, eventually arriving at the creature you just saw. His senses are incredible, particularly his hearing and sense of smell, so he can hunt in any weather, day or night. He's a tireless runner, and his jaws are among the most powerful in the world." Belkidar considered Briz for a moment. "His only drawback is his eagerness to kill. I'm forced to constantly remind him that we kill only what we need, nothing more."

"What do you mean? I thought *you* were Briz. Why would you have to remind yourself?"

"Any time a sorcerer assumes another form, he adopts the instincts of that animal – its essence, not just its shape."

"But you invented him. How can he have instincts of his own?"

"That's where it gets complicated. It's true Briz doesn't exist anywhere else in the world, but he does when I assume his form. And when I do, he's just as much a part of this world as you are. Through the centacycles, he's developed and refined his own instincts. Quite understandably, since much of his existence is spent hunting, that's what he knows best, and he does it exceedingly well. But his essence goes much deeper than that. He naturally becomes very excited during these hunts, not just because he's getting the chance to do something he's good at, but also because he's accomplishing what his creator intended. Being able to understand your creator's expectations – and then to be able to *fulfill* them – is exceptionally rewarding. I just need to control that aggression so it doesn't get out of hand."

Belkidar paused, then smiled. "I'm really quite proud of him. In fact, I should really set aside a few decacycles to let him explore his existence. I owe him that. Now, if you'll excuse me, after a successful hunt I always like to reward him by letting him to eat in his own form."

It wasn't long before Brohdan again heard shrieks followed by the unmistakable sounds of bones breaking between jaws. When Belkidar returned a half link later, he was once again in his own form.

"Any thoughts on how I can improve my sorcery?" Brohdan asked, tossing antlers to the edge of the field.

"Yes, I think so." He sat beneath the shade of a tall evergreen, resting the Staff across his lap. "You explained that you remove all emotion when you cast spells, but that limits your potential. It's always good to be in control of your emotions, but that doesn't mean you should be emotion*less* when you use sorcery. Like any undertaking, sorcery is fundamentally affected by emotions, and those emotions can be an ally or enemy. For example, imagine how a carpenter would perform if he's angry or frustrated compared to when he's content and focused. It's no different with sorcery. If you use your emotions constructively, the spell becomes alive with your character, but when you're emotionless, the spell lacks your distinctiveness. That's why the world's best sorcerers have been those with the finest character."

"It sounds complicated," he said, oblivious to Belkidar's joke.

The old man grunted before continuing. "Once you realize spells take on the characteristics of their creator, the concept's easier to understand."

They relaxed, each enjoying the respite. Birds noisily returned to their nests once Briz disappeared, and a warm breeze took the autumn chill from the shadows as they talked. Eventually, Belkidar stood. "We should make good time while we can."

"What do you mean?"

"None of the rest of our party can fly, so we can only go as fast as the horses can carry us. I believe I'll join them once we pick up our next colleague."

Brohdan laughed, then realized it wasn't a joke. "Why would you ride a horse when you can fly?"

"For a few reasons, but mainly for safety. I'd like be with the majority of the party in case we run into trouble. They may need me, and if I'm flying several linops away, I won't be of much use. Besides, I know you can take care of yourself."

"We'll see," Brohdan muttered uneasily. Dragon or not, his inexperience still made him feel vulnerable. It was the unknown that eroded his confidence.

Belkidar led the way. The large eagle flew quickly, and the pair made swift progress. They passed the gigantic peaks of the vast Cortusian range, and as with the Sichundars and Slatemores, he quickly adjusted to their frigid, unpredictable winds.

When the sun began to shine red, Belkidar decided to stop for the night. He chose a secluded valley in the foothills of the Cortusians' northwestern slopes. Soon after landing, he grew blurry in an increasingly familiar way, and before Brohdan's eyes, the powerful eagle had transformed into the seemingly frail old man.

"Refreshing, isn't it?" he asked, looking up into Brohdan's face.

"Absolutely. I haven't flown so many links since Krepli's conditioning drills, but that was always boring laps around camp."

The waning sunlight painted the tops of the trees red, but the base of the valley was already in shadow. "Are we spending the night here?"

"Yes, I thought we would. But we still have a link of daylight left, and I thought we'd use it to help fulfill my promise."

"Oh? I don't remember you promising me anything."

Belkidar smiled. "That's because I didn't. I promised your instructors, Krepli in particular, that I'd continue your training."

Brohdan nodded, his anxiety growing.

"Do you remember what I said about using your emotions?"

"Yes."

"Good. Remember, the spell's strength isn't the only thing that's limited by removing your emotions from the process, it limits its personality too. It's a very sterile way to do things."

"How can a spell have personality?"

"When cast properly, a spell has a life of its own – a life indebted to the sorcerer who created it. As a result, it'll do everything within its power to please you."

Belkidar noted his confusion. "All right, let's say I wanted to eat some fruit tonight. If I were to cast 'nurture' on that," Belkidar said as he pointed to a strange fruit-bearing tree with his Staff, "the spell would do everything within its power to succeed. Similarly, if I were to cast 'venom' on that squirrel, it would strive to kill it as efficiently as possible. A spell working on your behalf is significantly more effective than a spell with no ambition."

Brohdan nodded. "I've never heard of that theory before."

Belkidar chucked to himself as he remembered his own past. "It's much more than a theory, my friend. Anyway, let's see what we can do. Try casting 'steelskin' again, but include your personality this time. Just be yourself and don't try to hide anything. The spell will do the rest."

Brohdan closed his eyes in concentration, but this time he didn't try to exclude his emotions. As he focused on the spell's effect, he could feel his skin and scales harden. To his amazement, the result was much different than anything he'd experienced previously.

"Interesting, isn't it?"

"It's amazing! My skin and scales are so much tougher than before, but there's no weight to it!"

"That's the spell working *for* you. It obviously respects you, and it's trying to impress you."

Brohdan relaxed his concentration, releasing the spell. "So, if my emotions have that sort of effect on 'steelskin,' what would it do to 'cloak?'"

"See for yourself."

Brohdan repeated the process, freeing his emotions as he cast the spell. Once 'cloaked,' he opened his eyes and looked at Belkidar. "Can you see me?"

He smiled. "Of course, but I do have some experience with these things. And remember, casting 'cloak' won't make you completely invisible. You'd have to cast 'invisibility' for that."

"I don't feel any difference."

"That may be true, but the spell's doing a remarkable job. Before, it simply did what it was supposed to – transfer the light from one side of your body to the other, as I'm sure Krepli explained. But now the

spell actually *wants* to conceal you. The quality of the images'
projection is much improved, making you nearly invisible if you don't
move. And when you do, the spell attempts to predict those
movements, reducing the lag between the projected image and your
actual background."

Pleased, Brohdan released the spell.

"Now let's try 'fear,'" Belkidar suggested, "and remember the
delivery."

Brohdan concentrated. After a few drus, he looked at Belkidar.
"What do you think?"

"Much better! This time it was like you instantly appeared an elye
in front of my face a split dru after nothing was there. Well done!"

"Thank you. I never realized how emotions affected the spell."

"Not just your emotions, but your entire being. The spell feeds off
of who you are, and your emotions are only a small part of that."

Brohdan spent the next link practicing, but his exhaustion from the
day's long flight eventually caught up with him. He looked up,
entranced with the stars that filled the sky. Content, he silently walked
to the sorcerer, laid nearby, and joined him in sleep.

Early the following morning, the pair left the Cortusians and
entered the vast plains of western Drulop.

"Where are we going?" Brohdan asked.

"KelKinney," the large eagle squawked as he flew ahead.

"I've never heard of it. What's it like?"

"It's the north's largest port, only Brodor to the southeast is larger.
It's home to every type of sailor, but fishermen are most common.
KelKinney began as a small fishing village several kilacycles ago. It's
changed rather dramatically since then, but it's lost little of its original
personality. It's where I hope to find our next companion."

"What's he like?"

The eagle grinned mischievously. "You'll see. This person has many talents, some apparent, others…less so."

Their flight continued, and although their headwind gradually increased as they continued northwest, the duo still made good time. "The coast," Belkidar pointed out not long before sunset. "We don't have far to go now."

Brohdan studied the distant shoreline, then considered the large bird that flew ahead, wondering if his incredible sight was a result of being an eagle or his other talents.

"Let's descend. I don't want the sky as our backdrop."

That puzzled Brohdan. "Why don't you want to be seen?"

Belkidar paused a moment. "There's something you must understand, Brohdan. Most Men of this age don't believe dragons exist."

Brohdan was flabbergasted, almost forgetting to flap his wings. "What? Why? That's ridiculous!"

"I know, but dragons generally live in the south, where others are scarce. And remember, generations of Men have lived and died since the end of the War, so few have ever seen one, believing they were all killed by Jenkar and his hordes." He paused, clearing his throat as he considered how to continue. "Others believe dragons are simply a fantasy."

"A *fantasy*?"

Belkidar did his best to hide his grin, trying to remember if he'd ever heard such a high-pitched voice come from a creature so large. "I'm not defending them, I'm just preparing you for their reactions. If you're seen in certain parts of the world, many will panic, possibly even attack."

"So they compare me to unicorns? Or mermaids?"

A momentary pause. "Uh, Brohdan? You do realize both unicorns and mermaids exist, right?"

Brohdan stared at him for several heartbeats, half expecting Belkidar to be joking. "Really?"

"Absolutely. And I know you didn't mean to insult them, just as Men aren't trying to insult you. We're all simply unaware of certain things, so try not to judge them too harshly."

Deep down, he knew Belkidar was right. It wasn't their fault if they were raised believing dragons had all died in the War. Nor was it their fault if they were told dragons weren't real. But for some reason, the notion of his race's existence being regarded as nothing more than a fantasy nagged at him. "I'll try to keep an open mind."

"That's good advice for anybody."

Belkidar continued his descent toward the setting sun until he was a few elads above the treetops. When they approached the first settlements, Belkidar led Brohdan into a secluded clearing in the trees.

"Let's make camp here," Belkidar offered. "It won't take me long to find this person, but I may have some convincing to do before we return."

"I understand."

"Please be patient, and don't let any of the locals see you. If you get hungry, I noticed some elk not far to the south."

"Did you happen to see a cow or two?" Brohdan asked hopefully.

Belkidar laughed. "I did as a matter of fact, but the last thing we need right now is an angry mob coming after us." With that, the eagle gracefully leapt into the air, tucked his talons beneath his tail, and departed northwest toward the city.

Brohdan welcomed the calm serenity that night. After finding a large elk where Belkidar had indicated, he returned to the clearing and found a quiet area in a thick cropping of trees. Once nestled among the towering oaks, he tried to sleep. Before long, though, he realized sleep wasn't in his immediate future. He considered everything that had happened since he'd left his cave, but with the very idea of Sul Brul, his thoughts turned to Mikka. He wondered what she was doing at this precise moment, sighed as a pang of sadness anchored itself deep within his heart.

"This is ridiculous," he muttered under his breath. "You're a Broglia Black dragon, and you're laying here sighing about a female." He grunted, eventually falling into a fitful sleep, his thoughts on Mikka linops to the south.

KelKinney was a beautiful city. Having seen it grow from its infancy, Belkidar knew it well. He flew high above the streets, used his keen sight to locate Kiera's home beneath the moonless night sky, then landed silently within a cluster of nearby trees. He changed into his customary form, then walked briskly to her door. He knocked, then again more loudly when nobody answered, and was soon met with a few choice curses that remotely referred to the time of night.

"Kiera, please open the door," he replied, his gift making it sound as though he were in the same room. "An old man could easily catch a cold out here."

The door opened almost immediately, a short woman racing through it. "It *is* you!" she squealed, embracing the him.

He grunted at the impact, taking a step back to maintain his balance. "May I come in?"

"Of course! Of course! Please," she replied, frantically making space for him to pass.

"Thank you, my dear."

Kiera quickly closed the door behind him, refastened four locks, then led him into the common room. "Can I get you some tea?"

"No, but I thank you." He smiled. "It's good to see you again. I do apologize for the late hour, but I had little choice."

"Sounds interesting," she replied through the early stages of a grin.

"Actually, it *is* quite interesting, primarily due to the risk of torture and death."

Kiera snorted. "How can I help, Belkidar?"

"That means a lot to me, Kiera. It really does. But before you commit, you should hear the particulars."

She was already shaking her head. "Belkidar, I have my life because of you. Whatever you need, whenever you need it."

"You've always had a gift of exaggeration," he answered. "Our objective is to destroy Hildegard." Belkidar paused, giving her a chance to react. When he was greeted with nothing but a calm expression, he continued.

"It's a long story, so for now I'll make it brief. If you accept, we'll have mooncycles to fill in the details." He unconsciously looked around the room before continuing. "Hildegard stole the Jewel, and with two of the three Artifacts, the world is once again threatened by Jenkar's creation. We must act now, before his power grows beyond our ability to stop him."

"Just one question," she asked.

Belkidar arched a single eyebrow.

"Should I wear black or grey?"

The sorcerer laughed despite the topic. "I'd bring both," he managed. "And thank you."

Kiera smiled. "No need to thank me, Belkidar. It truly is the least I can do. Besides, this Quest sounds like something I'd hate to miss."

She went to another room, then quickly emerged wearing black pants and boots with a dark grey tunic that was partially covered by a dull, dark brown leather vest. She also carried a large pack that contained several items that Belkidar knew well.

"Did you already have that thing packed?" he asked after her swift return.

"Of course. You never know when you'd prefer to leave suddenly," she explained, flashing a pair of striking dimples.

"You still have the daggers, I presume?"

Kiera pulled and replaced no less than eight daggers from sheaths concealed throughout her clothing.

"I think we're ready then," he said, confident others remained hidden beneath her clothing. "One more thing. There will be a few others in our little party, one of which is waiting for us just beyond the outskirts of town."

"Why didn't he come with you?"

"Because his kind is rather uncommon in these parts."

Kiera stared at him, confused.

"Very well," he sighed. "Brohdan, the other member of our trio, is a dragon."

Kiera's laughter trailed off as she realized he was serious.

"Let me describe where you're to meet us."

After a few drus, Kiera had memorized the directions. "I'll be there in a few links."

"Very well. I'll fly overhead and make sure you're not followed."

Nodding, she opened the door for her old friend. After following him outside, she locked it before departing alone down the dark street. She smiled as she walked, noting a faint white-blue light among the shadows of the trees across the street.

Dawn arrived slowly the following morning. Brohdan rose, stretching as he leisurely made his way to the clearing, finding no evidence that Belkidar had returned during the night. Having lost all hope of sleep, he decided to at least make the time useful.

After settling comfortably back in the gully, he cast 'cloak.' As Belkidar explained, he cleared his mind, allowed his character to infuse his sorcery. He sat patiently, motionless.

It wasn't long before wildlife returned. Birds that he'd frightened away returned to their nests. Lizards scurried through dead leaves while squirrels raced along the branches overhead. After only a half link, his surroundings teemed with life.

He eventually got bored. Noticing a squirrel scouring for a meal along the forest floor, he focused his mind and cast 'fear.' It instantly dropped an acorn, sprinted up the nearest tree, trembling on the upper-most branch.

Then he spotted several deer in the distance, the intermediate trees blocking most of his view. He picked one female from the group and again cast 'fear,' this time targeting a location several elads beyond it. The female immediately darted in panic, alerting her companions as she fled from the spell's origin.

Brohdan continued practicing long into the morning. By the time he'd terrified several dozen creatures, a large eagle swooped down and landed only an elad from his nose. "Good morning."

"Hello Belkidar," Brohdan said as the bird blurred into a familiar form.

"I see you've been busy."

Brohdan nodded. "I'm starting to understand how they can be used."

"How so?"

"Well, I figured out how to scare one animal or several. I also learned how to make them flee in the direction I want. The more detail I cast the spell with, the more detailed the results. It's actually fun!"

The sorcerer laughed softly. "I envy you your discoveries." He looked around. "How'd you sleep?"

"Not well."

Belkidar nodded. "Don't worry, that'll get easier too."

His insight once again caught Brohdan off guard, but that too was becoming familiar. "Did you find our third member?"

"As a matter of fact, I did."

"That didn't take long. When will he join us?"

"He?" a feminine voice asked from the trees north of the clearing.

Startled, Brohdan reared up on his legs, spread his enormous wings, turned to face the unexpected voice. A bluish flame rose from his gaping jaws as he searched the forest for the intruder.

"Brohdan! Stop!" Belkidar shouted, quickly moving between them.

Although he heard Belkidar's shouts, his instincts were difficult to suppress. With some effort, he forced his gaze from the trees down to the sorcerer.

"You know, instincts like those are what give dragons a poor reputation," Belkidar said with a sigh. "The owner of that voice is our third member."

"Oh," Brohdan managed as he lowered himself.

"Er – Brohdan?" Belkidar asked. "How 'bout relaxing those fuel glands?" he suggested, motioning toward the flames that still trickled through the teeth of his upper jaw.

"Sorry."

"Thank you." Turning his attention to where Kiera had taken refuge among the trees, Belkidar continued in a slightly more pleasant tone. "Kiera, it's all right. You can come out now."

Slowly, and with the stealth of a cougar, Brohdan spotted a small woman.

"Brohdan, I'd like you to meet Kiera. Kiera, this is Brohdan."

Kiera said nothing, stared apprehensively at the huge beast that stood in the center of the field.

"Nice to meet you, Kiera," Brohdan offered, his deep voice resonating through her entire body.

"You really do exist," she whispered to herself.

Brohdan looked at Belkidar for an explanation.

The old man nodded. "Yes, but don't worry," he added, giving Brohdan a look that spoke volumes, "Brohdan is our friend."

Silently, Kiera looked to Belkidar, then back to the dragon.

"I'm sorry for overreacting," Brohdan said, following Belkidar's lead. "You startled me."

"I didn't mean to," Kiera said through a nervous laugh. "In my business, you learn to move quietly, and before you know it, it becomes normal."

"Brohdan," Belkidar interrupted, maneuvering the conversation away from the previous unpleasantries, "Kiera is an expert guide. She's been around the world more times than you've frightened squirrels."

Brohdan gave the old man a pained look as Kiera flashed him an equally curious one.

"She's also the best tracker I've ever seen," he continued before he was forced to explain. "There's not a better hand with a dagger in Tymoteu, and she knows how to get out of the most difficult of situations. All in all, I'd say Kiera will be a most valuable addition to our party."

Brohdan regarded the small human. She wasn't very tall, standing nearly an elye shorter than Belkidar. She had bright brown eyes and caramel hair that fell to her shoulders. As she approached them, he immediately noted the smoothness of her movements.

"I'm sorry, I'm usually not this quiet. I've just never seen a dragon before."

"I understand. Belkidar explained that not everyone will feel comfortable around me."

She laughed, a little less nervously Brohdan noted. Although her smile vanished quickly enough, he noticed her dimples lingered.

"Are either of you hungry?" Belkidar asked, relaxing a bit.

"I could always use a good meal," Kiera said.

Brohdan smiled. "I can see we're going to get along just fine."

"Thanks for the food," Kiera said as Belkidar finished eating.

"I'm not sure he can understand you when he's in that form," Brohdan offered as they watched Briz attack his food.

Belkidar soon changed back. "You're very welcome," Belkidar replied before turning to Brohdan. "Just because an animal wishes to continue his meal uninterrupted does not imply a lack of intelligence."

"Sorry. But it wasn't your silence that fooled me, it was your sloping forehead and protruding chin."

Kiera turned to hide her smile.

Belkidar let it pass. "Kiera, did you leave the horses where I asked?

"Yes, and I loaded two with supplies."

"Thank you. Brohdan, your presence may make the horses a bit edgy – say about 'panic' on the tension scale. Please keep your distance for a few days until they get accustomed to you. Also, if you fly too high when we're near populated areas, people will see your silhouette linops away."

"Got it. How will you reach me if we need to talk?"

"That's simple – 'communicate' is a handy spell that's adaptable to all types of situations. If you ever need to talk with me, simply focus on the message that you'd like to send."

"Sounds easy enough."

"It is, but when you do, don't visualize sentences or words, that takes too much time. Cast the spell so you send just the object of the message, not the message itself. It's much more efficient that way. Understand?"

"I think so."

"Very good." The sorcerer looked at both of his companions. "We'll make for Trisett next."

"Is it far?" Brohdan asked.

"Not quite as far as our journey from Sul Bru. It's on the border where Drulop, Ransu, and Charlov meet. But it'll take us longer to get there since the horses will set our pace going forward. I'm afraid my flying days are behind me for a while."

"That's all right," Brohdan decided. "I was getting a little tired of your tail feathers."

"What's wrong with my tail feathers?"

"Nothing, it's just when you've seen them for two days straight, they tend to get a bit tiresome."

Without saying a word, Belkidar turned and departed with Kiera toward the horses, twisting several times to inspect his backside.

Chapter 8
Batai

*Discipline is the soul of an army. It makes small
numbers formidable; procures success to the weak,
and esteem to all.*

George Washington

"I didn't think he'd be so..." Kiera began, unable to find the right words.

"Yes?" Belkidar asked, following her through the dense trees.

"Well, I didn't think he'd be so *amiable*," she finally admitted. "You know, dragons are supposed to be a myth, but today I meet one for the first time and find he's so personable."

Belkidar smiled. "Most are like that. They eat, sleep, cherish loved ones, and grieve those who are no longer with us. They tend to have poor reputations only from those who are intimidated by them – which, unfortunately, happens to be the majority of Men."

"I can imagine. When I surprised him, I felt a helplessness I hadn't experienced in a long time."

"No, I imagine you haven't," Belkidar replied, grinning. "Which is pretty remarkable if you think about it. With all of your escapades, I'm surprised you've survived this long."

"Escapades? Whatever do you mean, kind sir?"

He snorted.

"What's Brohdan going to do while we're riding?"

"Stay a good distance away from us, I hope. After a few days, I'm sure the horses will adjust. When they do, he can either walk with us or continue flying. Either way, we can only travel as fast as our slowest member."

"Won't he get lonely traveling so far with nobody to talk to?"

"I hadn't considered that. We'll tackle that as it comes," he finally decided. "With any luck, the horses will adjust quickly to having a dragon nearby."

They collected the horses and headed east, initially at a walk, then prodded them into a trot once they cleared the forest. Soon thereafter, Belkidar discovered Brohdan flying to the south. Too distant for the horses to detect, the two humans sat and watched the huge silhouette soar a few elads above the increasingly sparse trees.

"He really is an amazing creature," Kiera remarked.

"You have no idea."

She glanced at him. "Is there more I should know?"

"Brohdan isn't an ordinary dragon. He's a Broglia Black."

"He looks green to me."

"Yes, that's the way he began life, but now he's going through his grombit – a dragon's version of puberty, I suppose. Even as we speak, he's changing in many ways, and within the next few mooncycles his grombit will end. Among other things, his scales will turn black, and he'll grow to three times his pre-grombit size."

Kiera blinked a few moments before finding her voice. "How large was he then?"

"About half as large as he is now."

Several small ridgelines sloped from the Cortusians to the east, and Brohdan playfully flew between them as he weaved back and forth between their peaks. Every once in a while, Kiera winced as he headed directly toward a cliff, but without fail, he adjusted his giant wings and effortlessly turned a few moments before hitting them.

"It's difficult to imagine how he could become more graceful than that," she commented, her eyes glued to him.

"I know. It's just as difficult to imagine that he'll become deadlier, too."

Kiera nodded, recalling their initial meeting.

Brohdan managed to keep himself busy, realizing how tedious this journey would become if he didn't keep his mind occupied. Early in the day, he in and out of the small mountain ranges that dove off the scenic Cortusians. After a few links, though, this became tiresome, so he simply flew ahead of the four horses, landed some distance away, and waited for them to catch up. While this tactic left him more refreshed, it did nothing to alleviate his boredom.

After he flew ahead and began another lengthy wait, his thoughts inescapably turned to the friends and family he'd left behind. He thought about his parents and wondered how they were coping with his absence and the unknown circumstances that shrouded it. He guessed they'd be hunting about now somewhere north of the Sichundar Mountains. Brohdan also thought about the three younglings he shared grombit camp with. Methren, Albrogu, and Limbrin would presumably be together in Lukvia. He wondered if Limbrin had accepted the fact that he was not the only 'greater' dragon in their quartet.

He'd been content as a Dalluvian Green, at least until he completed that fateful journey south to the Sichundars. His heart still raced whenever he thought of those early mooncycles in grombit camp, and while he accepted his new life as a Broglia Black and the responsibilities that came with it, he'd never forget the suffering that defined his life back then. The anguish. The despair. The humiliation and helplessness. Those experiences helped shape him, and he knew he would forever compare future trials to that difficult period. He found strength from those experiences, and he vowed to use that strength throughout his life.

It happened just as the western skies turned crimson. Brohdan heard several riders approach from the east. "'Cloaking' and flying to his friends would take precious time, so he decided to try 'communicate' instead.

He closed his eyes and thought of the message he wanted to send Belkidar, remembering to send the object of the message, not the message itself.

"Please don't yell." Belkidar's message was tangible in his mind, as though he gazed at an idea.

"Sorry! But I wanted to tell you about the riders!"

"I got that part. Just don't yell anymore. It hurts my head when you do that." A pause. *"How many?"*

"It's hard to say from here. I'd say between twenty-five and thirty."

"Give me a moment."

As several of these tense 'moments' passed, Brohdan's anxiety swelled. He understood his might, but he also knew too well his utter lack of fighting experience.

"Stay out of sight," Belkidar's thoughts finally told him. *"I'll let you know if we need you."*

"How?" Brohdan asked as the riders passed his location and continued riding hard toward his friends.

Brohdan waited for Belkidar's reply, but none came. This only deepen his panic, but he forced himself to relax. After all, Belkidar was thousands of cycles old! And he'd never needed his help before.

"Help, Broh – "

Brohdan's instincts took over. With a great leap, he was a dozen elads in the air before his wings took over. He flew high, discovered where the riders had pinned down his friends, saw that Belkidar had been knocked to the ground. They left his limp body on the road before turning their attention toward Kiera.

They had her trapped in a small gully a few elads north of where Belkidar lay. Savoring the moment, most of the riders had dismounted and walked leisurely toward her. The four still on horseback blocked her escape. Considering Kiera's beauty, Brohdan didn't need to be human to understand what they had in mind.

The Broglia Black tucked his wings, dove toward the ground. Only a few elads above the road, he effortlessly climbed and descended, mirrored the rolling hills. In his mind, he could still see every minute detail of the surrounding area as if he were still high in the air. Just over the crest of the next hill, he would see Kiera down the gully to his right, the riders slowly making their way toward her from the very road he now followed.

In less than fifteen drus from the moment he'd received Belkidar's plea for help, Brohdan reached the final hill that separated him from the riders. As he climbed the long incline, he once again tasted the pungent fuel as it erupted from the back of his throat, felt the heat tickle his cheeks as the oncoming wind blew some of his flames backward.

Most of the riders never saw what killed them. Brohdan silently crested the hill, his incredible speed easily outpacing their ability to react. Kiera heard only the deep rumble of dragonfire as he streaked overhead, its heat blowing strands of hair from her face.

His fire first engulfed those on the eastern part of the road before continuing its deadly path west, directly through the mass of riders. Brohdan's liquid flames were so intense that man and horse alike were killed instantly, blackened bones protruding from legs or arms. Those that weren't directly in his fire's path were severely burned on the exposed side of their bodies before the force of his attack tossed them aside. The wounded screamed in voices so high they hardly seemed human. Only three attackers survived.

Brohdan leaned back and climbed into the darkening sky. He quickly slowed, momentarily stopped in mid-air. Just before falling back to the ground, he flapped his right wing upward and his left wing downward as he leaned right, pivoting fully around so that he faced the distant ground. With a single powerful flap, his immense speed returned as he fell.

He saw two of the three survivors bolting west, again opened his jaws, unleashed an inferno. The horses continued recklessly galloping in random directions after he blew their riders from their saddles. Then he leaning back, spread his wings wide, flared and landed, several elads from the lone survivor.

The rider leapt from his petrified horse and ran to where Belkidar still lay motionless on the ground. "Stay away!" he yelled, reaching for his hostage.

Brohdan lunged, falling forward onto his wing hooks, impaling him with his many razor-sharp teeth. With a sickening crunch, Kiera heard several of the man's bones splinter as Brohdan's jaws came together. Not wanting to taste this vile creature any longer, the man's body shot from his mouth as fire engulfed him. Smoke trailed his lifeless body before it landed with a thud, its arms flailing clumsily as it rolled to a stop. With a deafening roar, Brohdan purged the rage that had so quickly built up inside him.

He took several drus to calm himself before turning to Kiera. Despite the circumstances of their initial meeting and the gore that now surrounded her, she felt no fear as the dragon towered above her. She calmly walked onto the road, placed her hand on his leg. "Thank you Brohdan. You saved my life."

"You're welcome," he said, his voice still shaky. "Let's see how badly Belkidar's hurt."

"Right," she agreed, running to where he lay.

They found him lying face down. He had a lump on the back of his head, but as they turned him over to inspect for other injuries, they heard his curses.

"Are you all right?" Kiera asked softly.

"No," he answered gruffly. "I've got a headache that would kill a mountain troll."

Slowly, Belkidar opened his eyes and saw his two friends standing over him, their concern evident.

"Judging from the smell around here, I'd say either Brohdan took care of the attackers or Kiera's cooking again."

"Yup, he's all right," she said, then left to retrieve their horses.

"What happened?" Brohdan asked after Belkidar managed to sit.

"The leader stopped us and asked what business we had in this part of Drulop. Kiera told him we were traveling to see family in Kordare.

As she talked, I noticed some other riders surrounding us. I sent you a message, but I'm not sure I finished it."

"I got enough. How badly are you hurt? Maybe we should stop for the night."

"I'm not in any condition to ride far, but let's put some distance between us and this bloodshed."

"I found the horses!" Kiera shouted from some distance to the south. "Shall I bring them over?"

"No," Belkidar answered softly. "I think they've seen enough of Brohdan for one day. Salvage whatever horses you can while we take a moment to work things out."

"Okay. I'll also see what supplies they had while you two are guy-talking."

Belkidar shook his head. "Why don't you tell me what happened while I was out."

"It all happened so quickly," Brohdan admitted, replaying the events in his mind. "I got your message, or most of it anyway. I flew high enough to see what was going on, then dove back down and surprised them. There were only three after the first pass, so I turned around and came back for them."

"That's it?"

Brohdan nodded.

"Then why do you have blood down the sides of your jaw?" Belkidar asked, an eyebrow raised.

"The last one tried to take you hostage, and you were too close to risk fire." He shrugged.

"Well, I don't mean to sound ungrateful, but not much good can come from eating a human."

"I didn't exactly *eat* him."

"We both know that, but if a passerby happened to see you, what do you think he'd tell everyone at the pub tonight?" Belkidar let that prospect sink in. "Once you're given the 'man-eater' label, you'll spend the rest of your life hunted by humans. Trust me, Brohdan, that's no way to live. Next time, just step on the bastard."

"I think I will," Brohdan decided immediately.

"Aren't you two done yet?" Kiera asked.

"Almost! Just keep your pants on!" Belkidar yelled, then winced at the pain it caused.

In the distance, Brohdan distinctly heard some rather imaginative curses.

"One more thing," Belkidar said softly. "Have you ever killed anyone before?"

Brohdan looked into the sorcerer's eyes before returning his gaze to the ground. "No."

"Well, I have. It's never easy, and if you've got any conscience at all, it never will be. I've lost count of the people I've had to kill over the course of my life." His expression turned distant. "You'll have a lot of time to recount today's events. Don't be too hard on yourself. You did what was required."

Brohdan continued staring painfully at the ground.

"Thank you for saving my life today," the old man added.

Brohdan looked up, remained silent.

"Now let's get out of here."

Without a word, Brohdan took flight. He was beginning to more clearly understand the nature of the challenges that lay ahead, but he found comfort knowing he wouldn't have to face them alone.

"You let yourself get hit!" Kiera scolded softly, the horses in trail.

"I did no such thing!" Belkidar replied a bit too quickly.

"In all the cycles we've known each other – in all of our travels! – I've never seen a human strike you. Especially from a group so useless!"

"He got lucky."

Kiera snorted. "You wanted to test him."

Belkidar thought for a moment. "He must discover himself – his strength, his confidence, even a ruthlessness – to learn what it is to be a

Broglia. Those idiots just gave him the perfect opportunity. Besides, I knew you could handle them if needed."

They soon approached the small farm town of Kordare, a pleasant community located midway between KelKinney and the western slopes of the Cortusian Mountains. Kordarian farms stretched for linops in every direction.

"I love rural towns like this," Kiera said. "They're so refreshing."

"I couldn't agree more. I've seen so many people change over the cycles, life's temptations too many to resist. Farmers are the exception. They are today as they were eight thousand cycles ago. I admire that."

As they approached the town, Belkidar searched one last time for Brohdan. "Do you see our friend?"

"No, not for a while."

"I'm sure he's fine, but I think I'll check just to be safe." He appeared to stare into the distance, but Kiera realized he was doing much more than that.

"Where are you, my friend?"

"Several linaks east of the town, in the foothills."

"Good. Kiera and I won't be long. It's already dark, and I'd like to find shelter. My head's still throbbing." Belkidar relayed the information to Kiera.

"How are you feeling?" Kiera asked. "You look quite pale."

"That makes sense. I feel quite pale."

Brohdan rested on his stomach as he waited, tried unsuccessfully to keep this mind on something other than the attack on his friends and the killing that followed. He wondered if anybody would be able to tell that he was a murderer simply by looking at him. Would his parents be disappointed the next time they looked into his eyes? Would Mikka? Would she still feel the same way now that he'd killed for reasons other than food?

He forced himself to change the subject, but soon realized the impossibility of that task. So instead of running from it, he attacked it. He knew their deaths were the result of their choices, not his. And he was proud of the way Krepli and his instructors had prepared him for battle. If he needed any validation for those endless links of training, he now had it. His fire breath was much more effective than he'd imagined, and he hadn't yet developed his Broglia fire. He was also pleased with how quickly he was able to get to his friends' aid. If he'd been much longer, Kiera might have been injured. Or worse. But most importantly, he was there for his friends when they needed him most. It went much deeper than the 'thank you's' he received after the battle; their grateful expressions made him believe he truly belonged in this Quest. He realized he still had some things to sort out concerning the deaths of all those men, but in his heart, he knew he was a vital member of their group.

Kiera and Belkidar found the dark streets deserted. They saw several houses, each with lights shining from the windows as Kordare's families ate their evening meals.

"Typical farm town," Belkidar observed. "Everybody's on the same schedule. Get up before dawn, labor all day in the field, eat a delicious meal with your family, and then go to sleep so you can do it all again the next day."

"It sounds like you know something about it."

"In fact, I do. About five thousand cycles ago I spent forty-four cycles on a farm. I happened across a pleasant young couple recently married. After talking with them for a few links, Ed asked if I knew how to work with metal. I explained that I'd been a smith's apprentice some cycles before, and he offered me a job. I didn't have anything planned for the rest of the centacycle, so I gladly accepted." He smiled. "The time I spent on that farm with Ed and Beverly was one of the happiest periods of my life."

After riding through town, Belkidar nudged his horse into a trot. Kiera and the pack horses followed and, before long, they rendezvoused with a certain Broglia Black dragon.

"I'm glad you decided to join me," Brohdan said, his deep voice emanating from behind several hills that lay a hundred elads south of the road.

"Oh, quit feeling sorry for yourself," Belkidar answered. "At least your backside isn't chaffing like mine."

Brohdan laughed, but stopped when his friend came into view. "You don't look well. We should stop for the night."

"I agree with Brohdan," Kiera replied. "That blow to your head was worse than you're letting on. Let's find shelter over there," she offered, pointing to nearby hills that quickly grew into mountains as they continued south and east, eventually leading all the way to the majestic Cortusians.

"Since when were you two in charge?" Belkidar asked.

"Ever since you got knocked unconscious," Kiera replied.

"All right," he surrendered, "just don't get me killed before I get my senses back."

Brohdan maneuvered deeper into the hills before the horses could detect him. Kiera soon heard him offering directions, but knew he was too far away to be heard so clearly. Strange.

She immediately appreciated the location Brohdan had chosen. He had even cleared a circle of small trees in the center of where the hills formed a bowl, providing ideal concealment.

"Why don't you come over here, Brohdan?" Belkidar said. "I think the horses got a good view of you earlier today, and they must've caught your scent several times by now. Let's see how they react."

"I don't know. It's been a long day for everyone, and I don't feel like chasing after them."

"I think they'll be fine."

Kiera took a tighter grip on her reigns just in case.

Brohdan leisurely strolled toward the camp. Even though Belkidar knew why he was behaving this way, he couldn't help the chuckle that escaped his lips. The sight of a dragon walking nonchalantly was just too much.

Luckily, the horses responded to the dragon's presence in a similar manner. Once they recognized him, they paid him little attention and returned to their grazing.

Belkidar's chuckles grew into laughter. "Sometimes, I get the feeling we make things more difficult than they need to be."

"It seems Brohdan isn't so scary after all," Kiera managed, his laughter contagious. "Stay away from us, you brute!"

Brohdan grunted. "I think I'll head back to the comfortable cove I just came from."

"If you do, make sure you warn us first!" Kiera suggested, tears streaming down her cheeks now. "I don't think I could take that again!" This statement caused the two humans to begin another round of hysterics, only this time their laughter was at least two octaves higher than the first.

Brohdan found their amusement infectious, and he too began laughing. But when an adult dragon laughs hard enough, he can't help the fire or acid that inevitably escapes his jaws, similar to the tears that result from human laughter.

Belkidar was well aware of Brohdan's random fire, but he was helpless to stop his hysterics. "Brohdan! You're going to...terrify the horses...if you keep breathing fire like that!"

By now, Kiera was on her stomach pounding the ground as she tried to ease the pain in her gut.

"I know!" Brohdan cried. Unable to stop his fire, he found the only way to prevent panicking the horses was to leave. Sporadic light flashes followed him as he fled through the darkness. The humans, watching the hilarity through tears in their eyes, saturated the hillsides with another wave of laughter.

Several drus later, Brohdan returned. After settling down – and the horses finally got some peace and quiet – Kiera remembered something she couldn't explain. "Brohdan, when you gave me directions here, you sounded like you were a lot closer than you actually were."

That caught Brohdan by surprise. "Really?"

"He was nearly a quarter linak away," Belkidar offered.

"But then how did he sound so near?"

"I don't know," Brohdan admitted.

"It's a trait of Broglia Blacks," Belkidar explained. "Their vocal cords are much longer than other dragons'. A piece of cartilage in their larynx acts like a bridge against their vocal cords. When Brohdan speaks in a normal voice, this bridge is held in place, shortening them. But with the bridge retracted, they take on their full length, giving him a much deeper voice that can resonate over long distances. It's come to be known as 'ranging' over the cycles."

This puzzled Brohdan. "Krepli never explained that."

"That's understandable. Most Broglias never develop the ability. In fact, the last time I saw it was over three thousand cycles ago. Kainan was the wisest dragon I've ever known." Belkidar's gaze turned to the pair listening intently across the fire from where he sat. "But not because of his performances on the battlefield. His tactical intuition and his ability to always know right from wrong were second to none, despite the often-blurred lines of war." Belkidar's gaze turned distant again. "I learned much from him."

Silence filled the campsite as he recalled memories of long ago. "Perhaps I should get some sleep after all."

"He's finally making sense," Kiera sighed as she got to her feet. Within a few drus, she had prepared Belkidar's sleeping blankets and tucked him in for the night.

"Thank you."

She kissed his forehead. "You're welcome."

When Brohdan woke the next morning, he saw the others had already packed their sleeping gear neatly onto the pack horses.

"Good morning, Brohdan," Kiera greeted him. "It appears you slept well."

"Good morning. I did, thank you."

"We should be leaving soon," Belkidar said shortly.

"How's your head?" Brohdan asked, getting to his feet.

"He's fine," Kiera answered for him. "His stuff wouldn't be packed if he wasn't."

"Hmph," the old sorcerer managed as he finished the last of his preparations. They could faintly hear him mumble something as he climbed into his saddle. "Are you two planning to join me? We've still got a long way to go."

"There, there," Kiera said, nimbly climbing onto her horse. "You don't have to be so grumpy. I'm doing this for your own good."

"I never doubted you. In fact, I now understand why you're such a successful negotiator."

"Why Belkidar," she answered innocently, batting her eyelashes, "whatever do you mean?"

"I think you know exactly what I mean. Let's go before you manage to steal my horse."

The group made good time as they followed the road into the Cortusians. Brohdan, still wary of frightening the local residents, kept his distance, using the terrain to conceal himself.

The temperature dropped as their path climbed. Soon, the trees that were so common around Kordare vanished. After traveling for several more links, they encountered snow flurries that posed a cycle-round threat in this mountain pass.

They eventually stopped for their midday meal, taking care to stay hidden from the road. Food for the humans was carried easily enough on the pack horses, but the same couldn't be said for a dragon, especially one that would grow so quickly in the mooncycle to come.

After getting food from her pack, Kiera's attention shifted from Brohdan to his surroundings. "There's no game up here for Brohdan."

"True, but dragons only need to feed once every third day or so. Having said that, many packs adopted the custom of eating one or two smaller meals each day, Brohdan's included. But since leaving home, he's had little opportunity to maintain that custom."

Brohdan nodded. "I like it better this way. It's nice to have a full stomach. Plus, I actually look forward to hunting since I don't have to do it as often."

While his friends ate, Brohdan folded his wings and laid down, his chin resting on the ground as he watched Kiera prepare their meal of brown bread, cheese, and dried sausage.

"But this has to be boring for you. Wouldn't you rather fly ahead and wait for us near Trisett?" she asked while leaning her back against his shoulder, arranging her sandwich as she talked.

"No, I'd rather spend time with you guys."

"Aaww, you're so sweet!" she said, patting the scales near his wing hook.

Belkidar sighed as he bit into his sandwich.

"How long before we get there?" Brohdan asked.

"If we don't run into any storms up here, the trip down the east side of the mountains should be a quick one. From the bottom, it's only a day and a half."

"I think I'll pick up a new dagger while we're there," Kiera announced between bites.

"What happened to the old one?" Brohdan asked.

"Oh, just a little incident a few days before Belkidar found me in KelKinney. Let's just say that daggers and chainmail don't go together very well."

Brohdan knew appearances were many times misleading, but with Kiera the natural assumption of innocence, of helplessness even, was automatic. He found that he had to consciously remind himself that she was an experienced warrior. As she retrieved a severely nicked and slightly bent dagger from within her clothing, Brohdan saw that she was in fact nothing like what she appeared, realized that pretense was undoubtedly one of her many strengths.

He looked forward to meeting the other members of their group.

The weather for the next two days remained cooperative, and Belkidar's prediction proved accurate. The sun descended behind them, the mountains' shadows stretching eastward. And then, as they crested one final hill, Trisett appeared below them.

"There it is," Belkidar said, "the largest city of the North. Divided into thirds by Drulop, Ransu, and Charlov, it's the economic and cultural center of the entire Western Continent and, some would argue, the world."

Brohdan stared in wonder. "I've never seen anything like it! It's busier than I would've ever thought possible!"

"You should see the trading sector," Kiera offered.

Brohdan blinked in amazement. "Have you been there often?"

She nodded. "I've had a few opportunities to pass this way."

"I'm sure you have," Belkidar commented, "but it's been a while for me. I may need a guide with a more recent memory of the city."

"I don't know how much help I'll be. It's been almost two cycles since I've been here myself."

"Well, you've got me beat by – oh, let me think – about five hundred cycles."

"I see your point. Who exactly are you looking for, anyway?"

"You'll see. I think we should camp here tonight so we can get a fresh start in the morning."

"Why? We're almost there," Brohdan said, his gaze glued to the city.

"Trisett's so big that I think you've misjudged the distance. It'll take us the better part of the morning before we arrive at the city limits, and it may take a couple days after that before Kiera and I can find who we're looking for. Do you think you can keep yourself busy for that long?"

"I'm sure I can think of something," he replied with a straight face.

"I'm sure you can. Just don't let anybody see you doing it."

Brohdan said nothing, but then the mischievous grin that crept across his face conveyed more than was perhaps appropriate.

"I never realized how naughty dragons were," Kiera said.

"Kiera," Brohdan countered, "until a few days ago you didn't even know dragons *existed*!"

"That's true."

"If you two are quite finished, I think we should leave the road and find shelter for the night."

"Belkidar, that's the first thing you've said today that's made any sense at all," Kiera said, riding alongside Brohdan. "I think your head is finally clearing up."

All that could be heard from the sorcerer's wake was a few muttered curses as he rode into the darkness.

The next day came sooner than any of them wished. Brohdan remained lying on the cool, damp grass as the two humans packed their meager belongings onto their horses.

"You two have fun out there," Brohdan yawned. "Just try not to make too much noise as you leave," he added, settling his huge body into a more comfortable position.

"I see it's going to be another long day," Belkidar sighed, rolling his canvas sleeping mat.

"Brohdan, there are several ranchers on the other side of the city. I'm sure they wouldn't miss a cow or two," Kiera offered.

"You don't say. I just might have to take a taste – peek. I just might have to take a peek."

"You two are going to be the death of me yet," Belkidar moaned. "Brohdan, whatever you do, please don't get caught doing it. The last thing we need right now is for half of Trisett to be in a panic because some old rancher spotted a dragon eating his merchandise. We have much more important priorities than what's in your stomach."

"I know," he said seriously. "I'll make sure I won't be seen. In fact, I'll probably sleep most of the time you're away. Where should I meet you?"

"That's a good question. I think we'll travel to the northeast after we're finished here. Why not meet us on this same road a linop or two on the other side of Trisett? Let's say no later than tomorrow evening. If we're not there, you'll have to wait for us."

"I'll be there. If you need me, I'm sure I'll hear from you."

"Likewise," Belkidar agreed. "Shall we go, miss?" he said to Kiera.

"Of course. See you in a couple days, Brohdan. Don't do anything I wouldn't do!"

They led the horses from their campsite and up the hill that had concealed them from the road. Within drus they were back on their horses, making good time toward the city's west gate. As they approached it a few links later, Belkidar caught sight of several uniformed men.

"I hope they won't give us too much grief," Belkidar commented, indicating the dozen or so duty guards standing watch at the gate.

"Why would they?"

"Crime's been increasing lately," Belkidar explained, recalling the bandits. "Makes the guards wary."

"Leave it to me."

As they rode within talking distance, the situation looked bleak. "What's your business in Trisett?" the nearest guard asked Belkidar.

"To take my grandfather to see his daughter," Kiera answered.

"I see," the guard said, turning to look at her. "Why do you have all these supplies with you then?"

"It was a long journey from KelKinney," she said softly.

"Where does your mother live?"

"In the Ransu sector, on Koldobore Street."

"I've never heard of it. We'll check it out."

"Is that really necessary, Major?" Kiera asked, nudging her horse to where he stood.

"Sergeant, actually."

"Oh, I'm sorry," she said, positioning her horse directly in front of him. "Is there a difference?"

"Yes," he replied absently, his gaze slowly descending to her thigh, which auspiciously rested at eye level.

"Do you suppose you could make an exception?" she asked, skillfully nudging her horse so that her leg brushed against his chest. "As you can see, my grandfather is quite old. I'd really like to get him inside before it gets too hot." She turned around to look at him. "He's quite frail."

"I understand," the guard replied, neither taking his eyes off the woman's leg nor distancing himself from the contact. "You may proceed, miss."

"Thank you so much, Major. If you're ever on Koldobore Street, please look me up."

"Sergeant," he corrected her again as he watched her ride through the gate.

"Old? Frail?" Belkidar said once out of earshot.

"Oh, you know I was just offering the poor man an excuse to let us pass."

He smiled. "That was skillfully done."

"Why thank you, Grandfather."

"Cut it out."

"Whatever you say, Granddaddy."

Belkidar sighed, realizing the significance of this new development.

"Where are we headed?" she asked.

"The man we're looking for is Batai, the Captain of the Order of Paladins."

That sobered her. "Surely you don't mean *the* Batai?"

"The one and only."

Kiera stared at him in disbelief. "But with all of his responsibilities, you think he'll join us?"

"I can hope. The Paladin Order is the top echelon of Knights. As their Captain, he more than anyone is committed to the very foundation of what our Quest represents. I doubt convincing him will take much effort. Besides," he added almost as an afterthought, "we've known each other for several cycles. If all else fails, I'll collect on the favor he owes me."

"Oooo, that sounds interesting!"

"Never mind," he warned. "It happened a long time ago, and it's none of your business."

She let it pass. "I believe you'll find the Captain of the Order of Paladins near the castle. At least, that's where I'd want him if I was the king. Or the king's daughter."

"I know where his Order is based. I did mention that I've met this man, after all. It just so happens that I've never actually met him in Trisett. I have a distinct memory of this city as it stood five centacycles ago, but I'm afraid things may have changed since then."

"You think? You do realize these fine people have discovered fire since your last visit."

"If he's not there," he continued, doing his best to ignore her, "I may need your help in tracking him down."

"Grandfather, has anybody ever told you that you're grumpy in the morning?"

"Hmph," he mumbled, nudging his horse into a trot.

Trisett was just as Kiera remembered, its various merchants busily weaving their way through the maze of streets. On its outskirts, trash lined both sides of the road, but the residents seemed too preoccupied with their daily chores to take notice. The buildings were packed together, the structures nearly all two stories tall, the top floors serving as sleeping quarters for the merchants and their families. While most were built from brick, every once in a while, Kiera noticed a wooden one too.

As they made their way toward the city's center, the scenery gradually changed. The most obvious was the crowd. Belkidar had to take care not to trample businessmen as they mindlessly walked where they pleased, oftentimes right in front of his large horse. The trash that had been so common in the city's outskirts had gradually disappeared as they continued toward the castle. Apparently, the king liked his city tidy, but his business must not regularly take him far from his fortress.

Although similar in size, the buildings here were quite different from the previous ones Kiera had seen. For one thing, they were all neatly kept, and the paint on each looked new. There were large windows in nearly every store they passed, and the road had evolved from dirt to cobblestone.

After a link of dodging merchants and businessmen, Kiera saw the enormous castle peek from behind the buildings of a street corner. It was truly magnificent. She'd seen it several times before, of course, but it still took her breath away. Her attention was instantly drawn to its center, the main structure that dwarfed everything around it. From there, the castle spread into five wings, each ending with its own spire, all surrounded by a moat wider than twenty horses set nose to tail. A broad, thick drawbridge was already lowered, and many people scurried across it as they went about their daily routines.

"Must we enter the castle?" Kiera asked.

"I'm not certain. The Order of Paladins resides in the northern wing, so if Batai isn't in the city, that's where we're likely to find him."

"It'll take links to get through that crowd."

"I know. We'll avoid it if we can." He turned slightly to the right and continued up the road that led toward the castle. After another link of patient travel, they found themselves near the drawbridge.

"Let's figure out where Batai's hiding," Belkidar suggested.

It didn't take him long to find a soldier dressed in full body armor sitting on a beautiful mount near the drawbridge. The knight's silver armor was spotless, the late morning sun glistening off the immaculate metal. Even the horse had polished armor on its chest and neck. Belkidar casually rode directly toward him.

"Halt! State your business in the castle."

"You don't have to yell, son, I can hear just fine. Would you be so kind as to tell me where I might find Captain Batai? I've urgent business with him."

He laughed, a short and harsh sound. "The Captain of the Paladin Order has business with you?"

Belkidar stared at the young knight for several long moments, his face expressionless. "Son, I remember when your charge was to ensure peace and honor in our society. Tell me, when did it include bullying the weak?"

Kiera couldn't see much of the man's expression behind his lowered visor, but the change in his body language spoke volumes.

"Sir, you may find Captain Batai on Trisett's east side, assessing the quality of peasant housing."

"A noble task indeed. Perhaps you know which district?"

"The Norandre District, on Dyntor Street."

"Thank you. Your help has been invaluable," Belkidar said, bowing his head. With that, he nudged his horse east.

"You can be quite persuasive yourself," Kiera remarked.

"Cycles of practice."

"You know where we're going?"

"I do. We're headed toward the east side of Trisett, to Dyntor Street in the mighty Norandre District."

"You have no idea where that is, do you?"

"Of course not. The last time I was here, there was no such thing as a Norandre District, and that castle over there was no larger than my outhouse."

Kiera considered that. "Either the castle was quite a bit smaller than it stands today, or your facilities are perhaps a tad lavish."

"You're really going to try my patience today, aren't you? Now, if you wouldn't mind, kindly lead us to this Norandre District."

"Happily, Grandfather," she said, taking the lead. For some reason, his cheeks took on an unnatural red hue as she passed. "You look quite warm. Maybe you should seek shelter from the sun after all."

The color in the old man's cheeks deepened, yet despite his muddled curses, she was sure the corners of his mouth turned up ever so slightly.

It was mid-afternoon by the time Kiera guided him onto Dyntor Street. Identically-constructed houses painted either white or beige lined both sides of the long street, each with a small window in front and a chimney to one side. They were all made of wood and looked to be of good quality. As Belkidar looked down the street, he didn't recognize anybody from the Paladin Order. He silently took the lead and continued down one of the many short-cropped grass roads of the housing community. When he came to an intersection, he looked to his right but saw only a few women tending their yards. When he looked to his left, he saw a big man in glimmering armor sitting on the largest horse Kiera had ever seen. He leaned slightly down and to his right, apparently in conversation with another man who sat an elad below on his own warhorse.

"That's Batai," he told Kiera.

"Amazing," she said as her eyes met him for the first time. "The horse seems destined to have that man sit atop him."

"You don't know how true that is," he replied softly. "Batai!"

Batai straightened and peered over his shoulder, recognizing him immediately. Before he had a chance to adjust his reigns, the enormous animal had reared around and was galloping loudly toward them, Kiera feeling the impact of each hoof as they approached. When he was a few elads away, he leapt from his still-running horse and ran the remaining distance to greet his old friend.

"Belkidar!" he called, grabbing him in a bear hug and lifting him from his saddle. "It's been too long!"

"Batai," Belkidar said calmly, "if you don't put me down, you'll be spending the rest of your life shaving your back."

Laughing, Batai set him down. "You seemed to have gained a few pounds."

Belkidar let that pass. "You look well, Batai. I haven't heard from you in a while, so I assume you've been busy?"

"That's an understatement, and I thought it'd only get worse when I decided to check on the peasant quarters. I've been pleasantly surprised, though. Some need minor repairs, but for the most part they're in good order."

Kiera cleared her throat, making eye contact with Belkidar. Pausing to let him make the introductions, she finally decided to end the awkward silence herself. "Hello, I'm Kiera, a friend of Belkidar's."

"It's a pleasure to meet you, Kiera. I'm Batai, also Belkidar's friend."

"Nice to meet you." Her stare returned to the sorcerer.

"Oh, you both know me well enough to know I'm terrible at that sort of thing. You two are now acquainted, that's the important thing."

She grunted. "Batai, do these peasants have their houses maintained for them?"

"They do. Trisett, and the kingdom in general, is unique. In exchange for their honest work farming the fields, maintaining the streets, repairing city buildings, or any number of other royal occupations, the king provides them with shelter, clothing, rations, and stipend appropriate for the profession. Over the centacycles, we've found both sides prefer this relationship. After all, peasants primarily want stability and security for their families, and the king wants nothing more than honest work."

"They're free to work any job they wish?" she asked.

"Of course, assuming they're qualified. But if they choose to work for the kingdom, they receive the kingdom's benefits."

"It's so simple that I'm surprised nobody's thought of it sooner."

"Sorry," Belkidar said. "I was busy with other things."

This surprised Kiera. "Belkidar, I'm genuinely impressed!"

"Why thank you, young lady." He turned to Batai. "Do you have time to talk?"

"Of course. I have an office nearby." With that, he put his left boot in the stirrup of the enormous white horse and smoothly climbed into his lofty saddle. "Follow me. It's less than a linak." Batai started up the street where Belkidar and Kiera had first seen him talking with his subordinate.

As before, Batai's horse seemed to know exactly where to go, stopping next to the man with whom Batai had previously talked. "Lieutenant, continue the evaluations. If anything of significance arises, send word to me at once. I'll be at the Norandre office."

"I understand, sir." He saluted before leaving.

Batai led them to his office, a modest wooden structure similar to the countless peasant houses so common in this district. It had a simple window to the right of the lone entrance.

"It's not much, but then we don't really need much to do our jobs." With that, he opened the door for his guests.

Kiera entered and found the inside as plain as its exterior, with only two large rooms to the building. The one they entered had several desks with an ink and quill tidily placed toward the rear of each. A few carefully stacked scrolls and official-looking papers were also visible. The second room was filled with bunks and storage cabinets.

"Please, have a seat," Batai said as he motioned them to chairs. "If you'd like, we have water and food in the next room."

"Thank you," Kiera said. "I'd love something to eat if it wouldn't be too much trouble."

"No trouble at all. Just give me a moment," he said. Kiera was accustomed to neither the man in the armor nor the noise it made, yet she immediately felt that the sound perfectly suited him.

After a short time, Batai returned with their meals: ham, cheese, and bread. He left again and quickly returned with two cups and a small cask. "I wasn't sure if you'd prefer water or ale."

"Ale," Kiera and Belkidar replied simultaneously.

As his two guests ate, Batai asked about the purpose of their visit.

"Do you know of this?" Belkidar asked, extending the Staff in his right hand.

"Yes. You told me of it cycles ago."

Belkidar nodded. "Hildegard has recently stolen the Jewel from the Indifferent."

"It can't be!" Batai exclaimed, standing from the table. "He must be stopped at once. Let me assemble my men and we can end this now!"

"And you wondered if he would join us," Belkidar reminded Kiera. "Batai, there's one small problem. Through the centacycles, Hildegard's amassed millions. We'd have no chance."

"Then we must choose a different strategy, one he hasn't prepared for!"

"I've already done that, my friend. In fact, that's why we're here. I need you."

"Belkidar, you know you have my help, always," he said, taking is seat again.

"Your loyalty means much to me, Batai, and I'm afraid I'm in desperate need of it now. Hildegard may have the advantage of numbers, but I believe him to be vulnerable in one respect. If I can put together a small group, I think we'll offer challenges he didn't anticipate. Nonetheless, I've learned of Five Defenses that we must overcome; afterward, only Hildegard and his personal bodyguards will stand between us and the two Artifacts."

"Grandfather, after we retrieve the Artifacts, Hildegard's remaining forces may trap us within his fortress," Kiera observed between bites.

"Grandfather?" Batai asked.

"Never mind," he sighed. "I don't believe they will, Kiera. If we've gotten to that point, then we've not only destroyed Hildegard, but his Five Defenses as well. I doubt they'd stand against us. Regardless, the purpose of this Quest isn't to escape, it's to destroy Hildegard. Nothing else matters."

Batai nodded, silently considered their plan as Belkidar paced the room, the soft taps of the Staff becoming repetitive, soothing. "That raises a question. Apparently, the Headpiece has been the root of all this evil. It corrupted Krollum just as it had Jenkar so long ago. Will it not corrupt you as well?"

"It will," Belkidar confirmed. "That's why I must destroy it."

"But then the Staff of Power will be lost forever!" Kiera said.

"I know. I understand what the Staff of Power means, but the world will always be in danger as long as the Headpiece survives. Granted, the Staff of Power may be the greatest gift we'll ever know, but the Headpiece poses an even greater threat."

"What do you mean?" she asked.

"If we're successful, Hildegard and his bodyguards will have been defeated, leaving me as the world's only sorcerer. So if the Headpiece were to then corrupt me, who could stand against me? Hildegard and his evil are vulnerable only because another sorcerer can challenge him, but once either of us is destroyed, one survivor will remain, unopposed to do as he pleases. That's why our Quest is so critical." Belkidar thought for a moment. "The Headpiece must not be allowed to survive. The fate of the world rests upon that."

By the time they finished their meal, the sun had disappeared below the western horizon. They decided to spend the night on office cots, a luxury compared to the ground on which they'd surely sleep in the mooncycles to come. Before retiring for the night, however, Batai told his old friend what he'd been up to since they'd last seen each other.

"I'm very busy," he concluded, "but I thoroughly enjoy bringing order to the kingdom, and hope to the deprived."

"And you've performed your duties better than any in your ancient Order," Belkidar said sincerely.

"Thank you, my friend. From you, that means a lot."

Before long, all three were in bed. While Kiera and Belkidar soon fell into a deep slumber, Batai considered the opportunity before him. He finally found himself on the eve of another noble quest, but this Quest was the most important of all. Before long, he would battle to protect the helpless from unseen evil. Cycles had passed since he'd had the opportunity to pledge himself to such a worthy cause – since the last time he'd been in Belkidar's company, he realized – and the idleness since had frustrated him. He understood the importance of his current duties, but he missed that passion, the feeling of being truly alive, that he'd felt in cycles past. He hadn't risen to his current rank without the need to prove himself on the battlefield, and the battlefield was where he felt most comfortable. With a fire once again smoldering in his heart, he closed his eyes and, for the first time in ages, slept contentedly.

Batai woke early the following morning. He had several preparations to finalize before he felt comfortable leaving his numerous responsibilities to his subordinates. While the others slept in the next room, he quietly put his affairs in order as best he could, considering the short notice of his departure. He was surprised at how eager he was to leave them for the opportunities Belkidar's Quest afforded him.

Not long after sunrise, Belkidar and Kiera joined him. "Great timing," he said. "I'm just finishing. I trust you slept well?"

"Very well, thank you," Kiera answered groggily.

"I find after sleeping on the ground for a few nights, even a simple cot seems comfortable," Belkidar noted.

"I know the feeling well," Batai agreed.

He needed only a few more drus to finish his preparations. Once completed, he offered them food, standard rations of biscuits, sausage, cheese, and coffee. "Do you need any supplies before we depart?" he offered.

"As a matter of fact, I think we could use some restocking."

"Help yourself," he offered between bites.

"Thank you."

As Kiera leisurely finished her meal, Belkidar took the opportunity to fetch two leather saddlebags from the back room. He raided the food supplies and, after inspecting all of the woolen blankets, chose three for the journey. As she watched, Kiera realized the old man had learned to ignore proper manners such a long time ago that it would surprise even himself if he remembered any at all.

She regarded the knight as he began the tedious process of donning his armor. He was at least an elye taller than Belkidar with a broad chest and thick arms. His green eyes were complimented by his short, brown hair and, despite his muscular build, showed surprising flexibility as he pulled a hauberk over his head.

Batai decided to leave his full plate mail behind in favor of the lighter, less cumbersome chain mail that now covered his cotton undergarments. Lastly, he donned his travel uniform, its dull blue and dark gray wool much warmer and more subdued than the bright red and blue uniform he generally wore during city business. Finally, he packed his horse's immaculate armor along with his chest plate and helm for more serious occasions.

Kiera didn't take long to realize Belkidar was in a hurry. She wolfed down the last of her meal, impressing him. "That's more like it, lass," he said, patting her on the back.

"You're too kind," she managed, her mouth full.

As they stepped outside into the brisk morning air, Kiera realized for the first time the overwhelming size of Batai's stallion. He towered over the other horses, and while hers was larger than most, it resembled a foal next to the other beast. His hooves were almost half the size of a wagon wheel, and his head was nearly as long as her horse was tall! After watching Batai excitedly greet and then mount the imposing animal, she too climbed into her saddle.

"I've never seen a more extraordinary horse," she commented as they followed Belkidar east.

"I thank you," he answered modestly. "Einar is a charger. We have only eleven in our cavalry, plus eight mares in our stables. It's estimated that one in every two hundred thousand births results in a charger, but we've been blessed with a slightly higher percentage of late." He paused a moment to regard Einar, then continued as he stroked the animal's thick neck.

"Paladins form the upper tier of Knights. Together, we're the finest, most disciplined force in the world, and I'd match our cavalry against any in history." Batai paused suddenly. "I'm sorry if that sounded arrogant – I'm very proud of my men."

"I doubt neither your facts nor your sincerity, Batai. Please continue."

"With pleasure," he agreed, bowing. "Paladins are a subset within the Order of Knights, serving as trainers, mentors, and battle commanders. And among those, the king bestows a great privilege to a very select few, those who've risen above their peers with their integrity, resiliency, empathy – and above all, moral character. These few are given the opportunity to be paired with a charger, but it's the charger who decides if the bond is to be permanent."

"He's incredible," Kiera agreed, taking a moment to consider what she'd heard. "How else are chargers different?"

"Oh, in many ways. They're capable of much greater speeds, and their strength and endurance are legendary. Chargers are also fearless. A horse is fundamentally a prey animal, and so even an experienced warhorse will sometimes shy from danger. But chargers are unique in that they quite literally have no fear. They're totally committed to the paladin, and therefore totally committed to righteousness. But I think the greatest difference is their intelligence. After a paladin's been paired with a charger for a few mooncycles, an intuitive bond forms between them. Each is able to anticipate the other's needs which, as I'm sure you can imagine, offers an incredible advantage on the battlefield."

Kiera smiled. "I can't wait until Brohdan meets him."

"Brohdan?" he asked, looking first at Kiera, then Belkidar.

"I'm sorry," Belkidar said, slowing to allow Batai to catch up. "It must've slipped my mind. We've recruited one other member so far."

"Hmm, doesn't sound like a Trisett name."

"No," Belkidar agreed, "he comes from further south."

"Then why so eager to have Einar meet him? The southern provinces aren't known for their horses."

"That's true," Belkidar answered, barely stifling a grin. "In fact, Brohdan doesn't even have a horse. He doesn't need one."

Batai laughed. "I'm pretty sure he will on this Quest. Either that, or he better be able to run!"

"Oh, Brohdan doesn't usually run. He prefers to fly."

"Fly? Belkidar, you speak in riddles."

"Brohdan is a dragon."

Batai sat motionless in his saddle for form a long moment. "Your sense of humor rivals your other talents." Then he realized Belkidar was serious. "Belkidar, in the many cycles we've known each other, I've seen some very strange things. In fact, Briz still appears in nightmares from time to time."

"Will you never forgive me for that? I told you I was sorry. Besides, Briz's appetite can prove a little overwhelming at times."

"So you've told me."

"Don't be such a baby. He didn't do any permanent damage."

Batai let that pass. "As I was saying, I've witnessed many strange things on our travels, but you will not convince me that you've recruited a dragon to join our Quest. First of all, they don't exist. Secondly, even if they did, we'd end up in its stomach long before we reached the eastern shores!"

"My, you're quite an expert on a species that doesn't exist."

"Surely you don't believe in such fairytales?" he pleaded to Kiera, who trailed a few paces behind. A sly smile was all he received in reply. "What did I get myself into?"

"I almost forgot!" Kiera exclaimed. "Do you think I could pick up a new dagger or two while we're here."

"What exactly do you need?" Batai asked, gladly changing the subject.

Kiera opened her cloak and pulled out her ruined blade. "I had some trouble awhile back."

"That shouldn't be a problem. We'll pass one of my armories before we reach the East Gate. I'm happy to supply you with whatever you need."

"Why thank you, kind sir."

After a few links of nimbly picking their way through Trisett's citizens, they finally saw the enormous East Gate several hundred elads distant. "Three buildings ahead and to the left you'll find my armory. I'll escort you both inside. From there, please help yourself."

After dismounting in front of the large brick structure, Batai led them inside its only entrance. Kiera was immediately greeted with the familiar smell of leather and oil. She smiled, comforted.

"Good morning, Sergeant. These are my friends. Please see to their every need."

"Of course, sir," he replied, saluting. The armory supervisor then turned and faced Belkidar. "How can I help you, sir?"

"Thank you both," he replied, "but I do quite well with this," he explained, knocking his walking stick against the worn wooden floor.

"Sir, surely you can find a more suitable warstaff," the Sergeant offered. "We have a large selection of lances, javelins, spears, clubs, maces, batons, and similar weapons just over here," he offered, indicating the southwestern section of the armory.

"Son, I appreciate it, but I've had this Staff for quite some time now. I've grown quite accustomed to it."

"As you wish," he conceded, then turned his attention to Kiera. "What can I help you with, miss?"

"May I see your daggers and knives, please?"

"Of course. Right this way," he said, leading her to the end of the room.

"My, you have a large variety."

"Yes. The king spares no expense when it comes to the defense of his kingdom. What kind in particular were you looking for?"

"Well," she said as she removed several daggers from various locations, "I obviously need to replace this one. And I'm not particularly fond of the way these two leave their sheaths. You see?" she asked, repeatedly removing and replacing two daggers from their scabbards of boiled leather.

"Yes," he answered uncertainly after watching her arms blur through the demonstration. "Perhaps you'd prefer daggers with slightly shorter blades?"

"No, but thank you. Things become so tedious when the blade only partially pierces the heart." She pondered the problem for a moment. "Perhaps a better grip will help," she thought aloud as she tapped one of her dagger's flat blades against her lower lip.

"This could take all day," Belkidar moaned.

To his relief, Kiera had replaced six of her daggers within a link. She kept her two favorites, however, for sentimental reasons. "They may be old and worn," she explained to Batai as they exited the armory, "but they do bring back such fond memories."

Afraid to ask about the details, Batai wisely kept silent.

Chapter 9
Indira

This above all: to thine ownself be true.
And it must follow, as the night the day,
Thou canst not then be false to any man.

William Shakespeare, <u>Hamlet</u>

The guards at the East Gate immediately recognized Batai as he approached, towering over the currents of merchants and traders. They saluted in unison. He returned the gesture, pausing briefly to compliment the Sergeant on his men. A few drus later, Kiera glanced over her shoulder and saw the supervisor beaming. After the traffic thinned a linop beyond city, they nudged their horses into a trot.

"Brohdan, we've left Trisett."

"Good. I was getting bored."

"A few straggling merchants are still on the road, so please stay hidden. You should be able to join us in a few linaks."

"No problem. Were you successful?"

"Yes, he was eager to join us. But I'm afraid Kiera isn't be the only one who doesn't believe in dragons."

"You're joking."

"Just don't scare him too much. We do need his help."

They followed the main road, eventually turning left onto a narrow and seldom used path, overgrown with tall grass and saplings. They rode single file, Kiera scouting ahead with Batai bringing up the rear.

"All right," Belkidar finally said aloud. "It's safe for you to join us."

Batai moaned, shaking his head. "I'm not falling for this little joke of yours, Belkidar. There are no such things as dragons."

"If you say so. But you might want to tell that to Brohdan," he said, jerking his thumb over his shoulder. While the two men were talking, Brohdan had quietly landed on the road some distance behind.

With a sigh, Batai turned in his saddle. To his surprise, a dragon stared back at him. The thing was enormous! He walked with the help of his wings, the outer halves pointing skyward, his tail swaying side to side.

"Good morning. I'm Brohdan."

Kiera thought Batai had permanently lost his senses until his gibberish slowly evolved into normal speech. "It can't be," he said for the third time.

Belkidar smiled. "Dragons have been around for a very long time. In fact, their history predates humans' by at least a hundred thousand cycles."

Slowly, Batai regained his composure. "But how can they talk?"

"Human speech isn't difficult," Brohdan explained. "Long ago, we had a language of our own, but when we began interacting with Men, we found yours more efficient."

"You mean humans and dragons used to live together?"

"Of course," Belkidar explained, "that's what's so disappointing. Dragons and humans are very similar, and they have more in common than is widely known. But the War changed so much. Dragons – along with dwarves, elves, and a host of others – chose to live in isolation, to try and rebuild their societies after so many were killed. Over the generations, Men forgot, as they often do."

Batai considered Belkidar's words. "Brohdan, I hope you can forgive my ignorance."

"Of course, Batai. It's a pleasure to meet you. I've never met a paladin before."

Batai laughed. "Then we have something in common." He paused. "Tell me, are the stories true? Can you really breathe fire?"

"Yes," he answered unenthusiastically.

"You'll have to forgive him," Belkidar interjected. "Brohdan was forced to kill for the first time, but he did save our lives."

"I understand," Batai answered. "I still remember the first time I took a life."

"You do?" Brohdan asked. "That surprises me considering all the battles you must've been in."

"I'm afraid it doesn't work like that."

Brohdan paused. "How did you come to terms with it?" he asked, drawing alongside Einar.

"It took mooncycles, but in truth I still struggle with it from time to time. Taking a life is never easy, or at least it shouldn't be. I enjoy battle, the idea of testing myself against others, but I don't enjoy killing. But unfortunately, it's oftentimes the lesser sacrifice."

Brohdan silently considered this man, the dichotomy of his nature. He hated killing, and yet he chose a profession in which he must kill. A lot. "How can you enjoy battle when it requires you to kill?"

"That's a good question." He paused. "I love the process. To train for links – the early mornings, the sweat, the sore muscles, the bruises – each a test of your character, of your dedication and resolve. And then to be able to put those tests to use, to pit yourself against not just another man, but another collection of tests." He paused again, considering his past. "I'm lucky, because from a very early age, I've known what I wanted to do with my life. I live to spread light where there are only shadows. And so for me, the battlefield where I'm at peace."

Brohdan laughed, not unkindly. "You're a riddle, Batai. You hate killing, but love battle, and you're at peace while at war."

Batai laughed too. "Well, when you put it like that, maybe you're right."

Belkidar smiled. "You're not a riddle, Batai, except maybe for your love of early mornings."

Kiera stopped after another link, and they ate their midday meal in the shadow of a large oak. "Where are we headed next?" she asked Belkidar.

"Ætheldell, the Great Northern Forest."

"Really? To the elves?"

"As a matter of fact, yes."

"I've never been there," she explained, "but I've heard a few interesting stories."

"Me too, and I hope the tales about one elf in particular are even half true."

"You haven't met her?" Batai asked.

"Not yet."

Batai frowned. "Is it wise to recruit a stranger? They may have their own agenda."

"I'd normally agree with you, but elves are different. They have a unique perspective of the world, of life, that doesn't always agree with ours. But none of their kind has ever spoken a lie, it's as though they have an immunity to evil. Don't worry, if this elf chooses to join our Quest, she'll devote herself completely to it."

"I've always known elves to be a strange species, but I never knew they were so remarkable."

Belkidar nodded. "After the War, the Northern Elves returned to their homeland in Ætheldell where they've been isolated for thousands of cycles. In fact, it's quite possible the elf we seek believes humans to be nothing more than a myth," he added, stroking his long beard.

"Now you are joking," Kiera said.

The old man smiled.

They continued along the trail for the rest of the day. As darkness approached, they found an isolated place to camp a half linak east of the trail. Their meals eaten, Belkidar sat with his back against a fallen tree, the Staff resting across his lap. He described many of his experiences with elves, each of which impressed the others. "Elves have innate archery skills. Throughout their history, they've developed bows and bowstrings that make the human equivalents seem primitive."

"I've heard that, though I'd like to see it first-hand," Batai said. "Maybe I can share some of their techniques with my bowmen."

"How did you hear about this particular elf?" Kiera asked.

"I still keep in touch with the descendants of a few elves that fought with me during the War. They told me about a young elven girl with truly exceptional archery abilities, even by their standards. If the stories are accurate, I think she'll make a valuable addition to our group."

They rose with the sun the following morning. Brohdan was reluctant to wake even as the others started packing. Finally, and with great effort, he stood and yawned. Little shafts of flames swirled from his throat, his head and neck arched as he stretched. Batai's eyes grew wide as he caught his first glimpse of the legendary dragonfire.

"Good morning," Belkidar greeted him. "Your grombit's come a long way. I can still see green in your scales, but you'll be completely black in another half-mooncycle. And I think your horns will be finished even earlier."

"My barz is getting bigger too."

"Let me have a look."

"Just don't step on it," Brohdan murmured as he reluctantly swung his tail toward Belkidar.

"I never realized a dragon's tail was an area of weakness," Kiera remarked as she tied up her rolled sleeping canvas, putting her knee into it to keep it from spreading.

"Oh, they're not," Belkidar assured her. "At least, not normally. Brohdan isn't just an ordinary dragon, he's a Broglia Black." He described Broglias and their gombits.

"Tell me more about the blade," Kiera said, her eyes twinkling.

Belkidar smiled. "A Broglia's barz is unique, not seen anywhere else in nature. The blade will be three elads long, nearly a tenth of a Broglia's entire length. It's literally unbreakable, and it will never dull. For practice – or when he lost his temper – Balthasar used to cut down trees with one swing," he recalled, laughing.

After they finished packing, they walked the horses back to the trail, then continued northeast at a trot. "We're making good time," Belkidar said after a link, "we should reach the forest early tomorrow."

Their progress continued until afternoon thunderstorms appeared. Violent wind gusts descended from the Cortusian Mountains to the west and the Midrogru Mountains to the south. Heavy rain fell in sheets from the black clouds, restricting their visibility to just a few elads. Within a link, hail pelted them from seemingly all directions.

"Brohdan, see if you can find us some shelter!"

Brohdan nodded and took off, the gusting wind making flying difficult. He flew east but found nothing useful. He circled back as the hailstones increased in both size and volume, but couldn't find anything the way they had come either.

"Very well. Find refuge as best you can. We'll make due."

"Brohdan couldn't find shelter for us," Belkidar shouted over the continuous thunder of the walnut-sized hailstones crashing to the ground.

The three huddled together, bringing the nearly hysterical pack horses toward the center. Kiera covered her head with her arms as the hail grew in size.

Suddenly, a dark shape fell on them from high in the northwest. Batai quickly found his sword as Einar turned to face it. Relieved, he watched as Brohdan extended his enormous wings and gracefully touched down only a few elads away.

The Broglia Black, towering more than eleven elads above the tallest of his mounted companions, kept his wings extended after landing, pivoting so that they hung several elyes above his friends. Kiera looked up at the underside of his extended wing, noticed a slight change in the rumble of the hailstones.

"Nicely done!" Belkidar complimented.

Kiera realized something had happened. "Why did the sound change?"

Belkidar's smile grew. "Very perceptive. After landing, Brohdan cast a ward: 'steelskin.' Now, the hail would have a better chance of denting steel!"

"Nicely done indeed!" Batai said, running his hand along the dragon's scales.

By the time the horses were arranged beneath their makeshift shelter, the larger of the hailstones were as big as apples. They watched transfixed as each ice ball exploded with a loud 'pop,' creating a deafening rumble.

"Can't you do something about this?" Kiera asked Belkidar.

"I learned a long time ago how finicky weather can be. What I do now may change the weather patterns of the entire world for cycles to come. It may cause droughts in some regions, floods in others."

"I hadn't considered that."

"Neither had I the first time I tinkered with it. I had to travel all over the world – multiple times – before I fixed it. Took me mooncycles... Believe me, that's one mistake I won't make again."

"Did you travel in the form of animals?" Kiera asked.

"Sometimes."

"What's your favorite?" Batai asked.

"That's easy. Human."

"No, I meant other than your original form," he clarified.

"What makes you think this is my original form?" he asked through a wry smile.

"Well, I – I don't know, it's just that – when you first appeared to me – "

"I have several favorites. Eagles fly with such grace and confidence, it's hard for that to not rub off on you. Wolves have a loyalty to their pack that is truly unique. They also have excellent endurance; I love running links on end, my strength never fading. And a dolphin's personality is infectious. When you take their form, you can't help but have fun. In fact, I'm not so sure they know how *not* to have fun."

Kiera smiled as he described not just assuming the forms of other animals, but their personality as well. She imagined what it must be like, and soon found herself considering the advantages of becoming a fox.

"You're a marvel," Batai remarked. "Your talents baffle the mind."

"Thank you, but I simply have an ability that's not available to most. The same is true with your talents in battle, or Kiera's spying."

"*Spying?*" she objected, pried from her daydream. "I really wouldn't call it spying, Belkidar."

"Why not?" he asked. "Isn't that what you do?"

"Well, I suppose, but it has such a distasteful ring to it. I prefer to call it investigating."

"My mistake," the sorcerer replied, rolling his eyes.

"Apology accepted."

The storm continued for the better part of a link. Eventually, to everyone's surprise the hail stopped just as quickly as it began. Kiera peered out from beneath Brohdan's wing. The clouds still looked menacing, but they weren't as bad as before the hail started. "I think it's passed."

"I hope so," Batai replied. "It's going to take me days to pound these dents from my shield."

Brohdan slowly retracted his wings, folding them against his flanks.

"Thank you again, my friend," Batai said.

"Any time." For some reason, he had no trouble thanking others, but he felt uncomfortable when others offered him the same courtesy.

"Incredible," Kiera whispered, her eyes riveted to the nearby landscape. Thousands of hailstones littered the area, ranging in size from small pebbles to grapefruit. She wondered what a chunk that big would do to a human's skull, then nudged her horse to where Brohdan stood and gave his right leg a hug.

They slowly resumed their journey, marveling at the scene. Within a quarter link, sunlight lanced through the clouds, forcing them to squint as light reflected off ice. They made excellent time the rest of the day, eventually veering from the trail as evening approached.

Kiera once again prepared their meal, a habit the others appreciated. While she kept busy, Belkidar and Batai started a fire and set up the sleeping arrangements. Tonight, they simply laid out canvases and blankets for each of them, but when weather threatened, they carried a simple tent that could easily shelter six people.

"When do you think we'll reach the forest?" Kiera asked between spoonfuls of hot soup.

"By midday tomorrow, I hope. I'm not sure how long it'll take to find her clan, so I'd like to have some daylight left. That brings up another point," Belkidar said as he helped himself to another bowl. "Have either of you met an elf before?"

"No," they answered in unison.

"Then there's something you should know. They don't trust outsiders, especially since the War."

"What do you mean?" Kiera asked.

"Except for a few exceptions, they've lived alone in the forest. Over the thousands of cycles since the War, this seclusion evolved into a way of life. They've become comfortable there, and outsiders make them uneasy."

"I can relate," Brohdan admitted. "My pack in Lukvia is a small one, but I didn't realize just how small until after I left. Sometimes, it's still strange being part of a bigger world."

"Exactly," Belkidar agreed. "Which brings me to my point. I've visited them before, so they know me. You three are a different story, although I doubt Brohdan will cause concern."

"How can two humans make them more uncomfortable than a dragon? No offense, Brohdan," Kiera added quickly.

"None taken."

"Elves are most comfortable when they're able to live in alone in nature, without external influences complicating their beliefs. Most of the expectations and responsibilities that are part of our culture are lost on them. On the other hand, in the forest they perceive things other creatures cannot. Dragons have a similar culture, and similar values, so like elves, they're most comfortable living alone. That's why they'll accept Brohdan more easily than they will others – they realize that a hunger for money, power, or fame is what makes any creature truly dangerous."

"Like humans," Batai said, sighing.

"Like humans," Belkidar admitted.

"Why are you accepted then?" Kiera asked after a moment.

"Well, I've been a friend to the elves for thousands of cycles. They know me, and to an elf, that makes me something like an adopted cousin."

Brohdan unsuccessfully stifled a cough.

Belkidar scowled. "Fine. More like a great grandfather then."

Kiera chuckled. "But how can they go from not trusting you to making you part of their family?"

Belkidar's frown turned to a smile. "That's their nature. If they get the chance to know you, and if they come to trust you – to big 'ifs' by the way – then there's no middle ground. You're family. You're pack."

The next morning, Belkidar wasn't with the others when they woke. Kiera eventually found him sitting with his back against a tree not far from the horses. He sat motionless, eyes staring straight ahead.

"Are you all right?" she asked.

He didn't respond.

"Belkidar?" she asked a bit louder. "Are you okay?"

"Yes," he answered softly, then again, this time a little louder.

"What were you doing?"

He stood, using his walking stick to steady himself. "I was studying the different paths available to us."

"Using sorcery?"

"Yes, to help me see the outcomes a little clearer," he answered vaguely.

"Do you mind?" Brohdan asked. "Some of us are still trying to sleep," he added as he rolled over, crushing several small trees.

Belkidar smiled. "Brohdan's going through the last part of his grombit. He's growing quickly now, so he needs to sleep a lot and eat even more."

Batai had also risen and was busily packing their sleeping gear onto the pack horses. "I don't suppose you've cooked some food yet," he asked Kiera.

"No, actually I haven't," she said, sidestepping his taunt. "Would you care for some leftover soup? I think there's still some in the pot."

Brohdan coughed uncomfortably.

Batai went to the fire pit. "There's nothing left, but there *is* a large piece of the pot missing," he added, glancing at Brohdan.

Kiera and Belkidar looked first toward the ruined pot, and then at Brohdan.

He once again coughed uncomfortably. "That's weird."

A long silence passed before Brohdan coughed again. It was becoming obvious that his throat was unusually dry.

"Brohdan! How could you?" Kiera cried. "Now I have to cook! And without my favorite pot!"

"I'm sorry. I got hungry in the middle of the night, and I was too tired to hunt."

"But the soup wouldn't fill you up!"

"I wondered what human food tasted like. You're quite a skilled cook," he added smoothly.

"Flattery will get you everywhere, especially if you make it up to me."

"Give me a few drus," Brohdan said, standing. He spread his giant wings, then took off from the large crater than marked where he'd slept.

"I can't believe he ate my soup," she said, still surprised.

"I know. He doesn't even like potatoes," Belkidar agreed.

"But it wouldn't even be a small bite for him!"

"That's not the only reason he did it, you know. When you get used to it, you'll find a dragon's sense of humor is quite advanced. Strange for sure, but advanced nonetheless."

It wasn't long before Brohdan returned, flying low over the treetops and breathing wide flashes of fire as he approached. But his flames were so expansive, they didn't even singe the leaves.

"Look at him!" Batai called. "He's herding an elk toward us!"

When the terrified animal was only a few elads from the camp perimeter, Brohdan flapped his wings once more, rose into the air, then folded them along his flanks. As he fell, he extended his legs to absorb the impact. He came down with a thud, landing with the elk under the talons of his left foot.

Because of their tight schedule, they didn't have time to butcher the beast properly. Instead, Batai took his short sword and went to work. Although the meal wasn't fit to be served in one of Trisett's upscale restaurants, it was nonetheless delicious. Brohdan eagerly ate what the humans could not.

"Why didn't you just carry it here?" Batai asked as he finished.

"I can't. If I carry too much, I lose my balance when I try to fly."

He considered that. "So no rides, then?"

They left the campsite and continued northeast along the narrow trail. After several links, they crested one final hill where the vast forest finally came into view.

"How far does it stretch?" Brohdan asked.

"Many linops, all the way to the ocean."

"No wonder the elves can stay so secluded. It'll take us days to find them in there."

Batai agreed. "And I've heard elves can camouflage themselves like no other, especially among the woodlands. We could walk right past a dozen of them and never know."

"You're forgetting that I'm welcome there," Belkidar said. "Besides, I know where most of their villages are."

"What are they like?" Kiera asked.

"Incredible. Entire villages, built not just *into* the trees, but becoming a *part* of them."

The forest seemingly grew from one periphery to the other as they rode down the hill. When it filled their view completely, their progress seemed to stop. Belkidar had witnessed this phenomenon before, but he knew they would reach it soon enough.

After more than a link, Belkidar finally led them past the first few trees of Ætheldell. They walked into a soft breeze filled with the earthy smell of mushrooms and wet wood. Soon, the thick canopy left the forest floor in perpetual darkness, yet the trees weren't terribly dense. This heartened Brohdan, knowing he'd be able to walk with his friends.

"They'll sense us long before we see them, so please stay close," he explained, leading them deeper into the forest. They followed him for what seemed like links, but the little shafts of light that sneaked through the canopy showed it was only a little past midday.

Brohdan found the trees refreshing. In the past, he'd always had some sort of shelter. In Lukvia, he shared a cave with his parents. When he moved to the Sichundars and later Sul Brul, he took other caves for dwellings. Since then, he'd been outside every moment of every day, so it was nice to once again feel shade on his scales. He relished the cool damp air and sound of the swaying branches overhead as he carefully picked his way through the woodland.

"Stop," Belkidar announced calmly. "They surround us."

Kiera and Batai searched the forest, saw only trees. Brohdan extended his long neck and, after a few drus, detected an unfamiliar scent.

"Greetings!" Belkidar called loudly into the forest.

Silence.

"Shall we wait like this all afternoon?" he asked, only half joking. "We've known each other far too long to play these games."

"Indeed," a low, resonant voice responded from several elads in front of him. A tall elf stepped from behind a tree and cautiously made his way forward. "How are you, my friend?"

"I'm surviving. And you, Master Lodi?"

"Without complaint." He paused, his brown eyes drifting over the others. "Tell me, Belkidar, why do you travel with companions?"

The elf's speech amazed Kiera. Although Lodi spoke the same language, he spoke it in a flowing, sing-song way. Each word flowed smoothly into the next, and the break between sentences was just long enough to make her eager for his next words.

"I'm on a most difficult Quest, so I hope you'll forgive our intrusion. In fact, that's why I've come. I'm here to ask a great favor of your pack."

"Truly? What errand would force you to seek the assistance from anybody, even that of an elf?"

Belkidar looked around. "I'd prefer to continue this conversation someplace more…intimate."

"As you wish, Ancient Leader. You know you are forever welcome among us, as are your companions." Lodi whistled a loud, almost musical note. For a moment, Kiera thought the entire forest moved in unison as nearly fifty elves emerged from behind trees, bushes, and shrubs. Others appeared on branches high overhead, and a few from no shelter at all – it was only when they moved that they became distinguishable from their surroundings.

"You never cease to amaze me, Lodi," Belkidar complimented.

"Thank you," he replied, inclining his head. "If you would follow us, we shall lead you to our home."

Lodi turned and silently led them northeast. Belkidar followed with the others closely in trail, Batai taking the opportunity to regard these extraordinary creatures. An equal number of male and female elves surrounded them. The males appeared to average at least two elads in height, the females slightly shorter. Although taller than the average human, they were considerably thinner and less muscular. All had smooth, creamy skin, and while the vast majority had long, silky black hair, a few had blonde hair that glimmered gold when they walked through a random shaft of sunlight.

Batai understood first-hand how the leaves, twigs, and overhanging branches made moving silently through a forest difficult in the best of times, so he was amazed at the stealth and grace with which these creatures moved. They walked effortlessly, gracefully, yet made not the slightest sound.

Lodi led them for nearly a link before his village came into view, and what Kiera saw stunned her. Because their dwellings had been built near the tops of the ancient trees, even the lowest shelter sat over a hundred elads above the ground.

Brohdan discovered an elaborate network connecting the numerous dwellings. Hundreds of ladders were built into the trees nearly everywhere he looked, constructed not from fabricated timber but from living branches. Some spiraled tree trunks all the way to the ground while others were only long enough to reach an adjacent branch. He watched transfixed, its residents smoothly leaping from one branch to the next, its intricacy leading him to wonder how long it must've taken to build.

Lodi led them to what appeared to be the elves' communal center. Long, thick logs formed concentric rings around an enormous pit that accommodated a warm, crackling fire. It was obvious by the wear in both the ground and logs that this area had been in service for an incredibly long time.

"Please wait here," Lodi instructed, barely pausing as he continued through the commons area.

"Where do you think he's going?" Batai asked from atop his huge charger.

"He's probably gathering the elders," Belkidar replied. "Lodi's their chief warrior, not one of their pack leaders."

"Our responsibilities are similar, then. He's the Captain of their guards?"

"In a manner of speaking, yes."

"It seems elves are not so different from us after all."

"Not in most respects. But you must remember that you're not a typical human. Knights, like elves, are driven by honor. But while this is true for all elves, the same cannot be said for humans. I think you'll find them quite refreshing."

Batai nodded, impressed.

Lodi returned shortly with another elf in trail. His long, white hair framed a deeply wrinkled face, and he couldn't quite move with Lodi's grace. "Juron, this of course is Belkidar," he began. "Belkidar, I believe you know our leader."

"Indeed I do. It's a pleasure, as always, Master Juron."

Juron bowed slightly, his smile transforming his face into the purest expression of delight Kiera had ever seen. "It is ever good to see you, my old friend. Tell me, who are your companions?"

"Juron, this is my friend, Kiera. She's a very experienced guide and tracker."

"It is always a pleasure to meet friends of Belkidar. Welcome."

"Thank you. You have a very elaborate home."

"It is that, indeed," he agreed, "an enduring partnership, several thousand cycles old."

"This is Batai," Belkidar continued, "Captain of the Order of Paladins, the leader of all knights."

"It is an honor to meet any paladin," Juron said before Batai had a chance to greet him. "But to meet the Captain of such a respected fellowship is truly an honor."

"You are very kind, sir," Batai said, bowing.

Belkidar smiled. "Finally, I'd like to introduce Brohdan."

He'd had been standing several elads away. Although the trees were sparse enough for him to approach the central ring, he wanted neither to frighten the elves nor damage any of their structures.

"I'm very pleased to meet you," Brohdan said in his deep voice.

Juron didn't reply. He stared at him for a long moment, his brown eyes pensive, probing. Then, with a low, exaggerated bow, he spoke. "Revered Broglia Black, you are our most honored guest."

"Thank you, Master Juron," Brohdan replied, clearly uncomfortable.

It was only when Brohdan finished speaking that Juron rose. He then spoke softly to Lodi for a moment before turning his attention back to Brohdan. "I would be honored if you and your companions would join us for our meal tonight."

"We'd be happy to." He felt awkward receiving the focus of Juron's attention.

"Excellent. It has been our understanding that humans become uncomfortable living so far above the ground," he explained, his eyes darting toward his home. "Is this still true?"

Belkidar laughed. "I'm afraid so."

Juron smiled. "Then let us prepare suitable quarters for you down here."

"That would be most appreciated," Belkidar answered. "But please don't go out of your way. My business here shouldn't take long, and we are in somewhat of a hurry."

"I understand, we will not delay you any further than we must. But please allow us to feed and shelter you for the night, as any host should. We will have plenty of time to discuss your visit over tonight's meal."

"Thank you, we would be honored."

"Lodi will take you to your quarters and give you time to rest. We will meet again at sunset."

"Thank you, Juron," Belkidar said, bowing.

Juron nodded and left, then Lodi guided them deeper into the woods. After following a wide path for several drus, he turned to cross a small meadow. "If you need anything, please let us know." He then turned to face Brohdan. "Is this satisfactory?"

"Oh my, yes. I've plenty of room."

"Excellent, Master Brohdan. Now, if you will excuse me, I have some business I must attend to. I look forward to seeing you all at the feast tonight."

Brohdan watched as he disappeared into the forest. "Why do they treat me like that?"

"Because of who you are."

"It makes me uncomfortable."

"You have to understand their history. Kainan was the last Broglia the elves have known. He helped us defeat Jenkar during the War." Belkidar took a moment, sighed as he recalled events that shaped the world so long ago. "It's a very long and difficult story, but Kainan saved countless lives during the War. Some estimated that if it weren't for his bravery, his dedication, the entire elven species might've perished."

That shocked Brohdan. He never realized just how formidable a Broglia could be.

"Yes, Brohdan," Belkidar said, reading his expression. "Broglia Blacks have carved an indelible path through *all* of history, not just yours or mine." He smiled, its warmth tangible. "But don't let that trouble you. Just be yourself and do the best you can. Everything else will take care of itself."

"Good advice for us all," Batai concurred. "We can only affect what we can control."

"Exactly," Belkidar agreed before leading the others to one side of the clearing. There they found several large 'rooms,' the trees themselves forming the walls.

"I've never seen anything like it," Kiera whispered, stepping inside the nearest to inspect it more closely.

"Did they plant them this way?" Batai asked as he dismounted.

"Not exactly," Belkidar answered. "Elves have certain talents when it comes to nature. In this case, they simply encouraged the trees to grow in these particular groupings."

"How can you encourage a tree to grow in one place instead of another?" Batai asked skeptically.

"It's a talent unique to elves," he explained, shrugging. Then he looked past him, toward the sound of a nearby stream. "I think I'll go wash up," he said, disappearing into the forest.

"That man raises more questions than he answers."

Lodi arrived at sunset. "I trust I am not too early?"

"Not at all," Belkidar answered. "We were just practicing Brohdan's spells."

Lodi smiled, glancing at the dragon. "All is ready. I trust venison is agreeable?"

"We look forward to it," Batai answered.

"Excellent. Please follow me."

Batai quickly joined him as he led them back through the forest. "Belkidar told me you're the Captain of your guard."

"Yes. We are volunteers, sworn to defend our pack."

"I understand. I also volunteered to defend my people."

"You speak of the Order of Paladins," Lodi said, nodding. "I know of this fellowship, albeit only from reputation."

"From what Belkidar's explained, we share many responsibilities. If we have time, I'd love to talk with you. Perhaps we can learn from each other, to improve us both?"

Lodi nodded. "It would be an honor to learn from your Order."

As Batai and Lodi enthusiastically discussed their organizations, Belkidar talked with Brohdan.

"I can still see some green when the sun you're your scales just right, but otherwise they look completely black."

Brohdan nodded. "How much bigger do you think I'll get?"

"Several elads," he estimated.

Brohdan remained silent.

"Does that bother you?"

"No, I'm just not looking forward to being so big, that's all."

"Why not?"

Brohdan hesitated. "Being different just complicates things, and soon I'll be different from everyone else in the world. I'm still the same dragon I've always been, but I won't be treated like that anymore."

"I see," Belkidar said softly. "Those who knew you as a Dalluvian will adjust only as quickly as they're able. Nothing you do will change that, so it doesn't really matter if you stay this size or grow as big as a titan. Your friends and family will adjust in time, just be patient with them. And Brohdan?"

"Yes?"

"You're not the same dragon you've always been, and that has nothing to do with your appearance."

Juron sat on one of the long benches, the large fire crackling before him. "Welcome. I trust you are all hungry?"

"Most definitely," Kiera answered.

"Excellent. I prepared a private place where we may talk." Juron rose slowly and led them north into the woodland and the darkness within. After a quarter link they spotted a distant fire, it's shimmering orange struggling to reach their eyes through the many trees. Not long afterward, they arrived at an area similar to the one they'd just left, but this was considerably smaller and, if possible, appeared even more ancient. Smoke from the central fire greeted them, its warmth welcome.

"This is our council chamber," Juron explained. "Its members were slaughtered during the War, but this remains."

"We are honored," Belkidar said.

Juron took a seat, and the others joined him around the fire. Where the vast communal area promoted open discussion, this one's smaller size encouraged more intimate conversation. The six benches of the innermost circle measured two elads long, so that only five elads separated each from its counterpart across the fire.

Belkidar sat opposite Juron while Batai and Lodi occupied the two benches to the sorcerer's left and right, respectively. Kiera sat to Juron's left, the final bench to his right already occupied by two female elves. As Brohdan made himself comfortable behind the outer row of benches behind Belkidar, he regarded the two females. The one closest to Juron was shorter, although still nearly as tall as Belkidar. She had striking light-brown hair and wore a simple tunic and skirt with black hose. The nearer elf appeared younger and taller than the other, and the black hair that fell to her waist had several thin plaits that kept it from her face. Like all the elves he'd seen, her skin was pale, and the tops of her ears came to a rounded point, but it was her striking emerald eyes that stole his attention.

"The feast will be ready shortly. While we wait, will you tell me what brought you here?"

"Certainly," Belkidar said, casting a quick glance toward the two strangers.

Juron didn't miss it. "Concern yourself not with them. They are two of our most trusted kin. Here, you may discuss anything you feel necessary. I pledge my life on it."

"I thank you." Belkidar nodded respectfully toward the two strangers, then turned his attention back to Juron. "We've come to recruit an elf from your pack."

Juron smiled sadly, Brohdan instantly realizing he already knew the elf to whom Belkidar referred.

"I've heard of a very talented youth," Belkidar continued, "extremely skilled with a bow." He paused and looked at Lodi. "In fact, I've heard it's been over five hundred cycles since your pack has seen her equal."

"The rumor that has somehow found you is not accurate," Lodi objected.

Belkidar looked first at Juron, and then back to Lodi.

"She is the finest archer this pack has *ever* produced," he clarified, a slight smile curving the corners of his mouth. "But her talents extend beyond the bow. Even the deer do not perceive her approach. Her steps are silent to all creatures, her arrows always true."

"Tell me, Master Lodi, what is her name?" Belkidar asked.

Lodi looked to Juron, was greeted with a slight nod. "She is Indira, our most prized warrior."

"I'm afraid I must request her assistance in our Quest," Belkidar pressed. "I truly regret having to ask, but I assure you it is most critical."

Juron stared into the fire, considering Belkidar's request. "Indira is greatly respected within our pack, and it would affect us all if she were to leave, so I must ask why your need for her is greater than our own." The pride in Juron's tone was not difficult to miss.

"The Jewel was stolen from the Indifferent."

Juron's breath caught. "It is a very dark time, indeed. Hildegard?"

"Hildegard," the sorcerer confirmed, his voice barely audible above the crackling fire.

Juron stared into the fire, its flames casting flickering shadows across his face, accentuating each of his deep wrinkles. "It seems to me he has every advantage. He can simply wait until his army has grown to such overwhelming numbers that he can overrun every civilization in the world. Yet if we choose to attack, he has the advantage of defending his fortress against us. Either way, it is only a matter of time before he possesses the final Artifact." Juron allowed his gaze to drift from the fire to the Staff that rested across Belkidar's lap.

"You are of course correct on both counts," Belkidar agreed, "but another path lies before us." He outlined his plan, explaining the advantages as well as the dangers. "Once we defeat Hildegard and his Five Defenses, I plan to destroy the Headpiece before it corrupts anyone else."

"The odds seem against us," Lodi commented.

"What choice do we have?" Juron answered in place of Belkidar. "If we attempt nothing, we will most surely perish, but with Belkidar's plan we at least stand a chance." Juron then looked at the two female elves. "What do you think?"

They looked at one another. "His plan has merit," the younger elf offered. "If this is our only path, we must act."

"Indeed," Juron agreed. "Will you consent?" he asked her.

"I will, father."

Brohdan looked at her, then at Juron, silently chiding himself for not recognizing the likeness sooner.

"Juron, I had no idea the one I sought was your daughter," Belkidar said quickly. "If this sacrifice is too great, I will find another to take her place."

"Nay, Venerable One, there is no other. The rumors you heard are true, but they do not do her justice. You need her. My only choice is to bid my daughter farewell, and wish well your Quest." Tears formed in his tired eyes.

"Thank you, Juron. I understand too well the sacrifice you make."

He looked up from the fire, nodded slowly, his unshed tears twinkling in the fire light. "Yes. You more than any can make that claim."

Brohdan looked away, wanting to give him as much privacy as the circumstances allowed. So he turned his attention to Indira and noticed the elf seated next to her also had tears streaming down her cheeks. With a sudden realization, Brohdan understood the elf with the brown hair was Juron's mate, and that she too pledged her daughter to their Quest.

"Please, Ekkira," Belkidar told her, "I'll do everything in my power to keep her safe."

"You are very kind," she replied, her voice thick with emotion. "I expect you will do the same for all who accompany you."

"Unquestionably, with everything I am."

A great pride welled inside Brohdan, borne not from the great power to which Belkidar inferred, but from his loyalty.

Batai's attention was focused on Indira. He'd never known Belkidar to lie, but he discovered long ago that exaggeration was far from foreign to him. And so he wondered if he'd inflated her abilities, whether to bolster their confidence or persuade Juron to release her he did not know, nor did it matter. They needed an archer, someone with the ability to strike from a distance, he only hoped she was half as talented as he was led to believe.

Kiera watched Juron. His sadness nearly broke her heart, yet she knew the importance of his sacrifice. Indira put her arm around her mother's shoulders, a gesture that struck Kiera as ironic. They must band together to have any hope of defeating Hildegard, yet to do that, they must leave family and friends behind.

Their reveries were broken when several elves entered the council chamber, each offering generous portions of roasted meat. As they left the firelight, nearly a dozen others entered, struggling beneath the weight of an enormous wooden platter heaped with venison. After making their way to Brohdan, they wordlessly bowed to Juron and also took their leave, disappearing into the darkness.

Brohdan stared at the mammoth helping, smiling.

"I trust it is to your satisfaction?" Juron asked.

"It looks delicious! I think you'll spoil me if I stay here much longer."

Juron returned his smile. "Let us enjoy the food that has been prepared for us."

Most at the feast had never seen a dragon before, but nobody took offense to his eating habits. He stood, anchored his talons in one end of a particularly large buck, tore away the other half with his powerful jaws. His razor-sharp teeth severed sinew and flesh, the piercing cracks of breaking bone deafening. Like birds, he didn't chew, instead extended his long neck and swallowed the meat whole.

Brohdan finished well before the others. He laid back down and considered their small band. Belkidar's talents were obvious, and Batai's leadership and success in battle were legendary. He knew they would never get lost with Kiera guiding them, and they now had a skilled archer. They numbered only five, yet he was proud to be included in such a formidable group. "So," he said softly to Belkidar, who sat eating a few elyes in front of him, "I assume our party is complete?"

"Not quite," he answered. "I think we'll add one more, assuming he chooses to join us. He's got a few prejudices, all of them warranted." He paused, a little too long for Brohdan's comfort. "I hope I can reason with him," he added with little confidence.

A distant sound stole his attention. He raised his head high, cocking it slightly to better probe the darkness. To his delight, he heard another dozen elves struggling through the forest, all apparently straining beneath a sizeable burden.

Chapter 10
Gunnar

I am not bound to win, but I am bound to be true. I am not bound to succeed, but I am bound to live up to what light I have.

Abraham Lincoln

After the meal, the group socialized with their hosts. Batai spoke at length with Lodi, each becoming more animated as they learned about the other's order. In fact, upon Batai's return they coordinated for five of his Lieutenants and five of Lodi's Field Commanders to spend a mooncycle in the other's company. Afterward, they would take what they learned back to their respective orders, strengthening both in the process. It was the first such arrangement between Elves and Men, and it would become the first formal Elven expedition outside of the forest since the War.

Meanwhile, Kiera spoke with Indira and Ekkira. She didn't try to lift their spirits, not on the eve of their departure. Instead, they spoke of family, of pack. Kiera discovered much; like humans, they had close family ties, but their entire pack functioned as their family. She learned that a mother would care for several children from her pack, freeing others to hunt. Conversely, Indira was saddened to learn that Kiera never knew her parents, inferring that Belkidar was her closest friend, a surrogate father in fact. That pleased her.

Brohdan soon found himself surrounded by curious elves. They initially approached timidly, not from fear, but out of respect. But as soon as conversation began, nearly three dozen surrounded him, each waiting impatiently to ask him questions. Brohdan did his best to answer them, but he found their questions curious and lacked the background to answer many of them.

Belkidar spoke softly with Juron. They discussed Indira, and Belkidar did his best to assuage a father's concern. Juron explained the most suitable path south through the forest, Belkidar memorizing the instructions. Juron asked several questions about their Quest, and Belkidar did his best to answer them without jeopardizing its success. Juron nodded, appearing a little more encouraged with each detail.

Eventually, Lodi led them back to the meadow. It was an enjoyable evening, but they welcomed the chance to sleep before continuing their long journey.

They were greeted by a magnificent dawn. A thin mist exaggerated every shaft of sunlight that had somehow found its way through the thick canopy high overhead. With the darkness of night still looming in the background, the entire forest teemed with brilliant streaks of light.

A shadow moved amongst the shafts, momentarily severing one after another. Batai instinctively drew his massive sword, Einar turning to face the approaching shadow.

"There is no need for alarm," a feminine voice assured them from the darkness. As she entered the meadow, Batai realized it was Indira. "I have come to relay a message from my father. He awaits you in the commons area. Our entire pack has risen to see us off."

"We won't keep them any longer than necessary," Batai assured her. He turned and joined Kiera and Belkidar as they hurriedly packed their belongings onto the horses.

Brohdan sensed Indira's sorrow, but she hid it admirably. "I'm sorry for your sadness."

Her smile didn't reach her eyes. "Thank you." She paused. "I have never left this forest, nor my pack."

"I understand. The pack I come from is small, but I think we were closer for it. I left nearly three cycles ago, and sometimes still I find myself wishing I could go home."

Indira's face brightened at little.

"Maybe we can get through it together."

"I would like that, Brohdan. You are very considerate."

The compliment made him uncomfortable. "I'm happy to help. After all, we'll be each other's family during the mooncycles to come."

"It sounds as though I am leaving one pack for another."

"We're ready," Belkidar inadvertently interrupted.

"Please follow me." She led them toward the large communal area, a mixture of sorrow and excitement swelling in her. She was honored to be offered a place in this Quest, but dejected with leaving the only home she'd ever known. Yet Brohdan reminded her that these burdens weren't unique, and she was eager to get to know her companions.

Before she knew it, they had arrived.

Elves filled the entire area. Every bench circling the central fire was occupied, forcing dozens to stand beyond the outermost ring. Yet despite their hundreds, all was silent.

Juron greeted each of his guests, then addressed his pack, slowly walking around the fire as he spoke. "Courage is ever the measure of a soul, just as sacrifice is the measure of the pack left behind. Belkidar the Ancient asked for our help. We are honored to answer his call. We pledge Indira, our most cherished warrior, so they may defeat all who stand in their way. Let us wish them success in their Quest, for we all of us share their fate."

The entire pack stood, tapped the tips of their staves or bows once on the ground, bowed their heads, their shuffling sounds the only accompaniment to the crackling fire. Brohdan saw Ekkira stand from the front bench directly behind where Juron stood. Tears fell down her cheeks, and it appeared sleep had come sparingly.

"Thank you for your blessings, and for your sacrifice," Belkidar said softly to the hundreds. The elves leaned forward, straining to hear.

"We leave with a heavy heart, but rest assured we depart with conviction. We'll face many challenges, yet we shall not be deterred, we will not yield. You have my oath." He bowed low, then silently climbed onto his horse and rode south, Kiera and Batai in trail. Indira paused briefly, looked to Juron. She walked to him and embraced her father one final time before climbing into her saddle to follow the humans.

Brohdan lingered, couldn't help sympathizing with Juron and Ekkira. Although Indira's sorrow was a result of her own decision, her parents' helplessness was suddenly very clear to him. In that instant, he understood a glimmer of what his own parents experienced when they left him in Sul Brul. "Worry not, Juron. I'll watch over her."

He smiled. "Thank you, Brohdan. She must find her own way, but a Broglia's protection is most welcome." He extended his right hand.

Confused, Brohdan lowered his head, surprised when Juron placed his palm softly against his cheek.

"Take care of yourself, Brohdan. The world depends on it." The hundreds amassed in the hall held their breath, their leader momentarily frozen in time, his hand outstretched against the cheek of a Broglia Black. And then the moment passed.

Brohdan nodded. In the drus it had taken to catch up with the others, he had hardened his resolve, not just to uphold his pledge to protect Indira, but to justify Juron's respect.

It was dusk by the time Indira led them to the southern edge of the forest. "I know my home very well," she said softly, her voice rich, her cadence melodic, "but I fear I am not fit to lead any further."

"That's all right, Indira," Belkidar said comfortingly. "Kiera is well-traveled. She'll be our guide the rest of the way."

They set up camp that night, still sheltered beneath Ætheldell's towering trees. Indira told them stories of her home, of her pack, the others listening entranced. After a few links, however, their exhaustion forced them to their beds, the fire flickering faintly against the canopy high above.

They made excellent progress across the flat terrain south of the forest. At midday, they stopped to rest the horses. Thanks to Juron's generosity, they now had two additional pack horses loaded with supplies. They ate dried venison provided by the elves and cheese from Batai's stores.

"What sort of food is this?" Indira asked.

"It's called cheese," Kiera explained, "made from cow's milk."

"I've heard of such animals. They are also good to eat, are they not?"

All three humans turned to Brohdan. "They are. I'll have to introduce them to you when we get the chance. I'll even cook it for you if you'd like."

"No, please don't do that," Belkidar objected. "When dragons use their fire to cook, I can always taste their last meal. I really don't want a steak tinged with rodent."

Indira laughed in spite of her mood.

"I've never eaten a rodent in my life!" he said defensively, causing a new wave of laughter.

A half link later, they resumed their journey south. "Where are we headed next?" Batai asked.

"I think we'll try to add one final member."

"Try?" Kiera asked.

"Well, I'm not so sure he'll join us."

"Why not?"

"He hasn't exactly had good luck with others, so he lives by himself in the Midrogru Mountains. But he isn't out of the way, so it's worth a try. Assuming he doesn't try to kill us, of course."

"Who exactly are we talking about," Batai asked.

"Gunnar, the world's last giant."

His eyes grew wide. "I thought fanatics killed them all."

"Luckily for Gunnar, that's what most people believe. But he managed to escape, the human mob killing his family too preoccupied to notice. That was just over one hundred fifty cycles ago. Much later, I heard rumors of an enormous mountain troll there, one with pale skin. Following a hunch, I investigated."

"How can anyone confuse a giant with a mountain troll?" Kiera asked.

"Well, at the time, Gunnar wasn't fully grown."

"I cannot imagine he was happy to see you," Indira offered.

Belkidar smiled. "No. In fact, he spent several links trying to kill me."

"Poor Gunnar," Kiera sighed.

"Poor Gunnar? He threw boulders at me!"

"How did you survive?" Indira asked.

"Simple, I just teleported out of the way."

"Teleport? I am not familiar with this."

Belkidar's expression grew apprehensive. "Did your father tell you anything about me?"

"Yes. He said you are very old and that I should seriously consider any advice you gave me."

"How flattering. Is that all?"

"Yes."

"Oh, dear," he sighed. "What do you know of sorcery?"

"I have heard of it. It is a lost art that was known only by a few."

"Indira," Belkidar began carefully, "sorcery is very real. I don't imagine this will come easily to you, but I'm a sorcerer."

Indira gave him a long look but said nothing.

"Sorcery allows us to do things others cannot. In the case of Gunnar, it allowed me to vanish and reappear in another location."

"What happened?" Batai asked.

"Well, he eventually stopped long enough for me to explain. After that, he actually became civil. I've made it a point to check in on him from time to time."

They continued their journey in silence, each harboring some doubt about recruiting a giant whose contributions may prove more harmful than helpful. But by the time Kiera had prepared their evening meal, they had grown more comfortable with the idea, trusting in Belkidar's history with him.

"Tell me," Batai said, smoke from the fire drifting over his head, "what are giants like? I've heard stories, of course, but they can't be true."

"I wouldn't be so sure. Their strength is legendary, so much so that they were persecuted for the threat of it. They fought back, destroyed entire villages, but that only unified the humans against them. They were overwhelmed. When Gunnar dies, his race dies with him."

Indira listened intently. "This is the first I have heard of them."

Belkidar nodded. "They're similar to you or me, except as tall as four humans. And much broader."

"Incredible," Batai said, shaking his head.

"What's even more incredible is their strength – it's many times greater than their size would lead you to believe. Let's hope we don't see it first-hand tomorrow."

Kiera agreed. "I don't want to make him mad before he even gets to know me."

"Just let me do the talking and I'm sure he'll be the perfect host."

He was somewhat less than convincing.

Three days later they woke just after dawn, the coals still glowing red in their makeshift fire pit, the Midrogru Mountains looming around them. An overcast sky threatened rain as they began the day's journey, but the clouds gradually thinned, giving way to a clear blue sky.

Kiera guided them south, eventually stopping for their midday meal, their anxiety growing alongside the mountains they shadowed. Even Belkidar grew noticeably apprehensive.

After eating, Belkidar led them deeper into the mountains. He alone knew the way to the giant's home, and he wanted Gunnar to see him first, hoping that recognition would stave off any unpleasantness. But after repeatedly turning from one mountain trail to another, Kiera began doubting his sense of direction. "Are you sure you know where you're going?"

"Of course, my dear. Trust me."

"Only if I have to," she answered, smiling. Belkidar stifled a grin, knew better than to get in a smiling duel with her.

After what seemed like several links to Brohdan, Belkidar finally reigned in his horse. "We're getting close, so please stay further back. And when Gunnar appears, you must fight the urge to take up your weapons."

That confused them.

"You'll understand when the time comes. If he gets excited, dodge the boulders as best you can until I can calm him," he added, nudging his horse forward. At his signal, they followed him single-file through the narrow mountain trail.

He led them for the better part of a link, weaving through the towering peaks. Anticipation hovered like a mist, each wondering if an angry giant would surprise them around every turn.

The path veered sharply to the right, and Belkidar disappeared behind an outcropping of a stone. And then they heard shouting from around the corner, the cliff wall concealing its source.

"WHY DID YOU BRING THESE CREATURES HERE?" a deep voice asked. It was louder than any Brohdan had ever heard. It shook the ground, echoed from the mountain walls.

Still concealed from the others, Belkidar stopped his horse. "Hello Gunnar. I've come to talk with you."

"WHY DIDN'T YOU COME ALONE?"

"Gunnar, these are my friends, just as you are. We're on an urgent Quest, and I need your help."

An uncomfortable silence passed. Indira nervously flipped her thumb over her bowstring as they waited.

"I'll listen."

"Thank you. Please let me introduce you to the others."

After a pause, Brohdan felt footfalls vibrate through the ground. Belkidar appeared first. When he was halfway there, Gunnar rounded the corner, turned, strode toward them.

Kiera and Batai instinctively went for their weapons. The sight of such an imposing creature bearing down on them made them feel helpless, vulnerable. But they remembered Belkidar's warning, left their weapons untouched.

He was even bigger than they imagined. Belkidar rode a horse larger than most, yet he barely reached Gunnar's waist. His torso and upper thighs were covered in bearskins that hung over his left shoulder, secured around his waist with a wide strip of leather. He tied his long black hair behind him, his exposed arms, legs, and chest thick with muscles. His beard didn't quite hide his scowl.

Belkidar calmly approached, winked at Kiera, then dismounted and motioned for Gunnar to join him. The others followed his lead, sliding from their saddles.

"Gunnar, I'd like for you to meet Kiera. She's from the western side of the continent and is the best tracker I've ever known. She's also very good with daggers, scouting, and has even been known to wrestle now and again."

Gunnar said nothing, regarded the small woman in silence.

"This is Batai. He is the Captain of the Order of Paladins, the leader of all knights."

Gunnar stared at him for a long moment. "Knights came to our aid. While others butchered my family, they alone tried to help. But they were too few. Welcome to my home, Paladin."

"Thank you," Batai said, "I'm happy to meet you."

Belkidar continued. "This is Indira. She's the daughter of Juron, leader of the largest pack in Ætheldell."

Gunnar said nothing, so Belkidar continued. "Finally, this is Brohdan. He's from – "

"You're a Broglia." It was a statement, not a question.

"Yes," Brohdan replied, approaching the giant.

"I remember my father telling me stories of Kainan and the War. He believed we would've lost without him."

"I've heard similar stories."

Kiera watched, amazed. She'd never seen another creature half their size, and now they stood next to each other... Gunnar was stouter for his size, yet as tall as he was, he barely reached Brohdan's chest. And Brohdan wasn't even fully grown yet! Then she realized her jaw hung open, so she closed it as discreetly as she could under the circumstances.

"Why are you here?" Gunnar demanded, turning back to Belkidar.

"Are you familiar with the Staff of Power?"

"Of course. It was one of the stories my father used to tell me."

"Well, I've learned the Headpiece was responsible for corrupting Jenkar, and it's done the same to Krollum. He calls himself Hildegard now, and he stole the Jewel from the Indifferent."

Gunnar nodded. "History's a circle, Belkidar, you know this. Hildegard will bide his time until he can take the Staff."

"I wouldn't worry too much about that," he assured him, extending his walking stick for the giant to see.

Gunnar took a step back, shocked. "*You?* How?"

"Gunnar, this may be difficult for you, but I was the one who managed to disassemble the Staff of Power in the first place."

"That can't be. It happened thousands of cycles ago!"

"A little over seven thousand, actually."

He stared at Belkidar, then slowly lowered his gaze to his walking stick, its tip resting on the stone ground of his home. "Go on."

"You're right, of course. Hildegard seems content to wait as long as it takes, so we must intervene." He explained their plan.

"What'll happen if Hildegard's successful?"

"We all becomes slaves, living only to serve him."

He grunted. "Maybe that's what they deserve."

Belkidar was already shaking his head. "You don't believe that. And I know you'd never condemn the world to that fate because of an ignorant few."

Gunnar stared hard at Belkidar, eventually broke eye contact. He nodded once.

"You're with us, then?"

"I could never refuse you, Belkidar, not after all you've done for me."

The old man smiled, creasing the corners of his eyes. "Thank you. I wasn't very confident without you."

"That's encouraging," Kiera whispered to Batai.

"Are you confident now?" Gunnar asked.

"Not particularly."

Gunnar shook his head, his laugh infectious.

They followed Gunnar to his home, where he gathered some belongings for the journey, including a three-elad sword he carried in a scabbard that hung down his broad back. In his left hand he carried a small pack.

"Perhaps you wouldn't mind if I took that for you," Kiera offered, noting the near-panicked horses.

"Of course," Gunnar said, handing it to her. What appeared to be a small pack in his hands grew substantially in Kiera's. With surprising strength, she lifted it from his huge hand, carried it to the pack horses, and quickly rearranged their loads to make room for Gunnar's belongings.

Brohdan wondered how Gunnar would keep pace considering he was forced to walk while the others traveled on horseback, but he had no need for concern, his long strides easily matching the horses' pace.

North of the mountains, they had traveled through tall grass and even a few pines, but as they continued south along trails that climbed ever higher into the Midrogrus, the green grass slowly disappeared so all that remained was dirt and rocks. The trails appeared ancient, worn smooth into the rock of the mountains. "What were these paths used for?" Brohdan asked.

"Mining," Belkidar answered. "For thousands of cycles, Men and Dwarves mined gold, silver, and gemstones here, eventually picking it clean. About five hundred cycles ago, even the most optimistic of them left, seeking fortune elsewhere."

"Is that why Gunnar chose to live here?"

Belkidar nodded. "He realized these mountains offered two advantages – abandoned mines that he could use for shelter, and isolation from those who would see him killed."

The narrow trail slowed their pace, periodically looping back and forth as they climbed and descended the steeper slopes. Gunnar reassured them, explaining that the path grew wider a linop further to the south. It was mid-afternoon on the following day by the time they walked side-by-side, and Kiera took the opportunity to stop and eat.

"How much further before we reach the plains?" Batai asked, halfway through his corned beef and bread.

"We'll get there by tomorrow evening," Gunnar answered.

"Aren't you going to eat?" Kiera asked him.

"No, I ate this morning."

Batai sighed. "Brohdan doesn't average a meal a day, and now we find Gunnar also eats fewer meals than we do. Suddenly I feel fat."

"I noticed that too," Indira said quietly.

"What? That I'm fat?"

"Of course not!" she answered, her cheeks reddening. "Large carnivores tend to eat bigger meals, though less frequently."

Brohdan and Gunnar looked at each other. "I'm not a fan of vegetables," Brohdan said.

Gunnar scowled at the word. "Me neither. I'm partial to beef myself."

"I can see we're going to get along just fine," Brohdan said, patting his back with a wing.

"You like beef too?"

"It's a miracle a single cow survived," Kiera answered before Brohdan could.

He turned to where she sat, but instead of finding fear on her face, he discovered two very imposing dimples.

"Yes?" she asked innocently.

"Never mind."

It didn't take long to finish their meals, and before Brohdan knew it, they were heading south again. He let his mind drift. At first, he thought of his parents, and of Lukvia. He couldn't remember his home in as much detail as he could only a cycle ago, and that bothered him. Feeling guilty, he changed the subject and, inevitably, thought of Mikka. He cherished every detail he remembered of her, but each one caused him heartache. But he had grown used to pain long ago, so he savored the quiet moments that allowed him to think back to the time he'd spent with his mate.

Kiera continued leading them through the mountains, seemingly feeling her way as she went.

"I've never traveled this way before," Gunnar said.

"It'll be quicker than the mining trail," she explained.

"Are you sure?"

She smiled. And sure enough, Gunnar found himself on the south side of the final mountain range a full link sooner than he'd thought. "Impressive."

"Why thank you, kind sir."

They stopped two links later, long after the sun had disappeared behind the mountains to their right. "Belkidar, this looks like a good place to spend the night," Kiera explained. "We've got a creek nearby, and plenty of room for everyone to sleep."

"You're the boss."

It was a beautiful location, bordered by towering rock walls to their west and east. The trail had been narrow, but it opened up here, forming a large bowl before it narrowed again further to the south. After they dismounted and unloaded their gear, Indira took the horses to the stream. Kiera again prepared their evening meal while Batai, Belkidar, and Gunnar erected the large tent.

Brohdan, feeling a bit useless, flew off in search of firewood. Thinking there may be trees lower in elevation, he headed southwest over the descending terrain and soon discovered several in a valley to his right. He landed and gathered as much as he was able to carry, making several trips until there was enough wood to last them the night. Then he gathered a few logs together and blew a narrow stream of fire on them. But something was wrong. His fuel tasted different, bitter. And his flames were golden, not the blue and orange that he was used to. "Belki – "

Then he noticed the logs. They were ashes now, even though he ignited them only a few drus before. "Belkidar, I think you should see this."

The sorcerer joined him next to the dwindling flames. After a moment, he smiled. "It's your Broglia fire!"

That got everyone's attention, and they quickly gathered around him.

"What's Broglia fire?" Gunnar asked.

"It's dragonfire, but unique to Broglia Blacks. Other creatures can make fire, and so can I," he explained, turning a palm up where an apple-sized fireball grew bright. "But no creature can create fire half as intense as Broglia fire." He closed his hand, the fire winking out.

"Not even you?" Batai asked.

He shook his head. "Hundreds of sorcerers through the cycles have tried, and all failed. There's something unique about Broglia fuel that can't be reproduced."

Brohdan considered that, then looked at the ashes of what was to be their campfire. "Can I control how hot it is?" he asked, nodding toward the ashes.

"You only have Broglia fuel now, but you can control how much you use. You'll need less now – a *lot* less."

Brohdan gathered three more logs together, then blew a tiny fire stream toward them. They ignited immediately, and he was relieved to see that the logs remained, crackling in the shadows of their campsite.

"Just how hot can it get?" Gunnar asked, the flames' light flickering across his face.

Belkidar smiled. "Let's find out. Brohdan, I assume Krepli's training still includes practicing against rocks?"

Brohdan nodded. "Links of it."

"Would you mind trying that here, maybe against that?" he asked, pointing toward the rock walls to the west of their camp.

Brohdan walked to it, instantly recalling his grombit training with Krepli, Boseda, and Rouldra. They'd been excellent instructors, and he silently thanked them as he drew in a great breath.

Then he exhaled, blowing a tight stream of fire against the rock wall. It sounded deeper than before, and instead of blue and orange flames, his fire was golden-white, the color of the midday sun, and just as bright. The others drew back, the heat so intense it singed Gunnar's beard, despite standing several paces behind.

Brohdan continued, exhaling harder, forcing the stream tighter and tighter.

Kiera gasped, watched entranced as his fire bored *through* the rock, molten rivulets dripping to the ground. His fire reflected in five pairs of eyes, the first to see Broglia fire in over a centicycle.

Then he stopped, took a step back as the molten rock cooled, dimmed.

"That was awesome!" Gunnar roared, punching Brohdan softly on his chest. "Never seen anything like it!"

The others joined them, congratulating their friend. "Reminds me of Kainan," Belkidar said softly, his eyes distant. Then he smiled, and Brohdan couldn't help join him.

Before long, they resumed their chores. Batai finished setting up the tent, and Kiera hummed softy as she placed their food over the fire. Brohdan noticed how Gunnar sat subdued, mindlessly watching the flames. "Something bothering you?"

He grunted. "Haven't shared a meal with anyone in a long time."

"I know how you feel."

"You do?" He asked politely, but seemed unconvinced.

"Of all the creatures in the world, you and I are the only ones of our kind."

Gunnar looked from the fire, only a portion of the dragon's huge form flickering in its light.

"And neither one of us started out that way."

Gunnar nodded, returned his gaze to the fire. "I think that's the hardest part."

"When I learned that I was the next Broglia Black, everyone treated me differently. I still felt like the Dalluvian Green I'd always been, but that's not what people saw. Some felt threatened, others were jealous, but I think most just didn't know how to act around me. I was the same dragon I'd always been, but they couldn't see that."

"In some ways, it would've been easier if we never knew them at all," Gunnar whispered.

Brohdan nodded, ashamed that he'd considered that too.

"But that's a coward's way," Gunnar continued. "I'd rather remember them, remember what they stood for, than to avoid a little pain."

"The pain helps you remember, helps remind you of who you really are."

Gunnar looked up again, considered the creature across the fire from him. Pain. He knew it well, and it appeared Brohdan was no stranger to it either. "I struggle knowing their lives ended far too early, hundreds of cycles taken from us, *stolen* from us. Then I realize it's not just my family they stole from me, it's everything – friends I never met, mentors, a wife, children. Everything."

He paused, his eyes never leaving the fire. "A rage builds inside me, sometimes to the point I can't control it. But I will, because our Quest is too important. But more than that, I've dreamed of having a chance to show the world what giants are like, to leave our true legacy behind."

"To show the world that those murderers were just that – murderers," Brohdan said.

"Exactly." Just one word, but filled with emotion.

"It would've been so easy for you to retaliate, to avenge your family."

He snorted. "Don't think it's never crossed my mind," he said, his laugh bitter.

Brohdan smiled. "But you and I both know that's a trap. You'll get your revenge by leaving behind your legacy, a permanent reminder of who you were."

"Perfectly said," Belkidar agreed, staring into the fire. "An unfortunate consequence of long life is coping with the deaths of countless loved ones. I lived two hundred cycles before I gained your wisdom. Despite anything that happens, we ultimately choose how we live our lives. And so I chose to celebrate the time I shared with loved ones instead of mourning their losses. I was lucky to have known them in the first place, so why be selfish and only think about what I'd lost? It's not easy, but I still smile when I think of old friends and the time we spent together."

"Hmm," Indira whispered. "Next to your pain, mine is nothing. But I have also lost family, and already I am further from my home than I have ever been." She looked from Belkidar to Brohdan. "But I will try to do as you say."

Belkidar smiled. "Good for you, Indira. And from what your father told me, you have the strength and courage to do whatever you want."

Indira returned his smile, her beaming expression proved so striking, Brohdan thought it rivaled Kiera's.

They ate as darkness swallowed all but the area closest to the fire. "Gunnar," Kiera said, her tone dangerously playful, "I'd wager you're a decent wrestler."

"I suppose," he said carefully.

"How about giving me a try?"

"I really don't think that's a good idea."

"Why not?"

"It's...ah...too dark."

"Belkidar, can you please remedy that?"

Belkidar looked at Kiera, then at the giant. He consented, more concerned with her wrath than Gunnar's potential to injure her. The fire blazed suddenly, its reflections off the surrounding mountains akin to polished brass. Indira looked astounded, their campsite as bright as midday. The fire reflected in her dark eyes, her gaze finally settling on Belkidar, and she was left wondering if there were any limits to his ability.

"Thank you," Kiera said, looking up at Gunnar. "Better?"

"Kiera, I don't think this is a good idea."

"Too late. Belkidar's already exerted himself, and we wouldn't want an old man to do that for no reason, would we?"

Belkidar sighed, wisely said nothing.

"As you wish," Gunnar finally said, standing. They walked south to where their campsite grew widest.

"Give me a moment," Kiera said, meticulously removing several daggers from various parts of her clothing.

"Is that all?" Gunnar asked, a brow raised.

"Not quite," she answered, reaching into each boot. After counting on her fingers, she finally seemed satisfied.

"What's the objective?" Gunnar asked. "To kill you, or will minor injuries be sufficient?"

"Just play around a bit," Belkidar interrupted. "Remember our true goal here, and how an injury would impact that."

Gunnar crouched down, but judging by his demeanor, he wasn't exactly taking this seriously. Kiera felt him out, danced gracefully around him.

Brohdan watched the mismatched pair. Kiera, short even by human standards, stood even with Gunnar's bent knees. Batai watched intently, Indira's concern obvious. Belkidar seemed only to be waiting for the inevitable.

In a flash, Kiera made her move. She raced forward, slid the last few elads, used a scissors kick to nudge him off balance. Although perfectly executed, the giant didn't budge, stepped back from her, watched as she regained her feet.

Unperturbed, Kiera attacked with another leg-whip. As she again slid the final few elads, Gunnar braced himself, crouching slightly – exactly as Kiera had planned. About halfway through her slide, she nimbly regained her feet and leapt from his leveled right calf, using fistfuls of bearskin to pull herself up.

Gunnar reacted instantly, standing from his crouch to straighten his leg. But Kiera was ready, shifted her weight from her legs to her hands. With her feet dangling, she hauled herself hand-over-hand up his enormous back. By the time he realized she no longer needed his calf for support, she'd already positioned herself between his massive shoulder blades. He reached around, tried grab one of her legs, but she had already climbed to the top of his shoulders. Knowing her arms were too short, she sat on the back of his neck and circled her legs beneath his chin.

Gunnar fumbled slightly, carefully grabbed her legs, easily pulled her from his neck. A huge upside-down smile greeted him as he held her dangling.

"Got ya!"

Gunnar's laughter was uninhibited, contagious. "You did, at that," he agreed, carefully setting her on the ground. "Thanks for not using your daggers," he added, still laughing.

"Nah," she said, retrieving the first of them. "I couldn't hurt you! I like you too much."

That was too much for Gunnar. The others were helpless in joining him, and it took several drus before the laughter subsided.

As they made their way back to the fire, Belkidar returned the camp to its normal brightness. "I'd say we've had a full day."

Gunnar looked at him, nodded slightly. For the first time since he'd lost his family so long ago, he was happy.

Belkidar understood, nodded back. "Let's get some sleep. I want to put these mountains behind us tomorrow." The others left for the tent, but Gunnar and Brohdan were content to sleep by the fire. The giant had packed a long, thick canvas that he used as both bed and blanket.

"Sleep well," Brohdan said, his long neck circling the ground around him, nestling his chin near the base of his tail.

"Goodnight, Brohdan. And thank you."

Chapter 11
Fellowship

Courage. Kindness. Friendship. Character. These are
the qualities that define us as human beings, and
propel us, on occasion, to greatness.

R.J. Palacio, <u>Wonder</u>

As usual, Brohdan laid in his makeshift bed long after the others had risen, and through squinted eyes he saw the them packing their belongings. Sometimes, it's good to be a dragon. Humans carry way too much stuff.

Batai coaxed a fire from the coals, and they broke their fast with hot sausage and cheese. After smelling the meat cooking, Gunnar leaned toward the resting dragon. "I don't suppose you could find something more suitable for us?"

Brohdan smiled. "I think I could manage."

"You might want to hurry. If you don't find anything before Kiera starts to eat, we'll probably have to cook it ourselves."

Relieved, Gunnar watched as Brohdan appeared above the eastern wall a few moments later, a small doe in a rear talon. Then he took off again for his own meal.

Gunnar hoisted the animal and smiled coyly at Kiera, an eyebrow raised.

She'd never really considered giants prior to meeting Gunnar, but seeing one right in front of her with a childish grin just didn't seem natural. "Oh, all right," she sighed, "but you have to prepare it."

"Thank you, Kiera. You're very kind," he said, skinning the deer.

"Just don't tell anyone."

Before long, Brohdan returned. His satisfied expression spoke volumes.

"How many did you eat?" Gunnar asked.

"Six."

After the others had finished their meals, the cooking materials were cleaned in the nearby stream while the horses watered and packed. Soon, Kiera once again led them south.

For the next several links, they traveled in silence, sometimes forced to walk in single file when the trail narrowed. Brohdan noticed they were all drowsy, slumped in their saddles.

All except Kiera. She looked behind her, found the others half asleep. A mischievous smile, gone in a flash. "Trolls!" she shouted, her eyes fixated on the horizon.

Her cry nearly dislodged Belkidar from his saddle. Startled, Batai and Indira blinked first at Kiera, then to where she stared. Gunnar drew his great sword from the sheath behind his back, crouched in defensive stance. Brohdan glanced to where she stared, his wings spread and mouth open. Sounds of hastily-drawn weapons echoed off the mountainside.

After a few moments, they turned to Kiera, confused. "Rolls! I really feel like some *rolls* for our midday meal, don't you guys?"

Belkidar's curses were sputtered so quickly, Brohdan thought he invented half of them on the spot. Batai was also swearing, only he at least made some effort to keep his voice down. Either that or Belkidar's words were so loud, it only seemed that way. Finally, when Belkidar regained control of his speech, he turned his reddened face toward Kiera. "I suppose we all misunderstood you?"

"Whatever do you mean, sir?"

"It may very well be my advanced age, but it seemed to me you called '*trolls*.'"

"Oh, my. I guess 'rolls' does sound a bit like 'trolls.' I guess it's fortunate that I'm in the mood for rolls, isn't it? Because if trolls *were* on that mountain, we'd be dead."

Belkidar knew better than to argue. Although trolls were relatively rare in this area, a potential ambush by any creature would've been poorly met. More to the point, Belkidar knew Hildegard's unseen spies were a constant threat ever since he began recruiting members for this

Quest. "Maybe it is a good time to stop for a meal, now that you mention it."

To no one's surprise, Kiera didn't prepare any rolls. After finishing his small lunch, Batai turned toward the elf. "Indira, I understand you're pretty good with that bow."

"That is not for me to say," she answered, a twinkle in her emerald eyes.

"Care to give us an example?" he asked, his professional curiosity getting the better of him.

"What do you suggest?"

"Hmm." He looked around, found a fat, green lizard scaling a nearby rock. "Do you see that?"

"Yes." It was several dozen elads on the other side of the trail.

"Can you put an arrow through him?"

"Of course."

"Very well. If you put your first arrow through it, I'll eat it."

Batai had only just gotten the words out by the time Indira had taken an arrow from the quiver that rested down her slender back, nocked it, drew back her bowstring, and released it, all in one elegant motion. As Batai turned toward the sound she made, a soft thud immediately drew his attention back across the path. An arrow thrummed, embedded nearly an elye into the rock, while the lizard's twitching slowed, impaled through its heart.

"I understand they taste like chicken," Belkidar offered.

Batai slowly stood and walked to where his meal awaited him. "I don't imagine you'd cook this for me," he sheepishly asked Kiera.

"You'll probably mope the rest of the day if I don't."

At first, Batai looked as though he wouldn't keep his lunch down, but after tasting it, he seemed to enjoy it. "This really isn't too bad," he said, finishing the tail and starting on the legs.

"If you say so." Kiera turned away, squeamish.

"Let me know if you are still hungry," Indira said, lightly fingering the tip of one of her razor-sharp arrows, "I think I saw a frog near the stream."

"Thanks," Batai answered, his cheeks covered in lizard grease, "I think I've had enough."

Belkidar was still chuckling. "Batai, Indira's the finest archer I've ever met. Maybe the finest *anyone's* ever met."

"Oh, I don't doubt she's talented, but I was curious to see if she was really that much better than my bowmen."

Belkidar's chuckling continued.

When their meals of military rations – and one fat lizard – had been completed, the small group again weaved from one obscure trail to the next as Kiera led them toward the plains that lay south of the Midrogru Mountains. The links passed like those of the morning, except this time nobody dared slump in their saddles. At least once per link, Kiera glanced behind her to find several bright and alert faces staring back.

A couple of links before sunset, Kiera followed a gradual turn and found herself looking out over a broad plain. These rolling hills were covered in tall grass and were much greener than north of the Midrogrus had been, its stark contrast to the dull, brown of the mountains a welcome change. Relieved to put the mountains and their greater potential for ambush behind them, Kiera nudged her horse into a gallop, and it wasn't long before she heard the others keeping pace.

Then, without warning, a huge shadow enveloped them, but they relaxed when Brohdan passed overhead, watched as he disappeared beyond the next hill. Kiera dreamed of what it must feel like to soar so effortlessly, smiled as he descended out of sight. After a few drus, he reappeared far to her left, barely clearing the hill on his way back. She was reminded of a whale, but instead of the blue ocean water, he breached the green surface of the rolling grasslands.

"Are you having fun?" she asked as he passed above her in the opposite direction.

"Yes!"

"Please don't scare the horses!"

The others caught up and rode side-by-side. "Do you think we can make the forest before sunset?" Belkidar asked.

"Not unless you want to push the horses."

"No, they need rest. Besides, we're ahead of schedule."

"You doubted me?"

"Never."

"Well, there's a river ahead that runs down from the mountains. We'll cross it soon enough."

Belkidar nodded.

As they continued south, the trees gradually increased in both size and density. Brohdan heard the creek not long after seeing the first tree. It was a great location to spend the night since both water and firewood were plentiful.

Without much effort, Gunnar persuaded Brohdan to find them another meal, and he soon returned with a satisfied grin. "I found something interesting, but they're too big for me to carry back."

"What is it?"

"I'm not sure. I found them on the other side of the stream."

"Show me," Gunnar said, starting in that direction, "I'll carry one back for us."

"I think you'll need my help," Brohdan said, flying with such excitement he appeared to dance in midair.

In their absence, Belkidar and Batai set up the tent while Indira and Kiera gathered firewood. Soon, a fire blazed as Belkidar stood back, admiring his work.

"What are you so proud of?" Indira asked a half link later, poking him in the ribs.

"The tent."

"Belkidar, you must know the children of my pack are tasked with such things."

"Ah, but I haven't done one manually in nearly three thousand cycles," he explained, tapping his walking stick on the ground. "I'd like to see some kid do *that*!"

Indira said nothing, her smile slowly evolving into a smirk.

"I'll take the horses and water them at the creek," Batai offered.

"Would you like some help?" she asked, noting the empty water bags.

"I'd love some!"

Indira walked next to the paladin as Einar led the horses to the stream.

"I bet you can't wait until we reach the Glor Forest," he said. "I'd imagine it'll remind you of home."

"Yes," she agreed. "The mountains were interesting, but I prefer the woodland."

"As do I." He paused for a moment, considering her predicament. "I know we could never replace your family, Indira, but we're here if you ever need anything."

She smiled, nodded her appreciation. "We are familiar with Belkidar, but I had never met him until you arrived." She looked up, met his eyes. "Had you met any of our companions before?"

"No, only Belkidar. We've known each other for many cycles."

"How did you meet?

Batai took a moment, recalled their first meeting like it was yesterday. He smiled. "Belkidar's unlike anyone I've ever met. He cares so much for people, always looking for those who need his help the most." He paused, his smile widening. "I was nine when I met him. I lived with my parents in a small house on the outskirts of Trisett. My mother was pregnant, and both of my parents were hoping for a little girl. So was I, truth be told. I would've loved to have had a sister."

"What happened?" she asked tentatively, her voice soft.

"My father was a knight. One day his regiment was tasked to restore order to a neighboring district in Trisett. The people there were close to rioting because they felt cheated by the king." Batai shook his head. "The prince favored a noble in Trisett, so he showered her district with gifts. He wanted to win her heart, but failing that he knew it'd pressure her to marry him, else his gifts would stop, turning her district against her."

"As you might imagine, these gifts didn't please the neighboring districts, one eventually threatening riots. After my father's regiment arrived, most left and returned to their homes, but a large group remained. They grew belligerent, weapons appeared, and the knights were forced to defend themselves. Eventually, order was restored, but not before several townspeople were killed."

"Unbeknownst to them, the rioters had identified four of the knights. It took them three days to discover where they lived, and on the third night, they slipped into their homes and murdered them, along with their families."

"That is horrible!" She had stopped walking and stood motionless several paces behind. "How were you spared?"

Batai smiled weakly. "I wasn't home. I always knew I wanted to be a knight like my father, so I'd begged him relentlessly to train me with a sword. When I turned eight, he finally relented. I learned quickly from him, and after a cycle he decided I needed more dedicated instruction. We weren't rich, so you can imagine my surprise when he hired a tutor, an expert swordsman. I was training with him that night."

Batai saw the pain in Indira's eyes. He went back to her, put a big arm around her slender shoulders, once more led her toward the creek.

"Belkidar arrived that night. He took me in and raised me for two cycles before I was old enough to attend the military academy."

"But you were only eleven!"

Batai laughed. "You don't understand. I'd dreamt of going there, to help me eventually become a knight. True, I was still boy, but Belkidar persuaded the headmaster to accept me, even though I was three cycles too young."

Indira was impressed, with both Belkidar's compassion and Batai's aptitude.

"I completed the curriculum two cycles early, and after spending the next cycle in the service of my king, I earned my knighthood."

"So young?"

Batai looked down. "Well, I had motivation others didn't."

She understood. "What was Belkidar like as a father?"

"Oh, he never pretended to be my father. But he did claim to be my friend, first with his words, but always with his actions. He's an amazing person. I wouldn't be who I am today if it wasn't for him."

Indira was reminded of Batai's earlier offer to her. "That may be true, but I am sure Belkidar could make a similar claim."

Before long, Batai and Indira returned to the campsite. A few drus later, Brohdan approached from the northwest. "Where's Gunnar?" Kiera asked as he drew near.

"He's right behind me," Brohdan explained as he landed. "He's carrying it back for us."

"I thought it was too big for him to carry."

"It seems I underestimated him."

Just as Brohdan finished, Gunnar strolled toward them carrying an enormous carcass across his wide shoulders. Indira saw its thick legs bounce limply on either side of his head as he came into view, and it resembled nothing she'd ever seen.

"What is it?" Batai asked.

"I have no idea," Gunnar answered, dropping it by the fire.

"It's a hrundra ox," Belkidar said, approaching it. "They're related to the musk ox, only obviously much larger." The sorcerer walked around it. "He's actually a small one, only a few cycles old. When they're fully grown, they're nearly three elads at the shoulders."

"Well, I think this one's big enough," Batai offered. "I'd be surprised if all of us together could finish that thing tonight."

Gunnar giggled, looked over to Brohdan.

"Somehow, I don't think that's going to be a problem," Belkidar said, the two enormous creatures snickering behind him.

As it turned out, the only thing Batai had to worry about that night was finding enough food for himself. After Gunnar prepared the huge beast, he split it lengthwise into halves. Kiera actually seemed delighted to try her hand at cooking something so enormous, although she'd need Belkidar's help to prepare it in time for dinner. In the meantime, both Batai and Gunnar paced impatiently as the aroma of roasting meat saturated the area. Brohdan wasn't much better. He thoughtfully waited until his friends' meals had been cooked, flying circles around their camp to relieve his impatience.

Wanting to distract himself, Batai approached Indira. "I'll give you credit, it took skill to kill that lizard. But hitting a moving target requires even more, and to hit several requires greater skill yet."

She smiled, amused with his curiosity. "What did you have in mind?"

He turned to Brohdan. "Can I talk you into flushing some birds from the tall grass over there?" he asked, pointing toward a meadow several dozen elads to the south.

"Of course. You won't shoot me?"

"You have nothing to fear," Indira assured him.

Brohdan headed toward the field. When he was halfway there, all save Belkidar gasped when he disappeared.

No, that wasn't right. He didn't disappear exactly, but it was the next closest thing.

"What did he just – " Kiera began.

"I'll explain later," Belkidar whispered. "I believe he's ready."

"Are *you*?" Batai playfully asked Indira, who still sat near the fire.

"Always."

Batai nodded, unsheathed his sword and waved it high over his head. At that signal, Brohdan stood, released 'cloak' and, with his wings spread wide, cast 'fear' in the center of the field, causing several fowl to take flight.

Batai learned from his previous mistake. He was tempted to watch the birds, but he steadfastly ignored them to place his undivided attention on Indira. This time he wasn't going to miss a thing.

And he was lucky he did. When she saw the first bird take flight, she simultaneously grabbed her huge bow with her left hand and an arrow from the quiver along her back with her right. She brought the bow forward, nocked the arrow onto the thick bowstring. Then in one smooth motion, she drew it back with her right arm and leveled it with her left. Before Batai realized the first arrow had been released, she smoothly continued moving her right hand backward, over her shoulder. She selected a second arrow, nocked it, simultaneously drew back the string, released it. Her right hand never stopped, blurred as it moved between bow and quiver, her bowstring's song as unbroken as a lute's. Batai had never seen anything like it. After the third arrow, he could no longer recognize when she reached for an arrow or drew back her bowstring. Gunnar and Kiera were no better, stood dumbfounded next to him. In the space of two drus, Indira had emptied her small quiver of twelve arrows.

"Would you mind finding the birds?" Belkidar asked Brohdan, knowing his sensitive nose offered the quickest way to retrieve them.

"How many did you find?" Batai asked anxiously as Brohdan approached.

"Twelve."

Several moments of stunned silence.

"That was the most amazing display I've ever seen," Batai conceded. "Your talents are truly second to none."

Belkidar turned toward her, received a small nod. "To say Indira's bow is unique would be an understatement. Juron himself created it using techniques that predate the Staff of Power by thousands of cycles.

And yet despite creating it, Juron could never wield it. Only Elvorns can."

"Elvorns?" Kiera asked, confused.

"Elvorns are elves, but born with exceptionally rare skills. They're similar to Broglias in dragon societies, only not as rare, and they look like any of their kin. But appearances can be misleading, and that's particularly true when an Elvorn picks up a bow. They're no stronger than any other elf, but they can string and draw a bow that would be impossible for anyone else."

"Are you telling me Indira can string that bow?" Kiera asked incredulously, looking first at her slender friend, then at a thick bow that was nearly as tall as she was.

"Of course. Why would she carry a weapon that she was helpless to use? Or repair?"

Having survived many skirmishes, she of course knew the answer, but she was still surprised. The frame was as thick her leg, made of materials she couldn't recognize. And the bowstring was the thickest she'd ever seen.

"Well, it's no wonder I'm forced to eat my losses," Batai said. "At least no reptiles tonight." He gathered the birds, then with a practiced hand began removing their feathers.

Neither Brohdan nor Gunnar had eaten that well in ages. Kiera had prepared the ox to perfection, so much so that even Brohdan tried some of the cooked meat. After Batai had stuffed himself with four birds and a healthy share of the ox, he was amazed to see Gunnar still eating. Brohdan, of course, had finished his half long ago.

Within another link, they had all eaten their share and were ready for bed. But Brohdan slept fitfully that night, experiencing strange dreams where he found himself surrounded by hordes of hateful creatures. The dreams were made worse by how realistic they were, especially as he was forced to slaughter wave after wave. But for every enemy he killed, two more came rushing toward him. It was no use, he couldn't fend them off. They swarmed him, climbed on top of him, their combined weight pinning him to the ground.

He woke with a start. He searched the camp and, when satisfied they were safe, drifted back to sleep. His relief was short-lived, though, as other dreams just as vivid nagged him the rest of the night. Though unrested, he was happy to see the sunrise.

Indira noticed. "How did you sleep?"

"Not well," he replied through a yawn. "Nightmares. Hordes attacked me, more creatures than I could count. I didn't recognize half of them."

"What'd they look like?" Belkidar asked.

"Some resembled humans, but with a bull's head."

"Minotaurs," he grunted.

"Others seemed a combination of both humans and horses."

"Centaurs. Hildegard's apparently recruited several species native to Katja, which means his forces are larger than I'd anticipated. His human armies already outnumber Tymoteu's entire population, but with these additions, a full invasion would have no chance."

"But they were only dreams," Kiera pointed out.

"I'm not so sure. Broglias have been known portend future events through their dreams. They're sporadic, appearing at random, but always accurate."

"We have something similar in my pack," Indira admitted. "Sometimes an elf will dream the future. It happens very rarely, perhaps once in a generation, and none has ever accomplished it twice."

Belkidar stared at her. "In all my cycles, I've never knew that."

"I am not surprised. It is one of our most guarded secrets."

"And it will remain so," he assured her, then turned back to Brohdan. "What else did you see?"

"Gigantic, hairy creatures with long, shaggy fur and huge claws. There were only a dozen, but they were as fierce as the others combined."

"Gargantuids!" His tone revealed equal parts disgust and fear.

"They don't sound pleasant," Kiera observed.

"They're not," he confirmed, pacing the campsite, shifting the Staff from one hand to the other. "Gargantuids are usually docile creatures, preferring to live by themselves. But when disturbed, they're one of the most formidable foes you could imagine. A fully-grown gargantuid stands over eighteen elads tall, their claws more powerful than the jaws of most other creatures."

"Just a moment," Batai interrupted. "You're telling me these gargantuids are nearly as large as Brohdan?"

"Yes. And no. Remember, Brohdan still has a lot of growing to do before we reach Katja. He's perhaps twenty elads long now, but he'll be twenty-eight when his grombit is complete. But a dragon's frame is slender, otherwise it would hinder their ability to fly. Gargantuids don't have that limitation. They're powerfully built with unmatched strength."

"Sounds stimulating," Gunnar said, oiling his sword on the other side of the fire.

Belkidar sighed. "Did you see anything else?"

"I'm afraid so, robed figures in the background of every dream. Hoods covered their faces, but they all chanted something. Whatever they were doing didn't seem to have any effect on me – at least in my dream."

"The Jrelz, Hildegard's disciples," Belkidar explained. "Hildegard's actually arranged them into a surprisingly efficient hierarchy. The lesser experienced are trained by the more experienced. The Jrelz elders, often referred to as Jrelz Captains, receive their tutelage from Hildegard himself. They also serve as his personal assistants and guardians." Belkidar paused, shook his head. "It's a sad way to continue the ancient teachings."

"Well, we knew this wasn't going to be easy," Batai said. "At least we have an insight into Hildegard's plan, something we didn't have last night. And we still have plenty of time to prepare a counter-strategy."

Kiera was again struck by the paladin's confidence. Despite this troubling news, he always believed they would survive. No, not just survive. Succeed. Either he was perpetually optimistic to the point of insanity, or his skill on the battlefield was unmatched. Soon, she thought to herself, they'd all have the opportunity to prove their worth.

Once they emerged from the mountains, Brohdan once again ranged further from his friends, usually flying ahead to one side or the other searching for threats. But Belkidar wanted him hidden from others, and that forced him to fly lower, restricting the distance he could scout.

It was for this reason he missed the ambush. While he scouted a half linak to the south, a group of thieves sprang from the trees and bushes that lined the trail. Before Kiera had a chance to alert her companions, nearly a hundred men armed with daggers and swords surrounded them. Even Gunnar's presence failed to deter them.

A very large fat man stepped forward, the fact that he hadn't bathed in some time obvious. He had a bushy, black beard spotted with dead grass and small leaves. His soiled garments reeked of urine and old sweat. He studied them for a long moment. "You can make this easy. We want only your money, your horses, and your women. The rest may leave." He looked Gunnar up and down. "True, the large one may claim a few of my men, but we all know how this will end if you refuse my generosity."

Before Belkidar could respond, Gunnar charged, freeing his weapon in an instant. The bandits hesitated, awed by a sword whose length easily surpassed their height. Yet despite its size, Gunnar wielded it as though it weighed nothing. And it never slowed, its cold steel ripping through several enemies with each stroke, his free hand bashing others to the ground. In the first few drus of his attack, Gunnar had killed fifteen bandits.

Batai's hand found the handle of his own sword just as Gunnar's freed its scabbard, Einar already at a gallop despite trampling several thieves, the muscles in his chest flexing beneath his skin. The magnificence of Batai's sword matched Gunnar's, although not so much for its size but for the practiced way it was wielded, his combination of skill, training, and experience more art than butchery.

And yet for all of his ability, Einar's actions were equally remarkable. He perfectly anticipated Batai's intentions, trampling foes his rider ignored while simultaneously positioning himself to keep others within sword range. Belkidar realized this degree of teamwork between man and beast exceeded any he'd witnessed in several thousand cycles, as though one mind dictated the actions of both.

Kiera didn't hesitate. She sprang from her horse, rolled forward onto her knees, and with each hand threw a dagger that thudded into the chests of two enemies. In the next instant, she drew two longer knives while the nearest bandit lunged at her with his sword. Kiera smoothly sidestepped him, watched as his momentum carried him helplessly past, countered with a dagger to the back of his neck. He made no sound as Kiera smoothly pulled the knife free, blood spurting as he toppled at her feet.

She ducked under another swinging blade and drove both knives into the attacker's chest. With two others bearing down on her, she pulled the dead man toward her and rolled backward into a summersault, dragging the corpse with her. When she sat atop his body, she pulled her weapons free and threw them at the charging thieves. She drew two more unseen daggers just as the sternums of each thief cracked from the impacts.

Within drus of her initial attack, the quiver along Indira's back stood empty, two dozen men dead from arrows they'd never seen. And yet her bow continued humming. Fifty arrows had stood neatly in a hard leather quiver just in front of her right knee, another fifty to her left.

Belkidar watched his small group, realizing this may be his only chance to evaluate their performance before arriving on Katja. His only concession was the leader. At Gunnar's initial charge, white-blue light surrounded the fat man, and then he was gone, leaving only his odor behind. In an instant, he reappeared behind Belkidar, unconscious but still reeking.

The battle ended as quickly as it had begun. Indira had killed two dozen before Gunnar's sword had even found its first victim, while

Kiera, Batai, and Einar were already upon their first targets as it completed its initial swing. The majority of the survivors attempted to flee, but none could match the speed of Indira's arrows or the stamina of Batai's charger. Hildegard's involvement in this attack was remote, yet they couldn't risk any information getting back to him, so Batai and Gunnar searched for survivors as Indira's arrow found the last deserter.

"Nice little battle," Gunnar noted with a satisfied grin.

"Not bad indeed," Batai agreed, wiping his bloody sword on the tunic of a dead thief.

Kiera shook her head. "I'm not sure it was really worth all the nicks I just put in my daggers. It'll take links to sharpen them again."

"We're not quite finished," Belkidar interjected. "But before we continue, I want Brohdan to join us. This all happened so quickly I doubt he even realized we've stopped." The sorcerer's expression turned distant and, within a few drus, Brohdan landed nearby.

Belkidar raised his hand, postponing his questions for the moment. "Their leader is still alive, and I needed to establish Hildegard's involvement in this."

Slowly, they all turned to where the fat thief rested on his knees, sobbing for mercy to anyone who would listen. Just as slowly, they all turned back, stared at Belkidar.

"A simple ward."

Brohdan did his best to catch up. He surmised that they'd been attacked, and with relief discovered none of his friends had been injured. But he didn't understand how he could've missed all of these men, and he tried to convince himself that his five friends could've defeated them all so quickly.

Belkidar turned to the terrified survivor. "Why did you attack us?" The sorcerer's tone was friendly, inviting, as though they were old friends.

"I'm not a fool!" he answered, spittle flying from his chubby lips.

Indira watched carefully, anticipating Belkidar's anger, but his demeanor remained unchanged.

"I ask you to reconsider. Spare yourself a fate far worse than that of your men."

"I do not fear death."

"So be it." The sorcerer's gaze remained unchanged, but Indira slowly grasped a hint of the anguish that plagued the fat man. His face contorted, his sunken eyes widened, his mouth gaped in a disjointed, silent cry. Finally, his voice joined his expression, his initial moans transforming into a shrill scream. "Stop! Stop!" he shrieked in a pitch Brohdan had previously thought impossible of humans.

"Tell me why you attacked us," Belkidar calmly suggested.

"I was paid! Now take it away! Take it away!" Tears flowed over his portly cheeks and into his filthy beard.

"By whom?"

"I don't know! I don't know!" he screamed. "He wore a black robe, his face covered! Please! *Please!*"

"Where did your payment originate?"

"From Katja! Gul Krul! My orders came from Gul Krul!" Then he began laughing, hysterical. "You won't defeat him!" he added, his laughter growing alongside his convulsions. "Your way of life is over! My master will – " His seizures grew even more violent, cutting off his words. Within drus, he lay dead at Belkidar's feet.

"I don't think he was in the best of health," Belkidar sighed, taking a step back. "I must remember that."

"What was he talking about?" Brohdan asked, still confused.

"These men were hired by Hildegard. He wanted to kill us before we became too powerful, before we ever had the chance to steal back the Jewel." He stopped, nodded. "That's actually encouraging when you think about it."

"How exactly is that encouraging?" Kiera asked with forced patience.

"Simple. If we stood no chance at all, why would Hildegard bother hiring mercenaries? Perhaps our odds aren't as bad as I thought."

"Belkidar," Batai sighed, shaking his head, "you may be the greatest sorcerer in the world, but your motivational techniques could use some improvement."

"I'm afraid I still don't understand," Brohdan said. "How did Hildegard know we were here?"

"I believe it was an assumption on his part," Belkidar explained. "He knew I must challenge his theft of the Jewel, and he realized Brodor was the most likely port we'd use to gain passage to Katja. But he couldn't bring his own forces here, that'd be too reckless, and he wouldn't want to weaken his armies to do it. So he hired mercenaries. I'm sure there are more, probably along the main roads to Brodor." Belkidar thought for a moment. "Actually, I'd have done the same thing if I were in his position. I should've seen this coming."

"That's all right," Batai assured him, "we'd get complacent if we didn't have these little surprises along the way."

"Men," Kiera sighed toward Indira.

"How did I not see them?" Brohdan asked, frustrated that he hadn't detected the threat.

"Don't worry about it," Belkidar assured him. "We can handle this sort of thing. Besides, keeping you hidden is vital now. If you were seen and even one of these men escaped, Hildegard would know that we've recruited a Broglia."

"He's going to find out sooner or later," Kiera said.

"I'd prefer later," Belkidar replied. "Once Hildegard learns of Brohdan's involvement, he'll be forced to counter it, so the longer we keep it from him, the less time he'll have to prepare."

Brohdan nodded. "I'll do my best."

"It's only until we leave the continent. The ocean is vast, and most of the people on Katja live in Trillhell or Gul Krul, and we'll avoid them as long as possible."

They resumed their journey and soon found themselves among the trees of the Glor Forest. Although the path narrowed significantly, Brohdan managed to walk with the others when not flying. After a few links, they stopped for their midday meal. Kiera led them off the road where they unpacked some bread, cheese, and dried venison.

While the others ate, Brohdan felt a sharp pain in his barz. The pain increased tenfold, and he instinctively sniffed his tail.

Belkidar immediately realized what was happening. "Don't get too close!"

Brohdan looked at him.

"Your blade is fully grown," he explained quickly, "and it's forcing itself out."

Another stab of pain. "What do I do?"

"There are two schools of thought about that," the old man whimsically began. "Some preach that you should allow the blade to come through naturally, without any interference."

"What's the other?" Brohdan pleaded.

"You can extend the blade yourself, instantly slicing through your skin."

"They both sound painful."

"Oh, they are."

Brohdan winced. "I think I'll go for the second. How do I extend it?"

"Well, Balthasar told me he just tried to extend the tip of his tail."

"You mean Balthasar decided to cut through the barz too?"

"Of course. Why would anybody wait for it to happen on its own? That'd take days!"

Brohdan didn't hear a word as he considered Balthasar's technique. Then the pain grew sharply, overwhelming his thoughts. Brohdan responded instinctively, and his deafening roar accompanied a single, bloody, three-elad blade slicing through the end of his tail.

"I really can't believe how Broglias handle pain," Belkidar remarked, lowering his hands from his ears. "It's only a little cut."

Indira didn't agree, fearlessly rushing to examine his wound.

"Indira, it's never a good idea to pester a wounded dragon."

"But he needs help!" Brohdan stood in agony as Indira approached the long, bloody blade that glistened in the afternoon sun. "Brohdan, please retract that."

"I'll try." After only a moment, it disappeared back into his barz. He was surprised with how simple it was to extend or retract, as easy as opening or closing a talon.

Indira examined the wound. It was wide, his thick red blood pooling on the ground. She ordered Gunnar to fetch some water and Batai to start a fire. Obediently, the two men did as they were told.

"Do you know where I might find some water?" Gunnar asked Kiera.

"There's a small creek southeast of here. It may be a linak, though."

He shrugged, turned, picked up several water bags, and headed toward where she'd indicated.

Indira left Brohdan and foraged the surrounding area. After a few drus, she spotted something that apparently satisfied her. She strode quickly to a small bush near the base of a tree where dozens of small purple berries hung in clumps from its branches. She picked several clusters and brought them to where Batai tended a small fire in a makeshift pit. Just as she set the berries in a neat pile, Gunnar returned with all of the water containers filled. He brought them to Indira and set them next to the berries.

"Thank you both," she said, dismissing them. They took the hint and moved to where Kiera sat.

"What took you so long," Kiera asked as Gunnar sat next to her.

"The stream was at least a linak away, and – " He abruptly stopped when he saw her grinning up at him. The red of his cheeks somehow made it through his thick beard.

"I can help you with that, if you'd like," Belkidar offered. Without waiting for an answer, the water came to a boil. "But I don't know what all the fuss is about. This is natural. Brohdan will be fine."

"That may be, but his wound should be tended, as should his pain."
With that, Indira turned her back to him and began mashing the berries
with a rounded stone. Belkidar looked at Brohdan, their eyes met.
Then he allowed a little cry to escape his lips.

"Oh, you're pathetic," Belkidar said in disgust as he turned to join
the others. Belkidar realized what he was up to, but nobody else had a
clue. Brohdan cleverly dropped a cry here and a moan there at just the
right moment to tug at the heartstrings of the others. It seemed as
though the severity of Brohdan's pain went hand in hand with
Belkidar's sighs.

"You're pathetic!"

"But it hurts."

"Oh, quit that! You don't fool me."

Brohdan smiled slightly, turned toward the trees to conceal it.
When he turned back, even Belkidar was impressed with the agony
draped across his face.

"Pathetic," the sorcerer repeated aloud as he got up and went for a
walk.

When the berries were mashed into a paste, Indira mixed it with
hot water to make a salve that she applied to his wound, using two of
Belkidar's old cloaks to wrap it and keep the medicine in place.

Belkidar was not pleased when he returned.

"The stain will come out with the next wash. Besides, the berries
have a pleasant aroma," Indira added brightly.

Indira thought it best if they remained there until the following
morning, and Belkidar's insistence that they needn't waste an entire
afternoon had no effect. "We can make up the time later. What is most
important right now is Brohdan's health."

Belkidar could be heard mumbling several curses as he abruptly
left for another extended walk.

"At least he's going to be in excellent shape," Batai observed next
to Kiera and Gunnar. "By the time this is all over, I doubt he'll even
need a horse."

As strange as Brohdan looked with two of Belkidar's cloaks wrapped around the end of his tail, Belkidar's mood appeared even worse. But by sunset, he was forced to admit the rest came at a good time. Soon, they'd be through the forest and under the unforgiving sun of the Wruloric Wastelands. Halfway through a meal of fried ham, beans, and boiled potatoes, Batai turned toward him. "I've often wondered what happens to your clothes when you change forms."

"The same thing that happens to my Staff," he replied dryly.

"Oh, very funny."

"It's actually a simple process. When I change forms, I take the matter that makes up my body and rearrange it into the new form. I simply include my clothing and Staff in the process."

"Does that mean you lose the power of the Staff when you change forms?" Kiera asked.

"No, of course not. The Staff's power isn't restricted to the matter it's made of, it comes from its very existence. Shape-shifting could no more alter the power of the Staff than it could the soul of the sorcerer. My soul is the same in whatever form I choose, just like the Staff's."

"I never considered the possibility that an artifact has a soul," Kiera admitted.

"I can understand. And most artifacts don't, but a very few are more than the sum of its elements, just like us. These rare objects have a kind of consciousness, a soul if you will. The Staff is one of these few, as is the Jewel and Headpiece. Their consciousness isn't like yours or mine, but they do possess a will like we do. Some try to do good, others are more inclined toward evil. That's why it's so important that we stop Hildegard. He possesses two of the most powerful objects in the world, and with them he has become nearly invincible. If he were to somehow acquire this Staff..."

Their mood grew somber with Belkidar's explanation. Brohdan, with the sorcerer's cloaks still wrapped around his barz, considered what he'd just described. Before this evening, he'd never considered that an object might have a consciousness. "What type of influence do these Artifacts have?"

"I'm not really sure anymore. Seven thousand cycles ago, the Staff of Power was the most powerful object in the world, perhaps the entire universe. When I dismantled it into the three Artifacts, I was careful to ensure that each possessed no more power than another. They were as nearly matched as possible, but that was a long time ago. The Headpiece transformed Krollum into Hildegard, so we know its soul is tainted. The Staff and I have been together for so long now, we've grown quite close. I've taken on a few characteristics of the Staff's personality just as it's taken on several of mine."

"I hope it has a better sense of humor," Batai mumbled to Gunnar.

Belkidar wisely ignored it. "Seven thousand cycles ago, the Staff was uninterested with our realm, instead longing to rejoin its two brothers. On the other hand, I was very concerned with the world's day-to-day events. But the War changed much. Jenkar was a fellow sorcerer, and when the War finally came to an end, I felt keenly responsible for what had happened. I did everything I could to restore peace and prosperity. Over time, though, the Staff's indifference rubbed off on me; I no longer believe I was responsible for the War simply because one of my kind was. Likewise, the Staff grew fond of this world, of me."

"We've been together for a long time, and we've learned to complement each other's abilities. So to answer your question, Brohdan, every Artifact has its own distinct power, the extent of which depends on its connection with the sorcerer. As you might imagine, the strength of that relationship is influenced by how compatible the two are. The Staff and I work so well together because we're so similar – we both value honor and integrity, and we use our power for those purposes. There's no convincing needed, no working against each other, we just go about our business as though we were one mind. I seriously doubt Hildegard will ever reach that type of harmony with the Headpiece. That soul is evil, corrupted both Jenkar and Krollum, both good men. We know that soul was fundamentally different from Krollum's, so I don't think it's likely that a natural harmony exists between them."

"But it's not Krollum the Headpiece works with now, it's Hildegard," Brohdan pointed out.

"True, and I don't doubt their relationship is much stronger than Krollum's was. But Hildegard is still a product of Krollum, and I think that'll affect the strength of their relationship. I think it has to."

Brohdan considered that. Obviously, Belkidar was a very powerful sorcerer, but his power was even greater with the Staff working with him. "How do you know if Hildegard still has some of Krollum's honor? If he's completely turned to evil as the Headpiece obviously wants, then their relationship may become as strong as yours."

"But I don't believe it's possible to completely change the character of a being. Krollum was a good man, and he was my friend. I think Krollum still survives within Hildegard, if only as a shadow. When the time comes to face him, I don't think I'll be able to recognize any trace of him through the evil veil that is Hildegard, but just because I can't recognize him doesn't mean he's not there. Hildegard's been alive for thousands of cycles now, and that's no small feat for Krollum to overcome." He considered that before continuing. "No, I think there's still some of Krollum's honor in Hildegard, but I fear I'll never see it again."

The nearest branches trees adopted orange and red hues as the fire continued its monologue. Brohdan realized Belkidar's feelings for Krollum went deeper than he initially understood. Although it was a necessity, destroying Hildegard would most likely be the most difficult task Belkidar could face.

As the evening grew into night, the stars' shyness faded, as did the reservations of those around the fire. Huddled within its light, Brohdan looked into the eyes of his friends. He saw joy in Kiera's, peace in Indira's, serenity in Gunnar's. He smiled, recognizing the protection in Batai's as they periodically scanned the darkness. In Belkidar's, he saw wisdom, experience, paternal worry, but above all, kindness. They stared into the fire, each deep in thought. "Did you ever marry?"

"Yes. A very long time ago." He paused, didn't move for several long moments, and in his face Brohdan saw the happiness, the pain, of his past.

"I met Aelya around seven thousand cycles ago," he continued. "I was almost a thousand cycles old by then, and I'd been studying feverishly for the previous several hundred cycles in a cozy cave toward the southern tip of the Cortusian Mountains. Sorcery is not a simple task, and becoming adept with it requires knowledge, vast knowledge. The more a sorcerer understands, the more opportunities become available to him."

"I'd become anxious for a change in scenery after all those centacycles with little more than stone walls to look at. So I left my cave and traveled a few linaks to a small village east of the mountains. It's no longer there... After all this time, I don't even recall its name," he chuckled to himself.

"I was excited to interact with people again, and I happily waded through the village market – no doubt looking like an idiot – when I happened upon the most beautiful woman I'd ever seen. As she worked her way through the crowd, she cradled a tall basket of fruit under one arm not unlike a mother would carry a child. Half blinded by it, she walked right into me. I turned around, but my annoyance vanished in an instant. She apologized, and we talked as I helped her pick up her fruit. Her name was Aelya. She was nineteen and had lived in that small village all her life."

"We walked together, and she learned that I was new to her village, with no friends or family in the area. Still feeling guilty, she invited me to eat with her family that night. Of course, her parents adored me. I usually have that effect on older people," he added. When nobody laughed, he continued. "Anyway, Aelya and I spent a lot of time together after that, and we soon fell in love. It was the most natural thing I've ever done. But before I could take the next step and propose marriage, I felt that I had to tell her about me. But how do you tell someone you love that you're almost a thousand cycles old? I had no idea, but I eventually worked up the courage and just told her." A sheepish smile crossed his face. "And it didn't even bother her. I'd worked myself up for nothing."

"After that, I used sorcery more frequently around her. She was fascinated, so much so that she eventually asked if I could teach her. That one question changed my life. I'd never considered the idea of teaching – I'd had enough difficulty just learning myself! But before we could begin, I had to determine if she even possessed the ability. Not many people have a properly developed Linsilor Sorcerenic, so the likelihood of Aelya being able to learn was pretty small."

"But to my surprise, her Linsilor was incredibly developed! And so our lessons began, and through her inquisitive mind I soon realized how much I had yet to understand myself. Over the course of the next several cycles, Aelya progressed into a very powerful sorceress, teaching me far more than I could've ever taught her. Our relationship mirrored our developing talents, and before long, we married."

Brohdan smiled as he watched Belkidar's pride swell.

"Those were the happiest times of my life. Aelya and I wanted for nothing, and our sorcery skills grew at an incredible rate. First of all, she was a very gifted sorceress in her own right. But she had a unique perspective, looked at things in ways I never would've considered. And remember what I said earlier – sorcery skills go hand-in-hand with knowledge, so having a new perspective on things led to new ideas, new discoveries, and it accelerated both of our learning."

"But more than that, learning became fun again. Studying had always been so tedious. Don't get me wrong, I enjoyed the concepts. Determining why stars appeared to fall or discovering the mysteries of chemical properties interested me to no end. But the experiments… It wasn't enough to perform a few to prove or disprove a hypothesis. Hundreds were required – along with all of those detailed notes that followed. A few hundred cycles of that tedium would cause even the most enthusiastic scientist to consider a career change. With Aelya, though, I rediscovered the joy of learning again. She had such a spark about her, made me live every day to its fullest. With the success of our experiments, our understanding of the world grew, as did our sorcery."

The entire group remained silent as Belkidar stared into the fire. Brohdan sat opposite him, and it appeared as though its flames tickled his wrinkled face.

"During that time, Aelya experienced the most difficult period of her life. While we kept busy with our studies, her parents had grown old. One overcast morning her younger sister came to us and told Aelya that their parents had grown ill. We rushed to see them, but despite our talents, we were powerless to help. Aelya's mother died early the next morning. Just a half mooncycle afterward, her father followed."

"Aelya eventually outlived her entire family, seemingly without aging a day. As you might imagine, this is a very difficult time for any sorcerer. It's hard enough to cope with the death of somebody close to you, but when a sorcerer first experiences the passing of a loved one, that pain is accompanied by the realization that you'll not only outlive a few of your elder relatives, you'll survive their great, great grandchildren as well. You realize you'll experience the deaths of countless loved ones, and no matter how many children, grandchildren, nieces, nephews, aunts, uncles, cousins, or friends you may have, you can be sure you'll see each and every one of them die. That's a difficult reality to cope with, and many of my friends chose a life of solitude instead. For them, being alone was easier than coping with all of those deaths."

"Luckily, I was there to help her. Although she would eventually witness the death of her entire family, the same could not be said of her husband. I was her beacon because I was the one person that *would* be there. But as depressing as these times were, it brought us even closer together. We shared an ironic bond – each of us was the strength that supported the other, but the foundation of that strength was the very source of the problem. Our marriage wasn't typical, but it was built on ties as strong as any I've ever seen."

Kiera wiped tears away, tore her gaze from him to look into the fire. She couldn't help but imagine how similar flames must've flickered seven thousand cycles ago before Belkidar and his wife. And in that shared experience, she understood a glimmer of his pain.

"We continued our studies, traveling when we could, over the next four thousand cycles. During this time, of course, Jenkar's creation eventually led to war, which finally ended when Krollum, Aelya, and I dismantled the Staff of Power. Because we were married, it was mutually decided the two of us would only be responsible for one of the three Artifacts. Therefore, I was given the task of watching over the Staff while Krollum would take the Headpiece. After some discussion, we decided the Jewel would be protected by the Indifferent, relying on both their strength in numbers as well as their seclusion. They were actually made up of dozens of different tribes, all warlike, but perfectly content to stay isolated from the rest of the world. The only obstacle we had to overcome was convincing them that it was in their best interest to hide the Jewel. I flew down there and talked with their leader, the King of Tribes. Once he understood what was at stake, he agreed."

"Events slowed a great deal after that. Aelya and I gratefully reverted back to our lives before the War. The only major difference was an occasional trek to check on the other two Artifacts. That really wasn't a problem except for the fact that it was the only time the two of us were separated for more than a few links at a time. We couldn't risk any of the Artifacts being near each other again, so Aelya was forced to check on the Headpiece and Jewel without me."

"We both agreed that these trips would happen without the caretaker knowing because we didn't want Krollum or the Indifferent to change their routines. And to our relief, she always returned with good news. Both Artifacts were safe, secure."

"Aelya usually made these trips once every hundred cycles or so, depending on the global weather patterns and the progress of some of our larger experiments. You really wouldn't want to rush an

Antimitrigoritron Class Five experiment if you don't have to, after all. The journey typically took her a mooncycle."

"Something happened about three thousand cycles ago during one of her evaluations. This time, she planned to check on the Headpiece before making her way south to the Indifferent. But she was late getting back, and as the days mounted, my curiosity grew into concern. Although communication between continents is difficult, it's not entirely impossible. We'd done it on occasion when I needed her input on some of our more complicated experiments. But I wasn't able to reach her this time. I had no other choice, I left to find her."

"I took off and followed her planned route, first crossing the Celornorin Ocean and then half of Katja. I retraced my wife's path with ease, and I'm still not certain if that was the result of my sorcery or our intimacy. Regardless, I discovered her trail ended near Krollum's fortress. I had become frantic by then, maybe a little reckless. I knew I was bringing the Staff near another Artifact, but I went anyway."

"But I didn't venture too close. After the War, the last thing I wanted was a potential reunification of the Staff of Power, so meeting with Krollum was out of the question. My only recourse was to inspect the surrounding area to see if I could pick up her trail again. But I couldn't. Maybe she had intentionally concealed it, or was forced to leave the continent covertly? I decided to check Kaarlo, in case she got word that the Jewel was in danger. But when I got there, the Jewel was fine, and I still couldn't find any trace of my wife!"

"I had no choice. I returned home and retraced my steps, thousands of times. I scoured that trail to the tiniest detail and still found not the slightest clue." He grunted. "*That* was the clue I missed, the fact that there weren't any."

"Now, with Hildegard's theft of the Jewel, my wife's disappearance makes sense. It fits. I believe Krollum, who unbeknownst to me had become Hildegard, abducted Aelya to conceal his plans. He still needed thousands of cycles before he'd be ready to steal the Jewel, and if she could've reported his plan to me back then, three thousand cycles ago, we could've stopped him, and maybe save Krollum too. But when Aelya and I decided to conduct these evaluations in secret, we had no idea that Hildegard was actually taking steps to ensure his own plans remained hidden. In hindsight, I believe he allowed her to see only what he wanted her to, until his plans called for more drastic actions that he could no longer keep secret. Then he abducted her, killed her to keep his secrets. I couldn't save my wife because there was nobody left to save."

The crackling of the fire filled the silence, and Brohdan saw his sadness reflected on each of his friends' faces. He considered Belkidar's loss. Despite his loyalty to both the sorcerer and his happiness, he knew he didn't have the experience needed to truly understand his torment. "How could Hildegard hide so much?"

"I don't know," Belkidar answered softly. "More than anything, that puzzles me the most. I scoured Aelya's trail for centacycles afterward, never once finding anything that could be traced back to her disappearance. How can that be? I can't convince myself that he could remove all traces of her abduction. The very act of removing evidence only leaves more behind."

"Exactly," Batai agreed. "I've investigated many crimes, and we've always found evidence. So it must've been Hildegard's work. Somehow."

Brohdan considered the conversation. He lacked experience with both criminals and the process used to convict them. Throughout the long and sometimes difficult history of dragons, never had one committed a serious crime. Although similar to most intelligent species, they are very different in at least this regard – dragons are not drawn toward crime, because they are not driven by petty motives. This is true in every sense, whether it be self-advancement in status, wealth, ego, or even health. The most important thing a dragon can accomplish in his life is to better the pack, both his own and worldwide. So for a dragon to further his own status, he must first improve the status of his family and pack before he could advance individually. Even the arrogant actions of Gorduvian Golds can be traced back to this aspiration. And so Brohdan understood the concepts, but they were foreign to him – like having body hair. Or choosing to eat vegetables.

"What experience do you have, Batai?" Gunnar asked.

"The responsibility to build the case against an accused criminal falls to the Order of Knights, but when it deals with more substantial crimes, the Order of Paladins oversees the trial."

Gunnar nodded. "And you've never had trouble convicting anyone?"

"On occasion. It's rare, but it does happen. But a man's eyes are truly the window to his soul, regardless of the evidence – or lack thereof."

"Exactly," Belkidar agreed. "I didn't question Krollum because the Staff's security was my primary responsibility, it had to be, so I never had the chance to look him in the eyes. But the matter of his innocence is not in question – his theft of the Jewel proves his guilt."

"How do you know Aelya was killed?" Brohdan asked. "Maybe she was only taken captive."

"No, if Aelya had survived, I would've sensed her, especially considering the sorcery that's available to me. The fact that I couldn't leaves only one possibility."

The night's conversation occupied the whole of their thoughts, and long after midnight Belkidar finally went to bed. Brohdan, at last realizing how late it had become, felt his fatigue match his interest in Belkidar's past. As he lay drifting to sleep, he had vivid thoughts of a cruel sorcerer abducting a beautiful woman, and despite his pain, he knew he felt only a glimpse of what his friend was forced to endure every day of the past three thousand cycles. But it fortified his resolve. Although Hildegard had a distinct advantage in the size of his forces, he was hopelessly outmatched when it came to heart, determination, and an unconquerable soul.

The next morning they resumed their journey, the trees of the Glor Forest towering over them with each step. Thanks to Kiera's guidance, their progress remained swift, despite encountering a few dense patches in the woodland. By late morning on the second day, much of the forest lay behind them.

Just after midday, Kiera stopped for a meal. Gunnar searched for fresh water while Indira checked Brohdan's barz. She removed what had previously passed as Belkidar's clothing, surprised to discover it was nearly healed. "Incredible!"

"What's that?" Batai asked.

"Brohdan's wound! It is mended!"

"Naturally," Belkidar said. "As I've explained, this is a natural process. His barz was halfway healed before his blade even broke through."

Then he regarded Brohdan. With all that had happened during the previous mooncycles, he often lost track of his growth, despite his noticeably increased appetite. Wistful, he acknowledged that Brohdan was nearly a fully grown Broglia Black dragon, nearly ninety percent of his adult size. The undersized horns of his Dalluvian armor still lined the bridge of his nose, but it was much broader now. The ridge split into two rows, forming his brows as they traveled above his eyes, ending with two menacing horns at the upper rear of his skull. He'd grown several other horns too, each successively smaller as they continued down along the sides and top of his head. Similar armor grew along his neck, back and tail, but they too had grown in size.

Next to Brohdan, Gunnar seemed uncharacteristically small, barely reaching his shoulders. With his neck stretched to its full height, Belkidar estimated he'd be at least twice as tall as the giant. Now that his barz had matured, he could finally teach him the final lessons of his grombit. "Brohdan, you've really grown up quickly," he said, his voice filled with emotion.

Brohdan looked first at Belkidar and then down at his own body. It was true, he'd grown at an amazing rate. As he studied his chest, he

realized his scales had turned completely black. "How much more do
you think I'll grow?"

"Not much, thank goodness. I'd say you've got another few elads
in girth and several more in length, maybe another half mooncycle or
so."

"That is quite large," Indira said simply. "He must be the largest
creature in the world."

"Not quite. There are a few that are bigger, one in particular.
Now," he added, looking around their temporary camp, "we should
probably finish our meal and get back to the road. We've still got a
long way to go before we reach Brodor."

As had become the custom, Kiera took the lead and Batai brought
up the rear. Brohdan, still somewhat confined by the forest trees, often
scouted some distance ahead. Since the mercenaries' attack, though, he
frequently flew back and checked on his mates. Even Batai, who
sometimes trailed the others by several dozen elads, grew used an
enormous shadow enveloping him throughout the day. He'd look up
through the foliage and catch a glimpse of him, only elyes above the
treetops, and he couldn't help feel a warm sense of security knowing
they were allied with a Broglia Black dragon.

As the sun set and the darkness grew, Kiera led them a quarter
linak east of the trail. They stopped and made camp on the shores of a
loud creek.

"Indira, do you feel like honing your archery skills?" Belkidar
asked.

"I had not realized they were need of honing," she replied, smiling.

"Some of us learned from Batai's foolishness." Belkidar laughed
at Batai's grumbling behind him. "I just thought we could use some
fresh meat for tonight's meal. There are some bynowak beyond those
hills."

"Of course. However, I am curious – how did you know of their presence? You cannot see them, nor hear them."

"When you've taken the form of hundreds of different species thousands of times apiece, you retain many of their basic traits, even in your original form."

A confused expression was her only reply.

"I can smell them."

Indira inclined her brows. "I see."

"You don't seem convinced."

"I believe you, Ancient One. I just do not understand how one can smell anything further than three elyes from his nose when he reeks as badly as you do." She slid gracefully from her horse and pulled the huge bow from her back.

Kiera stifled a laugh. "I'm not sure which is more amazing – the thought of a sarcastic elf or you falling for her joke like a fish for a hooked worm."

Belkidar grunted, then slowly walked toward the stream. As he made his way through the thick trees, Brohdan saw him hold his hand out before the darkening horizon. A faint flash erupted from his upturned palm, and an instant later, a wedge of soap sat cradled in his hand. His mumbling continued.

Batai quickly cleared a large area of grass and leaves, then formed a large circle of rocks in the center. As Kiera made her final cooking preparations, Batai returned with a tall pile of firewood he'd collected from the area.

"Thanks Batai," she said. "Why don't you help Indira bring back our food?"

Batai wordlessly did as he was asked. Gunnar, carrying several water bags he'd just filled from the stream, passed the paladin on his way to the camp. "Where are you going?"

"To help Indira bring back our food."

"Give me a moment." He jogged the rest of the way to Kiera, the ground protesting each stride.

"Why don't you go and give…"

"...Indira some help. I'm already on my way."

"It's so nice when you have the men trained," she observed, filling a large pot with water.

Brohdan, not wanting to be part of Kiera's 'trained' flock, flew straight up through the foliage. He hovered a moment, pivoting to where he'd seen Indira depart, then disappeared beyond the treetops.

"Good choice!" Kiera shouted through a smile.

After a few drus, Brohdan saw where Indira prepared her hunt. She had almost finished climbing the back side of a steep hill, beyond which lay her prey. He carefully landed below the hilltop, concealing his presence. "I'll help carry back our food," he replied in his best 'whisper.' Unfortunately, because dragons have seldom required this ability, it sounded like throatier version of his normal voice.

"Thanks!" she replied softly, stopping an elye short of the summit. In Brohdan's short experience interacting with other species, he noted how noisily most of them advanced through life. Indira was the exception. Despite his heightened senses, he detected not a sound as she traveled through the tall grass and leaves. What made it even more astonishing was how naturally she went about it.

Before long, Batai and Gunnar caught up to him.

"Where's Indira?" Gunnar asked softly.

"Over the hill, stalking the bynowak."

"What do they look like?" Batai asked. "I'm not familiar with them."

"I'm not either," Brohdan replied. "I hope they're tasty, though."

"They are," Gunnar confirmed. "Probably the best meat you'll find."

That piqued his interest. "Continue," he 'whispered' eagerly.

"They're the largest members of the bovine family, a fully grown bull standing five elads at the shoulders. They generally resemble a cow, only on a much larger scale. Oh, and they're carnivorous."

"What?" Batai asked incredulously. "Does Indira know that?"

"I'm not sure. But I wouldn't worry about her. She can handle herself."

"Tell us more about the bynowak," Brohdan suggested.

Gunnar smiled. "They used to be more like cattle, but at some point in their evolution, they started hunting other animals. They eventually became quite good at it. Their once-bulky bodies became sleek, their height and length grew. Their mouths also grew longer and wider, and their teeth shifted from large molars to sharp daggers."

"Fascinating," Brohdan remarked. "How do you know so much about them?"

"Giants bred bynowak as work animals, in much the same way others keep horses."

"I imagine you would've had to watch them closely," Batai offered.

"No, they're loyal pack animals like dogs or wolves."

"I can't imagine giants would need much in the way of security."

Gunnar grunted softly. "You'd be surprised how many species felt threatened by us. It's ironic. We wanted only to live in peace, to be left alone, yet our presence posed such a threat that we were eventually hunted and exterminated. Bynowak protected us bravely during the early raids, but they were killed almost to extinction themselves, so we set the rest free. We were the true targets."

Batai shook his head. "I'm sorry."

"No need, my friend. You weren't even born when all of this happened."

"I know. But I can't help being disappointed with my kind."

"Humans aren't the only ones who regret parts of their history. Besides, I eventually realized it's not fair to judge an entire species based on the actions of a few."

Batai didn't appear convinced. "How can you forgive so much?"

Gunnar took a moment, considered his words. "I'm the last giant the world will ever know. If your actions were the final deeds of your entire species, how would you choose to live your life? Would you hunt down and kill every human you could? Even though only a few were responsible? That'd lead to a pretty short life, but worse yet, it'd justify their slaughtering." He shook his head. "No, I choose to live as my father and grandfather did. That's why I lived in the Midrogrus, so I wouldn't be forced to kill those that wanted me dead."

"Weren't you lonely?"

"Of course, but it was the only option I had. Before long, though, Belkidar found me." He stared out over the forest from his elevated vantage on the hillside. The sky was nearly black now, and a growing number of stars shone brightly. "That was a turning point in my life."

Brohdan's whispering was getting better. "Well, I admire you, Gunnar."

"So do I," Batai agreed. "I wish I knew more of your kind."

Gunnar's smile was the most genuine the paladin had ever seen. "That's why it was worth it."

"I'd better check on Indira," Brohdan said. "She's been gone for a bit."

"I really think she's fine," Gunnar repeated.

"I'm sure you're right, but I made a promise to her father that I don't intend to break." The black dragon rose effortlessly into the blackness, the soft ruffle of his beating wings the only indication that he was still nearby. Soon, even that vanished.

He climbed higher into the starlit sky, making certain he wouldn't alert Indira's prey. When he was only a pinprick against the stars, he leveled off and searched for his friend. He found her much sooner – and much more easily – than he'd expected. She was still making her way toward the bynowak, but based on their behavior, they would soon hunt. If Indira was to succeed, she had better take action soon.

At that instant she rose to a knee, pulled one of her long arrows from its quiver. This surprised him, because her prey still lay several hundred elads distant. She drew her bow, aimed, released the arrow, repeating the process five more times in the span of a dru. The bow still humming, Brohdan turned toward the bynowak and found three down, the others running frantically in all directions.

Indira was already walking to her quarry as Brohdan flew back to Gunnar and Batai. He approached, then spread his wings to slow his descent. He hovered effortlessly, rotating slightly to better face them. "She's done! Let's go!"

Batai and Gunnar stood awestruck as Brohdan's enormous form hung mere elads above them. Their clothing and hair were caught in his downdraft, and loose grass, leaves, and dirt scattered from where they stood. They didn't have time to enjoy it, though, as he excitedly left for his meal. He leaned over, descended quickly down the hillside toward camp, only a few elyes above the tall grass and rocks. His speed grew rapidly, then he arched is back, beat his wings *forward*, rotated into a backward summersault. When he was upside down, he flapped one wing up, the other down, rolled right-side up, then flew in the opposite direction, toward Indira.

Batai and Gunnar simultaneously looked from Brohdan's acrobatic display into each other's faces, each seeing the other's jaw hanging open. Wordlessly, they closed them, turned, and walked toward the summit, then to Indira.

Brohdan, of course, was already there when they arrived. Three large bynowak carcasses lay close to one another, each with an arrow embedded deep in its chest and a second just behind an ear.

"Very impressive, Indira," Gunnar remarked. "But how did you kill them so close together?"

"They were near the limit of my bow's range, so I shot each in the chest to keep them from fleeing."

"So why do they have another arrow in their heads, then?"

Indira looked perplexed, the answer obvious. "They are honorable creatures, so I wanted them to die quickly, painlessly."

Batai's eyebrows rose. "So you shot all three of them, and then shot all three of them again? Before the first even hit the ground?"

"Yes." Confusion still lingered in her expression. "Is that not what you would have done?"

"Indira," Gunnar answered, "I've never been that accurate with boulders." He smiled, then bent toward the nearest bynowak. "I'll take this one."

"Wait. I'll give you a hand," Batai offered.

Gunnar approached the animal from its belly, then squatted low, weaving on arm between its front legs and under its neck, the other between its hind legs and under its flank. Then he clamped a handful of its course hide in each fist, heaved the dead animal over his head to rest across his broad shoulders. Then he wrapped his arms around the outsides of the bynowak's front and hind legs before gazing down at his three friends. "Thanks Batai, but I can manage."

"I believe you. I can't believe what I just *saw*, but I believe you." He then considered the other two carcasses, deciding some assistance was required. He placed his thumb and forefinger to his lips and whistled a brief, shrill note. Within drus, Einar charged down the hill, stopping just short of Batai to look playfully into his eyes. "Later," he told him, stroking his neck, "right now we've got some work to do." He went to Einar's right side and retrieved a coil of rope from one of his many saddlebags. He made quick work of fastening one end around the bynowak and the other to Einar's saddle horn.

Brohdan bent over and took the third animal between his razor-sharp teeth, careful not to inadvertently begin his meal. "I hope you appreciate this remarkable display of willpower," he muttered between stationary jaws.

Indira, Gunnar, and Batai looked at him, then fell into hysterics, first because of his slurred speech, then from the saliva pouring from his jaws. Brohdan held out as long as he could but soon joined them. Still laughing, they were surprised when they arrived back at their campsite.

"What's so funny?" Belkidar asked, drying his thin hair.

His tone briefly halted their laughter, but after seeing the old man still wet from bathing, it returned even more intensely than before.

"I'm getting too old for this," Belkidar said, warming himself by the fire.

Belkidar's mood lightened when Kiera began cooking the meat. However, it'd take much too long to cook naturally, so he accelerated the process.

"If you wished, could you not cook the meat in a dru?" Indira asked.

"Yes, but the flavor suffers when you cook it too fast. It'll taste much better if it sits over the fire for a couple links."

"Brohdan, do you want me to cook yours too?" Kiera asked. "It wouldn't be any trouble."

"Thanks Kiera, but I don't like it burned."

"I don't *burn* it, I cook it."

"I like mine natural."

"Natural? You mean raw."

"It tastes better that way."

She screwed her nose up at the thought. "If you say so."

A mischievous grin crossed his face. "You mean this isn't appetizing?" he asked before sliding his dagger-like teeth into the bynowak. He tore off a huge slab of muscle, bloody sinew stretched tight. Still smiling, he brought his jaws together, severed it from the carcass, then swallowed it whole.

"Brohdan, I really don't understand how your kind ever evolved into an intelligent species."

They sat around the large fire, deep orange and crimson reflecting from the nearby trees. Content, Brohdan regarded each of his friends. Before he met them, they had their own lives, each with their own concerns. But now they shared the same priority. They were all sacrificing so much – perhaps their very lives – to ensure this Quest was successful. That alone distinguished them from most.

Brohdan suddenly realized a universal truth – those who sacrifice their lives for the good of others comprise a unique pack. At any given moment throughout history, a select few are willing to sacrifice

everything to preserve freedom. How many times had other creatures
sat around a similar fire, under these same stars, on the eve of battle?
He'd heard stories of heroes, songs sung in their honor. But he'd also
heard other stories, stories where heroes were shunned, not because
their sacrifices were less, but because their results were. Apparently,
more importance was placed on victory rather than the sacrifices
needed to ever achieve any hope of such an outcome.

Brohdan wondered how their Quest would be viewed, whether
their sacrifices would be recognized, regardless of the outcome. What
he and his friends would soon attempt reached far beyond the sacrifices
most others were willing to make. Yet, they weren't here for glory,
fame, or even wealth. For some reason, it mattered to him whether
their efforts would be appreciated in the end. Regardless of the
outcome, he wanted the sacrifices of these five friends to at least be
acknowledged by those they endeavored to save.

"Batai, you've dedicated your life to protect others. To protect
freedom. Have you ever been disappointed with how society reacted to
you? To your actions?"

"That's a tough one." He thought for a long moment. "I suppose,
but rarely. Why do you ask?"

"I'm not sure. I know it's not important, for some reason I want
society to appreciate the sacrifices we're making."

"Respect," he clarified softly. "Regardless of whether society
sympathizes, understands, or even agrees with what we're trying to
accomplish, they should at least respect what we're willing to sacrifice,
especially since they're made selflessly, for the benefit of others."

"Well said," Belkidar agreed.

The group watched in silence as Kiera tended the food. After
returning to her seat, Brohdan noticed the group shifted its attention
from her cooking to the fire, its tendrils sporadically licking the meat.
It was interesting, regardless of the creature – human, elf, giant, dragon,
male, female, it didn't matter – all seemed happier when they could
gaze into its flames.

"Brohdan, what was your childhood like?" Gunnar asked after several drus of silence.

"Not too different from most, I'd imagine. I grew up in Lukvia, a small community in southern Seamus. I lived with my parents in a large cave just north of the Sichundar Mountains."

"Did you have many friends?" Kiera asked.

"Yes, I suppose," he answered, remembering how Methren, Albrogu, and Limbrin had treated him before his grombit, and how they'd changed after learning he was the next Broglia. But after spending time with Belkidar, Kiera, Batai, Indira, and Gunnar, he hesitated to use the same word to describe them. "I grew up with three other dragons my age: Limbrin, Methren, and Albrogu. Albrogu and Methren are Klonduvian Reds, and Limbrin's a Gorduvian Gold. I was a Dalluvian Green."

"Whoa," Gunnar said, "how many different kinds of dragons are there?"

Brohdan smiled. "Four. Klonduvian Reds and Dalluvian Greens are the most common. Gorduvian Golds, considered by a few – usually the Golds – to be in a higher class than the Reds and Greens, are a little rarer."

"Are there many differences?" Kiera asked.

"A few. Color is the only real difference between Klonduvians and Dalluvians, but Gorduvians spit acid where the others breathe fire."

"How are Broglias different?" Gunnar asked. Belkidar smiled, and with prideful eyes watched as Brohdan described himself, his discomfort palpable.

He described the differences. "And Broglias are only born once every thousand cycles or so," he concluded.

Gunnar's brows raised. "I had no idea."

"Excuse me for interrupting, but the food's ready." Everyone shot to their feet and joined Kiera by the fire. They soon returned to their seats, most with a large steak or several ribs – or in Belkidar's case, both.

"How did you end up here?" Batai asked, resuming the conversation.

"Well, when my grombit began, things changed a lot."

"What exactly is a grombit?" Gunnar asked.

"It's when a dragon matures into adulthood, when we learn how to fly and breathe fire. Most complete their grombits in their own community, spending several links each day learning these new skills from their parents. But some dragons are sent to a grombit camp. I was one of them. Before I left, and even during the first few mooncycles I was there, I'd thought these camps were for dragons who needed more help than their parents could provide."

Indira noted the pain in his voice, in his expression, but her heart broke for what was left unsaid.

"Why were you sent there?" Gunnar asked.

"At the time, I assumed it was because of how clumsy I was, and I didn't blame them for that. I *was* clumsy, awkward. I was the first dragon in the history of the Lukvian pack to start my grombit late, and my childhood friends believed it was their duty to motivate me."

"What do you mean?" Indira asked, her anger and concern evident in her voice.

"Limbrin – the Gorduvian Gold – thought I needed more encouragement to start my grombit. In reality, he felt humiliated because I took the longest of all Lukvian dragons to start it. So he took his embarrassment and frustration out on me. I fought him of course, but being nearly a cycle older than me, he was already well into his grombit. I was only two-thirds his size, and he could fly and breathe acid." Brohdan shook his head. "I was no match."

"That must have been a horrible time for you."

"The worst of my life, not just because of Limbrin, because I hated being a disgrace to my pack. But most of all I hated the helplessness I felt by not being able to start my grombit when I thought I was ready for it."

"What do you mean?" Batai asked. "You weren't ready?"

"Yes, and no," he answered, glancing at Belkidar. "Remember, that was before I realized I was the next Broglia Black dragon, and I had no idea how different Broglia grombits were. They don't automatically begin like the others do, they start only when the dragon is prepared to *complete* it. So in hindsight, that period in my life – the pain and humiliation, the frustration – taught me what was important, and what wasn't. I'm a better Broglia because of it."

"I commend you, Brohdan," Indira remarked. "I am not sure I would have the same attitude."

Brohdan grunted. "Thanks, but it took me a while to gain that perspective. After it was determined I was the next Broglia, I spent nearly a cycle in the Lukvian grombit camp in the Sichundar Mountains, then two more in Sul Brul, one of the largest dragon communities."

"What did you learn there?" Gunnar asked between bites.

"To fly and to breathe fire, of course. I also learned how to cast a few spells."

At this point, Belkidar had heard enough. "I'm afraid Brohdan's being modest. His grombit represented a crucial time in his life, and it required a work ethic and dedication few creatures ever have to consider. And Brohdan showed those traits and more before he was even an adult. He changed from what he'd always known into a Broglia Black, the leader of all dragons, and the only one of his kind."

"His grombit was incredibly difficult. His body began a metamorphosis, growing to three times the size of a normal dragon and changing from emerald green to what you see here. He also had to learn sorcery and eventually how to use his barz. On top of that, he has a chance to develop skills that only a few Broglias ever have. Finally, and certainly most importantly, he started to realize the immense impact he'd have on his species, and indeed the entire world. Brohdan began to understand what he was capable of – and what would therefore be expected of him."

"That must've been hard for you," Gunnar noted, "especially since there was no one like you to help you through it."

Brohdan realized Gunnar was speaking from personal experience. "In an instant, I went from being a member of my pack to an icon, a role model, even though I looked and felt like the same Dalluvian I'd always been. Everybody treated me differently, even my parents."

"It was difficult for everybody," Belkidar agreed, "but for Brohdan most of all. His parents really coped well. In fact, I think they handled it better than any Broglia parents I've ever met."

That made Brohdan proud. "In my childhood, I had the perfect relationship with them. It's still strong, but I don't think they like the attention they get. And I don't blame them."

"I empathize with you," Indira offered. "I was in a similar period in my life when we discovered I was Elvorn. Despite that, my relationship with my family changed little. Perhaps that is because Elvorns are much more common than Broglias, and so my parents were not affected as much as yours. I could only imagine the heartache if that relationship changed, especially if it changed because of me."

"But it has changed," Belkidar corrected. "Indira, your relationship with your parents – and every other member of your pack – has been altered at every turn in your life." He turned his attention back to Brohdan.

"It would've been impossible for your relationship with your parents to stay the same, even if you stayed a Dalluvian Green. Relationships are a reflection of us, of who we are, so they change as we do."

Brohdan thought about that. "But if I'd remained a Dalluvian, my parents wouldn't view me any differently."

"Not so. You still would've entered and completed your grombit, so you would've become an adult, just as you have. They'd treat you differently today, even if you were a Dalluvian Green, not because you're a Broglia, but because you're an adult."

That realization shocked him. Methren, Albrogu, and Limbrin treated him differently because he was suddenly a Broglia instead of a Dalluvian, so he hastily assumed the same was true of his parents. Looking back, it was obvious they still respected him just as they always had. "Thank you, Belkidar. You've given me a lot to think about."

"My pleasure, Brohdan. I respect your parents a great deal."

"I was never fortunate enough to really know my parents," Gunnar said, "but if they were like yours, I'd be honored."

"You're right, of course," he agreed. "I guess I was too caught up in the pettiness of my friends."

By then, all had finished eating. "That was one of the finest meals I've ever eaten," Batai said.

"Why thank you, kind sir."

"I think she'll end up spoiling us," Belkidar agreed, patting his stomach.

They soon had their camp settled and their beds prepared. Brohdan licked the bones that remained from the feast as the others climbed into their sleeping blankets. He rested his chin on the cool ground, considered each of his friends as they drifted to sleep, amazed with how much his life had changed over the past three cycles.

Chapter 12
Szurgord

*We must humble ourselves before [others] so we may
learn from what others have lived. It is only when we
have added their expertise to our own that we can
truly excel towards our most ambitious goals and
reach our fullest potential.*

A.J. Darkholme, <u>Rise of the Morningstar</u>

When the morning sunlight managed its way through the trees of
the Glor Forest, it found each member of the group soundly asleep.
Eventually, Belkidar woke. After considering the angle of the shafts of
light, motes hovering in the distance, he shot into a sitting position.
"Everybody up! We should've been on the road links ago!"

Judging by his companions' reactions, his words must've moved
slowly though the brisk morning air. After a slightly more aggressive
reminder of the time, they slowly got out of their beds, all except
Brohdan. When the others had finished packing the pots, pans, dishes,
sleeping blankets, and the remaining items of their camp, Brohdan
wearily got to his feet.

Kiera led them back to the road, and the remaining links of
morning passed quickly. By afternoon, Kiera noticed the thinning
trees. "I think we should rest here, while we still have the forest to
shelter us."

"Very good," Belkidar agreed. "Besides, I think we could all use a
quick meal." Looking at Brohdan and Gunnar, he immediately realized
his mistake. "Well, *most* of us." Still full from the previous night's
feast, ham and cheese between slices of rye bread was more than
enough to tide them over until evening.

"What lies to the south?" Indira asked.

"Not much," Belkidar said through a mouthful of sandwich. "The Wruloric Wastelands. Linops upon linops of dry, flat land – mixed with a few rocks and twigs to break up the monotony."

She smiled, then became concerned. "I hope we have enough water for the horses."

"That isn't the only worry," he added. "Brohdan, as soon as we're clear of the forest, please fly ahead and search for anything that moves. I'm not too concerned about a few nomads here and there, but if you spot anything more significant, please let me know. With his mercenaries dead, Hildegard will deduce enough from their missing reports. He'll lack specifics, but he'll know where we've passed, and maybe where we're headed."

Before long, Kiera mounted her horse and led them out of the forest. Gunnar followed some distance behind, his presence forcing any enemy to think twice before attacking. Indira rode next, her position in the center of the column offering the best chance to use her bow unopposed. Belkidar followed, his watchful eyes never far from his friends. Batai rode last, his battle experience and mobility an enormous advantage as rear guard.

Brohdan scouted ahead, then glided west before eventually falling to the rear, noting the order and spacing of each member. *"I can see why you chose them."*

"Very perceptive. We each fill a need. Kiera's an expert scout and tracker. She's also very skilled in close combat and in talking her way through difficult situations, but her optimism is infectious, and that may prove most important. Gunnar's purpose is rather apparent, but I think you'll discover the perseverance and determination fortified during the cycles he spent alone in the Midrogrus even more valuable. Indira allows us to strike silently and from great distances, but her unique insight and perspective are invaluable. Batai's importance in battle is also obvious, but his commitment to righteousness will continuously set the standard for us. That, I fear, will be critical."

This confused Brohdan. *"Why? We're already united to defeat Hildegard's evil."*

"True, but this Quest will require us to make difficult decisions. What's at stake could justify any atrocity if we're desperate enough, but with him, we'll always choose the right path."

"I understand."

Belkidar paused a moment. *"Do you know why I needed you so badly?"*

Brohdan didn't take long to answer. *"Of course. I'm the only one who can fly and breathe fire."*

"Well, that's certainly true, but they're not your greatest strength." He smiled. *"Brohdan, your most important quality lies in your refreshing view of the world. You grew up among dragons, and that makes you unique – within this group, at least."*

"We are all of us jaded – save you. I've seen enough of humanity to know what lies in most people's hearts, and Batai battled countless enemies where he witnessed first-hand those deeds. Kiera's motives may be designed to help people, but her exploits primarily surround her with the unscrupulous. Indira's entire civilization chose isolation to escape the same corruption that exterminated Gunnar's entire race. Our suspicion and cynicism cannot be avoided, and perhaps that's a necessary consequence of our lives. But if we defeat Hildegard, your innocence – more than even your prowess in battle – will be the bedrock of that success."

"But how can innocence be valuable in war?"

He smiled again. *"If you knew the answer to that, my friend, much of your innocence would be lost."*

Brohdan continued scouting, distracted by his conversation with Belkidar. He couldn't understand how innocence could serve their Quest. He trusted Belkidar, but he hoped he wouldn't fail his friends when they needed him most.

Green gradually shifted to brown. Their noses, accustomed to the musty smell of the forest, were invaded by the hot winds of the wastelands. The grass disappeared, replaced by dry shrubs. With each of the horses' steps, soft fertile soil transformed into hard barren dirt.

As sunset loomed in the western sky, Brohdan discovered not a single tree ahead. He turned back, already missing the shade and scenery of the forest. As he faced south again, he realized their journey thus far had been easy. Soon, the intense heat of the coming days would be rivaled only by the vulnerability of this flat terrain.

Brohdan looked to his companions, realized the difficulty of their Quest changed nothing – their perseverance would ultimately define their success. With renewed determination, he spread his gigantic wings and took flight. The others turned to the west, watched him gracefully lift off the ground, the scarlet sun behind him. He remained low, accelerating beneath the strength of his wings. Then he arched his back, climbed vertically into the darkening heavens. The silhouette of a Broglia Black dragon coasting upward, his wings spread wide against the violet sky, was a sight none would soon forget.

Brohdan continued flying well into the night. His keen eyesight, coupled with the flatness of the terrain, allowed him to search from one distant horizon to the other. Confused, his night vision had seemingly improved over the course of the past mooncycle. Long after the others had fallen asleep, Brohdan finally landed and quietly made his way toward them. He initially recalled Belkidar's insinuations, how his innocence would benefit their Quest. But then he let his mind drift and, not surprisingly, soon found his attention resting on Mikka. With a heavy heart, he slowly fell into a deep slumber.

Morning came quickly for the entire group, but more swiftly still for the tired dragon. Kiera prepared a meal of salted pork and bread. Brohdan woke just as Batai finished eating.

"Good morning, my friend."

"Morning," Brohdan replied, stretching. "It seems I went to sleep only drus ago."

Batai smiled. "I can understand why. Spending half the night in the air can have that effect."

He felt embarrassed, having thought his flying had gone unnoticed.

"It's nothing to be ashamed of. But if I were you, I'd save those long nights for when we're on Katja."

"I'd like to, but I'm more comfortable when I can watch over us."

Batai nodded. "You're right. From now on, we'll split the night watch. If four of us stand guard each night in two-link shifts, we'd have an eight-link sleep period every night. We'd also have two nights off for every four nights we stand watch."

"That sounds perfect. When should we start?"

"I'm not familiar enough with these lands. Let's talk with Kiera and Belkidar later today."

The group swiftly disassembled the camp and rode southeast. Although the terrain wasn't too difficult to negotiate, Belkidar held the pace to conserve the horses' energy. By midmorning the temperature exceeded anything they'd experienced thus far.

"How hot does it get?" Gunnar asked over his shoulder, wiping the sweat from his forehead.

"Considerably hotter, I'm afraid. In fact, the Wruloric has the highest temperatures of any continent."

"Wonderful. At least it's autumn."

They continued southeast for the rest of the morning. Brohdan remained generally unaffected by the various types of terrain he'd witnessed since his departure from Lukvia. This wasteland, though, evoked a certain weariness in him. With all of this open land and so little life, he decided he preferred a greener place to live. Indira apparently agreed.

"I cannot recall hearing of any land like this. Does anything live here?"

"Only insects," Kiera answered.

"One species used to thrive here," Belkidar began. "Keviloks."

"I've never heard of them," Kiera said, wiping sweat from her face.

"I'm not surprised. They've not been heard from in over two hundred cycles."

"What killed them off?" Indira asked.

"I'm not so sure they were. In fact, I believe they're still alive and prospering, although most people assume they're extinct. Personally, I don't think they've been seen in the last two hundred cycles because few have been foolish enough to cross the Wruloric. Those that did have either gotten very lucky or very dead, neither of which provides a very good kevilok siting."

"Then why did you choose this path?" Indira asked.

"Because we're in a hurry. To go around the Wruloric would add many days to our journey. We can't afford that. Besides, I've amassed perhaps the most elite fighting element in the world. Surely you can manage the prospect of a few dozen keviloks that have been hibernating for two centacycles."

Batai looked to Indira and sighed. "Remind me to have a talk with that man."

"Makes sense," Gunnar said with a grunt. "We haven't accomplished anything yet."

"Typical," Kiera said as she turned her attention back to Belkidar. "Just what exactly do these keviloks look like?"

"They remind me of horned toads, but they have some significant differences. They're flat lizards with six legs, and rows of sharp horns line their backs. Their head also has a pair of horns, only those are flat, not cone-shaped like the others. They extend forward from the sides of their head, turn toward each other, then point forward again when they're about an elye apart. They use them for digging and fighting."

"Digging?" Batai interrupted.

"Yes. The soil is loose and sandy here, letting them burrow an elye or two below the ground. Like crocodiles, they stalk their victims by staying below the surface."

"What other exciting events do we have the pleasure of anticipating as we cross these exotic lands?" Kiera asked.

"Their jaws are very powerful," Belkidar continued, unperturbed. "They've been known to tear through the strongest armor as though it were beggars' rags. Really, keviloks are very ingenious little creatures," Belkidar added.

"Little? Just how *little* are they?" Kiera asked.

"I never got to that, did I?" the old man said, nudging his horse into a trot.

"No, you didn't," Kiera added, prodding her horse to keep pace. The others followed suit and trailed closely behind.

"They're not very big. Not really, when you compare them to some other creatures found in this world."

"How large are they?" Kiera demanded.

"They're a little bigger than a wolf. A large wolf."

"Wonderful."

"Just think of it as practice," Gunnar said with a smile as he walked next to her horse. "You do enjoy practicing, don't you?"

"I do," she said, matching his smile. "I'd offer you another chance, but I doubt you could fully recover from two such embarrassments."

"Ha!" Gunnar roared before reaching down and giving her back a pat. Although it was intended to be light, Kiera fought to remain in her saddle.

"How long to reach the other side of the Wruloric?" Indira asked.

"It'll take us two or three days to reach Fendurgin. If we travel faster than that, we run the risk of over-stressing the horses. If we take much longer, we'll run out of water."

"All right." Kiera maneuvered her horse toward the front of the group, the others falling into their customary positions. Brohdan took to the air and surveyed ahead. Despite the fact that keviloks were generally thought to be extinct, he nonetheless remained nearby. If anything did attack them, he realized his reaction time would be reduced considerably if the enemy attacked from below.

The pack traveled cautiously during the first few links, wary of a kevilok encounter, but their concern gradually waned. By early afternoon, they had made good progress and were ready for a quick meal. Kiera managed to find a dead tree and led the others to its meager shade. "This will have to do."

"It is better than nothing," Indira assured her. "It can at least cool the horses."

Unfortunately, Brohdan and Gunnar had no hope of enjoying the shade. In fact, once all of the horses were huddled beneath the branches, barely enough shelter remained for their four companions.

"I hope you're all comfortable under there," Gunnar said with a scowl.

"Oh my, yes," Kiera answered, flashing a sly smile. "Tell me kind sir, has the intensity of the sun diminished considerably?"

Brohdan, expecting the worst, turned his head and grimaced. To his surprise, the giant's grunt was accompanied with a smirk.

After Batai finished his meal, he turned to Belkidar. "Brohdan and I were talking this morning. We thought it'd be a good idea to post a night watch."

"What did you have in mind?"

He explained the plan, and all volunteered for the first watch. After a few drus, a rough scheduled had been arranged. "Fires will betray our position during the night, so unless we need one for warmth, I suggest we extinguish it before the first watch."

Belkidar nodded his agreement.

"I've been meaning to ask you something," Brohdan began, turning to the sorcerer. "My eyesight these past few nights seems to be different, clearer. Is that the result of my grombit?"

"It is," Belkidar explained, excited. "But it doesn't develop in all Broglias. You now have two types of vision. The first is the same as what we all have, the same as you've had since birth. Your eyes gather light and then transfer that information to your brain. The second type is much different. Sensors just above your ears gather heat from your surroundings. Your brain then overlays that information with the visual information from your eyes into one picture, which you interpret as your vision."

Confused expressions returned Belkidar's gaze.

"Everything you see emits heat, including that rock sitting in the sunlight, the trees of the Glor Forest, and our own bodies in the shade of this tree. But while the heat inside that rock fades after the sun sets, our body heat will not. When Brohdan looks at us during the day, he sees a combination of the sunlight that's reflected off of us and the heat that's generated by our bodies. Because the light's reflection creates a better image, Brohdan's brain places more emphasis on that. But after sunset, his brain realizes the image generated from the surrounding heat is more effective, so while the rest of us rely solely on reduced light, Brohdan unconsciously transfers the emphasis of his vision to heat."

"You mean Brohdan sees two of everything?" Batai asked. "One of light and one of heat?"

"No, not exactly. He sees one of everything like we do, only that single image is formed from two separate sources."

"Incredible."

"But wouldn't vision based on our body heat be less effective?" Kiera asked.

"That depends on our surroundings. If he looked at us now, then his heat-based vision would be horrible, because our body heat would be lost in the heat of the Wruloric. But imagine if we were in Ætheldell. At night."

Gunnar nodded. "We'd stand out like a beacon."

"Exactly."

Brohdan recalled his flight over the Sichundars when he'd searched for Dre's cave. From that experience, he discovered Broglias possessed keener vision than Dalluvians, but now he realized this new vision went much deeper than that. "Did you know about this?"

Belkidar nodded. "I had a hunch."

"Really? How?"

"I watched your heat sensors grow over the past mooncycle."

"Brohdan," Gunnar said, "you're truly the most amazing creature I've ever met."

Brohdan was speechless, but his expression revealed more than any words could. He was deeply thankful for such wonderful friends. He thought back on the first few mooncycles after arriving at grombit camp, and he couldn't help but feel grateful for the opportunities that now lay before him. The helplessness and frustration that accompanied each of his instructors' disappointed sighs and Limbrin's painful encouragements felt like they happened a lifetime ago. He was amazed with how far he'd come. He knew this journey would be dangerous, but he'd never before experienced friendships like these. For the first time in his life, he was part of something that was greater than his own existence, and he was honored to share those responsibilities with such admirable creatures. His pack.

"Thank you."

They rationed their supplies while crossing the Wruloric Wastelands, so it didn't take long to finish their meals. When Indira decided the horses were rested, Kiera again led them southeast.

They stopped several more times, but despite the stifling heat, the animals coped well. By evening, they were nearly halfway across. Kiera managed to find shelter for the night, making camp at the base of a large hill. Far from ideal, it was the best they could hope for. "I'm afraid dinner won't be much better," she sighed.

The group prepared early for bed, exhaustion prevailing over hunger. With a couple beats of his enormous wings, Brohdan perched himself at the hill's summit, overlooking the camp, scouring the wastelands for linops in every direction.

His time standing watch passed quickly. He thought first of their Quest and wondered how long it would take to finally stand before Hildegard. He knew several battles stood between this moment and that final conflict, and he wondered how they would fare in the challenges in between. He knew sorcery would have no effect on him, but the same couldn't be said for his friends.

That jolted him. Would any of them die? Or worse, how many? Such a loss would be unbearable. He'd already said goodbye to his parents. Leaving Mikka for an uncertain future was perhaps the most difficult thing he'd ever done. But neither could match the devastation of losing one of these friends.

Brohdan silently vowed that he wouldn't let anything happen to them. The solemn oath he made to Juron to protect his daughter now enveloped the entire group. Although defeating Hildegard and securing the fate of the Artifacts remained the ultimate goal, Brohdan pledged that this Quest's second goal was to protect his pack.

Brohdan lifted his head, using his long neck and exceptional vision to scour the surrounding area, detecting not a single creature for linaks in every direction. But in the next instant, he heard something moving *behind* him. He immediately turned, looked down the hill, saw a large form moving among his friends. Within drus, he got to his feet and opened his enormous jaws, flames licking the sides of his mouth. But after a moment, he realized it was just Gunnar getting to his feet. Apparently, it was time for the second watch. Somewhat embarrassingly, he closed his mouth and settled back onto the ground. Not long afterward, Gunnar greeted him on the summit, his huge sword in hand.

"Thank you," he told the dragon.

"For what?"

"For not burning me to a crisp."

Brohdan winced. "You saw that?"

"I did," he said, stroking his beard. "I also feel protective of them, as though it's my responsibility to keep them safe, but then I realize Belkidar recruited each of us for a reason. Trust me, if I'd been an enemy, I would've had four of Kiera's daggers and a quiver of Indira's arrows in me long before I knew what happened."

Brohdan nodded, knew he was right.

"How'd your watch go?"

"Fine, didn't see a thing out there."

"What did you do to pass the time?" Gunnar asked, taking a seat next to him.

"I was just thinking."

"About what?"

"Our Quest. How long it'll take before we defeat Hildegard."

Gunnar grunted a laugh. "I like your attitude. Most in our position would wonder how long it'll take to die."

Brohdan smiled. "Don't get me wrong, I know it'll be dangerous, but like you said, each of us is here for a reason."

Gunnar nodded. "What else kept you busy?"

"I thought of my parents, of course. And Mikka."

"Mikka?" Gunnar asked, momentarily shifting his gaze from the distant wastelands to Brohdan's dark eyes.

"A friend. I met her while training in Sul Brul. I only knew her for two cycles, but we grew close. It's hard to explain."

"She seems special to you."

"She is. When this is all over, I think we'll be happy together."

"Good, Brohdan, I'm happy for you. Being alone is no way to live."

"I'm sorry. I didn't mean to flaunt my past, my friendships."

"Stop that! Never pity me!" Gunnar said, louder than he'd intended. "It's not your fault I'm alone, so don't take responsibility for it."

"You're right. I didn't mean to offend you."

Gunnar nodded, understood.

"How did you cope?" Brohdan asked.

"Not very well at first. Not until Belkidar found me. I was only a child during the final battles between Giants and Men. My mother took me south and hid me in the mountains."

Brohdan noticed Gunnar's voice suddenly seemed far away.

"Like dragons, giants live longer than most. I was nearly fifteen cycles old, but I'd never traveled beyond my parent's supervision. By then, we knew we were doomed, so when the final battles began, my mother rushed me to the Midrogrus, left me inside a deserted mineshaft." Gunnar paused, gathered his emotions. Brohdan realized no amount of time would ever accomplish that.

"I'll never forget her last words to me." He paused, his memories replaying her words, her voice clear in his mind. *'Remain here, my Gunnar. I must go and fight alongside your father. If I can, I'll return for you. Farewell, my son. Remember always that I love you.'*

"She knew she'd never come back. We were overwhelmed, hordes trying to kill us, and by that time most of my kin were already gone. I don't know how I knew, but I realized I would never see my family again. I distinctly remember her running down the mountainside, and I watched from inside my damp home as she rushed to die alongside my father."

"She sounds like an extraordinary mother."

"She was. I can only imagine how difficult that choice must've been, to stay with her only son or fight alongside her mate. I remember my parents being very much in love, though. I have to admit, if ever I was lucky enough to find a relationship like theirs, I would've made the same decision."

Brohdan gave him a moment. "How did you manage to survive alone in those mountains?"

"It was hard. I didn't eat for days, but I did find a stream a half linak away, so luckily fresh water was always available. And I was still in shock. In the course of a few links, I'd lost everyone I'd ever known. I went from being a son, grandson, nephew, and friend to being completely alone. I think regaining the will to live was the hardest thing I've ever done. Whenever I've faced a difficult situation since then, I always compare it to those first few days I was alone in the Midrogrus. After that, nothing seems difficult."

"What eventually gave you that will to live?"

"The memory of my parents," Gunnar said simply. "I finally decided I wouldn't waste my parents' sacrifices on self-pity. So I devoted myself to honor their memories. Ever since then, I've tried to make them proud of me."

"You make it sound easy."

"Thanks, but like most things, it just came down to a choice. I chose to live."

"But you said you were a child. How did you learn to hunt?"

He grunted a laugh. "By making a lot of mistakes."

Brohdan smiled. "I happen to know hunting isn't that simple."

"When you're hungry enough, it becomes very simple. Remember, I hadn't eaten for days. When I finally decided to move forward with my life, my hunger became very...motivating."

"What did you hunt?"

"Mountain trolls," Gunnar answered, disgusted.

"I've heard they're pretty big."

"They're definitely not small. They're about six elads, twice as tall as I was."

"But you were a child. How did you ever manage to kill one?"

"In those days, mountain trolls were common in the Midrogrus. And since they're solitary creatures, I usually only had to fight one at a time. So I followed one to its cave. Once inside, it heard my footsteps. They're not the smartest creatures, and they're slow. We fought for a while, struggled against each other." He shrugged. "I eventually broke its neck."

"I'm amazed you attacked such a large creature – especially when you were only a child!"

"I was so hungry, Brohdan, and they were the only option. And I knew I was getting weaker with each day."

Brohdan noticed his sword. "Did you make that yourself?"

"Sure did, several decacycles ago, using an old forge I discovered in the mines. Troll hunting got a lot easier after that."

Brohdan laughed. "I can imagine."

"Trolls eventually fled the mountains, so that forced me to start exploring the areas outside the Midrogrus, mainly east, toward the ocean. Cycles later, I met Belkidar. He learned of a mountain troll sighting in the Midrogrus, but knowing they'd all fled by that point, he went to investigate. One morning as I left my cave, I saw this frail old human staring up at me from the bottom of the valley. Honestly, I never wanted to hurt him, but I was in no mood to be hunted and killed by some fanatic. So, I yelled for him to leave. When he refused, explained he was there only to talk, I tossed a couple boulders at him."

"You can understand my surprise when they flew off course, each one missing him by elads. And when one finally flew true, he vanished, only to reappear somewhere else. His laughter grew with my frustration. I was nearly out of boulders when he finally talked to me again."

"I reluctantly watched as he slowly made his way up to my cave. 'Nice decorations,' he said nodding toward a shattered boulder." Gunnar laughed. "He did have a unique sense of humor, I'll give him that."

"He only shared a little of his past that day, focusing more on how much he admired me. He even apologized for not realizing I was there sooner." He grunted. "His visits over the next few decacycles gave me a better idea of who he was."

"I met him under similar circumstances, three cycles ago."

"That's understandable. You never needed him until you entered your grombit. He was essentially my father, cycles after my real parents died."

"It's funny, in a way. Belkidar's served that role for both of us, maybe for all of us. He was there when you were forced to survive on your own, especially at such a young age. For me, he arrived just before I discovered I was a Broglia Black."

Gunnar nodded. "He's certainly filled a void in my life. Without him, I seriously doubt I'd be alive today. I tried my best to honor my parents and their sacrifices, but my anger and frustration constantly threatened to control my life. If it weren't for him, his wisdom, his patience with me, I think I would've eventually given in to that rage."

"I can only imagine. The first few mooncycles of grombit camp were hard enough, but they can't compare to the challenges you've faced. When this Quest is over, I at least have a chance to see my parents again. I just hope they'll understand why I misjudged them. I

can see now why they treated me differently, but I was too frustrated to
see it then."

"Oh, I'm sure they will, Brohdan. They know you better than
anyone."

Brohdan nodded.

"True, our childhoods were different, but they were also similar,"
Gunnar said. "Above all, we each felt abandoned during the most
difficult – and important – periods of our lives. Fortunately for us both,
Belkidar was there."

"I never looked at it that way before, but you're right. Do you
think he did that because he needed us for this Quest?"

"No. He helped me long before Hildegard stole the Jewel. He
didn't help us because he was expecting our help in return. He helped
us, just as I believe he's helped countless others throughout the
centacycles, because we needed it."

"He's a remarkable human. I don't understand how he can care for
so many different creatures, all at the same time."

"Well, he does have certain gifts. I'm sure he uses all sorts of
sorcery, but I'm not very familiar with that sort of thing. I'm a giant
after all."

Brohdan laughed quietly. "It's funny you should say that. I don't
think I've ever been viewed as a natural sorcerer. Quite the opposite."

"Really? I thought you could use it at will."

"I can, but only to a certain degree. And only a handful of spells,
but I needed cycles of practice just to use those."

"What spells can you cast?"

"'Steelskin' hardens my scales and skin. 'Cloak' makes me nearly
invisible, and 'fear' lets me frighten others."

"Can you cast them together? At the same time?"

"I had a hard enough time just learning to cast one spell at a time,"
he laughed. "Belkidar explained that a sorcerer must split his mind into
separate parts to do that, one for each spell."

"And Broglias can't do that?"

"No, I think only humans can. The powerful ones." He yawned.

"Why don't you get some sleep? I'm sure tomorrow will be just as exhausting."

"Good advice." Brohdan got to his feet and headed down the hill.

"Brohdan," Gunnar whispered, "good talking to you."

"Likewise." He quietly made his way to the southern edge of the campsite where he found a large area not far from the others. There he drifted to sleep, his last thoughts of how lucky he was to have found these friends.

They resumed their journey, links before sunrise, to avoid the coming heat. Still in the latter stages of his grombit, Brohdan was slow to rise.

They appreciated their early departure the moment the sun appeared over the horizon. As the light's intensity grew, Brohdan decided to fly closer to the ground. With no terrain to use for concealment, his silhouetted form against the bright sky would serve as a beacon to anybody within linops. He leaned forward and began a graceful dive, increasing the angle as he accelerated.

Kiera rode in her usual position in front and, with the brightening sky as a backdrop, watched Brohdan as he dove toward her. She was amazed with how easily he flew. He was at least twice the weight of the rest of the party combined, yet he seemed to soar effortlessly whenever he took to the skies. Nevertheless, as she watched his dive angle increase, she began to wonder if something was wrong.

To her relief, he leveled off when he was just a few elads away. She watched, mouth open, as he soared toward her. Her horse, having become accustomed to his presence, paid him little attention. Its rider, on the other hand, was thrilled with his awesome display. Flying faster than any creature she'd ever seen, Brohdan passed only a few elads above, his head, neck, body, and long tail disappearing behind her. His wake immediately followed, staggered her horse, forced Kiera to hold on tight for fear of tumbling backward from her saddle. Then she turned and watched as he slowly flapped his wings, passing over her friends.

After he'd passed over Batai and Einar, Brohdan banked sharply to his right and arched his back, his right wingtip nearly dragging along the ground before climbing higher into the air. When his momentum was gone, he was nearly upside down, fifty elads above the ground. With a few quick thrusts of his wings, he righted himself and hovered in place.

Kiera and Gunnar cheered loudly, Indira simply shook her head, amazed. Batai smiled as he and Einar gazed upward. Belkidar grunted, nudged his horse forward.

With exaggerated bows, Brohdan thanked his audience. He then descended from his hover and headed southeast to scout ahead of his mates.

"Nice display," Kiera said as he slowly passed to her left.

"Why thank – "

"But, if you ever scare me like that again, you will pay."

Brohdan laughed, but it came to an abrupt end with one look from Kiera.

There wasn't a cloud in the sky as the sun gradually distanced itself from the horizon. By midmorning, the heat once again became unbearable, and with his black scales, Brohdan felt the effects more than the others.

"Belkidar, I think now's a good time to take a rest," Kiera recommended over her shoulder. "Perhaps we can find some shade and get a bite to eat."

"Good idea."

They continued for the better part of the next link, but the only shade they could find was cast by elye-high shrubs that sporadically dotted the wasteland. "I don't think we'll find shelter anytime soon," she said weakly.

"We might as well stop here, then." Belkidar looked around disapprovingly. "This is a terrible position. We're out in the open."

"We must make do," Batai said. "Besides, it won't take long to water the horses."

"Hmph."

"Come on, Belkidar, it could be worse! We could be stuck in an office somewhere staring at stacks of parchments!"

They gathered the horses around Gunnar who had already untied one of the water bags. Kiera passed out cured sausage and nuts. "The salt should help."

Brohdan, feeling more than his share of exhaustion, laid down near the others, staying alert for danger. Within drus, something caught his eye. He initially thought the sand itself was alive as dozens of large mounds encircled them, still over a hundred elads distant. They all had at least one thing in common – they were approaching with incredible speed. He stood, instinctively spread his wings.

Batai acted. "Gather here! Form a circle, the horses in the middle! Don't let them get between us!" Einar went toward the center, the other horses following. Brohdan, much too large to work in such a confined space, remained some distance away.

Within drus, the first mound attacked. Indira was ready. The lizard sprang from under the sand just as her arrow pierced its scales. It fell, skidding several elyes short of their five-person ring.

"You call that the size of a wolf?" Kiera shouted.

"Well, a *large* wolf maybe," the sorcerer called back.

The dead kevilok was nearly two elads long, its entire body covered in scales that matched the color of the sand. A darker brown pattern made its way along its back, the perfect camouflage for the Wruloric. Its mouth hung open, revealing dagger-like teeth designed more for penetration than chewing. At the end of each of its six legs were enormous claws with long, flat nails. Just as Belkidar had said, a pair of flat horns grew from its head.

Their defensive circle held, but mounting a counterattack would put that in jeopardy. Their swords flashing, Gunnar and Batai killed several during the initial drus. Einar snorted angrily, forced to watch the battle that raged beyond his reach.

Kiera didn't use her throwing daggers, instead waited until the keviloks committed to an attack. She sidestepped each, drove a dagger deep into the base of their skulls.

Belkidar held the Staff high, created an intense sphere of white-blue light that hovered a few elyes above and before him, its low, coarse humming filling the gaps between Gunnar's elated battle cries, Einar's frustrated grunts, and the keviloks' furious shrieks. Each time one came near, the orb's intensity grew alongside its buzzing before a loud crack accompanied a blinding discharge. Each pulse threw a kevilok elads backward, most of their bodies burned away.

Unable to help his friends, Brohdan decided to take flight. At least he tried to, but just as he extended his wings, the sand beneath him erupted. Kiera watched, horrified, as a dozen creatures attached themselves to his wings, stomach, back, and neck.

"Brohdan! I'm coming!"

"NO!" he roared back. His one-word reply sounded more like a rabid animal's growl than something that could pass for speech.

Until that moment, she'd never seen him angry. None of them had. His rage was clearly directed toward their enemies, yet she couldn't sidestep the terror that pierced her like a winter night's chill. His fury saturated the area, drove hesitation in their enemy. But their tentativeness was short-lived.

The keviloks renewed their attack, three more leaping onto his black scales. With his long neck, he reached behind his shoulder and grabbed one clinging to his left wing. His jaws penetrated its scaly armor and, with its blood flowing from either side of his mouth, silenced its cries. Before it hit the ground, Brohdan was already plucking the second from between his wings. Bloody pieces rained down. Brohdan writhed to dislodge those that remained, and they eventually lost their grip and fell to the sand. But as soon as they landed, they immediately leapt back into the air, reattaching themselves to his back. This time, he was ready. The first kevilok to take flight was greeted with a three-elad blade, its whistling momentarily muted as it passed through its thick hide.

It didn't take long for the surviving keviloks to adapt, burrowing toward his belly to avoid his blade. Brohdan realized their strategy and in one motion retracted his blade and raised his barz high, then crashed it down onto the charging mounds, great plumes of sand flying in all directions. Time and again, he bashed at the burrowing keviloks, creating a deep rumble as though a thundercloud loomed overhead. Yet despite his relentless attacks, a few keviloks managed to avoid harm, leapt toward him the moment they materialized from the sand.

Belkidar smiled as the first of the creatures landed on Brohdan's right shoulder. The kevilok opened its mouth, displaying its vicious teeth.

"Your shoulder!" Kiera shouted helplessly as she fought off several others.

Her warning had come too late. The kevilok drove its head down toward Brohdan's shoulder, intent on tearing through his scales and flesh. But its thrust stopped abruptly, the crack of its shattered jaw ringing through the clamor of battle. Blood poured from its mouth, and several broken teeth skidded across Brohdan's scales.

Dazed, the kevilok fell from his shoulder. Brohdan, busy with another attack from his right, estimated where it had fallen, crushed it with a well-placed claw before taking to the air. Dozens leapt after him, bounced from his body like acorns against an oak. With a few powerful thrusts, he climbed higher, then hovered beyond their reach. He opened his massive jaws, blew thundering fire, its center surging forward while the flames along its outer edges curled back around themselves.

Brohdan spread his liquid fire wide, covering a large area. When he stopped, several bodies smoked lifelessly on the sand, a dozen isolated fires sending smoke into the sky. Those keviloks that had managed to survive quickly dove under the sand for protection.

Brohdan drew his next breath and attacked. This time, he kept his fire stream smaller than a wagon wheel, weaving it over the panicked mounds, soil exploding to either side.

His first fire attack left the carcasses blackened, burned alive by his liquid fire. But even with a passing spray, his second attack burned through the tops of their backs and deep into their bodies, despite having burrowed elyes under the sand. All that remained of each was a charred, hollowed shell. The one thing they had in common was a lingering stench that turned their stomachs.

When Brohdan had taken flight, he drew the majority of the keviloks away from his companions, and Batai didn't hesitate. He immediately launched a counterattack, shouting the order and moving forward. The others followed, enlarging the defensive circle.

Two keviloks leapt at him, one from either side. He swung his sword through the first, placed his left foot behind his right, accelerated its momentum. With his head rotating ahead of his weapon, Batai struck the second kevilok as the first fell lifelessly to the ground.

A large kevilok leapt toward Kiera. She dove forward, tucked her body, drew a dagger from each boot. Then she rolled onto a knee, held both daggers high. Caught off guard, the kevilok stared down as it soared over her, shrieked as her blades found its soft underbelly. Its entrails strewn across a dozen elads, the maimed animal attempted to stand. But Kiera's daggers were long, and it slumped back to the ground, its clouding eyes watching as she killed three more.

Gunnar's attacks weren't quite as agile. Initially, he used his massive sword, but he soon decided his enemy's horns and scales left too many nicks in his blade. He sheathed it as he stepped forward, caught a shrieking animal between its first and second pair of legs, stopping its jaws an elye from his face. He stared at it, watched its expression as he closed his hands around its chest, noted how blood trickled from its nostrils as he brought his hands together. He tossed it aside as he casually placed his right foot over an approaching mound, then shifted his vast weight onto it, forcing the breath from its lungs and several muffled fractures from the sand.

Indira's arrows accounted for more kills than everybody save Brohdan. While the others fanned out in their counterattack, she remained, her bow never silent. They burrowed toward the horses, launched themselves at her friends, her arrows finding each the instant they leapt from beneath the sand.

When Batai gave the order to go on the offensive, Belkidar sulked, clearly disappointed. He reluctantly held his Staff high, casually strolled forward as his orb descended, its color deepening from its original white-blue. When it stopped just an elad above the ground, it resembled the setting sun, discharging a crimson bolt whenever a kevilok approached. Each burned through the scales between its eyes, into its skull, causing violent convulsions before it stilled, whisps of smoke rising from its sockets.

The surviving keviloks fled. Belkidar released his cant, Kiera watching as the crimson sphere slowly shrank, the buzzing's pitch increasing until it vanished in a flash of white-blue light. In the meantime, Brohdan flew from his hover to where the majority of the lizards fled.

"Indira will take care of the rest."

"But I can fly them down in less than thirty drus."

"She can do it in a fraction of that time."

Batai, Gunnar, and Kiera turned to where Belkidar stood while Brohdan landed behind them. Indira took one of her large quivers and surveyed the retreating keviloks, closed her eyes and took a deep breath, feeling the dry autumn breeze against her cheeks.

Facing north, she released arrow after arrow high into the air, keeping her eyes to the distant ground, assessing the retreating mounds. She slowly pivoted clockwise as her bow hummed. After she had passed east, south, and west, she stopped when she once again faced north. In a span of only five drus, she'd used over half of her quiver of fifty arrows. Then she quietly walked to the others, placing her enormous bow over her back with its bowstring resting diagonally across her chest.

"Well?" Gunnar demanded. "Did you hit anything?"

"No," she said softly.

"No? How do you even know? It's impossible to follow your arrows when you shoot them so high."

"I know. Even I find it difficult. But it was the only option."

"What do you mean?" Kiera asked.

"The keviloks burrow away from us, so my arrows must penetrate not only their scales, but also the sand that conceals them."

"Makes sense," Batai agreed. "But you said you didn't hit any of them."

"No. Not yet."

"They're still in the air?" Gunnar asked, stunned.

"Give them another dru."

Then a yelp reached them from far to the north, others immediately following, winding their way clockwise to the east, down to the south, up to the west, and finally ending to the north again. At last, when the final wail died on the hot wind, silence once again blanketed the wastelands.

Gunnar, his eyes wide, pivoted where he stood as he followed the kevilok's cries. When the last was heard, he found himself facing Indira.

"If it would not be too much trouble, I could use some help retrieving my arrows," she said slyly, heading for her horse. Once salvaged, they shared water and a quick meal.

"Pretty good little fight," Gunnar said.

"It seemed like you were enjoying it," Kiera agreed. "Maybe a little too much?"

"Those little keviloks were well armored," Gunnar replied after swallowing a large gulp, fingering a deep notch in his sword. "They weren't worth the effort."

"I see," Kiera said with a lopsided smile.

Indira turned toward Belkidar. "I noticed you seemed a bit annoyed, especially when we took the offensive. What troubled you?"

"Nothing," he answered shortly.

"Come now," Batai agreed, "I noticed the same thing."

"I wasn't annoyed so much as disappointed. When we held our defensive position, the battle had the potential to be...interesting. But that changed once we went on the offensive."

"What're you talking about?" Kiera asked. "You preferred that we *not* kill them?"

"Of course not. It's just that sooner than any of you realize, we'll be on Katja, Hildegard's backyard. What we've encountered thus far is nothing compared to what we'll face there." He looked into their eyes. "I have no doubts about any of you – as individuals. But if we're to be successful in this Quest, we must learn to act as a team. We did that today. First, we formed a defensive circle to hold off their initial attack. Then, when Brohdan drew so many away from us, Batai assessed the situation and called for a counterattack. By taking the offensive, I knew the battle had been won."

"Then why were you disappointed?" Brohdan asked.

"Because I wanted to see how we would've handled some adversity before reaching Brodor and, ultimately, Katja. I find it quite difficult to evaluate our abilities when we kill our enemies so quickly."

"I apologize," Kiera began.

Belkidar noticed her smirk, unconsciously cringed.

"If I'd known you wanted us to struggle, I would've only used one dagger."

"Very funny. You know exactly what I mean."

"There's still one thing I don't understand," Batai confessed. "When they swarmed Brohdan, one made it past his barz and attacked his shoulder."

Indira agreed. "It seemed its jaw was broken."

Brohdan shrugged, feeling uncomfortable with the attention. "When I realized I couldn't stop them all, I cast 'steelskin.'"

Anxious to put the Wruloric behind them, Kiera was on her horse waiting for the others. "I swear, if any of you were any slower, I might as well unpack my sleeping blankets."

Gunnar grunted, scowling at the unforgiving landscape.

"Where else would you rather be? In some Midrogru cave?" She smiled. "Were you ever this free there? Did you ever feel this sense of purpose?"

"Well, no," he admitted. Although he was the only one who answered, none disagreed.

With the horses' welfare in mind, Kiera closely monitored their pace as she led them toward Fendurgin. By nightfall, the group had traveled a considerable distance.

"When do you suppose we'll reach Fendurgin?" Gunnar asked, chasing away the silence as they prepared camp.

"I suspect we'll be there early tomorrow afternoon."

"Good. I need a decent meal. Watching the rest of you eat is getting on my nerves."

Batai laughed. "How could somebody your size be jealous of such a pathetic meal?"

"Any food's better than no food, and that's especially true when you're as hungry as I am. If we don't get there tomorrow, I imagine we'll have one less pack horse."

Indira hadn't expected that. She leaned over to Belkidar in the darkness. "Is he serious?"

"Of course not." Then he glanced at Gunnar, stroking his beard. "At least, I don't think so."

"I'll take the first watch," Kiera offered.

Thankful, the others laid down, making themselves as comfortable as the conditions allowed. Within a few drus, Kiera was the only one awake.

They again woke before dawn, packing quickly. "I wouldn't mind getting into town a bit early so we can all find a nice place to bed down for the night," Belkidar said, climbing into his saddle.

"Bed?" Gunnar asked sarcastically. "I don't suppose they'd have one my size."

"No, I don't imagine they will," he agreed with mock sympathy.

"That's all right. I've never needed a bed before. What are we going to do about food?"

"I can manage that," Brohdan said cheerfully. "I haven't had much of a chance to hunt lately, so I'll take care of our meal tonight."

Gunnar suddenly flashed a mischievous smile as he turned toward the dragon. "What did you have in mind?" he asked as he wiped saliva from his lower lip.

"I'm not sure. What's around there?"

"Elk, deer, caribou, and some bison," Kiera answered.

"What sort of creature are these caribou?" Brohdan asked.

"They're a smaller version of elk," Belkidar explained. "A few thousand cycles ago, caribou used to congregate in the colder climates of the north. But as Men spread into their territory, they migrated south into less-populated regions. Since then, they've become acclimated to the warmer temperatures in the central and southern regions of Tymoteu."

"Thanks for the history lesson," Gunnar said. "What do they taste like?"

"I'm not sure," he admitted as he stroked his beard. "I wonder if Briz would enjoy them."

"Well, with any luck I'll let you know tonight," Gunnar said, winking toward his hunting partner.

Brohdan tried to return the gesture, but his winking experience apparently wasn't quite as extensive as the giant's. He contorted his face in several different directions, none even remotely resembling a wink.

Despite his best efforts, Gunnar couldn't prevent his hysterics, his contagious laughter spreading like a fire's warmth. Realizing what his face must've looked like, Brohdan joined him. The others, not realizing what had caused it, couldn't help but follow suit.

"Please," Gunnar pleaded, wiping tears from his bearded cheeks, "warn me if you ever try that again."

Still recovering, Brohdan only nodded.

The group departed with the recent amusement lingering in their thoughts, and their lighthearted mood helped pass the time quickly. After a few links heading southeast, Kiera was able to make out the highway that connected Fendurgin with the coastal town of Cordu to the northeast.

"Belkidar, I've found the highway."

"Excellent work, Kiera. How far north of Fendurgin are we?"

Kiera looked around, studied the landscape. "I'd say no more than a few dozen linaks."

"How can you be certain?" Batai asked, impressed.

"Well, you see that small range of hills to the east? Well, just beyond them lies a narrow stretch of trees. I once hid in there for several days while some gentlemen attempted to recoup some money I had won."

"Why would they do such a thing?" Belkidar asked sardonically, his expression confused.

"I'm not sure, really."

"Come now, my dear. You must have *some* idea."

"All right!" she confessed. "I won a lot of money in a friendly game of cards."

Belkidar stared at her.

"What?"

"I'm sorry," he replied innocently. "I didn't realize you were finished." His grin spoke volumes.

"Belkidar, it was a fair game. Those men just didn't have the necessary skills to win. I did."

"I see. They just weren't as good of cheaters as you were."

"Why, Belkidar!" Kiera replied, her expression hurtful. "I don't believe I've ever – "

"I'm sure you haven't," he interrupted. "But I appreciate your expertise," he added, nodding to the nearby road.

Disappointed she didn't evoke any sympathy from him, she at least appreciated the compliment.

"If you would be so kind to lead us to Fendurgin?" he asked.

Kiera silently nudged her horse down the highway, the others falling into place. Brohdan, still not comfortable showing himself in this region, flew a linak to the west.

She stayed on the road as they neared the outskirts, reasoning they'd be more conspicuous if they approached such a large city from the grasslands to the west than from this well-traveled road.

Brohdan had never seen such a large settlement in his life. Even from a distance of several linaks he was able to discern many tall buildings and sprawling markets. Its walls encompassed more area than all of Trisett, the largest human city he'd seen thus far. Without even thinking about it, he sent his thoughts to Belkidar.

"It's huge! I think it's even bigger than Trisett."

"It is. Trisett has more people if you include the nearby farmsteads, but Fendurgin covers more area. It's one of the oldest human cities in the world. Only KelKinney and Brodor are older."

"And Brodor is even larger?"

"Much. All of the commerce from Katja goes through there."

"Belkidar, what do you plan to accomplish here?" Kiera asked as they neared the city.

"As much as possible. Cities this size contain a wealth of information. I'd like to visit some of the finer drinking establishments to discover the latest."

"I'm sure *that's* the reason you'll visit those pubs!"

Belkidar looked hurt. "While I'll be the first to admit they may offer a certain benefit, ale is not my primary concern." He looked into Kiera's eyes for several long moments. "Fine. It's my secondary concern."

Kiera shook her head, laughed as she rode ahead.

"Do you have interests in Fendurgin?" Indira asked Batai.

"Actually, I do. The world's finest blacksmiths can be found here, and their quality is truly unmatched."

"Why are they so different?"

"Fendurgin is a very old city. In a way, the people who call it home are just as old. Generation after generation live and die in this community; it's virtually unheard of for a resident to leave. As a result, they've developed skills here that can't be found anywhere else."

"Fendurgians remain true to the old ways. When apprentices learn their trade in nearly every other community of the world, they eventually venture out to create their own business. That's their right. But in Fendurgin, the apprentice's responsibilities remain with his master until the master retires. The apprentice then becomes the master, eventually taking an apprentice of his own."

"An apprentice learns so much more when he works with a master tradesman for so long – not just more techniques, but how well each is perfected. So when the time comes for them to take over the responsibilities of their master, they don't have to spend time honing their abilities. They've already done that. Instead, they invest their time building on the knowledge that's been gained by previous generations. And because each master himself remained an apprentice for such a long period, the skills passed down are considerably more advanced than other communities. And remember, the apprentice turnover is low, so trades are learned and taught to very few apprentices. Therefore, the skills developed in Fendurgin are rarely learned outside these city walls."

Indira nodded. "It sounds like they follow the traditions of a pack."

Batai smiled, realized she was right. "I'm sure that's how your people learned to create such masterpieces," Batai said, motioning toward her bow.

Her smile showed both her gratitude toward his inference and her pride in her ancestry. "My pack discovered unique methods of forging bows several hundred generations ago. Other packs have become skilled in other areas."

"Can you tell us about your bow?" Kiera asked after letting the others catch up.

"Certainly," Indira began, hoisting it in her left hand. "There is none like it. Long ago, my ancestors learned to construct bows that perfectly enhance the skills of each archer."

"How so?" Batai asked. "Like how much tension they put on the string?"

"No, it goes far beyond that." She paused, trying to find the words. "Here," she finally said, handing it to him.

Caught off guard, Batai abruptly took her weapon. To his amazement, it was even heavier than it appeared. "How can you use something so heavy?"

"It is much less so in my hands," she replied softly. "You see, it was created for me. Draw it."

After rearranging himself in his saddle, he extended in his left arm, then pulled back on the thick bowstring. The Captain of the Order of Paladins barely managed an elye. He finally stopped, looked incredulously at the slender elf. "But I've seen you draw this a hundred times!"

"Yes. That is because it was created specifically for *me*. I doubt even Gunnar could draw it."

Batai quietly handed it back to her. "I'm afraid I don't understand," he admitted. "Do me a favor though," he added as she took the bow from his hands as though it weighed no more than a feather. "Draw back the bowstring."

Indira took the bow, extended her left arm, and easily drew the weapon to its full length.

Batai, still confused, noted the flexing of the bow's thick arms, considered the power that lay at her fingertips. "You are an extraordinary civilization."

"Thank you," she answered as she effortlessly guided the bowstring back into its resting position. "If you do not mind, I would like to go to the Fendurgin blacksmiths with you. I am curious to see them for myself."

"Of course. I'd be delighted."

Gunnar strode up alongside just as she replaced her bow across her back. "Did I hear my name?"

She nodded. "I told Batai that I doubted you could draw my bow."

"That?" Gunnar asked, jerking his thumb toward it.

"I could only manage an elye," Batai warned.

The giant was speechless. He looked first from the bow that lay innocently across her back, then to Batai. "You're having me on. She's able to pluck that thing like a harp. Surely you could do the same."

Batai grinned. "Would you like to make a wager on your chances?"

"Sure," Gunnar replied, a sly smile spreading across his face. "What'd you have in mind?"

"Let's say all the ale either of us could drink in one night."

"Done!" he replied immediately.

"Interesting," Indira observed, "I have not been included in this wager, yet the weapon is mine."

"Very well," Gunnar said. "If I can't draw that bow to its full length, I'll buy each of you as much ale as you wish for one night. If I succeed, Batai buys me ale one night, you buy the next."

"That sounds fair," Indira agreed with seemingly little emotion. Yet Batai noted the corners of her mouth curved upward ever so slightly.

"Good," Gunnar said between strides as he walked next to Einar. By now, of course, Kiera and Belkidar had heard enough of the conversation to take interest. Thanks to Belkidar's ability, it wasn't long before Brohdan joined them.

"Looks like you have an audience," Batai observed just as Brohdan settled behind a line of trees west of the highway, 'cloaked' to ensure he remained unseen.

"Fine by me," Gunnar replied, "just means there are more to witness your impending debts."

Indira stopped her horse, then handed him her bow.

"I'll try to not break it," he said seriously.

Suddenly, the bow seemed tiny in his enormous hands, and for the first time Batai considered how much ale a giant might drink in one night.

"Have you ever used one before?" Indira asked softly.

"No," he admitted.

"Which hand do you throw with?"

"Depends on the size of the boulder."

She smiled. "Which one is more comfortable for you?"

"My right."

"Very well. Hold the bow with your left hand, and draw the string with the three middle fingers of your right."

Gunnar pulled back on the string.

Brohdan was astounded, and by their expressions, so was everyone else. Gunnar's arm seemingly tripled in size as his muscles flexed under the enormous strain, his bearskins stretching precariously across his back. Yet despite his incredible strength, he only managed to pull the bowstring to half its full draw.

"Are we having some difficulty?" Batai asked.

"Never mind," Gunnar rumbled as he released it. After a deep breath, he tried again. Although his second attempt proved slightly better, the bowstring still stood over an elye from a full pull. With a fevered effort, he managed to hold it there, but could draw it no further. He finally conceded. "I don't understand," he said, handing it back to Indira.

"The elders of my pack created this specifically for me." She again demonstrated by smoothly drawing the bowstring to her cheek.

Gunnar watched as she held it for several moments before again guiding it back to its resting position. "I'm impressed, Indira. I had no idea your kin were so skilled. And I look forward to paying my debts tonight – just as long as I get a taste, too."

"I'm afraid I've got some bad news for a couple of you," Belkidar interjected. "I need two of you to stay outside the city while the rest of us take a look inside."

"Why do you want the women to stay out of the city?" Gunnar asked, feigning confusion.

"Please," Kiera answered through a grin, "you boys need us to keep you out of trouble."

Batai laughed. "I think you'd only add to whatever trouble we might to find."

"Why Batai, I'm sure I don't know what you're talking about."

It was Belkidar's turn to laugh. "Then would you mind telling us exactly how you won all that money that forced you into the trees just north of here?"

"I told you, I won that money in a friendly game of cards! Now, who did you want to stay outside the city?" she asked quickly.

"I originally thought Batai and I should," the old man quipped, "but the more I think about it, the more I like Gunnar's idea."

"Belkidar, you really need to work on your sense of humor," Kiera mumbled.

"I know, but I haven't found the time."

"But you're twenty thousand cycles old!"

"First of all," Belkidar began with a pained look, "I'm only a centacycle or two over eight thousand. Second, you have no idea how fast a few thousand cycles can fly by if you keep yourself busy."

"Busy? What could keep you busy for eighty centacycles?" Gunnar asked.

Belkidar smiled. "Let's just say I've kept busy doing many things, some of which include looking after people such as yourself."

Brohdan noticed Gunnar actually looked hurt.

"I didn't mean to suggest that you needed babysitting," he quickly amended. "Many creatures have needed my assistance for one reason or another. You fit into this category, and I was honored to help in any way I could. Each of you is unique for many reasons, but all of you are identical in at least one respect – you all endured difficult childhoods, forced to face circumstances that challenged you far more than most."

Brohdan realized for the first time the impact this apparently frail old man had on countless lives. He was awed by the responsibility Belkidar accepted without hesitation. Apparently, Gunnar was as well.

"I appreciate everything you've done for me, Belkidar. I don't know what would've happened to me if I never met you."

He smiled. "Your friendship has meant a lot to me too." He looked into each of their eyes. "You've all taught me so much, I'm not sure why I've been so blessed. For that, I'm truly grateful."

The others considered his words, and although honored by them, Belkidar didn't convince any of them that their contributions could even remotely match those he'd made in their lives.

Before Kiera neared the city, Brohdan and Gunnar took their leave. "We'll look for you in the trees beyond the southern gate," Belkidar explained as he continued riding toward Fendurgin. "I don't expect to spend more than two or three days inside."

"Sounds good," Brohdan agreed. "Just don't be alarmed if the neighboring communities see a giant and dragon sneaking through their villages."

Gunnar said nothing, but then speech wasn't really necessary considering the giggling that slowly followed Brohdan to the south.

"Why do I put myself in these predicaments?" Belkidar asked nobody as he followed the others toward the city gate.

Brohdan and Gunnar remained within the trees well beyond the city outskirts. After traveling well into the evening, they finally found themselves near the road that linked Fendurgin to Brodor further to the south. It didn't take long for Gunnar to find a secluded clearing.

"What's next on our agenda?" Brohdan asked.

Gunnar, having just made himself comfortable, managed to open an eye. "I think I'm doing it. Let's hunt tomorrow."

"Sounds good," the Broglia Black agreed as he too found a place to rest. There, the two huge creatures slept, only the occasional cry of a bird or rustle of a squirrel disturbing them.

"Do you think I'll find a better dagger than this one?" Kiera asked Batai.

"Yes, Kiera, I do."

"But this is one of my favorites!" she complained. "I had it made for me in Kordare. It fits my sheath perfectly!"

"Well then, perhaps you should have the local blacksmiths examine this sheath of yours. It'd be a shame if you weren't completely satisfied."

Indira did an admirable job suppressing her laughter. The same could not be said of Belkidar.

"I thought knights, and especially paladins, were men of honor. You should be ashamed of yourself."

"My lady," Batai began with an extravagant bow, "please accept my most sincere apologies."

Kiera stared at him, said nothing as she considered his sincerity.

"I meant you no disrespect," he continued. "Far be it from me to suggest when you should be satisfied."

This time, even Indira couldn't hold back her amusement.

Kiera turned quickly and offered her a surprised look. Despite herself, she too began laughing. "Indira, we're meant to stick together! You're not supposed to laugh at their jokes! Especially when the joke's on *me*!"

"I am sorry," she replied, wiping tears from her cheeks, "but Batai is just too much for me. The elves in my pack do not joke in this manner." Her smile was infectious.

"Oh my," Belkidar said, alarmed. "I'm going to pay dearly for this."

"What do you mean?" Indira asked, still recovering.

"When it's time for you to return to your family, I think I'll owe Juron a rather difficult explanation. I can just imagine you going home and cutting jokes like these. Your pack will be embarrassed, maybe even insulted."

"Oh, relax," she told the sorcerer. "Some of the elders may react that way, but it will not harm them. Who knows, they may even find it humorous."

Belkidar considered that for a moment. "Oh my…"

"Let's find a nice inn for the night," Kiera suggested. "I'd like to get an early start tomorrow."

"Well said," Belkidar agreed. "As soon as we find you a nice bed, I'm going to hit the local tavern."

"We've been in town for half a link and you're already thinking with your stomach! You're incorrigible!"

"Not really. But thank you. What I have in mind actually lies more in your arena. I'd like to gather some information while we have the chance. Brodor is certain to have Hildegard's spies scouring the city for news of our arrival, and while I'm sure they're in Fendurgin as well, I think the news we find here will be considerably more accurate than the misinformation we're sure to find in Brodor."

"That sounds reasonable," Kiera agreed. "If you don't mind, I'd like to tag along."

"Thanks all the same, Kiera, but I prefer to work alone."

Batai turned toward Indira. "Have you any experience in espionage?"

"No. Why do you ask?"

"No reason. You seem to have a perfect demeanor for it, that's all."

Indira looked at him for a long time, considering his words.

Belkidar soon led them into an inn he'd frequented several times over the cycles. It was a little smoky inside, but the hearth's warmth was welcomed. Within a few drus, the innkeeper came to the front desk. He was a short, fat man with a severely balding head. His clothes were dirty and unkept. "May I help you?" he asked, his eyes lingering on Batai's armor.

"Yes, you may," Belkidar said as he stepped from behind the large knight.

"Mr. Bowmont!" the fat man cried. "It's so good to have you back again! Please, this way," he offered as he hurried from behind his desk and led them down the hall. "It just so happens our finest rooms are available. Would that please you, sir?"

"Yes. Yes it would, thank you," Belkidar replied with much more dignity than was his custom. After the innkeeper had shown each to their rooms, Belkidar gave him a large tip.

"Thank you, sir! Thank you!" he cried, hurrying back down the hall.

"Belkidar, where do you get all of your money?" Batai asked. "You've never had a job for as long as I've known you."

"Dear, innocent Batai," he sighed. "There are many ways in this world to make money. The most common is to earn it – one way or another," he added as he turned toward Kiera. "Another is to do this." He opened his cloak and fished around in several of his numerous inner pockets before finding what he was looking for. After a moment, he removed his hand and opened it, revealing several round woodchips. Suddenly, a bright white-blue light flashed in his palm. It quickly faded, the woodchips replaced with gold coins. "Here," he said, handing the stack to Batai, "buy your weapons."

Batai took the gold from Belkidar, stunned.

"Now, if you'll excuse me, I'd like to change into something more appropriate for this evening's business." With that, the frail old man walked slowly into his room and shut the door.

Batai, standing with his hand still extended, finally closed his fingers around the fortune. "That man is amazing."

"Truly," Indira agreed before yawning. "I think I shall make it an early night. Are we still planning on visiting some smithies tomorrow?"

"Definitely," Batai confirmed. "Kiera, have you decided whether you're going to upgrade your daggers while we're here?"

"No, not really. I've heard of skilled blacksmiths here, but none that match your description."

"I'm not surprised," Batai answered. "They reserve their finest weapons for specific clients."

Kiera nodded. "I'd like to take a look."

"Sounds good," he said, stepping into his room. "Maybe by this time tomorrow you'll be quite satisfied with the day's events," he said, closing the door.

Kiera, realizing she'd just been had, smiled helplessly in her doorway.

"Goodnight," Indira said.

"Goodnight, Indira. See you tomorrow."

A few moments after they'd closed their doors, a greasy-haired man wearing torn rags emerged from Belkidar's room. "Ah, that's better," he said, closing the door behind him.

The next morning found Batai eager with the day's possibilities. He rose with the sun, quickly donned his armor. Although their circumstances probably didn't require such precautions, he never placed faith in chance. The metal of his armor glistened in the early morning sunlight that spilt the weather-worn shutters. He covered his chain mail with a blue and yellow tunic with red accents about the sleeves and neck. When the shafts of light struck him at just the right angle, glints of polished metal stole through his wool outer garments.

As he left his room, he paused momentarily outside Kiera's door as he wondered if it was still too early to wake his friends. Then he decided the purpose of their visit to Fendurgin lay in business, not in comfortable beds. He knocked on her door but heard no response. He knocked again. He tried Indira's room but again heard nothing. He finally received a response after knocking on Belkidar's.

"Go away."

"But we must make an early start to the day," Batai said through a grin.

"Early start? I already made an early start while you were fast asleep," the sorcerer explained from the darkness of his room. "Now, allow me the same courtesy before I do something I'll regret."

"As you wish. If I can ever find the women, we're going to visit some smithies today. Perhaps you can join us later."

"Perhaps. Now leave me alone."

Batai, still smirking, allowed the old man his sleep, but as he walked down the hall toward the stairs that led to the common room, he couldn't help feeling a little concerned with the women's absence. To his surprise, they were already there. Each was huddled over a large, nearly empty coffee mug.

"Well, it's about time," Kiera remarked over her cup.

"It's still early," Batai answered, shifting his scabbard so he could sit with his friends. "The sun's only been up a few drus."

"I know," Kiera said. "I watched it."

"Excellent! That means you're about ready. I know of a blacksmith not far from here. He has perhaps the finest reputation throughout the continent."

"Very good," Indira said as she took a sip. "I am eager to see these talents for myself."

"If what I've heard is accurate, I don't think you'll be disappointed."

"Who were you talking to in the hallway?" Kiera asked after a moment.

"Oh, just Belkidar's door. I think he's had a long night. I told him of our morning's plan in case he wanted to join us later."

"Good," Kiera observed. "He needs his sleep. The last thing we need is a grouchy leader."

"I wholeheartedly agree," Batai said.

"What kept him up so late?" Indira asked. "I thought he was to gather information from the local taverns."

"As far as I know, that's exactly what he did," Kiera said. "Gathering information like that is very delicate work. First, you have to blend in, then identify a patron who seems willing to talk. Choosing the right person is critical. Most drunks don't know anything useful in the first place, so risking exposure for something that's just a rumor is dangerous. But if he knows something worthwhile, you must befriend him in a way that lets you to lead the conversation while making it appear as though it flows naturally. It takes several discussions with many informants to piece together an accurate story. Trying to get too much information from one person is a common mistake, which typically doesn't end well. But if you do it correctly, it'll appear as though he just shared a friendly conversation with another of the pub's customers."

"I never realized spying was so complicated," Indira said. "We have no need for that in my pack. We need only post sentries to safeguard us."

"That's because elves are nearly impossible to spot in the woodlands," Batai remarked.

Kiera agreed. "I've only met a few of your kind, Indira, but I've never seen an elf's equal when it comes to blending into their surroundings."

"We have lived long amongst the woodlands, it is only natural that we have become accustomed to them."

"Well said," Kiera agreed. "Blending in is a useful skill. I'm sure Belkidar did an outstanding job of that last night."

"Perhaps that's why his head hurts so much this morning," Batai added as he got to his feet.

Indira smiled as she also rose from her chair. Kiera, just finishing her drink, trailed the others out the door.

"How did you hear of this blacksmith?" Indira asked as they mounted their horses behind the inn.

"Serving as a knight allows you to meet a lot of interesting people," Batai explained as he rode between his friends down the wide streets of the great city, Einar towering above the horses to either side. "Some wish to challenge us, to test themselves in battle."

"Men risk their lives in these challenges?"

"I suppose, but they seldom end in death. It's merely a way to challenge yourself, a way to validate your training, your dedication. During times of peace, when no battles exist to test your skill, these challenges are the only alternative. A knight may refuse, of course, but I've never heard of it."

"I've seen a few of them," Kiera remarked. "As I recall, the vast majority were lopsided in favor of the knights."

"What else would you expect?" Batai chortled.

"Exactly that," Kiera answered, her smile flashing in the orange dawn. Although Indira had seen her smile on a daily basis during their travels, she still found herself awed with her beauty.

"I imagine you've experienced some of these battles firsthand," Kiera continued.

"I have."

"Well?"

"Well what?"

"How did you fare in them?"

"Why didn't you just ask me that in the first place?"

"Batai, I'm becoming irritated."

"My goodness, somebody woke up on the wrong side of the bed this morning."

"Somebody's not going to be able to sleep on *any* side of the bed tonight if they don't get on with the story."

"Indira, I think Kiera's talking to you."

"I shall remain out of this one."

"Batai, please don't make me hurt you," Kiera said through clenched teeth.

"All right," Batai said with a laugh. "What did you want to know again?"

"I asked how you fared in the challenges."

"Oh, right. Thanks. I did okay. You must remember, many of these challengers were inexperienced. All had trained for cycles, some protected rich merchants, many others were notorious mercenaries, but few had ever experienced true combat."

"Why do they feel the need to challenge a knight then?" Indira asked.

"Because there comes recognition in defeating a knight. They covet a reputation, and that's the shortest path to one."

"That is a dangerous way to learn what only time and experience can teach."

"Well said," Kiera agreed.

"Over the cycles I battled against half a dozen challengers who used the most amazing weapons. When I blocked their attacks, I found my sword and shield took far more damage than I expected. So after defeating one of them, I asked about his sword. Through slurred words – the blow of my shield had caused him to bite through his tongue – he told me about a handful of blacksmiths here. They're able to forge steel that is many times harder than anywhere else. And from what I've learned, one of these blacksmiths is far more gifted than the others. His smithy is just around that corner," Batai explained as he pointed to a small alley to the right of the road.

Batai continued along the street and turned down the alley, soon coming to an unremarkable storefront where they dismounted. Only one window faced the narrow alley, and to its left stood a heavy door. The exterior walls were covered in white clay in need of thorough scrubbing. A small sign over the entrance was the only clue to the merchant's business.

"Szurgord's Smithy," Kiera read from the sign. "Sounds quaint."

"Very funny," Batai remarked as he removed his shield from Einar's left flank.

Just inside the door, their noses were assaulted with the thick smell of coal dust and molten steel. A large counter ran the width of the small room. Beyond it in the left corner sat a small square table and a single empty chair. A closed door stood opposite the table in the right corner.

Through the poorly lit structure Batai saw paperwork stacked on the table. "Orders," he sighed. "Looks like it'll be mooncycles before he'll get to our weapons."

Just then a large man entered the room from the rear door. His head was bald and appeared to be recently shaven, and he had the thickest arms Batai had ever seen. "How can I help you?" he asked in a deep, scratchy voice, not bothering to look at his customers as he retrieved an order from the table.

"I'm interested in your services."

"I'm sorry, but I've got too many orders stacked up. Come back next mooncycle and perhaps I can help you."

"I would if I could, but I'm only passing through. We won't be back for quite some time. We're in need of weapons, as soon as you can forge them."

The large man grunted as he dropped the order back onto the table, finally turning to face him. In an instant, his expression changed from shock to respect. Indira noted his eyes, so brown they appeared black, and they grew wider as they took in Batai and his poorly concealed armor. "You're a paladin?"

Batai nodded.

"I'm Szurgord, and this is my shop. I'd be honored to forge weapons for you."

"Sir, your reputation has spread throughout this continent and, I'm sure, far beyond. I've unfortunately faced your weapons in battle, so I know firsthand the quality of your work."

"I'm proud they made such a favorable impression. What do you need?"

"The finest weaponry you can make." He drew his sword and laid it across the counter. "A sword," Batai began, then placed his shield next to it, "and a shield." He looked down at Kiera. "My friend here would also like some daggers if that wouldn't be too much trouble."

Kiera removed several and placed them on the counter to the left of Batai's shield. "Well, six to be exact."

"I think I could manage that."

"And one more sword, if you don't mind," Batai added. Kiera shot him a curious look.

"Of course. Similar to the first?"

"Not quite," Batai answered, taking a sketch from an inside pocket of his tunic and placing it on the countertop. "As you can see, this one's...different. The handle's six elyes long, the blade sixteen. Also, as you can see here," Batai said, pointing to the drawing, "the base is much wider than normal."

"I understand," the smith replied, wondering why Batai would need such a massive weapon. He thought for a moment. "Return at sunset in two days."

"So soon?" Batai asked, stunned.

Szurgord smiled. "In many ways, I am like the weapons I create. My abilities, however insignificant compared to others in the world, are my own. Rest assured, your weapons will be ready."

Batai nodded. "Thank you, I truly appreciate your help. I can't overstate their importance in our Quest. Our fate may very well rest in your hands."

"If my talents help you in the slightest, noble paladin, my work will be justified."

Batai bowed respectfully, turned, and left the shop. Indira and Kiera followed him into the alley.

"I think we'll be quite pleased," Batai said, climbing into his saddle.

"So do I," Kiera said as she too mounted her horse. "I'd sure like to know how he's able to create such extraordinary weapons, though."

"And so quickly," Indira agreed. Then she paused. "Why are you having a sword made for Gunnar?"

"Well, since he couldn't join us, I thought it'd be a nice way to repay him. I just hope he'll like it."

"Why would he not?"

Batai considered Gunnar, his past. "He made his sword with his own hands, and it's helped keep him alive for a long time. In a way, it's been his only companion."

Belkidar was awake in his room by the time the others returned.

"Did you discover anything interesting last night?" Kiera asked once inside.

"I did."

"Well?" Batai prompted.

"I'd rather not discuss it where there are so many ears. Besides, I haven't confirmed anything yet. How did it go at the smithy?"

"Fine. Our new weapons will be ready in two days." Batai said dismissively. "Belkidar, we're far from prying ears. Tell us what you've heard."

"Not yet. By the time you receive your new weapons, I'll have discovered all there is to know. I'll explain everything once we meet up with the others. Now, where can we get a decent meal?"

That night, Batai, Kiera, and Indira ate at a nice tavern. Belkidar, on the other hand, once again disappeared into the darker corners of the city.

Like the sorcerer, Brohdan and Gunnar remained busy that night.

"I'm hungry," Brohdan said, his stomach rumbling.

"Me too. Feel like hunting?"

"I thought you'd never ask."

Because the sky was not yet dark, Brohdan didn't want to fly and risk being seen. "Let's see," he said, considering their options. "Would you like me to flush something toward you?"

"I suppose that would work, but I feel like more of a challenge tonight." Gunnar stroked his black beard. "Tell you what, I'll take care of our food tonight." With that, he slipped away into the darkening forest.

Brohdan, a little surprised by Gunnar's sudden departure, quietly returned to their shelter among the trees. He found himself alone for the first time in days, and he soon thought of Mikka, shocked that the thought of her no longer caused him pain. Instead, he found peace. That realization amazed him. He lay among the tall trees, watched it grow dark as he recalled every detail of the time he'd spent with her.

Gunnar didn't have time for such reflections. He found himself in a large ravine that led toward the Celornorin Ocean. As he made his way down the center of the valley, he soon heard animal cries coming from the top of the southern ridgeline. He stopped for a moment, listening. They perplexed him, sounding like they were made in harmony with at least one other voice. Despite the length and complexity of each cry, the voices remained in perfect unison.

Shortly after they ended, Gunnar heard another exchange from the northern ridge. He suddenly realized the two groups were communicating with one another. The revelation hit him like a boulder – they were hunting, and he was their prey.

He thrust the tip of his sword into the ground, grabbed a handful of dirt. He slowly rubbed it between his hands as he considered his situation. Then he retrieved his weapon, and not a moment too soon.

The first attacks came from south. He turned to greet several creatures resembling extremely large wolves, but they definitely weren't wolves. Each had three heads supported by a broad, muscular neck. Instantly, Gunnar realized they were cerebi, an ancient relative of wolves, but at nearly two elads tall, they easily dwarfed their smaller cousins. He silently scolded himself, too late realizing why their calls were so perfectly synchronized.

The first cerebus charged. With a flick of his sword, Gunnar severed its right front leg, and it yelped in three-part harmony as it limped clear. After fending off a second, he realized those on the northern ridge had made their way down the steep embankment. Within moments, he was surrounded by nearly two dozen of them.

Their second day in Fendurgin passed in much the same way as the first. Belkidar spent most of the morning recovering from the previous night's events while Batai, Indira, and Kiera took some time to enjoy the ancient city. They explored the eastern region known primarily for its trades, then the northern districts famous for its arts and crafts. The southern region was Fendurgin's economic center, and it teemed with everything from fresh produce and fish markets to questionable precious metal and gem dealers. Kiera experienced a familiar, deep-rooted solace once they strayed into the western district, within which originated most of the city's corruption. Politics influenced nearly every transaction, and distrusting eyes were common. Kiera sighed contentedly, feeling at home.

They eventually ate lunch in the outside courtyard of a quiet tavern. "You know, this expedition of ours suddenly resembles a well-needed vacation," Kiera said, sipping an ale beneath a large oak.

"It's been nice here," Batai agreed.

"Something tells me we should enjoy it while we can," Indira said, smiling.

"You're right," Batai said, setting his empty tankard on the table. "I've had – business – over there, and I can attest to Belkidar's concern."

"What took you there?" Indira asked.

Batai smiled at a barmaid as she placed another ale before him. "Pirates began raiding some of our towns along the coast. After investigating, we discovered they originated from the eastern continent, so I led some of my men over there to let them know we didn't appreciate such hospitality from our neighbors." His satisfied grin revealed considerably more than his brief explanation. "But I wasn't there long, and I only visited a few coastal towns."

"Well, I trust Belkidar," the elf concluded. "If anybody could lead us to victory, it is him."

"Agreed," Kiera said, raising her drink. "To Mr. Bowmont."

Batai raised his tankard to hers. Indira stared at them.

"We call it a toast," Kiera explained. "We touch our glasses together to honor our friend."

"I see," Indira replied softly, following suit.

After a few more drinks, they resumed their exploration of the large city. They reminisced past experiences, both pleasant and difficult, each realizing how much they had in common despite their very different backgrounds.

That night Belkidar donned a different appearance. Instead of a smelly drunk dressed in rags, he now resembled a wealthy aristocrat. His clothing was absolutely immaculate. He had a charcoal jacket and pants with black boots, gloves, and vest. We wore a scarlet shirt beneath the latter, and his charcoal hat included subtle scarlet features. With the exception of darker hair and a beardless face, his physical appearance remained nearly unchanged. When the others finally found their way back to the inn, they found an identical note waiting for each of them in their rooms.

> *I'm sure you're all having fun. Don't forget our*
> *purpose. I'll be busy tonight confirming the validity of*
> *my information. We should be safe here, but don't*
> *attract unnecessary attention. I won't return until late*
> *tonight but will nonetheless accompany you when you*
> *retrieve your purchases tomorrow.*

Be careful.
Bellolicious

"That is one disturbed man," Kiera said after they had congregated in Batai's room.

"Bellolicious?" Batai asked nobody in particular for the fourth time.

"He certainly is unique," Indira agreed.

That night they stayed at the inn. They went to the common area for a meal and drinks but soon found the quality of both to be less than desirable.

"Maybe we should just call it a night," Kiera said, standing.

"You're right," Batai agreed, also rising. "Bellolicious won't return for several more links. We might as well wait until tomorrow for any news."

"It seems a pity to call it a night already," Indira remarked.

"Tell me about it," Kiera grumbled.

"Perhaps we could venture into the city, if only for a short period?" she suggested coyly.

"Don't tempt me, Indira."

Indira returned her smile, considering the potential of the night ahead. "The extra sleep would do us good," she finally relented.

Although nobody noticed it, Batai's face took on a decidedly relieved expression.

They unenthusiastically headed to their rooms. "I wonder how our friends are managing," Batai said.

"I'll wager they're having more fun than we are tonight," Kiera answered.

"No doubt," Indira agreed. "How could they not?"

Due to both their early night and their anticipated meeting with Szurgord, all except Belkidar rose with the sun. As had become the custom, the trio met early to break their fast in the inn's common area. Belkidar, also as usual, was fast asleep.

"Are you excited?" Indira asked Batai.

"About what?"

"About collecting your weapons from Szurgord this evening!"

"Oh, that. I guess so."

"You'd never know it," Kiera quipped. "I can't wait until I get my hands on those daggers! I only hope they suit my sheaths. I do hate it when drawing a blade is slowed by a poor fit."

Batai looked at the small woman, his expression revealing much more than could any words.

"Do you have a problem?" Kiera asked.

"I didn't say a word!"

"No, but then you really didn't need to."

"What shall we do until Belkidar wakes?" Indira asked, unsuccessfully suppressing a smile.

"Let's find someplace that serves better food," Batai suggested.

"But Belkidar wants us to remain inconspicuous," Kiera reminded him.

"I know, but some of these small inns barely serve more than a dozen customers at a time. And there's at least three times that many here." Batai's grin grew wider. "That'd actually make us *less* conspicuous."

"You know," Kiera said, her dimples flashing, "I think you're onto something. Let's see if we can find one that serves dessert," she added, heading for the door.

Batai quickly got to his feet and followed, Indira bringing up the rear. "We will pay for this when Belkidar finds out," she said softly. She wasn't sure if Kiera or Batai heard her, however, because by the time she'd finished, the others were already out the door.

Belkidar wasn't nearly as upset as Indira had feared. By the time he'd finally found them, his friends were ready to order their evening meal. "I thought I might find you here," the sorcerer grumbled as he stood between where Kiera and Indira sat at an inn table.

"How did you know we'd be here?" Kiera asked innocently.

"Because it serves the best food in town. When are your supplies going to be ready?"

"At sunset," Batai said after a sip of his ale. "We were planning to meet Szurgord after a nice meal. Care to join us?"

"Well, since I'm here."

During a sizeable meal and several ales, Belkidar told them very generally what he had discovered over the course of the past three nights. "The purpose of our journey hasn't changed," he said quietly, "but I'm afraid our future host knows quite a bit more about us than I'd previously thought."

"How can he know anything about us?" Indira asked quietly, nibbling on large shrimp.

"While we were…occupied, others were taking great pains to scout us." He looked into their faces. "I'll get into more detail when we meet up with the others."

They finished their meal in silence, the crackling fire in the old hearth the only sound. Each realized their enemy had collected vital information about them, information that would make their Quest even more difficult. Belkidar had planned to use an element of surprise for as long as possible, and although that advantage wouldn't last forever, maintaining some level of deception would've made their journey that much easier. But now that Hildegard had discovered some of their strengths and weaknesses, their Quest would prove much more difficult. There would be no easy steps along this road.

Belkidar finally stood. "Please allow me," he offered as the waiter approached the table. Indira, seated to Belkidar's right, noticed a faint light emerge from one of his jacket's deep pockets.

"Keep the change my good man," he offered, dropping several gold coins into the waiter's hand.

"Thank you, sir!"

"You're quite welcome. I've not had a finer meal in quite some time. Please share this with the chef."

"As you wish!" he said, rushing to the kitchen.

"That was very generous," Kiera offered as she rose from her chair.

"Not really. Sometimes, money really does grow on trees. Besides, in two links those coins will revert back to wood." With that he led the group out of the restaurant and into the street.

"Surely you cannot be serious!" Indira said, rushing to join him outside.

Belkidar smiled coyly as he mounted his horse. "My dear, do you really think I'm capable of such horrid things?"

"I certainly hope not," she said, smoothly climbing into her saddle. To her relief, any doubts were squashed with a pat on her back as he rode by.

Batai mounted Einar and guided them to Szurgord. Leading the other horses slowly down the smaller and less populated streets, Einar nimbly weaved his way to the smithy. Finally, after what seemed like links to the anxious group, Batai turned a familiar corner and found the small alley that fronted Szurgord's workshop. Batai waited patiently while his friends tied up their horses, Einar standing untethered next to him.

"Ah, good timing," Szurgord said as they entered.

Batai greeted him, extending his right hand. "Good evening, Szurgord. It's nice to see you again."

They grasped forearms. "And you. Welcome back."

"Thank you. I trust you had no difficulties?"

"Only with the large sword. It was almost too long for my forge!" he said, laughing. He bent down and removed a package from behind the counter. It was neatly wrapped in a cloth blackened by the polishing of metal. He set it on the countertop and slowly unfolded it, revealing in stages an immaculate sword, its finish reflecting the fires from the wall sconces more clearly than any mirror Batai had ever seen.

"I took the liberty of widening it at the hilt," Szurgord explained as he hoisted the weapon and offered it handle-first. "I think you'll find its balance improved."

Batai accepted it and performed a few practiced strokes, his expression evolving from fascination to amazement as he guided the weapon through the air. He finally laid it back on the counter. "You're truly an artist."

"You are most kind, sir," he replied, bending again behind the counter. The package he carefully set beside the sword was much larger than the first. Again, Szurgord meticulously folded the cloth aside.

Batai stared down at a flawless shield, its mirrored finish resembling the sword next to it. He noticed how large it was, at least half again as big as his old one. Into the boss, Szurgord had fashioned an enormous horse, and to Batai's astonishment, the two-dimensional image somehow resembled the energetic Einar to an impossible degree.

"Go ahead," Szurgord offered, nodding toward it. "It's not as heavy as it looks."

Batai took the shield, surprised to find it weighed half of what he'd expected. He turned and inspected the back, confused.

"It's my own recipe," Szurgord proudly explained.

"Incredible," Batai whispered. Kiera and Indira watched from a distance as Batai studied the polished metal. Belkidar stood silently in the corner, watching.

"Strap it on," Szurgord suggested. "I'd like to fit it while you're here."

Once completed, it suited Batai better than any shield he'd ever owned. He extended his arm, then pulled it close. Kiera stood amazed, for Szurgord had somehow created a shield that mated perfectly to Batai's body. Then he raised it, bringing the rim upward and forward in several attacking strokes. Astonished, Batai removed the shield and leaned it carefully against the counter. "Incredible."

"I'm glad you like it," Szurgord said, his eyes alive. "My lady?"

Kiera excitedly approached the counter. The smith again bent over and placed three small packages on the countertop. He kept two near but placed the third directly in front of her. "Be my guest," he offered.

Indira watched as Kiera's nimble fingers made quick work of the cloth, then gripped two identical daggers, their handles perfectly sized for her small hands. The blades were straight and viciously sharp. She twirled them, familiarizing herself with their weight and balance. "They're perfect," she said almost to herself, then reluctantly returned them to the cloth.

"Thank you. They're the most balanced throwing daggers I've ever created." He slid them aside, then pushed a second bundle toward her. "I designed these for quite another purpose."

Again, Kiera's fingers quickly revealed its contents. The first two daggers were quite small – the blades were only slightly longer than their handles – but these were far different. While these handles were a little longer, their elye-long blades ended in a serrated barb. The blades were relatively wide at the tang, but slowly narrowed along their length. Then, each widened again near its tip, forming a barb that resembled half of an arrow's head which encompassed the final quarter-elye of the blade. Kiera held them with their spines resting against the underside of her forearms. They fit her perfectly.

"They'll defend against swords or axes, and everything in between." Then he pushed the final package toward her. "I designed the last pair for close combat."

Intrigued, Kiera unwrapped it and soon held two daggers with noticeably curved edges. These were just as long as the second pair but seemed slightly shorter due to the curvature of the blades.

"You'll not find a sharper blade in the world. I guarantee it."

"Sir, I have no doubt," Kiera said, studying the blade's elegant arc.

"I also took the liberty of making some sheaths. I lined them with – "

"Thank you," Kiera said, mesmerized, slowly turning the daggers to examine them from all angles.

Szurgord smiled. "The last one was most challenging," he continued, lifting a large package from the floor behind the counter. Batai and Kiera cleared the countertop to make room for Gunnar's sword. Even with their help, it was much too large for the counter. Szurgord laid it diagonally so its handle rested near Batai.

The knight pulled the cloth away. They stood in silence, staring at Szurgord's masterpiece. It was enormous, magnificent, literally taking up their entire view. The handle was two elads long by itself, the blade stretching to almost three times that. Szurgord had etched intricate designs just above the hilt where it was well over an elye wide. On one side, he created a portrait of a solitary boy standing among several mountains, alone save for the sun to the east and the moon to the west, the boy's twin shadows somehow resembling a contented couple. On the other side stood a large man hoisting a sword over his head in front of a beautiful woodland background. The length of the depicted sword extended an elye down the very blade of Gunnar's extraordinary weapon. The look on the man's face revealed more than a picture ought to portray, his triumph and inner peace palpable.

Despite Szurgord's special 'recipe,' Batai struggled to lift it, his hands appearing tiny gripping the massive handle. After turning it to view it from all angles, he set it carefully back on the counter. "Szurgord, your skills are phenomenal," he said, rewrapping it in cloth. "I've worked with countless blacksmiths in my life, but I've never seen work like this. Not ever. I didn't even know it was possible."

"You're far too kind. But to fully appreciate these weapons, you have to do more than just look at them! Please, come with me."

They followed him through the rear door, Kiera bouncing in her excitement. Belkidar and Indira followed loosely behind, enjoying their friends' youthful exuberance.

The rear room of Szurgord's shop was enormous. A huge forge sat to their left, and further toward the rear wall sat the largest anvil Batai had ever seen. Two large tubs sat next to it. As Batai gazed to his right, the room transformed into a practice arena. There were straw figures equipped with various weapons and shields. At least a dozen logs stood in the near right corner, their ends secured in round holes in the floor, seemingly forming a small forest. Several wooden targets hung the length of the right wall, some of which still had daggers and arrows protruding from previous tests. In the far-right corner Batai noticed several marble columns, but they were too short to be useful for any architect. They were also in considerable disrepair, each having several nicks and gashes in the once-smooth surface. "What are those used for?"

"Funny you should mention them," Szurgord answered. "Attack one."

Batai glanced at his beautiful sword. "Never!"

"Trust me," Szurgord softly assured him.

Batai, torn between trusting the smith and his own instincts, looked from Szurgord to the marble columns. They had obviously been used for just this sort of test; the nicks in the marble were precisely the height of sword strokes.

"Go on!" Szurgord bellowed from the middle of the room.

Batai held his sword up, noting the contrast between its flawless, mirrored finish and the dull, battered surface of the old marble. It was difficult, but in the end, his trust in Szurgord prevailed. "As you wish."

He approached the nearest column, readied his sword, then swung it in a powerful arc, putting his body behind the blow. The piercing crash of metal and marble rang through the building, fragments erupting from the impact. Batai took a step back as the air cleared and, after a few moments, reluctantly raised his sword to better inspect the damage. To his surprise, the weapon remained flawless. "I don't understand."

Szurgord walked toward him, his pride evident. He continued past Batai and stopped just short of the target.

Batai studied the column, his awe intensifying as he realized his single stroke had sliced through the entire elad-wide pillar. With only one finger, Szurgord toppled the massive structure, its top half crashing to the floor.

Batai returned his attention to the sword. He twisted his wrist, inspected one side, then the other. Then he slowly lowered it, stared again at the blacksmith.

"Batai, Captain of the Paladin Order." Szurgord's gravelly voice filled every corner of the enormous room.

"You knew?" he asked, his eyes still wide.

"I recognized you from the first moment I saw you. I knew immediately, whatever your quest, you'd need the finest weapons this world has ever seen. So that's what I tried to make."

"Sir, you've done an amazing job of it."

"Thank you." He walked to the knight, took the sword and inspected the blade just as Batai had done a moment earlier. "Its edges will never dull, regardless of what you strike. These blades will remain as they are now, forever, immune to the passage of time."

"How can that be?"

"Come now," Szurgord said with a grin, "you don't really expect me to reveal all of my secrets, do you? It's taken generations to discover them, to hone the skills to make them useful. During these centacycles, my predecessors guarded and improved this process, each waiting for the time to finally put this knowledge to use. That time is now."

Batai nodded. "These aren't like the weapons I faced in challenges."

"No, these are...unique. When I recognized you, I understood their potential in your hands. Though you may face your own quest, mine is simple – to create the world's finest weapons for those few who fight history's most important battles. And while I don't need the details, why you'd need such a large sword is beyond me," he added almost to himself. Then his eyes returned to the paladin's. "I'm not surprised you've never come across weapons like these, because there *are* no other weapons like these."

Batai stared at him as those words sunk in.

"Unlike most of the people of Fendurgin, I took several cycles of my youth to travel far beyond this city. I've been in every type of smithy in the world, studying them, because I knew there'd come a time when I'd need to forge weapons, *these* weapons. And whenever that time came, I would not fail. After returning home, I explored hundreds of techniques from thousands of different smiths from across the continent. That knowledge, coupled with the experience gained from my father and the generations before him, provided a foundation that led me to new ideas, new techniques. For many cycles, I've practiced in secret, refining them. Then, when I saw you – a man renowned for his honor, his integrity – appear in my shop, I knew that time had come."

Belkidar had remained in the background, but now strode forward. "Do you know who I am?"

Szurgord studied him, then shook his head. "I don't think so."

"Well, I'm very pleased to meet you. I used to know one of your ancestors."

"Oh?" Szurgord said with a note of skepticism. "One of my grandparents?"

"In a manner of speaking. I was a good friend of your great, great, great – oh, let's just say lots of greats – grandfather."

Szurgord's eyebrows rose, disbelief spreading across his face like a shadow.

"His name was Szorbirg, and he was a dear friend for over six centacycles. Szorbirg was also a sorcerer, but he studied a very specific branch of alchemy, eventually focusing on metalwork." Szurgord watched his eyes grow distant.

"Fighting by my side in the War against Jenkar, Szorbirg battled seven of Jenkar's apprentices, but he always stayed one step ahead. I was only a quarter linak away, but I was in a similar situation. I managed to kill four of my attackers, but eight remained. Looking back, I should've fled then, come to his aid, but I was young and stupid. So I stayed until I killed the rest of them."

Belkidar slowly shook his head. "I didn't realize Jenkar was baiting Szorbirg. While his sorcerers kept him occupied, Jenkar had four gargantuids flank him. They circled behind, then descended on him. He never saw what killed him. They tore his body limb from limb as Jenkar's sorcerers watched, laughing."

"When I finally teleported to where I'd last seen my friend, Jenkar's seven apprentices were still chuckling. I won't describe the despicable acts the gargantuids were committing. Fury consumed me. Some might argue the actions I took next were even worse than what happened to Szorbirg." He paused, lost in his thoughts. "Nearly a mooncycle passed before their bodies had decomposed enough to kill them."

After several moments, Szurgord found his voice. "You fought in the War? But how can that be?"

"The same way that you're able to forge weapons that slice through marble columns."

"Who *are* you?"

"I'm sorry. I should've introduced myself. My name is Belkidar. It really is a pleasure to meet you. You look remarkably like him."

"Belkidar? As in the Sorcerer? I've heard those stories."

"Oh? I hope they were accurate."

"But they're only stories!"

"Belkidar, do you mind if I try my daggers now?" Kiera asked.

"You really believe he's Belkidar the Sorcerer, don't you?" Szurgord asked her. Then he turned toward Batai and Indira, saw the same certainty. "You all do."

"Of course we do," Kiera said offhandedly as she eagerly fingered the point of one of her new daggers. "This *is* Belkidar, Szurgord. He's telling the truth."

"If you're right, then one of my ancestors – Szorbirg – was also a sorcerer."

"That's right," Belkidar confirmed. "He was perhaps the finest alchemist the world has ever known. I believe that's the reason you're so adept at metalwork yourself. Certain traits are passed down, you know."

Szurgord considered that for several moments.

"There you have it," Kiera interrupted. "It's settled then. Szurgord's a genius blacksmith because one of his ancestors was a sorcerer and an alchemist. Now let's see if I can do as well as Batai did on that marble." Kiera took one of her throwing daggers in each hand, then cocked her right arm. Batai, however, was slightly quicker.

"Szurgord, today you've made your family proud, justified their endless links in front of a hot furnace. I can't describe our Quest to you, but you should know it's directly related to Szorbirg's death. I pledge I'll do everything in my power to avenge that death, and it will be accomplished with metal forged from his own blood."

"Well said," Belkidar agreed.

Szurgord smiled, slowly nodded. "My task is complete then. Thank you, Batai. You've given me peace."

Although she respected the significance of the moment, Kiera had heard enough conversation for the time being. She turned toward the tallest marble column, then in a flash threw a dagger. It whistled softly as it spun end over end, a glimmering star in the waning sunlight. Then it struck the column, sliding easily into the marble to its hilt, a brilliant note hanging in the air.

Distracted from their conversation, the other looked to the column, trying to discover the source of the tone.

Kiera threw the second dagger, and it embedded itself a half-elye next to the first. With a satisfied grin, she walked quickly to the target and pulled both weapons free. "My dear Szurgord, you've really outdone yourself. I could get used to these," she added, turning her back to the column. "Yes, I do believe I could become quite accustomed to these marvelous little toys," she repeated to herself as she measured twenty paces before letting two more daggers fly.

"My friend," Batai said to Szurgord as he reached into the inner pockets of his tunic, "weapons of this quality are priceless, but I'd still like to offer payment," he explained, removing a leather pouch stuffed with the gold coins Belkidar had created.

"Batai, you know full well money wasn't what motivated me."

"Of course," he answered. "Be that as it may, Belkidar here is also uniquely talented. As a result, we rarely have need for money." He smiled as he placed the bag on a short marble column, the coins clinking loudly through the leather. "Besides, carrying such a burden would only hinder us."

Chapter 13
Brodor

*A pessimist is one who makes difficulties of his
opportunities and an optimist is one who makes
opportunities of his difficulties.*

Harry Truman

The darkness of early morning found them well rested, each having
already packed their belongings and gathered outside a link before
sunrise, the sound of crickets and cicadas deafening compared to the
peaceful inn. They mounted their horses and turned toward the city's
southern gate.

"I'm going to miss this place," Kiera remarked as they traveled
swiftly through the deserted streets.

"Why is that?" Indira asked.

"It reminds me of Kordare. Fendurgin is much larger, of course,
but it has a similar feel."

"I know exactly what you mean. Certain regions of Ætheldell
remind me of home."

Einar came up alongside, an enormous shadow in the darkness. "I
don't understand," Batai said, "why some areas but not others?"

Indira gave him a look of incomprehension, as though the answer
was obvious. "Parts of a forest are not unlike parts of a city. Each of
your buildings is different, making each neighborhood distinct. In a
forest, every tree is unique. I can close my eyes on a calm day and
sense exactly what they feel."

"Trees feel?" Kiera asked incredulously.

"Of course they do. They're alive, just like any one of us. Why
would they not?"

"Because they don't have brains for a start."

"Feelings do not come from the mind, they come from the soul."

Kiera had no answer to that, considered the notion that trees had emotions. Finally, as they neared the southern gate, she accepted there was considerably more to a forest than she had understood. "I'll try to keep an open mind, but it's going to take me a while to accept the idea that trees have souls."

Indira smiled. "I understand. It has taken me a long time to accept the buildings of your cities also have souls."

Shocked, Kiera blinked several times, not knowing how to reply.

Indira said nothing, but her slight smirk spoke volumes.

Kiera burst into laughter, relieved more than anything. Indira soon joined her.

Batai looked at them before giving Belkidar a quizzical look.

"I've learned many things over the course of my life. One of them is to never ask questions like the one you're about to ask. Instead, just feel fortunate they're occupied with something other than why your beard is too long."

Despite the old man's advice, Batai couldn't help but laugh.

Only a few links passed before they reached the general area where they expected to meet up with their large friends. They rode through a magnificent sunrise, its warmth a welcomed change from the chill of the pre-dawn coastal breeze. They traveled quickly along the highway that led from Fendurgin to Brodor, initially crossing the small plains south of the city and through the sweet smell of bluegrass, then into the trees beyond. Not long after, Kiera led them into the wilderness west of the road where they were greeted with the scents of moss and wild ginger.

"What's the problem?" Belkidar asked Kiera.

"Who said anything about a problem?"

"Why have we stopped?" he asked slowly, his patience waning.

"Listen."

They sat motionlessly atop their horses, a smile forming on Indira's face. After what seemed like an eternity, Belkidar's impatience broke the silence.

"What exactly are we supposed to hear?"

"Is that not snoring?" Indira asked.

"Yes. Two sets, to be exact."

Belkidar strained again, then heard an uncommonly low rumble coming from the distant trees. His slow recognition was too much for Kiera to pass up. She stared at him but remarkably said nothing.

"My hearing isn't as good as it used to be," he explained.

Kiera smiled, nodded slowly in agreement.

"Listen, kid, you'll be lucky to hear as half as well as I do by the time you're half my age."

Kiera chuckled, knowing she had no hope of living that long. "As you say, Grandfather." Then she led the others through the woods to greet their sleeping friends, their snoring growing louder as they approached. After traveling nearly half a linak, she finally found them fast asleep, hidden within a dense cluster of trees.

Brohdan heard their approach. He raised his long neck, his eyes glowing amber in the deep shadows beneath the trees. "Gunnar, they're here."

Gunnar's eyes opened a crack, spotted his friends, then rolled over and drifted back to sleep.

"Forgive him," Brohdan said quietly. "He's been a little busy these past few days."

Indira inspected their campsite. "It appears so," she concluded, taking in the numerous skeletons scattered about the clearing.

"Gunnar's an excellent hunter."

"Do you mind keeping it down?" the hunter asked.

"I'm afraid we must be on our way," Belkidar answered. "We've got linops to cover before nightfall."

Gunnar slowly rose to a sitting position, blinking in the morning sun. "What took you so long?"

"I had some business to take care of. I'll explain on the road."

He nodded, then rose to his feet. "Is everything all right?"

"We'll see."

Gunnar gave Batai a questioning look.

"He's been evasive since we left Fendurgin."

He shrugged. "Give me a moment." He wiped down his sword before returning it to is scabbard, then fastened its leather straps across his chest. Next, he retrieved the empty water containers from the pack horses before joining Brohdan next to a small stream.

Batai noticed his sword, but postponed that topic, instead focusing on the many skeletons that littered their camp, "There seems to be more skulls than usual."

Gunnar smiled coyly as he returned the filled water containers to the pack horses. "They were hunting me."

Batai grunted. "I can't think of many creatures that'd be that foolish. Especially with Brohdan at your side."

"He wasn't with me."

"Still," Kiera agreed, "what would have the courage – or stupidity – to attack a giant?"

"Cerebi."

"Impossible!" Belkidar said. "They've been extinct since the War!"

"Apparently not." He explained how they surrounded him, calling to each other in perfect harmony.

"What did you do?" Indira asked.

"The only thing I could – defend myself. It was weird, though. The more I killed, the more determined the rest became."

"In what way?" Belkidar asked.

"They came at me in coordinated attacks, which isn't surprising since wolves do the same thing. But when I killed the first three or four, the others grew even more determined. The more I killed, the more aggressive they became. I would've expected them to eventually give up, but instead I had to kill every last one."

Belkidar nodded slowly as he listened. "Anything else?"

He thought for a moment. "Yes. I'm not fond of dog. Too stringy."

"Briz would appreciate that. But this only confirms what I learned." He paused, considering how the discovery of cerebi fit into what he'd heard in Fendurgin.

Batai broke the silence. "Well, I'm glad you still know how to use a sword. After the keviloks, I was beginning to think you had no use for them."

He shrugged.

"We happened to meet a most interesting person in Fendurgin." He paused, noticing Gunnar's expression change from annoyed patience to mounting curiosity.

"Well?" he thundered.

Batai told him about the weapons he'd encountered in some of his challenges, then explained Fendurgin's reputation for blacksmiths, one in particular. "I took the opportunity to pay this man a visit. It wasn't a waste of time."

"Did he make something for you?" Gunnar asked, excited.

"I'm getting to that."

"Oh, Batai! Just tell him!" Kiera squeaked.

"That's what I'm doing, Kiera. These things have a certain decorum."

"Batai – " Kiera growled through clenched teeth.

"As I was saying," he interrupted, "we paid this blacksmith a visit. He took our orders and said they'd be ready in only two days. When we returned, Belkidar joined us. We ordered nine weapons in all, and Szurgord presented them to us in turn." As he talked, he pulled his sword from its scabbard and offered it to Gunnar.

Batai gave him time to examine it, watched as he turned it over in his big hands, noticed the smile spread across his face. "Needless to say, we were impressed," he said, eventually taking it back. "Next, Szurgord presented me with a shield." He unstrapped it from Einar's left side and again offered it to Gunnar.

"I ordered six daggers," Kiera continued, drawing each pair from their sheaths as she explained their purpose.

"You only have six now?" Gunnar asked, giving Batai his shield back.

"Of course not! I kept a some of my old ones, my favorites. Plus a few more that you don't need to know about."

Gunnar smiled, then looked confused. "But that's only eight. Where's the last one?"

"Right here," Batai explained, patting Einar's flank.

"What do you need besides a sword and shield?"

Batai dismounted, then unstrapped the huge weapon. "This definitely wasn't made for me," he said, handing it up to him.

Despite the blankets that concealed it, Gunnar immediately recognized what Szurgord must've created. "I don't know what to say."

"Say you'll unwrap it!" Kiera suggested, bouncing in her saddle.

Still stunned, Gunnar slowly removed the blankets. In his hands, what had always appeared ridiculously oversized now seemed appropriate, perfect. He gripped the handle and slowly slid it from its scabbard, his eyes growing wider as more of the flawless metal was revealed. He looked in succession from Batai, Kiera and then Indira, remained silent as they rested on Belkidar. His expression conveyed more appreciation than could any words. Then he took several moments, studying each depiction Szurgord had inscribed for him. "Thank you," he managed, his voice hoarse.

"Try it on that," Kiera offered, indicating a half-buried boulder.

"No! Never!"

Batai smiled, remembering his own hesitation. "Trust us, Gunnar. This is no ordinary blade."

Gunnar met his gaze, then slowly walked to the edge of the clearing. Gripping the sword with both hands, he raised it, then brought it down in a brutal arc. The long blade whirred through the air, becoming only slightly louder as it passed through the stone, a soft ringing the only lasting sound.

Gunnar stood frozen, his sword held before him, stunned. Then he turned to the boulder. It too appeared unchanged, but then he noticed a thin line running diagonally across its surface. He took his left hand from the sword's handle and pushed, the muscles of his arm and back flexing as the top of the stone toppled to the ground. Then he returned his eyes to the sword. "It's not even scratched!"

"That's what makes Szurgord so unique," Batai replied. "But I know how much your old sword means to you."

Gunnar smiled. "True, it is sentimental, but I'll cherish this one for the rest of my life," he said, looking at each of his friends. "Thank you."

"Let's continue this conversation on the road," Belkidar gruffly suggested.

After loading Gunnar's old sword and scabbard onto Einar, Belkidar maneuvered his horse next to Gunnar as Kiera led them back to the road. "We're likely to have a lot of company thanks to all of the trade between Fendurgin and Brodor. Would you mind going with Brohdan?"

"Of course not. I'll be around if you need me."

The group made excellent progress throughout the remainder of the day, Gunnar actually having to make an effort to keep pace as he navigated the woodland. As sunset loomed, they searched for a secluded area to spend the night. With Brohdan's help, they didn't have to search long.

"I found a nice basin."

"Excellent. Where?"

"Go east, past a small ridgeline. I'll guide you as you get closer."

"Kiera, head east into the trees. Brohdan's found our campsite."

"Yes, Grandfather."

As Brohdan guided the group nearly a linak through the trees, he also took the opportunity to track down Gunnar and explain the plan.

"I'll see you there," he replied, turning his massive shoulders toward the northeast. Brohdan then took flight to update the others' progress.

To his relief they were heading directly for the basin. He turned
north and flew far enough away to remain undetected. He then turned
to the southeast and flew directly toward the group from their rear.
Hugging the treetops, he passed just above the pack horses, Batai,
Belkidar, Indira, and finally Kiera. None ducked their head in response
to his antics, even the horses having long ago become accustomed to
his flying. Once he passed Kiera, he continued in the same direction
toward the basin, confirming their course.

Gunnar was the first to arrive, a low rumble from deep within
Brohdan's throat signaling his location. The others arrived a few drus
later. Kiera immediately scoured the area before dismounting, but
Batai knew better. "Brohdan, anything around?"

"Nothing of interest."

"Thank you. Belkidar, do you think this will suffice?"

"Yes," he answered shortly.

"Is everything all right?" Brohdan asked him.

"I'm not sure," he answered before dismounting and unrolling his
sleeping canvas.

Indira and Batai did the same. In the meantime, Gunnar collected
firewood and stacked it toward one side of the camp. After clearing a
large area, he dug a shallow pit where he laid out some of the wood.

Once finished, Brohdan extended his neck toward it, then blew a
small fire stream onto the logs. It cast a dim glow over the area, the
nearby foliage adopting an orange hue in the early evening darkness.
His liquid flames clung to the wood, and soon a welcomed fire cracked
in the depths of the secluded basin.

"Thanks!" Gunnar said as he retrieved two medium-sized logs
from the wood he'd collected. Indira caught up with him as he
carefully placed them over the flames.

"Would you mind helping me hunt?"

"Of course not. Just give me a moment to get my sword."

She smiled, embarrassed. "I need your help carrying our prey, not
killing it."

"Oh."

"I'm sorry. I have gone too long without hunting. I hope you understand."

"Of course I do," he answered, thinking back to his encounter with the cerebi.

Indira led him through the trees, and although the sun had set long ago, the half-moon helped Gunnar navigate the rocky terrain.

"Do you see them?" she asked a half link later, her voice mingling with the swaying tree branches above, the teeming insects below.

Gunnar shook his head.

"Let's see if we can get closer without scaring them off."

Gunnar smiled to himself, then followed her as quietly as he could, but the utter silence of her movements put his to shame.

She swiftly made her way south of where the sounds originated, Gunnar realizing she was carefully circling her way downwind. Then she turned north. After a few drus, they crested a small hill, beyond which stood several deer. Gunnar lay down next to her.

"How many do you think you could carry?" she whispered.

Gunnar grinned. "As many as you can kill."

She nodded once, nocking an arrow.

"How are you going to hit them from here?"

"Through the heart," she replied, confused.

"From this far away? Through all those trees? In this darkness?"

"It is only a few hundred elads. As for the trees, there are many paths an arrow can travel," she explained, motioning toward the grazing deer.

Gunnar shook his head but said nothing.

Indira drew back her bowstring, aimed slightly down at the distant deer, and released the arrow. Before it found its target, she had released two more.

Gunnar struggled to keep up, quickly moving his head side to side as he tried to watch both Indira and her arrows. He soon abandoned it, instead concentrating on just her arrows and their path through the tangle of trees, branches, and leaves.

She shot her first three arrows in short succession, but released the next volley at uneven intervals. Gunnar knew why. The first three found their targets standing motionless, grazing on the wet grass. But there wasn't enough time to kill a fourth deer that way, since by then her first arrow would've struck home, panicking the others.

Gunnar instantly recognized the genius of her second volley. The trees and branches that lay between her and the deer significantly restricted her options, so she monitored the handful of slender paths through them, smoothly fired arrow after arrow as she anticipated the deers' panicked movements. Gunnar watched in awe as each arrow thudded home.

And then it was over. Indira stood, watched the remaining deer flee through the trees.

Gunnar slowly rose to his feet, still processing what he'd just seen.

Before long they reached the first deer. Gunnar surveyed the area and failed to find a single stray arrow. "Didn't you miss even once?"

"Of course not! Not since I was a very young girl." Indira added more softly.

Gunnar noted the pain in her voice. "I'm sorry. I didn't mean to offend you."

Indira shook her head. "No, I am the one who should apologize."

Gunnar let the subject drop and followed her from deer to deer. Indira retrieved her arrows, examining each while wiping it clean. Most of the time, she simply put it back into her quiver, but a few forced the slightest of scowls. Eventually, Gunnar's curiosity got the better of him. "What in the world are you looking at?"

She shook her head. "Do you see this?" she asked, handing the arrow up to him.

"The tip?"

"The scuff on it."

"Yeah," he said, handing it back to her.

"It scraped against the ribcage."

"So?"

"I should have done better," she said, her disappointment surprising him.

"Indira, you shot this animal when it was panicking and unpredictable. From over four hundred elads away. Using a tiny path through thousands of branches. In the dark! I don't understand how you could even *see* the ribcage, so how can you be upset with yourself for being less than a finger width off?"

"That can be the difference between success and failure. I was aiming for the heart, not the ribcage."

Gunnar had never seen her like this. "What's wrong?"

She paused. The moonlight shimmered down her long, black hair, exaggerating her pale skin. "When I was a young girl, my friends and I went to fetch water from a nearby stream. Just as we knelt with our waterskins, we were attacked by wolves. They were like skeletons, starving and desperate. By the time I realized what was happening, they were already on Keluvi. My friends ran, all except Jovina and I. We shot three, but could not save her. The rest turned on us. Jovina was closer, they attacked her next. We shot at least ten arrows at them, but as they got closer, she fled. I killed three more as they chased her, but it was the one I missed..." Indira looked down, silent for a long time.

"The wolf leapt on her back as she ran, his weight causing her to stumble. I shot it as she fell, still remember its yelp as it landed next to her. In tears, I ran to Jovina, only to find her blood pooling beneath her. The wolf bit her neck, clung there as she stumbled and fell."

"Indira, you were only a girl, I'm sure you did the best you could."

"No. From that moment, I decided I would never miss again. I owe Jovina that at least."

"Maybe. But I've never believed a person was guilty when an honest effort was made."

"But I had never truly dedicated myself toward anything before her death. Since then, I have." She raised her head. "Let us take these to Kiera."

Gunnar nodded. He stacked the deer carcasses and heaved them into his arms before turning back to the camp. Indira fell in step next to him.

"I don't like how you torture yourself with something that happened cycles ago. Not even Belkidar is perfect. Imagine if he let past mistakes haunt him." He shook his head. "Sooner or later you must make peace with yourself. And with Jovina."

She said nothing for several moments, Gunnar's footfalls loud against the silent forest. "It is not easy."

"Regrets never are," he agreed, recalling his own past. "But you've got friends here."

She thought of his horrific childhood, distantly understood the obstacles he was forced to overcome. She reached up, gently touched his huge arm with her small hand.

Kiera had the fire blazing when they returned. He took the deer to the edge of the basin where he quickly prepared each before taking them two-by-two to where Kiera waited next to a small stack of long metal rods. "Belkidar's work?"

Kiera nodded. "He made them from dead tree branches."

He fastened the meat to them, then leveled each on pairs of long stakes that Batai had pounded into the ground. With Belkidar's help, Kiera soon had four deer cooking over the large fire, Gunnar having left the remaining six for Brohdan. But she quickly realized the task of constantly rotating the meat was more than she could handle. "I could use some help here!" she demanded as she frantically went from one rotisserie to the next.

"All you had to do was ask," Belkidar said.

Kiera returned her gaze to the deer where she saw them slowly rotating above the fire. "You could've done that a quarter link ago!"

"True, but then we would've missed the entertainment."

Kiera let it go, more relieved than annoyed, and took a seat next to Brohdan.

"Are you ever going to explain what you discovered in Fendurgin?" Batai asked.

"Now's a good time." Belkidar took a seat with his back against a large oak, the Staff resting comfortably across his lap, his face flickering in the firelight. "As I think you know, my main reason for going through Fendurgin was to gather information, specifically on what lies in wait for us once we reach Katja. What I discovered was not encouraging."

"During the first two nights, I disguised myself as a commoner, a rather poor one at that. I went to a few shady pubs and talked with people deep into the night. That's the best way to get accurate information, by the way. But the key is to blend in. If you don't, you're just wasting your time. In that case, you might as well – "

"Belkidar. What did you find?" Kiera asked.

"Oh, sorry. I got distracted. But when you're my age, you tend to notice some of society's peculiarities that others miss."

"Belkidar!"

"Right. The first night I talked with some miners who work just outside the city. I learned many things. For example, the cost of ore is going up, yet they don't see any of the profits."

"Belkidar," Kiera said through clenched teeth.

"Right. Over several – dozen – ales, they told me a handful of people with strange accents had come through asking if anyone had seen a very old man with a long white beard."

"That doesn't necessarily mean they were looking for you," Batai pointed out.

"True enough. They also asked if anyone had seen a man who stood over eight elads tall."

"Oh."

"Somehow Hildegard discovered that we have Gunnar with us. In hindsight, I think he learned that when we fought the keviloks in the Wruloric Wastelands. If so, that battle was only a distraction, a way to occupy us while his spies observed unnoticed. I'm now convinced the bandits we fought west of Trisett was also planned."

Brohdan nodded. "I can't imagine he got an accurate report since all of those men were killed."

"On the contrary," Batai interjected, "the fact he didn't receive any report at all was telling."

"Exactly," Belkidar agreed.

"I wonder if Gunnar's cerebi were Hildegard's idea too," Indira offered.

"If Gunnar hadn't found them, I'm sure they would've ambushed us on our way to Brodor."

"Hold on," Kiera said. "If Hildegard had spies in the Wruloric, then he knows all about us. Including Brohdan!"

"I have no doubt. By the time we reach his fortress in Gul Krul, we can be sure of one thing – he'll be prepared for a Broglia Black, as well as a giant, an archer, a spy, and the Captain of the Order of Paladins."

They considered that, each having believed the presence of a Broglia Black, if unaccounted for, would all but guarantee victory. Now they realized how hollow that strategy had been.

Finally, Indira spoke. "What could Hildegard recruit to compete against a Broglia?"

"That's just it. I'm not sure, and that's what worries me. He knows a great deal about our strengths and objectives, but we know very little about his. We know we must face the Five Defenses he devised centacycles ago. Once we defeat them, we must make our way to his fortress where we'll most likely face his sorcerer apprentices. There, of course, I must face Hildegard. Now we must also consider whatever he's planning for Brohdan."

She nodded. "That explains why you appeared as a commoner, but why did you dress as a noble during our final night there?"

"For two reasons. During the second night, I heard about a very exclusive party being thrown by one of Fendurgin's more influential politicians. By attending the event, I hoped to gather information not generally available in pubs."

"Were you invited?" Batai asked.

"Of course not. They don't know me. And even if they did, I didn't go as myself."

"Then why weren't you turned away?"

He smiled, looked at Kiera, an eyebrow raised. She explained. "If you act as though you belong there – as though the festivities couldn't possibly take place without you – then you're guaranteed to be accepted at any stuffy party. Especially if it's thrown by politicians."

Belkidar's smile widened. "And that's exactly what I did. At first, those snobs didn't know what to think, but the more I acted like a pompous fool, the more accepted I became. After a link, I was the guest of honor," he added, chuckling.

"What was the second reason for going?" Indira asked.

"Simple – those types of parties generally serve the finest ales. At any rate, I discovered a great deal. Within a few links, both host and guest were drunk, and leading their conversations was actually a lot easier than the ones with the exhausted commoners in those filthy pubs. Maybe the rich are easily swayed by anyone projecting power. Or, perhaps the people in the pubs become more opinionated as they drink?"

"Belkidar! What did you discover at this party?" Kiera demanded.

"Considering how frequently he gets sidetracked, it is a wonder he was able to lead these conversations at all," Indira whispered to Brohdan.

"I heard that, miss. Now, as I was *trying* to say, my goal initially was to determine the status of trade in the city. As I expected, the bulk of it stems from the many ties that exist between Brodor and Fendurgin. Also, many of these gentlemen earned their wealth from trading with the other cities of Tymoteu. But I was more interested in trade between Brodor and Katja."

"We all know Brodor is the largest sea port in the world. In fact, that's precisely why we're departing there for Katja – its sheer volume of shipping will help conceal us. Now, where was I?" he asked, his smile directed at Kiera.

"I'm not sure. I must've dozed off."

"Oh, yes. Trade between the two continents has never really flourished since the War. Even still, business has waned considerably in recent mooncycles. I tried to find the reason, but none at the party could offer an explanation. I'm curious as to what ideas we can come up with."

Gunnar was the first to speak. "Pirates?

Batai nodded. "Or maybe it just became more economical to trade here, on Tymoteu. The overhead would be far less."

"Both excellent ideas," Belkidar agreed. "I thought of them too, so I dropped a few hints to make it appear as though my intoxicated friends came up with them. Unfortunately, both were quickly dismissed."

"The traders of Katja expect war," Kiera offered quietly. "Did you ask specifically about the status of the weapons trade?"

"In fact I did. To my surprise, it's increased dramatically."

"That's it, then," she sighed. "Traders are scrambling to find a profit in the only sector they can – weapons."

"Unfortunately, that's the same conclusion I came up with, and it certainly doesn't bode well for us. Rumors must've slowly trickled down from Hildegard's inner circle to Katja's traders. That means he's known of our intentions for quite a while, and we can be sure he's used that time to fortify his Defenses and refine his strategy."

"Well, nobody ever said this was going to be easy," Brohdan offered. "If you think about it, this really doesn't change anything. I must face an enemy whose abilities likely rival my own. And you know what? That doesn't bother me. I never expected this to be easy."

"Well said," Batai agreed. "He's right. Hildegard may have learned more about us, but all we could've ever done anyway is worry about what we can control. Our focus should be on us, not him."

Gunnar was shaking his head. "You all speak as though this doesn't even bother you. Well, it bothers me! Don't you understand? Hildegard will have found something to rival Brohdan!"

That forced the others to silence, the fire's crackling and occasional pops the only sounds. Then Gunnar stood. "Why didn't he bother to find something to rival *me*?"

The group breathed a collective sigh of relief. "How could he possibly find anything to challenge you?" Kiera asked.

Belkidar smiled, then considered their options. "I'm pretty confident we know Hildegard's general plan, even if we don't know the specifics. We can finalize some of our strategy while we're crossing the ocean, but most of the details will have to be worked out once we get there and see things for ourselves. I'm a little tempted to try and get more information in Brodor, but I really don't think there's much more we can discover from here. Besides, if we're spotted, we'll give Hildegard the one piece of information he doesn't yet have – our schedule." He paused, shook his head. "Let's not linger in Brodor. We can make our way down to the main port. I'll buy a ship, we can load it with whatever supplies we might need and head out to sea. Brohdan can meet up with us once it's safe."

"Where should I meet you?" Gunnar asked.

"Let's rendezvous a few linops north of Brodor. If we meet at night, we can get pretty close to shore, but you'll have to swim the rest of the way. We'll be fine as long as we get far enough out to sea before sunrise."

They removed the deer from the rotisseries and began eating. Brohdan quickly finished his half-dozen while Gunnar enjoyed three of the four that Kiera had cooked. When the others had difficulties eating even half of theirs, Gunnar graciously finished it for them.

It was at that moment Brohdan realized there's a certain contentedness in having a plan, even a half-formulated one. An uncertain future breeds insecurity and doubt, but now theirs was clear. Brohdan enjoyed his meal while he listened to their conversation. He knew there was danger in his future, danger he couldn't yet fathom, but sharing it with these friends strengthened his resolve.

The next morning proved colder than usual, made worse considering winter lay less than a mooncycle away, but they eventually managed to pry themselves from their warm sleeping blankets and pack their belongings.

"I'll be east of the road," Gunnar said.

"Right," Kiera answered, climbing into her saddle. "Watch yourself."

"You too." Brohdan followed him through the trees, careful not to topple any of them.

"I guess it's just us, then," Batai said as Einar turned toward the road. "Shall we?"

"Of course," Kiera answered, leading them back to the highway. Belkidar filed in quietly behind Indira.

"You are quiet," she noticed.

"I'm not much of a morning person."

"But mornings are beautiful! It is the beginning of a new day, a time when you realize it is totally up to you where it may lead."

"Hmph. It's people like you that give them a bad name," he mumbled to himself as he drew his cloak closer around his shoulders.

Indira looked at him for a moment, then turned and laughed softly to herself, her green eyes sparkling in the dawn sunlight.

They soon reached the road and, once there, made swift progress. Belkidar communicated with Brohdan several times throughout the day. Because Gunnar's journey through the forest offered more challenges, he wanted to make sure they didn't outpace him. To his surprise, that didn't seem to be an issue. More times than not, Brohdan reported that Gunnar was actually ahead of them.

"How can that be?" the sorcerer asked.

"The road weaves around the terrain. Gunnar's path is more...direct."

"How direct can it be with all those trees in the way?"

"Maybe you should take a look for yourself."

"Good idea. It's been a while since I spread my wings."

"I'm going ahead to take a look," Belkidar told the others. "I'll meet up with you later."

"Be careful," Kiera answered, "I'm sure we'll see more traffic as we get closer to Brodor." But she wasn't sure if he understood her, for as she finished, she saw a bright, white-blue light hover over his saddle. She was able to discern a vague silhouette within it, but it lasted less than a dru. Then the light vanished, revealing a familiar eagle perched on Belkidar's saddle. He jumped into the air, spread his wings, tucked his talons beneath his tail, and climbed effortlessly into the blue sky. "Incredible."

"I can only imagine what that must be like," Indira agreed.

"Where is he now?" Belkidar asked.

"Just ahead," Brohdan answered behind him.

"Why don't you take the lead since you know where we're headed."

Brohdan nosed over, flapping his enormous wings. "Let me know if I go too fast for you."

"I'm sure I'll be fine."

Taking advantage of the eagle's incredible sight, Belkidar detected movement several thousand elads ahead. As they flew closer, it became clear exactly how Gunnar was able to move so quickly through the forest. He jogged tirelessly, weaving around the larger trees and trampling those that where smaller and more flexible, that latter springing back up once he passed over them. "Nicely done!"

"He jogs like that for a half link or so, then walks for a couple," Brohdan explained. "Every once in a while, he'll come across a group of bigger trees. He has to go around those, but they're not very common."

"We'll reach Brodor sooner than I thought," he replied, banking to the west. "I'll catch up with the others and let them know. As long as we don't have any delays, we should reach Brodor's northern outskirts in two days. Keep in touch."

Belkidar's estimate was accurate. After forty links, Kiera found herself nearing Brodor's northern settlements. "I'm afraid the road will become a lot busier if we go much further."

"Very well." His eyes turned distant. *"Please meet up with Gunnar and ask him to make his way east and find someplace we can rendezvous in two night's time. Make sure you send me an accurate description since you won't be around to guide us back to it."*

"Will do."

"Meet up with us in three or four days. That'll give us enough time to put some distance between us and Brodor's other ships." He paused. *"And Brohdan?"*

"Yes?"

"Be safe."

"See you soon. Just make sure you don't sink before I get there."

"I'll do what I can," the sorcerer replied with a smile.

"You'll do what?" Kiera asked, confused.

"My perpetual job of keeping you out of trouble. We're to meet Gunnar in two nights, Brohdan in three."

"Will he be able to find us?" Indira asked.

"I'm sure of it. I just hope we have the same luck finding Gunnar."

Late afternoon on the next day, Indira crested a gently rolling hill, revealing Tymoteu's most populated city. "Magnificent! I have never seen anything like it!"

"That's because there *is* nothing else like it," Belkidar answered.

"I never imagined there could be this many people living together. What causes so many to live in one place?"

"Jobs, mostly," Kiera explained.

"Exactly," Belkidar agreed. "Many centacycles ago, Brodor established itself in two economic areas – fishing and trade. While KelKinney is a very successful fishing community in its own right, Brodor long ago established itself as the dominant fishing industry on this continent. When trade opportunities with Katja opened several centacycles ago, Brodor was the first to initiate contact. That one decision has paid dividends to this day, making it the world's chief trading hub."

They continued for another half link, then decided to make camp before the road became too crowded. "In the morning, we can make our way to one of the smaller ports, buy our ship, then head out."

"Why not leave at night?" Kiera asked.

Belkidar shook his head. "That'd help keep us hidden, but few set out at night. Morning's when the fishing is best, and it keeps the traders safer from pirates. If we wait until morning, we'll blend in with the other ships and hopefully slip out unnoticed."

"But won't that work against us when we come back to pick up Gunnar? You know, at night?"

"Not unless we're spotted. We'll stay in remote waters far to the north of Brodor, away from all of the shipping routes."

Kiera nodded, thinking the plan through. "You think of everything, don't you?"

"No, not everything. Like what's to eat tonight."

"Don't worry about that. I saved some dried sausage and cheese for a special occasion."

"I knew I brought you for a reason."

"We're setting up for the night about a linak north of the city gates. Tomorrow morning we'll buy a ship and head out with the local fishermen and traders. After dusk, we'll turn around and head back to pick up Gunnar – if we know where that happens to be."

"Don't worry, we'll choose a cove that you'll find easily enough."

It didn't take long for Gunnar to find a place where they could stretch out unseen during the night. "I'll see you tomorrow," he managed as he fell asleep.

"I hope so," Brohdan answered, smiling as he watched his friend pass into unconsciousness.

Chapter 14
The Celornorin Ocean

We are what we repeatedly do. Excellence, therefore,
is not an act but a habit.

Aristotle

The rising sun was magnificent, its light glimmering on a calm Celornorin Ocean. Brohdan and Gunnar were heading toward it, the trees' long shadows becoming lost in the lingering darkness behind them. They traveled in silence, both enjoying the serenity of the morning, and of their friendship.

"Do you actually plan on buying a ship today?"

"Look, this is my specialty, Belkidar," Kiera replied shortly. "You'd be amazed how far a little patience can get you."

"But if we don't buy one soon, we'll miss the outgoing wave!"

"Relax. Really, Belkidar, I'm shocked you haven't died of a heart attack by now," she said, blinking innocently as she approached the morning's fourth vendor.

To his relief, this one offered a ship that met her expectations. Within a quarter link, she had negotiated the sale.

"I'm very impressed," Batai said. "But why barter at all when we have Belkidar with us?"

"You assume the price is the goal," Kiera said, her dimples flashing in the morning sun.

"Ah, you enjoy the game of it. I can see why, too. That was a better price than I could've gotten."

"Well, I had several advantages."

"Oh?" he asked, knowing full well he was taking the bait.

"I've found most salesmen become uncomfortable when the pace and direction of the conversation is dictated by the customer."

"Uh-huh," he said doubtfully, staring at her.

"I've also realized the nature of a man is to feel protective of a woman. I simply use that weakness against him."

A slow smile spread across his face. "I feel sorry for your future husband," he added as he walked with Einar to where their newly-acquired ship lay bobbing in the clear blue water.

Gunnar led them down the coast. They kept to the trees as they searched for a location that was large enough to conceal themselves, but also easily identifiable from the ocean. "I'm hungry," he said, ducking below a tree branch.

"Me too. Let's see if we can find something to eat."

Before long, Batai had familiarized himself with the ship. "All we need now is a crew."

"Never mind that," Belkidar said, waving his hand. "Just stand on the deck like you know what you're doing."

"Very funny." He waited. "Well?"

"I've taken care of my part," Belkidar answered, showing considerable effort to stay awake.

"There's no wind, and nobody to man the oars."

"What would you do if there were?" he asked, pulling his hat down over his face.

"I'd give them the order to row, of course."

"So do it."

Batai did, feeling a little awkward shouting orders to empty rowing stations, but the oars responded in unison. Then the ship began to move. After completing a leisurely turn, they headed east, out of the bay. Batai looked incredulously at the sorcerer.

"Anyone who happens to see us will see a normal ship with its normal complement," Belkidar assured him.

"Nicely done," Batai said.

"Why thank you. Just head out to sea with the other ships. If you need to adjust the sails, simply give the order. But please don't go too quickly; we still need to make our way back to pick up Gunnar and return to sea before dawn."

"Leave it to me."

"That was delicious," Gunnar said. "What was it?"

"I'm not sure," Brohdan answered, using his tongue to dislodge a morsel from between his sharp teeth. "Whatever it was, it tasted a lot like chicken."

"I noticed that too."

"We should probably find that cove now," Brohdan said, stretching.

"All right. But I hope this doesn't take too long. I could really use a nap."

Batai followed the loose formation of ships as they headed out to sea. With Belkidar's help, a sudden leak low in the bow appeared shortly after midday. To all those who passed by, several men appeared to be feverishly repairing it before the ship took on too much water. Now and again, another ship's captain stopped and offered his assistance. Batai refused each time, politely explaining that they had everything under control. Shortly after sunset, they were utterly alone. He turned and headed back toward land.

As they continued south along the coast, Brohdan noticed a large boulder jutting from the water at the mouth of a small bay, its beaches filled with beautiful white sand. "I think that'd be noticeable from sea, don't you?"

"Definitely." He looked around before making himself comfortable in the cool shade of the tall trees.

"I may not be here when you wake up."

"Oh? Why?"

"I can't risk being seen tomorrow morning. I'll head out once it gets dark."

"Of course. You'll tell Belkidar?" he asked, motioning toward the bay.

"Sure." He paused. "Take care of yourself."

"I will. Make sure you do the same."

"Belkidar, we've found a nice spot for you to rendezvous with Gunnar."

"Very good. We've just turned back toward land."

"We're approximately three linops north of Brodor." He described the cove with white sand, the boulder at its mouth.

"I understand. We'll head several linops north of the city just to make sure we're not seen, then go south along the coastline until we see your landmark. Tell Gunnar to meet us as far out to sea as possible. The sooner we can head back, the better off we'll be."

"That's already his plan." He paused. *"Once we meet up again, do you think the ship can take my weight if I need to rest for a few links?"*

"No, not even close."

"Are you sure I can make it from one continent to the other?"

"Brohdan, you have more strength than you realize."

"If you say so," he replied uneasily.

"I do. Now, get some sleep. I'll see you soon."

He soon found a spot not far from where Gunnar lay snoring. As he drifted off, he imagined both the distance of the coming voyage and the depth of the water that spanned it.

Gunnar woke in the dark of the night, the sound of the surf eventually persuading him that he was no longer in his Midrogru cave. He turned to Brohdan but saw that he'd already left. He felt a pang of loneliness, an all-too familiar sensation, and he marveled at the thought. For the first time since he joined this Quest, he felt alone. He was amazed at how quickly he'd grown accustomed to having friends, especially after living by himself for so long. He'd grown close to all of them, but Brohdan in particular. In many ways, he was the sibling he'd never had.

He rose, walked toward the rhythmic sound of the waves. He took a knee, cupped his massive hands and rinsed his face. He stood again and surveyed the horizon, the water cascading through the maze of his beard. Despite the faint starlight, the boulder stood like a beacon against the dark horizon.

He slid his new sword from its scabbard, held it so that it reflected the night sky, veiled by neither moon nor cloud. He stared at the stars through Szurgord's steel, contemplating the long cycles he spent alone in his cave. He was surprised at how difficult it was to find emotions that had proven so overpowering not that long ago. But once remembered, they came rushing back. He considered both his old life and the one that now lay before him, realized his existence was nothing more than a reflection of countless choices, each like a star that shaped the night sky. Gunnar took comfort in that thought, for if his destiny was even partially affected by choice, he knew his former helplessness would have no place in it.

Batai navigated back toward the Western Continent, Belkidar's talents responsible for much of their swift progress. The large vessel carved a path through the water in a way Batai had never before witnessed, their enormous wake a testament to the depths of his powers.

Indira stood next to Kiera at the bow, their hair blowing in the wind. "Do you have any regrets?" she asked softly.

"Yes, a few," Kiera admitted. "You?"

"I have often wondered what my life would be like had I left home sooner, when I was younger."

"I think that's common. Most people never leave the city they were born in, and your home is many times larger than any in the world."

"And yet I cannot help think there are many things I missed by not exploring it until now. A city offers a variety experiences, far more than my home."

Kiera thought about that. "I'm not so sure. You've learned so many things the average human knows nothing about." She paused. "I've been fortunate because I have had a lot of experiences, each invaluable, and I'm a stronger person today because of them. But they came with a price. I didn't grow up in a family like yours. Both of my parents were killed when I was just a girl, and to make a living, I had to work at a very young age. I didn't have any practical skills, so I started on farms owned by people who'd been friends of my parents. They were very good to me, and I remember working hard to repay their kindness, but they gave me far more than I could've ever worked off."

"As I grew older, I decided I wanted more from life. So when I was thirteen, I left the farms and headed out on my own. I took as much food as I could, but it didn't take long to realize how unsympathetic life could be. I regret that I resorted to stealing food when I couldn't find work, but I learned quickly enough. I was also becoming a woman, and it didn't take me long to realize how often people underestimate us – and how to manipulate that. I learned very early how to negotiate my way through life, and that's how I ended up where I am today."

"I envy you."

Kiera nodded. "And I envy your childhood, your relationships with your family and friends. I would trade all of what I learned for a chance to see my parents, if for only a moment."

Indira closed her eyes, knew she was right.

"Each of us would go back and change things if we could. That's part of life. But remember, everything you've ever experienced made you who you are today – and that's one of the most genuine, caring people I've ever met."

She looked down. "Thank you, Kiera, you have given me a lot to think about."

"What are friends for?"

Brohdan couldn't sleep, the daunting task of flying across the Celornorin Ocean making him restless. He finally decided to start it instead of spending the night worrying about it.

As he flew out to sea, he thought of Mikka, remembering the links they'd spent together. The rhythmic flapping of his wings his only companion, he thought of the final night he spent with his mate. Although he wouldn't allow himself to admit it until this Quest has been fulfilled, deep down he longed for a life with her.

Brohdan, one of the most powerful creatures to ever live in this world, flew further into the night.

"Land ahead," Batai called softly to his friends.

"Where do you think we are?" Belkidar asked, walking to his side.

"I'm guessing we're about three and a half linaks north of Brodor."

"Guessing?"

"Well, I'm not a sorcerer. Why do you even need to ask? Why don't you just – " he suggested, flipping is hand effeminately in the air.

"First of all, real sorcerers don't need to wave their hands. And if they did, it certainly wouldn't look like that."

Batai made no reply, save a slight smirk. He continued on a westerly heading until the features of land became more distinct.

"Don't get too close," Belkidar warned.

"You don't actually think we can be seen in this darkness, do you?"

"Not by the people here, but some in Hildegard's forces may have ways of seeing what others cannot. Besides, we're close enough to find Gunnar."

Batai turned the ship south and slowly slipped through the dark waters, the crew huddling starboard to search for their friend.

Gunnar walked into the bay. When the water reached his massive chest, he stopped and looked out to sea. The boulder sat only a few elads ahead, and he slowly waded into deeper water until he finally reached it. At a depth taller than three humans, Gunnar's head was still well above the surface as he stretched a hand to touch the rock. It was smooth, cool to his touch, soothing him. He maneuvered to its seaward side, then removed his sword and cut a long diagonal slash into the white stone. He repeated it five times so that six parallel lines marked the smooth surface, one for each member of their Quest. He paused a moment, then added a seventh, for Einar. He leaned his back against them, stared across the vast ocean, the starlight dancing on countless waves. He was surprised with how much he was looking forward to reuniting with his friends, and he hoped all seven slashes would be represented when at last their Quest was over.

Brohdan climbed high through the cool air, considered where his life had taken him since he left Sul Brul. He marveled at the huge disparity between his dull, routine pre-grombit life in Lukvia and the one that now led him to perhaps history's most significant event. Then he thought back on his first few mooncycles in the Sichundar Mountains, how he'd felt like a helpless spectator in his own life.

He continued climbing silently into the night sky. Despite his exceptional sight, the details of the surface eventually merged into hazy shapes. He continued climbing toward the stars and, after nearly a link, finally leveled off. Even at this incredible altitude, he couldn't see Katja's coastline. Realizing he had many days of flying ahead, he extended his massive wings, gliding silently through the night.

Batai continued south along Tymoteu's eastern coastline, all searching for the lone boulder that Brohdan had earlier described.

"Any sign yet?" Batai asked Kiera.

"No, not yet. Are you sure you know where we are?"

"Of course I do. We're on the ocean."

"I see something," Indira said quietly, pointing toward the distant coast.

"What is it?" Belkidar asked, quickly making his way to her.

"Something pale in the distance. It could be a rock."

Kiera joined them, strained to see what Indira studied, knowing it was futile.

Batai turned toward it, and as they drew nearer, Indira nodded. "That matches Brohdan's description."

They drifted closer still, soundlessly, then something caught Kiera's attention. "The rock's moving!"

Indira shook her head. "No, it is only – "

"But it is!" Kiera interrupted. "Look at it!"

"That is Gunnar. He was only leaning against it."

"Oh. That would've been my next guess."

Gunnar took only a few drus to make his way to the others, swimming the final elads. As he approached, he raised his right arm along the side of the ship. In one smooth motion, he reached into the cat's hole, the gap through which the anchor chain rides, and pulled himself up, causing the entire vessel to list severely. The four passengers nearly fell overboard before finding something to grab. Once aboard, the ship rocked back and forth, the others bracing themselves until it finally settled.

"Hello," Gunnar quietly greeted them.

"Sink any good ships lately?" Batai asked, finally releasing his death grip on the wheel.

Gunnar smiled, shaking water from his hair.

"It's good to see you again," Batai said, taking Gunnar's arm, the others greeting him in turn.

"How did you learn to swim so well?" Kiera asked. "Didn't you spend most of your life in the Midrogrus?"

"I did, but there was a mountain lake not far from my cave. It's pretty isolated, tough to reach. I spent a lot of time there."

"Would you like me to find you something to dry yourself?" Indira asked, stepping back from the growing puddle.

"Thanks," he replied, giving Belkidar a sideward glance, "but I'll manage."

"Fine," he sighed. Accompanied by an exaggerated wave of his hand, steam began rising from Gunnar's clothing. Almost as quickly as it had begun, he was dry.

"How'd you do that?" Gunnar asked.

"Effortlessly."

"But how did you keep his clothes from burning?" Batai asked.

"Never mind that!" Kiera butted in. "How did you keep *Gunnar* from burning?"

"You're making it more complicated than it needs to be," Belkidar explained. "Why does the temperature of the water and his clothing have to be connected?"

"Because it is always so," Indira said softly.

"Maybe in nature," he agreed, leaning on his Staff. "It's the difference between nature's path and my own. They don't always have to be the same."

The others just stared at him, trying to understand.

"Batai, would you be so kind as to take us back out to sea?"

"Of course." Within moments, a long wake trailed behind, their hair blowing in the wind.

"How long will you risk this speed?" Indira asked Belkidar.

"Until sunrise."

She nodded. "That makes sense. The time we would save is not worth the risk."

Belkidar looked into her young eyes. "Your wisdom never ceases to amaze me."

"Thank you," she replied, her face turning scarlet.

Brohdan stretched his wings, descending surprisingly little as glided through the cool night air. Soon, a familiar 'voice' interrupted his reverie.

"Brohdan, we've found Gunnar. You chose the perfect location."

"Thank you."

"We've got about four links before sunrise, which is more than we'll need."

"Very good."

Belkidar paused. *"Are you busy?"*

"No. Why do you ask?"

"You seem preoccupied."

"Well, maybe a little. I climbed pretty high so I could conserve energy. I never realized I could glide this well."

"Of course you can. You're a dragon after all."

"What do you mean?"

"Well, dragons are unlike any other flyers in the world, in part because their physique is so poorly suited for flight. Unlike birds or

even bats, they can't carry any useful weight. Also, they're rather clumsy; their heads and tails bob up and down when they flap their wings, and worse yet – "

"Belkidar, do you have a point?"

"Of course I do. I always do. Because of these...issues, your wings are far bigger than they'd normally be, which explains why you can glide so well."

Brohdan nodded. *"Where do you expect to land on Katja?"*

"We'll circle to the southeast where there's a small pass in the mountains. It's the only accessible place on the entire continent that's secluded."

"Won't Hildegard expect that?"

"I'm sure of it, but we have little choice. We can probably expect the battles to begin shortly after landing."

"The First Defense?"

"Most likely." He paused. *"You can catch up with us tomorrow night."*

"Let me know if you need anything, or if your plans change."

"I will. Take care."

"You too."

Belkidar took a final look around, then found a place on the forward deck to lie down. Just as he was drifting to sleep, a voice greeted him. It was not audible.

"You don't expect to defeat me, do you?" the thin voice asked.

"Of course I do."

"My old friend, you cannot endure what I have planned. Go back. Go back now."

"I have never been your friend, Hildegard. Mine died long ago."

"Krollum still lives, only now he serves me."

"I'll see you soon enough. Now if you'll excuse me, I'd like to get some sleep." With that, Belkidar closed all access to his mind, but it wasn't so easy to separate his thoughts from that short conversation. One thing was now certain – their arrival was not only expected, it was confirmed.

"This is finally coming back to me," Batai remarked the following morning.

"It's about time," Kiera replied. "I thought my sea sickness would never pass."

Batai only smiled.

"I have never been on waters like these before, but so far my stomach has not been affected," Indira said.

"Why thank you, my lady," Batai said with an exaggerated bow.

"What are we having for our morning meal?" Gunnar asked as he stumbled to his feet, weary from sleep. "I'm starving."

"Well, I made sure the ship came with some fishing gear. It's stowed below. Give me a moment."

Before long, Kiera emerged with a fishing rod. In Gunnar's hands, it looked like a toy. "I'm not sure this thing's big enough to pick fish from my teeth."

"It'll be fine," Batai assured him. "It actually looks to be an excellent pole."

"If you say so," he said, taking the equipment to the aft rail.

"I should warn you," Batai added, "any fish you catch this far out to sea may be pretty big,"

Gunnar laughed, deep and affable, but said nothing.

The next few links passed without much luck. Then the fishing pole that looked so small in his hands was nearly pulled from them. He crouched, fought to regain his balance.

"Hold onto it!" Kiera yelled.

"I am!" Gunnar growled back.

"Don't let the line break!" Batai added, watching from the helm.

"Please!" Gunnar said as nicely as he could, "I'll bring him in. Just let me do it!"

In the meantime, Belkidar woke and casually walked aft to where Gunnar fought against the rod. By all accounts, it was a huge catch.

"Whoa!" Gunnar said, nearly dropping it.

"What happened?" Kiera asked.

"Nothing. It's nothing. It just gave me a shock or something."

Then the rod grew to over seven elads in length, its thickness tripling. Even the fishing line grew in diameter. Kiera looked back at the sorcerer.

"What?" he asked innocently.

"Don't you help him!"

"It would've broken."

"Uh-huh."

"If you've all finished," Gunnar said, turning from his friends to the waters beyond the ship's railing. He planted his feet, pulled back on the rod. Thanks to Belkidar, it barely flexed, despite the enormous strain.

"Now, reel in the line as you let the rod fall forward again!" Kiera explained.

Frustrated with their jabbering, Gunnar held the rod to her with his right hand, his arm extended, the muscles along the length of his arm and back bulging. "You want to do this?"

Stunned, she looked from the stressed rod to the arm that held it motionlessly in place. It seemed to triple in size. At least. "Ah, no. You're doing fine."

He nodded once, then turned back toward the water.

"It must not be as large as we had thought," Indira whispered to Belkidar.

"I wouldn't be so sure."

She thought back to how Gunnar held the rod with one hand, then considered how he drew the fish closer with apparently little effort. She shook her head but said nothing more.

They watched him work, and after a half link, a pale shape slowly materialized beneath the surface. After another few drus, its thrashing foamed the water. It was enormous. When he finally pulled it from the ocean, only Belkidar seemed calm.

"Look at those teeth!" Kiera said.

Batai stepped closer. It looked like a huge shark, but was stouter, its nose blunter. The front of its dorsal fin was straight, gradually slanting down the length of its broad back, disappearing an elye or two ahead of its tail – which thrashed violently side to side as Gunnar hoisted it out of the water. Then, suddenly, it calmed.

"Has he given up?" Gunnar asked, disappointed.

"No," Belkidar answered.

"Why has it stopped?" Batai asked.

"Because for the first time in its life, it is out of its element," Indira answered softly.

"Precisely," Belkidar agreed, nodding. "Hrulg may dominate the ocean, but they've never been out of the water, never felt their full weight."

Gunnar vaguely listened, focusing more on hoisting the creature onto the deck without injuring his friends. He held the rod high with his left hand, dragging the hrulg's bottom half over the aft railing. He slid his sword free with his right hand, then swung it, severing its head. Its body crashed to the deck, thick scarlet mixing with dripping salt water. "I hope they're tasty."

"Oh, they are, at least when I took the form of a sperm whale. I just hope the taste transfers."

"Transfers?" Kiera asked.

"Yes. From a sperm whale to a human."

"Why wouldn't it transfer? It's the same food."

"True, but just like tastes vary from person to person, they also vary from species to species. For instance, I couldn't stop eating spiders when I took the form of a pragrin, a rare bird that lives in the southern regions of Seamus and Gladar. I particularly enjoyed the crunch of tarantulas," the old man added almost to himself.

Kiera said nothing, forced to wonder what a spider might taste like. "I see."

"What's the best way to cook them?" Gunnar asked.

"Oh, I ate them raw."

Batai noted Kiera's squeamishness. "Spiders, or hrulg?"

"Both."

"Leave it to me," Kiera announced, happy to distract herself from their conversation.

"You were right," Indira said to Belkidar, noting how small Kiera looked next to the headless hrulg. "Giants are wonderous creatures."

He smiled sadly. "They are indeed."

With Belkidar's help, Kiera cooked the hrulg without burning the old ship. After a link, it was ready.

"Looks great!" Gunnar said excitedly, nearly running to where the food lay prepared.

"Thank you," Kiera replied. "I hope it tastes as good as it looks." Judging by how quickly he ate, she didn't think it would matter much.

After everyone had taken a share, Gunnar came back for seconds. "Kiera, you have an unparalleled talent with food."

Belkidar agreed. "Not bad. Not bad at all. Less salty than I remember."

"Well, you're not eating this one with a mouthful of seawater."

"That might have something to do with it."

Brohdan flew links into the evening before he first spotted a vessel on the open water. He had glided during the night, but now flew much closer to the surface, making it easy to evade.

He wondered what Hildegard had planned for him. He wasn't afraid, more curious about his future, and whether he would measure up. He continued on, toward his destiny.

"Hrulg tastes a lot like chicken, but a lot greasier," Batai remarked later that night as he sat against the railing. "I feel like a steak tonight." He frowned at the tiny, isolated island that was their ship. "Pity."

"Oh, come now," Indira said, patting his broad back. "I am sure we can find something to your liking. Fish perhaps?"

"Are you trying to be funny?" he asked, looking up into her green eyes.

Gunnar grunted a laugh. "I'm not sure if she's trying or not, but I think she's succeeding."

The rest of the evening passed without spotting another vessel. As darkness consumed them, Belkidar again increased their speed.

"Do you risk anything by using sorcery?" Kiera asked as they sat together. "To our Quest, I mean."

"Good question. It depends on a few factors. The more significant the use, or how I apply it, the easier it is to detect. But proximity is the biggest factor."

Kiera raised an eyebrow.

"Not to worry. The ability to focus wind or move water isn't substantial enough for Hildegard to notice. Also, I'm quite good at blending this sort of thing with natural events."

"Natural events?" Batai asked.

"Sure. Water currents are actually quite common throughout the Celornorin Ocean. And wind gusts happen every day, all over the world. I simply mask my actions with these natural events."

"So that is how you do it," Indira noted with a smile, her black hair blown from her face. "You use both wind and water currents."

Belkidar nodded, returning her smile.

"Can't you simply make us go faster by thinking it?" Kiera asked.

"It doesn't work like that. Sorcery doesn't allow me to do impossible things, it's simply a means to do possible things in an alternate way. And what's truly possible is what's most often misunderstood. It's easy to assume something's impossible if you never see it happen, and while that's sometimes true, it's far less common than you may think. Drying Gunnar's clothes without heating them is a perfect example. This is the same thing I explained to Brohdan when he was in his grombit. Don't let your past experiences limit your imagination and, thus, your sorcery. There are only two true limitations: nature and the sorcerer's own abilities."

"Nature places a very tangible limit on what I can and cannot do, but good sorcerers don't make assumptions about where those limits are. Instead, we use our imagination to find alternate ways to do things. Occasionally, we reach a dead end, where natural laws make something impossible, but again, that's pretty rare."

"The second limitation, of course, is determined by my own abilities, and it just so happens that this isn't a very tangible limit," he continued, searching for a reaction to his dry humor. After finding none, he continued. "I'm lucky because my Linsilor Sorcerenic happens to be pretty advanced, so my potential is rarely limited by my own abilities. Nature, of course, isn't so selective."

"I see," Batai said seriously. "So you cannot, for instance, turn me into a goat for saying your breath smells like hrulg intestines."

"Well, actually I could. That's what I was talking about. Just because you've never seen a fully grown man turn into a goat doesn't mean it's not possible."

"Ugh!" Kiera yelled. "You sure are an ugly goat! Turn him back before he jumps overboard!"

Bewildered, Batai held his arms out, checking to make sure they hadn't changed. Then he dropped them, shaking his head.

"Sorry," she managed between fits of laughter. Indira was also having trouble controlling herself.

"Women," Gunnar said.

"Changing your form into a goat's isn't limited by nature. You've seen me change forms many times."

"But how can it be possible to change into a goat?" Batai asked, ignoring their snickering.

"Well, I wouldn't actually change *you* into a goat. I'd simply change your *form* into a goat's. See the difference?"

"I suppose so, but isn't it superficial?"

"No! Quite the opposite. If I were to change *you* into a goat, you'd have all the attributes of that creature – its intellect and personality. By simply changing your form, you retain all of your human attributes. So when I change into an eagle's form, I'm still able to make the same decisions I would in human form, but I gain all of physical abilities of an eagle."

"But how does nature allow you to change forms?" Indira asked.

"Well, to understand that you must first understand how matter is assembled."

Kiera looked impressed, realized her vulnerability too late.

"No need. I'll explain," Belkidar whispered loudly to her. Her reddened cheeks revealed everything her voice did not.

"A few thousand cycles ago, I had the good fortune to meet Nichah, a common man who worked a large farm in central Drulop. He was the most inquisitive person I've ever met. It's a shame his Linsilor hadn't developed, because I think he would've made some of Men's greatest discoveries if he could've extended his life."

"As I helped him work his farm one spring morning, he asked about the nature of matter. 'Why is iron hard and wood soft?' I'd never really thought about it before, so I told him I'd find out." He paused, a long moment passed. "I eventually discovered the answer, but it came a cycle to the day after Nichah's death. His lands, along with all of the farms in the area, fell victim to a massive flood. I'd been away, researching, doing experiments. He saved his family, but at the cost of his own life. I spent the better part of the next two decacycles helping his wife raise those beautiful children."

He stopped again, lost in the past, the sound of the waves and the smell of salt water eventually bringing him back. "Matter is comprised of tiny building blocks, and their number and arrangement determine the nature of a material. So to change my form to an eagle's, I need only rearrange those building blocks in my body."

"Sounds complicated," Gunnar remarked.

"It is. It took me a cycle just to change a grasshopper's form into a cricket's. But with practice I got better and better, eventually learning how to change my own form – as well as those of others." As he finished, Kiera noticed a light shimmer to her right. When she looked, she saw a goat sitting on its haunches where Batai had once sat. She gasped, startled, before regaining her composure and hiding her laughter behind a small hand.

Batai, not realizing what had just happened, simply looked from the sorcerer to Kiera. Shaking his head, he looked to Gunnar. "Women," he said in an unfamiliar voice, instantly realizing what had happened. To everyone's surprise, he simply got to his hooves, walked over to Kiera, and bit her on her backside. Belkidar led the laughter as Kiera jumped to her feet, rubbing buttocks.

"That's not funny!" she yelled. "I'm going to have a bruise there!"

Batai couldn't control himself, his high-pitched goat laughter soaring above the others'. This, of course, only made their hysterics worse. Even Kiera couldn't help herself. Finally, when Belkidar had recovered, he changed Batai back.

"That was an experience!" Batai said.

Indira nodded, wiping tears from her eyes. "It must be a wonder to take the form of another creature."

"I suppose so, but I was talking about having a mouthful of Kiera's backside."

The laughter began again. This time, Gunnar's imitation of Batai's goat laughs could be heard from linaks away.

Brohdan flew tirelessly beneath the cloudless sky, amazed that even the most distant stars appeared just out of reach, all seemingly watching in earnest as his fate drew ever closer. He looked toward the horizon, but it was lost somewhere between the ocean of stars above and the calm water below.

He flew links on end, contemplated the unexplored depths that passed in silence beneath him, wondered what creatures lived their entire lives without ever seeing the light of day. And yet they were linked with him, with his friends, because despite their apparent detachment from this world, Hildegard's evil would inevitably infect all the world's creatures should their Quest fail.

Then he looked up, fascinated by the endless expanse. The

enormity of the ocean below was infinitesimal when compared to the stars. Even when he was young, the night sky had intrigued him. But now with no distractions, he studied them, savored their beauty, their mystery, wondering what strange events were taking place in the far-reaching places of the universe.

Over the next several links, he rarely took his eyes off the heavens. He saw several shooting stars, a few of which ended their spectacular journey in distant ocean waters. He also searched for threats, but only discovered the heat signatures of two other vessels, both of which were linops distant.

The next day passed without incident. Brohdan turned just in time to see the sun sink below the vast waters of the Celornorin Ocean, welcoming both the serenity and security the darkness would soon provide. One by one, the stars began winning their battle for the sky. Like a line of marching soldiers, the brilliance in the darkening east advanced on the lingering light in the west. Eventually, the sunlight surrendered the day's final battle, and darkness once again celebrated its victory with an ardent display of stars, galaxies, meteoroids, nebulae, planets, and comets.

Brohdan once again lost himself in the mysteries of the night sky. With all of the unknowns that surrounded him, what creature could ever predict the outcome of their Quest? If that myriad of stars existed beyond comprehension, surely it wasn't impossible for a small group of determined warriors to overcome such evil. It was that very thought that struck at his soul. Several linaks passed before he was willing to consider the thought that had so briefly surfaced in his mind.

If the water below and the sky above contain countless undiscovered possibilities, what limit does Hildegard have in discovering something to outmatch a Broglia in battle?

"Brohdan, are you awake?"

Belkidar's message startled him from his thoughts just as dawn's first colors appeared above the horizon. *"Of course. I'm flying after all."*

"What does that have to do with sleeping?"

"Everything," he answered, suddenly unsure.

"Let's talk about that another day. We're making better progress than I'd anticipated. You're free to join us at your leisure."

Brohdan was overjoyed. Although he'd missed his friends, the topic of the previous night made his isolation uncomfortable. *"I'm on my way!"* Then he paused. *"Where are you?"*

"Right here."

Brohdan suddenly knew exactly where they were, as if he'd seen it from high above the water. He turned slightly to the south, increasing his speed. *"How'd you do that?"*

"Remember when I described the basic principle of how sorcerers communicate? This is no different. You don't send words – that's inefficient and takes too long – instead, you send thoughts. Pictures. Ideas. Whatever's the root of your message."

"So you sent me a picture of where you are?"

"In part. I sent a picture of where we both are, in relation to each other. Otherwise, you wouldn't know which direction to fly."

"But how did you know where I was?"

"I don't – I mean, I didn't."

"I don't understand."

"Don't take this the wrong way, Brohdan, but...novices...allow a lot of information to leak into their messages."

"Leak? How?"

"Your brain manages everything you think and do, it connects every part of your existence. So it's easy to accidentally include other information in your messages. In a way, it's like any normal conversation. Body language and inflection can express more than words, sometimes even contradict them. Likewise, it's possible for

your mind to transfer unintended information into your messages, including your flight orientation, your fondness of the night sky, and even your current position over the water."

Brohdan was quiet for some time. *"Then you also know of..."*

"Yes. But don't worry. You'll see her again if I have anything to do with it."

Less than a link later, Indira made her way up the stairs and onto the deck, the sun just emerging above the horizon. She stretched, the salty air still a novel sensation.

She enjoyed these rare times by herself, moments that allowed her to reflect without distraction. Her gift was undeniable, but what was she to do with it? Was it simply the product of chance, or was there a purpose behind it? And if so, does that not imply a destiny?

She watched the sun, a red sliver above the calm water, its reflection brightening her face, warming her heart. She turned left, a magnificent violet arc running from horizon to horizon, north to south, separating night and day. She continued turning, admired those stars that stubbornly remained.

Her eyesight was far too precise to have missed it.

Indira's gaze had initially passed over a slight movement, then she found it again. She reached for her bow, nearly calling for the others, then recognized the dark speck above the distant horizon.

It only took a few drus before her friend was within earshot. He passed north of her, continued east before banking to his right. She watched him pass over, only a few elads above the ship's mast, surprised at how much their reunion comforted her.

Brohdan slowed as he drew alongside, his wing's slow, methodically beating complimenting the slapping water against the hull.

"Good morning," she said softly to her friend. "I am happy to see you again."

"Good morning, Indira. I'm happy to be back!"

"Anything interesting happen while you were away?"

"No, but it gave me time to think."

"I know what you mean. That is when I find peace with myself."

"Me too." He paused. "But sometimes answers are hard to find."

Indira nodded but said nothing. Her own times to herself had raised more questions than answers.

"Don't get me wrong," Brohdan continued, inadvertently startling her from her thoughts, "I'm happy to be back. The days I spent alone made me appreciate how lucky I am to have found you."

"Likewise," she whispered almost to herself. Then she smiled. "But I am not the only one who has missed you!" She nocked an arrow, only partially drew back her bowstring, then released it toward the top of the ship's mast. A loud bell tolled from somewhere high in the forest of sails and ropes.

Afterward, she still stared toward the sky. After several drus, she smoothly reached out her right hand and plucked the falling arrow from the air. She inspected before replacing it in her quiver. "That ought to do it."

Before long, Gunnar ran from where he'd slept near the stern. "Where's the attack coming from?" he demanded in a hoarse voice, drawing his sword.

Then Batai emerged from below, nearly taking out the support beam of the ship's crew quarters ceiling with his head as he emerged from the darkness. Kiera trailed closely behind.

"Look at what I found!" Indira said.

Gunnar looked up at his friend. "I missed you. We weren't the same without you."

"Thank you. I've missed you too."

Kiera stopped next to Gunnar. "You were gone too long," she said shortly. "Don't do that again."

"I'll try not to."

"Did you have a chance to eat?" Batai asked.

"No. I spent the days trying to stay out of sight. I didn't see much, not until I headed over here."

"Must've been the shipping lanes," Kiera explained. "They offer more protection from pirates."

"Interesting," Batai said, stroking his beard. "I'll have to investigate once I get back to Trisett."

"I'm sure you will," Belkidar said as he made his way to the railing. "Brohdan, it's nice to see you again."

"And you. "Have a nice nap?"

"Dandy."

They spent the day talking, sharing what they'd experienced while separated. Brohdan filled in his friends on his solitary journey across the ocean, describing how he could spend links deep in thought, eventually being able to fly without even thinking about it.

Likewise, the others described the adventures that Brohdan had missed. Even Gunnar found these stories interesting since many took place in Brodor. Batai proudly boasted of Kiera's haggling talents, exaggerating only a little when he described her ability to somehow legally 'steal' their vessel. Belkidar was persuaded to explain how he shortened their travel time to Katja. Kiera beamed when she described Gunnar's victory over the mighty hrulg, Indira enthusiastically describing the ensuing feast. Brohdan, having not eaten for a few days now, felt his stomach churn.

As night fell, the party slowly dispersed to their beds. Indira remained.

"I can stay and talk if you would like."

"Thank you, Indira, but I'll be fine. Besides, you should sleep. Take advantage of not having to post guards during the night. I'm sure that won't last long."

"Okay," she agreed, "but promise to let me know if you need anything."

"I promise."

She nodded, then went below.

Now that his grombit was complete, Brohdan knew he needed far less sleep than other creatures, and that made him appreciate Indira's offer all the more. She was caring, selfless. They all were, all consistently putting each other's wishes above their own. He smiled, knew that in many ways he was still young to this world, but he'd found enough wisdom to comprehend the rarity of finding true friends and the preciousness inherent in those relationships.

Having seemingly bid Indira goodnight only moments before, Brohdan was startled from his thoughts by the foreshadowing of another sunrise. One by one, his sleepy friends greeted him. Kiera silently pulled a tuna from its holding tank, lopped off its head, and began preparing it for their morning meal.

"Caught it the other day," Gunnar said in a gruff voice. "Last one, I think."

Brohdan looked at him and then back at the tuna. "Shame."

He watched as they ate, Kiera the last to finish.

"Did you save some for me?" Brohdan asked.

"Why sure. We're keeping yours down there," she answered, motioning to the ocean's depths.

"Enough chit chat," Belkidar said, taking a seat next to where Brohdan flew. The others joined him. "I'm very pleased with our progress. We've managed to assemble everyone and leave Tymoteu, all without any hiccups."

"Hiccups?" Batai asked. "Didn't you hear Gunnar a few days ago?"

"I never thought he'd stop!" Kiera agreed.

Gunnar stood silently, a smirk passing slowly across his face.

Belkidar smiled, his steel-blue eyes twinkling in the morning light. "Think of all we've experienced to get here, alone on the ocean, and we didn't suffer a single injury – or worse. Hildegard tried, and though he sent people against us, we were able to defeat them and evade the rest."

He paused, looked into their eyes. "Hildegard contacted me. He gained little, but that shows he's at least aware of our progress."

"But does that not show he can monitor our voyage across the ocean and onto Katja?" Indira asked.

"Yes. And no. The closer we get to him, the more effective his sorcery becomes. But the same is true for me – *my* sorcery becomes more effective against him, too. I've taken steps to make sure he can't discover anything significant about us, but when you're dealing with a sorcerer as powerful as Hildegard, I'm sure he'll be able to discover some information."

"Like what?" Brohdan asked in his low, resonant voice.

"He will know you are hiding something," Indira offered.

"Very true," Belkidar said, nodding, "but he'll be able to determine more than that. For instance, he'll be able to track me to a certain extent."

Batai grimaced. "What else?"

"My mood. Our perceived progress, in general terms. The frequency and power of my sorcery use. That sort of thing."

The group remained silent for some time before Brohdan spoke. "If he can learn details about our progress, can't you discover anything about his plans?"

"Well, we can only discover information through the other's actions, and I'm afraid we have a lot more to hide than he does. We're sailing across the Celornorin Ocean trying to arrive unseen into his backyard, all while evading his spies. He completed his actions long ago when he created his Five Defenses and molded the continent to suit them."

Brohdan considered that. "How can I shield my actions against him?"

Belkidar turned to him, his expression cautious. "There's...um...no need." He sighed. "Don't take this the wrong way, but your sorcery isn't great enough to be noticed."

Brohdan blinked, flapped his wings once, twice.

"Think of it like a huge spider web, one that covers the world. The closer two spiders come together, the more they'll each feel the web move. And the harder either one shakes the web, the easier it is for the other to detect."

"That makes sense," Brohdan said.

"Well, with your sorcery, you can't vibrate the web very much. Barely at all, in fact."

"Oh."

The group felt a surge in their speed, watched the ship's wake grow. Belkidar stood and faced the dawn, his white hair blown from his sunlit face. "Time is of the essence now. Hildegard's already sensed my presence, so we might as well take advantage of that setback. I can reduce our voyage to Katja five-fold; anything more would shake the web too much, and I won't risk him gaining more information."

"So I'm guessing we'll get there in about three quarters of a mooncycle now?" Batai asked.

"I hope a bit less," Belkidar answered.

"That is still a long time for Brohdan to go without sleep," Indira said.

"Not really. Dragons in general, and Broglia Blacks in particular, have endurances far beyond other creatures. Now that he's an adult, he could quite easily go a mooncycle without sleep."

"You'd never know it," Kiera said, smiling.

"Ah, but you've only known him during his grombit."

"These winds will help," Brohdan said. "And when I get tired, I can always glide."

"And you can swim," Belkidar added.

"Swim?" Brohdan, Batai, and Kiera asked.

"Sure. Dragons are excellent swimmers."

"Have you never tried?" asked Indira.

"Well, sure. But only in lakes. Shallow ones."

"For a dragon, maybe," Kiera joked.

Brohdan returned her smile, but his numerous sharp teeth portrayed a decidedly different impression.

"Well, dragons are actually quite good at flying under the water," Belkidar explained. "But as with anything, there are pros and cons."

"Such as?" Kiera asked impatiently after several moments without elaboration.

"Such as his anatomy," he continued with a smile. "Swimming will let him rest some of his muscles – the ones his wings use to keep him in the air – but he'll use others even more."

"The ones that push him forward," Batai said.

"Exactly. But if he alternates between swimming and flying, he'll have little trouble keeping up."

"Why's that?" Kiera asked.

"Because dragons are nearly as graceful under the water as they are above it," Belkidar answered.

"Why don't you get some food, then?" Gunnar asked. "And while you're at it, find something for me?"

"I'll try," Brohdan said before climbing higher into the sky. Then he suddenly leaned forward, tucked his wings against his body, and dove into cold waters of the Celornorin Ocean. The resulting wave was enough to make even the most experienced sailor take notice. Batai immediately got to his feet and ran toward the helm.

"Never mind," Belkidar said calmly. "I'll take care of it."

Batai stopped and turned, watched approaching wave. The others also turned in anticipation of his sorcery, but all they saw was the huge wave grow closer. Soon, it became apparent that, if Belkidar's intentions were to reduce the size of the wave, he was failing miserably.

"It's still approaching rather quickly," Kiera observed.

"It is."

"And it hasn't gotten any smaller," she pointed out.

"I think you may be correct."

Kiera nervously looked back to the water just in time to see the enormous wave crash against the side of the ship. But the vessel didn't budge, steadfastly remaining upright without so much as a sway to either side. Once at the crest, they plummeted down the backside, causing everyone to feel their stomachs surge into their throats.

"Why didn't you do something?" Kiera demanded.

"We're not sinking, are we?"

"Why didn't you just get rid of the wave?"

"That would've alerted our future host. Besides, that was too much fun to pass up."

Indira laughed. Gunnar, Batai, and Kiera looked like they might explode. Belkidar simply looked over the ship's railing. "I wonder how he's doing down there."

Once underwater, Brohdan spread his wings and explored the ocean's depths. He was immediately confronted with several revelations. He knew the water must be cold, yet his body somehow protected him. He also discovered that he could not only hear many of the ocean's inhabitants, he could estimate their location as well. And while he knew how to swim from his childhood tramps in the Lukvian lakes, he couldn't remember being this good at it.

He explored, diving deeper and deeper. Soon, all sunlight vanished, but not the heat patterns of his prey. He swam after a large fish, extended his neck, easily plucked it from the black water. He ate another three before bringing the fifth to the surface.

An enormous bow wave caught Gunnar's attention. Then the surface exploded as Brohdan literally flew from the water, torrents rushing from his flapping wings and swaying tail as he climbed into the sky.

He found the ship and flew toward it. As he approached, he came to a hover and waited for them to come alongside, then gently laid the fish onto the deck. A huge smile crossed Gunnar's face as he lifted it. "Thank you!" It didn't take him long to prepare it, nor for Kiera to cook it thanks to some help from Belkidar.

"Did you eat?" Indira asked Brohdan.

"Yeah, I've already had four. I think they're giving me gas."

Batai could've been a little less obvious as he rearranged his seat to the opposite railing from where Brohdan flew.

"How did your swim go?" Kiera asked.

"Good. Great, actually. Better than I ever remember swimming before."

Belkidar nodded. "You're not the same dragon who began his grombit cycles ago. You're several times bigger and far stronger. Plus, your endurance is beyond compare. Simply put, you're now a Broglia Black. The days of being a Dalluvian Green are behind you."

"Well, I still have the same personality."

"Good point," he conceded, "and may I say it'll serve you well."

The compliment made him feel uncomfortable, and he was glad when Indira broke the silence.

"How did the hunt go? Was it very different beneath the water?"

"It was. As I went deeper, the sunlight faded until it was completely black, but I could still see – I think better than the fish, because they weren't very hard to catch."

"Did you have any trouble holding your breath that long?" Batai asked.

"No, actually I didn't." He thought about that, then turned to Belkidar.

"You can go nearly a link without breathing, but you'd need time to recover before doing it again. Broglias' lungs are extremely large for their bodies, which is one of the reasons you have such good endurance." Belkidar looked torn for a moment, then continued. "Perhaps Mikka already knows of this."

Brohdan, sensing more questions were imminent, quickly dove into the water.

"What was that about," Kiera asked.

"You'll have to ask him."

"Oh, I plan to," Kiera said softly. "I plan to."

Brohdan continued hunting, his confidence growing with each link. Kiera and Indira watched as he frequently came into view racing after his prey, using his wings to accelerate in an instant or change directions in a flash.

Meanwhile, Batai, Gunnar, and Belkidar were all happily sampling the assortment of ales that somehow found their way aboard during their brief stay in Brodor.

"This is a good stout," Batai said as he refilled his stein from one of the many kegs.

"It is," Belkidar agreed. "I discovered it over five hundred cycles ago just outside of Kordare. That village no longer exists, but this recipe fortunately found its way to a talented brewer just inside the city. I must admit," he added as he rose unsteadily to refill his own mug, "I'm their favorite customer."

"Well, I can understand why," Gunnar said. "You must've had more than the rest of the world combined."

"That may be true, but it's a distinction I will undoubtedly pass to you if you keep drinking them by the keg."

Batai, at least, appreciated Belkidar's subtlety as he watched Gunnar drain his keg and reach for another.

Later that evening, everybody on board took advantage of the vast supply of ale and wine. Indira, having never experienced such a wide variety, explored the different flavors, preferring the summer ales of central Charlov and the rosés of southern Gladar. Kiera, of course, was right at home drinking with her friends. In fact, Batai realized he may be in trouble if a competition ever arose.

Once everybody had a chance to down a pint or six, they found their way below deck and one by one fell asleep. Gunnar sat near his makeshift bed facing his friend. "It's good to see you again."

"Thank you. It's good to be back. But I did enjoy the time alone. It let me put some things into perspective."

"Such as?"

"I realized I spent too much time worrying about things that really weren't important. The time I spent trying to start my grombit was the lowest point in my life. But as cruel as Limbrin was...the helplessness, the humiliation, they were even worse."

Brohdan took a moment to consider his past. Gunnar was content to wait, listening to his wings flap in the darkness above and the waves slap against the hull below.

"Over the past few nights, I realized it doesn't really matter if I changed or not. They treated me differently because their *perception* of me changed."

"But you can't help that. You can't blame yourself for the ignorance of others."

"True," Brohdan admitted, "but somehow that doesn't make it any easier."

"I know what you mean. When you're so isolated to begin with, forgiving becomes difficult."

"So does forgetting. I understand why they treated me that way, but it was still disappointing."

"I didn't have friends at that age, but I do know what it feels like to be an outcast, to be different than everybody else. It's a difficult situation, but you can only do the best with what you've got."

"You amaze me, Gunnar. I just realized that last night."

"Yeah, but I've had decacycles to think about these things, and it took me a lot longer to figure out than it took you. We do have an advantage, though."

"What's that?"

"Just as I'm the world's only giant, you're the only Broglia Black. Indira's skills make her unique, Kiera's the lone female in her profession, and Batai doesn't have peer on the battlefield, or in any community of Men. And Belkidar...well, Belkidar truly is a freak."

Brohdan couldn't help but laugh. "That he is, but he's *our* freak."

"Exactly! Regardless of our success against Hildegard and his Five Defenses, this Quest has done what we couldn't – it's torn away everything that made us different from everyone else, all the things that forced us to be isolated in our own lives. It forced a handful of outcasts to work toward one goal. It brought us together."

"Then we've already won." He again looked at the stars and felt at peace. He was content, in part because he belonged to something greater than himself. Not just their Quest, but to these people, his friends. He looked down at Gunnar who now lay comfortably across the hard wooden deck. It was that wood – difficult for most, but not nearly as hard as the stone ground of his past – that brought tears of pride to his eyes.

They experienced several highs and lows during the next half-mooncycle. Just after dawn on the following morning, at least three dozen porpoises appeared, darting in and out of their bow wave. They watched in wonder as Belkidar joined them, his behavior so natural, none would ever suspect he was anything else. But on the eighth night, they witnessed firsthand the terror of a hurricane. Waves swelled to sixteen elads, their tiny vessel soaring over each before plummeting back down again. Brohdan chose the ocean's depths to the peril above, yet thanks to Belkidar neither ship nor crew were ever in any danger, but the seasickness most experienced seemed real enough. Then, after several exhausting links, they finally emerged from the storm's wrath, and as their reward, they witnessed one of the most spectacular sunrises any had ever seen.

With a winter moon reflecting in the background on the twenty-fifth evening at sea, Indira noticed Belkidar had assumed a familiar look.

"I see you're progressing nicely."

"I think so," Belkidar replied lightly.

"You should turn back. Now. You've no hope of success."

"Then why are you wasting your time talking to me?"

"Because we're friends."

"No. Never yours. I was, and am, Krollum's."

"I am Krollum. He is me. You should know this."

"I know this all too well. You killed him with your birth."

"We are one in the same."

"You need some perspective."

Hildegard paused a long moment. *"How exactly do you plan to defeat me?"*

"Convincingly."

"I know you, Belkidar, and I've had thousands of cycles to prepare for anything you might try."

"That's what will make our victory all the sweeter."

"You're still a fool."

"Some things never change."

"Bad news?" Indira asked once Belkidar's attention returned.

"No, I don't think so. But he knows we're getting closer."

"What's our next move?" Batai asked.

"Nothing's changed. We have no choice."

Brohdan remained silent for several drus, considered the links he'd internalized their impending battles. "I'm ready for whatever Hildegard has planned." He said it humbly, matter-of-factly.

Belkidar looked from Brohdan to the eastern horizon. "We'll each discover our own worth soon enough."

Bedtime came early that night. Belkidar's conversation with Hildegard loomed in each of their minds, and everyone seemed content to end this day so they could begin the next anew.

Indira was the last to descend the stairs. She looked back and saw Gunnar snoring, then turned toward Brohdan and watched as he easily kept pace with the ship's unnatural speed. She knew he would soon scout linops ahead, and she marveled at his strength. He approached three quarters of a mooncycle without sleep, yet he continued flying as though he had just departed Tymoteu. "You shall be fine."

Chapter 15
Katja

*Only those who will risk going too far can possibly
find out how far it is possible to go.*

T.S. Eliot

Brohdan saw it several links before sunrise, climbed a thousand elads above the ocean for confirmation. Then he dove back to a safer altitude, scouring the horizon for threats as he descended. Having finally sighted Katja was a cause for relief and a source of anxiety. He was happy at the thought of finally getting some sleep, but he also realized the fate of the entire world would be decided here.

Batai was headed directly for the continent's southern tip. Brohdan initially recognized only vague features, but more details gradually appeared as he continued flying toward it. He looked left and followed the coastline as it stretched into the darkness, discerning a faint glow far to the north. He couldn't yet see the source of the light, but he guessed it came from a coastal city.

Then he turned his attention to the coastline itself. Although his sight wasn't as precise as it was during the day, it didn't take long to realize the unforgiving shorelines precluded any possibility of docking a ship. Angry waves crashed against sheer cliffs, and huge rocks littered the shallow waters below their hundred-elad summits.

"Belkidar, you must wake."

"I'm coming."

"What is it?" he asked as Brohdan landed in the water nearby.

"Katja. There's nowhere to dock, but I think there's a city further to the north."

"I understand." Belkidar took his Staff and struck it once against the deck, a muffled thud reverberated through the wood. Gunnar immediately stirred, and within moments, the others came racing up the stairs and into the crisp night air.

"Brohdan's spotted land, and thanks to Batai's navigation, we're on course. As I'd suspected, the terrain along the shoreline provides only a couple of suitable landing sites. Trillhell, the largest and most populated city, lies further to the north, but that'd be much too crowded for comfort, so we'll continue to the southeastern side as planned."

Gunnar was shaking his head. "I still don't understand why Hildegard would secure his entire shoreline, yet leave that spot open."

"When Hildegard shaped Katja's landscape to bolster his defenses, I believe he still needed a way to covertly travel to and from his home. His theft of the Jewel is a perfect example. Several hundred thousand people live in Trillhell, too many for him to evade. So he preserved a secluded piece of coastline to conduct his business, and the uninhabited region in the southeastern corner served his purposes nicely. Just as I hope it does for us."

"And I don't think it's as vulnerable as it appears," Batai agreed. "Hildegard must know enemy forces wouldn't land at Trillhell, so we should expect some sort of resistance after we land."

Brohdan, quiet during the conversation thus far, finally spoke. "I may've caused more harm than good."

"What do you mean?" Kiera demanded, admittedly a bit too adamantly.

"Hildegard strengthened his plans because of me."

"First of all," she began with an almost motherly tone, "you're a part of us. Secondly, you bring infinitely more strength to our cause than Hildegard could ever counter."

"Unquestionably," Batai agreed. "Brohdan, you're the most formidable creature I've ever seen. Yet you have such sincerity, such honor. You're invaluable, regardless of what Hildegard's planned."

"I appreciate your faith in me, but I won't be as satisfied until I prove my worth."

"Damn right," Belkidar agreed. "The same can be said for us all. A worthy song has never been written about a warrior's potential." He paused, reeled in his emotions. "You're no different than the rest of us, Brohdan. I've been fighting evil for thousands of cycles, but I'm never satisfied with what I might do tomorrow."

"I just hope I don't disappoint you," Brohdan said to his friends, but to Belkidar specifically.

"Do your best," he answered, looking each in the eyes. "Do that, and I'll be proud of you, all of you, regardless of the outcome. And I vow to do the same."

The weather remained cooperative, and Batai had little trouble navigating around the southern tip, keeping enough distance to avoid detection. At dusk on the third day after spotting land, they had turned northeast alongside the continent's eastern coast.

"I'd like to reach land while it's dark," Belkidar explained during their evening meal. "Tonight would be ideal since the moon is new."

"How much further?" Indira asked.

"Not long – another few dozen linaks or so. With any luck, we'll find the beach in a link or so."

"How?" Gunnar asked.

"I've already spoken with Brohdan. He'll fly ahead, near the coastline, searching for the narrow pass through the mountains. The beach isn't much bigger than this ship."

"Should we expect resistance before then?" Indira asked.

"I doubt they'd tip their hand before we reach land, especially since they can't know whether we bring an armada of warships or not. But considering how limited our options are, I believe the first of his Five Defenses will be somewhere nearby."

"We'll be ready," Gunnar said confidently. "So long as I've eaten first."

The group finished their meals, and soon thereafter, Brohdan silently departed for Katja's cold shores. In the meantime, the others made preparations for their short voyage to the beach, loading their smaller landing craft with their packs and supplies.

"How are you coming along?" Belkidar asked.

"Fine. I'm flying east of the mountains along the coast, below the tops to make sure I stay hidden. So far, though, all I've seen is – "

Silence. *"What?"* Belkidar asked.

"I found the beach!"

"Where?"

"About ten linaks west-northwest of you."

"Right. Please stay there and make sure we anchor in a good spot. Nice work."

Brohdan descended rapidly and leveled off just a few elads above the waves. Although he had been without sleep for nearly a mooncycle, he found himself alert, anxious to be back on land again.

"Brohdan's found the beach," Belkidar told the others. "We'll drop anchor shortly. Let's make sure we're ready."

"Right," Kiera said as she put the last of the packs in the boat. "I think we're just about there."

Brohdan watched the ship make its way up the coast. It appeared tiny, but he knew it moved with unnatural speed. *"That's a good spot."*

"Thanks. We'll see you soon."

Belkidar, Kiera, Indira, and Batai quickly repositioned themselves in the landing craft and headed for shore. With Einar and all of their supplies also on board, no room remained for a giant, so Gunnar was forced to swim. The distance was easily a linak or more, but he seemed indifferent to the task. Once his friends were safely en route, he checked the ship one last time before diving into the ocean.

He quickly gained on them, passing well to the north, but his wake still rocked their boat. By the time the others were halfway to the beach, Gunnar stood and waded the rest of the way.

Brohdan approached from further inland and landed in the water several elads next to him, his talons finally reacquainted with a solid surface.

"Long flight?" Gunnar asked.

"You could say that." He paused, watched their friends row closer. "Hildegard's Five Defenses await us."

"They do," Gunnar replied, peering through the narrow gap in the mountains.

"We must prove worthy of their trust," Brohdan said, looking into his friend's dark eyes.

Gunnar returned his gaze, immediately understood. "We owe him that."

Gunnar met the others a few hundred elads from shore and pulled them the rest of the way. They collected their belongings, shouldered their packs, and gathered on the beach. "We can't leave anything that can be traced back to us," Batai said. "Brohdan, do you think you could help?"

"Of course." He took flight, quickly covering the distance between the beach and the anchored ship. He landed on the aft deck, still beating his wings so that the vessel bore only a fraction of his weight. Then he extended the blade from his barz and drove it down through the wood. He repeated this twice more, breaking apart the aft portion of the ship, his weight accelerating its descent. Soon, he was forced to take flight as it disappeared into the black water.

He returned to the beach and settled in front of their small landing craft, nudging it to deeper water with his nose. Then he took to the air again, tucked his wings, and fell onto the boat, crushing it.

After he rejoined his friends, Gunnar couldn't wipe the smile from his face. "Did you have fun?"

"Maybe a little," he admitted, shaking water from his scales.

Batai turned to the gap in the mountains. "You know, despite how predictable our path is, we do have a few advantages. First, we have Brohdan. He can fly into the night sky and scout ahead of us. With his unique vision, he can discover things Hildegard assumed would be hidden. And just as importantly, we know he has Five Defenses, the first of which is likely nearby. He's lost the element of surprise."

"Beautiful," Kiera agreed. "Simple, yet brilliant."

Chapter 16
The First Defense

*Why should I fear death? If I am, death is not. If
death is, I am not. Why should I fear that which
cannot exist when I do?*

Epicurus

Kiera led them slowly into the narrow coastal pass, the eastern skies still black. Each remained alert, ears probing the silence, eyes combing the darkness. After nearly two links, they still found no sign of enemy forces.

After another linak, Kiera turned back toward the others. "If you want a break, now's the time. We have about a link before dawn, enough time to find shelter."

Indira was still searching the darkness. "The First Defense could be anywhere. Is it wise to rest here?"

"We can't go on forever," Batai explained, "and if Hildegard's forces wanted to contest our arrival, they would've done it by now."

Belkidar nodded. "I still think the First Defense will show itself soon enough, but Batai's right – we'll be better prepared for it if we're rested."

And so Kiera led them further north, deeper into the mountains. Before long, she rounded a low ridge to discover a wide copse of trees. "This should do nicely."

"Brohdan, we'd like to make camp here. Can you please scout the area?"

He 'cloaked,' then flew north, higher into the mountains, taking his time to search every gulley. Then he circled counterclockwise, his night vision detecting only a few nocturnal animals. *"It's clear for linops in every direction."*

"Thank you. Now please join us and get some sleep. You've earned it. The rest of us will split the watch."

They settled beneath the trees as dawn threatened the eastern sky. Batai posted two sentries, each on a hilltop overlooking east or west of their camp to warn of any ambush. As the others prepared their sleeping blankets, Brohdan was already fast asleep.

They alternated sleeping and standing watch over the next several links, taking great care to not disturb him as they walked past. The deep rumble of his heavy breathing vibrated through their boots, resonated through their bodies, mingled with the gratification they felt for finally being able to repay his tireless devotion.

When Belkidar woke him, Brohdan was surprised to see the sun sinking below the western mountains. "How long was I out?"

"Links," Belkidar answered, smiling. "You needed the rest. Besides, we thought it best if we traveled by night."

Kiera resumed their path beneath the steep cliffs, steadily moving deeper into the pass. As darkness once again consumed them, their progress slowed, yet they stuck to the foothills as Brohdan scouted for enemies. As the links passed, they eventually discovered a distant glow further inland.

"A city?" Indira suggested.

"It's the Southern Camp," Belkidar explained, "the primary base for Hildegard's southern army. He has similar camps throughout the continent, each a fort as large as a city, their primary mission to search for and destroy any and all threats. They send regular reports to Hildegard."

Gunnar felt at home in the highlands. He breathed deeply, savored the chilly air. "How far inland do these mountains go?"

"Linops," Belkidar answered, "eventually turning north to form Lake Mamate's eastern shoreline. When Krollum first discovered it, he made it into the gem of the continent, a sanctuary. But Hildegard had a different plan, used it as a sort of laboratory for his demented imagination. Local fishermen soon realized the creatures there were hazardous to their health. Lake Mamate eventually became its nickname and, over the centacycles, Krollum's name for it was forgotten."

"You plan to cross it?" Gunnar asked.

"I don't think we have any other choice. We're on the southeast corner of the continent, and Gul Krul lies at its center. Regardless of what decisions we make, we must travel north and west. We can't go too far west because we'd never bypass the Southern Camp unnoticed."

"Can we fight our way through?" Kiera asked.

"Maybe, but even if we survive, we'll have alerted Hildegard and the rest of his forces. By the time we made it halfway to Gul Krul, we'd have six or seven million after us." He shook his head. "No, we have no choice. I'd rather avoid Hildegard's hordes, even if that means we remain a little more predictable."

Belkidar considered their options. "A large river empties into Lake Mamate about halfway up its western coast. We could follow that, but it'd eventually lead us to the Northern Plains and Hildegard's central army. There's another tributary further to the south, but it's too close to the Southern Camp for it to be any use. So I think we'll take our chances on the lake. It's surrounded by mountains several thousand elads high, so whatever we may find there, we'll at least be able to deal with it in seclusion. Plus, if we stay near the western coast, we can find places to make land if needed."

"Mountain lakes are deep," Gunnar offered. "No telling what might be down there."

Belkidar nodded. "True, but I'd rather put my trust in our strengths than Hildegard's, and battling his armies is exactly what he wants. We must get to Gul Krul without starting another War. Stealth gives us an advantage, that's why there's only six of us after all." He turned to face Kiera. "Are you familiar with the settlements south of the lake?"

"Vaguely," she answered coyly.

"Good, we need supplies. Now let's see if we can get there without being spotted."

As dawn loomed behind them, Kiera continued a northwesterly heading through the mountains' southern foothills. She stayed in the long shadows, using the darkness for as long as she could. Gunnar kept a watchful eye ahead, as Batai did behind. Brohdan flew to the north, staying well below the peaks.

Indira listened, the wind sounding strange to her. In Ætheldell, it caressed the trees, weaving life with its currents. Here, it battered rocks and stripped bark, siphoning life with each gust. To the ears of an elf, it seemed as though – "

In an instant, she had an arrow nocked, then sent it into the darkness. Belkidar, walking several paces behind her, clutched the Staff tighter as the arrow disappeared from sight. "We are under attack!" she cried, another arrow whistling from her bow.

A piercing shriek abruptly ended the stillness in those peaceful moments before dawn. They drew their weapons, had their backs to one another by the time her second arrow forced another cry from the darkness. Brohdan soon hovered nearby.

"What makes noises like that?" Batai asked.

"So that's what he's got in mind," Belkidar said. "I've not heard their kind for kilacycles."

"What exactly is *their* kind?" Kiera demanded, her patience fading.

"Orcs. They were bred for slave labor, but Jenkar also used them to enforce some of his less popular laws. But that was before the War!"

"I am unfamiliar with them," Indira stated calmly.

"They're dim-witted and small, just over half the height of humans, but they have surprising strength and stamina for their size. They used small axes to hack at their enemies, but they can throw them if needed."

Just as Belkidar finished his hurried description, an immense sea of reeking bodies flowed over the higher terrain several hundred elads to the north. It appeared as though an enormous wave of an angry ocean had just crested a beach. They ran feverishly, grunting and shrieking as they descended toward them.

"Stay together!" Batai shouted.

Then Brohdan leaned forward from his hover, accelerating toward the advancing throng. He flew above the range of their axes, revealing his silhouette to his enemies.

The horde slowed from their furious sprint to an indecisive jog. Then they stopped, shouting at each other in a strange tongue, pointing toward the sky.

"How many are there?" Belkidar asked.

Brohdan flew north, directly over their center, amazed with how long it took to reach their rear ranks. *"Thousands! They stretch deep into the mountains."*

"When you attack, work your way from the edges toward their center. Above all, make sure they don't advance any further. Indira only has so many arrows, and I'd hate to use them all during the first few drus."

Brohdan turned east, flanking the orcs so that he wouldn't scatter them toward his companions. Before long, he'd completely circled their eastern lines, returning to where he'd started. He hovered there, alone, bridging the quarter linak that separated his friends from the endless orc sea. Then he filled his great lungs, tasted the pungent fuel as it sprayed from his glands, felt the intense heat as his igniters birthed an inferno.

He flew north, circled east, then back down and around to the west. The survivors ran in all directions, some even into Brohdan's path. They crashed into each other, toppled one another to the ground.

Brohdan saw that they were scattering, so he altered his strategy. He blew liquid flames, surrounded the throng with a wall of fire, his fuel burning hot long after it sprayed the ground. With the orcs entrapped, Brohdan spread his fire wide, sacrificing some of its intensity so that it covered a much wider area. Yet it was still Broglia fire, its fury melting metal axe heads as easily as orc bones. The dirt of the rocky ground flew high into the air with each pass. Orc bodies were blown into one another and often several elads above the ground as he completed pass after pass, his fire's deep rumbling reverberating through the foothills.

In all of his battles, Batai had never witnessed anything like it. He stared, transfixed, half in wonder and half in horror, as orc carcasses were blown aside like dolls. It seemed surreal, his fire wall illuminating the darkened valleys of the foothills, every attack eliciting dazzling reflections, their sheer volume vibrating deep in their chests.

And then several spears struck the ground to their east. Simultaneously, dozens of huge, green creatures with gigantic clubs trotted from the west. "Stand ready!" Batai yelled, turning toward the imminent sunrise, his armor glowing orange. "Gunnar, Kiera – ogres from the west! Indira – we'll take the centaurs!"

Remaining between them, Belkidar turned briefly to face the orcs. *"We've got company. Continue your attack, ours will begin shortly."*

Indira struck first, her arrows killing dozens of centaurs, their throwing spears still clutched in their hands. Seated silently atop Einar, Batai watched, studied his foes. The centaurs' lower half resembled a horse's body, and the human torsos that rose from their front hips were just as hairy. Each had what appeared to be a horse's mane that ran from their heads down their backs, and thick, bushy eyebrows and large, flat noses made them only distantly resemble humans.

Batai had spent his entire life around horses, but he'd never encountered any with temperaments like these. They approached with such hatred that Batai scarcely recognized any relation at all. Einar also sensed the evil in them, pulled against the reins that Batai held softly in his hand. Relatives or not, these creatures betrayed everything a horse was meant to represent.

Indira released over a hundred arrows in the initial moments of the attack, yet those that survived converged on her with great speed. Batai nodded once to her, and she adjusted her strategy accordingly.

And then Einar charged the approaching horde, Batai's sword held ready. Eager for battle, he hit full stride only a few elads from where he'd stood, closing the distance in a flash. Their heads were nearly level with Einar's, but he outweighed them three-fold. Batai brought his sword down, cut through the chest of his first victim, the momentum of Szurgord's blade unhindered by ligaments or bone.

Einar raced on, creating a wide path as he trampled dozens to the ground, the rumble of his hooves like thunder from low clouds. They'd reached a hundred elads into the horde before panic set in, a further insult to the charger. He veered right, crashed into the thickest of the centaur throng, Batai hearing bones crack under the magnificent collisions. Einar's legs kept churning, accelerating through them, his breast armor turning red as each broken body fell to the ground and slid beneath him. Batai soon realized his attendance was proving unnecessary. "Save some for me!"

Einar turned his head, revealing large, excited eyes and wide, flared nostrils.

"Fine, but remember my sacrifice."

Roughly a half-linak to the northeast, a small band of centaur scouts watched the battle unfold. Their Master had not prepared them for such formidable creatures, but they knew that fact would not save them, even if they were to escape with their lives. Torn between being slaughtered on this battlefield or murdered in Gul Krul, they hastily formulated a new plan.

Gunnar and Kiera faced a completely different battle to the west. While hundreds of centaurs formed the eastern flank of Hildegard's First Defense, only several dozen ogres made up its western flank. They were an elye or two shorter than Gunnar and, although not as muscular, actually outweighed him. Each carried an enormous club, at least three elads long, scarred from cycles of use.

"Whenever you're ready," Gunnar said, watching the ogres lumber up the hill.

"Now's as good a time as any."

Gunnar smiled as he drew his weapon, Kiera jogging to keep pace. His long strides covered the distance to five of them in drus. He brought his sword down on top of the lead ogre's head, embedding it into its chest. He pulled it out, the blade singing as it came free. He charged the second, knocked it off balance and smoothly severed its head before the other three could close.

Meanwhile, Kiera approached an ogre several elads to Gunnar's left, waited for it to attack. It looked like a mismatch, the ogre at least three times her height and twenty times her weight. With a dumb smile, it brought its club down in a crashing blow, but just as it fell, Kiera sprinted two steps, slid between its legs.

The heavy club missed, forcing the ogre off balance. Kiera grabbed a handful of the creature's tattered leggings and scaled its backside, climbing hand-over-hand to reach its broad back, then its shoulders. She steadied herself by squeezing its head between her knees, then slid a barbed dagger into its skull behind its ear. It went in with a muffled squelch, causing violent spasms as it toppled forward. Kiera got to her feet, using the embedded dagger to steady herself against its convulsions. Just before it landed, she leapt from its shoulders, sliding her dagger free. She landed in a somersault, rolled to her feet as the grey-green corpse crashed with a deafening thud.

Ogre scouts higher in the northeast foothills watched dumbly as the giant tore through their comrades. Fury grew in them, and they grabbed their clubs, ready to join the battle. But creatures approaching from the west stopped them before they could attack.

Most centaurs fled Einar, instead hurling their spears from a safer distance as he descended into the troughs of the rolling hills. Indira watched as he maneuvered through them, chasing down one after another. Hundreds lay dead, either mangled by Einar's tireless strength or Indira's unparalleled accuracy.

As Batai's sword came down on another exhausted centaur, Indira noticed a few huddled together behind a hill, hidden from his sight. They were beyond her bow's range, yet she watched intently as one moved slowly toward the top of the hill. Einar and Batai continued their assault on the remaining centaurs, moving lower in the rolling hills toward the foreground of Indira's view. In the background, she watched in horror as the lone centaur slowly crested the hill. She nocked an arrow and effortlessly drew her bow, her eyes focused on the centaur, her subconscious noting the currents through the tall grass, the way the smoke rose from Brohdan's fire.

Still several dozen elads away, the centaur watched as the charger chased down more of his comrades. He was their chieftain, the one who was supposed to lead them. Now was his only chance. He drew back, sent two spears racing down toward the knight.

Still out of range, Indira's counterattack was immediate, her bow thrumming twice before falling silent. Then she took a large quiver from her pack and sprinted toward the small band of centaurs that were still hidden from her friends.

Belkidar understood, knew she could take care of herself. He grunted softly, then turned his attention to the many ogres that still fought to the west.

Batai realized the attack too late. He saw his enemy's smirk a moment before the spear, knew he was killed. It fell from above, moving far too fast to evade. And then he noticed a flash to his left. Before he had time to turn his head, the object streaked from the fringe of his vision to its center, striking the centaur's spear. He watched in disbelief as Indira's arrow cut through the thick shaft, stared with wide eyes as both pieces fell harmlessly to the ground to either side of Einar's path.

He turned to thank her only to discover a second spear, then watched another arrow deflect its path. He raised his sword in thanks, Einar ignoring the temptation to retaliate. They continued their pursuit of the larger centaur group fleeing further to the east, knowing Indira could easily hunt down those that should've killed him.

The centaur leader had played its hand, the only one that had been available to it. Its small band turned and fled north, further into the foothills of the mountains and away from the pursuing elf.

As Gunnar was busy dispatching the remaining three ogres from his initial attack, seven others had encircled him. They grunted and snorted to each other, then closed on him.

Kiera, facing a lone ogre to his right, once again dodged a fatal blow. She leapt onto its thigh, then dove across the top of its chest. Its hand fumbled at its throat, discovered two deep gashes as she landed gracefully with a forward roll. It fell to its knees, dark blood spurting down its body, watched as she sprinted toward the giant.

Then Kiera's vision exploded with blinding light, then in an instant faded to black. She numbly felt her cheek scrape against dirt, her listless arms slide to her sides before skidding to a stop. Dazed, she struggled onto an elbow as her sight slowly returned. Ignoring her mounting nausea, she turned her head back to the ogre whose throat she had just slashed. It smiled triumphantly as it swayed on its knees. She shook her head defiantly, then saw its club resting only an elad or two behind her, its length easily surpassing her height.

Kiera turned back and saw the huge creature topple to the ground. Then she struggled to a knee, fighting to regain her balance, unaware of the two ogres approaching from behind.

Gunnar hadn't witnessed Kiera's attack that killed the ogre, but he did see its final act. His concern for her, now lying dazed with two ogres closing on her, gave his seven attackers the advantage. The nearest crashed its club into his forearm, his immaculate sword clanging to the ground.

Fury grew in him like a summer storm. Irritated by his mistake and terrified for his friend, he grew enraged, opened himself to his cycles of anger and frustration. Of loneliness and helplessness. The world faded, became only his enemies. He no longer noticed the sun's heat on his neck or the sweat that trickled down his back. He was no longer haunted by his childhood, nor his mother's final words. All was now, this moment, nothing else. All was savagery, ferocity, rage.

With a single stride, he stepped inside the ogre's next attack. In one fluid motion, he took its head in his hands and twisted. A pop, then wet, sickening crunches. He let go, let the corpse fall to the ground. He maneuvered around the back of the next, swung his fist hard at its back. He heard a muffled crack as its legs went limp, but he caught it, held it for an instant before slinging it toward another. The approaching ogre dodged to its left, but Gunnar was already there, his fist cracking into its jaw, dislocating it. It fell to its knees, stunned, as blood poured from its mouth. As it tried to determine what had gone wrong with its jaw, it heard a loud collision, noticed one of his mates abruptly land nearby, watched as it slid several elads before coming to rest beside him. Whatever had caused his jaw to break had apparently also caused his mate's right ear to bleed.

Gunnar ducked beneath a club, smoothly stepped toward the fifth ogre, swung his fist up. It collided with the underside of its jaw, reverberated along the surrounding foothills, and fragments of teeth joined blood and saliva in the pre-dawn light. Gunnar ignored the last two ogres, sprinted toward those that still threatened Kiera.

He launched himself, knocking both on their backs and landing flat on his chest. He scrambled to his feet, then reached down and grabbed the nearest, one hand clenched around its neck, the other around the inside of its thigh. Then he lifted the dazed creature off the ground, his grip eliciting a muffled crunch from its throat.

Kiera knelt in shock, her mind reeling. Her friend had hoisted an ogre – a creature weighing more than seven horses and standing nearly as tall as he did – high above his head! His eyes were mad with rage, the muscles along his back tore at his clothing as the ogre twitched in his fists. With a low, feral grunt, he threw the creature headlong toward the other, knocking it back to the ground where it lay motionlessly beneath the weight of the first.

Gunnar knelt beside his dazed friend. "Are you all right?" he thundered in an uneven, adrenaline-filled voice.

"I think so," she managed, rising to her feet. "But I'll feel a lot better after I find my daggers."

Gunnar chuckled, despite himself. Then he rose, his eyes focusing on the two remaining ogres from his previous fight. "They're mine."

"Fine. You go play. I won't be long."

Gunnar charged the first, feinted left, dodged a whirling club, stepped behind it. He swung hard, breaking ribs and doubling it over. Then he crashed his elbow into the back of its head, and it fell half-conscious at his feet.

The second ogre paused and looked down on its companion. Gunnar slowly planted his boot on the creature's throat. It gargled under his weight, sighed once, then fell limp.

Outraged, the second ogre roared as it raised club and lumbered forward. Gunnar caught its forearm before its swing had any momentum, but with its other hand, it similarly locked onto Gunnar.

With each other's forearms clasped, they circled one another, parlaying for position. When Gunnar's face came into view, Kiera saw that he was – *smiling!* Stunned, she realized he was toying with the beast, despite its fury over the death of its companion. Then Gunnar tightened his grip. The ogre howled, its hands instinctively opening. Gunnar jerked it forward, and it staggered off balance. He spun behind it, covered its mouth with his right hand, his left opposite it behind its head. Then he twisted.

In an instant, the ogre's arms went from reaching for Gunnar's head to hanging uselessly at its sides. Kiera could see its neck was badly dislocated; its chest still faced away from him, but its blank eyes stared at Gunnar as it collapsed to the ground.

He quickly turned and retrieved his sword. "I think the last three fled west!"

"I'm right behind you!" In reality, though, she had no hope of keeping up. Within moments, Gunnar disappeared beyond the crest of a hill. By the time she could see him again, he'd already impaled two and was in the process of finishing the third.

In the meantime, Belkidar stood in the center of the battlefield. To the north, Brohdan was flying low, his fire flashing intermittently as he flew down the remaining orcs. Indira had left his side to chase down a small band of centaurs while Einar finished off the rest. To his left, Gunnar and Kiera pursued the last of the fleeing ogres. He felt a surge of confidence, a wave of pride. They'd fared extremely well, and they hadn't even needed his help, which offered Hildegard no additional knowledge through the defeat of his First Defense. He smiled, despite knowing their path only grew more difficult.

Before long, after the remaining creatures had been hunted down, they made their way to Belkidar. Brohdan landed nearby, the old man forced to shield his eyes from the dirt that swirled from his wings. The low sun glimmered through the particles, the dragon's shadow its only blemish.

"Good little battle," Gunnar offered.

"What took you so long?" Kiera asked Batai as he made his way up the sloping terrain.

"Einar was a bit slow."

The charger grunted, shaking his head.

"Where's Indira?" Brohdan asked.

"She finished a small band higher in the foothills," Batai explained. "She shouldn't be too far behind us."

The others nodded, waiting for her to crest one of the lower hills.

A dru passed. Then two. Three.

"I'll go," Brohdan said, already several elads into the air.

They watched anxiously as he flew toward the general location Batai had indicated. When he turned back and searched a different area, their hearts fell. When he turned again, panic set it.

"Where is she?" Gunnar shouted.

"Stay calm," Belkidar answered, although his anxiety was evident in his uneven voice. "Brohdan will find her."

After several more drus, Brohdan still searched. A half-link passed, the others helping him. After two links, they still had not found her.

"Where could she have gone?" Kiera asked frantically.

"I don't know," Belkidar said softly. "She chased only a handful of centaurs, and she could've killed them long before ever getting in range of their spears."

"Did you find any tracks?" Brohdan asked.

"Too many," Kiera answered. "It's impossible to find hers after this battle."

"We can track her if we moved further into the mountains, where there aren't as many," Batai offered, hopeful.

"Perhaps," Belkidar answered, "if they weren't made of rock."

Batai understood. If Indira made it to those mountains, she'd be impossible to find.

"Can't you find her by seeing her heat?" Gunnar asked Brohdan.

"I could if she were here."

Gunnar's face contorted, and he slammed his huge fist into the ground as he bellowed his rage. "I'll kill them ALL!"

Belkidar sighed. "No, you won't. None of us will."

"What?!?" Gunnar and Kiera demanded together. Batai nodded, lowered his head, his right hand covering his eyes.

"This Quest is more important than any one of us. It's more important than *all* of us!" Belkidar explained, suddenly looking more like a frail old man than a powerful sorcerer. "I assembled this group for a reason, you can all take care of yourselves. Hildegard will eventually hear of this battle, and we can't spend days searching for Indira while he fortifies his plans. We all knew the risks, and I know any one of you would rather give your life than be the reason our Quest failed."

The others lowered their heads, knew he was right.

"I promised Juron I'd protect her," Brohdan said softly.

"She saved my life today," Batai added, slowly stroking Einar's neck. "Both of ours."

"She may yet live," Belkidar said, strength returning to his voice. "Don't underestimate her."

Gunnar had remained silent trying to get his temper under control. Kiera went to him and put a hand on his leg. "What will we do?" he finally asked.

"Exactly what we discussed. Indira knows we plan to cross Lake Mamate, so that's what we'll do. If she's still alive, perhaps she can meet up with us."

After a few moments, they silently turned and resumed their journey. As they left, Einar quietly made his way to where Indira's pack still lay on the ground. Batai retrieved it and stowed it next to his own before remounting and following his friends toward their fate.

They despondently continued through the foothills beneath the tall mountains, each realizing the finality that each step signified. They missed Indira, and while they realized their strength was significantly reduced without her, they missed her friendship far more than they could ever miss her abilities on the battlefield. They knew in their hearts that Indira's impact extended far beyond her archery skills, and they were lesser for her absence.

Yet their Quest still awaited them, and the fate of the world didn't discriminate against their successes or failures. For this reason, after several links Belkidar decided the group needed a short break, each taking the opportunity to rest and eat a small meal.

"I don't think I recovered all of her arrows," Batai said to no one.

"That's okay," Belkidar answered softly, "I can easily make more."

"Really?" Gunnar asked. "Why didn't you do it earlier?"

"She never used so many before," he answered with a shrug. "You performed incredibly well, by the way," he added sincerely.

"Oh?" Kiera began. "You weren't too busy to watch?"

Batai noted her attempt at humor, admired her leadership.

"I didn't want Hildegard to discover anything more than he already knows. And the closer we get to Gul Krul, the more he'll be able to learn. Besides you guys didn't need me."

The group remained silent for some time. Finally, Batai spoke. "Indira was the only one who could strike our enemies at a distance – at least, without using sorcery." His implication was obvious.

Belkidar nodded once. "I'll use it if I need to."

His companions suddenly realized the significance of their loss in the battles to come. If they ever needed to attack from a distance, Hildegard was sure to learn far more than they would prefer.

"Do you know what advantage that would give him?" Kiera asked.

"Not precisely, but if it happens during the next Defense, the advantage he gains will almost certainly prove insurmountable."

"Why?" Gunnar asked.

"Because of the time he'd have to act on the information he learns. We still have a long road ahead of us, and that gives Hildegard too much time to perfect his strategy, especially now that we have a glaring weakness. Remember, our entire Quest depends on using a small force to circumvent his assumption that only an all-out war could defeat him. That information is precious. The longer I wait to use sorcery, the less time he has available to him, so his advantage is reduced with each passing day."

Another silence enveloped them. Brohdan considered the past several links, replaying the battle over and over in his mind. "I can't be sure, but a few orcs may have escaped into the mountains."

"That's okay, I doubt they'll be a problem."

"Well," Gunnar said in his low voice, a wide grin on his face, "I'm not sure about the orcs, but I *am* sure about the ogres. None escaped."

Batai took his lead. "Well, perhaps if our foes more closely resembled big green sloths, we could've tracked them down too."

Gunnar just smiled.

Belkidar appreciated their attempts to pull the group out of the shock that still lingered from Indira's absence. "Considering the circumstances, I'm not too concerned with any creatures that managed to escape. Hildegard created these Defenses centacycles ago. These creatures you fought today – orcs, centaurs, and ogres – were put in place several dozen generations ago. They were initially bred in these mountains for a single purpose: to patrol this area and kill all intruders. They pass down their responsibilities and hatred of outsiders from one generation to the next."

"What a pitiful life," Gunnar remarked softly.

"Hildegard's system does offer a few advantages," Belkidar continued. "First, these creatures appeared to operate independently of his main armies. That autonomy benefits Hildegard, but we gain a few advantages as well. For instance, they were poorly trained. None were battle-tested and all frightened much too easily. Their only responsibility was to kill any intruders that traveled through their domain. Hildegard bestowed them life for just that purpose. Now, after numerous generations had guarded this very pass, their time had finally come. And they failed. I doubt very much the few that survived will be rushing to tell their master of their incompetence. More likely than not, they'll return to their dwellings and pray Hildegard never discovers them."

Batai nodded at Belkidar's logic. "Since there's no general these creatures report to, his other forces will be none the wiser. If any survivors won't report their failure themselves, and since there are no battle commanders to do it, I doubt Hildegard will be getting any updates on our progress."

"At least for now," Brohdan added.

"At least for now," Belkidar agreed. "I think it's safe to assume that each Defense will prove more difficult than the last, so I expect our enemies will become more formidable with each battle. Even if they too lack experience, their talents alone will carry them further."

Batai stroked Einar's neck, encouraged by his words. "I'm proud of the way we worked together. We should enjoy this victory, because we've got a tough road ahead."

Belkidar nodded. "Let's put this battlefield behind us." His blue-grey eyes squinted toward the sun. "It's nearing midday. We can talk more about this tonight, but for now let's move."

Batai turned back toward the battlefield, now several linaks behind them, watched the crows gather for their feast. Brohdan also took one last look, and he was suddenly amazed with his indifference. Before leaving Sul Brul, he'd never killed beyond the necessity to hunt, but this Quest had taught him the grim reality of battle. Now, as he considered the thousands of blackened corpses that stretched deep into the hills, his lack of emotion troubled him. He desperately wanted to destroy Hildegard and his evil, but at what cost?

Two links after sunset, they found a shallow depression in which to sleep. They took turns standing watch, yet when the time came, each slept fitfully. Kiera dreamt of a sister she never had, Gunnar of a lost sibling, one he couldn't protect. Belkidar dreamt of a daughter – too young, too innocent, too precious; Batai of a comrade in arms, a spark of light in utter darkness. A friend.

Brohdan also dreamt of a sister, his pack. His charge. His failure.

Chapter 17
The Second Defense

If you're going through hell, keep going.

Winston Churchill

They proceeded in silence toward Lake Mamate, their progress swift despite lacking horses. Brohdan scouted around them, mostly staying to their northwest to remain concealed from the Southern Camp.

After seven nights, Kiera noticed a few birds in the distance, and as the links passed, their numbers grew. "We're getting close," she said during their midday meal on the following day.

"Our first task is to buy a boat," Belkidar began. "If we can find one big enough, a few horses would also be helpful."

"I'll take care of that," Kiera offered. "I'd like Batai to go with me, but the rest of you should stay hidden."

"You're right," Belkidar agreed, "we shouldn't be seen together. While you're in town, we'll go north into the mountains east of the lake and wait for your signal."

Gunnar was nodding. "We need to rendezvous far enough away where nobody will see us."

"Good point," Kiera agreed. "If we go far enough north, the shore veers to the east, behind some mountains. That'll provide cover from the settlements."

"I can help you find each other again," Brohdan offered, "but I shouldn't fly during the day while we're in sight of the villages."

"Agreed," Belkidar said. "For now, let's plan to rendezvous there, behind those mountains. Brohdan can relay any changes."

After taking a few more drus to enjoy the rare break, Batai offered for Kiera to join him atop Einar. Once mounted behind him, they departed quickly to the west.

"We should get going too," Belkidar suggested. "Either we make Kiera's rendezvous or we'll never hear the end it."

Gunnar took the lead, feeling comfortable as he climbed deeper into the mountains despite being several thousand linops from his adopted home. Using the Staff as a walking stick, Belkidar followed. Brohdan flew ahead, searching for potential enemies while guiding Gunnar onto the swiftest path through the mountains.

"What's your plan?" Batai asked.

"To find a boat and a few horses, of course," she replied just behind his left ear.

"Thanks. How exactly do you plan to do that?"

"I'm not sure yet. I probably won't know until I talk with the owner. My only concern is getting one with a big enough bedroom."

Batai laughed. "You're definitely one of a kind."

Brohdan guided the others almost due north, following a relatively gentle path through the steep terrain. Gunnar was impressed with the scenery, despite his time in the Midrogrus. They walked beneath pines and spruce, their aromas a welcomed change from the battlefield.

"If we continue this pace, we should make the lake in four days," Belkidar estimated.

"I hope Kiera is doing just as well," Gunnar offered.

Einar quietly entered one of the many small encampments situated along Lake Mamate's southern shores. Batai and Kiera looked in wonder at the enormous body of water and the austere mountains that formed its eastern and western shores. Although Batai couldn't see far enough to confirm it, he assumed similar mountains formed its northern shoreline as well.

"I never tire of this," Kiera said. "It's like we're looking through a window into another world."

Batai's eyes traced the line of mountains to either side. "I've never seen anything like it." Then a thought occurred to him. "I have no idea how we're going to meet up with the others," he said, studying the eastern shoreline. "Those cliffs continue for as far as I can see."

"Some must be five hundred elads high."

"We'll have to find the lowest point and hope that's where they'll be waiting for us."

"First thing's first," Kiera said as she smoothly dismounted the huge charger. "We've got some business to take care of." She walked forward, reaching high to run her hand under the length of Einar's neck and head.

"How would you like us to help?" Batai asked.

"Actually, I think my chances are best if I work alone."

Batai considered that, realizing a small woman haggling by herself offered unique opportunities. But he also understood the dangers. In the end, he trusted her. "I'll be mingling if you need me."

Kiera, now standing alone on the outskirts of the encampment, pulled her hood over her hair, lowered her head into the gusting wind, and walked toward the unsuspecting settlement.

The sun set early there, thanks to the towering mountains to the west. Batai approached the water, and as the evening darkness engulfed him, he noticed a large boat tied to a long pier bobbing slowly with the small waves. He studied it, wondering what type of fish such a large vessel might hunt. Then he saw a sailor make his way above deck and took the opportunity to see if he could learn anything about their impending journey across the lake.

"Good evening!" Batai said as Einar neared the boat.

The sailor said nothing, continuing his chores in silence.

Batai became slightly irritated with his poor manners. "I said good evening."

Again, the sailor ignored him.

Now more angry than irritated, Batai guided Einar to the ship's stern, giving the rude sailor one final chance for a pleasant conversation. "Perhaps you didn't hear my previous greetings," he said with forced patience.

"Oh, I heard you, Batai, I was just too busy to answer," Kiera said as she pulled in a mooring line.

"Kiera!" Batai said in shock. "But, how did you – "

"Shhh! Not so loud!"

"But how did you manage to steal this ship so quickly?"

"First of all, I didn't *steal* it! I simply managed to procure it in a game of cards."

"So quickly?" he asked again.

"We're in a hurry, are we not? Besides, these imbeciles aren't worth any more of my time. Now, if you'd kindly get yourself aboard and take care of the horses, we can be on our way."

"Horses?"

The next few links passed quickly for the busy duo. After loading the ship with fresh water and supplies, they slowly disembarked and made their way north. With the help of a cooperative breeze, they guided the vessel forward, using only a fraction of the sails to keep their workload manageable. As midnight approached, they found themselves alone on the water.

Gunnar continued for another link, finally finding level ground to make camp. Brohdan joined them, forced to sit a short distance away where the trees were less dense. He watched his friends, both fast asleep. They were his pack, his family. But his pack was already one member short, and they still had four Defenses to go. As he kept watch, he sent a silent apology to Juron, wondered if one of them would someday have to do the same for Mikka.

That night, Batai navigated toward the center of the lake, hesitant to turn east until they were well clear of the settlements. That would add at least a day to their travels, but it was worth it. Besides, he knew Belkidar and Gunnar needed time to make their rendezvous, so he stayed patient, his goal to sail beyond the local fishing waters before sunrise. "I doubt we'll get much sleep tonight."

"That's all right. You can use the time to tell me about your travels."

The two continued slowly north, trading stories from their considerable travels. Kiera was amazed with Batai's past, not just his battle experience, but what he'd often been forced to endure. Similarly, he was impressed with Kiera's adventures, especially considering her relative youth.

Three days passed. Gunnar and Belkidar continued north through the mountains. The scenery was as beautiful as it was demanding, but Brohdan's scouting reduced their efforts considerably. Batai and Kiera faced their own struggles. They took turns at the helm, the other managing the sails or preparing their meals. They anchored each night to sleep, but only for a few links since that was the best time to travel unnoticed. Finally, at dawn on the fourth day, Batai spotted the bend in the shoreline where it turned east. They were getting close.

Gunnar rose quietly, walking to the edge of their campsite to where his waterskin hung on a branch. When he returned, he saw Belkidar rising from his sleeping blankets.

"Where's Brohdan?"

"He's scouting ahead," Gunnar answered in his deep rumble.

"I see," he said as he rummaged in his pack, finally finding the dried meat he'd been searching for. He'd just completed his small meal when Brohdan landed a few dozen elads away. He appeared concerned. "Is there a problem?"

"For me? No. For you, I think so."

"What is it?" Gunnar asked.

"As you know, the lake lies only a few linaks ahead."

"That's good," he remarked, confused.

"True, but it's at least a hundred elads below us.

"What?" Belkidar asked.

"We're on a mountain. We've been climbing higher and higher ever since we left the others. Unfortunately, the water level stayed the same," he added with a smirk. "I think you're going to have to jump."

"I hope this isn't too entertaining for you," Belkidar said after a few curses.

"Why not just change yourself into something that can fly us down?" Gunnar asked.

"Too much sorcery to risk, especially considering Gul Krul lies just on the other side of the lake." He lowered his head, considered their options. "We should be fine if the cliff's only fifty elads or so."

"I'll see what I can find," Brohdan said, extending his wings.

"Isn't this lake dangerous?" Gunnar asked.

"Yes," Belkidar grunted, apparently annoyed at something. "But we won't be in the water long."

They packed their meager supplies, and within a quarter link, Brohdan returned, unable to conceal his smile.

"Oh, no," Belkidar grumbled, shaking his head. "I don't want to hear it."

"It's actually good news. I discovered a small vessel only a quarter linak from the mountains."

"That is good news. Any suitable cliffs around?" Belkidar asked.

"A couple that must be seventy elads. I'll see if I can find a shorter one."

"Please do, but we shouldn't linger too long. If you can't find any within a link, don't bother."

"Right." He departed again, Gunnar and Belkidar following. After a quarter link, he returned, landing on a nearby pinnacle. "I found another cliff," he said in his deep voice as they passed beneath him. "It may be a little shorter, but not much."

"That'll have to do. Please let the others know the plan."

Brohdan leapt from the mountaintop, spread his wings as he fell, and soared through a cut in the ridgeline. The others followed, albeit less gracefully.

"I could use a swim," Gunnar commented, adjusting his large pack.

"Speak for yourself."

"You don't like swimming?"

"Absolutely. As a dolphin."

"When did you wake?" Kiera asked as she sat up from her sleeping blankets.

"About a link ago. I wanted to search for them."

"By yourself?"

Batai smiled. "The winds were light."

"But we decided to take a short nap only if we *both* got some rest."

"I couldn't sleep." He turned, pointing toward the distant cliffs. "Looks like they're the lowest in the area. With any luck, that's where they'll be."

"Good," she answered, getting to her feet. "Care for some food?"

Halfway through their modest meal, a wave rocked the boat. "Wind?" Kiera asked.

"No, something else caused that," he answered, heading toward the bow, Kiera closely behind. They searched the water but found nothing.

"Good morning," Brohdan said from behind them, his head protruding from the water.

"Good morning, Brohdan!" Kiera answered, her concern forgotten.

"I see you found a nice boat."

"That was her doing," Batai said. "Just don't ask how she managed it."

"It was nothing," she explained vaguely. "Do you know where we're to meet the others?"

The dragon turned his head, creating more waves. "Right there," he said, nodding toward the saddle in the mountains.

"When are we to fish them out of the water?" Batai asked, unable to hide his grin.

"In about a link."

"That soon? You made better time than I thought."

"Are they really going to jump?" Kiera asked, grinning.

"Yes, and Belkidar isn't exactly thrilled about it."

"Well, there's nothing like a morning swim to brighten your day!" she exclaimed.

Gunnar led Belkidar quickly through the mountains. The path Brohdan chose was still steep, but much less so than the surrounding terrain. Within a link, he discovered evidence of water on the horizon. As he continued, Lake Mamate opened before him like a trap door.

"Found it," he said with a smirk over his shoulder.

Belkidar took a moment, admiring the beauty of the lake and the cliffs that made up its shoreline. "Pity Hildegard had to ruin it with his experiments. It'll take eons for nature to reclaim what she's lost."

"I think I see the others," Gunnar announced, pointing to an approaching vessel.

"Hmm, that's a fairly large boat for these parts. I wonder how she managed it."

"I'm sure we'll find out soon enough," Gunnar said. "Let's prep our belongings for the jump."

"You're really looking forward to this, aren't you?"

"Sure. It'll be fun."

"Hmph." He mumbled some more curses as he removed his pack. "Please toss these toward Kiera's latest bounty. We can fetch them on our way there."

"Won't they sink?"

"I don't think so."

"You used sorcery?"

"Yes."

"But you said Gul Krul was too close!"

"I did this almost a mooncycle ago, before we left Brodor."

"Oh. I suppose that's okay."

Belkidar sighed. "You've spent too much time with Kiera."

"They've made it to the edge," Brohdan told the others.

"Excellent," Batai said. "We should be in position within a few drus."

"I'll update Belkidar." Then he disappeared from sight, only to explode from the water, creating thousands of tiny ripples as drops were flung from his powerful wings.

Belkidar watched him approach. "They'll be ready," Brohdan explained.

"Very good, but why not just send me your thoughts?"

"We're safe behind the mountains like we planned. Besides, I wanted to watch."

Belkidar again cursed under his breath as Gunnar giggled in the background.

"You're not afraid of heights, are you?" Brohdan asked.

"Of course not!" the old man replied loudly. "At least, not when I have wings."

"You've got to be joking!" Gunnar said.

"Listen, I spent the past eight thousand cycles with wings, whenever I needed them! They give you a sense of control, security. Falling doesn't."

"Don't worry, Belkidar. Once gravity takes over, you'll be fine."

"Thanks for that."

"Don't be so touchy," he said, tossing the first pack over the cliff. "I was only joking." He threw the others, watching them land near the boat with a splash. Then he turned to Brohdan. "Is it cold?"

"No, not for me at least," he answered, his grin aimed toward Belkidar.

"I guess I'll find out soon enough. Are they ready?"

"Yup. Kiera's waiting impatiently in the bow."

Gunnar measured a few paces from the cliff, then turned back, his smile huge. "See you on the other side!" Then he sprinted toward the water, planted his left foot only elyes from the edge and appeared to take flight. But just as he'd predicted, gravity took over, the cliff face racing behind him.

Brohdan watched while Belkidar stood a few paces from the edge, then smiled as he saw his huge friend tuck his knees to his chest. An instant later, the water exploded, the spray seemingly reaching halfway up the cliff. Kiera and Batai braced themselves as the huge wave approached.

Within drus, Gunnar was seen swimming toward the boat. On his way, he collected their packs, tossing them aboard one-by-one. Then he hoisted himself onto the stern using large ropes Batai had secured onto the deck. He shook water from his hair and beard, then gave Belkidar a cheerful wave, the boat taking a long time to settle.

Brohdan's grin never faded. "I guess that means it's your turn now."

Belkidar looked first at the nauseatingly jovial dragon and then at the distant lake below. The sorcerer slowly approached the cliff, paused a moment, then jumped. Brohdan was surprised to see so little hesitation. He looked down and watched, almost feeling sorry for him as he sped toward the water.

The impression was somewhat different for those on the boat. They stared transfixed as the sorcerer clumsily fell. Belkidar, perhaps the most powerful creature in the world, plummeted feet-first with most of his robe flying above his head, his skinny legs bare. Gunnar, Batai, and Kiera watched through tears, no longer trying to hide their amusement. Much like a horse must occasionally be put down to end its suffering, Belkidar's entry into Lake Mamate was an act of compassion.

Nobody said a word as Gunnar helped Belkidar out of the water. Kiera couldn't help likening his sodden appearance to a dog after receiving a detested bath. His beard hung awkwardly from his chin, his robes clung to his legs, and his thin white hair dripped loudly against the awkward silence. He brusquely took a large cloth from Batai and began drying himself.

Brohdan approached and landed smoothly in the water. "Is everybody okay?" he asked, breaking the silence.

"I think so," Batai replied with some difficulty.

"Some of us more than others," Kiera shrieked, no longer able to hold back her hysterics. Batai and Gunnar quickly followed suit.

"What did I miss?" Brohdan asked.

"More than you will ever know," Gunnar managed.

"I never knew you had such exquisite legs," Kiera said.

Belkidar smiled. "I never said it would be graceful," he explained, shaking the water from his ears.

Once everybody recovered from Belkidar's fall from grace, Batai took the helm and headed northwest toward the center of the lake.

"Head north," Belkidar said.

"But we planned to sail up the western coastline, to stay hidden from Gul Krul."

"True, but that was before we lost Indira. If she survived, she'll be in those mountains somewhere," he explained, nodding to the east.

"You're sure she wouldn't follow our trail to the encampments?"

"Not entirely," Belkidar admitted. He bowed his head, considered each possibility, then opened his tired eyes and continued. "If she didn't make it, we accept more risk of being seen if we stay in the east. But if she somehow survived, we know she'll try to make it here, to Lake Mamate. She knows an elf would attract unwanted attention, so I think she'll stick to the mountains."

"Why do we risk more by staying on the east side of the lake?" Gunnar asked. "Wouldn't it be better to stay as far from Gul Krul as possible?"

"Not necessarily. That's what Hildegard would expect. And staying on the east side keeps us in view of Hildegard's scouts in the west. But if we sail up the western shoreline, staying below the mountains, we'll be hidden from Gul Krul and its spies."

"Will we run into anyone on the way?"

"I doubt it. Lake Mamate has a fierce reputation, so few venture far from shore. Fishermen are the only ones on the water, but Batai passed beyond their fishing grounds three days ago."

A long moment passed. "How long before we abandon her?" Kiera asked softly, staring into the eastern mountains.

Belkidar looked down again, sighed. "A couple days. Then we must turn west before we cross north of the river mouth. That'll be when we're most vulnerable, so we'll need the cover of the western mountains."

Batai nodded. "Are you willing to risk sorcery so close to Gul Krul?"

"A little, but not until we turn west. It's just like when we crossed the Celornorin, the sorcery needed to alter water currents and wind direction is relatively insignificant. I doubt Hildegard will even notice it, and even if he does, he'll gain nothing."

The remainder of the day passed quickly, each taking turns searching as the mountains drifted by. By nightfall, they had prepared simple meals of dried venison and potatoes that Kiera had acquired from the southern settlements.

"So tell me, how exactly did you manage this?" Belkidar asked, tapping his Staff onto the ship's deck.

"Don't forget the horses," Batai added.

"Horses?" Belkidar asked, set to enjoy a good story.

"It was nothing, really," Kiera said. "Let's just say those poor saps don't know the first thing about poker."

"Well, I would imagine not," Belkidar agreed. "Outside influences are limited, especially those from Tymoteu."

"That's a shame," Kiera said, dismissing the news. "Perhaps if they'd given my offer more thought, they'd still own a boat."

"Were they cocky?" Gunnar asked.

"In the beginning."

"What did you bet?" Batai asked.

"A pair of my daggers. After I showed them what Szurgord's steel could do, they were more than happy to wager eight horses."

"I'm sure they weren't as happy after you won," Gunnar suggested.

"Not so much. But that didn't stop them from trying to win their horses back. So I asked what else they had to wager, and after a few whispered discussions, they offered a boat. After taking a look at it, I agreed to bet the eight horses along with four daggers for the boat and some supplies."

"How'd they take losing a second time?"

"Not very well. I had to show them Szurgord's work one more time before they let me leave."

"You didn't kill anybody, I hope," Belkidar said. "We don't need the attention."

"Of course not. But I did show them how smoothly my daggers pass through all sorts of clothing. They looked pretty silly running away in just their boots."

"Remind me to never play poker with you," Gunnar said, slowly shaking his head.

"Did they ever have a chance?" Batai asked.

"Of course not!" Kiera said. "First of all, I'm a better card player than they'll ever be."

"Second of all," Belkidar continued for her, "the half dozen cards she has strategically placed throughout her clothing all but guarantee victory."

"Oh, I didn't even need those."

"Like I said," Gunnar whispered to the paladin, still shaking his head, "never let me play cards with that woman."

Everyone save Brohdan had a refreshing night's sleep. The next day passed in much the same manner, each taking turns searching the eastern mountains for their friend. The winds were favorable, so Belkidar's assistance wasn't yet necessary.

During the quiet links of the night, Brohdan once again allowed his mind to drift, but Indira was all he could think about. He knew the odds of her still being alive were miniscule, especially since he failed to find any trace of her so soon after the battle had ended. What could've happened to her? They couldn't find her body, but with all of the corpses that littered the battlefield, that wasn't a surprise.

She was part of his pack, and her loss was too permanent – too *final* – for him to think about so soon after losing her, so he eventually forced his thoughts from one lost friend to another: Mikka. He wanted her to be happy, and he wondered if she had perhaps chosen the same path as her father. He hoped so. Her struggles in her own grombit would only help her relate to her students, and he knew Boseda would teach her everything he knew.

Brohdan understood that he needed Mikka in his life before he could ever be truly happy. But he knew the odds. He was on a Quest unlike any in history. He chose to meet his enemies on the battlefield, and because these enemies were both plentiful and formidable, he deeply regretted that he'd probably never see her again, a prospect made ever more likely with Indira's loss. He was haunted by the fact that he *intentionally* chose a course which took him further and further from his mate. He didn't regret his choice to confront Hildegard, but he felt guilty that his decisions hurt someone he so genuinely loved.

Their second dawn on Lake Mamate came too quickly. The huge dragon dipped his head below the lake's surface, raised it, and shook the water from his scales. The cold refreshed him, but his mood from the previous night was not so easily rejuvenated. Indira's loss still haunted him, and the thought of Mikka and their potential life together still lingered in the corners of his mind.

Soon, the others made their way from the ship's bowels. Belkidar was the last to emerge. "I hope everyone slept well last night," he growled, "because we have another long day ahead of us."

"What's on the agenda?" Kiera asked in a perky voice.

"Sailing," he replied, glaring at her dimples.

"Did Grandfather have a bad night?"

He ignored her, his face unusually grave. "We can't spend any more time searching for her."

Gunnar stared at him with disbelieving eyes. Batai looked down, his anger surpassed only by his helplessness.

"We're too vulnerable here, and we can't give Hildegard any more time to fortify his plans."

Brohdan couldn't help notice the single tear that fell into his beard.

Batai looked up, stared into the mountains, willing his eyes to find her.

"Head west, Batai."

The paladin stood frozen, his eyes still focused to the east.

Belkidar walked to him, placed a frail hand on a wide shoulder. "We must move on. That's what she'd want."

Batai nodded once, then silently left for the helm. Within drus, he pointed the bow west, and their speed increased three-fold. Gunnar and Kiera stood together in the stern, watching the eastern mountains shrink, then disappear.

Three days later, the towering mountains of Lake Mamate's western shores came into view. By midday, they found themselves sheltered beneath them. Batai turned north, and Belkidar slowed their pace as they drew ever closer to Gul Krul.

"It's even more imposing than the eastern shore," Kiera noted.

"Austere," Gunnar agreed, staring up at them. "I've seen my share of mountains, but these are unique."

"Hildegard made it so," Belkidar explained. "Unless you can fly, you're forced to go around them. And for good reason; Gul Krul lies only a few linops to the west."

"So we're getting close," Brohdan said.

"Yes and no. It may only be a few linops away, but thanks to Hildegard's precautions, we still have a long way to go."

Batai unrolled a rough map of the area that Kiera had obtained with the boat, and the others gathered around. "I'd estimate our position to be here."

Belkidar studied it for several moments, then nodded. "Agreed."

"I'll follow the cliffs until we approach the river mouth, here," he explained, sliding his finger halfway up the coast. "I'll swing wide there to make sure we're not seen. Once we're north of the river, we can take shelter under the mountains again."

Belkidar nodded slowly, admiring how naturally leadership came to him. He understood firsthand the rarity of the skill, to be able to take command without imposing doubt, disparity, or envy in others. To align everyone's personal and shared ambitions toward a singular, collective goal is an art, and in this regard, Batai was the greatest artist Belkidar had ever seen.

Brohdan scouted ahead as the sun swept across the sky, only his head and neck protruding from the water. Batai positioned the others to best search for threats. Belkidar stood in the bow scanning ahead and to port while Kiera and Gunnar searched from the stern and starboard, respectively. Batai guided the vessel through the deepening shadows of the mountains, exploring for any signs of danger.

Brohdan, of course, was in a much better position to discover potential threats. His heightened senses would alert him if any enemies drew near, the water amplifying any sounds made by the lake's residents. Yet despite these advantages, he couldn't detect the small waves that slowly converged on the boat, nor could he distinguish the sounds of his enemies from the millions of other creatures that lived in those waters. And he couldn't have known they were moving into the jaws of their trap.

An enormous six-headed creature emerged from the surface of Lake Mamate not far ahead of where Brohdan slowly swam. The Broglia Black immediately took flight, the resulting mist illuminating the large vortices that trailed his wingtips as he gained altitude. From the air, he realized there were actually four of these mammoth creatures, and they surrounded the boat. He dove toward the one that blocked their path to the north. *"There're four of them!"*

"Hydras!" Belkidar called, raising his Staff. He didn't want to use sorcery, especially this close to Gul Krul, so for now all they could do was wait and hope Brohdan could slow them.

"How do we kill them?" Gunnar asked.

"Their hide is hard, like armor. Our only chance is to take out as many of their heads as we can; even a single brain will keep its vital organs functioning."

"How do we do that?" Kiera asked.

"I don't know," Belkidar answered, working the Staff in his hands. "Brohdan can do it, but he won't have enough time to kill all four before they reach us."

"Sorcery, then?" Batai asked.

Belkidar studied his enemies, turning from one to the other, judged how long it'd take before they converged on the boat. "Not yet, but I'll have no choice if they get much closer."

The others understood. Their Quest hung in the balance, their odds of success fading with each elye gained by the hydras. Any significant sorcery this close to Gul Krul would provide Hildegard with everything he needed to defeat them.

"Brohdan, unless I use sorcery, you're our only hope. You must destroy or sever all six heads to kill them. And you must hurry!"

The concern evident in Belkidar's message alarmed him, added a sharp edge to his fury. He flapped his powerful wings, increasing his airspeed as he dove toward his enemy. As he approached, he realized the hydra was larger than he originally thought. Much larger. Each neck rose at least twenty elads above the surface, and he could only guess at what lay below. It had scales instead of skin, but they appeared much tougher than his. Not entirely sure how effective his fire would be, he nonetheless blew an intense stream toward one of its heads. Then he beat his wings harder, exploded through the billowing smoke, staying just beyond its reach. As he climbed higher, he peered around and saw the creature dip its head into the water, extinguishing the flames, continuing unharmed through the smoke.

Brohdan turned and again dove toward it. As he neared, he arched his back, flapped his enormous wings, climbed just out of reach of its many jaws. As he did so, he let his tail continue down along his previous path and, at the last moment, extended his blade. Because he'd begun to climb into the sky while his barz continued to swing down toward his enemy, his tail acted like a whip. He barely heard the blade penetrate its scales, but he clearly felt it pass through its spine. Then he banked hard, flapped his wings once, twice, used the turn to help keep his barz from striking his belly in its follow-through, his eyes never leaving the hydra. He watched as one of its heads and the upper third of its neck slid into the water, blood spurting from the stub that remained.

The others anxiously measured Brohdan's progress, and despite his success, every pass took precious time. Belkidar watched as his friend severed the hydra's fourth head, his forehead creased, his index finger tapping the weathered wood of the Staff. It was taking too long. He knew what must be done, and in doing so, he chose to die later, perhaps in Gul Krul, instead of today, on Lake Mamate. Resolved, he raised his Staff high, faced the hydra to their west, silently apologizing to his friends. But an instant before he attacked, he noticed a flash streak overhead, racing toward the east. Before he could turn to investigate, he discovered it was only the first of a dozen, all originating from atop the western mountain cliffs high above the water.

"She's alive!" he yelled, turning to see her arrows lance through the eyes of the eastern hydra. Twelve arrows, twelve eyes, all striking nearly simultaneously, its six shrieks fighting for dominance as its spasms turned the waters white.

The others weren't as quick to realize what had happened, but after Belkidar's elated cry, they instantly understood. Batai, Gunnar, and Kiera turned from where the hydra fell thrashing into the water, stared in disbelief toward the western cliffs. There, on a distant mountaintop, with the afternoon sun at her back, they saw the silhouette of a friend.

Brohdan had just severed the sixth and final head of the northern hydra. With grim determination, he turned to the southeast, yet to his astonishment, he saw its final two heads sink below the surface. *"You used sorcery?!?"*

"No! Indira saved us!"

Brohdan's heart leapt. He roared, deep and long, rolling in midair despite the circumstances. He couldn't believe she was still alive! And that she had somehow made it all the way here to save them! With renewed determination, he climbed higher, prepared his next attack.

Indira had studied the hydras after they'd appeared far below, and at first it was simple to predict their movements. But after witnessing the deaths of their comrades, the last two acted sporadically, moving their long necks unpredictably as they swam ever closer to the boat and her pack. She watched from high above as Brohdan's first attack against her nearest foe failed, the hydra dodging his blade at the last moment.

She turned to the southern hydra, drew her bowstring as she studied the swaying movements of its six heads. She took an uncharacteristically long moment before releasing her arrow, then instantly nocked and released a second. Then she watched, patiently awaiting the results that she'd use to hone her next volley.

The first arrow headed directly for one of the creature's eyes, but at the last moment, it veered left, the arrow glancing harmlessly off its scales only an elye from its mark. The second arrow found more success, piercing through an eye of a neighboring head. An earsplitting screech, then it slumped forward, its neck hanging limply, its head dangling in the cold water.

The creature's five remaining heads moved frantically, and she again took a long moment to recognize its patterns. Then her bowstring hummed, the hydra never seeing the tiny projectile. Another shriek pierced the cool breeze, another head swung limply, but it continued onward, straight for her friends.

Kiera watched Brohdan fly overhead toward the western hydra. Distracted, she barely noticed a silvery flash in her periphery. She instinctively ducked, drew two daggers, faintly registered the whir of Gunnar's massive blade as it swung less than an elye beside her right ear.

Gunnar hadn't realized what flew from the water, yet he unconsciously drew his sword and in the same movement swung it down. The small creature raced across the boat, an elad above the deck, just a flash of silver, but Gunnar's blade was faster. Two silver-blue pieces skidded across the ship's worn wooden deck.

"Knifylm!" Belkidar said.

"What?" Gunnar asked, his sword still held ready.

"They look like small fish, but they're actually distant relatives of birds. Their wings are sharp as razors, equally dangerous in the air or water."

"So they attack with their wings?" Kiera asked.

"Yes. They'll swarm you if you let them."

She nodded, replacing her barbed daggers with the curved blades. "Then let's not let them."

Having become more familiar with the hydras' movements, Indira found increasing success with each volley. She smoothed the fletching as she selected another arrow, unconsciously felt the worn wooden handle press firmly into her calloused hand as she drew. Her long, black hair that fell down her slender back slanted north, yet no white spray topped the waves far below. She released her bowstring, was comforted by the vibrations that resonated up her arm. Then she rested her bow on her bare left foot, waited patiently for eleven drus, a corner of her mouth curving slightly as another shriek startled birds from the nearby trees.

Unfortunately, the knifylm attacking her friends multiplied thirtyfold with each arrow. By the time she killed the hydra's third head, Gunnar, Kiera, and Batai were doing everything they could to protect themselves from the treacherous creatures that swarmed the boat.

Due to both the size of Gunnar's sword and his aggressiveness in battle, Kiera and Batai left him to defend the ship's bow, protecting their northern flank. Meanwhile, Batai defended against attacks from the southeast while Kiera did the same to the southwest. Belkidar stood in the center, his Staff held ready.

Like Indira, Brohdan gained more insight with each attack. Severed hydra heads attached to various lengths of neck tumbled clumsily into the reddening water. Soon, only three remained. He climbed a hundred elads above the lake, banked steeply to his right, readying himself for another pass as the creature moved closer to his friends.

Belkidar watched Gunnar's sword flash through the sun's afternoon light, smiled with pride despite the handful of cuts on his forearms. Their attacks were constant now, each taking flight the moment they left the water. Gunnar's huge blade was in constant motion, killing three or four with a swing from his shoulder, then one or two with a turn of his wrist. When the swarms grew denser, he swung the flat of his blade into them, never slowing its momentum, killing dozens with each broad swing.

Kiera's curved blades only killed single enemies with each swing, yet her attacks were so numerous Belkidar could barely keep up. She spent just as much time rolling or somersaulting on the deck as she did on her feet, smoothly dodging the lightning-quick creatures, deftly countering each attack, many so precise that, although dead, the knifylm continued along their original trajectories as they passed lifelessly overhead.

Batai's attacks were a combination of Kiera's precision and Gunnar's might, yet they were keenly those of a knight. Alternating between sword and shield, he accounted for more kills than either of his friends. He used his sword to cut through a silver flash while swinging his huge shield in a backward arc, crashing it through a large swarm, crushing them under his boots as they fell dazed to the deck. By the time Indira had killed her second hydra, the paladin's death toll numbered well over three hundred.

Brohdan attacked the western hydra several more times, distracting it with his fire, each culminating with a whipping attack of his blade. The surviving three heads had numbly watched their brothers tumble ungracefully down their shared body before disappearing below the water's surface. Those that remained grew panicked, lunging desperately as he passed nearby. Brohdan dodged them, countered with his blade. Now, with half of the hydra's means of attack sinking into Lake Mamate's depths, he turned and attacked from the south. His blade easily sliced through the creature's fourth neck, but this time, he maintained its momentum, adjusted its path. A hydra's skull was much too dense for an arrow, even from Indira's mighty bow, but the same could not be said of a Broglia Black's blade. As a result, just as she dispatched the southern hydra, the western hydra's fifth neck slumped toward the water, a diagonal portion of its skull sliding grotesquely from its head.

The sixth and final head snapped at him, but Brohdan flapped his wings, rolled upside down, dodged its jaws at the last moment. Then he righted himself, now directly over a neck stretched taut from lunging, and embedded his talons deep into thick scales and tense muscle. The hydra roared in frustration, its neck bending down beneath the Broglia's weight. Brohdan flapped his wings, steadied himself as he sank his teeth into its neck, tearing out its throat and cutting short its roar. Then he beat his wings more forcefully, pulling its neck tight before unleashing Broglia fire. It burned through the wound in an instant, and then Brohdan suddenly flew free, the charred remains of its neck and head still in his talons. By the time the hydra had disappeared into its watery grave, Brohdan had already covered half the distance to his friends.

Belkidar noted a whisper of sorcery as Brohdan approached, then watched as he unleashed a brilliant inferno. He sprayed liquid flames across the water, giving the boat a wide margin. A firestorm raged on the surface, a dozen small fire tornados sprouting from the heat, a narrow gap to the north the only shelter.

Accustomed to the cold water, the silver-blue creatures near the surface or in the air had no chance. Those that were further underwater survived, diving deeper to flee his fire. Brohdan dove after them, yet his still-burning fire didn't seem to mind the wave that resulted, riding high atop the crest and low in the trough that followed.

Once the wave passed beneath them, Brohdan's friends peered over the side and watched as the dark blue depths sporadically turned gold, the color of a midday sun, enormous bubbles rising to the surface several drus after each attack. Finally, after nearly a quarter link, Brohdan emerged, flapped his enormous wings, and took flight. Water cascaded from his black scales as his satisfied smile conveyed all that was needed to his friends below.

"I didn't know he could breathe fire under water," Gunnar said to himself.

"Neither did I," Belkidar admitted.

As Kiera and Gunnar dispensed with the last remaining knifylm, Batai took the helm and headed for the gap in the fire that Brohdan had left to the north. Once clear of the smoke, Belkidar surveyed the area, not surprised when he found it. *"Brohdan, there's a boat about a linop or so north of us, near the shore. Please introduce yourself."*

Brohdan turned, dove back into the water, swam toward the western shoreline. Then he flew from the lake, an explosion of black scales and white water. They watched as he neared the boat, squinted at the ferocity of his flames. Then he flew up and down the coast, searching for enemy scouts. Once satisfied, he turned, climbed higher into the sky, heading toward his lost friend.

He was ecstatic that Indira was alive! But his happiness didn't last long. Once on the cliff, Brohdan for the first time began to understand the depths of her suffering. Her face was a canvas of bruises, her left eye swollen closed. She was barefoot, her clothing in tatters, scarcely covering her too-thin body. Blood marked several rips in her tunic, and she leaned heavily on her bow for support.

Brohdan's anger rekindled in an instant, flames poured from his jaws while a rumbling, guttural growl resonated deep from within his chest.

"It is okay!" Indira said quickly, limping to his side. Her arms couldn't wrap halfway around his leg, yet she took comfort from his warm scales. "I am safe now."

It took all of Brohdan's self-control and several long moments to suppress his rage. When he was finally able to speak, he forced his eyes back to his friend. "What happened?" he asked, his voice a growl.

"It is a long story, perhaps best told when we are all together."

"I'm sorry, Indira, you're right. I'm just happy to see you."

Indira answering smile re-opened a cut in her lip, but she didn't seem to mind. She appeared hesitant to let go of his leg, and that Brohdan didn't seem to mind. He sheltered her with his wing, content to have his pack whole again.

Eventually, Gunnar's booming voice reached them from far below, and Indira finally let go of Brohdan to waive to her friends.

"The cliffs are pretty high here," Brohdan said. "Want me to find someplace lower?"

"No thank you, this is fine. I would be grateful if you could carry my bow for me, though."

Brohdan considered it, knew it didn't approach the limits of what he could carry in flight. "I'd be honored."

Indira smiled her reply. She handed it to him, Brohdan taking it gently in his talons. Then she approached the cliff and, without a moment's hesitation, calmly dove over the edge. She was obviously much more powerful than her slender body would suggest, her trajectory taking her far from the cliff face. Her dive was the epitome of grace, of beauty. She descended headfirst, virtually flying through the evening air, her body soaring through the crimson of sunset into the shadows of the mountains.

Brohdan watched in wonder as she entered with hardly a splash, then immediately arched her back, converting her vertical momentum into horizontal velocity, leaving a long trail of bubbles behind. Her speed eventually waned, but by then she was already near the ship. She surfaced, took a breath, then swam the remaining distance to her friends, nimbly climbing the rope Gunnar had tossed into the water for her. Kiera greeted her with a large cloth, and the men anxiously stepped from one foot to the other as they waited their turn to welcome back their friend. Soon Brohdan hovered next to them, carefully offered back her bow.

"Thank you."

"You're welcome. Give me a moment," he added before disappearing below the surface Within drus, he had resurfaced with a large fish in his mouth and another in each claw.

Indira's reaction was instant, her friends immediately realizing how little she must've eaten since she was lost. Gunnar took the fish, prepared them at the stern while Batai carefully started a fire a few paces away. Belkidar was tempted to help but decided against it, instead walking to where Gunnar worked. "Do you mind cutting a few slices thin to start?"

Gunnar was about to protest, then understood. "Of course."

The first few morsels were cooked in drus and on Indira's wooden plate before she had a chance to get comfortable. By the time she had eaten them, Kiera had nearly finished cooking larger ones. With food in her stomach, she sat back, closed her eyes, sighed deeply. "It is good to be back."

"It's good to have you back." Belkidar answered.

Once they had all eaten and Batai had resumed their course north along the western shoreline, they gathered around the helm while Brohdan swam silently a few elads to starboard. To no one's surprise, Kiera's acquisition had somehow included a cask of ale, so most had a well-earned tankard in their hands as they settled down. The sun had descended below the western mountain cliffs a link earlier, and they wrapped blankets around themselves to keep warm.

"Do you need anything?" Gunnar asked her.

"No, but I thank you."

Just then, Batai emerged from below deck where he was seeing to Einar and the horses. "I believe you forgot something," he said, a smile of relief more than mirth.

Indira couldn't believe it. She took her pack from the him, amazed that he'd still believed in her, despite her failure.

"Welcome home," he told her, putting an arm around her shoulders.

Tears welled in her eyes, and she looked in turn at each of her friends before nodding once, disbelief written across her face.

Several long moments passed as they considered the final drus of the First Defense. Finally, Kiera broke the silence with the simple question that was on all of their minds. "What happened?"

Indira took a small sip of ale before answering. "What is the last you saw?"

Batai answered immediately. "You saved my life. And then you chased after those that almost killed Einar and me."

Indira nodded. "I followed them for a quarter linak, had nearly gotten within range. I remember cresting a steep hill, then everything went black. I woke later with my wrists and ankles bound. I realized I was being carried, and we did not slow for several links. When we finally stopped, the centaur captain lit a small fire for their evening meal. That is when I pieced together what had happened."

Indira paused a moment. "In the firelight, I counted five centaurs and four ogres. I believe when the centaurs attacked Batai, they were laying a trap, knowing one of us would pursue them whether they killed him or not. So when I crested the hill, the ogres were waiting for me. I think they wanted me alive as some kind of peace offering to Hildegard."

Belkidar nodded, his frustration evident. "I should've anticipated this," he chastised himself. "I saw they were getting more and more desperate as their chances faded. Taking one of us back to Hildegard for questioning would've been the only thing that could've saved them."

Indira nodded. "I think that was their original plan, but they were very angry with me, bitter, terrified that they had failed Hildegard."

"What did they do?" Gunnar asked, his voice becoming dangerous.

Indira closed her eyes. "They wanted information, which gave them the excuse they needed. Every time we stopped to eat or rest."

The others remained silent, Indira recognizing the anger and guilt in their expressions. None met her eyes. "Please do not blame yourselves. It was my fault."

"It was *not* your fault," Belkidar said, much louder than he'd intended.

"I am fine, that is the most important thing." Then she smiled, comforting them despite her many injuries. "We all knew the risks, and if this is the worst that happens, we should consider ourselves fortunate."

"We searched for you," Kiera said, eventually finding her voice. "Where did they take you?"

"Into a cave," she answered softly. "I am not certain where they entered it from, but they carried me for links. Then we surfaced again, I am not sure how many days later. They beat me, knocking me unconscious. Many times. I think that is when they crossed to the western mountains, south of the settlements, and they could not risk me calling for help."

She paused, took another drink. "It was dark when I finally woke again. I saw that we were in another cave, but this one evolved into a maze. I eventually recognized it as an enormous mine, with shafts so deep I could not see the bottoms. Ancient equipment still hung from high ceilings, and we passed huge dormitories with hundreds of stone beds and a meeting hall that was so vast, light from our torches never touched its walls."

"Of course," Belkidar sighed. "When Hildegard built Gul Krul, he needed a lot of materials, and the mountains west of Lake Mamate provided everything he needed. He mined them continuously for nearly two hundred cycles to build it. But I didn't realize those mines traveled this far south."

"They do not. Others must have tunneled to them from the southern edge of the mountains."

Belkidar nodded. "And that's how they planned to take you to Gul Krul without being seen."

"How did you escape?" Batai asked.

Indira immediately looked down, unable to face her friends. She took another sip of ale, and it seemed to Batai that she did this to delay answering. "You don't have to recall everything tonight," he comforted her. "Besides, you must be exhausted. Kiera's already prepared your bed."

"Thank you, but I feel much better after eating." She paused, looked up, met his eyes. "I am...ashamed."

"Why?" Gunnar demanded. "Because you were caught? That could've happened to any of us!"

She smiled weakly. "No, because of how I escaped."

They had not expected that.

"After we entered the mines, they still beat me, but not to the point of unconsciousness. So I studied them, searched for ways to escape. It seemed hopeless. The ogres were enormous, and two were always guarding me. The centaur captain had taken my bow, never allowing anyone near it. But the more I studied them, the more I learned."

"They did not sleep much, perhaps one night in two, I assume because of their desperation to reach Hildegard. And so their exhaustion grew by the day. When they did stop, the two ogres guarding me took turns sleeping. Before long, neither could stay awake."

"That was days after my abduction, and by then, the blood from my wrists let me stretch the leather straps. So the next time they stopped to sleep, I freed my hands, then my ankles. Their small fire was only embers by then, but that was enough for me to see. I approached the furthest ogre, drew its sword." Indira paused, looked at Belkidar. "Are you familiar with them?"

"Ogre lieutenants carry them, as a symbol of their rank."

She nodded. "It was very sharp."

"I wish I could've seen that!" Kiera said, confused as to why she'd feel ashamed. "I remember when we first met you and how your pack was able to blend into their surroundings, some when they should've been in plain sight. And that was in the middle of the day!" The thought of Indira, alone with the centaurs and ogres, in a cave lit by dying embers... "They had no chance!"

"No."

"You didn't leave?" Gunnar asked.

"No."

Belkidar understood, tried to end the conversation when she spoke.

"I killed the ogres first. It was easier than I thought. Two quick slashes across their throats while they slept. The second managed to stand despite its shock, so I severed a kneecap, pulled its sword free as it fell. They couldn't scream anymore, but their gurgling surprised me. I did not think it would be that loud. Still, it took time for the centaurs to wake, and by then, I had already killed the other two ogres."

Shame again forced her gaze from her friends. When she continued, she stared at the wood planks of the deck, her fingers white around her stein. "Every movement reopened a wound, reminded me of what they did to me. I had never been so angry in my life."

She paused, took a deep breath. "With the ogres dying, I turned to where the centaurs roused. I do not think they could see as well as I could." She snorted bitterly recalling Kiera's earlier observation, the gesture somehow alien to her, disturbing even. "I do not believe they would have seen me had they a bonfire. So I took my time."

"Two of the centaurs had gotten up. They whispered to each other, trying to figure out where the ogres had gone, not sure if they should risk angering their captain by waking him. I circled behind and cut their hind legs out from beneath them. They screamed, fell clumsily, writhing as they tried to stand. I stepped forward, forced the blades into their backs, through their chests. The other three were awake now, spreading out in the darkness to find me. They called out, explaining what they would do to me."

"It was just noise. I approached one, it did not even know I was there. I slid a sword into its stomach, slicing down as I stepped away. Its innards splashed onto the stone floor, and its cries provided the perfect diversion to reach the last two. They went to investigate, slipped on entrails as they scrambled to put their backs to one another."

"I circled them in the darkness, not making a sound. They cursed me, then pleaded, offering me my bow if I would just leave. Still I circled, then walked beside one, swung a sword into its throat. I left it there, and it clanked loudly as it hit the ground. One centaur remained, the captain."

"It was panicking, stabbing into the darkness with it spears, begging for its life. I asked, 'Why should I spare you after everything you did to me?' It threw one of his spears where my voice had been, but it missed, skidded on the ground, the noise taking a long time to fade against stone walls. It clung to its final spear as though it were life itself. I circled behind it and whispered, 'Where were you taking me?'"

"In a flash, it swung its spear backward, a whirring arc in the darkness. But I was no longer there."

"'Where?'" I asked again, cutting down through its weapon and the fingers that held it." Tears spilled down her cheeks now, her voice trembling. "I was enraged, so I swung again, severed its front legs, just below the knees. It fell awkwardly, screaming. I reached down, wrapped my fingers around its throat, lifted it from the ground, its stubs writhing, its spurting blood warming my cold feet. It tried to scramble away with its hind legs, but the blood made the rock slippery, and my grip was strong. 'Where were you *taking* me?'"

"'To Gul Krul! To Hildegard!'"

"'Does he know about us? About your defeat?'"

"'No!'"

"I squeezed harder, felt its muscles spasm beneath my grip."

"'I would've told him everything, but only after we delivered you! So he'd show us mercy!'"

"It was a coward. 'Tell me about Gul Krul, its defenses.'"

"'I don't know. I've never been there!'"

"I believed him, doubted they had contact with Hildegard for centuries, but still I slid the ogre's short sword a hand-breadth into its abdomen. *'Tell me!'*"

"It shrieked, cried, its words barely recognizable. 'I don't know! *I don't know!*'"

"I slid the sword up, slowly, through its intestines, into its stomach, watching its eyes as the metal separated its flesh. 'Then what good are you?'" I released it, let it fall, knew its leaking stomach would make its death long and painful."

She paused again, taking another deep breath, her gaze still not meeting the others. "I still had my sense of direction, so I took the largest corridors that led east, toward the lake. The further I traveled, the less stale the air became. From there, it was just a matter of finding a shaft to the surface. It took me almost two days, but I finally found one, then headed here."

The others remained silent for several moments. "How long ago was that?" Batai asked.

"Two days."

"You've been waiting here for two days?" he asked, surprised.

"Yes. Why?"

"Nothing," he said, shaking his head. "Indira, you are a wonder."

"I do not feel so," she answered softly, looking down again.

"You did what you had to do!" Gunnar said.

Belkidar nodded. "You had to kill them, not just to escape, but to prevent them from going to Gul Krul. You saved us!"

Indira's tears had stopped. She slowly raised her head and faced her friends. "You do not understand. I do not feel guilty for killing them."

The others returned her gaze, confused. "Then why?" Brohdan asked.

Indira's voice was steady, cold, her eyes smoldering. "Because of how much I *enjoyed* it."

Belkidar wanted his friends to enjoy their recent success, but he understood there would be more difficult challenges ahead. Shortly after sunset, he watched the others slowly descend the stairs that led to the lower deck.

"Will she be okay?" Brohdan asked softly, still swimming slowly alongside the ship.

"Yes, she's stronger than she knows. But it'll take time."

Brohdan nodded, recalling when the bandits attacked Kiera and Belkidar, and afterward how difficult it was to think of anything else. "How can we help her?"

Belkidar smiled. "Just be there when she needs you, just as you always have."

Shortly after the stars had enveloped the sky, Indira quietly emerged from below and walked to where Belkidar and Brohdan were in quiet conversation. Not wanting to intrude, she went to the starboard railing and watched as Brohdan swam effortlessly in the black water. Seeing her, he swam closer, and she put a hand on his cheek. "It is good to be back," she whispered.

The three talked well into the night, discussing topics that ranged from the origins of the stars to the comfort of a shared meal. They compared Brohdan's adolescent clumsiness and Belkidar's awkward teenage cycles to the innate grace that elves possess from birth. Indira disputed such claims, of course, but her humility didn't sway them. Belkidar made them laugh, telling tales of his youth and how he had always managed to avoid getting punished as a child, despite constantly getting into trouble. Indira described her childhood, and Brohdan was surprised to hear how similar hers had been to his own. Eventually, a few links before dawn, Indira again went below decks, and Brohdan hoped this time sleep would find her.

At mid-morning on the next day, Belkidar gathered everyone near the helm. He smiled, despite his exhaustion. "I just wanted to congratulate you. It's been a long road to get here, you should be proud."

Gunnar nodded. "Yesterday, the boat that Brohdan sunk. Were they Hildegard's scouts?"

"Yes. The mountains are impassable, so the river was the most effective way to travel between here and Gul Krul." He paused, thinking. "Hildegard's smart to avoid using sorcery to monitor his Defenses, he knows that'd give me insight into his plans."

"But now he won't receive *any* updates," Kiera noted.

"True," Batai agreed. "He knows we mean to confront him, and that means defeating his Five Defenses first. I doubt a lack of reports from his scouts will fool him long."

Belkidar smiled again, then slid down the railing before pulling his hat over his eyes. "That may be, but I'll take any advantage I can get."

They spent the rest of the day taking inventory of their vessel and supplies. Batai guided them north, paralleling the western mountain cliffs of the lake, while Belkidar searched for potential threats. Indira searched through her pack and silently thanked Batai for his thoughtfulness. Except for one missing quiver, all of her arrows were neatly packed on one of the horses and were even waterproofed with oiled canvas. Brohdan hunted for them, and Gunnar prepared the fish while Kiera cooked it over a small fire. Before they knew it, the sun had descended beyond the western cliffs, and the stars soon appeared against a blackening sky. As the warmth faded, they gathered to eat their evening meal and discuss the plans for the days ahead.

"I'd like to have our feet back on land as soon as possible," Belkidar said softly.

"It won't be easy," Kiera said. "The entire northern shoreline is sheer cliff. In my travels, though, I just so happened to stumble on a path that leads to the Great Drulg Swamp on the other side."

"Why would you need a path like that?" Gunnar asked incredulously.

"I didn't," she answered innocently.

"You never used it before?"

"Of course not. Why would I?"

He shook his head. "I'll have to get you drunk before I get any information out of you."

"Anyway, I've heard the trail is difficult," she continued. "It's narrow in certain areas and steep in others, but whoever made it certainly knew what they were doing. Steps have been carved into the cliffs, so our progress should be swift, all things considered. The path begins diagonally, running northeast through the mountains, so it's virtually invisible if you're looking at it from the water."

"After scaling it, the path continues east before turning west. That marks the halfway point. It gets easier from there, mostly downhill into the southern marshes of the Great Drulg Swamp."

"Which sounds lovely," Gunnar said.

"Not so much. We'll need help if we're to cross it," she explained, staring at Belkidar."

"I'll take care of it," he assured her. "Just get us to that trail of yours. I can't risk going any faster, but we'll be getting close in three days or so."

"Great," Brohdan said. "Just knowing more of those hydras could be swimming below me..."

"I don't think they'll be bothering you any time soon," Gunnar assured him. "If they're smart, I think they'll avoid dragons and elves as much as possible."

The next two days passed uneventfully. They gave the large river mouth a wide birth, then took shelter beneath the tall mountains again. Belkidar closely monitored his sorcery, choosing a slower pace as they sailed further and further north. And they tended Indira, knowing some injuries took longer to heal than others.

Brohdan spent the nights in the air to better search for threats. He carefully remained below the tops of the mountains, casting 'cloak' to ensure he remained hidden. He occasionally circled behind them and toward the center of the lake, but he spent most of his time searching ahead and a short distance into the mountains, frequently discovering the body heat of mountain goats and nesting birds but little else.

He marked the passage of time by the soft periodic flaps of his wings through the chilly night air and the subdued claps of the waves against the ship's wooden hull. He flew on, intent on avoiding any thought of what Indira had suffered, and failing miserably. She was strong, perhaps the strongest person he'd ever met. He couldn't imagine how she had survived, alone against five centaurs and four ogres. And he thought about perspective, about how he could be so proud of her for many of the same reasons she felt ashamed.

Chapter 18
The Third Defense

It's not that I'm so smart, it's just that I stay with
problems longer.

Albert Einstein

"What?" Kiera demanded, slowly rising to a sitting position.

"You must wake," Belkidar whispered again, a reassuring hand on her shoulder. "We're nearly there."

"All right. Let's have a look." She got nimbly to her feet, alert, climbed the worn stairs onto the deck and made her way to the ship's port railing. The mountains that lined Lake Mamate's northern shores were slowly drifting by, only a few hundred elads distant. "When was sunset?"

"Three links ago," Brohdan replied in his deep voice.

Kiera nodded and turned to her left. She studied the shoreline that ran west, judging their distance from where it turned south. Then she looked right, searched where the mountains disappeared into the eastern horizon. "Another three linaks or so."

"Want me to scout ahead?" Brohdan asked.

"No thank you, just in case it's become more popular since my last visit."

Belkidar woke the others. As the ship neared Kiera's unseen destination, they prepared their belongings and brought the horses from below deck. Before long, they were packed and ready to go. The only remaining necessity was for Kiera to find the veiled corridor through the mountains.

"Are you sure we haven't passed it?" Gunnar asked.

"I'm sure. We've got another linak to go." Then, after a few drus, something piqued her interest. "Slower," she said to both Belkidar and Batai. "We're getting close."

"How can you tell?" Brohdan asked. "The mountains all look the same to me, just rocks and cliffs."

"You can start to see differences the more you practice looking for them," she whispered, keeping a watchful eye on the cliffs. "Perhaps when this is over, I can – " She stopped, stared at the mountains ahead. "That's it. Right there."

The others looked to where she pointed but saw nothing. Batai adjusted their course using Kiera's whispered inputs, and the ship coasted silently toward the towering cliffs. Brohdan was relegated to keeping only his nostrils above the surface of the black water in case they encountered strangers. Finally, as they coasted within a dozen elads, a path slowly materialized in the darkness.

"Incredible," Batai said, "I've never seen anything like it."

"I do not think many have," Indira agreed.

As they drew closer, Gunnar turned to his small guide. "It's just a column of notches!"

"Well, we have to start somewhere, don't we? Besides, it's not like it's completely vertical. See how they're camouflaged behind those ledges?"

"Ingenious," Batai said. "It appears perfectly natural unless you see it from exactly this direction."

"Exactly, but they form a ladder up the mountain. Once we're at the top, the trail gets a little easier."

When the boat was only elyes from the rock face, Brohdan held it carefully in place. They arched their necks, staring at the stone indentations that seemingly climbed into the sky, weaving unevenly to the right as they disappeared into the darkness. Then Indira donned her pack and adjusted the bow across her back. The others quickly followed, silently making their way to the vessel's port railing. Kiera, however, went below and brought up the other supplies she'd won from her poker games.

"What are those?" Gunnar asked.

"This is how you're going to bring the horses to the top."

"Oh," he said, resigned.

"These canvas tarps are of good quality, the ropes even better. I'll stay on the ship while the rest of you make your way up. Once at the top, Gunnar can lower the rope. After I secure it to the canvas, you can hoist them up one by one. It should only take a link, so we'll be on our way well before sunrise."

"I hope the horses will cooperate," Brohdan said. "It's a long fall if they panic."

"Einar will take care of that," Batai assured him.

"Really?"

"Absolutely. Chargers have a unique relationship with horses, serving as both leader and guardian. They'll be fine."

"Einar sounds like my father," Indira admitted.

Batai laughed softly, comforted to see even a glimpse of her humor return.

Indira sprang from the ship's deck to the top of the narrow wooden railing. Pausing a moment as the ship bobbed in the water, she timed her next leap perfectly, soaring several elads to the fifth foothold above the surface.

Batai watched her swiftly ascend the ladder, marveling at her gracefulness. "Looks easy enough," he joked as Gunnar positioned himself in front of the path. Then he leaned over the ship's side, grabbed onto the same foothold Indira had leapt to, and pulled himself up. He reached for the next handhold, using every fourth or fifth notch to scale the cliff.

"I'll go next," Belkidar said, climbing onto the deck's railing. With the Staff secured in a small leather sheath sewn into his pack, he smoothly stepped from the railing to the cliff face, then began the long climb, albeit at a considerably slower pace.

As the sorcerer disappeared into the darkness, Batai approached his partner of so many battles, reaching high to place a hand on his broad neck. Kiera watched in wonder, still amazed with how Einar could make Batai look so small. Then he went to the ancient ladder, transferred his weight from wood to stone, and began his ascent.

Kiera took the heavy canvas tarp and laid it across the deserted deck, then went to the rear of the ship and led the first horse to it. As she began securing the canvas, the horse took an uneasy step backward, but only an elye before backing into Einar. He grunted, then nudged the horse back into place.

Its ears pinned back, the horse reluctantly stood motionless as Kiera quickly tied the two rear corners of the canvas together above the animal's hips, then the two front corners across its shoulders. She next rested a large wooden beam gently along the length of its back, beneath the tied corners of the canvas tarp, then secured the canvas corners to it. By the time she'd prepared her makeshift litter, Indira had already made it to the top of the cliffs.

Despite the lingering pain from her recent trials, she welcomed the climb, felt energized by the exertion. After scaling over the ledge, she prepared a brace from a dead tree. She used a branch and a large rock to leverage it from the ground, then to move it to the top of the stone ladder. She repeated the process twice more, then sat and waited for Gunnar to emerge from his climb.

"Did you have to make it look so easy?" he whispered, hoisting himself over the top. "I used the handholds five at a time and I still couldn't keep up!"

"Sorry. Next time I shall make it appear more difficult."

Gunnar grunted as he got to his feet, then slowly shook his head as he discovered she'd already prepared three large trees for their winch. "How did you..." He looked from the nearby logs, neatly laid next to the ledge, to where Indira calmly sat. "Never mind."

She smiled, the reminders of a few bruises still visible. "You must to conserve your strength. The horses are depending on you."

"They have nothing to fear," he said, removing his massive pack and retrieving Kiera's rope. He quickly examined their lengths one last time before securing one to the thick, overhanging branch of a nearby tree.

Gunnar then went to work on the winch foundation, first using his sword to sharpen the ends to better drive them into the ground. With his back facing the cliffs, he raised the first diagonally so its upper end extended slightly beyond the cliff and over the water far below. Indira had seen him work before, but she was still amazed to see his muscles flex beneath the weight of the tree.

After a quarter link, Gunnar had constructed a makeshift 'A' frame using the two smaller trees to form an inverted 'V' to support the largest of the three trees, one tip embedded deep into the ground, the other extending diagonally several elads beyond the cliffs. He secured them together with the shorter lengths of rope. He saved the longest, guiding it through a notch that he'd cut in the tip of the longest tree, then letting it fall to Kiera far below. Belkidar and Batai watched it pass below them as they labored up the path.

It landed a few elads beyond the bow, but Brohdan repositioned the boat and it was soon within Kiera's reach. She quickly tied it to the wooden beam still resting atop the horse's back, then gave it three solid tugs. Within drus, the first horse rose from the deck, Einar grunting one last time.

In the meantime, Belkidar made it to the top, gracelessly climbing over the edge. Within a few drus, Batai joined them. "Not a bad climb," he said, inspecting the view below.

"Quite invigorating," Belkidar agreed, "just so long as we don't have to jump back down."

Gunnar effortlessly pulled the first horse to the top of the cliffs, Indira informing him when it drew near. Once above the summit, Batai and Indira pulled on the canvas litter as Gunnar lowered it onto the ground. As Batai led it away, Gunnar lowered the empty litter back down to Kiera.

They repeated the process until the remaining seven horses and Einar had been hoisted safely to the summit. Once Einar was en route, Kiera collected her pack and the few remaining supplies before approaching the ladder.

Each of the stone indentations appeared ancient. Although some remained in remarkably good condition, most had been worn more by the elements than travelers. Dozens had been eroded so severely that they slanted precariously toward the water far below. The others had just finished loading the pack horses as Indira helped her over the top. "Beautiful, is it not?"

Kiera turned to face the lake. The stars were perfectly reflected in the calm water, and the mirrored peaks stretched their way inverted to the south. "It truly is, despite Hildegard's meddling."

Just then, Brohdan flew vertically up the cliff face, passing only a few elyes beyond their noses. Kiera jumped back, startled, but Indira laughed, delighted by his sudden appearance. Her long hair flew back as Brohdan flapped his enormous wings, then his tail disappeared above as though it were the end of a rope being hoisted from the bottom of a well. "Speaking of beautiful."

Belkidar, standing several elads behind them, grunted a bit louder than was necessary as he finished preparing his horse for the ride ahead.

Kiera smiled. "Oh Grandfather, you know in my eyes you'll always be the strangest creature in the world."

Belkidar grunted again, Indira unable to suppress her laughter.

Kiera turned, walked from the ledge toward her horse, pausing to give Belkidar a kiss on his cheek as she passed. Although he wouldn't admit it, his mood improved noticeably as they prepared for the journey ahead.

After Einar strode away, Belkidar watched as Gunnar dismantled the winch. "If memory serves, you're quite good at throwing large objects, particularly toward old objects."

Gunnar didn't reply, but the thought of their first encounter brought a sheepish smile to his face. Then he lifted the largest of the three trees and heaved it over the side, the others rushing over to watch. After several drus, it struck the center of the ship, the sound taking a long time to reach their ears. Within moments, only flotsam remained.

"Nice," Belkidar said as he turned and left the cliff's edge.

Gunnar tossed the remainder of his 'A' frame into Lake Mamate's dark waters, each satisfying splash making him smile. Kiera took one more look at her poker spoils, sighed, then turned for her horse. "Some evidence remains, but at least it won't stick out like a club amidst four hearts."

"Always the professional," Belkidar said, mounted his horse.

They started their journey toward the Great Drulg Swamp, each silently taking their positions in their familiar column. Almost immediately, they lost sight of the lake as they followed a low valley, the trail weaving beneath the towering mountain peaks like a river. The scent of pine was strong, the early morning air cold in the deep shadows. Unfortunately, they were eventually forced to cross several ridgelines, many of which were a challenge for the horses, who apparently hadn't received the best care from their previous owners. They tired quickly, and despite Einar's support, they were forced to make frequent stops to let them rest.

The ancient trail was often dangerous, the mountains inhospitable, the terrain relentless. In some cases, the path climbed near-vertical ascents; other times, it descended sharply, the well-placed footholds all that prevented them from falling several hundred elads to their deaths.

To minimize how often they were forced to stop, Gunnar and Einar bore the majority of their supplies, the others carrying what they could to help quicken their pace. But their packs grew lighter as they climbed, the plummeting winter temperatures forcing them to don more and more of the furs Kiera had acquired in town. Free of their burdens, Batai tied the pack horses in a line behind Einar, whose guidance proved invaluable.

Near evening on the fifth day, Kiera reached the western bend in the path. She led them to a familiar cove, concealed from the seldom-used trail, sheltered from the worst of the frigid gusts.

"This is the halfway point?" Batai asked through numb lips, his speech slurred.

"Yes," Kiera acknowledged. "It's also the highest. From here, the path begins a gradual descent to the Great Drulg Swamp." Then she turned to stare at Belkidar.

"Don't worry about the swamp," he assured her.

"You're not worried about Hildegard?" Brohdan asked.

"Not if I do it correctly," he answered before drinking some water.

Kiera finished her small meal and laid back against her sleeping furs, gazing at the dark silhouettes of the towering peaks, her breath smoking in the cold. Of all the places she'd seen in the world, nothing came close to its austerity.

"They're his design," Belkidar explained.

"Creating them must've taken centacycles."

"At least. Hildegard's been preparing a long time. I think he created these mountains for two purposes. First, he wanted to enclose Lake Mamate so he could experiment without interruption. But I think the second reason is what really drove him to create this," he added, his arm sweeping across the dozens of jagged peaks, their summits touching the sky.

"Any invasion would have no chance of crossing these mountains. If an army of Tymoteu or the Indifferent throngs of Kaarlo ever wished to invade Gul Krul from the east or south, these mountains would slow their progress to a crawl, and even if they *could* somehow negotiate them, winter would stall their supply trains for mooncycles."

Batai nodded. "They funnel an invading force toward his armies."

"A daunting task to say the least," Belkidar agreed.

"How do you know he has not prepared for a small group like us?" Indira asked as she watered the horses.

"I don't, but based on Hildegard's own actions, I highly doubt that thought's ever crossed his mind. For instance, these mountains were designed to thwart an entire invasion, not a small group. It's the same with the millions that comprise his armies. And so far his Defenses were meant to defeat a large number of individually weak creatures."

He paused, shaking his head. "Imagine how easily those orcs could've overwhelmed a conventional army. Or how devastating the hydras would've been to a flotilla. *That's* what they were designed for, not to stop a group like us."

Brohdan had thus far remained quiet. "But he's sure to adjust his strategy now that his spies have reported back to him. We know he'll have something planned for me."

"There's nothing in this world that could ever challenge you, Brohdan," Kiera assured him.

"That may be true," Belkidar agreed weakly, "but remember, Hildegard has both the Headpiece and the Jewel now. We can't underestimate his ability to find a worthy opponent for Brohdan."

The others remained silent, imagining what type of creature could match a Broglia.

They resumed their journey shortly after dawn, Kiera slowly leading them west through the gradually descending terrain. Although the mountains remained rugged, the path was noticeably less challenging than it had been over the past few days. By evening, the frigid temperatures had finally relented.

"We should reach the swamp tomorrow," Kiera said.

"Very good. Let's find someplace to spend the night before it gets too dark."

"A small gully lies ahead," Indira offered, focusing where the others could not.

They made camp there, missing neither the freezing temperatures nor unrelenting winds from the mountains' heights. Belkidar pulled some cured sausage from his pack. "I'll take the watch tonight."

The others began to protest, but he cut them off. "I need to assess Hildegard's strategies. Maybe I can discover a few things that'll help."

Brohdan began softly snoring before the others had even become comfortable in their sleeping blankets. Soon, everyone except Belkidar was fast asleep.

He sat with his back to a tree, motionless, a statue in the darkness. His head rested against the bark, his wrinkled hands on the Staff, and despite his eyes being closed, he saw.

The next morning came quickly, but the long sleep refreshed the group, especially considering they'd spent the majority of the previous nights trekking through the mountains.

"Today will be a good day," Kiera said as she finished securing her belongings onto a pack horse.

"What makes you say that?" Gunnar asked.

"Because today we'll finally put this cursed trail behind us."

He smiled. "It wasn't that bad."

"That's easy for you to say. This was your first time."

An eyebrow rose. "How many times have you passed through here?"

"This is the ninth time, I think?" she said after a moment. "I lost count after I was nearly killed on the third one."

"Fall down a cliff?" he asked, only half serious.

"Nearly, but not because I slipped. I had half the Southern Camp after me."

"Why did you – "

"Never mind, Gunnar," Belkidar interrupted. "Trust me. You don't want to know."

He thought about that. "Something tells me you're right."

Within a few links, the ground gradually leveled after descending toward the swamp, its pungent odor growing alongside its stifling humidity. Unfortunately, as the terrain became more accommodating, the visibility did not. By late afternoon, Kiera could only see a hundred elads in any direction.

"We must be careful," she said softly, turning to the others. "Even on good days, I've never seen anything that approached good visibility here, and it won't change until we emerge onto the Thrud Wastelands to the northwest."

"Ideal conditions for an ambush," Gunnar said.

Indira nodded. "We must lean on our other senses."

"Let's tighten the formation," Batai suggested. "We may be more vulnerable for an ambush, but at least we'll all be aware it."

"And Brohdan?" Indira asked.

"He's fine," Belkidar assured her. "The mist will limit his heat vision, but not to the same degree. He'll still be able to fly."

"That dragon impresses me more every day," Kiera said. "But he still isn't as remarkable as Belkidar," she added hastily.

He wisely let that pass and continued riding silently ahead of Einar. Indira may have been mistaken, but through the fog she could've sworn she saw a smirk pass over his lips.

The ground grew soggier as they traveled. By evening, thick mud left stains halfway up the horses' shins.

"Belkidar," Kiera began, "I think if you're going to do something to help us through this quagmire, now would be a good time."

"If you insist."

They noticed a change in neither his expression nor his movements, yet within drus, the mud that once measured over an elye deep began drying with each step. Soon, the ground nearly resembled the Wruloric.

"How'd you do that?" Batai asked softly, his voice carrying eerily through the mist.

"Simple. I just moved the water."

"To where?" Kiera asked.

"Behind us."

He looked at them, but received only blank stares.

"I moved the water from the ground directly below us to the ground we've just passed over. If you could see a dozen elads behind Batai, you'd realize the water is still here, it's just following us."

"To prevent Hildegard from learning anything," Indira remarked, impressed.

"Precisely. Moving liquid is easy, it *wants* to flow. So I just 'flowed' it behind us," he added, smiling. When the others didn't react to his play on words, his smile disappeared shortly before his muttered grunts carried through the fog.

Thanks to Belkidar, the group made excellent time as they headed northwest through the wetlands, a stark contrast to how slowly they'd moved through the mountains. Mosquitoes became their only complaint, but once again, Belkidar provided an elegant solution.

"They hate the smell of Wilderberry flowers," he explained through a satisfied grin.

"Ingenious," Kiera agreed. "Belkidar, you really are the most inspiring creature I've ever met."

"Hmph."

Unfortunately, the mist didn't have such a simple cure. "I could move it, or even lift it a few dozen elads, but that'd require far more sorcery than we can risk."

Most of the sun's light failed to reach the ground, so they traveled in what seemed like perpetual dusk, and estimating the time became difficult. However, as the sun disappeared below the unseen horizon, the swamp became exceptionally dark. With neither the moon nor stars to illuminate their way, Kiera found navigating through the quagmire nearly impossible.

"I think we're still headed northwest," she said during a short rest, "but I can't be certain."

Indira nodded. "Perhaps we can remain here until – " She paused, her eyes focused into the thick fog. "A creature approaches. It is quite large," she added, now smiling.

"Brohdan," Gunnar guessed, matching her smile.

Within drus, the Broglia's shadow materialized overhead, his dark silhouette landed seemingly in slow motion through the mist. "I saw you stop and thought I could help."

He led them for two links before they set up camp. He'd gotten plenty of sleep the previous night, and considering how well he could see compared to the others, he offered to take the first watch. They were grateful, collapsing in their sleeping blankets almost immediately, the time they'd needed the warmth of their thick furs seeming a lifetime ago. When dawn came, Brohdan still stood guard over his friends.

"Why did you not wake one of us?" Indira asked through a satisfying stretch.

"I wasn't tired, and I figured you needed the sleep more than I did."

"We appreciate your sacrifice," she said.

The others woke and quickly packed their sparse belongings. Kiera handed out dried meat and water for their morning meal. Belkidar moved some of the surrounding water into a large puddle to let the horses drink before starting the day's journey.

"Won't the water harm them?" Batai asked.

"Maybe, if I hadn't taken precautions."

"Such as?"

"I simply moved the water – and nothing else – for them to drink. So anything harmful was left behind in the soil."

"Very good, Belkidar," he decided with a nod.

"I'm thrilled you approve."

"When did you want me to head west?" Brohdan asked Kiera.

"Not too much longer. I'd estimate we're a quarter of the way through the swamp, thanks to Belkidar's help. But we need to be careful where we make our turn, so let's keep going northwest for a little while."

"Why? It doesn't look like we'll find any breaks in the mist, regardless of where we turn."

"True, but I'm worried about after. When we emerge from the swamp, we can't be too far north and risk detection by the Northern Camp or too far south and risk exposure to Gul Krul."

The morning light was predictably dim, and so Brohdan's unique abilities proved essential. What they could see wasn't exactly scenic. Thick, green marsh water surrounded them, and slimy, leafless trees grew dense in some areas yet surprisingly barren in others. A pungent, stale odor hung in the air, and although the temperature was only warm, the humidity made for a very uncomfortable journey.

Brohdan maintained a quick pace, each probing the mist more with their ears than their eyes. Then Indira heard a faint *whfff* approach at great speed, and in a flash slid down the left side of her horse. The object passed within an elye of her right elbow before continuing harmlessly through the heavy fog.

"Stand ready!" After sliding back into her saddle, she nocked and released an arrow in one smooth stroke, using the same trajectory to extrapolate the location of her unseen enemy. After an unnervingly short period, an ear-piercing cry echoed in the mist, distantly reminiscent of the hydras' several days before, only octaves higher.

"Wyverns!" Belkidar called. "They're large flying reptiles that have poison-tipped thorns at the tips of their tails, launched by whipping them toward their enemies."

But it was too late for Gunnar. Multiple thorns the size of crossbow bolts where embedded deep into his back and behind his legs.

"NO!" Kiera cried, running frantically toward him, the mist swirling behind her. She quickly pulled them from his back, careful to not let any scratch her.

"I'll be all right," he told her gruffly, attempting to rise from his knees.

"Gunnar's been hit!" Brohdan said, taking flight. Belkidar noticed the faint murmur of 'steelskin' as the angry Broglia Black flew northeast toward the wyvern's cries. It wasn't easy to distinguish their body heat from the surrounding swamp, but when he climbed a high enough, he found them.

"They're dozens of them," he 'ranged' back to his friends. To the others, his voice seemed to come from all directions, as though it were part of the mist that surrounded them. "About a hundred elads northeast of you."

Indira waited with an arrow nocked, Brohdan's dragonfire struggling to reach her eyes. She watched in wonder, the tiny water droplets refracting the flames countless times. It resembled a fantastic fireworks display, a stark contrast to the wyverns' horrific, tortured screams.

"Behind us!" Indira said, pivoting in her saddle to face southwest.

"What is it?" Batai asked, turning with her.

"I am unsure, but many creatures approach through the water."

Belkidar grimaced. "Through the water, or *on* it?"

Indira stared at him, disbelief in her eyes, but as the sounds painted an increasingly accurate picture, she understood. "*On* the water!"

"Lilkes," he explained, his concern obvious. "They're lizards the size of small dogs, but exceptionally quick and agile – so nimble, in fact, that they can run on water. Their sharp teeth and claws can shred any one of us in drus."

"Sounds vicious," Batai said, calmly searching the fog.

"Brohdan, we could use your fire over here," Belkidar said aloud to keep the others apprised of his plan, then used sorcery to update Brohdan on their new enemies. He didn't answer, but his immediate over-flight provided all the confirmation they needed. Gunnar, still conscious, watched as his huge silhouette passed overhead.

Indira searched their flanks, anticipating the wyverns continued attacks. With Batai in her right periphery, she saw Brohdan's familiar glow through the reflection in his immaculate armor. She fingered the fletching with her thumb, waiting.

Kiera had pulled nearly thirty spikes from Gunnar's back and legs, but he refused to stay out of the battle. He drew his sword and, under the circumstances, politely shoved Kiera into the quagmire as he disappeared into the fog, the water not quite reaching his knees.

"I can't stop Gunnar! He's attacking the wyverns!" Kiera yelled.

"Kiera – " Belkidar began, still facing where the lilkes advanced from the southwest.

"You can't just let him go!" she interrupted. "He was hit by dozens of them!"

"But Kiera, let me – "

"Belkidar, DO SOMETHING!"

"Kiera, giants are immune to all poisons."

Kiera stood dumbfounded. "Oh. Well now I know that."

"I doubt you will believe this," Indira interrupted, "but more creatures approach from the northwest."

"What do you hear?" Belkidar asked, dragging his attention from the lilkes.

"It sounds like..." She listened intently once more before continuing. "It cannot be. They sound like *trees*!"

"Venom woods," Belkidar said, alarmed. "They're technically trees, I suppose. This soil has been soft and muddy for thousands of cycles, and with Hildegard's invaluable assistance, a certain species slowly developed the ability to move through its waters."

"But that means they're sentient," Batai noted, incredulous. "Surely Hildegard couldn't bestow *that* to them."

Indira was shaking her head, still facing the unseen lilkes. "Trees have always been self-aware, since the dawn of time. Most simply lack the ability to communicate with them. But they have always lived in harmony with nature. I am amazed even Hildegard could alter that."

Belkidar slowly shook his head. "Like water running over stone, Hildegard's…persuasion…over thousands and thousands of cycles can have drastic results. Regardless, we must defend ourselves. These enemies are slow, but very powerful."

Kiera, Indira, Batai, and Belkidar remained watchful on the artificially dry soil of the Great Drulg Swamp. Indira listened for any clues as Gunnar charged toward the remaining wyverns. The others watched as the yellow and gold of Brohdan's fire attacks reached them through the fog.

Gunnar reached the wyverns in drus. Several charred corpses littered the oily trees of the marshy terrain. He knelt and studied one. It was nearly six elads long with large leathery wings, but it was thinly built, designed for flight, not strength.

He continued into the mist, slowly, listening for movement. The swamp water muffled his footfalls, but it also kept him from moving silently. He paused after every fourth or fifth step, probing the thick fog with his ears. Then he heard something. A splash. Another. Then bird-like chatter, coming from several directions. And then they attacked.

The first flew at him through the dense fog, realizing too late its enemy wasn't exactly defenseless. Gunnar's long blade easily sliced diagonally through its body, its wings stopping in mid-stroke, its two halves tumbling into murky water.

Three more attacked, the first using every elye of its long neck to snap at him, but Gunnar was faster. A second flew at him from behind as Gunnar flicked his wrist, smoothly cut through the neck of the first. Its head plopped into the water, its body convulsed, violent tremors shuddering through its wings and what remained of its neck.

He turned, ducked just in time as the second wyvern flew over, its neck lowered, its jaws wide, but Gunnar's sword was longer. He extended it, smoothly severed a wing. It fell awkwardly behind him, but he had no time to watch.

The third closed on him from his right flank. He turned, charged it, took several thorns to his upper body, used the flat of his blade to protect his face, then impaled it through the chest. Holding his sword flat over the ground, Gunnar held it up, studied it as it writhed. Between shrieks of agony, it lunged at him, its needle-like teeth snapping with each attack. When its cries became unbearable, he let it slide from his sword, shifted his weight over it, let the dark water silence it. He then returned to the one he'd hobbled, still struggling, splashing as it attempted flight without its missing wing. He approached it from behind, an unconscious grunt escaping his lips as he severed its long neck just above its torso.

An unconscious grunt escaped Belkidar's lips as he watched Brohdan's fire moved ever closer. "Gunnar, we're going to have our hands full here," he said in a voice that carried to the giant's ears. "When you're done with the wyverns, please make your way to our northwest, in the direction we were headed before the attack. We've got trees approaching, and they too have poison to deal with." He turned back toward Brohdan, wishing his enemies were fewer, their advantage smaller.

Brohdan turned back toward the lilkes, wishing they were fewer, their advantage smaller. Their speed, agility, and sheer numbers made killing all of them impossible. At first, Brohdan tried to herd them away from his friends like he'd done with the orcs during the First

Defense, yet despite using a wide stream, dozens maneuvered around his fire, racing toward the only dry patch in the Great Drulg Swamp.

In a last effort to thin their numbers, the Broglia flew to the others, turned in midair, and met the lilkes' advance with a long, intense breath. Batai stood in amazement, the deep rumbling of his attack lasting no less than one hundred drus. But when it finally did end, the wave of lilkes surged against his landlocked friends.

Indira's bow hummed while the others waited, Batai calmly stroking Einar's neck, Kiera impatiently thumbing a dagger while watching the stream of arrows that left her bow. She smiled, shook her head, unable to keep Indira's arm in focus as it blurred from bowstring to quiver and back again.

Even more remarkable was the brief period she had to aim and release each arrow. Because of the thick fog, Indira couldn't see the lilkes until they were close, and when she did, they approached in a frenzy, weaving diagonally across each other's paths, a wave of chaos. Yet she never missed, killing creature after creature, many of which Kiera couldn't yet see. But their numbers again proved overwhelming.

"There are more than I can kill," she said, her bow never slowing. "Get ready."

"It's about time," Batai said, sword in hand. Einar, apparently thinking the same, shook his head, snorted eagerly.

With her two barbed daggers in hand, Kiera crouched, waited for the first of the lizards to appear. She didn't have to wait long. Through the fog, she saw what initially appeared to be a wave in the swamp water, then realized the green ripple was actually the savage lilkes racing toward her, each screeching faintly, the collective effect growing deafening.

At that instant, Brohdan materialized above them, hovered directly over Kiera, his wings momentarily arched backward as he unleashed his fire, its brilliance like a sun. He turned his head side to side, the force blowing the lilke horde backward, burnt carcasses skidding along the water's surface before sinking. The heat was nearly unbearable, yet it was familiar, a refuge.

But his attack eventually ended, and he again disappeared, the lilkes renewed attack coming almost immediately. When they closed to within a few elads, their movements became even more erratic. Some jumped toward their faces, others stayed low, skimming the water's surface. Some feigned one way, then at the last instant leapt to attack a neighbor.

Finally, Batai and Einar were able to join the battle. He used shield and sword, bashing and cutting through their onslaught. They flew from his shield, their crumpled bodies amassing unseen under the swamp water to his left. His sword he barely swung, letting their fury and aggression do the work.

Several elads to his right, Kiera jumped, rolled, lunged, side-stepped, and ducked her enemies, countering their attacks with one of her sharp daggers. All was silver arcs, whirring flashes, piercing shrieks. She was never stationary, always attacking, each strike planned four or five steps ahead.

Indira adjusted her strategy, letting Batai and Kiera battle the nearby lilkes while she thinned the horde beyond their sight. Arrow after arrow disappeared into the fog, faint cries answering each.

The wave advanced, unstoppable.

Gunnar advanced, unstoppable. He cut through the wyverns, their poison useless, their teeth and claws worthless against the reach of his sword. But it was taking far too long, their speed and apprehension slowing his work, delaying his priority. He knew he must intercept trees to the northwest, before their poison threatened his friends. Frustrated, he abandoned the last of them, sprinted into the mist, shouting an update to Belkidar as he ran.

Belkidar sent an update to Brohan as he watched.

"Brohdan, can you please see to the last of the wyverns?"

Brohdan abandoned his attacks against the lilkes' rear flanks. He barely cleared the short trees, accelerated rapidly, but it would still take him drus to reach them.

The lilkes adapted, more and more racing along the water's surface to avoid Batai, attacking Einar instead. But there was no way for them to know he was just as capable, just as deadly. He moved from side to side, reared high, bashing the frenzied lizards with his enormous breast plating, crushing them with hooves nearly twice their size.

Kiera outmaneuvered them, waiting for each to commit to an attack before countering with a quick thrust, an upward stab, a short sweep, a flicked wrist. With Brohdan's sporadic illuminations in the background, Belkidar watched with a proud smile and a furrowed brow.

Gunnar heard the venom woods long before he saw them, surprised with how many had gathered in the mist. He bent, retrieved a wet branch, considered the irony; they'd discovered the freedom of movement, only to walk willingly to their deaths.

He held the branch before him, shielded his body, charged the nearest. It stopped, swept a long branch forward as if in slow motion, released a salvo of elye-long thorns. More trees attacked, swinging dozens of branches, each a bombardment.

His log was far too small to shield his entire body, but it freed his sword-arm while protecting his eyes. He doggedly advanced, forming a giant-sized silhouette through each wall of thorns, their thuds against his makeshift shield loud in his ears, his blood oozing from his exposed arms and legs.

Kiera blurred into the dense mist, killed several lilkes while dodging the attacks of others. She sliced open the belly of one as she rolled, evading the attacks of two others, surprised to come face-to-face with a fourth. It didn't hesitate, charged with open jaws, met her dagger with its skull as the two she'd previously avoided pounced from her flanks.

Her attacks were swift, immediate, but her mind was faster, fast enough to recognize her mistake, her helplessness. The unseen lilke had delayed her for an instant, but that was enough. The other two converged on her, simultaneously, their jaws a handbreadth from her flesh.

And then they were flung away, as though leaves in a gust.

She blinked, examined the closest, saw the hole that ran from its right shoulder to its left hip. The second lay not far away, a bloody arrow imbedded in its chest. She stood, glanced at her friend.

Indira smiled, her bow humming, her arrows drawing a near-continuous shriek from the mist.

Kiera couldn't believe it. With a single arrow, Indira had saved her from both creatures. But she didn't have time to dwell. She continued her onslaught, her daggers reflecting Brohdan's distant flames. She felt an occasional breeze, unconcerned by the arrows that darted within a finger-width of her body.

Although Batai and Einar had each other to rely on, Indira monitored their progress as well, and what she saw stunned her. She'd initially witnessed two creatures independently fighting the waves of lilkes. Einar repeatedly reared high, alternately used his armor to quell leaping attacks while stomping others from below. Meanwhile, Batai clung to the lurching charger with his knees, using his shield to bash soaring lizards to his left, cutting down with his sword to his right. But as she took a moment to consider what she saw, she realized its true significance.

Einar, not having the luxury to see what his companion was doing, reeled on his hind legs not for his own sake, but for Batai's. Whenever he was in need, Einar instinctively maneuvered his own body, putting Batai in perfect position for the kill while leaving himself vulnerable.

But Batai had the same connection with his charger, slaughtering every lilke that attempted to take advantage of Einar's vulnerability. Indira could no longer distinguish between susceptibility and strength. She initially thought Batai was protecting Einar, but she then realized it was Einar who took advantage of the lilkes attacking Batai. As soon as she felt confident in that perception, she realized it was Batai who killed them when they foolishly attacked Einar.

She smiled, shook her head, concluded this was nature's perfect example of symbiosis. Batai and Einar were one. Each intuitively attacked the enemy when they mistakenly perceived a weakness in the other, each creating a strength on which the other was able to capitalize.

Gunnar soon realized the trees had two methods of attack. First, they shot hundreds of venom spikes from their long branches, but once he drew closer, they tried to bash him with those same limbs. Neither proved particularly successful against a giant.

Hundreds of spikes covered his shoulders, arms, and legs, but the poison proved harmless. And he easily negotiated their swinging limbs, leaping over some, ducking others, using his sword to cut through the rest. He closed the distance, sprinting from one tree to the next, his blade easily slicing dense trunks and swinging branches.

By the time he'd progressed halfway through the forest, those toward the rear realized they were outmatched. In their panic, they attempted escape, their retreat sluggish at best. Gunnar chased them down, still dodging long, lumbering limbs, smoothly sliding his blade through the base of their great trunks. Gunnar's sword was drenched with slimy swamp water, but he had long ago become accustomed to handling a slippery weapon. They fell silently, splashed in the thick marsh water, once again motionless in the Great Drulg Swamp.

Kiera's daggers were drenched in lilke blood, but she had long ago become accustomed to handling slippery weapons. Batai and Einar also made quick work of those attacking from the southeast. Indira's attacks altered between intermittently helping her friends and killing lilkes more distant. Belkidar observed from the center of the battlefield, his Staff ready.

Gunnar returned, arriving just in time to see Kiera's daggers slice through the final four lilkes, the others slowly making their way to Belkidar. He joined them.

"Let us help you!" Indira said, rushing to him.

"Did you manage to dodge even one?" Kiera asked.

Gunnar just smiled.

"Be careful," Belkidar warned, "even the slightest prick would kill any one of us."

Gunnar had removed most of the thorns, but he couldn't reach them all. Indira and Kiera carefully pulled dozens from his back, his blood matting his clothing.

Just then, an earsplitting roar echoed through the swamp. A few drus later, Brohdan landed behind Gunnar, a wyvern corpse sagging in each rear talon, another dangling from his mouth.

"Frustrating, aren't they?" Gunnar said.

Brohdan threw them aside. "They wouldn't stay still long enough for me to kill them!"

In the meantime, while Einar rounded up the horses, Batai prepared meat, cheese, and bread. By the time he'd finished, Gunnar was finally free of thorns. They sat on the artificially dried ground and ate slowly, silently replaying the battle in their minds.

"Three down," Batai said.

"And without needing Belkidar's help!" Kiera added.

Indira nodded. "I only hope our fortunes continue."

"I can't say for certain," Belkidar replied. "These Defenses are indeed becoming more difficult, and who knows what the Fourth will be like. But we're also getting closer and closer to Hildegard, so even if we do need my sorcery, he won't have much time to use whatever information he may learn."

They took their time, discussed the battle so that they might perform better in the future. Brohdan felt exhausted, yet surprisingly calm. They had just defeated Hildegard's Third Defense, again without need of their mightiest member. And they were still safe – all of them! He knew greater challenges awaited, but for now, he savored their victory.

Once rested, Brohdan again led them through the mist, slowly veering according to Kiera's estimates. The others followed in their tightened formation, and with the ground dry beneath them, they again made excellent progress, stopping shortly after sunset.

"I'll stand watch tonight," Belkidar offered.

"I'm fine," Brohdan insisted. "You need the rest more than I do."

"I'm not some frail old man, and learning to go without sleep is hardly the most difficult thing I've done."

"I don't imagine it is," Brohdan reluctantly agreed. He leaned his head to where Gunnar prepared a shallow fire pit, the wet logs instantly succumbing to his flames. Kiera had a small meal nearly cooked by the time the others had set up camp. They finished it in silence, Brohdan realizing everyone was ready to put the exhausting day behind them.

Brohdan watched as each of his friends slipped into their blankets and quickly drifted to sleep. Belkidar, still sitting with the Staff laying across his lap, was of course the exception. He wondered if either of the two remaining Defenses would require his intervention, a part of him eager to finally see him use his gift in earnest.

Then he turned his gaze upward, expecting to see a night sky filled with countless stars, but he saw only the thick, gloomy fog. Disappointed, he returned his chin to the ground, closed his eyes, and slowly drifted to sleep. The last thing he remembered was the thought of Mikka, and he wondered if she was able to see the stars this night.

Chapter 19
The Fourth Defense

*Adversity is like a strong wind. It tears away from us
all but the things that cannot be torn, so that we see
ourselves as we really are.*

Arthur Golden

Belkidar let the others sleep well into the morning. They'd
definitely earned it. Besides, he'd been busy. As he'd done two nights
prior, he again divided his mind into three distinct areas. In the first, he
vigilantly watched over the camp, prepared to greet any fool that might
attack his friends in the darkness. He let the second slip into a deep
slumber, and although this type of rest proved less effective than
conventional sleep, his body and mind would still be refreshed in the
morning.

He used the third part to think, his mind racing, examining details,
extrapolating possibilities. He deliberated on many topics, including
the likeliness of his need for sorcery in the coming Defenses, the
consequences if it was indeed required, the potential success in these
future battles, and the present state of the group. But he spent the
majority of the night assessing what type of creature Hildegard had
doubtlessly prepared for Brohdan.

Belkidar recalled each detail of his existence, cataloguing every
type of creature Hildegard could potentially create, summon, convince,
or coerce to fight on his behalf. He re-witnessed every experiment he'd
conducted with Aelya. He recalled the thousands of scrolls and books
he'd studied, re-read some in his mind's eye as though they lay before
him. He re-introduced himself to the countless creatures he'd
encountered through the course of his long life. Finally, as the sun rose
unseen into the eastern skies, he reluctantly arrived at a single bitter
conclusion.

Hildegard had discovered Brohdan's presence only recently when considering the centacycles he spent arranging his theft of the Jewel, but ample time remained for him to prepare any one of a handful of creatures to oppose him. But few could match a Broglia Black. After comparing those against the ones he could summon in the time it takes to travel from the Wruloric Wastelands to Gul Krul, Belkidar confirmed his worst fear.

Indira began stirring from her night's sleep. He tore himself from his thoughts, merged the three parts of his mind. He donned a false smile, wanting more time to consider the options available to him.

But in truth, he was frightened. This creature had never faced a Broglia Black in battle, yet it easily matched their successes. The process required to create one was tremendously complex, and history's account of their existence revealed a rarity that rivals even the exceptional Broglia's. But when summoned correctly, they have wrought destruction the world had never before witnessed.

After breaking their fast, Brohdan guided them to the western borders of the Great Drulg Swamp. With Belkidar's ability to dry the ground, he maintained a swift pace, the horses trotting to keep up. By late afternoon, the mist slowly began thinning, the air becoming a little less acrid.

"We're getting close," Gunnar said.

"Two more links I think," Kiera agreed, "but we should stay in the swamp until nightfall."

"Good idea," Belkidar said. "I'm sure Hildegard positioned scouts throughout the continent, and without sorcery, there's no way I can determine where they are. And now that we near Gul Krul, anything they discover will get to him much sooner than it could before."

"So we travel by night?" Gunnar asked.

"I think so. And Brohdan? I think you should 'cloak' during the day."

Brohdan nodded, thinking about the spell and its limitations. "Are the Thrud Wastelands similar to the Wruloric?"

"They are, both pretty constant, monotonous. 'Cloak' should work fine."

"Any thoughts on how we're going to conceal me?" Gunnar asked.

Belkidar smiled. "The same way as the rest of us. We'll travel by night as much as possible and as fast as the horses can manage." He shrugged. "That's all we can do without sorcery."

Indira turned to Kiera. "How long do you expect our journey across Thrud Wastelands to take?"

"A little more than three days. Four if we're forced to take a detour or two."

They stayed there for another link, taking the opportunity to eat and rest the horses. As dusk approached, Brohdan led them to the fringes of the swamp, then took to the air to scout ahead.

Once night had fallen, Kiera led them into the vast wastelands, the mist slowly yielding to a clear, moonless sky. They paused, breathed in the crisp winter air, rejuvenated by the stars in the sky, the oppression of the swamp lifting with the fog.

Kiera's pace was swift, covering as much distance as possible before sunrise. The horses, having spent several days in Indira's care, were much better prepared for the journey across the Thrud Wastelands, their struggles through Lake Mamate's harsh mountains a distant memory.

Kiera initially headed west, then slowly curved southwest to stay equidistant from the Northern Camp to her right and Gul Krul to her left. They stopped a few times to rest the horses, and when the sun's first rays appeared above the horizon, she led them to a shallow gully beneath a low hill. It wasn't ideal, but it would at least conceal them if any of Hildegard's scouts passed nearby. After rearranging the horses, Gunnar found enough room to stretch out. Soon, even the horses were asleep.

Brohdan, of course, was the exception. Now 'cloaked,' he found a secluded area nearby. He watched over his friends, staying motionless

to maximize the spell's effectiveness. He studied the impending dawn
to the east, then looked west, watched as the stars disappeared one by
one. They seemed invincible just a few short links ago, overwhelming
the entire night sky. But as he watched the final star succumb to the
sun's might, he hoped it wasn't a prophesy of their own fate beneath
the shadow of Hildegard's evil.

They resumed their journey at dusk, Brohdan remaining 'cloaked'
until well after dark. Kiera remained several linops from Hildegard's
fortress, turning more and more south as the links passed. Then, as
dawn threatened in the east, Brohdan swooped down and landed ahead
of the column.

"We walked into an ambush! There are two groups in the hills –
one to the southeast, the other northwest."

"What do they look like?" Belkidar asked quickly.

"Two creatures in each group. One's very tall – at least an elad
taller than Gunnar. They have huge bows and only one eye."

"Cyclopes!" Belkidar said, disgusted. "Most were killed during the
War, and the survivors begrudged those who fared better, a resentment
that's only grown through the cycles. They're ruthless, killing for the
pleasure of it. I doubt they needed much enticement from Hildegard."

"What does the second creature look like?" Batai asked.

"They're also tall, at least six elads from hooves to horns. Their
body and arms appear human, albeit a hairy one, but everything else is
looks like a bull. And I could see their red eyes, even from where I was
flying."

"Minotaurs. It appears your dreams heading to the Glor Forest
were accurate after all." He shook his head. "They also fought with
Jenkar during the War. Even back then, the two creatures worked well
together, an alliance that's apparently persevered through the
centacycles."

Belkidar paused, his eyes searching the hills. "A cyclops is an expert marksman, their ten-elad frame perfectly suited for their bows – which are eight elads themselves. If they keep to the same strategy they used during the War, the minotaurs will engage us while the cyclopes stay in the high ground, picking us off one by one. And judging from Brohdan's report, their attacks will come from opposite directions."

"Won't they kill minotaurs as well?" Gunnar asked.

He nodded. "If we'd been an army, each of the two minotaur groups would've blocked their ends of this valley, pinning us in, freeing the cyclopes to bombard us from the tops of both plateaus. But we're more agile than an army, so the minotaurs will have to engage us. They won't hesitate. They take pride when they die in battle, believing it's the only way to for their soul to survive, to be reborn as another minotaur warrior. And so they have no fear, no hesitation, only rage."

Batai nodded, assessing their predicament, his eyes taking in the narrow valley, the higher terrain. "The cyclopes must be contested."

"I'll take one group," Brohdan offered.

"I will hunt the second," Indira said, her voice soft.

Batai considered it, couldn't help remember what happened the last time she was isolated in battle. But he knew that wasn't her fault, knew she could take care of herself. He met her eyes, hiding neither his concern, nor his faith. "Be careful."

"Always," she replied, her smile revealing relief, gratitude, resolve. "Brohdan, where are the cyclopes to the southeast?" she asked, taking several quivers from one of the pack horses.

Brohdan described their position while Batai organized the others. Then Belkidar spoke, looking each in the eyes. "I can't underestimate how well they work together. When things begin to stray from their original plan, they'll form contingencies. We must do the same."

They nodded, then Brohdan took flight, heading toward the higher terrain to the northwest.

"Brohdan!" Belkidar called. "You're not 'cloaked!'"

"If I'm to occupy the cyclopes, I'd like for them to see me. I'm an inviting target after all!"

"Very well," he said, watching him gain speed. Then he felt the faint whisper of 'steelskin.' With a smile that only partially concealed his pride, he turned and watched Indira gallop to the southeast.

Batai assessed their surroundings, looked down the path they'd ridden to get there, then further to the southwest where they'd been traveling. Higher terrain bordered them to either side, long plateaus from which the cyclopes planned to attack. "Belkidar, I think we'll need your help with this one. You and Kiera form a line there," he said, facing them down the valley to the southwest. "Gunnar and I will meet them here," he finished, his eyes fixed to the northeast.

Kiera smiled, Batai's confidence contagious. He took charge, methodically organized their defenses, calmly planned their strategies. He formed them into a square, with each pair putting their backs to the other, spaced so they wouldn't hinder their partner. Einar needed room to maneuver, as did Kiera. They also gave Gunnar's sword a wide margin.

Then she was torn from her thoughts. Low, savage grunts and wild, hysterical howls resonated from the southwest, their answering calls coming almost immediately from the northeast. A low rumble was felt more than heard, becoming deafening as they neared. Finally, they crested a rolling hill, and the minotaur horde came into full view, their thunderous hooves striking the hard ground, saliva flying from jeering maws.

Gunnar studied them as he pulled his sword free, noted their long, two-bladed battle axes. He moved his right arm through wide, sweeping strokes, the rising sun making his sword glow orange against a violet sky. He jerked his neck sideways, eliciting two pops, his smile nearly hidden by his thick beard.

Batai sat calmly atop Einar, ran his left hand down his broad neck, felt his excitement through his mailed gauntlets. He unfastened his shield, meticulously attached it to his left arm, then drew his weapon. He gazed down at both Kiera and Belkidar, then up at Gunnar. "We must focus on our own responsibilities, trust in each other to defend their own quadrant."

"Agreed," Kiera said, keeping her eyes fixed to the southwest even as the minotaurs converged on Gunnar and Batai from the northeast.

"This is where we make our impression on Hildegard," Batai said quietly.

Belkidar nodded. "Today will send the chill of doubt down his spine."

"If he even has one," Gunnar added.

The minotaurs followed what appeared to be their leader. It was considerably larger than the rest, its horns at least two elyes longer than the others', its irises shimmering red around black pupils against the pre-dawn shadows. It frothed at the mouth, cursing as it sprinted far ahead of the horde.

When it was a few elads away, Gunnar sprinted toward it, the minotaur raising its axe as saliva streamed from its jaws and mucus flew from its nostrils. But in just three strides, Gunnar had already neared full speed, so its axe was still rising when his shoulder exploded into its chest. Its sternum crushed, Gunnar reached for its throat with his left hand, held it high, muffled crunches escaping his fist. He roared, threw it down like a doll, followed it with his sword. Then he returned to his position in their defensive formation, each footprint trailing the chiefton's blood. The horde, still several dozen elads distant, never slowed.

Einar stood a few paces away, his unbridled enthusiasm making Batai's heart swell. Then he charged the nearest foe, his acceleration and sheer size overwhelming the minotaur. It brought its axe back far too late, utterly unprepared as Einar bowled it over, knocking it on its back. He never slowed, charged another, crashing a hoof over its confused expression. Surrounded by chaos, Batai clearly heard its skull crack beneath Einar's bulk, its body twitching in a growing crimson pool.

To the minotaurs, the charger fought as one of them. He rampaged through their ranks, grunting and snorting with wide, excited eyes. But he couldn't have been more different. They couldn't have known he maneuvered with a plan, incited them to attack only to have their jaw broken by the rim of an upthrusted shield or their flesh opened by the cold edge of an arching sword. The battle glory was upon him, and to the minotaurs, he fought like one of them.

Indira raced southeast, towing the pack horses behind her. Before long, she reached the plateau Brohdan had described, standing at least fifty elads above the surrounding basin. Its top ran northeast-southwest, forming a perfect vantage for a ranged ambush. Her friends were at least four hundred elads away, but the cyclopes' powerful bows and elevated position would render that distance trivial. She quietly rode to the mesa's southwest tip where she smoothly dismounted and tied the horses to a tree. Then she climbed.

A shelf had formed halfway to its summit, and she crept along it until she reached its southern tip. She continued, easily negotiated a jagged outcropping until she could peer behind the mesa. What she saw surprised her.

Brohdan's description was accurate, if incomplete. The cyclopes numbered more than fifty, each at least ten elads tall, waiting on a lower shelf roughly a third of the way up the plateau. She saw their plan in her mind's eye, watched them receive their cue, charge to the summit to launch arrows the size of spears. Their single eyes seemed oversized, conveyed an utter lack of compassion she'd never before seen, prompted the same pitiless rage that had welled in her during her captivity in the mines.

Indira closed her eyes, took a deep breath, held it. She felt the wind skirt the mesa, became a part of it, flowed with it around the terrain, through the cyclopes, rocking the dry undergrowth at its base. Then she pulled her bow from her back and smoothly nocked an arrow. She leaned around the ledge, let the first arrow fly, releasing fifteen more by the time it had completed half of its hundred-elad flight.

The first arrow hit its mark, penetrated a cyclops through his lone eye, continued through the rear of its large head. Its legs buckled, fell in a heap, silent. Eight more fell by the time the others realized they were under attack, but her arrows were far faster, crumpled six more to the ground.

"We're under atta – " a large cyclops bellowed, only to be met by Indira's sixteenth arrow. But its final words were enough to scramble the others, using boulders for shelter.

Indira released another short volley, killing nine more as they fled for cover. Then she leaned back behind the ledge, nearly half of her enemies killed. She closed her eyes again, saw with preternatural clarity where each hid. She smiled.

Brohdan flew north to flank the other cyclops band, then spotted the dust cloud rising from the horde of minotaurs as they thundered toward his friends. But he couldn't let that distract him, knew he had to eliminate the threat of the cyclopes and their arrows. So he hugged the terrain, keeping higher ground between himself and the source of the dust. He turned northwest, descended behind a low hill, then recognized the ridgeline behind which the cyclopes hid.

Brohdan climbed twenty elads as he approached the final turn. He banked hard, flying at speeds few could match, rounded the ridgeline's tip, appeared from nowhere to see them arguing over which was going to kill the most of his friends.

There was nothing they could do.

He was a shadow that streaked overhead, momentarily obscuring the dwindling stars, silent save the deep rumbling of his fire, the flames brilliant in the early dawn. It chased away the lingering darkness, reflected from rock walls, cracked stone, melted arrowheads, disintegrated sinew and bone. Death came slower for those further from its path. They scrambled in shock, crawled to nowhere, their arms or legs withered to charred stubs. Of the nearly sixty cyclopes that had gathered there, only six survived. Two readied their weapons, launched five-elad arrows, the others searching for bows whose strings hadn't snapped from the inferno's heat.

Brohdan arched his back, coasted into the sky. Then he leaned sideways, flapped his wings in opposite directions, dove head-long toward the ground, his speed surging. He again tasted pungent fuel, felt the intensity blossom in his jaws, killed four more before landing between the two survivors.

"You failed," Brohdan said. The one behind him launched an arrow at his back. It clanked against his hardened scales, fell in pieces amongst the blackened corpses. He extended his blade, his tail a blur, smoothly cut the creature in two, never taking his eyes from the first.

It nodded, conceding the point, its head reaching Brohdan's shoulders. "True, but with you here, your friends will die." Its voice was deep, its accent strange, harsh. "But don't worry, they'll hoard the females. Especially the elf." It smiled.

Brohdan was airborne in a flash, his tail whipping around as he turned, his blade singing as it passed through the repulsive creature. This time he 'cloaked' to stay hidden from the minotaurs, letting him take the most direct route to where Indira battled the other cyclops band. He trusted her, but facing several dozen cyclopes was a difficult task for nearly anyone, let alone an elf a less than a third of their height and a tenth of their weight. And he would never forget the promise he made to Juron.

In the meantime, the second group of minotaurs appeared, closing the jaws of their trap. Still a hundred elads away, Kiera calmly made her final preparations. "I think I'm ready," she decided, each dagger inspected and returned lovingly to their sheaths.

"I should hope so," Belkidar mocked as Gunnar beheaded a minotaur not far behind them.

"Are you?"

"Sure. Why do you ask?"

"I've just never seen you fight before. I guess I'm not sure what to expect."

"My dear, I've unfortunately witnessed more battles than the rest of the world combined. Don't worry about me," he added, distracted by a large stone a few elads away. She watched as he calmly strode forward, bent over, and with some effort lifted the head-sized rock with both hands, his Staff tucked awkwardly under an arm. Satisfied, he carried it back to where he'd previously stood.

"What in the world are you going to do with that?"

"I learned a long time ago to avoid fighting if at all possible."

"I don't understand."

"Prepare yourself," Belkidar said, nodding to the southwest where their enemies approached.

"Right." She watched as the snorting, thundering minotaurs broke into a sprint after seeing how few their opponents numbered.

Belkidar cradled the large stone in his right hand and took up the Staff with his left. As the minotaurs bore down on them, Kiera watched from several paces away as he closed his eyes and removed his hand from beneath the rock. To her surprise, it didn't fall, instead hovered motionless two elads above the ground.

When Belkidar opened his eyes, Kiera barely recognized him. His normal compassion was gone, replaced by a cold viciousness – not evil, but just as ruthless. In an instant, Belkidar had transformed from a frail old man into the embodiment of strength, into a being like nothing she'd ever seen. He physically stood neither taller nor broader, but the ancient creature radiated power, towered over the battlefield, his will as engulfing as Broglia fire. She returned her attention to her enemies, and when they closed to within a dozen elads, Belkidar unleashed his fury.

The stone that had been hovering beside his right shoulder accelerated to incredible speed, instantaneously, silently, covering the distance in less than a heartbeat. The minotaurs had no time to react.

It plunged into the charging horde, moved faster than anything Kiera had ever seen, much faster, having already traveled elads before bodies were flung high into the air. The delay was almost comical, a wave of flailing bodies crashing to the ground long after the stone had come to an unnaturally abrupt stop. At least a dozen were killed on its first pass, then Belkidar sent it on another.

The minotaurs were experienced warriors, but they had no idea how to combat this enemy. The stone flew a perfect line, the collisions never prodding it off course. And they were magnificent, each accompanied by sickeningly dull thuds, the muffled crack of shattered bones, or the spray of blood from torn limbs.

Kiera instinctively ducked as the bloodied stone raced toward her, saw it pause in midair a few elads from Belkidar's expressionless face, then watched as he again sent it through the dwindling horde. After completing its third pass, the minotaurs realized it'd soon return, so they fled – straight toward where Kiera stood.

"Finally!" she said, spinning a dagger in her right hand.

"Patience, my friend," Belkidar replied, sending his stone on its fourth trip.

His tone was calm, almost peaceful, but she knew him better than most, detected the fury raging inside him. Then the nearest minotaur charged, its horns towering more than four elads above her. With the spine of Szurgord's barbed daggers pressed beneath her forearms, their razor tips extending slightly beyond her bent elbows, Kiera dove under it, slashed at its legs before rolling to her knees. It shrieked, fell horribly, its weight buckling its shins where she'd cut.

A second minotaur charged, was nearly on top of her, his enormous axe raised high. In a flash, Kiera flung a dagger, rolled backward next to where the first lay writhing on its back, silenced it with a practiced thrust, her blade sliding smoothly into its sternum. The second toppled forward, his horns falling an elye from her face as she pulled her dagger from its forehead.

Gunnar and Batai were deep in battle when Belkidar's stone began its first flight. Einar moved lithely, threaded a path through the horde while putting Batai in perfect position for sword or shield. He ignored some, knowing full well Einar would manage them in due time. They moved as one, foiling a flanking attempt, funneling others toward Gunnar, always securing their quadrant in their defensive formation.

Nearly three times as tall as a man, the tips of the minotaur's horns struggled to reach Gunnar's shoulders. In their frenzy, they swarmed him, attacked from all directions, their grunting and cursing a chorus. Each met his cold blade, dawn's violet reflecting in every swing. But they never paused, trampling over dead comrades in their lust for blood.

One dove at him from behind, its horns buckling his knees as he fell. Gunnar rolled to his back, narrowly avoided a falling axe, swung his sword in an arc, severed legs before another minotaur crashed into them. Its knees thudded into his chest, pinned him to the ground. Gunnar wrapped his fist around a horn, drove its head into the ground, used it to leverage himself back to his feet. Enraged, he swung the creature by its horn, broke bones with its body. The survivors drew back, gave him a wide berth.

Gunnar held the corpse at arm's length, let it dangle from his fist. He bellowed at them, taunted them, invited them to attack, threw the body at them in disgust when they hesitated. But when he bent to retrieve his sword, the bravest of them charged. It swung its axe down, but Gunnar rolled underneath, abandoning his sword. It brought its axe back again, but Gunnar stepped inside its swing, brought his elbow down hard, shattered its clavicle. It bellowed, dropped its weapon. Gunnar caught it, chopped down with it, splintered a kneecap, then

swung it high, embedded it in its head. For a brief moment it stood
frozen, then toppled onto its back, the axe handle sliding from Gunnar's
hand. He again bent to retrieve his sword, smiled when none objected.

The surviving cyclopes took shelter behind a line of small
boulders, calling to one another in a strange tongue. They cursed their
unseen enemies, each other, their impotence.

Indira listened while she took stock. She had used less than a third
of her quiver and still had three in reserve. She drank from her water
skin, then peered around the corner, slowly, searching for weaknesses.
A cloud of arrows exploded from the cyclopes below, most flying
overhead toward the mesa's summit, others far to her left. She recalled
Belkidar's warning about their marksmanship and smiled. They had no
idea where she hid.

She nocked an arrow, drew back her bow, carefully leaned past the
ledge. Her green eyes saw every curve of the landscape, every tree and
shrub. They noted the distance and differences in elevation, her mind
subconsciously calculating trajectories. And they detected a soiled
boot, a protruding elbow, a sweat-beaded forehead. As the sun
emerged above the eastern horizon, Indira released two arrows in quick
succession. The first penetrated an exposed shoulder. It immediately
stood in agony, instinctively reached for the source of the pain, saw the
second arrow an instant before it exploded through the back of its head.

The other cyclopes froze, unsettled by what they'd just witnessed.
They stared at their comrade, its crimson blood soaking the dry soil of
the Thrud Wastelands. Then they took more care to conceal their tall
bodies behind the boulders, the noise of their shuffling exceeded only
by their cursing.

Some succeeded, eleven did not, the boulders too small to
completely shield them from her elevated position. Her mind raced,
weighed options, calculated outcomes, settled on a sequence for her

attack, all in a heartbeat. Then she filled her favorite quiver full of arrows, nocked the first, and again drew her bow.

She released eleven arrows in a flash, her left hand pausing briefly over each cyclops, her right blurring between bowstring and quiver. Her bow hummed, just as much a part of her as her beating heart. Then she released a second barrage, her left hand following the same sequence as the first, the entire process taking less than three drus.

Indira's first volley struck eleven cyclopes and, somewhat amusingly, elicited shrieks in the same rapid sequence as they jostled behind their concealment. Over the next dru, her second barrage silenced them, eleven bodies collapsing, disappearing again behind the boulders, their sequential thuds creating a brief rumble through the ground.

The minotaurs were overmatched, yet their battle rage lived on, despite the sorcerer's damnable stone. They grunted forward, cried their family names, cursed the humans, soared in the air, fell mutilated to the ground. And each time the stone passed safely overhead, their temporary relief abruptly ended when Kiera gashed a throat, severed a hamstring, or disemboweled the survivors. As a result, only two minotaurs remained after its sixth pass. Belkidar let the bloodied stone thump to the ground as he watched them retreat into the hills.

"What about that last two?" Kiera asked.

"I want to pay my respects to an old friend." Then a familiar white-blue aura encompassed him. A moment later, Briz towered an elye above her. His low growl resonated through her body, then he loped away, his six legs covering elads with easy strides. But to her confusion, he went north instead of northwest where the minotaur pair fled.

Brohdan passed well north of his friends just as Belkidar's stone completed its third pass. Then he turned south, staying low in the hills, eventually recognizing the mesa behind which the other cyclopes hid. He released 'cloak' and climbed higher above the ground, searching for the best way to assist Indira.

Cyclopes are not stupid creatures, but instincts are difficult to suppress, especially when an arrow splinters a clavicle or thuds quivering into a kneecap. After her last volley, Indira estimated only twelve remained, but they were taking great care to avoid the same fate as their mates. She searched for vulnerabilities, found none, considered the possibility that she'd have to abandon the high ground to finish them off.

Then a huge shadow passed overhead, straight into the rising sun. Without moving, Indira rolled her eyes up, instantly recognized her friend. His timing was perfect. She drew back her bow and waited.

As Brohdan flew over the battlefield, the cyclopes watched in horror, praying the dragon would continue past them, their anxiety marring their concealment. In a flash, Indira released fifteen arrows, then took shelter again, awaiting their outcome.

She didn't have to wait long. Brohdan's sudden appearance caused only half of them to show their heads, so she was forced to kill the others by any means necessary. She impaled three through the heart, their hands clutching at their chests as they fell shrieking. Two others had their necks sliced open after reacting to an arrow in an elbow or hip, their blood spurting through trembling fingers. But the last proved more of a challenge, offering only a tiny window to attack.

The cyclops wondered how many enemies it faced, but it was more concerned with their unnatural accuracy. It had watched its comrades fall, taking more care to conceal itself with each. It struggled to keep its panic at bay, frantically tried to discover how it could escape the same fate. Then it saw the black dragon fly across the battlefield. It was the last thing it remembered.

It initially heard a loud crack as an arrow passed through its chin, the sound deafening as it reverberated through its broken jaw. It had repeatedly told itself to withstand whatever pain was to come, and at all costs remain hidden, but despite that, it numbly rose to its knees, bringing both hands to where the searing pain resonated through its body. It didn't realize the last of its comrades were being killed. It didn't notice its fingers probing where its chin had once been, nor the arrow as it burst through the back of its skull. The last of the cyclops fell limply to the ground, its fingers still probing its shattered face for answers.

A group of minotaurs tried to surround him, but Einar bolted through them toward four others. He dodged the first attack which Batai immediately blocked with his shield, then beheaded the creature with an arching sword as Einar collided with another. It had just raised its axe with both hands, was vaulted backward, crushed by a hoof to its chest. Batai feigned a downward swing against the third, and with its axe held high, instead lowered his blade, extended it an elye as Einar's momentum carried it across its neck. Its blood sprayed Einar's flank as he charged the fourth, bashing it against the left side of his chest armor. The minotaur spun where it stood, stayed upright, met Szurgord's shield, shattering its face.

Batai looked back, prepared for another charge. Instead, Einar paused, and he gently stroked the back of his neck. They waited there, watched the magnificence, the splendor. His might, his glory.

Gunnar faced the last five minotaurs, nodded toward them, for they persevered despite over a hundred of their kin lay dead. He wondered if their souls would in fact return to this world, for they'd fought bravely. But courage alone wouldn't see them through this day.

They circled, surrounded him, attacked in unison. With his sword held low, Gunnar swung it toward the first, slicing it in two, continued its momentum, rotating his arm so his blade pointed toward the brightening sky. He pivoted his feet, slammed his fist into the second, shattering the side of its head. He followed through, and now gripping the handle with both hands, brought it down, splitting the third from the top of its left shoulder through its right hip, sending a severed horn flying. He released the sword with his right hand and, despite lacking the space to step into his punch, smashed the fourth before it could bring down its axe. His fist cracked its sternum, caved in its chest. The creature fell backward, gasping for the air its collapsed lungs could not find. It writhed on the ground, struggling, suffocating.

Gunnar dodged the huge axe of the last minotaur, stepped back. He looked into its red eyes, saw no fear, only hatred, the purest malevolence he'd ever seen. This was completely different than the malice he remembered in the humans, the ones who'd ended his race. Theirs was a hatred spurred by fear, by ignorance. The creature was foul, wicked, wholly evil.

It shouted something at him, a foreign warcry, then attacked. Gunnar stepped back, let its axe swing in front of him once, twice, then on the third caught its arm against his side. He lurched it up, cracked its elbow, heard its axe fall behind him. It tried to pull away, to get enough space to impale him with its horns, but Gunnar held it close. He raised his sword, slid it slowly down, into the top of its chest, through the small of its back. Still he held it close, felt its spasms through his own body, felt it go limp like a sack of wheat. Then he released it, let his sword slide free as it fell.

Batai and Gunnar joined Kiera, their eyes following hers as she watched the last two minotaurs flee.

"Where's Belkidar?" Batai asked.

"You mean Briz," she corrected. "He ran off to the north."

"Why would he go that way when the minotaurs – "

Gunnar's question was answered mid-sentence as Briz appeared in front of the minotaurs, cutting off their escape. He stood there, his head held low, his eyes fixed on his enemies.

Briz was a large carnivore, yet his shoulders didn't even reach half the minotaurs' height. That fact seemed to encourage them. Both readied their axes, taunting him with curses and jeers.

Then Briz let loose a long, savage growl, exposing his enormous fangs and forcing Kiera to cover her ears. He repeatedly clinched and released his foreclaws, his bloodlust palpable.

That proved too much for the smaller of the minotaurs. It bolted back the way it'd come, leaving its larger companion to face Briz alone. To its credit, it paused only a moment before attacking.

But Briz was bred for killing, and as the minotaur brought its axe down, he charged beneath it, took out its legs. Aided by the downward swing of its heavy axe, the minotaur toppled forward onto its face. Its snout and right eye socket shattered, the minotaur rolled onto its back, fumbling for its axe, but to its surprise, the strange creature was already standing over it. Briz stepped onto its chest, snarling, staring into its red eyes, his hot breath on its skin, his saliva falling onto its face.

Kiera watched them in silence, each frozen for completely different reasons. Then the minotaur moved for its axe. Briz clamped his jaws around its upper bicep, easily pulled it from its socket, its sinew stretching before ripping audibly from the joint. The minotaur howled, screamed, cursed as Briz held it down, his foreclaws digging into its chest. Then he closed his jaws around its throat, silencing it with a vicious tug, its half-severed head bouncing back to the ground.

Briz lifted his nose into the breeze, immediately located his fleeing enemy. He sprinted forward, using his forelegs to help accelerate, then to maintain his balance, his speed unmatched. He ran diagonally from where it fled, flanked it, then crashed into it, clamping his jaws around his right hip. The pelvis is a sturdy bone, and so when Briz planted all six claws into the dirt of the Thrud Wastelands, the minotaur had little choice but to stop with him. Briz opened his jaws, instantly re-clamped them to improve his grip, this time encompassing the minotaur's entire pelvis. He lifted it, shook it brutally from side to side, his saliva flying in all directions, his primal growls emphasizing each searing jerk. The minotaur screamed, but soon its cries turned to silent pants, pain overwhelming terror. Eventually, Briz' enthusiasm prevailed, the creature flying from his jaws.

Unable to walk, the minotaur used its arms to scramble away, but Briz was created to kill. He padded to where it struggled, stepped on its heaving back, sank four long fangs into its skull. The minotaur stiffened, its body rigid as a log, then went limp as Briz' jaws came together with a sickening crunch.

Briz sniffed at what remained of its head, pawed at the back of its neck. He leapt from its back and circled the carcass, his nose first to the ground, then in the air. Satisfied, he finally abandoned it, trotting to the others. Once there, the white-blue aura reappeared, leaving Belkidar standing next to them.

The three stared at the old man, horrific expressions on their faces. "What?"

"That was truly gruesome," Kiera finally managed.

"Come on. It wasn't that bad."

"Belkidar, you still have some of its brains in your beard!"

"Oh. Yes. I suppose that may be true. I'll wash it out once Indira returns with the pack horses."

"You think they'll need our help?" Gunnar asked as Belkidar felt for the sticky wetness in his beard.

"No," Belkidar began, walking over to him. "Brohdan will have made quick work of his lot, and since he's not here, I'm sure he's with Indira." He approached Gunnar's inverted sword, its tip on the ground, Kiera noting how it stood over twice his height. He gazed into its flawless steel, picked brains out of his hair. "What took you two so long?"

Gunnar turned for the first time to examine the opposite half of the battlefield. Impressed, he looked down at the sorcerer. "Not bad."

"Not bad?" Kiera demanded. "He only left eight for me!"

"How exactly did you manage that?" Batai asked as he dismounted next to Belkidar, running his hand along Einar's flank.

"Simple," he answered just as a bloody stone hovered and stopped an elye behind Batai's head. "Take a look," he added, nodding behind him.

Batai turned and was surprised to see a battered, reddened stone roughly the size of his helmet staring him in the face. Speechless, he turned back and looked at Belkidar.

"Like I said – simple. The Thrud Wastelands is rich in iron, so I just manipulated the existing magnetic field to move the rock wherever I wished," he concluded, shrugging his shoulders.

Brohdan arrived to see his friends in the middle of the gory field, the carnage a tribute to their might.

"Where's Indira?" Belkidar asked.

"She's coming. I found her just in time to see her kill the last of cyclopes. She never missed, not once, even though most hid behind boulders. She was amazing."

Then she appeared, cresting a distant hill, leading the pack horses behind her. Soon, she rode up beside them. "Good battle," she said simply.

"That's what we heard," Belkidar replied, smiling.

"What is *that* in your *beard*?" she asked, horrified.

"Never mind. I'll wash it out soon enough."

Indira nodded uneasily. After taking note of the battlefield, her eyes found Belkidar's bloodied stone. She raised a single eyebrow.

"I'll explain on our way to Gul Krul. For now, let's just say it involved a bit of sorcery, so I'd like to be on our way before Hildegard's minions arrive to find his Fourth Defense in ruins."

"Agreed," Batai said. "Shall we?" he added, turning to Kiera.

"Of course."

As they mounted their horses, Gunnar bent down, using the garment of a fallen minotaur to wipe his sword clean. Then he looked up, watched his friends resume their journey before looking one last time at Hildegard's Fourth Defense. "Good battle indeed."

Chapter 20
The Fifth Defense

There is purity in violence, in the desperate struggle to
pull life from death, that surpasses any philosopher's
sere quest for truth. – Caine

Matthew Woodring Stover, <u>Heroes Die</u>

They departed in a single file, their progress swift, taking only brief respites throughout the day. By dusk, Kiera was headed almost due south, their arc around Gul Krul nearly complete. Speed was of the essence now, but she knew unknown creatures of the last Defense loomed ahead, and she vowed to discover them before they could do her friends harm.

Gunnar followed her by several elads, his long strides easily keeping pace with her horse. The handle of his sword extended an elye above his head, dimly reflecting the growing starlight. He was relaxed, surrounded by family, and he felt a belonging he'd never before known.

Indira rode behind, felt his fulfilment, his gratification, as though it were her own. Belkidar had refilled all of her quivers, and so she rode contentedly atop her horse, searching the darkness for enemies.

Belkidar rode with his Staff secured in a hard sheath of boiled leather. He'd strapped it to his saddle diagonally so that he could rest his right hand on its old, familiar wood, his left hand loosely holding the reigns of his horse. He'd washed his beard earlier in the day.

Batai and Einar brought up the rear, their bond their strength, a constant source of fulfillment. He often spoke quietly to Einar, conveyed his appreciation, his fortune in somehow finding such a rare friend.

Brohdan used the growing darkness to scout the desolate terrain. He generally flew ahead, his sight their greatest advantage during the night. He remembered the time after they'd lost Indira, his grief, his helplessness. He knew their most difficult battles still lay ahead, realized the danger associated with each, so he savored the moment, when they were complete.

"Belkidar," Indira began, "do you think Hildegard learned anything from the last battle?"

"Because of his antics with the stone?" Kiera asked.

She smiled, but Belkidar only scowled. "The planet's magnetic field was already in place, so it's not like I had to create it myself, I just had to alter it a little. Still, I'm sure he learned some things."

"How much will he have learned from Briz?" Batai asked softly from the rear.

"About as much as my manipulation of the magnetic field. They have similar footprints, because just as the magnetic field was already there, so was my body."

"Why didn't you use the stone to kill those last two minotaurs?" Gunnar asked.

Belkidar paused a moment. "Briz has been a loyal friend. Since the day I created him, all he's ever done is try to make me proud. He deserved a role in this Quest. Besides, I think he did quite well," he added almost to himself.

"What type of information could Hildegard have learned?" Batai asked.

"That's difficult to say. It depends on many things, such as his diligence at the time I used sorcery, my own ability to minimize its footprint, how long I used it, and many others. So the specific knowledge that can be gained is seldom the same. For instance, yesterday he may have learned my mood, but tomorrow he might learn our position, or our vulnerabilities."

"You've seen me use sorcery to communicate with Brohdan. That's possible because sorcery intimately links all sorcerers together. Just as the water of the Celornorin Ocean connects a whale to the north with a sea lion to the south, the medium of sorcery inherently links all sorcerers. Therefore, whenever a Linsilor is used, a bridge connecting that Linsilor with all others temporarily exists. Like when a whale calls to a mate, any creature within linaks can gain information from that sound. Distance, direction, mood, intent – they can all be derived through the water. The same is true of sorcery, only instead of water, sorcery itself is the medium. The main difference is the link disappears as soon as the sorcery ends."

"Can you gain any knowledge of Hildegard when you use sorcery?" Batai asked.

"Unfortunately no, just as the whale learns nothing from those that hear its calls."

"Why then does Brohdan's sorcery not link his mind with Hildegard's?" Indira asked.

"It does. We're all inherently connected, a truth that hasn't even slightly changed since the dawn of sorcery. But the more the Linsilor is used – meaning, the more sorcery is required to reach an objective – the stronger the bridge becomes. Brohdan's capable of casting a handful of spells, but none require significant use of a Linsilor. So the medium is weak, like trying to see linaks in the fog of the Great Drulg Swamp. No matter how hard you try, you can only see a few dozen elads. The same is true with Brohdan's sorcery – Hildegard could try to discover something, but the medium isn't strong enough to allow it."

"Do you expect him to adjust his plans based on whatever he's learned?" Gunnar asked.

"He may tweak a few things, but he doesn't have the time to make any major changes. And more importantly, he committed to this plan a long time ago. He's no fool. He won't abandon a campaign he'd so carefully prepared over kilacycles."

"Shouldn't we hurry then, to limit what he *can* change?"

"Absolutely, and we don't have much further to go. We will, of course, meet his Fifth Defense sometime between now and the gates of his fortress. And that brings me to another topic."

He paused, his outline barely visible in the light of the crescent moon. "Ever since Brohdan's dream, I've wondered how the Jrelz fit into Hildegard's plans. Along with the Jrelz Captains, they form the backbone of his dominion over these lands, so they must figure in his strategy somehow."

Batai thought about that. "Well, we only have his last Defense left, plus whatever he's got waiting for us at Gul Krul."

"Exactly," Belkidar agreed. "I think the Jrelz will show themselves near his fortress, so there's a good chance they'll be part of the Fifth Defense."

Batai nodded. "And so you believe they'll attack somewhere near Gul Krul."

"It makes sense. His last Defense should be his strongest, and it'd be easy to monitor if he keeps its creatures nearby."

"What about the Jrelz Captains?" Kiera asked.

"Their primary purpose is to protect their master, so we probably won't see them until we battle Hildegard in Gul Krul. That'll be a challenge. I still believe Hildegard will wait until then to reveal whatever he has planned for Brohdan, so the rest of us shouldn't count on his help during the final battle."

"What threats do the Jrelz pose?" Indira asked.

"They're relatively inexperienced and therefore not particularly advanced in their sorcery. They must tie words to their cants and wards to better engage their Linsilors, so they prefer to keep their enemies at a distance. But if given no alternative, they're adept at hand-to-hand combat. The staffs they use to amplify their sorcery can be pulled apart into two swords. Both have long handles – half the length of their staff – because each handle serves as the scabbard for the opposite sword. Wielded in both hands, they've spent countless links mastering their combat arts before they begin their sorcery training in earnest."

"The Jrelz Captains are trained by Hildegard himself, and in return, they protect him and instruct the Jrelz. While even the Jrelz Captains lack Hildegard's ability – compensating for eight thousand cycles is difficult, after all – they're still quite formidable."

"How many Jrelz can we expect?" Batai asked.

"Hildegard typically trains a dozen Captains. There will be many more apprentices."

Batai played the battle in his mind, considered various strategies. "Indira must engage them while Gunnar, Kiera, and I charge their position."

"A good plan," Belkidar said, "as long as Indira can keep them from using sorcery until you reach them."

Indira's smile widened.

To everyone's relief, the cool night breeze energized both rider and horse. They rapidly traversed the flat terrain north of the continent's lone highway that connected Northern Trillhell to Gul Krul.

Brohdan constantly kept the others in sight. He looked south, faintly detecting the collective heat generated by a group of farmers hauling their produce along the highway. As he turned back to the north, he caught a glimpse of the heavens.

He felt a powerful connection with the night sky. It was his solace in the first few mooncycles at grombit camp, and now it was the most tangible link he still shared with Mikka. Though an ocean away, they could both look up and see these same stars. And while a great distance separated them, it was nothing compared to the expanse that lay between them and the distant stars. And yet the stars prevailed. That gave Brohdan hope, because so long as the stars shone in the night sky, he'd forever be connected with his mate.

After nearly four links of hard riding, Kiera brought them to a halt. Brohdan, flying slightly to the east, joined them in the darkness of the vast wastelands.

"Is something wrong?" he asked after landing a few elads downwind to minimize the dust he blew toward them.

"No, everything's fine. We only have a few more links of darkness, and we're only a link from the highway. If we're to get any rest, now's the time."

"Is there shelter near?" Indira asked.

"Yes," Brohdan replied. "A few large boulders just over a linak to our southwest."

"Excellent," Kiera agreed. "We're only planning to sleep until dawn, so that should be perfect."

After a few drus, Kiera faintly saw the boulders in the starlight. They were larger than she'd imagined and would easily shelter them from the main road.

Brohdan turned to the others. "I'll take the watch."

"Are you sure?" Indira asked.

He nodded. "I got an entire night's sleep before we left the swamp."

It didn't take them long to unroll their sleeping blankets. Belkidar, the last to lie beneath them, took one last look around before closing his eyes. Before long, even the enormity of the coming events succumbed to the exhaustion of the previous days.

Brohdan 'cloaked' before climbing the large rock formation, an island in the otherwise flat terrain. His thoughts turned to his past. He remembered the frustration and pain he endured in the Sichundars when he was unable to begin his grombit. He recalled each of the beatings he'd suffered from Limbrin, his body not yet strong enough to fend off his brutality. He couldn't help but think how far he'd come, how the humiliation and pain he endured were worth it, just so he could have one chance to rid Hildegard's evil from this world. Although difficult, the agony he endured back then couldn't even remotely compare to the suffering he'd experience should any one of his friends fall in the coming links.

Then his thoughts turned to Mikka, knew the next day would determine not only their destiny, but the fate of the entire world. Ever since he'd met Belkidar and learned of Hildegard's theft of the Jewel, Brohdan realized his fate would be decided by some critical battle on a faraway continent. As he watched over his friends, he realized that time had finally arrived. No longer did his future hang in the balance of some distant outcome; the defining moment of his life, and that of the world, lay only a few links away.

Brohdan harbored no trepidation, and that surprised him. Instead, he felt relieved that the opportunity to forever end both Hildegard's evil and his own destiny's uncertainty was finally in his grasp.

Belkidar woke as the sun emerged above the horizon.

"Good morning," Brohdan said in his version of a whisper.

"I certainly hope so," he replied, sitting up. "Anything to report?"

"No, all quiet."

After waking the others, Belkidar silently watched his comrades as they re-rolled their bedding and packed them onto the horses. He saw Gunnar stretch widely before sitting and inspecting his sword, his manner practiced, relaxed. He observed Kiera and Batai as they completed the final preparations of their morning meal, their banter and quick wit making him smile. Then he turned and studied Indira as she efficiently took inventory of her many arrows before meticulously inspecting her large bow. Satisfied, she swung it over her shoulder in a smooth, practiced motion, letting it rest across her chest as she gracefully walked toward Einar. The charger melted as she slowly ran her hand down the underside of his broad neck, his eyes half closed, his ears low.

Then Belkidar turned to Brohdan. He sat just below the summit of the rock formation, his gaze scouring the surrounding landscape. He took several moments to study his eyes, didn't need sorcery to know his friend was prepared for whatever lay ahead.

Belkidar recalled the first time they'd met. Over three cycles ago, it seemed only a mooncycle since that fateful day next to the river north of the Sichundar grombit camp. He remembered Brohdan's initial distrust of him, when he actually tried to kill him with his tail. He chuckled, despite himself.

He jumped when Kiera offered him bread, cheese, and dry sausage for the second time. "Sorry," he said, accepting the meal from her.

"Are you all right?" she asked.

"Never better."

"If you say so," she said before offering food to the others in turn.

Belkidar returned to his thoughts. He knew he was prepared to meet Hildegard in Gul Krul. What's more, he knew his friends were too.

They sat together, eating and talking of the battles to come. "The strength of the first three Defenses centered on sheer numbers," Belkidar said. "The orcs, knifylm, lilkes – they were intended to overwhelm an army, an invasion. But the Fourth Defense was different. The cyclopes and minotaurs were well trained, and they used a battle-tested strategy. If not for Brohdan's scouting abilities, we very well could've lost that one. I think we can expect more of the same with Hildegard's Fifth Defense. The Jrelz, for example, offer unique challenges."

"Can you elaborate on that?" Batai asked. "Most of us have never fought sorcerers before."

"Very well," Belkidar agreed, knowing full well that Batai and Einar were in fact the only ones who'd previously encountered them in battle. "The first thing you should know is how to kill them. Unless you're talking about an extremely powerful sorcerer – "

"Like you?" Kiera interrupted.

"Yes, like me," Belkidar answered shortly. "And like Hildegard. As I was saying, the Jrelz are inexperienced, all around thousand cycles old, so they can be killed like any other person. They will, of course, present dangers others do not, but that shouldn't alter your strategy much."

"I understand," Indira said. "How do we kill Hildegard?"

"You can't, most likely. He's simply too experienced, too powerful." He looked down for a moment. "That's why I must face him alone."

"What?" Kiera demanded. "Not a chance. We fight him together!"

Belkidar was shaking his head. "You know how much respect I have for each of you, but Hildegard's lived long enough to master a great many things, one of which is death. Throughout the eight thousand cycles of our lives, we've each come to understand what it takes to cause death, and to prevent it. Swords, axes, arrows – they're all the same, and after studying long enough, revelations take place."

"You're telling me that if I slid my sword into Hildegard's heart, he'd survive?" Gunnar asked, incredulous.

"Not exactly. What I'm trying to explain is more basic. Your sword, Indira's arrows – they'd never get close to him. There are simply too many ways he could stop you from coming within a hundred elads, most of which ends with you dying. That's why I must face him alone. And remember, killing me won't be easy for him either, so he won't be able to attack the rest of you so long as I remain alive."

The others nodded, grudgingly accepting his logic.

Belkidar continued. "While I battle Hildegard, you must engage the Jrelz Captains." He remained silent for quite some time. "That brings me to you, Brohdan."

"I'm now certain the entire battle with the keviloks was conceived for the sole purpose of scouting us and our capabilities. I'm sure learning of Brohdan was a surprise. I wish I could've seen his face," he added with a grunt.

"Other than you, and perhaps Hildegard, what in this world could challenge Brohdan?" Kiera asked.

"And of them, how many could he recruit in such a short period?" Indira added.

"I've asked myself those same two questions countless times, and I could only come up with one answer. A titan."

"They're not real!" Kiera said more loudly than she'd intended.

"That's what we used to think about dragons," Batai pointed out.

"Titans are indeed real," Belkidar said. "First conceived by Jenkar a thousand cycles before he forged the Staff of Power, they can only be summoned by an exceptionally powerful sorcerer. The world was a different place then. There had never been a war, and sorcerers were more concerned with their thirst for knowledge, not killing each other. That's when titans were conceived."

"Originally created to protect enormous vaults of knowledge – the products of hundreds of sorcerers throughout the kilacycles – Jenkar later used titans for his own purposes. Toward the end of the War, after the Staff of Power had corrupted his every thought, Jenkar created three to fight by his side. Dozens of dragons and sorcerers lost their lives before they were finally destroyed. But they proved their worth. Some of us have never forgotten."

"What are they like?" Gunnar asked.

"They're enormous, fashioned in the likeness of a human, but on a much larger scale. If my memory serves, they stood at least thirty-five elads tall. By comparison, Brohdan's length from head to tail is twenty-eight elads. And with their size comes unparalleled strength. They have no sorcery, but Jenkar bestowed in them the ability to harness the static electricity around them, discharged as bolts of lightning."

"How did Kainan fare against them?" Brohdan asked.

"Good question. He didn't. Kainan battled Jenkar's other forces, and it was debated for centacycles whether he should've confronted the titans instead. I could see the wisdom in that, but losing him would've cost us the War."

"They're two of the most dominant creatures the world has ever known. While a Broglia has a natural life that extends beyond a thousand cycles, a titan lives only a few mooncycles. They're the product of sorcery and aren't meant to exist in this world. The great sorcerers before the War took turns summoning them, but Jenkar was the last. Krollum, Aelya, and I saw what they were capable of, so we agreed to never again create such a dangerous creature, at least not until the source of Jenkar's corruption was destroyed."

"What effect will their lightning have on me?"

"I don't know Brohdan, I'm sorry. A Broglia Black has never encountered a titan, neither in peace nor war. Your natural resistance to all forms of sorcery may help protect you, but a titan's electricity isn't sorcery, so your resistances may not help at all."

Brohdan's expression failed to reveal his true feelings. He was actually relieved, his likely adversary finally identified. And despite those uncertainties, he never once believed this Quest would be easy.

"You've given each of us our responsibilities," Batai said. "Now we must fulfill them."

Gunnar nodded. "And we can't rest on our previous success."

"I know we would be of little use to you," Indira said to Brohdan and Belkidar, "but if you should need us, we will fight by your side."

"Damn right," Kiera agreed.

"Thank you," Belkidar said. "Of that I have no doubt, but as Batai said, we each have our responsibilities. If we're to achieve our ultimate goal, we must each complete our own tasks. Brohdan must conquer the titan. I shall defeat Hildegard. And you four – "

An objecting grunt echoed through the darkness of the early dawn.

"My apologies," Belkidar corrected, grinning. "As I was saying, you *five* must defeat the Jrelz Captains."

Einar grunted his approval, and Batai raised his hand to rest it on his shoulder. "But let's not forget, all this is for naught if we don't get past the Fifth Defense."

"Good point," Gunnar agreed. "Let's get on with that."

Kiera mounted her horse with the others following suit, then quickly led them from behind the boulders and resumed their journey south toward the highway.

Brohdan shimmered into the background as leapt into the air, considered the irony that the featureless terrain that'd make concealment nearly impossible without sorcery only enhanced his use of it.

When only a half link had passed, Kiera turned and headed east. "I want to stay out of sight from anyone on the highway," she explained before Belkidar could ask the question that had already formed on his lips.

"Very well."

They continued east for another half link across the desolate wastelands, the heat of the morning sun already a nuisance.

"I can see parts of Gul Krul," Indira said.

"In that case, its guards will see us soon," Belkidar explained. "Stay alert, the final Defense can't be far."

Just as he finished the last syllable, Indira sensed the faintest tremor resonating through her saddle. "They come!"

"Who?" Gunnar asked, searching the horizons.

"Several creatures, from the south. They are enormous!"

Just then, Brohdan landed behind Batai, releasing 'cloak.' "There are twelve of them, the ones I saw in my dreams."

Belkidar winced. "Gargantuids," he said simply. "Extremely rare creatures that I'd thought extinct. They resemble gorillas with short, stubby necks and long, powerful arms, their strength far greater than their size would imply. But unlike gorillas, their mouths overflow with sharp teeth and four large fangs, and their huge three-fingered claws have opposable thumbs. Oh, and they like to eat their enemies," he added, almost as an afterthought.

"Sounds like fun," Kiera mumbled to nobody in particular.

"What else?" Gunnar asked Brohdan.

"Nothing. Just those gargantuids."

"There must be more," Indira said, surveying the horizons.

"Yes, but where?" Belkidar asked sourly.

"How long before the gargantuids get here?" Batai asked, his eyes scouring the southern horizon.

"They're still at least a linak south of the highway," Brohdan answered, "but they're moving fast. I'd say less than a quarter link."

"Very well," Batai said. "We charge the gargantuids."

"What?" Kiera asked. "That'll put the battle directly over the highway!"

"So be it. The rest of the Defense hasn't made its presence known, maybe they're not even here yet, so we should attack the ones we know about as quickly as possible. The more gargantuids we kill now, the less we'll have to deal with when the rest of Hildegard's final Defense reveals themselves."

Belkidar nodded. "Batai's right. To the south, and swiftly!"

They galloped ahead, and before long, they saw a large, well-prepared road in the distance, and beyond it the hazy forms of the gargantuids.

"Enormous creatures," Kiera said to Gunnar.

"Yes, they are."

"Over twice your height," she pointed out.

"So it would appear."

"And considerably heavier, from the looks of it."

"Yup."

"And meaner," she added.

"Well, at least they can't be as mean as you," Gunnar said, his face stoic.

She grunted as she removed two of her daggers, her dimples betraying her otherwise annoyed expression.

Dozens of early morning merchants from Trillhell first noticed the small group of warriors to the north of the highway. Inevitably, though, the gargantuids to the south demanded their undivided attention. Even the most dedicated salesman quickly turned and scurried from their approach, all apparently valuing their lives more than their morning's revenue. Within a few drus, the highway was deserted. The sun slowly continued its climb into the clear eastern skies as the dust raised by the final terrified merchant settled back onto the barren road.

There was no realistic way to prepare for seeing gargantuids for the first time, their shaggy grey fur somehow making them appear even larger than they were. They towered over everything they passed, grunting, snorting, and growling in deep, gravelly voices, shaking the very ground as they approached.

Kiera stopped and smoothly dismounted, Belkidar joining her. Indira and Batai remained in their saddles, preparing their weapons. After a couple of snorts from Einar, the other horses turned and fled back to the north.

Just then, the dozen gargantuids slowed from a run to a walk as they neared the highway, reducing the previous earthquake to just a large tremor. Then they stopped, still a hundred elads away, surprised with how few adversaries stood across from them.

"Where are the rest of the condemned?" the largest and nearest asked, its voice sounding more like a growl than speech. It stared down at them, its animosity plain, the cruelty it projected reminding Kiera of the minotaurs.

"The rest?" Belkidar asked.

"We wouldn't have been awakened for so few. Where are the rest?"

"I'm afraid it's just the six of us."

"Six?" the huge creature snorted.

Belkidar feigned confusion, appearing old and frail. "Yes. Six."

"The small female is one," the gargantuid began as though talking to its own youngling, pointing toward Kiera with an over-sized arm. "The skinny elf is two. The knight makes three. That large man is four. And you, old man, makes five," it concluded, its derisive grin revealing more of its teeth.

"You forgot Brohdan," Belkidar answered simply, nodding toward a point above and behind it.

The beast paused, his expression frozen, then turned to where Belkidar indicated.

Far too late.

Brohdan dove on his enemy, his wings tucked back, a black blur against the blue sky. As he closed, he extended his wings, the muscles across his chest rippling beneath his scales. He rotated his hips, flapped once, twice, then extended his blade.

Brohdan used his incredible speed to drive his blade deep into its flesh. And instant later, his talons thudded into its back, the hooks of his wings crashed onto its shoulders, all straining under the force of the impact.

The largest creature of the Fifth Defense flew forward, landed on its face with astonishing force, skidded to the highway before finally coming to a stop. The same tremor that shook Brohdan's five companions continued for linops through the compact soil of the Thrud Wastelands.

To his friends on the other side of the road, the epic collision seemed to occur in slow motion. They watched in awe, witnessing the attack from a far different perspective. Brohdan's dive was steep, wild, yet at the last moment he spread his wings, somehow held them extended. They stared with wide eyes and open jaws as an elad of his blade exploded from the gargantuid's chest, scattering blood and bone across the dry ground. The gargantuid's knees buckled, its arms flung backward, and Brohdan's fire joined his ear-splitting roar as he rode it to the ground.

The remaining gargantuids stood frozen, shocked, their leader killed in the first moments of battle. Killed by a Broglia Black.

"As I tried to explain," Belkidar continued, "there are six of us. Perhaps awakening you was warranted after all?"

The gargantuids stared first at their fallen leader, then at the Broglia Black. Gunnar, never having been accused of being particularly patient, took advantage of their hesitation. He charged, Indira having already embedded nearly twenty arrows into the nearest gargantuid's eyes and throat by the time he'd drawn his sword. Surprised, it turned its head and raised its arms to protect its face.

Gunnar brought his sword back, Indira's arrows streaking only elyes above his head. He pivoted, planted his leg, whipped his blade in a double-handed swing, his head barely reaching the gargantuid's chest. Szurgord's steel sliced through both bones of its lower leg, buckled it just below the knee, the sound like twin detonations, scattering bone fragments across the ground.

It howled in shock and pain, lost its balance, tried to use its ruined leg for support, its lower half dangling, and fell cursing in a heap. It writhed on the ground, reaching first for its leg, then at the giant who had mangled it.

Gunnar swiped its grasps away with his sword, severed long claws, drew more curses. He circled around to its shoulders, and still holding his sword with both hands, swung it down through the side of its stubby neck, the resulting gush nearly knocking him to the ground.

Kiera spotted a group of creatures descending toward them, far to her right. "We've got company!" she warned, nodding to the west. "Birds?"

"No, griffins!" Belkidar corrected.

"I always believed them to be aligned with good, not evil," Indira said, still focusing on the battle across the highway.

"They were once the noblest of creatures," Belkidar confirmed, shaking his head sadly. "There is endless corruption in that Headpiece. First Jenkar, then Krollum. Now this, after countless centacycles of honor..."

He updated Brohdan who'd been circling the south of the gargantuids. *"I'm afraid you must eliminate them, Brohdan. They can't be allowed to attack the rest of us while we battle the gargantuids."*

"I understand." He turned, gained airspeed as he climbed, flew into the brightening sky as it became increasingly littered with the profiles of the once-honorable creatures.

While Indira and Gunnar attacked the northern-most gargantuid and Kiera watched Brohdan climb west toward the griffins, Einar and Batai flanked the gargantuids to the east. They proved more agile than Batai had assumed, but Einar's speed and stamina prevailed. He raced around them, dodging in and out of their reach, his grunts taunting, his mane flying. They lunged for him, turned in circles to protect their backs, bumped in to one another in their eagerness to catch him.

Their recklessness grew with their frustration, focusing ever more on killing him than protecting themselves. That's when Einar maneuvered within range of Batai's sword, deftly dodged an enormous swinging claw as he bolted behind another. Batai swung, his blade severing the tendon above its heel, continued its momentum as Einar swerved around it, detached the other. The hobbled creature roared in fury, fell backward, its outstretched claws narrowly missing the speeding charger as it crashed to the ground.

This loss further enraged the other gargantuids, and they cursed in a foreign tongue as they chased after him. Einar tirelessly provoked them, turning the gargantuids from a single, unified pack into several disorganized individuals.

Gunnar immediately appreciated Einar's brilliance, quickly made his way through the swarming gargantuid pack to Batai's first victim.

He approached it carefully, waited until it fell from another futile attempt to stand, then charged. He drove every elye of his five-elad blade directly into the top of its skull, almost immediately losing his grip as the gargantuid broke into violent convulsions. Another saw his death blow, realized he was defenseless, growled a war cry as it attacked. Gunnar paused, waited, then found the handle of his sword, ripped it through the top of the corpse's head, up into the charging gargantuid's closing jaws. The last elad of his blade cut through its lower jaw, severed teeth, sang loudly as it came free. Gunnar dove with it, slid on the ground, barely evaded the crashing beast. Then he sprang back to his feet, rushed to where it fell, ended its curses with another blow.

"Prepare yourself," Belkidar told Kiera.

She looked first to the sorcerer, then toward the east where he gazed. She watched as faint wisps flickered several dozen elads from where they stood. Indira, her arrows distracting the gargantuids, didn't seem to notice as they increased in size and intensity.

"Hold on," Belkidar said with a grin.

Suddenly, Kiera felt herself being lifted from the ground, her hair flying around her shoulders and face as though she were in a sudden storm. She looked at her feet and was surprised to find them still on the ground. She gazed at the gargantuids, then toward the points of light still intensifying to her left, both becoming increasingly washed out by the white-blue light that enveloped her.

Just as quickly as it had appeared, the aura vanished. In that instant, the lights that were once forming in the distance now surrounded her. She turned to Belkidar.

He didn't speak, just nodded to the southwest. Kiera turned and was startled to see Gunnar, Batai, and Einar battling the gargantuids, now over a hundred elads away. "Why?"

"These are the Jrelz. They hope for a ranged battle, so I brought the fight to them."

Kiera drew her daggers, crouched slightly, balanced on the balls of her feet. As the whisps materialized into human shapes, her daggers flashed, gashed a throat, punctured a lung, whirled to pierce a sternum, none comprehending what had killed him.

In striking contrast, Belkidar remained motionless, the sea of sorcerers materializing around him. His Staff held high, a spark appeared an elye above him, then swelled into a fire overhead, fell as an inferno around him. It burned orange-red, too brilliant to behold, its deafening roar sealing himself from the world.

Then he walked among his enemies.

His fire scorched them, charred their bodies, their screams octaves higher than Kiera had thought possible. But she never stopped, her immaculate blades flashing in the dawn, slicing throats, removing limbs, thudding into chests, eliciting moans from the dying, pleas from the living.

The abruptness of their attacks initially befuddled the Jrelz, but their training soon took over. Those near Kiera slid their blades free, those near Belkidar died, the rest worked their Linsilors.

Nearly half of the Jrelz attempted to materialize elsewhere, far from the woman's daggers, even further from the master's sorcery. Yet when they reappeared, they stood in the same place they were before. Some tried again, only to find the same result. Then they saw the master's smile.

Angered, they raised their staffs while their brothers burned, formed orbs of yellow flames, shafts of stunning light, bolts of searing intensity, racing from every direction toward the master sorcerer.

His fire shield absorbed it all, made it burn brighter, stoked its intensity, widened his smile.

It didn't take long for Brohdan to reach the griffins, and as he drew closer, he realized there were nearly three dozen of them. Their bodies resembled lions, their head and wings eagles. Twice the size of a large stallion, their size surprised him, more than nine elads long, their wingspans at least seventeen. He admired them, wished fate would've offered an alternative. But Hildegard's evil had touched many, and this was but one instance of what the world would look like should their Quest fail.

They climbed higher as he approached. Brohdan flapped his enormous wings, easily matched their altitude. When they came within a few hundred elads, they spread out, their squawks piercing his ears, their powerful talons extended as they accelerated toward him.

They surrounded him, and he let them, allowed them to draw ever closer before he unleashed his fire. He kept its stream wide, knowing they'd be rendered flightless if his burning fuel touched enough of their frail feathers. He headed toward the center of the flock, flew among them, sprayed his liquid flames in all directions.

Over half fell victim to his Broglia fire, fell smoking, shrieking, to the ground.

Their arrogance gone, the remaining eight gargantuids adapted, placed their backs to one another, maintained their defensive formation as they slowly advanced on Indira. Einar initially attempted to lure one or two out by using himself as bait, but even Indira's arrows couldn't pry them from their circle. They continued toward her, all the while cursing their enemies, growling their fury.

Gunnar tried a different strategy. Because they kept their backs to one another, the one at the rear was forced to walk backward as they marched north, limiting its agility. Also, attacking that one would be the least noticed by the others, especially by those in the front who were more concerned with reaching Indira.

Batai and Einar continued their attempts to bait the eastern flank out of position, so Gunnar was alone in his attempt to breech the gargantuid defense. He looked down his blade, then at the southernmost creature in the ring. It sneered at him, inviting him to attack.

Gunnar charged.

The gargantuid swung at him. Gunnar ducked its claw, then planted his foot, anchored himself as it swung again. He raised his sword just in time, Szurgord's steel passing through its fur, claw, and bones as it sped in the opposite direction. The gargantuid roared, its three long fingers falling to the ground. Two short nubs remained, its thumb and inner wrist severed.

Gunnar bolted toward its weakened flank, the wounded gargantuid distracted by the blood pulsing from its injury. But it saw him, took a small step to its side as it brought its good claw forward, directly toward the charging giant.

Gunnar appeared not to notice, sprinted straight toward it. Then, at the last moment, he raised his sword, braced it upright with both hands as he dove for the ground. The gargantuid's arm soared above him, its claw grasping only steel, its wake fluttering his black hair. The blade cut deep into its palm, continued smoothly through its thick bones before finally exiting through the outside of its forearm, only elyes from its elbow.

Gunnar jumped to his feet, but not before he was once again drenched in blood. He advanced, easily dodged a feeble swing of a mangled claw, worked himself closer to its legs. Then he swung again, reduced the length of its right leg by four elads.

It fell awkwardly, shrieking in pain, but Gunnar ignored it, raced into the gargantuids' defensive ring. The nearest watched him, then with a frustrated growl, finally broke formation to face him.

Gunnar advanced on it, swung wildly at its feet, but it easily backed away from his attacks – straight into Batai's sword, who slashed at the back of its legs, hobbled it as Indira's seemingly endless barrage distracted those that faced her. Unable to stand, the gargantuid fell backward, roared as its head thudded to the ground, stiffened as Batai's sword slid deep into its skull.

The defensive alignment was broken. With their backs still facing one another, the surviving gargantuids were slow to recognize the breach, hesitated for a critical moment, torn between attacking or defending, eliminating the source of those infuriating arrows from without or the blood-stained swords from within.

Gunnar did not hesitate. He raced around the inside of the circle, maiming three before the others reacted. As the last trio finally regrouped, Einar and Batai approached Gunnar's side.

Belkidar's fire shield rumbled, the dead bodies shimmering almost unrecognizable from its heat. He walked casually through them, among them, smothered any hope they still held of casting even the most rudimentary spell.

Kiera quite happy battled those who remained beyond his fire's reach, encouraged that they'd been relegated to a more familiar form of combat. She rolled, ducked, dodged, and weaved through their thinning ranks, sent two daggers flying, drew another as she scissors-kicked a tall sorcerer with a thin beard, slid it into his temple as his fall knocked the air from his lungs. She side-stepped a falling sword, parried another, her dagger nearly cutting it in two. She blurred underneath a silver flash, severed a leg above the knee, opened the belly of another as two more sorcerers charged.

She rolled onto her knees, ducking one sword, blocking the second with her dagger. Then she shot to her feet, embedded its twin into a neck, pivoted toward the first as she again sank to her knees, detaching his kneecap. He fell to the ground screaming, then stiffened as he felt two icicles enter his body, one through his right kidney, the other through his left lung.

A third charged her, lost three teeth to the heel of her boot, two fingers an instant later to her dagger. He staggered back, hadn't yet taken a second step before he saw his blood spray from beneath his chin, two dimples flash in his periphery.

Four sorcerers sprinted toward her, each from a different direction. She threw both daggers at the sorcerers approaching from the north and east, heard their handles thud into their chests as she pulled Szurgord's two barb-tipped daggers from their concealed sheaths. She rolled backward and to her left, toward the fat sorcerer charging from the west, closing the distance in a flash. She raised a dagger over her left shoulder as she completed her backward somersault, the sorcerer only elads away.

He knew she'd killed him, knew there was no way he could avoid her blade, so he decided to take her life as payment for his own. With his sword already held high, he brought it down as he helplessly impaled himself on her weapon. At the last moment, with her back still facing him, she raised her other dagger, leveled it above her head, its spine resting against her upturned forearm. As if in slow motion, the Jrelz saw his sword collide with the dagger, saw it sever his blade in two. Then the woman raised her other dagger, its barbed tip slicing up through his chest. The gutted Jrelz toppled to his left, his entrails splashing to the ground as Kiera prepared for the fourth sorcerer still approaching from her right.

He was already on her, swung first one sword, then the other. Kiera leaned to her right and fell to a knee, dodged both flashing blades, calmly drove a dagger between his ribs as he completed his follow-through. The Jrelz toppled backward, graciously removing himself from her blade.

After Brohdan's initial attack, the griffins adapted, altered their strategy. They dove at him in coordinated attacks, usually three or four at a time and always from opposite directions. He cast 'steelskin,' used his long neck to help repel attacks from above and below, from his flanks and rear. His fire bursts lit the sky, resembling an aerial ballet more than a battle.

He remained patient, recalled the endless links of high hover practices and countless laps around the Sichundar grombit camp, knew he must prevent them from reaching his friends. But he couldn't stop every attack, and when a griffin clamped its jaws around his ankle, it nearly cracked its lower beak, squawking loudly as it dove away. Others followed, continued their strike-and-run strategy, received similar injuries. They were the fortunate ones.

Most never had the opportunity to use their beaks or talons, Brohdan's fire thwarting them when they were still elads away. His short bursts flew with great speed, initially knocking them out of their flight path before the flames took effect, spreading quickly whenever a trace of his burning fuel touched their beautiful feathers. Most survived the fire, but it stole their ability to fly, and they fell squawking to the ground, delayed thuds marking each impact.

Indira provided overwatch for all three battles. She initially aided Gunnar when he attacked the gargantuids, streaming an endless volley toward the grunting beasts, distracting them so he could get close enough for his sword. When the gargantuids turned and kept pace with Einar as he raced through their ranks, she embedded arrows into their opposite shoulder or hip, causing them to hesitate or turn in the wrong direction.

Within drus of Gunnar's initial attack, two other battles broke out on the Thrud Wastelands several linaks from Gul Krul's doorstep. Belkidar and Kiera vanished, then instantaneously reappeared over a hundred elads to the east. Moments later, numerous enemies materialized around their locations. To make matters worse, Brohdan was forced to single-handedly combat nearly forty griffins above the barren wastelands to the west.

The griffins fought beyond her range, but the Jrelz did not. While Gunnar slit the throats of the gargantuids that had fallen from Batai's sharp blade, Indira turned and released a short, dense barrage toward the sorcerers. Then she turned back, assisted Einar, her bow never silent.

Kiera battled four sorcerers, felt a wisp blow her hair a fraction of a dru before two of her foes fell to the ground. She smiled, turned to see bloodied arrow tips protruding from their heads. The remaining two Jrelz also turned, paused as they considered where the arrows had come from, felt cold steel before all went black.

Nine gargantuid carcasses lay scattered across the barren wastelands, an enormous pool of blood beneath each, overwhelming the dry, dense ground, reflecting the sporadic brilliance of a Broglia Black's fire. His acrobatic reactions to the griffins' lightning-quick maneuvers underscored the ease with which he flew, as though the twenty-eight elad creature obeyed a different, less restrictive set of physical laws. He flapped his huge wings once, twice, rolled onto his side, then tucked them against his body, dove a hundred elads before extending them to level off. He simultaneously burned a charging griffin, dodged another as it closed from beneath his right wing, and embedded his blade into the skull of a third that dove from above.

Nearly twenty griffins survived his initial attack, but only seven remained. They fought on, endured his fire, evaded his blade, gallantly mounted one final assault.

Brohdan watched as they surrounded him, flew in erratic patterns to avoid his flames. Then, as if reacting to some unseen cue, they turned toward him, charged, some diving from high above, others closing fast from below. They came from all directions, timing their attack perfectly. Brohdan initially used his fire to turn them back, but there were too many, coming far too fast. He braced himself.

The final three gargantuids grouped together, watching their enemies. They showed their huge, menacing teeth, opened and closed their powerful claws, growling and cursing, inviting them to attack.

Gunnar slowly circled around them, dividing their attention. Then Indira released four arrows toward the nearest. It was focused on Einar, wary of Batai's sword, kept the giant in his periphery, and was completely unprepared when her arrows pierced its flesh.

The first two lodged into the rear of its eyes, so it didn't see the next two penetrate his shaggy fur to breach a jugular. It howled in agony as it brought one hand to his useless eyes, the other to its seeping neck, attempting to determine what had caused the warm sensation now pulsing down the front of its massive chest.

Gunnar reacted in an instant, charged the wounded beast, driving his sword deep into its bloodied torso. The other two gargantuids turned to investigate, giving Einar the window he needed. He raced in front of them, brought Batai's sword in range. He swung it slowly as Einar sped past, cutting deep into their shins, the bones breaking outward beneath their massive weight. Kiera, still in the midst of battling the Jrelz, distinctly heard the deafening cracks as the gargantuids lost any hope of victory. One beast collapsed in a heap, falling onto its back and pinning its mangled legs beneath it. The second fell forward, extending its arms to break its fall.

Gunnar killed the first creature, so he was behind the other two when Batai lamed them. He saw the first collapse, then sprinted toward the second, leapt onto its back as it fell forward, drove his sword to its hilt through the back of the gargantuid's skull as he rode it to the ground. With the creature's head bowed from the force of the sword's impact, the elad of Gunnar's blade that had exited through its forehead was the first to hit the ground. Then he pulled its free, slowly, wiping it on its matted fur. He hopped from its back, then turned toward perhaps the world's final living gargantuid.

Einar approached it. The gargantuid's broken legs were pinned under its immense body, and it writhed in pain as it cursed its enemies. Batai remained beyond its grasping claws, stared into its hateful eyes, felt its evil permeate the area around it like a fog. Then he threw his sword.

The gargantuid watched helplessly as it streaked toward its head, knew full well it was breathing its final breath.

The sword glistened orange in the dawn as it soared end-over-end, slid silently into its head, stopping only when its broad handle thudded into its thick skull. The beast's writhing and cursing stopped immediately, replaced by violent seizures, then stillness. The last of Hildegard's gargantuids lay dead.

Although expert swordsmen, the surviving Jrelz could match neither Kiera's agility nor Belkidar's sorcery. Just as Indira released the four arrows that had blinded the first of the three gargantuids, Belkidar's fire shield killed its final victim. Then he turned to Kiera who was in the midst of battling the last two sorcerers several elads away.

The first attacked her, trying to make up for all of his lost comrades with one well-placed swing. Kiera ducked it, threw the dagger in her left hand, its impact jerking his head backward. His swords clanged loudly against the ground an instant before his limp body joined them.

The second sorcerer, realizing she now had one less dagger than before, attacked. She blocked his sword with her blade, leaned to her left as she kicked, drove her shin into his midsection, doubling him over. Then she brought her right hand down, easing her blade into the back of his head.

The remaining seven griffins attacked, all from different directions. Brohdan managed to kill two with his fire, but the rest sped toward him, each weighing more than a horse, their impacts simultaneous. One crashed the crown of its head directly into Brohdan's temple, another rose from beneath and collided into his jaw. Brohdan dodged the third, but it was still able to cling to his left wing before colliding with one of its mates. The final two attacked from his rear flanks, rammed into him just below his ribcage. 'Steelskin' protected his skin and scales, but the violence of the collisions dazed him as much as the griffins.

All six creatures fell from the sky, slowly drifted apart, each in various stages of consciousness. One of Brohdan's wings was extended, so he rotated slowly as he fell, corkscrewing toward the ground. The two griffins that had rammed into his head were knocked completely unconscious, accelerating as they fell head-first. The other three slowly flapped their wings as if by instinct, only faintly aware of the ground that rushed toward them.

Brohdan was in a haze. He fought to rid himself of the darkening swells that smothered him, struggled to keep his mind from drowning in them. He dimly recalled the crashing blows, but for some reason couldn't estimate how much time had lapsed since. Slowly, colors appeared again, first the browns of the terrain below, then the yellows and reds of the griffins around him. He gradually comprehended the images of a rotating horizon, became faintly aware of the cool breeze rushing past his sensitive nose. He felt the trailing edges of his wings flap loosely in the slipstream and his barz flutter at the end of his long tail.

His mind slowly roused, as if from a dream. Then the sunlight pierced his eyes, woke him with a jolt. He spread his wings, leveled off less than thirty elads from the ground, glided in a wide arc, watched the five noble creatures plummet to their deaths.

Gunnar walked alongside Einar as they waded through the gargantuid carcasses. "Good battle."

"I am not so sure," Indira replied.

"Oh?"

"It shall take me days to replace all of my arrows," she explained, nodding to several empty quivers.

Gunnar nodded to the sea of burnt Jrelz bodies. "I'm sure Belkidar can help with that," he explained, patting Einar's neck as he considered the impact of his sorcery.

Belkidar and Kiera appeared an instant later, her smile relieved, infectious. After a few drus, they watched Brohdan land a few elads away. Belkidar approached him. "How are you?"

"I'm fine."

Belkidar nodded uncertainly. "This was the most difficult battle yet, and you had the toughest task of all. Fighting three dozen griffins is hard enough, but knowing they would've been the first to join our Quest if not for Hildegard made it that much harder. Just realize that each of them fought his evil, even while they were fighting you. They kept their honor by giving him a much tougher battle than they could've possibly given us."

"I saw it in their eyes," Brohdan said softly.

"You cannot help but admire them," Indira whispered.

"It was strange to see them fight against us," Batai admitted.

Belkidar nodded, his eyes flashing. "That's a glimpse into Hildegard's reality, and it's exactly why we must finish this Quest!"

Chapter 21
Hildegard

My first wish is to see this plague of mankind, war,
banished from the earth.

George Washington

They ate a quick meal while Einar retrieved the horses. The Fifth
Defense took place only a few linaks from Hildegard's fortress, making
stealth no longer necessary. Kiera led them quickly, following the
well-traveled highway to Gul Krul and the Quest's final confrontation.
Likewise, Brohdan flew higher than he'd done in the past, wanting to
scout further ahead as they neared Hildegard's fortress.

"How did you do that?" Indira asked over her right shoulder after
discovering her packed quivers.

"Elegantly."

"You may prove quite handy," she decided, inspecting the arrows.

Belkidar smiled from atop his galloping horse, reflecting on how
far she'd come since they first met in Ætheldell.

"We're definitely within range of their scouts," Belkidar said after
nearly a link of swift riding. "I don't expect any surprises until we
reach his fortress, but let's keep our guard up." After another half link,
he called for a quick break.

Batai passed around rations from a saddlebag he'd taken from one
of the pack horses. "Think of how far we've come, the sacrifices we've
all made – just so we could have this opportunity."

Indira nodded as she sipped her water, silently considered each of
her friends before her gaze finally rested on Belkidar. "I must share

something." She paused, the sun's brilliance reflecting in her long black hair, penetrated the incredible depths of her emerald eyes.

"We do not know what fate awaits us in Hildegard's fortress, so I want to take this opportunity to thank you. You each have an eternal place in my heart, and I can no longer imagine a life without you. Regardless of our Quest's outcome, I will forever cherish the time I spent with you."

Her friends were speechless. Batai silently nodded his agreement, realizing he'd never forged friendships like these in all of his travels. True, they were courageous, noble – much like those he'd fought alongside in the past – but they were also genuine, caring almost to a fault. And most of all, they were loyal, utterly dependable in the most difficult circumstances. Like his family had been.

Kiera was also silent, but perhaps that had more to do with the tears welling in her eyes. She too treasured these friendships, especially since her travels typically required the antithesis of companionship. She knew her true life's value would be measured not with the trivial success she attained through her work, but in the bonds she left behind.

Belkidar simply placed his hand on the young elf's shoulder, his firm grip conveying far more than words. He'd met a wide variety of creatures in his long life, befriended thousands of them, and to his amazement, only one compared to these. With equal parts sorrow and contentment, he realized Aelya would've also deeply cherished these friends.

Gunnar was initially stunned, for despite his best efforts, he couldn't understand how her sentiment could so closely mirror his own. His old life seemed foreign to him now, his isolation barely remembered. He'd dreamt of having friends, but he'd never actually expected it. How could he? And these were far more than friends, more than anything he had a right to deserve. He raised his eyes, met hers and nodded.

The oath Brohdan had pledged to Juron initially surged to the forefront of his thoughts, but an overwhelming pride quickly wrung every other emotion from his mind. Perhaps more naïve than the others, Indira understood life's fundamental essence that Hildegard's evil could never truly eradicate. The friendships forged through their travels, through their hardships and sacrifices, would endure the ultimate test of time, and whether their Quest proved successful or not, their actions in defiance of tyranny would forever bind them together.

They resumed their journey, soon cresting a gentle slope in the road. Hildegard's fortress slowly revealed itself, its flawless black marble contrasting sharply with the dull, beige soil of the surrounding wastelands and the towering, snow-capped mountains encompassing Lake Mamate further to the southeast. A tall tower rose from each corner of the rectangular structure, and a fifth rose from its center, dwarfing the others. "That's where Hildegard lives," Belkidar explained, pointing his Staff toward the soaring spire.

"I've never seen anything like it," Gunnar admitted.

"That's because there *is* nothing else like it."

More of Gul Krul's details gradually revealed themselves as they rode closer. A wide moat surrounded the fortress, and long black banners snapped in the breeze atop each of its five spires.

"The moat's deep, at least two hundred elads to the black waters below. There are only two ways to cross it. This highway leads to a drawbridge, reinforced with steel to support the massive wagons and carts that supply the citadel."

"What's the second?" Gunnar asked.

"Flight, of course," he answered, glancing toward Brohdan.

"Well, the rest of us will need that drawbridge lowered," Batai said. "What kind of resistance can we expect?"

"The city's defense is the responsibility of the Jrelz Captains, and they employ thousands to support Hildegard's empire. Most work in and around Gul Krul, interacting with the local merchants and traders, manning the catapults and other defenses, supervising the local businesses, and providing general labor to support his stronghold. The men operating the drawbridge won't be a problem."

"You do not expect Hildegard to engage us outside his fortress?" Indira asked.

"No, but I can't be sure." He paused. "I used to know Krollum quite well, of course. He was an overly dramatic sort of fellow – always very accommodating whenever Aelya and I visited his tower before the War, almost to the point of making his guests feel uncomfortable. If Hildegard still possesses any shred of my friend, he'll allow us entry into his fortress before we commence with the unpleasantries. After all, whether I face him within the castle or without makes little difference. Likewise, the Jrelz Captains are just as powerful inside as they are outside, and Brohdan's battle with the titan obviously won't be affected either way. No, I think Krollum's affection for polite hospitality will override any objections that may exist in Hildegard." He paused. "But be ready just in case."

"Won't we have to contend with his armies?" Kiera asked.

"No, I think they'll stay where they are in case we're just a diversion."

"And I doubt they'd remain loyal to Hildegard after he's been defeated," Batai pointed out.

"I certainly hope not. Hildegard has forced their loyalty for thousands of cycles. A hundred generations have lived and died beneath his ruthlessness, but there's no way to predict their reaction to his death. They may disband and celebrate, or they may avenge him. Hopefully we'll find out."

"Swell," Kiera sighed as she examined one of her flawless blades.

The enormity of Gul Krul lurked only a few hundred elads before them. After mooncycles of travel, through relentless rain and merciless heat, endless links on horseback, countless cold meals followed by just as many cold nights, the Quest's Volunteers had finally arrived at Gul

Krul. They didn't hesitate, rode straight toward its drawbridge and to their destinies beyond.

Belkidar took the lead, followed closely by Gunnar, Indira, Kiera, and Batai. Brohdan abandoned any thought of stealth and flew ahead to inspect the closed drawbridge and its operating mechanisms. Nearly two hundred men, ironically all wearing black clothing identifying them as Hildegard's guards, scurried about in fear beneath his black silhouette.

He landed gracefully atop the drawbridge's black marble frame, his wing wrapped around the portcullis within, his wing hook scoring deep into the marble. Left alone by Hildegard's terrified subordinates – perhaps in part due to the flames that trickled from his raised lips – Brohdan extended his blade and easily sliced one of the two heavy chains holding it closed. It rocked slightly, groaning in protest, and when he cut the second chain, it slowly swung outward. It gained momentum as it fell, its crash thundering through the castle's foundation.

"Hildegard probably knows we're here," Kiera muttered to Batai.

Brohdan took flight and scouted beyond their view. Believing the dragon had left, Hildegard's guards slowly returned from where they hid. They examined the severed chains and fallen bridge, then formed a defensive barricade as their superiors screamed orders. Well over a hundred men blocked the drawbridge, each armed with either a broadsword or halberd. Their short, squatty sergeant confidently stood at the center of the drawbridge, behind his troops. "What brings you to my master's home?"

"That's none of your concern," Belkidar answered. "Step aside."

"I think you'd better look at our numbers, friend," he suggested, taking a hard look at Gunnar. "He may do your will, but he can't possibly account for my legion."

Belkidar shot Gunnar a look. It was difficult to misinterpret. Gunnar released the long handle of his sword, reluctantly let it slide back into its scabbard. Then Belkidar returned his attention to the arrogant sergeant. "Very well."

His cocky grin widened before he saw what appeared to be a small ripple in the ground just ahead of the frail old man. Then, in an instant the ripple grew into a two-elad wave that raced toward him with unnatural speed. Its approach sapped the balance from his army, forced even the nimblest to the ground, then carried the entire throng to the brink of the moat. He watched as it swept every last man over the edge, their screams echoing up the sheer walls as they fell. Their impacts spared them the fate of drowning.

Gunnar smiled, nodded a thanks to Belkidar, pulled his sword free as he strode forward. He stopped in front of the sergeant and, holding the sword with his right hand, wrapped the other around his plump body. Then he effortlessly lifted him, brought the man's eyes level with his own. "I do my own will."

Judging by his reddening face, Gunnar perhaps clutched him tighter than was necessary. "You deserve the same fate as those you were meant to lead." He swung the now hysterical man over the side of the drawbridge, slowly, then held him suspended, his feet dangling over the abyss. He paused, gave him a long moment to consider his fate, then opened his huge hand. The sergeant fell, screamed for his life, disappeared into the darkness below.

"I think he wet himself," Gunnar said with a scowl, wiping his palm against his clothing.

"We're entering Gul Krul."

Brohdan re-materialized in an instant, roared in his eagerness, once again landed atop the portcullis frame that had a moment ago anchored the massive drawbridge chains. His tail swayed from side to side as they passed beneath him.

"Welcome to my home," a loud, distinct voice boomed, seemingly originating from every corner of the fortress. "Please greet me at the far end of the courtyard."

"It appears a part of Krollum indeed survives," Indira observed.

"Maybe," Belkidar said warily. "Let's not keep our host waiting." He nudged his horse into a trot. "Brohdan, please remain out of sight. I have no doubt Hildegard knows you're here, but I'd rather he not know your exact whereabouts."

He nodded, watched them disappear into the cloisters of the courtyard beyond. His eyes lingered there as he considered them, his pack, and he renewed his vow to do everything in his power to protect them in this final battle. Then he turned, a growl vibrating from deep within his chest, blue flames rising from his jaws, then leapt from the portcullis, disappearing beyond the citadel walls.

Belkidar headed directly across the long axis of the magnificent oval courtyard. It was completely open to the clear sky and was obviously tended to on a daily basis. Perfectly manicured grass stretched to the black marble walls encircling them, its lush green a stark contrast to the veined black that surrounded it. Multiple marble walkways were laid throughout, intersecting one another, linking the many doorways connecting the various sections of Gul Krul to this communal court. The four lesser towers loomed from the distant corners of the large fortress, connected by towering walls of black marble.

The main tower, attempting to touch the sky from the citadel's center, rose from the far end of the courtyard. Its base was massive, housing both Hildegard and his servants. Approximately nine elads above its massive foundation, a five-elad overhang extended outward, then gradually narrowed as it rose to the heavens. Nearly twenty elads from its pointed summit, it once again jutted out, and Belkidar knew this bulb was actually a vault, safeguarding the tremendous wealth of knowledge Hildegard had amassed during the eight thousand cycles of his life.

Belkidar continued across the courtyard, his eyes noting every detail. He rode slowly, leading the others along the black footpath, the horses' hooves inordinately loud in the otherwise silent courtyard. He stopped a few dozen elads short of the tower's entrance.

"Welcome, my friend," Hildegard said to his ancient acquaintance. He sat on a large, extravagant chair within the cool shade of the overhanging ceiling that encircled the base of his tower. He faced the entrance to his fortress, allowing him to observe every elye of their arrival.

His magnificent robes were made of an unnaturally pure black silk, and intricate gold and silver patterns glistened across its sleeves, neck, and hem. Although Kiera knew them to be peers, the brawny Hildegard had bottomless black eyes, his countenance a polar opposite to Belkidar's geniality. Their only notable similarity was the equally white hair that emerged from their wide-brimmed hats.

"You are not my friend, Hildegard," Belkidar replied, dismounting.

"Surely you recognize some remnants of Krollum. Does that not make us friends?" He rose from his throne, slowly made his way into the sunlight.

Belkidar smiled, but his expression was sad, remorseful. "It's true, I do see Krollum in you. But you are not him."

Hildegard said nothing, but his sneer widened, showing more of his teeth. It seemed forced, like a lion trying to smile.

"You know why we're here," Belkidar continued.

"Of course I do. You're going to kill me."

"Not unless I have to. I'd rather you abandon this nonsense. Restore this world to its natural evolution."

"I *am* its natural evolution! If you can't accept that, you must become part of its history."

"I already am."

Hildegard chuckled at the truth of it. "So you are. So are we both."

"At least forfeit the Headpiece. You must know *that's* the source of all this! Krollum may yet live!"

"Krollum was weak!" he spat. "It was the Headpiece that enlightened the fool! I'll never surrender that which created me."

"Do we have no other recourse?" Belkidar asked, his arms spread wide, his voice sincere, his eyes searching.

"No." Then he motioned toward the far end of the courtyard. Twelve men entered, each from a different doorway. They wore identical robes, each black with red trim, signifying their superiority in the Order of Jrelz.

"Very well."

Hildegard raised the Headpiece in his right hand, the Jewel in his left. Kiera, Gunnar, Indira, and Batai made their way to where the Jrelz Captains had congregated toward the western end of the courtyard. Belkidar stood rooted to the ground, his eyes fixed on Hildegard.

A tangible anticipation filled the air, a flammable vapor awaiting the faintest spark. Hildegard smirked, pleased. "Belkidar, I never took you for a fool, but you must've known I've been aware of your progress. Your innovative if desperate strategy initially caught me by surprise, for I must admit the idea of such a modest attempt never occurred to me. Indeed, your trek through my Five Defenses impressed even me. But your success ends here." Hildegard's eyes studied him, searched for clues. He found none.

"I know of the Broglia. He'll suffer the same fate as the rest of you."

As he finished, a colossal human figure emerged from where he'd been concealed beyond the tall eastern walls of the citadel. The towering creature turned slowly, then approached Gul Krul's outer walls, shaking its very foundation with his every step. With the majestic mountains surrounding Lake Mamate as a backdrop, the titan stopped fifty elads from the fortress walls, awaiting orders from his master.

He was even larger than Belkidar remembered. He was truly enormous, standing at least thirty-five elads, literally head and shoulders above the castle's eastern walls. He wore a metal helmet, each side of which bore a metallic representation of a lightning bolt slanted backward toward the skies. He was magnificent, clothed in a simple beige and gold tunic that left his muscular arms bare. In his left hand he carried perhaps the world's largest shield. Adorned with silver trim, its polished bronze was fashioned in a slender crest that extended from his shoulders to his knees. His eyes glowed white, never blinking, his expression neither compassionate nor hostile.

"My doomed friends, you must now realize, I see all. I've always been one step ahead of you, Belkidar. You simply lack the intelligence necessary to – "

Brohdan exploded from behind the central tower, his enormous wings pounding, adding to his incredible speed. He was a black streak racing above the black walls, nearly too fast for their eyes to follow, heading straight for the titan.

"Kill the dragon!" Hildegard shrieked, providing his requisite order.

Now having a purpose to his existence, the titan turned to face the charging dragon. But Brohdan was moving far too fast, was already upon him, giving him no time to raise his shield. He flapped his wings once, twice, aligned his body vertically, struck simultaneously with his claws and wing hooks. Both razor-sharp talons pierced deep into his flesh. A titan's mass was at least three times a Broglia's, but Brohdan's incredible speed at the moment of impact resulted in a massive collision that was more felt than heard, sending clouds of dust from Gul Krul's ancient marble ceilings.

The titan repositioned his right leg behind him to absorb Brohdan's momentum, but the collision lifted him from his feet. He flew backward, lowered his right arm to break his fall, Brohdan's talons still embedded deep into the muscles of his chest and midsection. Brohdan clung there, rode him to the ground, roared with surprising rage. The titan landed on his back, skidded elads, sent another shockwave through Gul Krul and his shield skidding behind his head.

The Jrelz Captains spread out, leisurely formed a rough line to face their enemies. "I am Grealm, leader of the Order of Jrelz. Regrettably, my master prevents me from facing a worthy opponent. Killing Belkidar would've validated my training, confirmed my talents. Alas, I'm relegated to executing his underlings, a task hardly worth my time." He sighed, flicked his wrist toward a subordinate.

The sorcerer next to Grealm smiled, raised his staff high, mumbled an incantation of war. An ember formed an elad from his face, swelled in size, grew into a miniature sun, its brilliance too intense to behold. It streaked forward, unabated, unresisted, straight toward his enemies.

Where it winked out like a candle.

The twelve sorcerers blinked, their mouths agape, their eyes disbelieving. Then they raised their staffs as one, each conjured balls of fire, arcs of white phosphorus, bolts of blinding silver, beams of piercing violet. Death raced forward, covered the nearly thirty elads separating them in a flash, only Indira's impossibly quick reflexes enabling her to flinch.

Each cant wilted, vanishing before their eyes.

Gunnar wasted little time wondering how he'd survived. He charged Grealm, his five-elad blade helping traverse the distance seemingly as quickly as their sorcery had only a moment earlier. It whirred through the air, silently passed through Grealm's neck. His body slumped, his knees crashed to the ground, dislodging his head and sending it rolling in a circle. A black, ethereal mist oozed from his corpse, faded into nothingness as his blood stained the green grass.

Hildegard attacked, his face twisting in rage. Twin beams flowed from his Artifacts, buzzed like a thousand bees, both black as oil, arching toward Belkidar. Just as they bore down on him, the streams bent slightly, sped harmlessly around, continued behind him until impacting the interior wall of his courtyard. The marble evaporated, fumes rising slowly as the marble melted and fell in clumps to the walkway below.

"I see you've improved," Hildegard complimented.

"Actually, I *have* studied since we last met, but until now I've had surprisingly little need for war cants."

"I can't say I know what you mean." He attacked again, this time unleashing a stream as wide as his head, a bottomless shadow, its depths incalculable, draining the life from everything around it. It pained the eyes to behold, even heat and light failed to escape its touch.

Belkidar tilted his Staff forward, sent a brilliant white-blue star into the shadow, simultaneously attacked independent of his Artifact. He manipulated the planet's gravity, sent Hildegard racing upward, flying headlong toward the underside of his tower's overhang.

Hildegard's eyes grew wide an instant before his motion slowed. He hung there, his disbelief lingering, before smoothly landing where he'd once stood. "Impressive. Perhaps you'll prove more challenging than Aelya. I always held her in such high regard," he sighed almost to himself. "But when her childish meddling finally forced my hand, all she could do was utter your despicable name."

He motioned toward an antechamber at the base of his tower, and to Belkidar's total astonishment, Aelya emerged from the darkness within.

By the time the titan skidded to a stop, Brohdan's three-elad blade had pierced his right thigh once and his lower abdomen twice, each attack so savage his barz disappeared into the wound with each thrust. But the titan recovered quickly, grabbed Brohdan below his shoulders, pinning his wings awkwardly against his body, his hands crushing him like a vice. The titan tossed him aside as though he were a child's toy, sending the twenty-eight elad Broglia Black soaring end over end.

He tumbled nearly eighty elads before he could react, then righted himself, spread his wings, smoothly transitioned into flight. He circled high above, watched his enormous foe regain his feet, inspect his wounds, then emotionlessly retrieve his shield.

Not knowing if it would protect him, Brohdan cast 'steelskin.' It was obvious he couldn't match the titan's strength, knew he must avoid getting close. Then Brohdan saw him extend his right arm, raise it straight toward him.

The titan drew the static electricity from the surrounding air, the blinding light escaping his closed fist an instant before he opened it, his palm facing outward. A deafening thunderclap rattled Gul Krul, shook the towers, echoed off marble walls as the bolt streaked toward Brohdan, far too fast for even a Broglia to follow.

Brohdan instantly tucked his wings, dove toward the ground, his abrupt reaction causing the bolt to pass an elye above his left wing. The titan's second bolt followed almost immediately after the first, struck Brohdan on his left hip, the force throwing him badly out of his flight path. He again reacted in an instant, instinctively adjusted his wings and swung his tail to regain his balance. But the titan was faster.

With another deafening clap, the third lightning bolt struck Brohdan's chest, the next two on the undersides of his left wing and throat as he desperately tried to maintain flight. Still seventy elads above the ground, he instinctively flapped his wings, his flight erratic, struggling to maintain consciousness.

The titan's next attack struck him just behind his left temple, the blow jolting his head and long neck backward. With the thunderclap still resonating through Gul Krul, Brohdan spiraled helplessly to the ground, a nauseating thud accompanying his impact several hundred elads to the southeast.

Limping, the wounded titan slowly walked to where Brohdan's body lay unmoving.

Indira followed Gunnar's lead, released eleven arrows by the time Grealm's blood tainted his sword. The quickest of the surviving Captains reacted just in time, stammered a ward of flames. A blinding orange-red dot appeared above him, fell rumbling around them as Indira's arrows raced through the air, its heat reducing her final four to ash long before it encountered his fire. But he wasn't fast enough, the first seven passing through the foreheads of his companions, each resulting in the discharge of another dark, ghostly miasma. Gunnar, having just completed the follow-through that had beheaded Grealm, dove to safety.

The four surviving sorcerers huddled within their protective shell, their voices harsh, their words rushed as they tried to determine the source of their impotence. But their enemies were just as confused, unsure as to what had initially saved them, and what actions might jeopardize that safety. And so the two quartets paused, stared at one another through the undulating flames, each waiting for the slightest opening to end the stalemate.

"Aelya!" Belkidar called as his wife emerged from the antechamber.

Hildegard laughed. "Maybe you're a fool after all, Belkidar. I killed Aelya long ago, before her silly inspections could threaten my plans. She was always so *thorough*." He smirked, extended a familiar, welcoming arm toward her, his satisfied smile like a gaping reptile. She went to him, bowed her head in acquiescence, then moved away to face Belkidar.

"You left me no choice. I abducted her during her last visit, an act rendered trivial by the Headpiece. Honestly, Belkidar, why would you send her here so defenseless? Without an Artifact, she had no chance!"

He laughed again, but Belkidar didn't hear. He reeled back, unable to process his allegations. "Aelya?" he asked weakly, staring at the woman who now stood several elads to Hildegard's left.

"Aelya is dead!" Hildegard spat, then turned to her, his smile returning. "I'd like you to meet Phaylyn. Like Krollum, Aelya was sacrificed so that Phaylyn may live."

"No, no, no, *no*. It can't be. I searched for you!"

"Yes, and if you weren't so pathetic, I might've found it amusing." He shook his head sadly. "I hid her, far beyond your reach."

Belkidar was slowly recovering from his shock. "That's impossible. It's been three thousand cycles! You couldn't have hidden her that long."

"No, of course not, but I didn't have to. I needed only hide her long enough for the combined wisdom of the Headpiece and I to birth Phaylyn. After that, there was no Aelya for you to find."

"Of course," Belkidar said, his face stricken, his eyes tired.

"And now you begin to see, Belkidar. Finally! Between Phaylyn and I, armed with the Headpiece and Jewel, you cannot win. But there is an alternative to death, my old friend."

Belkidar said nothing, just blinked at the sound of thunder.

"Link with the Headpiece. I beg you. Within a few days, you'll begin to see things more clearly. There's no need for you to die! All I ask is that you surrender the Staff. Do that, and I'll spare you!"

Belkidar shook his head, slowly, his steel-blue eyes meeting Hildegard's black ones. "You know I'll never surrender to its evil, Hildegard. Had Krollum known better, do you honestly think he would've chosen this fate? Or Aelya? If she hadn't been held against her will, she would've never submitted to this, to its corruption."

For the first time, Phaylyn spoke. "Its soul is not corrupt, Belkidar, it just sees with remarkable clairvoyance. Link with it, and join with me as you once did."

Belkidar hadn't heard her voice in over three thousand cycles, but hearing her now sent a chill down his spine. Her voice resembled his wife's, but it had an element that sounded detached. Cold. Heartless.

"I've never joined with you, only with my wife." Belkidar raised his Staff. "Let's end this."

Brohdan had instinctively kept his wings partially extended, spiraling away from the titan and slowing his fall. But just as 'steelskin' was powerless to protect him from the griffins' ramming blows, it couldn't protect him from the titan's lightning strikes. Nor the ground's impact.

He lay motionless on the rocky terrain. All was black. He couldn't tell if his eyes were open or closed, whether he was alive or dead. Then he heard something. He could almost recognize it, but it came from far away. But as he strained, it drew closer. Low, savage. Harsh, vicious. Familiar. It was him. He was growling his defiance, deep and guttural, willing himself back to consciousness. He rose unsteadily, supported by his wing hooks, immediately fell onto his side.

But images slowly started to replace the black. The blurry brown landscape. The hazy snow-topped mountains. The marble spires with their snapping banners. The bright sun, eclipsed by a towering titan.

Indira sent several arrows to probe for vulnerabilities in their fire ward. With the ineffectiveness of their initial attacks still fresh in their minds, the sorcerers flinched as each arrow sped toward their faces, their confidence swelling with the incineration of each.

Belkidar released two streams of sorcery, one each toward Hildegard and Phaylyn, both of whom responded immediately. Hildegard's blood-red met Belkidar's white-blue, an intense orange aura blossoming from their union. Phaylyn's stream was a vibrant purple, creating a brilliant magenta when it met Belkidar's. But he battled Hildegard with only one Artifact while is enemy enjoyed the benefit of two. More critically, he was forced to divide his power between two opponents while they could both focus the sum of theirs against him. As a result, the orange convergence slowly, inexorably, drifted toward Belkidar. The pulsing magenta remained nearly stationary, but it too crept slowly toward him.

Hildegard's concentration was written in his expression, but with Phaylyn's assistance, he recognized the inevitability of the battle. "You had your chance, my naïve friend."

Belkidar said nothing, watched as the orange union of their sorcery slid ever closer, knew Hildegard was right. He poured every ounce of his power against them, but he wasn't strong enough to defeat them both. He looked at Phaylyn, saw the Headpiece's evil in what had once been his wife. Her expression remained emotionless, but he could plainly see the malevolence in her eyes.

Construing Hildegard's nature was a much simpler matter. He sneered as he forced his sorcery nearer, his black eyes flashing, and Belkidar immediately understood how this battle would end.

Then he thought of his companions. Despite the power he summoned to fight the combined strength of these two sorcerers, he knew he was utterly powerless to overcome the guilt, the sorrow, he experienced at the thought of failing them. His friends. No, his family. They depended on him to defeat Hildegard, and they battled even now to ensure he had that very opportunity. They sacrificed so much in their pasts, and he'd led them to believe this Quest was worthy of those sacrifices. And for what? To let them down when his support was needed the most? To fail them this close to the end? But he *had* failed them, there was nothing he could do to alter that truth.

Death was only two elads away now, and Belkidar knew his end had come. He looked away from Hildegard, from his taunting smile, turned to Aelya. He knew she was dead, but he wanted her image to be the last thing he saw before passing beyond this life. He looked into her eyes as Hildegard's sorcery moved closer still, and he smiled knowing he would die viewing at least a small glimpse of the happiness this life had afforded him.

To his utter amazement, *Aelya* smiled back. Before he could react, she turned, and in a flash shifted her sorcery steam from Belkidar to Hildegard, both of whom were caught completely unprepared. Hildegard was focusing his undivided attention toward his enemy, but empowered by his two Artifacts, was somewhat protected from her unfocused sorcery. Nevertheless, he was jolted backwards under the might of Aelya's attack, momentarily diverted from Belkidar as he took several steps to regain his balance. But he was quick to recover, mainly due to the brevity of the encounter.

Also caught off guard, Belkidar's reaction was instantaneous, immediately ceasing the sorcery stream he'd used to attack Phaylyn. But it was too late; Aelya's actions had been too sudden, too final. No longer having Phaylyn's sorcery to resist it, Belkidar's white-blue stream bolted toward Aelya just as her stream struck Hildegard. But she lacked the protection of his two Artifacts. Belkidar's sorcery lifted her from her feet, threw her backward. Her body crashed against the black marble of Hildegard's courtyard wall, fell in a heap to the cold walkway below.

Their attacks never faltered, but Aelya's actions stunned both sorcerers. Hildegard couldn't believe Aelya still possessed the strength to resist the Headpiece, a strength he could never fathom, especially after three thousand cycles! Belkidar, still staring at his wife's motionless body, understood with haunting clarity that he was the one who had killed her. The fact that she voluntarily sacrificed herself so her husband could finally defeat her abductor did little to suppress the fury that erupted in him.

An overpowering rage consumed him. Where there once stood a seemingly tired, besieged old man, the form of an exceptionally powerful being stood staring at his wife. Although Belkidar physically remained unchanged, he towered over Hildegard, over the courtyard, over Gul Krul. He replayed his wife's sacrifice in his mind, became even more enraged. His Linsilor Sorcerenic manipulated reality to a level never before realized and, with the Staff's assistance, sought to end his evil once and for all.

A dark grey shaft replaced his previous white-blue stream. Hildegard fought back, channeled his sorcery through the Headpiece and Jewel. Laboring, he managed to scatter Belkidar's deadly beam moments before it reached the Jewel. Hildegard held the Artifacts before him, beads of sweat forming on his furrowed brow, desperate in his assault. Slowly, he pushed Belkidar's sorcery back, first an elye, then two.

Then, in an instant, Belkidar transformed his cant from a dull grey shadow to an immensely brilliant light. Exceedingly narrow, its faint blue hue instantly illuminated every corner of Gul Krul.

Hildegard reacted to Belkidar's new strategy, countered with an equally intense black beam, used first the Headpiece to focus his power, then used the Jewel to intensify it further.

The union of their conflicting sorcery generated an incredibly deep, reverberating hum, its decreasing pitch and rising volume reaching unnatural levels. The sound became unbearable, diving to frequencies that were better felt than heard. Its tone continued to plummet, draining all sound for linaks in every direction. As the titan limped slowly toward the fallen dragon, each of his colossal steps continued shaking the ground, but made not the slightest sound. The fire ward that had burned with a deafening rumble suddenly fell silent as it blazed. The apprehensive, staccato sentences of the Jrelz Captains within it were tapped from their throats, their silent syllables mouthed but unheard.

Then, drus after the hum siphoned all sound from the region, an incredibly massive blast shook Gul Krul. The utter silence had lasted only a moment, the contrast of the ensuing explosion like looking at the sun after a long sleep. Two of Hildegard's corner towers buckled, collapsed upon themselves, crumbled to the ground. It disintegrated the various statues that once lined the outer walls of the courtyard, felled airborne birds, their lifeless bodies thudding to the ground. It extinguished the fire shield that encompassed the surviving Jrelz

Captains, knocked them from their feet, tossing them several elads before they skidded to a stop. Kiera, Indira, and Gunnar were also thrown backwards, but Einar and Batai, partially shielded by Gunnar's huge form, were spared much of the blast's force.

Despite the enormity of the detonation, both Belkidar and Hildegard used their Linsilors to stabilize themselves and preserve their balance. Belkidar stepped forward, leaned into his Staff, pushed back Hildegard's sorcery, the violet-blue aura separating his brilliant white and Hildegard's cold black sliding slowly toward his one-time friend.

Sweat flowed freely from Hildegard's temples, streamed down his back and into the silk of his robes. His anger grew alongside his desperation, his sole purpose to push the deadly fusion back toward his enemy. His face wildly distorted, he summoned the sum of his eight thousand-cycle life – all of the wisdom gained from his endless studies, the cruelty instilled by the Headpiece, his devotion to that corrupted soul, the ruthlessness that grew with each murder, the regret that he could never seem to abolish. He used all of himself, halted Belkidar's sorcery two elads from where he held the Jewel.

Belkidar opened his eyes, regarded his enemy. Hildegard met his stare, held it. Belkidar searched his eyes for even the slightest residue of his old friend. He found none, sensed only selfishness, malevolence, an insatiable thirst for power. He renewed his attack, forced the violet convergence forward.

Taking one last moment to clear his head, Brohdan took a deep breath, spread his wings and took flight, accelerating as he hugged the ground, increasing his distance from the titan.

Still a quarter linak away, the titan stopped and watched him depart. He raised his hand again, then dropped it, knew the dragon was flying too low, too erratically. He waited.

Brohdan flew faster and faster, his wings beating frantically, still only a dozen elads above the ground. He knew he'd be exposed to the titan's lightning as soon as he climbed higher, so he flew as fast as he could, summoning every bit of the strength he'd developed as a result of Krepli's seemingly endless training sessions, all the while circling south of Gul Krul. Now links away, he arched his back and climbed high, traded much of his incredible speed for altitude, his wings never slowing, bolted higher and higher, sheltered behind Hildegard's central tower.

The titan had lost sight of Brohdan drus earlier, his altitude too low, his distance too great. He searched for him, eventually saw a black silhouette rocket into the sky from behind his master's tower. Then nothing.

Brohdan abandoned 'steelskin,' saw first-hand how little it protected him from the titan's attacks. Instead, he cast 'cloak,' hoping it would offer a greater advantage, knowing the clear blue sky would improve its effectiveness. He stayed high, closed the distance by flying unpredictably, angling east of where he stood, then west, but always north toward the titan, his course never the same for long.

The titan's white eyes flared, saw more than most, gathered electricity from the air.

Brohdan saw the lightning flashes long before he heard the thunder, but he flew too high, his movements too random. The bolts streaked by, never closer than a few elads.

When Brohdan neared the titan's location, he leaned forward, violently flapped his huge wings, descended rapidly. Then he partially tucked them against his body, minimizing the area exposed to both the onrushing wind and the streaking lightning. Brohdan plummeted, a blurred meteorite flashing toward the titan, gaining speed as he descended.

The titan realized the dragon's intent, raised the shield in his left hand as he drew in more static electricity with his right. The bolt shot from his hand, another thunderclap rocked the citadel, drew in more electricity.

Because his speed helped close the distance even faster, Brohdan knew he'd have very little time to react to the titan's bolts. So he didn't wait, adjusted his partially tucked wings, veered instantaneously up, down, left, right. The titan sent a chain of thunderous claps through the region, the bolts streaked by, one after the other, some passing less than an elye from his body. Still Brohdan descended, knowing he flew far too fast for his breath to push his fire into the onrushing wind.

The titan remembered their first encounter, the blood still oozing from his injuries. As Brohdan drew near, he raised his shield, braced it with both hands, readied himself for the impact.

Brohdan kept his tail within his slipstream, extended the three-elad blade from his barz. The titan hid most of his body behind his enormous shield, but that didn't matter. At the last moment, he extended his wings, somehow held them against the rushing wind, the muscles across his deep chest and back straining beneath his thick scales, and pulled himself out of the steep dive. Then he flapped once, twice, climbed over the titan's head while letting his tail continue downward. The whipping motion snapped his barz forward just as his blade reached the bottom of its swing, embedding itself in the lower right edge of the titan's shield.

But Brohdan continued flapping his wings, continued climbing away, pulling his tail taut, dragging his blade up through the colossal shield, filling the courtyard with an earsplitting screech. Then it was pulled free.

The titan maintained his feet, his shield nearly in ruins, blood pooling beneath him. He angled his shield forward, saw the blood where he'd used his arm to brace himself against the dragon's attack, saw his right hand, wrist, and half of his forearm fall the last five elads to the ground.

Both quartets still lay on the floor, drus after the massive shock wave drove them to the ground. Kiera, Gunnar and Indira looked to be unconscious, yet the Jrelz Captains were already stirring. But thanks to Gunnar shielding them, Einar and Batai were the first to react. Still recovering, Batai instinctively grabbed Einar's saddle horn an instant before the huge charger got to his feet. Batai slid his left foot into its stirrup, was easily hoisted into his saddle, Einar already in mid-gallop by the time he settled his right foot. By his fifth stride, he was moving faster than any horse; by his sixth, any charger. Batai felt Einar's muscles bunch then release, bunch then release, felt the same urgency, realized the vulnerability of his friends, knew he must get to the sorcerers at any cost.

As they approached, one Jrelz Captain staggered to his feet. He stumbled as he turned, nearly fell, then raised his eyes to see an enormous horse veer slightly toward him, already in a full gallop, an armored knight pulling free his sword. He instinctively touched the tip of his staff to the ground, muttered a few words. A bright orange-red pinpoint of light flashed before him along the ground, several elads ahead of where Einar sprinted.

Einar leapt at the same time Batai crouched in his stirrups, exploded from the ground, soared high into the air. And not a moment too soon. The light shimmered with heat, scorched the grass in an instant, grew outward along the ground, swelled into a blanket of molten fire, melting the marble walkways.

The sorcerer stood several elads away, watched as a second Jrelz unsteadily rose to his feet. He turned back to them, mocking his sympathy.

The heat was unbearable, even from high above. Batai felt it through his greaves. Einar's hair along his legs and stomach wilted, his skin turned red, then blistered. Then he reached the height of his leap, started to descend, the flame's rumbling loud in their ears. Batai knew it would be close, knew their landing would be within elyes of the boiling fire. Then he looked up to see the Jrelz drag his staff's tip along the ground, the blanket of fire mimicking the motion, extending the area of death below.

Then he sensed something in Einar. Irritation. Frustration. Disappointment in failing him. Batai smiled sadly, ran his mailed glove along his neck, conveyed his deep pride, his eternal friendship. Then he threw his sword, followed it with a leap from his saddle.

His weapon spun as if in slow motion, end over end, almost as slowly as Einar descended toward the fire. It struck true, nearly cut the Jrelz in half as Einar landed an elad short, the bottom half of his leg incinerated, his bones protruding black from his knee. He stumbled, fell with a sickening thud, his momentum carrying him clear of the fire.

Batai soared beyond him, crashed shield-first into the second Jrelz, narrowly prevented another cant of war. His shield crushed his sternum, sent him flying backwards, his blood spraying with every labored breath. Batai landed next to him, staggered quickly his feet. Only to face the third Jrelz, smiling from six elads away.

Fire instantly enveloped Batai, charred the surface of his once-immaculate armor, made its edges glow red. His beard flashed, was gone in an instant, turning the skin of his face and neck an angry red, blisters turning black. He took one labored step backward, half turned, only to see the fourth Jrelz Captain behind him, his staff already raised high.

Then Batai smiled, watched Einar charge the sorcerer from behind, limping awkwardly, courageously, his belly black, his stub oozing blood. His massive, broken body crashed into the fourth sorcerer, fell on top of him, smeared his body as he slid to an elye from where Batai stood. Einar lay there, motionless, blood pouring from his ears, his eyes vacant, the leather straps ahead of his stirrup chewed through.

The third sorcerer laughed from behind Batai, four elads away, but it might as well have been a linak. "Imagine that," he mocked, "a knight without his sword." He leaned forward, spoke softly. "After I kill you, I'll take my time burning the others." He laughed again as he raised his staff, beginning the cant that would kill him.

Then, in one smooth stroke, his body charred, his muscles spasming, his body broken, Batai pulled Gunnar's old sword free from its scabbard along Einar's flank, whirled it around, its tip slicing through the sorcerer's neck, grating against bone.

Batai's body continued whirling around as his knees collapsed. He sprawled face-first onto the ground, Gunnar's massive sword skidding from his right hand, his left coming to rest against Einar's neck.

Brohdan knew the titan was still dangerous, knew he must at all costs remain beyond his reach. But without his lightning, he didn't have to fly nearly as fast, could therefore alter his strategy. Now a few hundred elads away, he raised his head and arched his back, climbed high into the air. He coasted up, his wings tucked close, a black silhouette against the blue sky, let his momentum fade, then swept his right wing forward and his left wing backward, leaned to his right. He pivoted in midair, soon looked straight down toward the ground, then flapped his wings, accelerated rapidly as he fell back toward his wounded foe.

The titan raised his damaged shield, his blood pooling at his feet, waiting.

Brohdan opened his mouth, once more tasted his pungent fuel, unconsciously fired his igniters. His huge lungs forced the fuel from of his mouth, the fire not entirely ignited until it was several elads away, the liquid clear and thick before turning blue, then orange, then gold. He continued the onslaught as he flapped his wings, passed over the titan, his neck arched low, his liquid flames engulfing him, burning long after he climbed toward the sky. Thick black smoke rose into the air, confirming a Broglia Black fought near Gul Krul.

The titan stood in an inferno, the pain overwhelming, incapacitating. He numbly dropped his melting shield, fell to his knees, his face still expressionless, his eyes glowing bright from the within the flames. He muttered not a word, not a groan or cry, but couldn't help writhe beneath the agony.

Brohdan quickly dove toward him, extended his blade, removed his head as he sped past. Then he turned, watched as the corpse of his greatest adversary slumped forward and disappeared into the flames.

Belkidar took a deep breath, abandoned the idea that he could save Krollum, tore his thoughts from Aelya and her sacrifice. He pushed his brilliant white-blue forward, forced Hildegard's black stream backward, the violet-blue aura moving ever closer to the Jewel, the second Artifact he used to channel his sorcery.

Hildegard's panic grew alongside the approaching nexus, its crackling growing ever louder in his ears. He took an involuntary step backward, then two, his eyes wide, his forehead drenched, his sneer gone. His concentration crumbled beneath his fear, helplessly watched as Belkidar's sorcery moved even closer. Two elads, then one. An elye. Less.

Then, for the first time in nearly seven thousand cycles, Belkidar's will touched the Jewel, merged with its soul.

It shone with the brilliance of a star, its previous dull black forgotten. Its soul came alive, embraced Belkidar's will, honed it, focused it like a magnifying crystal. Now employing two Artifacts, Belkidar's power surged forward, assaulted the Headpiece in a flash.

Its corrupted soul balked at Belkidar's sorcery, fought against his will. Nevertheless, he controlled it, prevented Hildegard from using it, rendering it useless to both owner and master.

Belkidar's gaze penetrated his enemy's eyes at the exact moment his peaceful white-blue stream struck the center of his forehead. It bored through his skin, skull, and brain, at last caressed his Linsilor Sorcerenic. At that instant, Hildegard ceased to exist. His power was broken, released enough energy to instantly disintegrate everything within a linak of his Linsilor. The explosion was magnificent, brilliant, deafening, its shockwave racing outward, toppling trees linaks beyond the blast.

Belkidar stood motionless, his feet less than an elye from the precipice, the eastern half of Gul Krul a smoking crater. His ward glowed white-blue, cast an elye before him and running a linop in every direction, it safeguarded the western half of Gul Krul even as the explosion annihilated everything within a half-linak radius to the east.

Behind him, Belkidar's companions were still staggering to their feet, dimly watched the final moments of his victory, their disbelief written across their faces. Brohdan heard the explosion but had no idea what had caused it. He took to the air, immediately saw the crater, appearing as though an enormous being had taken a spade and torn away the eastern half of the citadel, leaving the western half completely intact. He flew faster, his fear mounting, was relieved beyond words when he saw Belkidar standing at the crater's edge.

Resting against the Staff, the world's oldest creature stood at the very edge of the black marble that had previously served as the western foundation of Hildegard's main tower. He looked up beyond the enormous crater, toward the majestic mountains that formed Lake Mamate's western borders, took a moment for himself. Brohdan watched as he eventually turned and, with difficulty, made his way to the southern end of the courtyard.

Brohdan shifted his gaze, found the others. But something was wrong. He flew faster, dove toward them, Kiera noticing his alarm. She turned to where he stared, saw charred metal, broken bodies. "NOOOOOO!"

She raced to him, the others following, Brohdan landing not far away. Gunnar knelt next to them, tears matting his beard, carefully lifted Batai's limp body, then just as carefully laid him back down. Anger flashed in his eyes, crashed his huge fist through marble, sent pieces of the sidewalk flying. Kiera bent over his body, inconsolable, yet it was Indira's cries that were the most wrenching.

Brohdan stared down at them, at their grieving, at the lifeless bodies of his friends, as if it were fake, a mere story told to pass the time. Then it hit him. The shock and anger. The misery. The helplessness. He extended his long neck, raised his head high, roared, tried to purge the fury, the anguish. But he knew that was impossible, knew they'd be his companions for the rest of his life.

"Why?" Kiera asked, her sobs racking her small body.

Indira raised her head, noted the bodies of the sorcerers. "There were four left when we were knocked unconscious. Now there are none."

"How?" Gunnar growled.

"I do not know," she admitted through her tears, running her hand softly against his disfigured face, "but they fought through hell to save us."

"What knocked you unconscious?" Brohdan asked, his voice unsteady.

"I don't know," Gunnar answered, shifting his attention to where Belkidar had faced Hildegard.

They turned with him, reluctantly left Batai's side to investigate. Indira was the first to spot him, kneeling over a woman's body. They took a few steps toward him, but in their silence, they heard his whispered sobs. They stopped, dropped their eyes, felt only a fraction of his pain.

"I didn't think you lived," Belkidar sobbed, holding the woman's hands in his own. "How could I be so stupid?"

"No, my husband," she answered, her voice barely audible, thick with pain. "Don't blame yourself. We couldn't bring the Staff near the other two Artifacts. We had no other choice."

"I'm sorry, Aelya. I was supposed to be there for you, always."

Aelya moved her husband's hands until they rested over her heart. "You have been. Every day."

Her grasp slackened. She looked up, smiled as a tear fell down her cheek.

"I love you, my wife. Forever."

Aelya's smile widened, unaffected by her pain. "I love you too, my husband. Forever." And then her eyes went vacant, her grasp loosened, her head lolled backward.

Belkidar's sobs increased, watched as a brilliant white mist rose from her body and was slowly lost in the sunlight. He bent over her, gently laid her head against the ground, softly kissed her lips. Only after a long while did his sobs lessen.

Indira approached him, gently placed her hand on his shoulder. She said nothing, her hand solid against his robes, warming his skin, the caress of a friend. Of a daughter.

Belkidar eventually rose to a knee, wiped his face with a handkerchief. "She saved me. Saved us all."

Kiera ran to him, embraced him in a desperate hug. Belkidar instantly knew something was wrong. "Where's Batai?"

She held him tighter, felt his sobs.

"No. Please, no."

They stayed there for a long time, huddled together in their grief. They didn't speak, Gunnar silently carrying Aelya's body to where Batai and Einar rested.

Eventually, Belkidar got to his feet and went to them. He lifted his wife's body, carried her to a section of the courtyard unmolested by their battle, laid her gently in the lush grass. Then he summoned a shovel and began digging. Kiera's heart broke as she watched Belkidar bury his wife.

"Can you make another one of those?" Gunnar asked.

Belkidar paused, nodded.

Gunnar joined him, the rhythmic grating of the shovels the only sound.

Chapter 22
Corollary

Fall seven times and stand up eight.

Japanese Proverb

How can anyone feel two opposing emotions so strongly? The loss of Batai and Einar saddened him beyond thought, a darkness that swallowed him like the swells of an angry ocean. Cold. Uncaring. Not ruthless – impassionate, apathetic. An indifference that somehow deepened his pain. And then to see Belkidar finally reunite with his wife, only to have her die in his arms…

But another part of him rejoiced. They'd completed their Quest, beyond all hope, beyond all reason. Hildegard was killed, the Jewel destroyed! The world was finally free from their evil!

And yet a part of him felt empty, as though their loss severed a piece of his soul, never to be filled. Never to be healed.

They won.

So why did he feal so defeated?

Afterward, they left the courtyard and crossed the drawbridge to find hundreds of farmers and traders congregating along the highway.

Belkidar took a deep breath, then approached. "Fear not!" he began, magnifying his voice so even the furthest could hear his words. "Hildegard, the merciless tyrant who for centacycles worked you and your ancestors to early graves, is dead."

The crowd stirred, uneasy with such words. Belkidar watched as their restlessness grew.

"Nonsense!" a man yelled, his face lost in the masses.

"Who could kill a sorcerer?" another asked.

"A stronger one!" Gunnar bellowed. He did not need sorcery to be heard.

"I am Belkidar, and these are…" He paused, smiled. "…my family. You are safe."

They laughed, mocked him. "Belkidar's just a story we tell our children, to give them hope!"

Brohdan raised his head, glared at them from high above, silenced them in an instant.

"He does not lie!" Indira called before Belkidar could reply, her voice clear, like a bell chime carried to the farmer furthest afield. Kiera glanced at Gunnar, saw her surprise mirrored on his face. "Belkidar is real! He led us through Hildegard's Defenses to here, Gul Krul, where we destroyed him!"

Murmurs grew in the crowd, only a few at first, but multiplying, starting first with some elders in the front, then trickling back through the rest.

"Prove it," one of the oldest challenged.

"We just did," Belkidar answered. "Now if you'll excuse me, we're in need of rest. And some ale, if there's any to be had."

The hundreds parted as he walked onto the road, the others following. Brohdan took flight, flying only elads above the crowd, his shadow enveloping them. He circled north, found the pack horses and herded them back toward the others.

As Belkidar neared the rear of the horde, a short stocky man approached, his thick red beard contrasting sharply with his thinning hair. "I'm Haeme. Ah own a pub. Ain't much, but yer welcome ta stay as long as ya like."

"Thank you," Belkidar answered. "Are you sure your wife won't mind?"

"Ne'er bin married. They don't seem ta like th' ale as much as Ah do."

"Don't suppose you've got some on you?" Belkidar pressed.

"'Fraid not. Drank it during yer speech." Then he looked up, watched as Brohdan landed nearby. "Not sure where yer big fella's gonna stay," he said to nobody in particular.

"I'll be fine outside."

Apparently, the presence of a dragon wasn't enough to faze Haeme, but he nearly knocked Indira from her saddle when he spoke. "He talks?"

"Sure does," Belkidar answered. "Cooks a mean steak too."

He led them a half link along the highway before turning south, following a worn path that ended in a small village. The Dirty Pub sat at its center. "Like Ah said, not much, but the kegs're full."

"Music to my ears," Belkidar said, his legs moving twice as fast as his walking stick.

Brohdan soon had a large fire blazing in a wide pit Gunnar had dug several elads behind the pub. They sat around it, made themselves comfortable as the stars began piercing holes in the darkening veil to the east. Before long, a thin crescent moon slowly emerged above the peaks bordering Lake Mamate.

It didn't appear as though Haeme had a staff to help him with his pub, yet within drus he carried out a huge pot of mutton stew. He shooed Gunnar away when he tried to help him hang it over the fire, but gladly accepted his help when he brought six kegs outside.

They ate together and shared a pint, but after the last bowl was scraped clean, Haeme labored to his feet. "'Tis ne'er ma wish to overstay ma welcome. If yer be who ya say ya are, I'm forever in yer debt. If yer not, well, at least ya gave that sorcerer bastard a new view."

"Thank you for everything," Kiera said as they watched him disappear into his pub. Then she turned to Belkidar. "I don't think he's exactly rich, but that didn't stop him from treating us like kings."

"Already taken care of," Belkidar replied between gulps of a particularly good stout, hoisting a fat leather pouch, its drawstring pulled tight.

Their conversation eventually turned to their recent victory, yet despite their enormous success, their words were spoken softly, their manner subdued. The fire comforted them, yet they were exhausted, and they'd suffered far too much to celebrate.

Wanting to delay the others' recounting for as long as possible, Brohdan first described his battle with the titan. He went into great detail, explaining the rage he felt during his initial attack, the ease with which the titan tossed him aside, his lightning bolts that struck like anvils. He described how he tried to clear his head after crashing to the ground, then told them of his strategy to sever the titan's right hand, thus robbing him of his most dangerous weapon. He took his time, explained how the titan never showed anger or pain, and how gallantly he fought to the end. "After he lost his lightning, he must've known he would die, yet he fought on."

"That's the essence of a titan," Belkidar said. "They're neither good nor evil, but absolutely loyal to their creator. Many have interpreted this as blind obedience, but nothing could be further from the truth. A titan chooses to defend his master, chooses to continue fighting when there's no hope of victory, not because he has no alternative, but because he understands the debt he owes his creator."

"Admirable," Gunnar replied after a moment, his deep voice adding to the cracking of the fire.

"Truly," Indira agreed. "Dangerous, but honorable."

A long moment passed. "I tried to end it as quickly as I could," Brohdan eventually continued. "He didn't deserve to suffer. I ask myself if I would've acted that honorably."

"You already have," Belkidar said.

Brohdan said nothing, uncomfortable with his compliment.

Kiera refilled her enormous mug, then through a foamy mustache told the others of their encounter with the Jrelz Captains. She too went into great detail, pausing several times to let the stabs of misery pass, then circled back to the parts she didn't understand.

"I'll answer all of your questions as I describe my battle with Hildegard. But first I need to top off my ale," he said.

He continued after returning to his seat before the fire. "I hoped to recognize some good in him, to see if Krollum still lived." He shook his head. "But he spent too many centacycles with the Headpiece. I defended myself against his initial attacks, then countered with one of my own."

"What did you do?" Indira asked.

"I tried to ram his head through his living quarters."

"Elegant."

"Thank you. But it didn't work. That's when he summoned Phaylyn." He paused as he retrieved his handkerchief.

"Hildegard explained what happened to Aelya, confirmed how he'd abducted her during one of her inspections. What I didn't understand was how quickly both the Headpiece and Hildegard could turn her, a fraction of the time the Headpiece alone needed to corrupt Jenkar or Krollum. He initially used sorcery to shield her from me, but that was no longer necessary when Phaylyn emerged. That whole time, I searched for my wife, never realizing that evidence of Phaylyn could've led me straight to her."

"Aelya fought them every day since, but she couldn't overcome their combined strength. That changed when I confronted Hildegard, because that forced him to divide his power between us. With his control over her weakened, she finally broke free, the last thing he ever expected."

Belkidar paused, his eyes distant. "I was beaten. I had only the Staff to counter Hildegard's Headpiece and Jewel, and there was also Phaylyn to contend with. I wasn't strong enough, knew there was nothing I could do to stop them. The guilt was unbearable."

"Guilt? For what?" Indira asked.

He smiled, but there was only sadness there. "Of failing you, for trusting me only to let you down when you needed me most. But that's when Aelya broke free. She redirected her sorcery, attacked Hildegard, but she did it so abruptly, I couldn't react fast enough..."

"She couldn't hesitate and risk tipping her hand," Gunnar said softly.

Belkidar nodded, silent, ran his handkerchief across his cheeks again, the fire's reflection dancing across his face. After several long moments, he continued.

"After I killed her, I unleashed the most heinous, evil cant I could muster. But almost immediately I realized my mistake, conjured instead a glimpse of what the world would be like without the likes of Hildegard and his evil. He fought it with his own vision – despondency, anguish, suffering – everything the soul of the Headpiece yearned for. And so we battled each other through these two destinies, each trying to impose our will on the other." He paused, took a long draught from his stein.

"How were the Artifacts used?" Indira asked, filling the silence.

"Good question. Just as a magnifying crystal focuses the sun's light into a smaller, more intense beam, we use Artifacts to focus our sorcery's energy, to intensify our spells."

"But Hildegard had two Artifacts," Brohdan pointed out. "Didn't that strengthen his sorcery even more?"

"Yes. And no. He first used the Headpiece to focus his power, and since its corrupted soul mirrored his own, they worked in harmony. But the Jewel's soul was still pure, so it fought against him, limited how much it helped him."

"In what way?" Gunnar asked. "You said an Artifact has no choice but to serve its owner."

"True, but they're not like us, they have no free will like we do. They must serve, but the effectiveness of that service can vary, just like ours can. For example, a happy employee works more efficiently than a disgruntled one. Both are technically loyal to their employer since they both labor on his behalf, yet their productivity can be very different."

He finished his ale, and Gunnar refilled his stein with a dark porter. He nodded his thanks as he continued. "When our sorcery met, their incompatibility created a nexus, a physical manifestation of our conflicting realities. It was chaos incarnate, drained all sound from the region, eventually releasing a shock wave before reaching a state of equilibrium. That's what extinguished the Jrelz' fire ward."

"No longer having to contend with Phaylyn, I pushed Hildegard's sorcery back, forcing the nexus to the Jewel. At that instant, its soul felt two wills, was bound to serve them both, but the efficiency in how it served each couldn't have been more different."

"The Jewel's soul is like the Staff's. Each is unique, but they have similar morals. So when the Jewel perceived my will, it became reinvigorated, eager to help me. I pushed Hildegard's will back, robbed him of the Jewel. Now armed with two Artifacts, it took only a moment to force the nexus to the Headpiece, seizing his final Artifact, one he'd known for thousands of cycles. The nexus accelerated toward him, penetrated his head and finally his Linsilor Sorcerenic, the source of his power. When that happened, Hildegard ceased to exist."

"Ceased to exist?" Kiera asked, incredulous. "His death disintegrated half of Gul Krul!"

"He was a powerful sorcerer," Belkidar said, shrugging. "Hildegard died the instant the nexus reached his Linsilor, extinguished the consciousness that contained his power, releasing the energy he'd gained through the eight thousand cycles of his life."

"Why were we not destroyed?" Indira asked.

"Once I took control of the Jewel, I realized the outcome of the battle had been determined, so I cast a ward of invulnerability. It's an invisible field that extends in all directions, its size and strength dependent on the sorcerer who casts it."

Kiera nodded. "That explains how we survived Hildegard's death, but how did we survive the Jrelz Captains?"

"I cast 'sanctuary' when Hildegard motioned for them to enter the courtyard, a ward that siphons the power from most cants of war."

"*Most?*" Gunnar asked, his brows raised.

Belkidar shrugged again before taking another drink.

The others stared into the fire as they replayed the battle in their minds. "It is a shame you could not save the Jewel," Indira said, her lilting voice soft, somehow perfectly complimenting the fire's crackling.

"It is," Belkidar admitted. "My first responsibility was to defeat Hildegard and destroy the Headpiece, but I do regret that I couldn't save the Jewel. Although not the Staff of Power, two Artifacts would've helped bring a new reality to this world. Now, that'll take centacycles."

"But that fate still lives, if delayed," Indira noted. "Perhaps that will give the rest of us time to build something we can be proud of."

"Exactly," Brohdan agreed. "With Hildegard and the Headpiece gone, the three continents can finally work together again, like before the War."

"You're right, of course, but I'd have liked for you all to have seen it."

"We shall see it," Indira offered, "through you."

"That you will." He raised his tankard, the others joining him.

The fire crackled in silence for several long moments before Gunnar spoke. "Should we set up a watch tonight? In case Hildegard's armies retaliate?"

"Good thinking, but there's no need."

"How do you know?"

Belkidar said nothing, instead tapped his head.

"What about his tower?" Kiera asked. "I'm sure you would've liked to snoop in there for a centacycle or two."

"First of all, I don't snoop. But if I did, that would've made for some interesting reading."

They spent the night huddled together beneath the clear, starlit sky. Brohdan wasn't sleepy, habitually watched over his friends. His gaze rarely left the heavens as he considered the honor of the griffins and the loyalty of the titan. He thought of Batai and Einar, remembered the days and nights he was fortunate enough to have spent with them. He silently thanked them for their sacrifice, hoped he would live a life half as honorable. Then his mind turned to Mikka.

The thought of her instantly sent a wave of anticipation through him. Their Quest was finally over! The morning's light would usher with it the first day of his journey home. Soon, he would look upon her for the first time since he'd trained in Sul Brul so long ago.

Despite his excitement, the day's exhausting events finally took its toll. Only a couple of links before sunrise, the Broglia Black slowly drifted to sleep, content knowing their Quest was finally over, thrilled that he'd soon be reunited with his mate.

Chapter 23
Reunion

*We cannot tell the precise moment when friendship is
formed. As in filling a vessel drop by drop, there is at
last a drop which makes it run over; so in a series of
kindnesses there is at last one which makes the heart
run over.*

Ray Bradbury, Fahrenheit 451

Dawn came swiftly, and judging by the way their heads ached, a few wondered if they'd received battle wounds they hadn't noticed. Soon, Haeme joined them outside.

"Got some eggs, bacon, an' toast fer ya's. Comin' up in a few drus," he added before turning and disappearing back into his pub.

They ate slowly, enjoying the feeling of not having the weight of the world looming over their every decision.

"When did ya plan on leavin'?"

"As soon as possible," Brohdan replied a bit too quickly.

"We have family and friends that we haven't seen in a while," Kiera explained. "Most don't even know if we're alive or dead."

"Say no more," Haeme replied. "Ah understand. Jus' happy ta have ya spend the night."

"We cannot thank you enough for your hospitality," Indira said.

"And the ale," Belkidar added between mouthfuls of bacon.

"Think nothin' of it. But tell me somethin', if ya don't mind. Is Hildegard really dead?"

"He is."

Haeme shook his head. "Hard ter 'magine ya so few could do what the rest darit no."

Belkidar nodded. "That's how we beat him."

Haeme thought about that, but it made little sense. "If ya say so," he finally decided before standing and heading back inside.

"How were you planning on getting back to Tymoteu?" Gunnar asked.

"I've got an idea."

"What are you planning?" Kiera asked, a curious smile spreading slowly across her face.

"You'll see. All in good time."

They eventually helped Haeme clean up from the previous night, then departed The Dirty Pub after thanking its gracious owner one last time. The last to leave, Belkidar left a few heavy bags where Haeme was certain to find them. They rode north along the small path that led back to the highway. For a welcomed change, they rode side-by-side.

"Well?" Kiera finally asked.

"Well what?"

"Oh, come on!"

"Very well. But first we need to find shelter. There are thousands of people in these small villages. Merchants buy and sell goods that were carted from Trillhell but have been deemed unworthy for sale in Hildegard's fortress. Farmers toil the infertile lands, somehow providing the local populace with fresh produce. In fact, I remember a story – "

"Belkidar!"

"Right. There will be sorcery involved in our voyage home, and I don't wish it to worry these people any more than we already have."

"Fine," she sighed.

"What will all those people do without the markets of Gul Krul to support them?" Indira asked.

"They'll thrive. Hildegard is gone forever – it feels good to say that – but the need for trading goods and services isn't going anywhere. These people will flourish."

Indira smiled, nodded slightly as they continued along the highway. After traveling another half link, Belkidar at last seemed satisfied. He led them north of the road and eventually into some rolling hills. Once concealed, he finally explained his plan.

"Throughout this long journey, each of you wondered what it must be like to take the form of another creature. Today you'll find out."

"What?" Kiera demanded, perhaps a bit louder than she'd intended.

"I distinctly remember you marveling at how I changed into an eagle's form as we traveled from Fendurgin to Brodor. If memory serves, you sat in awe atop your horse, wondering what it must be like to soar through the air," Belkidar pointed out, his mischievous grin boring into her.

"Well – I suppose – yes. But that certainly does *not* mean I ever intended to find out!"

"I would love to fly as a bird!" Indira said, her eyes wide.

"It's really a simple spell once you get the hang of it. It just takes so long to master. Wouldn't want to inadvertently transform one of you into something I couldn't undo."

Judging by their expressions, they didn't appreciate his humor.

"Seriously, there's nothing to worry about," he began again. Somehow the smirk he failed to conceal didn't help his cause. "Everybody, off your horses. Considering it's your first time, I'll transform each of you individually, but I'd first like the horses to make their way back to Haeme."

"I'm sure he'll appreciate the gesture, but how do you know they'll return there?" Kiera asked.

"I'll take care of it," he assured her.

The others, still affected by the previously night's – and morning's – consumption of alcohol, gingerly dismounted and gathered the few belongings they desired.

"Now, who'd like to go first?"

Indira quickly raised her hand.

"Very well, my dear," Belkidar said with a smile. "Do you have any particular bird in mind?"

"I always dreamed of being a hawk."

"It would be my pleasure."

It took only a moment before Indira felt as though she was being lifted off the ground. Her long black hair flew everywhere, and a white-blue light shrouded her as she fought her instincts, dropping her right hand to her side after initially reaching for an arrow. She knew better, knew she was safe, yet Belkidar's enormous power alarmed her, his Linsilor working far beyond her understanding.

Although it seemed much longer to her, his white-blue light grew brighter as his spell's energy surged – only to vanish in an instant, revealing a beautiful golden hawk. Her immaculate feathers glowed magnificently in the brilliant sunlight, her deep golden eyes observing far more than could even an elf.

"Amazing!" she squawked. "Everything is so clear!"

"Another happy customer," Belkidar sighed, smiling. "Who's next?"

"All right!" Gunnar bellowed. "Just don't turn me into something that likes vegetables!"

"Would I do that to you?" Belkidar asked between giggles. His huge form instantly shimmered into a small seagull. Needless to say, his friends – in both human and bird form – were completely unprepared, their laughter filling the area around them.

"My, you look delicious," Indira squawked as she hopped over to inspect him.

"And you, my dear?" Belkidar asked Kiera.

"A bald eagle."

"A fine choice."

Her incredible vision also took her by surprise, and she spent several moments examining everything around her.

Belkidar gathered them nearby. "I have a feeling the winds will be extremely favorable during our flight, but it'll still take a day and a half to get back – a difficult proposition to say the least considering this'll be your first time flying. So I've taken a few steps to make sure your strength and stamina are up to the task. The ability to fly doesn't come easily, and I can't instill all of the knowledge and experience you'd need to make this flight effortless, especially when you weren't born with those instincts. Besides," he added with a smile, "where would the fun be if I could?"

He demonstrated several takeoffs before his friends practiced them one at a time. They did their best to mimic him, but all failed, crashing ungracefully back to the ground.

Belkidar watched them. He was tired. Tired of war. Of sacrifices and death. Of putting on false masks, pretending to be fine. Tired of living. But as he watched his friends, he felt their elation as they learned to fly, recalled his own struggles thousands of cycles ago as though it were yesterday. They supported each other, encouraged one another, laughed at their own mistakes, yet each attempt yielded slightly better results. He experienced their fulfillment as they slowly mastered their new forms, almost reliving it for the first time himself.

After two links, he knew they were ready. "If anyone needs a break along the way, fly close to the water so I can change your form into a fish's. Then, after you've properly rested amidst the shark infested waters of the Celornorin Ocean, I'll transform you back so we may continue our flight."

With that, the ancient eagle leapt into the air, spread his huge wings, tucked his talons beneath his tail, and gracefully took to the skies. Brohdan remained on the ground and watched his enthusiastic friends follow. Each successfully took to the air and, albeit less gracefully, followed the eagle west.

They flew in a predictably loose formation, and to nobody's surprise, Indira fared the best. Kiera and Gunnar were an entirely different matter, yet despite their clumsiness, Belkidar enjoyed watching them the most. They technically flew, but spent more time falling or climbing back to altitude than they did in level flight, frantically correcting one mistake after another. He watched as Kiera recovered from a terrifying dive only to suffer another from the laughter caused by the first. Gunnar and Indira laughed with her, then nearly collided as she shot between them.

"Seeing their happiness reminds me of my first flight," Brohdan said.

"Me too, and that's saying something."

They flew into a breathtaking sunset, its red and violet reflecting for linops below them. When its light faded, they were treated to another momentous display, the stars so clear they seemed close enough to touch, as though they could run their hand through them like the blue waters of a glacial lake.

With only the periodic flapping of wings to mark the passage of time, the heavens treated them to an incredible display of vivid galaxies, streaking comets, intense novae, and vibrant nebulae. Although Belkidar aided their progress across the water, all were grateful that he hadn't tampered with the speed of the passing night. Nevertheless, dawn's first light appeared long before they wished.

"We should see Tymoteu in a link or two," Belkidar announced.

"That soon?" Kiera asked.

"I didn't think you liked the idea of changing forms."

"Well, that was before I tried it."

"Then I'm sorry to say our progress has been swift. We should arrive in Sul Brul within five or six links."

The others savored the precious time that remained. Indira treasured the sensation of the wind passing smoothly over her feathers while Kiera and Gunnar silently took turns mimicking each other's movements. Brohdan, having the fortune to enjoy flight whenever he wished, experienced perhaps the group's greatest fulfillment through the happiness of his friends. He smiled as he watched their joyful expressions, desperately hoped their future would bring equal fulfillment throughout the course of their own lives.

To those flying for the first time, the inevitable appearance of Sul Brul was a depressing sight, but for Brohdan, finally seeing Mikka's home couldn't have been more exhilarating.

Belkidar instructed the others as they approached. He flew ahead, serving as the model for them to imitate. While each did an admirable job, only Indira touched down solely on her talons. Gunnar stopped too high and fell onto his tail feathers while Kiera carried too much speed as she neared the ground, toppling forward and skidding to an ungraceful stop. Brohdan trailed them by elads, landed well short to make sure the wind from his enormous wings didn't overwhelm them.

"Not bad!" Belkidar complimented before returning them to their original forms. To their surprise, it took several unsteady moments before they once again felt comfortable with their natural legs. Gunnar took an extra moment to ensure Belkidar hadn't inadvertently added – or subtracted – anything important. Then they thanked him, Indira embracing him, Kiera kissing him on the cheek.

"You're all very welcome. It was the least I could do to repay your sacrifices."

"Come now, Belkidar," Indira replied, "we volunteered for this Quest not as a favor to you, but because it was our duty."

"Absolutely," Gunnar agreed, "but I'm relieved it's over."

"Me too," Belkidar confirmed. "But I wonder…"

"What?" Indira asked after a long moment.

Belkidar stroked his beard, his face pensive. "It's true Hildegard and the Headpiece are gone, but for thousands of cycles their corruption helped shape this world. How much evil can we withstand before it fundamentally changes us?"

They paused, considered his words. Then Brohdan looked to a familiar ridgeline, the sun highlighting its peaks.

"Yes, how foolish of us," Belkidar said. "You've earned this."

Brohdan nodded, recalled the countless links he'd dreamt of this moment. But just before he spread his wings, he turned back to them. "Will you be staying awhile?"

"Absolutely. Dragons once again played a decisive role in the preservation of peace, and I think we at least owe them a recounting of what they helped accomplish."

They watched as he took off. "I don't think I'll ever grow tired of seeing that," Kiera remarked.

Reaching a familiar valley, Brohdan dove toward Boseda's dwelling, then landed smoothly outside his cave.

Boseda heard him land. "Brohdan! You're alive!" he said, hastening toward the towering dragon. "You completed your Quest?"

"Just two days ago. Belkidar's here, along with the rest of our party. He plans to tell everyone about it tonight."

"I'm looking forward to it!" his former instructor said, then paused. "Where are my manners? I'd invite you in, but I'm afraid you're too big to be comfortable."

"Thank you, but I'm fine." Brohdan awkwardly rearranged the way his wings were folded against his body. "Is Mikka home?"

"Oh, I'm afraid she doesn't live here anymore."

He stared into Boseda's eyes, paralyzed.

"She left over a mooncycle ago, not long after you left actually. Now she lives just over the next ridge."

Brohdan exhaled the breath he hadn't realized he'd be holding.

"She's missed you very much."

"The thought of her is what kept me going."

After politely excusing himself, Brohdan took flight and headed toward his mate. He searched the valley Boseda had indicated and found only one cave suitable for a dragon. He quickly descended and landed just outside. "Hello?"

There was no answer.

Brohdan waited a moment before trying again.

"Oh, just a moment please."

Brohdan's anxiety tripled upon hearing her voice, then stared transfixed as she slowly materialized from the shadows of her cave.

She was even more beautiful than he remembered.

"Brohdan!" she shouted, sprinting toward him. "You're alive!"

He couldn't believe it. After so many lonely nights, after witnessing the horrors of battle and the devastation of lost friends, he finally looked upon his mate once again. Her beauty still managed to take his breath away.

They held their Hongi a long time, still not quite believing this moment was real. They spent the next several links together, Brohdan again finding himself infatuated with each of her movements, and he marveled at the way she gracefully accomplished even the most ordinary tasks. They both realized that, despite the insecurity of the previous mooncycles, a new dawn approached in which their past suffering would only deepen the happiness to come.

"Let's find somewhere to spend the night," Belkidar announced. "Most of the dragons passing through Sul Brul take shelter in those caves up there," he explained, pointing to the southeast.

He led them there, and soon nearly a dozen caves came into view. "If memory serves, that's one of the larger ones," he explained, looking up the face of the ridge, "and one of the lowest."

"I have never slept in a cave before," Indira noted.

Gunnar smiled. "A word of advice – try to get a corner near the back. Much less drafty."

Belkidar's memory was accurate, the cave large enough to comfortably shelter twice their number. It took only a few drus to arrange their belongings.

"I think it's time I paid a visit to the elders," Belkidar explained. "You guys stay here and make sure the cave doesn't move."

"I'll do what I can," Gunnar said, relaxing in the warm sunlight, the rumbles of his snores echoing in the valley long before Belkidar's eagle form disappeared from view.

"What are your plans?" Kiera asked Indira.

"I thought I would explore until Belkidar returns."

"Mind if I join you?"

They were careful not to disturb the dragons until Belkidar had met with the elders, but they couldn't help run into a few, all of whom immediately recognized Indira as an elf. That realization encouraged the dragons, and although a few were still hesitant, most approached them unreservedly, asking them about their lives outside of Sul Brul. But most of the time they simply explored, content to spend time in each other's company without a battle looming or the world's fate resting on their shoulders.

Belkidar announced himself to the elders, and as he'd expected, a feast was quickly arranged. During the celebration, he planned to describe every detail of the Quest before nearly two dozen of Sul Brul's elders. It was nearly sunset by the time all of the preparations had been made and Belkidar returned to his friends.

Dusk came just as quickly for the others, but especially for Mikka and Brohdan. The two discussed what each had experienced during their separation. He knew Belkidar would soon explain their Quest during the night's festivities, so he instead described the vast Celornorin Ocean and the immense beauty of the night skies, the unbearable heat of the Wruloric and the snow-capped mountains surrounding Lake Mamate. He conveyed his early self-doubt despite the considerable support he received from his friends and the grief he experienced from taking so many lives. That saddened her, but her

smile returned when he described the continual strength he found
whenever he thought of her. Finally, as the sun sank low in the west,
they slowly made their way to the center of Sul Brul.

Most of the elders were already there. An enormous fire had been
prepared, with cords of wood piled high in the growing darkness
beyond the fire's reach. He saw many familiar faces. Krepli, Boseda,
and even Rouldra excitedly approached, taking turns to congratulate
him on his success. He was comforted to be with them again, Rouldra
included. As they talked, he realized she'd become a little less
insulting. Maybe.

"You must tell us what happened!" Krepli said. "Did you use
'steelskin'? Or 'cloak'?"

"I did, many times."

"I look forward to Belkidar's accounting!"

Just then, Belkidar led Brohdan's companions down to where the
fire blazed. Each wore unfamiliar clothing, no doubt the result of his
unique skills. Indira had a tunic of rich dark green and matching pants,
a black shirt and brown leather boots. For the first time since Brohdan
had met her, Kiera abandoned her drab clothing for a beautiful black
cloak, its sleeves and neckline adorned with elaborate grey accents.
Gunnar had also shed his old clothing for the occasion, replaced by a
simple black tunic and matching pants. Belkidar decided on his
favorite robes of the deepest blue Brohdan had ever seen, intricate
silver patterning his sleeves and hem.

"You look handsome," Brohdan told him.

"Thank you. It was Aelya's favorite."

Brohdan took his time introducing his friends. It was surreal, their
silhouettes dark against the flames, growing in size from a small
woman to an elf, sorcerer, and eventually a giant, his height greater
than even the dragons when seated on their haunches. Brohdan, of
course, towered over everyone, and he watched with delight as his

friends became acquainted with the dragons from his past. They enjoyed it just as much, for prior to this Quest only Belkidar had ever seen a dragon.

Everyone found a comfortable position around the blazing fire. Soon afterward, four dragons placed huge wooden platters around the fire pit. The meal included a wide variety of delicious food, including roasted pork, lamb, deer and, of course, beef. Those that preferred cooked food appreciated their thoughtfulness. Belkidar waited until the majority had completed their meals, not wanting to appear rude by interrupting something that had obviously taken so much effort to prepare.

"My friends. The journey has been long and difficult, but I'm honored to announce that Hildegard has been destroyed!"

The eruption of the dragons' deep, elated growls took Kiera by surprise.

"But it was not a simple matter, and it unfortunately required great sacrifices. When Brohdan and I first left Sul Brul a few mooncycles ago, we traveled north to KelKinney. To quicken our pace, I transformed myself into an eagle."

"Show us!" a female dragon implored from the opposite side of the fire.

"Maybe later," he replied, actually looking embarrassed. He continued, explaining their Quest in exceptional detail. His hosts listened intently for links as he described every minute aspect, including the unselfishness of his companions, the diverse circumstances in which they fought, the strengths and numbers of their enemies, the various paths that frequently lay before them, the logic they used to choose the right ones, the challenges posed by each of Hildegard's Defenses, and the final battle in which they forever freed the world of Hildegard's evil.

Throughout his incredibly detailed chronicle, Brohdan wondered if Belkidar hadn't at times delved into his unique abilities. Inevitably, and always at just the right moment, he heard the faint ringing of swords against axes, the excruciating shrieks of wyverns, the hysterics

that frequently surfaced in their affable group, the reassuring hum of
Indira's bow, the deafening sound of minotaur hooves, the deep growl-
like speech of the gargantuids, the claps of thunder against marble
walls, and even the scornful laughs of Hildegard himself. Finally, only
a few links from dawn, Belkidar finished his account.

"You are heroes to us all," Krepli began. "Once again, humans,
elves, giants, and dragons have proven their honor on a common
battlefield. Let us never forget this day, to forever remember how
together we remain strong, and how through friendship we found
peace."

"Well said, Master Krepli," Belkidar agreed. "Well said, indeed."

Gunnar raised his drink. "A toast. To Einar. To Batai, my friend.
Two of the bravest warriors this world has ever seen."

Indira, Kiera, and Belkidar raised their cups to his in silence, a
stark contrast to the dragons' resonant growls. Their rumbling tribute
seemingly originated from the darkness, surrounded them, filled them,
so deep it vibrated in their chests, pulled at their hearts. Then as one
they fell silent, considered all their guests had endured, honored those
who paid the ultimate price for their peace. Finally, Brohdan spoke.

"The time I spent with these extraordinary friends will remain with
me for the rest of my life. Yet despite Belkidar's exceptional account,
our experiences are truly indescribable. These people accepted me, as a
friend, as a comrade, unconditionally. They showed me what self-
sacrifice looks like, and why duty is a burden worth those sacrifices.
Yet my fortunes don't end there."

He turned to Belkidar. "Mikka and I have become lifemates."

Belkidar smiled, the fire's light reflecting from his face and beard,
his blue robes glowing.

"I'm so happy for you both!" Boseda said. "Mikka, I know how
hard these past mooncycles have been, and I know he'll make you
happy. And Brohdan, I recognized your character from the first
moment I met you, and I treasured the two cycles we spent together
more than you know," he concluded, his emotions getting the better of
him.

Each of Brohdan's companions excitedly approached to personally congratulate the two dragons. Afterwards, they settled back into easy conversation. Kiera told everyone of Brohdan's exceptional swimming, for once not even tempted to exaggerate one of her stories. Indira smiled, then described how Brohdan's barz finally showed itself, her smirk widening at Belkidar's scowl as she detailed his ruined robes. Gunnar was persuaded to once again imitate Batai's goat laughs, his high-pitched laughter smoothly transitioning to a deep, affable chuckle before trailing off entirely at the memory of his friend.

They shared stories for another few links, Brohdan enjoying every moment with his friends. He savored the smell of the food, the crackling of the fire, the brilliant stars, the simple companionship – all reminding him of their long journey, and how remarkably rare these friendships had become. But their celebration unfortunately had to end.

"Belkidar's taking the rest of us home at dawn," Kiera explained. She paused a long moment. "You've been a constant source of strength and inspiration for me, Brohdan. For all of us. Thank you for always giving us hope, even when we had no cause for it," she added, tears falling down her cheeks.

Brohdan lowered his head, stared into her eyes. "Thank you, Kiera, for your acceptance, for your genuineness. For the comfort of warm food after traveling links in the rain. For your continual optimism. And for somehow guiding us through Hildegard's hatred."

She hugged him, kissed his cheek before disappearing into the darkness.

"You will forever be welcome in my pack," Indira said. "Thank you for always watching over us, even when we could not see." She looked up into her friend's eyes before softly continuing. "I know of your promise to my father. You have fulfilled your vow, and for that I will always be grateful."

"It was my honor, Indira. I'm just sorry I couldn't stop the cent – "

She raised her hand to his jaw, placed rough callouses against rough scales, silencing him. "We all made sacrifices, and we are all of us stronger for them." She smiled, trailed her hand against his jaw as she departed.

Gunnar approached next, his face serious. "Before we met, I felt certain of one truth in this world – I was alone, and nothing would ever change that. Then I met you, and I realized I wasn't so unique after all. But more importantly, I found a brother. It's been an honor fighting by your side."

"The honor was mine, Gunnar. I leaned on you, on your strength – not in your arms or back – but in your character, in your friendship. You taught so much, to persevere no matter how difficult the circumstances. I learned that being the only one of your kind can be an asset, not a burden."

Then Belkidar approached, the seemingly frail old man leaning heavily on his Staff. He looked up into Brohdan's eyes, considered him for a long moment. "This is where you're meant to be. Live happily."

Brohdan looked down on him as tears welled in his large eyes. He silently nodded as his emotions stole his voice.

"I'll visit you soon."

They returned to their caves, leaving the elders to discuss their Quest and to celebrate Hildegard's defeat. But soon, even the most excited had departed to get a link or two of sleep before dawn.

By midmorning, Brohdan's friends were ready to depart.

"Brohdan, I'm taking the others home."

"When will I see you again?"

"Not long. Enjoy yourself in my absence."

"I'll try," Brohdan replied sarcastically.

"Does everybody have their belongings?" Belkidar asked.

"Yes, Grandfather."

"Very well," he replied, even as their bodies were engulfed in a familiar white-blue light. An instant later, each once again resembled a feathered creature, although unlike the previous occasion, this time they all took the same form.

"A griffin's honor is truly inspirational. Savor it, let it become part of you, and consider how they used that honor to fight Hildegard, even as they fought Brohdan."

Thanks again to Belkidar's assistance, they found themselves approaching KelKinney early that afternoon. While their landings were improving, they were still far from graceful. Once back in their natural forms, Gunnar approached Kiera. "*This* is your home?"

"Yes. Why?" she asked defensively.

"Nothing. I just thought it'd be bigger."

"At last count, she owns fourteen of these little houses throughout the continent," Belkidar explained.

"A girl's gotta make a living."

Gunnar laughed, then lifted her into his huge arms. "You are truly a warrior. Thank you for leading us through hell and back," he said, embracing her. "It was an honor."

"Thank you, Gunnar. I'll miss our wrestling matches," she grunted as he gave her one final squeeze. Then she whispered into his ear before he set her down. "Take advantage of the opportunity that lies before you."

He nodded, confused, then made way for Indira.

"Looking after all these men was not an easy task," she said, smiling.

"It certainly wasn't," Kiera agreed, pulling her close. "Your archery skills are incredible, but your friendship is far rarer. I have no doubt you were meant to take part in this Quest."

"Thank you, Kiera. I have questioned my purpose, but no longer. Please visit me whenever you can."

"I will, my friend. I promise."

"Belkidar," Kiera said before the sorcerer could speak, "early in our Quest, I wondered why you included me. Batai, Gunnar, Indira, Brohdan – they were obvious choices, but – "

"So were you, my dear."

"I tried my best for you," she whispered, unable to stop her tears.

"And it was more than I could've ever hoped for. You truly did lead us through hell and back. For that, we're all in your debt."

Kiera leapt forward, embracing him. "I'll miss you. You've been the only father I've ever known."

"As I will continue to be," he said, gently stroking her hair.

After several drus, she was finally able to let go, then quickly disappeared into her modest home.

Belkidar watched her go, his tears contrasting with his smile, then silently transformed the others back into a griffin's form. They followed him east, toward Ætheldell, and arrived a couple links before nightfall. Belkidar chose to lead them into a sizable prairie, offering ample space to control their crashes.

"Indira, would you like to lead us to your pack?" he asked after they'd all been returned to their natural forms.

"Sure!" she answered, eager to be reunited with her parents. It promised to be a beautiful evening. The waning sunlight slanted through the trees, birds sang overhead, and a refreshing breeze swayed the high branches, carrying the smell old bark and new saplings. Indira's excitement grew with each step, but after a quarter link, she finally slowed, then came to a stop. "Father! I've returned!" she called into the vast, seemingly empty forest.

That confused Gunnar, and he nearly voiced his concern when something caught his eye. He turned, his hand twitching for the handle of his sword, then relaxed when he recognized them. Where they had initially been invisible to his eye, four elves now walked toward them. "Where did they come from?" he whispered to Belkidar.

"Their home."

An old elf led them. He didn't pause, didn't even speak, just walked to Indira and embraced her. She stayed in his arms for several long moments. "I thought I would never see you again, my daughter."

Indira was too emotional to speak, and so she just held him. Then they separated, tears on both of their faces.

"Father, you of course know Belkidar," she began, smiling despite her tears.

"As always, I am honored, Venerable One. Thank you for returning my daughter to me."

"Master Juron, I think it is she who returned us," he replied, bowing.

"Father, this is Gunnar."

"It is my pleasure to meet you," Juron said without hesitation, bowing low.

Gunnar was initially taken aback, but he recovered quickly. "I'm honored to meet Indira's father, for she was truly the eye that watched over us all."

He smiled, his pride obvious. "Would you care to join us for our evening meal?" Juron offered.

"Yes, thank you," Belkidar said.

"Lodi, would you be so kind as to lead our friends to the feast?"

The elven captain approached, and after bowing silently to Belkidar, turned and led them deeper into the forest. After a half link, he stopped next to a modest fire set in an ancient pit. Its warmth was welcome, its smoke rising nearly vertically through a small opening in the canopy. The scent of pine was strong, and its six benches formed an intimate setting.

"Juron, Indira, and a few others shall join you shortly."

"Thank you, Lodi. I hope you'll be joining us as well?"

"Of course! I would never miss such an occasion!" he replied, motioning for them to sit. Then he left them, vanishing into the darkening forest.

They made themselves comfortable, and although Gunnar chose the largest of the benches, the wood nonetheless creaked loudly beneath his weight.

After a few moments, Juron arrived followed closely by his wife Ekkira and their daughter. Lodi trailed behind, and they each took seats on the logs opposite Belkidar and Gunnar. Soon, two elves brought them drinks while seven others carried their meals. Juron thanked them before they disappeared back into the forest.

"Our Quest was long and difficult, but we were victorious!" Belkidar began. Thus, he once again told the story of how he and his companions traveled to Brodor, crossed the Celornorin Ocean, overcame Hildegard's Five Defenses, and eventually destroyed his evil forever. Belkidar paid them the same compliment he had the dragons, took his time, spared no detail, for the world owed elves a similar debt.

Juron listened intently to his incredibly vivid narrative, felt as though he suffered with them, fought alongside them during each battle. It was the same for Ekkira, the firelight revealing her wet checks or wide eyes. Her laughter mirrored Indira's from a mooncycle past, experiencing her fulfillment as though it were her own.

Then, after nearly six links, his tale ended. Gunnar watched as Juron summoned an elf who'd somehow stood invisible a short distance behind. After a quick conversation, he gracefully departed and, to Belkidar's delight, soon returned with large deerskins plump with rich elven wine. As the fire crackled into the night, Juron asked Belkidar several questions about their Quest, many of which dealt with Brohdan. "He was true to his word."

"He was," Belkidar agreed. "He protected your daughter as though she were his own. Indeed, he watched over us all."

"A truly worthy successor in the noble line of Broglias."

"I've been fortunate to have known eight thousand cycles of Broglias, including Balthasar, Kantor, Gorldalev, Thordlow, Shohtor, and even Kainan. But Brohdan impressed me the most with his sincere desire to improve the world, and his incredible ability to make those desires reality."

They talked well into the night. Gunnar, having just met Indira's pack, was content to sit quietly in the background, the flickering firelight struggling to illuminate his huge form. He contemplated Kiera's last words to him, knew the fulfillment he now experienced stood in stark contrast to the loneliness that had previously defined his life. He painfully recalled the times he'd spent alone in the Midrogru Mountains, the seemingly endless cycles where he woke, hunted, ate, and slept in solitude. He then thought of the past mooncycles, knew the time he'd spent with Kiera, Batai, Indira, Brohdan, and Belkidar was the happiest of his life. If fact, he couldn't remember being this happy since his parents were still alive. He thought back to Kiera's words.

'Take advantage of the opportunity that lies before you.'

Gunnar suddenly realized he was staring blankly into the fire. He looked up and saw Indira talking happily with her mother while Lodi listened intently to Belkidar as he described the importance of properly aging certain types of ale. Juron watched, one hand resting gently in the middle of Indira's back, the other wrapped around a deerskin.

And then it came to him, the realization hitting him like a hammer.

He turned to Belkidar, knew he'd seek his counsel when the moment was right. For now, he grabbed another helping of venison, filled his wooden bucket with wine, and contentedly joined his friends in conversation.

The feast finally concluded with dawn only links away. The skies were clear and the weather warm, and they chose to sleep among the trees beneath the waning stars.

"You will have some solitude here," Lodi said, bowing as he took his leave.

"Thank you for your hospitality," Gunnar said as he left.

"It is my pleasure, Gunnar."

He joined Belkidar in preparing his sleeping blankets, thinking as he worked. "I've got something to ask, and I want you to be completely honest with me."

"Of course," he replied, curious. "What is it?"

"My home in the Midrogrus has been…less than ideal, to say the least. The time I've spent with friends revealed parts of me I never knew existed. For the first time in my life, I understand the significance of friendship – and the worthlessness of life without it."

Belkidar nodded slowly as he spoke.

"Kiera realized this, told me to take advantage of this opportunity, but I had no idea what she meant. Not until the feast." He paused, deep in thought. "Belkidar, would it be possible if I stayed here? To live with the elves?"

He smiled. "My friend, as you've seen, elves are a truly remarkable species. They've taught me many things, perhaps the most extraordinary of which is the way they unconditionally accept others. So long as they prove worthy, of course."

"That was one of the first things I noticed about them. When Indira introduced me to her father, he didn't even blink when he first saw me. I can count on one hand how many times that's happened in my life."

Belkidar nodded. "I understand, and yes, they'd take you in without question, especially considering how you've already demonstrated your character through our Quest. But you must understand what you're asking. Elves prefer their seclusion, so if you live among them, you must agree to live as they do."

"Seclusion among friends is exactly what I want."

"Then I have no doubt you'll be happy here. How could you not? You share so many of the same qualities that are essential to their society – loyalty to friends, dedication to values, willingness to work, and honor above all."

Gunnar nodded. "Who should I talk to?"

"Juron must decide. I'll arrange a meeting later in the morning after we've all gotten some sleep." He paused. "If you don't mind, I'd like to be there as well."

"Of course, Belkidar. I'd have it no other way."

Gunnar didn't wake until the sun's midmorning light touched his bearded face. He sat up, stretched in its warmth, then saw Belkidar approach from the forest.

"Juron will see you," he explained enthusiastically. "In a link."

"Thanks. That'll give me just enough time to fit in a meal."

"You know, you may just eat these poor elves out of their forest."

Belkidar led him to where Juron sat beside a warm fire. To Gunnar's surprise, Indira was there as well. They sat, Gunnar facing Juron while Belkidar, seated to his left, sat across from Indira.

"Master Gunnar, it is good to see you again. How may I help you?"

Gunnar lowered his head, his eyes lingering on the flames. "Thank you for seeing me." He paused, then looked into Juron's eyes. "As I'm sure you know, my family – my entire race – was hunted and killed. Afterward, I lived alone. Had Belkidar not intervened, I'm certain that's how my life would've passed. But this Quest introduced me to parts of myself I never knew existed. For the first time since my parents were alive, I came to understand unconditional friendship, where others would willingly sacrifice their lives to protect me. Their *family*."

He paused in thought, knew something more fundamental had taken place. "During the decacycles I lived among the Midrogru Mountains, I intentionally chose a life of solitude so I could survive without having to kill those that wanted me dead. But during this Quest, I realized I could shape my own destiny, and for the first time, I was content."

"Hildegard's evil is gone, and I'm proud I had something to do with that. But at the same time, I'm saddened with the prospect of returning to my old life." He paused again, surprised that his time in the Midrogrus seemed a lifetime ago. "Master Juron, it is my sincere wish to remain here, in Ætheldell, and live as a member of your pack."

Juron nodded, considering his words. "You inherited a most difficult life, Gunnar, and for most, survival would be their only measure of success. But you not only survived, you lived honorably. I sympathize with you, but my greatest responsibility lies to my pack." He turned to Belkidar.

"My daughter recommended this very possibility after last night's feast. I trust her judgment, but I would also hear your thoughts, if you would share them."

Belkidar couldn't conceal his surprise, and he momentarily held Indira's gaze before answering. "Master Juron, your daughter is wise. I've known Gunnar nearly his entire life, and he shares many traits that are so important to you and your pack." He turned to look at Gunnar, smiled, then met Juron's eyes. "Gunnar would only add to the prosperity of your pack, and he'd leave them better for it."

Juron smiled. "Then the matter is settled. Gunnar, I gladly welcome you into our pack!"

Gunnar was stunned, the sudden realization that he'd forever live among friends overwhelmed him. Tears disappeared into his thick beard as his dark eyes reflected the morning's fire. "I won't disappoint you," he said at last to Juron, but somehow directing his words more toward Belkidar.

"Congratulations, Gunnar!" Indira said a bit too loudly as she rushed to embrace him.

"Thank you, Indira. I just hope I don't let you down," he said in a low voice.

"I think that would be impossible," she whispered, overcome with emotion, thrilled to have him as a brother, relieved to know he would never again be alone.

"I know you'll be happy here, Gunnar," Belkidar said. "Adapting to their customs will take time, but I have no doubt you'll be a blessing to them, just as you were to us."

"Thank you," Gunnar replied softly. "I owe you so much, Belkidar. I'm not sure I'll ever be able to express my gratitude."

"No need, my friend," he said, waving the compliment away.

"I'd still be alone in an abandoned Midrogru mine if it weren't for you."

"Gunnar, I know you. Your integrity, loyalty, and generosity govern everything you do. If anything, I simply found an opportunity for you to show that to the rest of the world. You've earned this! Never believe differently."

He nodded once, then left to thank Juron.

"Indira, you are a most insightful creature," Belkidar said. "It seems I'm the only one who hadn't considered this possibility."

Indira smiled. "He is already family, Belkidar."

Belkidar embraced her. "I must leave now. Please watch over him, just as you've watched over us all. I'll see you soon."

"You had better," she said, fighting back tears. "My life surely would have been incomplete had you not included me in this Quest. Thank you for trusting me."

"You didn't need this Quest to understand your purpose in life, but I'm glad it gave you the opportunity to find peace. But now that it's over, you must discover the person you're destined to become."

She held his embrace for several moments as she considered his words. Finally, and with considerable regret, she allowed Belkidar to leave.

"My dear friends, it's been a sincere pleasure to have shared these past mooncycles with you. Farewell, and be happy," he said as he shimmered into nothingness.

Gunnar walked with Indira to the communal area so Juron could announce the news to the rest of his pack. As he walked, he pulled his enormous sword from the scabbard down his back. "Do you suppose I'll ever use this again?"

"I hope only for hunting," Indira replied, her smile wide, her excitement obvious.

As he walked with her, he regarded his sword, but this time as a work of art, not a tool. He first admired the immaculate metalwork at the tip before letting his gaze to fall down the blade, its edge still razor-sharp. His eyes rested on one of the portraits Szurgord designed near the hilt. There he saw a reflection of his past self, a lonely boy standing among many mountains. He then turned the blade over and studied the second portrait.

And froze in his tracks.

On his blade was another familiar depiction, but until now he had no idea of its significance. He saw a man completely content with his life, standing among friends, hoisting a sword high, his inner peace infectious. And in the background stood the interwoven trees of a great forest.

Chapter 24
Resolution

*And once the storm is over, you won't remember how
you made it through, how you managed to survive. You
won't even be sure whether the storm is really over.
But one thing is certain. When you come out of the
storm, you won't be the same person who walked in.*

Haruki Murakami

The day after Belkidar and his friends departed north for
KelKinney, Brohdan and Mikka headed south for Lukvia. They took
their time flying under the clear sky, stopping often just to enjoy each
other's company.

Brohdan in particular enjoyed life without the enormity of the
Quest constantly affecting his every decision. He savored the serenity
of knowing Hildegard's evil was gone forever, yet a part of him
wondered if that evil somehow survived, like a lingering infection in a
wound mended.

When they arrived in Lukvia, it was as though he had never left.
He guided Mikka so they both landed by the lake near Brohdan's old
cave. He paused there, savoring the moment. Eventually, he walked to
where his parents lived.

The cave was precisely as he remembered it, and although it
appeared smaller, he was surprised to see that he'd still be able to fit
inside. He approached the entrance from the side so he could stay
hidden from those within. "Good afternoon," he said loudly, altering
his voice.

"My Brohdan!" Grediva shouted as she half ran-half flew from the shadows.

Surprised she'd recognized his 'disguised' voice, he stood motionless beside the cave's entrance, watched unnoticed as his mother frantically emerged. After finally discovering him, she smothered him with her affection. Brohdan's smile portrayed a hint of fear, for she nearly caused more injuries than all of Hildegard's hordes combined.

Brohdeck soon followed his wife out of the shadows. Once Grediva had finally, if only temporarily, completed greeting her son, Brohdeck at last had the opportunity to do the same. However, he saved Brohdan a similar fate, instead calmly touching his nose to his son's.

"Mom," he began, looking into his mother's watery eyes, "Dad. I'm sure you remember Mikka."

"Of course, darling!" Grediva managed between sobs. "How are you, my dear?"

"Fine, thank you."

Brohdan's realized his mouth was unusually dry. "I've got something to tell you." He turned to look at Mikka before continuing. "Mikka and I have become lifemates."

"Ooohhhh," Grediva cried, starting the cycle all over again.

"Congratulations, son! And to you, my daughter," he said, touching his nose and forehead to hers.

Grediva had finally recovered enough to congratulate them, but still found it difficult to articulate words, so she settled for giving each a sloppy Hongi.

The remainder of the day offered the perfect conclusion to Brohdan's long journey. He spent links describing every detail of the Quest to his eager parents, spending the majority of the time talking about his companions, Batai in particular. They weren't quite as modest, so after he finished, he spent considerably more time answering a slew of questions, all revolving around their son.

They asked how he coped with being so far from his pack and about his feelings when forced to fight and kill creatures that, under ɔrmal circumstances, would've been his allies. Some questions were difficult to answer, and often his responses were short. Fortunately, they still knew him in ways others never could, so they abandoned the painful topics and turned instead to more pleasant ones.

The family talked for the majority of the night. When all of his parents' questions had been exhausted, Brohdan began a barrage of his own. He was thrilled to be lying in front of his cave again, catching up with everything that had happened during his lengthy absence. But eventually their exhaustion forced them inside, each drifting to sleep, content in being reunited with loved ones.

Brohdan rose with the sun. He quietly left his cave, dawn's red and violet glistening against his countless scales. He walked to the lake, taking his time, enjoying an old ritual. Once there, he sat by the water's edge, comforted by the familiar scent of moss and sweet grass. He wasn't sure how long he'd been reminiscing when he heard a familiar whisper behind him. He smiled. "Hello, Belkidar."

"Hello, Brohdan, it's good to see you again. I don't mean to intrude, but I wanted to talk with you before I pay a visit to a humpback whale I know."

Brohdan raised an eyebrow.

"She's a friend," he explained, shrugging.

"What will you do afterward?"

"Well, I've actually given that some thought," he said, sitting next to his friend. "I'm the world's last sorcerer. Perhaps it's time to change that."

"You're an excellent instructor, Belkidar."

"Thank you," he replied sincerely, "but that's not why I'm here. I know you still grieve over a few things that happened during our Quest."

Brohdan nodded, remained silent for a long moment. "Batai," he whispered.

"Yes. And others as well. The griffins, the titan – you had to kill them if our Quest had any hope of succeeding. You must make peace with yourself."

"I understand. But I wish there was another way."

"So do I. But you acted honorably, and that's never something you should feel guilty about. The griffins sacrificed themselves for the sake of the world. They couldn't overcome Hildegard's control, yet they fought him to their deaths." He thought for a moment before continuing. "If you had to choose between sacrificing yourself for the sake of the Quest or living and watching it fail, which would you choose?"

"The Quest," Brohdan answered immediately.

"Exactly! It's the same choice Batai and Einar made. It's the same choice you made a dozen times, the first of which is when you agreed to join the Quest in the first place. You did it again when you took flight to battle the griffins, and again when you fought the titan. But more importantly, you chose the Quest's success over your own wishes when you bid farewell to Mikka, for neither of us knew if you'd ever see her again. And in that way, you and the griffins are the same. They sacrificed themselves to help us defeat Hildegard, to help us find peace. Each of us was prepared to make that same sacrifice many times over during our Quest." He paused, thinking.

"Brohdan, I've lived eight thousand cycles, and I learned a very long time ago to never let things trouble me if they happened beyond my control. You must understand this." He looked down, his eyes distant. It was a long time before he continued.

"Batai died. So did Einar. I killed my wife. But I'm at peace because I know they willingly sacrificed themselves so we could once and for all defeat Hildegard and forever end the evil that threatened this world. Despite my power, I was helpless to prevent Aelya's death, so I choose to move on with my life in a way that would make her proud of me. You must do the same."

"Focusing on the things you can control is really what life's all about. It's normal to get frustrated when life forces you to make

It decisions, but that doesn't mean you should feel guilty about
,m. That'll only erode your happiness. Trust me. You have a very
long life ahead of you, Brohdan, far longer than your friends and
family. If you don't cast aside your unfounded guilt and regret, the
grief that will accumulate over your long life will destroy you."

He stopped a moment, considered his past. "Having long life is a
blessing. But if you let it, it can also be a curse. Watching far too
many loved ones grow old and die… It never gets easier, yet it's
unavoidable. You must learn from my mistakes. Instead of regretting
things that happened beyond your control, find solace in your
perseverance, in battling through those difficult situations. Instead of
mourning the loss of friends and family, celebrate the lives of those you
loved, and be content in the fact that you were fortunate to have known
them at all. All the while, live life so that on your own deathbed, you
can look back on your life with no regrets. Live each moment as
though it were the last. Take nothing for granted, because nothing lasts
forever."

Brohdan remained silent, his gaze fixed on the calm, clear water of
the lake. "I'll try to cast my guilt aside, to live my life so that I have no
regrets."

"Very good," Belkidar said, relieved to hear his friend would
eventually rise above the circumstances that had been the source of so
much anguish.

"Something else still confuses me," Brohdan admitted. "After the
final battle, we flew from Katja to Sul Brul in just two days. Why
didn't you just have us fly directly to Gul Krul in the first place?"

Belkidar smiled as he looked up into Brohdan's deep eyes. "For
many reasons. First, it takes considerable sorcery to change all of our
forms, so Hildegard would've known the moment we entered his
domain. True, our progress would've been swift, but he would've
known our precise location, numbers, and intent by the time we made it
halfway across the ocean. Besides, we needed those Five Defenses."

"What do you mean?"

"We had to work as a team to simultaneously defeat Hildegard, his Jrelz Captains, and the titan, but forging that degree of teamwork over the course of a two-day flight from Tymoteu to Gul Krul would've been impossible."

"Think back to each of Hildegard's Five Defenses. When we first battled the centaurs, ogres and orcs, our ability to work as a productive team – to accurately anticipate each other's intentions while protecting their vulnerabilities – was in its infancy. But our teamwork grew. I witnessed our progress as we battled the hydras and knifylm on Lake Mamate, and later the wyverns, lilkes, and venom woods in the dense mist of the Great Drulg Swamp. When we defeated the cyclopes and minotaurs on the Thrud Wastelands, I knew we were getting close. The way we battled the gargantuids, Jrelz, and griffins in the Fifth Defense convinced me we were finally ready to face whatever Hildegard had prepared for us."

"But those battles were far more important than just giving us a chance to learn each other's nuances and tendencies. That familiarity certainly helped, but it can't explain how we performed far beyond the sum of our parts." He smiled.

"The reason for our success, the advantage that Hildegard could never anticipate, could never understand, was the relationships we formed with each other. We didn't just fight to defeat Hildegard, we fought for each other. We were all willing to sacrifice ourselves for the sake of our friends, and that common trait allowed us to conquer what an army could not. Ironically, his Five Defenses focused the power that ultimately led to his destruction."

Belkidar took a moment before continuing. "We undertook a Quest to forever rid this world of Hildegard's evil, but that certainly wasn't the only quest that was completed over the course of our travels. Sometimes, facing adversity is the only way to know enough of yourself to truly find peace. The lessons you learned that allowed you to start your grombit, coupled with the friendships you forged since we left Sul Brul, shall accompany you throughout your long life. You have an extremely fulfilling life ahead of you, Brohdan. Be happy," he said as a familiar light shimmered around his body. "I'm proud of you," he added just as the aura's intensity overwhelmed him. In the next instant, the peaceful white-blue light disappeared, leaving only Brohdan and his thoughts.

Brohdan spent nearly a link contemplating Belkidar's words. He recalled what Dre told him during his visit to his cave in the southern Sichundar Mountains so long ago. According to that old Gorduvian, a Broglia Black will not begin his grombit until he's completely prepared for the trials that await him, for Broglias must endure their species' most difficult challenges. Dre believed Brohdan had physically matured enough to begin his grombit, so he reasoned that perhaps his behavior and decision making had been lacking. Indeed, his grombit began only after he learned to ignore the ridicule and judgments of others.

Dre also explained that a Broglia Black must fundamentally be a leader. All other dragons instinctively look up to a Broglia, and because there exists only one in the world at any given time, he must understand the difference between being liked by those he leads and being respected by them. Every Broglia is confronted with a tremendous opportunity, a responsibility to lead their entire species, to single-handedly advance nearly every aspect of their society. And they must hold themselves accountable.

Brohdan remembered the apprehension he'd felt after discovering his fate. The idea of leading his entire species was incredibly daunting, and at the time he wondered how he would ever acquire the wisdom necessary to fulfill such a destiny.

As he sat along the lakeshore and considered Dre's comments, he took a moment to compare them to what Belkidar had just told him. The sorcerer explained, albeit somewhat cryptically, that the adversity Brohdan had endured may serve other, more obscure purposes than the obvious destruction of Hildegard and his evil. He then overlaid that premise with the information Dre had given him over three cycles earlier. In a flash, he understood.

The suddenness of Brohdan's revelation rivaled Belkidar's instantaneous obliteration of Hildegard and Gul Krul's eastern districts. In a moment of exceptional clarity, he finally understood what all Broglia Blacks must – life, like leadership, embodies an intrinsic dichotomy. Each perfectly combines individual struggles with selfless cooperation, indifferent tragedy with unbridled euphoria, rigid authority with indulgent compassion, and even profound loneliness with incredible friendships. To successfully blend these seemingly opposing qualities, he must constantly incorporate honor and virtue, for they alone lead to contentment, to a life without regret. Brohdan finally found peace, for not a doubt lingered in his mind that he would become a worthy leader of his species.

Brohdan stood and returned to his cave. He entered its cool shadows and silently made his way to where Mikka slept. He laid down beside her, only slightly stirring his lifemate from her slumber. Brohdan let his mind drift to the remarkable friendships he'd forged with Kiera, Batai, Gunnar, Indira, and Belkidar. He then thought of the countless times he looked up to the stars, wondering if he'd ever get the chance to see Mikka again.

Realizing he was exactly where he wanted to be, Brohdan closed his eyes, content, and fell asleep.

The End.

Epilogue

If there ever comes a day when we can't be together,
keep me in your heart, I'll stay there forever.

A.A. Milne

It didn't take long for Brohdan to find the cave again. He landed nearby, relieved to find him still alive.

"Brohdan!" he managed, slowly emerging into the sunlight.

"It's good to see you again, Dre."

"And you. What brings you here?"

Brohdan smiled. Dre hadn't changed a bit. His scales were still unusually pale, and he still moved gingerly, finding the same spot to warm himself in the morning light. "A couple things." He described their Quest, Dre asking many questions throughout. Although his talent couldn't match Belkidar's, Dre was nonetheless impressed.

"I'm sorry," he said. "The world mourns the loss of any paladin, but Batai most dearly."

"Thank you. I felt I owed you a recounting of our journey, but I'm also here to ask a favor."

"Oh?" Dre asked.

"I'd like you to gather some dragons and establish a new pack on Katja."

Dre's golden eyes widened with surprise. "But I thought you said Hildegard was destroyed, that his evil is gone forever."

"It's true that he's gone, but I fear his evil may linger. Some remnants of his First Defense survived, and there may be others. And there are still the millions that make up his armies – the Northern and Southern Camps, and his main army in the Northern Plains." Brohdan paused, and Dre couldn't help notice the concern in his eyes.

"What aren't you telling me?"

Brohdan smiled uneasily. "Nothing that I can confirm. I just have a feeling. Hildegard's evil, the corruption in the Headpiece, they're not easily dismissed – nor forgotten."

"And you think dragons would help contain that evil?"

Brohdan nodded. "I think you'd help emphasize that following in Hildegard's footsteps would not be in anyone's best interest."

Dre smiled. "Where would we live?"

"The mountains west of Lake Mamate."

"Why there?"

"Hildegard molded them to be impassable, to force us around them to get to Gul Krul. You'll be safe there, at least until the land returns to her natural state. But long before that happens, it's my hope that the people of Katja will come to accept you, that they'll come to admire what we stand for."

Dre considered that for a long while. "It's a good plan, Brohdan. A great one. But I fear I'm too old to make the journey."

Brohdan nodded. "Not to worry, Belkidar can help with that. Besides, there's no one better suited to lead a new pack, especially one as important as this."

"Very well, I'll start making the arrangements. Do you have any dragons in mind besides me?"

"No, I'll leave that to you."

Dre smiled. "You've grown a lot since we last met. I look forward to serving you."

Brohdan returned to his cave, Mikka meeting him as he landed. "Welcome back. Did it go well?"

"It did. Dre's as loyal as ever."

"That's good to hear," she said, her voice anxious.

Brohdan approached her, alarmed. "What is it?" he asked, expecting the worst.

"It's nothing Brohdan. It's just that…"

"Yes?" he asked, his anxiety growing.

She smiled. "I'm pregnant."

Brohdan froze, then smiled with her. He'd never been happier! He rushed to her, touched his nose to hers. Then she looked up at him. "Do you have any ideas for a name?"

Brohdan's smile widened. "I do."

Made in the USA
Coppell, TX
21 September 2021